Beyond God's Realm

David Barnett

Published by New Generation Publishing in 2020

Copyright © David Barnett 2020

First Edition

ISBN
     Paperback   978-1-80031-648-5
     Hardback   977-1-80031-647-8

www.newgeneration-publishing.com

New Generation Publishing

Dedication

This book is dedicated to our son-in-law
Christopher Cullum
1961 -2019
Victim of Leukaemia
Husband to, Karen
Father to, Joshua and Charlotte

Acknowledgments

Atlas Edition	Kings and Queens of England
History Files	Life in Anglo Saxon Britain
Kaye Jones	The Medieval Anarchy
Orderic Vitalis	Account Battle of Lincoln
Timeline	King Stephen
Timeline	Empress Matilda
Wikipedia	A host of relevant information

Typical Norman Mote and Bailey Castle

Prologue

"Please God, don't let me die now." Henry silently prayed. "More time. I need a little more time." But over the past three or four days he had grown rapidly weaker and by now he was virtually paralysed. Even the drawing of a breath took prodigious effort.

"Lampreys! It was the lampreys," his physician had told him. Henry loved lamprey and had gluttonously gorged himself at the Royal Feast a week ago. Almost straight after he had been violently and continuously sick. His strength had been sapped by ferocious retching. When there was nothing left to be spewed, save his very toenails, came the convulsions which rendered periods of unconsciousness while his body thrashed involuntarily.

It was not for himself that he made this survival prayer but for his infant grandson. Young Henry was only three years old, and that was much too young to become King of England and Duke of Normandy. Death now would leave Maude, the infant's mother to rule. Rule at least until the boy was old enough to take the crown. But a woman ruler had never been heard of in all Norman history and there would undoubtedly be strong opposition. Henry knew that, and to ensure continuity he had gathered all his Nobles together and had them swear fealty to Matilda (Maude), his daughter.

"Sire, Sire." someone was demanding his attention.

Henry opened his eyes into the dimly lit room. Grim faced men stood silently among the shadows. The dancing flame from the fire flickered fleeting shadows down the side of their faces seemingly contorting features into gargoyle-like masks. Henry wondered if they could be the minions of the devil come to claim his soul.

"Sire." The demanding voice said again. "Who will you name as your successor?"

Henry slowly turned his head towards the Archbishop of Amiens. "You shouldn't need to ask," he feebly replied. God damn the man. He knew well that all had sworn the oath to support Maude. "Robert. Where's Robert?"

"I am here Father," Robert said as he took Henry's hand and settled on the bed at his side. Robert Earl of Gloucester was the eldest of Henry's many children, but all except William and Maude were born outside wedlock. William had died in a shipwreck at sea leaving only Maude to

1

continue the royal line. Henry wanted to instruct Robert to make sure that all the nobility honoured their fealty, but he was too tired, too weak to speak.

"Will you name Stephen as your successor?" the Archbishop spoke again.

Henry felt anger grow in his breast. That same anger that had made brave men tremble before him during the thirty-five years as England's King. That anger lent him a modicum of strength and he tried to reply in a stern voice. But, "Stephen only nephew," was all he could weakly reply.

"Did he just name his nephew as his successor?" Henry heard Hugh Bigod exclaim. "He did! He named Stephen!"

"He did not!" Robert retorted hotly. "He pointed out only that Stephen is a nephew and not a direct descendant."

Henry was relieved and tried to squeeze Robert's hand in gratitude. Henry knew that Robert would have made a good king, but he was born a bastard and would be even less acceptable than a woman. But then William the bastard Duke of Normandy, Henry's father, had ruled England for twenty-one years. However, he had taken the throne by force considering it to be his right.

The sainted Saxon King, Edward the Confessor, had promised William the crown after his death, but at his very end he reneged on that promise. A bastard could not be king and instead had named the Saxon, Harold Godwineson. But a furious William crossed the English Channel in 1066 while Harold was in the north of the country fighting Vikings. William took full advantage of Harold's absence to strengthen his position at Hastings, so that by the time Harold arrived with his travel and battle-weary troops, William held a formidable position of strength. William the Conqueror defeated Harold and subjugated the Saxons by filling the country with Norman nobility and a fighting army.

By now Henry was so very very tired, and it seemed as if nothing mattered anymore so he closed his eyes. His body then lapsed into twitching spasms before laying very still eyes staring wide and jaw dropped agape.

"Physician?" Robert demanded.

From the shadows the Royal Physician stepped forward to hold a glass very close to Henry's face with one hand while searching his wrist for a pulse with his other. Finding neither pulse nor breath upon the glass he stepped away. Then looking over to John Fitzgilbert, he gave a brief nod. The Archbishop, meanwhile, began to administer the last rites to the king.

John Fitzgilbert had been Henry's Royal Marshal and confidante many years and now he had just one last duty to perform for his dead king. He left the room and made his way to the Great Hall where many more nobles waited. The room gradually fell silent as Fitzgilbert made his way to the king's throne. Standing on the bottom step he turned to face expectant faces.

"The King is dead. Long live the Queen," He loudly proclaimed.

"Long live the Queen came the enthusiastic reply. But not from everybody.

* * *

Empress Matilda (Maude)
Castle Anjou, France. 3rd December 1135

The town of Angers in the region of Anjou is dissected by the River Maine. East and west are joined together by a solitary wooden bridge spanning the wide river. On the eastern side the great imposing Cathedral of St Aubin, and close by the Castle. This castle is the ancient ancestral home of the Angevin's.

From the window of her chamber, Maude looked down from the keep into the inner bailey below where her husband Geoffrey Plantagenet, Count of Anjou, was leading out a small party on a stag hunt. She was as pleased to see him go as he was to escape her company. Their marriage was a tempestuous alliance, and only minimum efforts were made for the sake of appearances to disguise their variance.

Maude was dressed in the sombre attire that was fitting for a daughter in mourning. However, the mourning dress was more to pay homage to protocol than any real sorrow. She had not wished her father's death, but neither did she particularly mourn his passing. He had always heartlessly used her as a political pawn, a bargaining tool to further advantageous alliances. She had received the news yesterday of his death, and for the very first time in her life she could look forward to a future which promised complete independence and a freedom which she had never experienced in her thirty-three years.

She was aged just twelve when Henry had married his daughter to the Holy Roman Emperor Henry V of Germany, giving Maude the courtesy titles of Empress and Queen of Germany. Just eleven years later Henry died leaving Maude a widow. Without any children to cement a case to remain as Germany's Queen Mother, Maude returned to England. Less than two years later Henry arranged another marriage for his daughter, by then aged twenty-five, to the fifteen-year-old Geoffrey. The marriage was a strategic one cementing an Alliance between Normandy and Anjou against any threat from the King of France.

But from the very onset the marriage was beset with troubles because neither Geoffrey nor Maude wanted the marriage. Maude found Geoffrey to be an inexperienced spoiled brat. From the very onset Geoffrey went out of his way to make things as unpleasant for Maude as he could. "Whilst Maude publicly very subservient to her husband, did her best to exact revenge in private. Nevertheless, there was a son produced in their marriage, Henry, and another child within her belly.

Unusually, this morning, Geoffrey had been pleasant towards her, even giving her a squeeze and a kiss before leaving for the day's hunt. Maude was not fooled. She could guess easily what was running through her husband's mind. When Maude claimed her right as England's Queen then she as a woman would be subservient to her husband and the natural order was for Geoffrey to become king. He would be expecting to be Geoffrey, King of England, Duke of Normandy and Count of Anjou. Maude permitted herself a wry smile, he was going to be extremely disappointed.

At this time, the child within her anchored her in Anjou. So it suited her purpose, for now, to humour him. But as soon as the child was born and weaned off to a wet nurse, she would cross the channel and claim her throne. She would take young Henry with her as heir to the throne of England. That was his birth right. Once she was crowned, she would make proclamation to disbar Geoffrey Count of Anjou from ever setting foot in England. After that she would have no master, instead all would bend knee to her and carry out her bidding.

Maude turned away from the window and sighed, all this was yet a number of months away. She resolved to hide her impatience and play out the time circumspectly until the blissful day arrived. Until then she must continue the façade of a dutiful wife and go through the apathetic motions expected of a Count's Lady.

At this present time she could enthuse no particular interest in female trivia, but she did need to exhibit a false disposition of indifference. So, imposing herself to lady-like pursuits she picked up her sewing and joined her maid who sat quietly working her own embroidery.

"My Lord Geoffrey has left for the day." She needlessly informed the maid. "All should be quiet while daylight remains." Maybe beyond that, if he were to visit one of his whores, she added in thought only.

* * *

Stephen De Blois
Guildford Castle 15th December 1135

The log fire burned fiercely in the inglenook fireplace but the mood around it was as sombre as the bleak cold and wet weather outside the castle. The plan to put Stephen on the throne of England instead of his cousin Maude had started disappointingly.

"Not too much of a disaster," Geoffrey de Mandeville said. "It should have been anticipated. After all, the Patron of Dover and Canterbury is Robert of Gloucester."

"Aye. He'll be no friend to us." Waleron Beaumont agreed.

"When you have the crown then you should make those townspeople pay dearly for the insult." Waleron's twin brother Robert said angrily. "The audacity of those peasants! Shutting the town gates and refusing entry to their King."

"Aye!" Stephen spoke for the first time. "But the major disappointment was that the Archbishop William Corbiel did not recognise my claim."

"There is Henry!" Robert went on, nodding towards Stephen's younger brother. "He is Bishop of Winchester and you could easily elevate him to Archbishop deposing William Corbiel."

"It would need approval from the Pope," Henry pointed out. "But it could be done."

Stephen glanced at his brother and knew that from the moment the usurp plans had been made months ago, that was precisely where his brother's ambitions lay. He was a greedy man and as Archbishop he would considerably increase his already prodigious wealth. More importantly when at last he entered into God's Kingdom, then an Archbishop would outrank even a king, and his position in the hear-after would be well assured for all eternity. Henry had started to preach in his sermons that it was against God's Holy Scriptures that a woman should dictate a man. How then could a woman become ruler and dominate all men in her realm? It was a valid point and prodded at men's unease about a female monarch. The intention was to further Stephen's claim to the crown, at the same time he was enhancing his own prospects. Without doubt he expected to be well rewarded, as would all his supporters.

"Let us wait and see how Hugh Bigod fare's before we start any retaliation." De Mandeville added restraint to the discussion.

Hugh Bigod had remained at Canterbury to beg an audience with the Archbishop. He hoped to convince him that King Henry in the last moments of his life had named Stephen as his successor. Bigod worked hard to convince all that was what the dying Henry had said. Stephen didn't believe it; he knew his uncle too well and could not imagine Henry releasing all from their oaths. 'I was there, and you weren't, my Lord.' Bigod had pointed out to quell Stephen's doubt.

That was true, and Stephen envied him that. He had respected and admired the old tyrant that was his uncle, and Henry had treated him as if he were a son instead of a nephew, keeping him at his Royal Court. Stephen's benevolent and easy-going nature had made him a popular figure among the nobility of the court, and several had intimated that when the time came, he would be preferred to Maude as England's monarch.

On hearing the news of the kings death, it was these influences that had motivated Stephen to leave Blois and sail immediately for England. He was aided and abetted by the Beaumont's, Mandeville, Bigod and his brother Henry. However, when they had landed at Dover, instead of receiving the expected acclamation they had found the gates of the town closed to them. Moving on to Canterbury they had found the same reaction. Hoping that the reception would be different in London they had travelled on until they reached Guildford. Here within thirty miles of London they paused and had taken shelter in the castle.

Acting prudently, Stephen had sent on an advance party under the command of Simon de Senlis to London in order to gauge the reaction they were likely to receive. Now they waited for news.

It was mid-morning the next day, when Simon de Senlis returned with the news that the people of London were waiting to greet him as their king. After making careful ostentatious preparation, Stephen rode to London the following day at the head of his small cavalcade and entered the city to a rapturous welcome from the townspeople.

On 22nd December 1135 Stephen was crowned King of England by William Corbiel Archbishop of Canterbury. The Archbishop, realising his own vulnerability, and not entirely convinced by Bigod's story, also mindful of his own oath to King Henry, accepted the alternative. After all, oaths made under duress, were not valid.

Chapter 1

Scorrenstone, June 1139

The day was hot, it was Sunday and the nearest thing to a day of rest for a Saxon villager. Ardron sat on the shaded side of the wattle fence looking down to the river Avon at the bottom of the steep sided valley. A dense row of willows lined the riverbank, and from somewhere within the security of the trees canopies a heron took flight. Its large wings flapped lazily as it languidly gained height and curved in Ardron's direction. He did not have his bow with him, so Ardron lifted an imagined weapon, pulled back on the non-existent string and released the imaginary arrow to bring the great bird down. Then he watched as the bird continued its onward flight, oblivious to the fictitious disaster that had befallen it.

"Good shot," Swidhurn said clapping his hands mockingly.

Ardron leaned back to see the big man leaning on the fence above him. "I'll save a leg for you," he countered to pass off his embarrassment.

"Are you alone?" Swidhurn asked.

"For the moment."

"Where's your brother?"

"Esmond will be here soon. He's changing from his church clothes."

Swidhurn said nothing, but he swung down the billhook he carried to wedge in the top of one of the supporting posts. Then he pulled the sheepskin tunic over his head. "It's too hot to work beneath that," he said, as he discarded it over the fence. He was a heavy-set man in his mid-twenties with large muscles across his chest and upper arms. His powerful physique had been honed and developed by the long hours that he worked as the village ironworker. His unkempt hair hung down both sides of his face almost to his shoulders whilst his heavy black beard added to the wild man appearance. "We may as well get started," he said as he re-claimed the billhook.

"Aye," Ardron agreed less than enthusiastically, then picked up his own billhook and both men made their way down the steep bank to the river. The willows had been well coppiced and over the years had provided the village with a bountiful supply of straight and supple poles. They took a few moments to slowly stroll among the willows selecting a suitable tree on which to start work.

"This one," Ardron suggested and waited for Swidhurn's agreement. When it came Ardron too peeled off his sheepskin. Of similar age to Swidhurn, his physique was much less than Swidhurn's bulky mass. It did, however, bear testament to a life of hard labour. His frame was thin almost to a point of emancipation but his muscles hard and toned, well able to withstand the long rigorous work hours. His dark hair hung onto his shoulders and was controlled only by a tight headband. His beard, however, unlike his hair was trimmed, almost neatly. Both men set to work chopping off poles.

Twenty minutes later they were joined by Ardron's younger brother Esmond and his friend Cerdic. Ardron paused to watch as the pair lopped happily down the steep bank to the meadow below in good spirits. 'And why wouldn't they be? Ardron silently questioned himself. Esmond was soon to wed to the delectable Hildi, and Cerdic as Esmond life-long and staunch friend, would be happy for him.

"Find yourself a tree," Ardron said with a wave of his arm, "And start cutting." It was a needless instruction because not only did Esmond know exactly what to do, he also had the motivation.

The poles they were to cut would be wattled together to form the basis of a wall in the construction of a bucolic house for Esmond and his bride. Once wattled tightly and then firmed into position they would be plastered over thickly with a mixture of mud, straw and animal dung to form a stout barrier against all the elements.

For more than an hour they worked hacking and chopping off suitable poles then tossing them into a pile. Eventually Ardron straightened his back giving it a brief respite. He studied the pile harvested and decided that perhaps they had enough to complete one wall. "Enough," he said bringing the cutting to an end. He got no argument from anybody, and they dropped tiredly to the ground in front of the pile surveying the result. It had been hot and thirsty work and Swidhurn picked up the water skin took a generous swallow then passed it around. The need now was to move the pile up the steep bank into the village. They discussed their options, but there was only one realistic option and that was to hump the pile up the hill manually.

The village of Scorrenstone was sited atop the hill on a flat plateau. The river Avon bordered its southern end and curled around its western edge. It was a typical Saxon village with around a hundred residents. All were Churls, for there were no slaves in this village. Before the Norman Conquest, seventy-three years earlier, Scorrenstone had been at the very heart of the large estates owned by the Saxon Thegne, John, son of John Rattlebone. But as a penalty for showing loyalty to Harold Godwinson and fighting alongside his king at Hastings, John had found all his estates confiscated by William the Norman Conqueror. Ardron was a direct descendant of John son of John Rattlebone, but it would be his elder brother Redwald who would become thegne after his father, Wolfstan. Not that the title was of any real status anymore. The title Thegne of Scorrenstone in this instance was degraded simply to be a village head.

8

"The sooner we get started the sooner we get finished," Ardron said getting to his feet to set the example. The four friends then began to separate the poles into small manageable piles. However, horseplay developed between the younger two and they began a mock sword fight using a couple of the shorter poles.

Swidhurn paused briefly and watched. "Do you think your young brother is enough of an adult to be marrying my sister?" he asked Ardron with a sigh.

Ardron watched the duelling pair then shrugged without replying.

"Why is it that your younger brother marries before you?" Swidhurn went on.

Ardron shrugged. "I suppose I am not yet ready," he said.

"No," Swidhurn nodded knowingly. "You're too busy taking your favours where you can," he added with a scoff.

"Perhaps you misjudge me, my friend." Ardron defended.

"Really?"

"Well__." He didn't have time to finish what it was he was about to say because Cerdic suddenly dropped his make-believe sword. "Normans," he said pointing down river.

A quarter of a mile away about to cross the rustic bridge a party of mounted Norman's headed towards the village.

Ardron shaded his eyes to examine the party; it was a sizable force of perhaps fifty. At its head four knights led the column, while a pair of carts brought up the rear. A standard of blue and grey streamed and rippled in the breeze. It was a livery that Ardron did not recognise. It was seldom a happy event when such a party of Normans came to the village.

Ardron spoke passable French which hardly anyone else in the village did. His father would need his assistance. "Stay here," he briefly charged and hurried up the hill to the village.

The Norman's were already in the village when Ardron arrived and clandestinely he studied the band as he made his way along the side to the front. At the head those four knights were armed, helmeted and wore hauberks. When Normans arrived wearing the hauberk chain mail chemises it was seldom a social visit. These armed men were either in-bound towards trouble or out-bound away from it. At the head of the column his father Wolfstan was attempting to bid a Saxon welcome. However, the knight at the head neither spoke English nor was interested.

"Is this Burbage part of Bishop Roger's Salisbury's estate?" he kept demanding in French.

"It is," Ardron interceded.

The knight looked at Ardron and said nothing. Then he half raised his arm in a lazy wave giving the sergens permission to move forward. The other knights at the front then spurred their horse forward knocking

9

Wolfstan to the ground and rode over him. This was a signal for mayhem to erupt.

In groups of three or four, the Normans scattered as a bomb burst and began to pillage the village. They chased livestock, slaughtered it where they found it then dragged the carcases to their carts. Some on foot chased chickens wringing the necks of those they caught. Others raided the villager's home and took what food or valuables they could find. Intimidation by well-armed and well trained sergens deterred any resistance. Where they did find a modicum of resistance it was brutally put down.

Ardron's immediate concern had been for his father's welfare and he had quickly moved to his rescue, dragging him clear of galloping hooves. Wolfstan back on his feet, but in much pain from horse kicked ribs, was beside himself with rage. With an old warriors attitude he moved forward and with indomitable spirit shouted for someone to bring him a sword. Ardron grabbed his arm and pulled him back just in time to avoid being knocked over by stampeded horses. This time it was village horses that were being driven away and in the lead was Wolfstan's own charger, Rattlebone.

"No no. Not Rattlebone," Wolfstan shouted in dismay.

The village was not horse rich, having no more than a dozen in the entire village, but the big bay was Wolfstan's pride. He had named him after the village legend Sir John Rattlebone who with his mighty sword had been the scourge of the Danish. The big stallion Rattlebone stood seventeen hands high with huge shoulder muscles and powerful rear quarters. Although necessity decided that the animal was often used as a labourer, his value lay in stud duties for he stamped his mark on all of his offspring. So much so that neighbouring villages often brought mares to be covered by him, which provided a useful income for Scorrenstone. But now they could do nothing but watch as the horses disappeared down the road and out of the village.

It was a woman's scream that brought Ardron's attention back to the horror that was happening in the village. Hildi ran down the road being pursued by two Norman's sergens on horse-back. One leaned over and made a grab for her, but she managed to squirm free, leaving the Norman with only a handful of wimple. She wasn't so lucky with the second rider, he grabbed her by her long fair hair and dragged her close alongside his horse. With her feet barely touching the floor he half lifted half dragged her towards the knight who sat astride his horse just watching the mayhem.

"Sir Robert," the sergen called dragging Hildi alongside. "This one will provide us with good sport this evening."

The knight glanced down almost disinterested, then after nodding said. "Bring her along."

Ardron was already halfway there running hard. He came up on the blind side of the sergen and putting both hands under his foot tried to tip the man out of the saddle. But the Norman was a good horseman, and he managed to keep his balance. However, holding Hildi with one hand and trying to control a prancing horse with the other he could do nothing about Ardron's persistence. Ardron then managed to get a good grip of the man's clothing and this time pulled hard. The man began to fall towards him.

Whether he heard something or simply just sensed the danger, Ardron glanced sharply to his right in time to see the knight almost on him and the iron spiked ball of a mace swinging at him. It hit him at the side of his head lifting him off his feet. With a rushing sound in his ears he lay in a dazed stupor unable to move at all. Completely paralysed, he could do nothing about the prancing hooves inches from his face, nor the screams and shouts of mayhem.

Eventually, someone started to drag him off the road. After getting him clear, Swidhurn lifted him to rest his back against a tree and then began pressing leaves against the wound to stem the bleeding.

"Your sister." Ardron tried to tell him about Hildi, but Swidhurn either didn't hear or didn't understand. He then became aware of the strong smell of smoke. The Norman's had fired the village, and fire was a horror in a Saxon village where all the houses have straw roofs. He tried to curse them, and the mothers that had born such hell spawn. But he was slipping into unconsciousness as a black ring started on the periphery of his vision and began closing in.

"Stay with me. Stay with me." Swidhurn instructed.

* * *

The brightness of a sunny morning streamed in through the open shutters when Ardron opened his eyes. Beyond these shafts of light the room was shadowy, and as his eyes became accustomed to the contrast, he could see that he was alone. He half rolled onto his shoulder and looked across the room, recognising the place as Redwald's house. The rough-hewn seats and bench had been neatly stacked in the corner indicating that Redwald and his family had left to begin their daily chores. In the middle of the room was the fire trough, but there was no fire. Only the ashes from the night before and that was not unusual. It would only be lit when Acha, Redwald's wife, began her cooking duties.

He moved to sit up and immediately felt the agony of the swelling that was the side of his head. Gingerly, he touched the spot to find his head swathed in cloths that acted as bandages. He swung his legs down from the cot and then had to sit awhile until the giddiness passed. When he tried to stand the giddiness returned, involuntarily he put out his hand and found a wall on which to steady himself.

"Christ on the cross. What are you trying to do?" Acha scolded as she entered and saw him on his feet swaying unsteadily. "Sit you back down," she said taking his arm. Ardron gave her no argument.

Once he had settled back on the cot, she poured a pitcher of milk then sitting by his side handed it to him.

"What happened?" he asked.

"You don't remember?"

"Up to the time I passed out I do. But what happened after?"

"Nothing good. I'll get Redwald, he can tell you."

She paused only to put on her wimple and left. Acha was a comely woman, easy on the eye with a quiet calm disposition. She had been Redwald's wife almost five years and had borne him two children. Ardron held her in high regard and had often thought that when the time came for him to marry, if he could find her equal then he would be well satisfied.

A few minutes later Redwald entered, having to stoop slightly to come through the doorway. He paused and studied his brother for a moment. "Well brother it's good to see you in your senses," he said as he sat at his side. There was no doubting that they were brothers, but for an age difference of around three years they could have passed as twins.

"What news?" Ardron asked.

"A lot. None of it good." Redwald replied. He paused gathering his thoughts not sure where to begin. "The Norman's pillaged the village stealing what food and valuables they could find. They slaughtered about half our live-stock and took it with them. From sheer malice they torched half-a-dozen homes and struck down any who resisted."

"Was anyone killed?"

"No but some, like you, were injured."

"Who were these barbarians?" Ardron asked.

"We don't know. Not yet we don't." Redwald paused. "That's not the worst of it," he added almost apologetically. "They took away two of our women-folk."

Ardron remembered Hildi and trying to go to her aid. "Hildi?"

"Yes Hildi. And Edyo."

"Edyo? Young Edyo."

"Yes," Redwald confirmed.

"Oh no," Ardron groaned. "She is no more than fourteen." Then he remembered his brother Esmond and his attachment to Hildi. "Esmond! What of Esmond?"

"He took off after the Normans yesterday."

"On his own?"

"Along with Cerdic."

"You should have stopped them. What could they achieve?"

"You know Esmond. There was just no stopping him. But they were on foot. So it's unlikely that they will catch up to the Normans."

It was understandable, Ardron allowed in thought, but didn't say as much.

"How are you feeling?" Redwald asked.

Ardron touched the sore spot tenderly. "Not too bad."

Redwald looked at him quizzically. "Father and I could do with your help this morning, if you are feeling well enough."

"To do what?"

"Father intends to go this morning to Malmesbury Castle to report the attack, and appeal to the Castellan to do something. We need your French speaking ability."

"How will you get there?" Ardron asked remembering seeing the horses being driven off.

"By cart! Rattlebone found his way back last night and brought three mares and a young colt with him."

"I'm well enough," Ardron decided.

It was close on midday by the time Wolfstan, Redwald and Ardron started the five miles trip to Malmesbury Castle. Only halfway there and the imposing Abbey at Malmesbury dominated the skyline. Built at the highest point overlooking the surrounding countryside its four wings and two towers, imposed itself on the surrounding landscape with massive autonomy. Close by in its north-west, was the castle. Although this castle of mote and bailey was not insubstantial, it was nevertheless dwarfed in comparison to the abbey. A stout wooden palisade defended the castle bailey with the steep mote at the far end. Atop the mote, extensively constructed, was the castle keep where the dignitaries lived and conducted business.

Malmesbury was one of four castles owned by Roger, the Bishop of Salisbury, the others being at Sarum, Devizes and Salisbury. However, the Bishop spent most his time living in the Bishop's Palace at Salisbury or counting the nations riches at Devizes.

Roger had been King Henry's justiciar collecting and securing, at Devizes, all England's rentals and taxes due to the king. Such an elevated position made him one of the most powerful men in Norman England. Indeed, such was his power that whenever Henry had been out of England in France, Roger had acted king. Additionally, his influence as Bishop of Salisbury also collected homage from all the surrounding ecclesiastical Parishes. A man with that amount of financial power would have to be either a fool, or very honest, not to make himself one of the richest and pampered men in England. Roger, Bishop of Salisbury was neither. He had

13

used his corrupt influence to further his wealth by appointing his two nephews as Bishops of Lincoln and Ely.

However, the three Saxon's would not have to plead their case to the Bishop. He had appointed Walter de Pinkney as castellan to administer the Malmesbury district in his absence. It would be to Walter or his younger brother Roger, to whom they would have to make their report.

By early afternoon they had reached Malmesbury and crossed the bridge over the Avon. Here to the south of the town there was a convergence of two rivers, the Avon from the west, and the Ingleburn from the east. The two rivers flowed either side of a large rocky outcrop into the convergence. The steep cliff like faces of the hills formed a natural defence, and strategically built upon the top of this outcrop, were the abbey and the castle.

Most of the day had waned and it was early evening by the time they were admitted into the great chamber within the castle keep, for an audience with the castellan. De Pinkney sat on a large ornately carved wooden seat upon a raised dais with the pretentiousness of a king. His brother Roger stood slightly behind with his arm casually resting on the back of the chair.

Wolfstan began to introduce himself but was cut short by the interpreter.

"Sir Walter, knows who you are."

"Bring forward the boar," de Pinkney then demanded of two lackeys skulking at the back of the chamber.

Although Ardron understood the French language his father had instructed him to pretend he did not. He had reasoned that there might be some advantage to be gained if the Norman's were not aware of it,

The lackeys brought forward a dead boar on a shield with an arrow protruding from its ribcage and laid it in front of the dais.

"Ask him; as the thegne of his district what does he know of this."

"Nothing," Wolfstan answered after the translation.

"Ask him again and this time point out that it is a Saxon arrow sticking in the pig."

"My Lord," Wolfstan replied. "I know nothing of this. My people all know well Forest Law. It is against the king's law for Saxon's to hunt or even scavenge in the forests. Respectfully, I would point out that there are several villages in this burbage. The culprit could have come from any one of them. But I will assure you he was not from Scorrenstone."

"Do you think he tells the truth?" Sir Walter muttered to his brother.

Roger's teeth bit his bottom lip thoughtfully. "Probably not!"

Sir Walter deliberately allowed the silence to protract. "What brings him here today," he eventually asked of the translator.

Wolfstan then described to the translator what had occurred the day before in the village. The telling of which was long and protracted since the translator had to keep stopping him in order to translate to Sir Walter.

"Ask him if the pillagers sported a livery," Sir Walter asked.

"Blue and grey quarters," the answer.

"Do we know this livery?" Walter asked his brother who disinterestedly shrugged and slowly shook his head.

"Why do we need to concern ourselves with Saxon woes?" Roger de Pinkney queried his brother, with exasperation.

"Clerk," Sir Walter summoned.

"Sir," the answer was immediate. Ardron watched a slight and timid looking man get up from his desk in the corner behind the dais.

"Bring your accounts leger," he summoned without even glancing his way.

The timid man picked up the leger and hurried across to the dais.

"Scorrenstone. Tell me about Scorrenstone."

The clerk held the leger awkwardly and thumbed the pages quickly. Then using his knee for support under the leger he opened out the big book fully.

"Scorrenstone rents approximately one eighth of a hide from my Lord Bishop with a population of around one hundred Saxon's. None are serfs, all free men. Scorrenstone is obliged to supply to my Lord Bishop twenty Vassals, as and when, required and all to be of fit and fighting age." He then went on to list all grown produce and all livestock that the village had to supply to the castle quarterly.

Walter de Pinkney waited patiently until the clerk had finished. "So, do you see brother?" he said turning towards Roger. "If they don't have the ability to fill their obligations then we are shorted, and we then have two options. We can appeal to the Bishop to accept less than his due. And that, you know of course, he will never accept. So it then befalls on us to make up the shortfall. That is why we can't allow any trespassers to pillage villages under our Burbage."

The conversation was entirely in French but Ardron had listened intently. Their concern was solely for their own benefit, and they had not a jot of concern for the two kidnapped women. Exasperated, a quiet sigh escaped.

"Have a care brother," Roger said staring at Ardron. "That one understands what we are saying."

Both men stared at Ardron. He still wore a rag bound tightly around his head and by this time his bloodshot eye was surrounded by black and purple

"You, pig face." Sir Walter said.

Ardron stared back with a blank expression.

"Your mother must have lain with the boars in the forest for you to get a face like that." He went on.

Acting dumbly, Ardron pointed at his own chest. "Are they talking to me?" he asked the interpreter.

"Yes they are."

"What are they saying?"

"They are asking if you can speak French."

Ardron held up his hand with his finger and thumb very slightly apart indicating that his knowledge of French was only very small. "Very little."

Both brothers stared at him suspiciously trying to make up their minds. Suddenly an agitated courier blustered into the chamber making the matter irrelevant. Unceremoniously, he approached the dais, "Sir Walter," he said. "If it pleases, I have urgent news."

Clearly not impressed by the man's lack of respect Walter glared at him. "This had better be important," he almost growled.

"Sir, if it pleases you, I have to inform you that Roger, Bishop of Salisbury, has been arrested by King Stephen." The courier blurted,

The surprise on Sir Walter's face was plain to see and the news brought him to his feet. "On what charge?" he demanded.

"I don't know. But he, along with his nephews, were summoned to attend King Stephen's court at Oxford. Shortly after their arrival the king ordered all three arrested.

"All three?

"All three, Sir. However only two were detained. Bishop Roger and the Lincoln Bishop, Alexander. Nigel of Ely received some prior warning, and he fled before the sergens arrived. The king then marched on Devizes Castle to take charge of the treasury. "Indeed, he is probably there now."

A moment of stunned silence followed which was eventually broken by Roger who calmly said. "That begs an interesting question. What of us? And to whom do we now owe allegiance?"

"All power and possessions owned by the Bishop of Salisbury, except those ordained by the church, have been seized by the king." The courier answered the question.

"That then must include this castle. It can be only a matter of time before the king, or someone sent by him, arrives here." Roger said to his brother.

"Aye, And what then?" Walter replied. Then remembering the Saxon's before him said to the interpreter. "Get rid of these Saxon's. Tell them I'll look into their problem."

Outside the keep and still within the bailey, Wolfstan looked enquiringly at Ardron. "Did you get any of that?" he asked.

"Pretty much all of it." Ardron said. Then he proceeded to relate what he had heard. There was no sympathy for the bishop, nor was there any elation. In effect it would mean very little to the Saxon community. They would simply swap one master for another. But on the journey home they were pretty much agreed, they could expect no help from the Normans. Houses could be rebuilt; food shortages could be endured and live-stock re-bred. Hardships there were to come, and they would have to be borne. But it was the two kidnapped women that was the major concern. Even though it was getting late by the time they reached Scorrenstone there was still a little daylight left. Ardron got down from the cart and began to unharness the horse.

"Leave that," Redwald said taking over. "You should go and get some rest."

Ardron, silently thankful, allowed him to take over.

As he stepped back and walked with his father they were greeted by Esmond.

"Esmond!" Wolfstan greeted his youngest son. "What news?"

Esmond shook his head sadly. "We followed those Normans south for about ten miles before we lost their trail north of Chippenham. We went into Chippenham, but they had not been sighted' so they did not pass through the town. I'm afraid we lost them father," he added crestfallen.

Wolfstan placed a consoling arm across his son's shoulders. "Never mind son we have an idea where they might have gone."

* * *

Early the next morning Wolfstan convened a meeting in the village meeting house. In pre-Norman days this house had been the meeting hall for the Thegne's whole estate in this corner of Wiltshire. The stone-built house had, like the village Scorrenstone, not only degraded greatly in importance but its previous grandiose appearance had faded into mediocrity. Inside, the great hall had been sectioned with the bigger part becoming shelter for the village animals. Now, as the majority of villagers crowded into the restricted space, it was inadequate. Nevertheless, all those who wanted to be there managed to squeeze in.

Wolfstan addressed the meetings by describing the situation and the indifferent reaction of their Norman superiors. Although the pillaged supplies were a concern which affected everybody, it was the two kidnapped girls that was the immediate priority. He then stated his intention to send a small party to find the two women and to bring them home. Even as he spoke, he knew it was an immense task. Firstly, the party would have to find the girls. Then after that they would have to either negotiate their release or affect some sort of clandestine rescue. But at this stage all that could be done was to select the rescue team.

There were no shortage of volunteers, but in the end, it was Wolfstan's decision who should go. He accepted the argument from his youngest son, Esmond, that he should go because Hildi was his intended bride. After all, it would not look particularly re-assuring if he were not in the party that rescued her. Even though he was loathed to lose the services of the village ironworker, he accepted Swidhurn argument that, he as Hildi's brother, should also be there. However, he rejected the argument from Durwin, Edyo's father, that because he had no son to send, then he should himself be in the party. Wolfstan could see his point and held a deal of sympathy for him. However, he was not a young man, and this would be a young man's mission. There would be a lot of long and hard riding. Then, if they did manage to find the girls, who could say what action the rescue team might have to carry out. He also rejected Redwald's claim that as the Thegne's eldest son, he should lead the team. Instead he turned to Ardron because he could speak French.

* * *

Along with his young brother, Ardron had almost finished their preparations when Swidhurn entered the hut with his pack. Carrying beneath his arm, something was concealed in a blanket. Wordlessly, he laid down his pack then crossed over to the cot, on which he laid the blanket. Then carefully, he began to unwrap it. Ardron, slightly behind him, looked over his shoulder and snatched a surprised breath when Swidhurn revealed an exceptionally fine sword indeed. He held the broad sword up, and lovingly turned it slowly to be appreciated. And appreciated it was. Satisfied with the silent reaction he handed it over to Ardron.

Straight, flat and double edged it was almost as long as a tall man's leg. The hilt was waisted and embellished with silver decoration in the form of knot-work. The pommel on the end resembled an acorn, and its added weight shifted the point of balance a little higher up the weapon, making it easier to handle. A shallow groove ran down the centre of the blade reducing its weight whilst not compromising thickness.

"What a beautiful sword," Ardron muttered. "Truly, Swidhurn, you are a craftsman."

"It took many hours work flattening out iron strips before twisting together for strength and purity. Then it was shape, temper and cool over and over again. After that came the decoration. Yes, it took weeks."

Holding the weapon with both hands Ardron swished the sword around and marvelled at its balance. "Truly this is the work of an artist." He noticed then the sword's tip. The normal construction of sword tips flattened to a rounded end giving the point strength. This one, however.

tapered to a fine point." He lowered the sword until the tip was before his face, then looked questioningly at Swidhurn.

Swidhurn nodded understanding the unasked question. "I have a theory," he said. "A sharp point has a much better chance of piercing a hauberk. I have tested it!" He added, responding to Ardron's dubious glance. "If enough force is applied it will pierce chainmail. Another admiring glance then reluctantly he handed it back.

"No no," Swidhurn said holding up both hands as a refusal. "It's yours."

Ardron looked at the weapon again truly it was a wonderful gift. "I can't take this," he said with a sigh.

"Why not? Of us three you have the best sword skill."

That might be true but even then, he did not consider himself to be a master swordsman. Indirectly he owed any skill to Roger Bishop of Salisbury. It was Roger who had decreed that his subject vassals be trained to a basic sergen standard. Not through any generosity of spirit but purely in the interest of self-preservation. Any fighting force that he might have to put together either for defence or intimidation would be a strong one. Ardron had undergone his training at Malmesbury Castle, and whilst there he had been befriended by a young Norman soldier, William Grugy. It was William who had taught him to speak French, and it was William, who through endless hours of practice had mentored Ardron's sword skills. Up to that point, Ardron had used a sword only to chop, slash or stab. In return, Ardron had tutored William in the use of the Saxon long bow. The disadvantage of the French crossbow was in the loading. The shaft needed to be placed beneath the feet in order to pull the string back over the latch, then the shorter arrow placed onto the breach. The Saxon long bow could fire three arrows to one by the Norman crossbow. During the time spent at the castle Ardron and William had become good friends, but soon after Ardron had completed the training and returned to Scorrenstone, William had been moved to the Castle Sarum.

Ardron brandished the sword around once more feeling the balance, truly it was a wonderful weapon. "This sword belongs to a warrior. I don't deserve it."

"Before this mission is over you might have to prove yourself to be a warrior," Swidhurn said

Ardron held the sword straight out before him and peered along its length. It was true and straight, its edge honed to a hair's width. "Swidhurn," he said coming to a decision. "I will take this, and with my grateful thanks, but when we return with the girls then you must take it back."

Swidhurn shrugged and replied with a non-committal. "We will see!"

Ardron sheathed the sword in his baldric and hoisted the harness over his shoulder then fastened it across his chest. With the broad sword safely slanted across his back, he was ready to go. He ripped the bandages from his head, deciding that they were not needed. Then each man picked up his own pack and went outside.

By this time, the morning had moved on towards noon, and in the bright sunlight a small party of well-wishers had gathered. Wolfstan stood at the head of the three readied horses, and then led his prized charger, Rattlebone, forward. He then held out the reins to Ardron.

"He's not the fastest, but he will still be galloping after the others have collapsed," he said. "Look after him and he'll look after you."

Feeling exalted, Ardron almost apologetically took the reins. His father then clasped him in a warm bear hug before turning to his youngest son. Then clasped him to his bosom also. He looked over the young man's shoulder and said to Ardron. "Look after this one too. Make sure you bring him home safely."

Each man loaded his pack across their horse's and mounted ready to leave. Ardron paused not knowing what to say, if anything. Then deciding that there was nothing to say he looked round to his two companions. They too were ready.

"God," Wolfstan now with arms raised offered a brief prayer to the heavens. "Look kindly on these thy envoys protect them and grant a favourable outcome to this righteous mission."

Ardron wheeled the big horse's head and spurred him forward. With the small crowd of villagers waving and shouting good luck wishes the search began.

Chapter 2

Melksham Royal Forest

At first his befuddled senses couldn't tell him where he was. The dampness around him and the strong smell of wood smoke only added to his confusion. Ardron opened his eyes to see tree canopies above him and rough grass beneath him. It took only a second for him to remember. They had travelled south from Scorrenstone passed to the west of Chippenham, crossed the Avon by the village of Lacock, and, when darkness had fallen, made their camp in the Royal Forest of Melksham. He sat up and looked around. His brother's blanket was empty, and Swidhurn crouched over a newly lit campfire which was smoking excessively.

"Where's Esmond?" he asked sleepily.

"Oh, so you're awake at last." Swidhurn said. "Esmond? He's out searching for breakfast."

Ardron yawned heavily and gingerly touched his stiff and swollen face. He got slowly to his feet and pulled his blanket tightly across his shoulders as shelter from the fresh morning air. "We have oats for porridge," he muttered.

"Aye we do. But he thought he might find some bird eggs or maybe some forest fruits."

Ardron sat down close to the smoking fire and watched the flames struggling to establish themselves. "I want to press on into Devizes as soon as we can," he said as much to himself as to Swidhurn.

"Seven or eight miles," Swidhurn muttered using a stick to poke the fire. "Do you think we'll find the girls there?"

Ardron shrugged, "Perhaps," he said. He was not optimistic, but he kept his own counsel.

"We don't even know who we are looking for."

"No," Ardron agreed. "Our only clue is that blue and grey quartered livery. Perhaps we'll get lucky. Or maybe we'll find somebody who knows that livery." He shrugged again with a degree of scepticism.

"Damn the Normans to hell. In fact hell-fire-damnation might be too good for those Normans that we seek," Swidhurn hissed bitterly.

Ardron did not reply, but silently agreed. Kidnappers, robbers and rapists they were for certain, but Saxons could not easily get justice in this Norman world. He looked beyond Swidhurn a few yards to the track that they hoped would lead to Devizes to see Esmond appear suddenly.

"Riders," he called running towards them. Then as he got nearer, "Norman riders coming this way," he pointed over his shoulder.

Both Ardron and Swidhurn were on their feet instantly. "How many?" Ardron asked.

"Six! Seven? I'm not sure."

Unsure of the situation, Ardron decided it would be better to avoid them, but then the smoking fire betrayed their presence. "Quickly, gather your belongings and hide in the brush." Hastily the pair gathered their piles under their arms, and then stumbled into the security of the bushes.

Ardron settled at the campfire placing his sword close to hand. He hoped to convince the riders that he was alone, and so glanced round to make sure there was nothing to suggest otherwise. Then he spotted the horses. He leapt to his feet, unhitched the reins and led them towards the bushes. Esmond realising the situation ran from cover and took the reins from Ardron.

"Make sure you keep them quiet." Ardron instructed. Almost before he had re-settled by the campfire the riders came into view. They were six, a knight, his squire and four sergens.

As soon as they saw the campfire and Ardron sitting by its side, they wheeled their horses off the track and came over to where he sat nonchalantly poking at the fire with a stick.

The knight at the head of the small party leaned forward over his horse's head and gently patted its neck. "What are you doing here, Saxon?" He asked.

"Just passing through bound for Devizes, Sir Knight."

"And no doubt stealing game while you are here."

"No Sir. I take nothing from the forest."

"Except, of course, the wood from which you made your fire."

Most certainly that was petty but Ardron had no answer.

The knight dismounted and walked over to Ardron. "What happened to your face?"

Self-consciously, Ardron touched the tender bruises. "A Norman's mace," he muttered.

For a moment, the knight stared at him, then deciding that it was of little consequence, said. "I am Baron Humphrey de Bohun of Trowbridge. This Forest and all the surrounding area are part of my Burbage from the king. So peasant," he raised his voice. "On your feet when I address you."

Ardron got to his feet. "I am sorry Baron I did not know. And I will happily pay for the wood I have used."

De Bohun studied him a moment, then his eyes fell on the sword by Ardron's foot. The sword was still in the scabbard, but the silver decorated hilt was clearly visible. "Is that your sword?"

"It is."

"Such a fine-looking sword, stolen no doubt."

"No Sir."

"If it is yours, then you should be able to use it. So, let us just see." He drew his own sword and held it two handed in the raised position. "Draw your sword, Saxon."

"Sir, I have no quarrel with you."

But he was belligerent. "Draw your sword, peasant, or as God is my witness, I'll carve you in two where you stand."

Reluctantly Ardron drew the sword. Slowly and almost lazily de Bohun brought his sword down first on Ardron's left and then on his right, which he parried easily. Then for a moment he held the sword pointing direct at Ardron, before making a thrust. Once again, Ardron easily deflected the sword point while moving clear.

De Bohun stood back a moment then said. "At least Saxon, you know how to defend yourself." Then he came in for another attack left right and left again, but this time at a much-increased speed. So much so that Ardron panicked slightly as he back peddled blocking and deflecting the attacks. But he was taken completely by surprise when the knight swung his sword at his head. He felt the blade brush through his hair, and he knew, that if he had wanted, de Bohun could have laid his sword across his neck. He was fighting for his very life against an accomplished swordsman.

In shock, Ardron paused for a moment and de Bohun dropped his guard. Ardron seized his chance leaping forward and thrusting at the unguarded chest. But de Bohun danced sideways and brought the flat of his sword across Ardron's back with a loud slap. He was being tormented like a mouse caught by a cat.

Ardron skipped clear and took refuge behind a tree. For a few seconds he managed to keep the tree between him and his tormentor, bobbing first one way and then the other. Eventually, however, he was forced back from the tree and had to leave its sanctuary. Once again, he was back-peddling and desperately fending off the Norman's attacks. De Bohun paused a moment arrogantly twirling his sword in front of Ardron's face, then he suddenly lunged forward. Ardron drew himself upright and turned sideways on, deflecting the sword to pass harmlessly by. Acting on instinct he spun round completely and found an exposed back in front of him, but he did not slice it open. Instead he used the flat of his sword to slap de Bohun's back.

There was absolute astonishment written all over the Norman's face when he turned once again to face Ardron. But he composed himself quickly and attacked with even more venom. Once again Ardron gave ground, hard pressed to keep the sword from his body. Then there was an opening but only for an instant. He raised his sword high and brought it down onto de Bohun. But de Bohun had dodged away and he found his sword being helped on its downward trajectory by de Bohun's sword. When the tip hit the ground, he found the other sword still forcing his downward, and it was ripped from his grasp. Now with the Norman's sword at his throat, Ardron moved slowly backwards until he felt his back against the tree. He could go no further. But he did not see his death in de Bohun's eyes, only a satisfied triumph. He realised that to the Norman it had been nothing more than an exercise.

"Hold off your arrows," he shouted in English.

"So Saxon you now plead for your life." Clearly, de Bohun spoke no English.

"No Sir, I do not," Ardron said in French.

"Nevertheless, you have it." de Bohun said after a short pause, then he withdrew his sword. "You were seconds from death, and you didn't plead for your life?" It was said sarcastically, as he slid his sword into its scabbard. Clearly, he didn't believe him.

"You can come out now," Ardron said in English once more.

From their hide in the bushes both Swidhurn and Esmond emerged with arrows strung in their bows. But the bows were now lowered. Instantly, the sergens kicked their horses forward to intercept the new threat to their Lord.

"Hold off there," de Bohun ordered his soldiers.

"So you see, Sir, you too were seconds from death." Ardron explained.

De Bohun shook his head ruefully and picked up Ardron's sword. "There is more to you Saxon than meets the eye," he said as he handed over the sword. "Tell me, I'm curious," he went on. "We both know that I could have slaughtered you at any time I liked. And yet through my own arrogance I gifted you a chance. A chance to save your very life! But you didn't take it! Why not?"

Ardron stared at the man for a moment, then after a shrug replied. "I don't know." And it was true he didn't.

"Where are you men from?"

"Scorrenstone."

"Scorrenstone?" de Bohun furrowed his brow in thought. "Isn't that somewhere near Malmesbury? You are a long way out of your stamping ground."

"Yes, Sir."

"And you journey on to Devizes?" More a question than a statement.

Ardron then went on to describe the circumstances that had placed them on this journey, while de Bohun listened intently.

"Renauld," he addressed his young squire. "Do we know this livery of blue and grey quarters?"

"No Sir." The squire slowly shook his head. "And yet," he suddenly brightened as an idea came to him. "There is the blue and silver of the Fleming, Robert Fitzhubert."

De Bohun looked at Ardron. "Could the livery have been blue and silver?"

Maybe it was, but he wasn't sure. He asked the question of Swidhurn and Esmond. Esmond confessed that he didn't actually see the colours, but Swidhurn also thought it could have been.

"Perhaps it was," Ardron replied.

"How about the knight's coat of arms? Did you see that?"

Ardron just stared back somewhat confused. "His coat of arms?"

"Yes the knights family crest. He would have had it on his shield."

Ardron cast his mind back to that morning, and in his mind eye he recalled the nonchalant knight sitting on his horse, and the way he lazily waved his arm forward given his men permission to start the rampage. His other arm was hidden behind the shield that he held. "Blue shield with three heraldic animals," he muttered.

De Bohun glanced at his squire.

"What sort of animals?" The squire questioned.

Ardron was at a loss. "I don't know."

"If they were rampant lions, then it was Robert Fitzhubert." The squire addressed his master.

Then Ardron remembered the sergen addressing the knight as Sir Robert. "I do believe his name was Sir Robert."

"It does sound rather like a deed that Fitzhubert would inflict on the helpless." De Bohun said. "He is a man completely without scruples." He added with more than a hint of contempt. Putting a leg in the stirrup he prepared to mount his horse. "Come to my castle at Trowbridge tonight. I will see you fed, and perhaps I can help with your search." When mounted he waited for Ardron's response.

"Thank you, Sir Humphrey. We would be grateful for any assistance you can give."

"Find my Constable, Sir Francis de Aumale, when you arrive. I'll tell him to expect you." De Bohun wheeled his horse, then as an after-thought looked back and said. "Saxon, you owe me a grout for the firewood."

***

Trowbridge

It was the first time Ardron had ever been to Trowbridge. They approached from the south, across common land, and entered a town which was situated upon a steep sloping bank overlooking the river, Biss. The shallow river bordered the south and west of the town, with the castle occupying the highest point. Of standard Norman design the castle consisted mote and bailey, with a man-made moat encircling the whole assembly.

The trio crossed the rustic bridge and entered through a large and deep portico. Inside the bailey was congested with bucolic constructed shelters, which doubled as workshops and living quarters. Towering above this confusion of disorder was the mote, with a stone-built keep atop of the man-made hill. An inner keep enclosed the mote top, as added protection for the keep.

"We need to find the constable," Ardron said.

"We need to stable the horses," Esmond muttered.

Ardron glanced at his young brother; clearly, he was still in bad humour. Esmond had disagreed with the plan to come to Trowbridge, instead he argued to press on to Devizes. "We are wasting time," he had said.

Ardron had overruled his opinion, presenting the counter argument that if the women were not there what would they do then? De Bohun was a better option he might be in a position to furnish more reliable information.

It was Swidhurn who smoothed the situation to a degree. He had placed a comforting arm around Esmond and spoke softly and sympathetically. "Esmond," he said. "I know what you fear for my sister, and I understand what you are feeling inside. This is now the third day since the girls were kidnapped, and I am afraid to tell you that what you fear the most for Hildi has, by now, almost certainly happened. You have to accept that. Our priority now is to rescue them both as soon as possible. Rushing blindly around the country will not be the quickest way." Esmond it seemed had grudgingly accepted that, nevertheless, it did nothing to lighten his pique.

But Esmond did have a point about the stable need for their horses. So Ardron dismounted handed over his reins to Swidhurn and left them to seek out the stabling, while he went in search of Francis de Aumale. Eventually he found him inside the keep.

"Yes," de Aumale said looking rather disgruntled. "I have been warned of your arrival." Clearly the man wasn't really pleased at having to accommodate Saxon's. "Sir Humphrey will see you this evening after dining. In the meantime, you can find yourselves a corner somewhere to bed down in the sergens quarters. And__," the next words almost gagged in his throat. "He says that this evening you may eat with the castle servants."

Ardron stared back at him somewhat nonplussed without speaking; he had no idea of Norman protocol.

"It means," de Aumale said with a hint of exasperation, "That you have been privileged. You will wait outside the great hall with the castle-servants until the masters have finished dining. When they have left, and only then, will you be allowed in to partake your fill from that which is left on the tables." Scrounging among the leftovers did not sound much of a privilege to Ardron, but he said nothing. "Be here at sunset," the Constable added curtly, then moved away to tend more important duties.

However, the scrounging among the leftovers turned out to be very opulent in comparison to the Saxon village way of life. The castle servants moved in an orderly fashion along the long table selectively choosing from an array of carefully prepared dishes. The three Saxons tagged, self-consciously, at the very end of the file and picked shyly at a lot of food they did not recognise.

It was early evening when de Aumale came to find Ardron. "Sir Humphrey will see you now," he said, and led the way to the Baron's private chamber in the upper reaches of the keep.

Inside the rotund room the Baron sat to one side of an inglenook fireplace with two Irish wolfhounds at his feet. On the opposite side of the fireplace, staring down hypnotically, into the dancing flames stood another Norman noble.

"The Saxon is here, Sir Humphrey," de Aumale announced.

De Bohun leaned back in his chair and waved Ardron over to where he sat. "This Miles," he said addressing the standing Norman. "Is the Saxon that I spoke of." The man looked over towards Ardron with only limited interest.

"This is Sir Miles Fitzwalter, Sheriff of Gloucester and Earl of Hereford," de Bohun informed Ardron. "He is also my father-in-law. Relate your story to him, Saxon."

Miles listened without comment as Ardron went briefly through the events again. When he had finished Miles looked towards de Bohun. "Could be Fitzhubert. Or then it could be any of the kings supporters," he said.

"Yes," de Bohun agreed as he got from his chair and moved to pour wine. However, the constable seeing his intention beat him to it and began to pour for him. "Pour four," de Bohun muttered. He then offered the first to Miles and the second to Ardron. When everybody was charged, he waited a moment then lifted the pewter in a toast. "To the Empress Maude," he said.

"Aye, may she soon arrive to claim her crown." Miles added.

Ardron sipped the wine and then struggled to control his expression as the gingered wine burned the back of his throat.

"This man you seek, what is your intention if you find him?" Miles asked.

Ardron shrugged. "First to rescue the two kidnapped girls and then, perhaps, to seek some sort of justice for his crimes."

Miles laughed out loud. "If it is Fitzhubert you seek there can be no justice other than that you wreak yourself, and I would say that you are ill equipped to that end."

"Nevertheless, there must be something that can be done. Even if we have to appeal to the king."

"The king?" Miles said with surprise. Then shaking his head moved to a seat and made himself comfortable. "Let me explain a few things, my young Saxon friend," he said.

"This king is finding his usurped crown to be something of a poisoned chalice. Rebellion and insurrection are everywhere. He has very little time to rule as a king should. Instead, he spends his time travelling around the country trying to put down insurrection. First the Scottish King David, who is the Empress Maude's uncle, invades the north so regularly that Stephen was forced into a bad treaty. In return for peace he gave away Cumbria to the scots king, and made his son, Henry, Lord of Carlisle and Doncaster and Earl of Huntingdon. He was forced into that because his army were needed at Exeter, where Sir Baldwin de Reviers, Earl of Devon, had seized Exeter castle. It took a three-month siege before the garrison eventually surrendered, and only then because Stephen promised them safe passage out of the country.

Meanwhile, Empress Maude and her husband, Geoffrey, were asserting her rights in Normandy by taking from Stephen the castles of Exemes, Domfort and Argentan. Stephen could not ignore the developing chaos in his Duchy. So he crossed the channel trying to re-occupy Argentan. While he was away the scots king broke the treaty and invaded England, pillaging Northumberland. Stephen was forced to return. And so to settle the Normandy disputes he bribed Geoffrey with 2000 Marks to betray his own wife and stay behind his own Angevin borders.

Stephen's army then met the Scots in Yorkshire. Although they won the battle, and in order to placate David's territorial ambitions, Stephen granted his son Henry a further Earldom. That of Northumberland. But then Stephen faced more revolts right here in the west, at Hereford, Shrewsbury and Harptree. He laid successful sieges to all those castles.

So you see, my young Saxon friend, this king has to keep an army at arms or at a state of readiness. That is expensive, and the probable reason why he seized control of his own treasury at Devizes. Now you can understand why his supporters can pillage freely at their leisure. They see it as part of their reward, and the king can hardly discipline them harshly for fear of losing their support. Instead he turns a blind eye to these excesses.

Now this man Robert Fitzhubert, he is a Flemish mercenary, and has a very powerful connection. His cousin is non-other than William de Ypres. And William de Ypres is the king's right hand. How then can Stephen discipline Fitzhubert without alienating de Ypres?" He shook his head slowly answering his own question. "There will be no retribution from the king, because Fitzhubert has the protection of de Ypres'"

Although he was aware that King Stephen travelled the country squashing rebellion, Ardron had not fully appreciated the politics that went with it. Nor had he concerned himself that much about it. It was a Norman problem, and a problem of their own making. It was only when their squabbling seeped down to affect the mundane existence of the Saxon proletariat was there any need to take interest.

"Even so," he said, "I must do what I can."

"Of course," de Bohun agreed. "The gallantry code of a knight demands that you do what you can to rescue your womenfolk. So from that aspect I applaud your venture."

'The gallantry code of a knight?' Ardron silently thought. 'It was a gallant Norman knight that kidnapped the girls.' His deadpan face gave away nothing of his thoughts.

"Even though you are not a Norman knight," de Bohun went on. "You display the same ideals." He glanced at Miles. "We may be able to locate Fitzhubert's whereabouts for you. If I do manage that, do you have a plan?"

"No Sir Humphrey. At this stage I do not. I shall have to wait and appraise the situation before I can do that."

"Of course," de Bohun agreed. He glanced at Miles. "Tomorrow morning," he went on, "Sir Miles will return to his castle at South Cerney."

"And on the way," Miles took over the conversation. "I will call in at Castle Combe before going on the Cerney. If I have any news of the whereabouts of Fitzhubert, I will despatch a rider back here with that information."

Ardron had just enough time to mutter his thanks before de Bohun continued. "And I will despatch a rider to the castles at Devizes and Ludgershall. Another will go to Sir Brien's castle at Wallingford and a third to Bristol. With that amount of spread there will surely be news of the whereabouts of this man."

It was extraordinarily gracious of these two men. Ardron knew that it would take many days for the Saxon trio to cover that amount of ground. "I have no words that can express my gratitude, Sir."

"Don't speak of it. Call it a debt paid because you did not slice open my back when you had the opportunity." De Bohun said. "But it could take a couple or three days for the messengers to return. So in the meantime stay in and around the castle to await any news."

***

It is the Roman Catholic Church that decides the appropriate time for Normans to take breakfast, and that is after the completion of morning mass. It is around mid-morning when everyone ceases activities to sit down and take a casual breakfast. Although the custom was alien to the three Saxon's they were, nevertheless, obliged to observe the ritual of their hosts. Sitting at a long trestle table among the castle sergens they picked frivolously at the unfamiliar fare before them. Ardron was pleased when breakfast ended, and he went immediately to the stables where he began to meticulously groom Rattlebone. To him it was a labour of love, and he talked endlessly to the big stallion as he worked.

"That is a very fine animal," de Bohun said.

So engrossed was Ardron that he hadn't seen the Baron approach. "Yes Sir, he is," he replied stopping to stroke the animal's nose.

The Baron stood back a pace or two and slowly walked around Rattlebone. "Hmm," he said. "Big and strong. He'd make a very fine charger, indeed. I don't suppose you want to sell him?"

"He's not for sale."

"I'd give you a very fair price."

"He's not mine to sell, and even if he were, I would never sell him. Would I, big fellow?" he addressed the horse as he affectionately patted its neck.

The baron was silent a moment then accepted Ardron's decision. "I came to inform you that the messengers have gone out and that Sir Miles left early this morning. So all that there is to do, is to await the returns. Meanwhile, Saxon, you have an exceptionally fine horse and a very fine sword too. But if you don't improve those sword skills someone will take them both from you. Get your sword, we have time for a lesson."

For over an hour they practised with the baron frequently stopping practise to criticise and to amend some of Ardron's faults. Ardron was a quick learner and he could feel his skills improve with the invaluable lessons being taught. At the end of the session de Bohun was guardedly complimentary about Ardron's ability.

"Where did you learn to wield a sword?" he asked as they walked back to the stable.

Ardron explained that it was part of the Bishop of Salisbury's tenancy condition that villages supply a number of fighting men, and that those men be trained to an effective standard. He then went on to explain how a befriended sergen at Malmesbury had given him extra tuition.

"You were well trained, and your abilities are above standard," de Bohun said as he made himself comfortable on a straw bale. Carefully he slid his sword into its scabbard. "You are young, quick and agile. I would say that you need only lots of practice to become a master with the sword. However, you may be lacking one important feature. You need to develop a ruthless streak. A killer instinct! You can dance around passing up many opportunities, but it will take only one mistake for your opponent to slash

30

you open. As it was with you and I, two days ago in the forest. I underestimated you, choosing only to torment and belittle you. But you didn't know that. As far as you were concerned you were in combat for your very life. And yet when your opportunity came you did not take it. If it had been for real, then I would have recovered from that to kill you off very quickly." He stood and gathered up his sword and scabbard. "Do you think you could kill a man in a sword fight?"

"If I was fighting for my life and there was enough anger in my heart, I think I could." He thought of Fitzhubert and decided that in his case he could, and very easily.

De Bohun stared at him thoughtfully contemplating Ardron's reply. "I could arrange for my sergen arms trainer to give you more sword lessons if you wish."

Ardron had no particular pressing engagement, and since he was obliged to await here for news, he gratefully accepted the offer.

Two days later and in possession of information, Ardron took his leave of Baron Humphrey de Bohun, and the three Saxon's left Trowbridge for Winchester. The messenger had returned yesterday with the news from the Ludgershall Castellan, Sir John Fitzgilbert, that Fitzhubert had passed across his estate bound for Winchester three days before.

"What's at Winchester?" Ardron had queried

De Bohun could only shrug and make a guess. "The king's brother, Henry, is Bishop there perhaps Fitzhubert was about the king's business."

But that was only speculation and of little consequence. Fitzhubert had gone on to Winchester and so the pursuit would be to Winchester. By late afternoon they had reached the village of Ludgershall, but they did not stop. Instead they passed to its north and entered the forest of Chute where they made camp for the night.

"Tomorrow, we should be in Winchester," Swidhurn said without taking his eyes from the pot bubbling on the campfire. "Do you have a plan?"

"Assuming Fitzhubert is still there," Esmond cut in tersely.

Ardron ignored his young brother. "No I don't. Not at this stage. I do know that we need to be very cautious about our enquiries, lest word should find its way to those we seek. T'would do us no good at all to pre-warn our quarry that he is being sought. But you are right, Esmond," He acknowledged his brother's remark. "We need first to establish that Fitzhubert is there. Then to establish that it is indeed he that we seek. If all is as we hope, then we need to find exactly where Hildi and Edyo are being kept. After that, maybe then we can make a plan."

Swidhurn reached for a wooden platter. "If we do manage a successful rescue do you think we will be pursued?" he asked as he spooned a helping of gruel onto the platter and handed it to Esmond.

31

"I don't know," Ardron replied rubbing his brow tiredly. "I wouldn't think so. After all the girls are probably no more than amusement to the kidnappers."

"But if they see them as possessions?" Esmond questioned.

"Then they probably would come after us," Ardron replied. "I don't have any answers." He went on somewhat exasperated. "We can only deal with the situation as it occurs."

"Yes," Swidhurn agreed sensing Ardron's pique. "Have some gruel," and he offered him a platter. "I have an idea that might help."

"I am open to any suggestions," Ardron said.

"On our arrival in Winchester, what if I set up as a travelling iron-worker touting for business? That would give us a good reason for being there, and with contact with the locals we can ask discreet questions."

"That is a smart plan," Ardron approved. "But do you have your tools with you?

"I have brought one or two basic tools in case a situation arose where I might need them."

"Will you have enough?"

Swidhurn nodded slowly. "I can manage."

"Then we have the first part of a plan. What say you Esmond?" Ardron sought his brothers input.

Esmond spread his arms. "It's the best we have."

The three fell silent each alone with his thoughts as they ate gruel.

It was Esmond who saw him first, quietly standing watching on the fringe of the clearing. He wore a brown knee length woollen shirt belted tightly at the waist. Beneath the shirt he had grey trouser that were cross gartered below the knee. His fair hair hung around his head untidily and partly covered his mud smeared face. There was no beard, for he was little more than a boy.

"We have a visitor," Esmond said quietly.

All three turned in the direction he indicated and stared at the boy. He just stood staring back making no movement.

"Are you hungry boy?" Ardron called. There was no indication that he had even heard.

Ardron held up his platter towards Swidhurn. "Put some gruel on here." Then he held it up and offered it towards the boy. "Come and eat." Still no movement. "Come," Ardron tried again. This time the boy moved nervously towards them. "Here sit," Ardron said when he was near. For a moment or two the boy hesitated then his hunger overcame his caution and he sat down taking the platter from Ardron and began to eat hungrily.

The trio glanced at each other but contained their curiosity while he ate. Then they began to talk amongst themselves ignoring the boy deliberately in order to settle any insecurity that he might be feeling.

32

"Where are you from?" it was Swidhurn who asked the first question.

"Ludgershall,"

"What's your name," Ardron asked.

"Adelfrid, Sir."

"Alright Adelfrid, you're among friends so relax."

"Ludgershall is not so far away," Swidhurn went on. "Why are you out here at this time?"

"I am on my way back. I have been to Newbury."

"Rather than travel on into the darkness you can stay here tonight. If you wish." Ardron invited.

"No sir. I cannot," he replied with some agitation. "I must get back to Ludgershall."

"What is it that is so urgent?" Esmond asked.

"My father's life!"

The remark was greeted with stunned silence. "Explain?" Ardron said.

Adelfrid bowed his head wiped his finger across the platter collecting the last of the gruel then licked his finger clean. When he looked up Ardron could see the tears that glistened in his eyes.

"My father works in the church at Ludgershall and has done for many years. His duties are as maintenance or grave-digger or even as a cleaner. Anything and everything the priest has a mind to task him. But two days ago my father was accused of stealing by the priest. And it's just not true. My father would never steal anything and most certainly not from God." His eyes appealed his father's innocence.

"Alright," Ardron calmed placing his hand gently on his shoulder. "What is he accused of stealing?"

"A gold chalice studded with diamonds,"

"Phew," Esmond whistled. "That is a very selective thief, for certain."

Adelfrid stared at him with some hostility.

"I didn't mean your father," Esmond added hastily. "I mean whoever that thief maybe. It sounds a valuable item."

"It was a gift from the Lady Aline to the church." Adelfrid explained.

"Lady Aline?" Ardron queried.

"Yes Lady Aline," Adelfrid said. "She is a very devout woman and often makes such gifts to the church. She is the wife of John Fitzgilbert and he as the King's Marshall is a rich man and he can indulge such excesses by his wife."

"When was the item stolen and why do they think that your father took it?" Swidhurn asked.

"When, no one knows for certain. It was the Lady Aline asking its whereabouts after it was not used during an Extreme Unction."

"Extreme Unction?" Esmond queried.

"The last rites," Ardron explained. "The chalice would be used to hold oil or holy water or something, and a priest uses it to anoint the sign of the cross on the gravely ill or newly deceased. Go on," he pressed Adelfrid.

"The priest organised a search of the churches treasures after he couldn't find it and concluded that it was stolen. My father has keys to the church and so he became the chief suspect. The priest made the accusation and demanded he be hung. Fitzgilbert, however, asked for proof. A search was made of our home and although they did not find the chalice, they did fine a silver frankincense boat which branded my father a thief."

"Where did the boat come from?"

Adelfrid shook his head bewildered. "I don't know. I don't believe my father is a thief."

"Could it have been deliberately put there?" Swidhurn asked.

"I think it must have been," Adelfrid replied. "Anyway, I don't think Fitzgilbert was entirely convinced and so he rejected calls for my father to be hung and offered him Wager of Battel. But that's not much of a chance because my father is an old man."

"What is Wager of Battel?" Esmond queried.

"Wager of Battel," Ardron explained, "Is trial by combat, the theory being that God will decide who is innocent."

"A priest cannot kill and so he cannot take part in a Wager of Battel," Adelfrid went on. "So he named a champion to take his place. He named Sir Albert Casteneau who is a renowned knight, and my father would have no chance against him even if God were on his side. Because the priest named a champion Fitzgilbert allowed my father to name a champion also. So I went immediately to Newbury to find my eldest brother and ask him to be father's champion. But he wasn't there and is believed to be in London. So either I or my father will have to fight this knight."

"When does this take place?" Ardron asked.

"Tomorrow at noon."

"Tomorrow?" Ardron leaned back and looked skywards lost in thought. It was a clear summer's night with millions of stars visible in the heavens. It mattered not what distresses and misfortunes befell people on earth, the stars had, and would ever, continue to twinkle in complete indifference. And why should the stars have concern at all since all the problems are inflicted upon human beings by human beings. "We are but fleas on the back of a stray dog and deserving no more consideration," he involuntarily muttered his thoughts.

"What was that?" Swidhurn asked.

"Nothing just thoughts." Ardron passed it off. "Adelfrid, what is your father's name?"

"Welfwulf."

Ardron nodded. "You must stay here tonight and get a good night's sleep," he said. "There will be time enough tomorrow for you to reach Ludgershall."

Long after the others slept Ardron continued to stare into the fading embers of the campfire. He could not be certain that Adelfrid's father had not taken the chalice, but it seemed most unlikely. After all if a lowly Saxon had stolen such a valuable piece what could he do with it? He couldn't sell it, except to a rich man. Even if he were to prise out the diamonds and melt down the gold there would still be questions to be answered when he tried to sell. Unless it was for community gain and therefore a shared profit. But then the man would have to be stupid to steal from the church where he held a key. Suspicion would most certainly fall upon him.

The next question in Ardron's mind came when he thought of the priest. Why had he not missed the chalice when performing Extreme Unction? It had taken a question from the Lady Aline for him to realise that he hadn't used the valuable chalice. Or perhaps it was that he didn't always use the best chalice. There were no answers to be found in the dying embers of a campfire he thought with a sigh.

"You intend to go to Ludgershall tomorrow don't you?"

Ardron looked up as Swidhurn made himself comfortable beside him at the fire. "Yes," he said.

"Why? This is no concern of yours and we have our own mission to concentrate on."

"You are right. But, nevertheless, I cannot in all conscience allow an innocent to hang while I do nothing."

"How do you know he's innocent?"

"Well I don't for certain. But common sense screams it is not probable that he is guilty. I will have to do my best to find out."

"Why bother? You don't know this man and there must be others much closer who should be doing something."

"It's the time we live in, isn't it? Life is valueless and in-particular Saxon life."

"You don't intend to be this man's champion surely." Ardron didn't answer because at this stage he didn't know what he intended. "You may be a fine swordsman, Swidhurn went on. "But there are many Norman's better than you, and plenty who are experienced at killing people. This Albert Casteneau is probably one of them."

"You talk so much sense Swidhurn, but my mind is made up. And for your peace of mind I don't intend to get involved in a Wager of Battel if I can help it."

Swidhurn shook his head dubiously. "And what of our mission?"

35

"I want you and Esmond to press on to Winchester tomorrow and proceed with your plan. If it is God's will, then I will join you within two or three days. If I don't turn up, then you must continue the rescue without me. And may God grant you success."

Swidhurn sighed heavily. "Give me your sword. Let me hone its edge."

***

There was still two hours before noon when Ardron rode into Ludgershall Castle with Adelfrid riding double behind him. They lost no time in finding the castle constable and explained their presence in the cause of Welfwulf. It was a further thirty minutes after that before they were brought into the presence of John Fitzgilbert.

Fitzgilbert stood quietly gazing from the window. He wore a short tunic of grey over a long tunic of blue. Over his left shoulder hung a red cloak fastened by a sizable silver brooch. His hand patted the head of a wolfhound which leaned affectionately against his leg. He turned his attention from the window view and silently appraised Ardron.

In the middle of the room a priest stood staring curiously at Ardron. His hands were linked across his middle resting on a sizable belly. He wore a brown cassock buttoned from neck to his sandaled feet. Perched on the back of his head, a small skull cap. He was not particularly old but would not see his fortieth year again. Next to him, a much taller and younger man, he was also dressed in a full-length tunic, but his, unlike Fitzgilbert's, was patterned in red and yellow squares. He regarded Ardron with the hint of a disdainful smile.

"Who are you?" Fitzgilbert asked.

"I am Ardron. A Saxon from the village of Scorrenstone."

"You're a long way from home, Saxon. Why are you here?"

"I am here to plead the case of Welfwulf."

Fitzgilbert sighed and moved away from the dog. "We are well passed that. Now we only require the Wager of Battel to prove or disprove his innocence. Are you here to be this man's champion?"

Ardron was on the spot. He was being sucked in to do battle for his life in the cause of a man who he had yet to see. But he did still have a plan. "If we have to resort to that then I will."

"We do have to resort to that, he replied." Then he turned his attention to his constable who had remained by the door. "Admit the old man," he said.

Moments later the constable returned leading a slight man of meagre physique, his arms and legs in chains. Ardron studied the man for whom he had set himself up as rescuer. Welfwulf was a man well into his fifties with wild unkempt hair and beard. His knee length shirt of green was old faded and grimy. He stared around the room with a confused air and it was only when he saw Adelfrid did the concerned expression leave his face.

"Old man," Fitzgilbert said. "This man has offered to be your champion. Do you accept him?"

Welfwulf looked even more confused. "What did he say?" he asked Adelfrid. Clearly his command of French was limited.

"Sir, I don't think his French is very good," Ardron said to Fitzgilbert.

"He," Fitzgilbert said pointing at Ardron, "Will be your champion." Do you accept him?"

"May I try, Sir John?" Ardron asked.

"Go ahead," he replied with a brief wave of an exasperated arm.

Ardron turned his attention to Welfwulf. "Welfwulf," he said in English. "I am here on your behalf to champion your cause if you will accept me."

"Why?" Welfwulf replied.

It was a good question and briefly Ardron asked himself the same question. "Because your son is convinced of your innocence and he has convinced me."

The old man shook his head dubiously. "You would risk your very life for a perfect stranger?"

Ardron looked around and glanced at the expressionless priest, he didn't like this fat pompous priest, and he made up his mind then that it was he who was probably the guilty person. He could see why he would want this old man blamed and then dead. It would put him in the clear.

"If you can't beat this man," Welfwulf nodded at Casteneau, "Then the outcome will be the same and you will also have died in a futile deed."

Ardron nodded agreement. "And yet," he said, "perhaps I have a way where no one need die today. "He accepts me," Ardron addressed Fitzgilbert pre-empting Welfwulf's answer.

"Then all that remains is for my constable to arrange it. I assume it will be a free choice of weapons."

"No Sir John," Ardron interrupted. "If it pleases you, I would specify the weapons to be used."

"For a moment Fitzgilbert was surprised. "Well that's not usual, but then as the accused it is your right."

"Then I choose turnips."

The statement was greeted in stony silence. Fitzgilbert recovered quickly. "Did you say turnips?"

"That I did!"

More surprised silence and then Fitzgilbert asked. "How will the combat be decided?"

"By a clean hit to the head from a thrown turnip,"

Fitzgilbert began to grin. "Then turnips it will be."

"Sir John. I protest." The priest objected. "It makes a mockery of the whole charge."

"Aye, that it does, and maybe it is fitting," Fitzgilbert replied.

From that remark Ardron surmised that he too was not convinced of Welfwulf's guilt.

"I too protest," Casteneau spoke up. "It would be unfitting for an esteemed Norman knight to be seen in combat throwing around turnips."

"Do you withdraw?" Fitzgilbert challenged.

Casteneau unsure of his position glanced at the priest.

"No we do not. We are convinced of the man's guilt. And I would see him hung for stealing from God's own house," the priest answered.

"Then it is settled," Fitzgilbert decided. "But, Saxon, do not think this Battel is any less serious, the man still forfeits his life should you lose."

"Yes Sir John."

Fitzgilbert turned his attention to his constable. "Benet, make the arrangements for noon." Then not directed at anyone in particular he said, "At least we should see some unique entertainment."

"What is happening?" A thoroughly confused Welfwulf asked.

Soon after noon the combatants and their supporters faced each other across a roped area just outside the castle bailey. Inside that roped area turnips had been scattered at random.

A carnival like atmosphere pervaded among the local spectators. Reports of the pending spectacle of combat by turnips had spread through the local townspeople, and with an atmosphere that belied the fact that a man's life depended upon the outcome, there was a clamour to watch. Ardron was also in good humour feeling that he would be much more relaxed about the absurdity of the combat than Casteneau, and this he saw as an advantage. Additionally this was a game in which he was not unfamiliar. During his adolescence years when helping to harvest the village's turnips, it was not unusual for this type of horseplay to develop among the youngsters. The elders had usually tolerated the idiocy of youth for a short time before putting an end to the fun. However, not in his wildest dreams had he ever envisaged playing this childish game with someone's life at stake.

"Combatants," the constable summoned both parties to face Sir John Fitzgilbert.

"Ardron wriggled the baldric from his back and handed the sword over to Adelfrid for safe keeping then walked over to face Fitzgilbert.

To afford a better view of the proceedings Fitzgilbert stood, with his wife Lady Aline, upon a dais raised three-foot above ground level. "Are you both prepared?" he asked.

"Sir John, I protest." Casteneau appealed. "It is just too humiliating for a renowned knight such as I to take part in such a farcical combat."

"Do you wish to withdraw?"

There was a moments silence while Casteneau considered his option then he replied sadly. "No Sir, I cannot."

"Then let the combat begin." Fitzgilbert said.

"One clean hit about the head with thrown turnip will decide the victor," the constable clarified the situation. "Go then to your seconds and when the fanfare ends the combat is begun."

It started cagily with both opponents picking up a couple of turnips then advancing cautiously towards each other, before and from a safe distance, hurling the turnips. From the distance they were thrown more in hope than any real hopes of scoring. After a couple of minutes of cautious circling and over-optimistic throwing, Ardron decided that it was time to get the bout started seriously. Armed with a turnip in both hands he charged at Casteneau. At first Casteneau stood his ground and then when he realised that Ardron intended to bear right down on him he tossed a turnip towards him then retreated rapidly. Ardron continued to close in on him and when close he threw the first turnip. It hit Casteneau on the back. The second was fended off with an arm. Ardron continued his run past the Norman then with a grin wheeled away to safety and picked up two more turnips.

Casteneau's long gown was proving a handicap to his mobility, while Ardron's pants, cross gartered below the knee, gave him no such handicap. Learning from Ardron's charge Casteneau tried the same tactics, except he spent his turnips too soon, and then realised that he was unarmed. He was almost face to face with Ardron who still had two turnips in his hands. He turned and retreated at a gallop with Ardron in pursuit. As he ran, he trod on his long gown which caused him to stumble. Deciding the best way to avoid that happening again he, lifted his gown, and ran like a noble lady. That sparked jeering and laughter from the spectators. With Ardron close behind Casteneau then made the mistake of taking a second to pick up another turnip. But before he had straightened Ardron was on him, and with a well-placed foot in the Norman's backside gave him a hefty shove.

Casteneau tumbled forward, but managed to find a leg, and then another, to keep him on his feet. But he stumbled uncontrollably. It was to no avail as Ardron barged into him knocking him to the floor. Casteneau then started a desperate scramble to get away on all fours. He glanced up to see Ardron poised over him with a raised turnip. He raised an elbow and successfully defended his head, but in a flash Ardron leapt over him and threw the other turnip from the other side. It struck Casteneau on the back of his head.

"A clean hit." The constable decided, and the contest was ended quickly.

Ardron's victory was greeted by cheering from a high-spirited the crowd. Briefly he acknowledged their praise and then turned to offer an assisting hand to Casteneau who was still on the ground. But scowling bad temperedly, Casteneau knocked it away and rolled clear before getting to his feet.

It mattered not; the contest was over. Welfwulf's innocence was proved. He would not hang. Ardron made his way back towards Adelfrid waving and grinning to the applauding crowd. He was greeted with huge grins and back slapping from both Welfwulf and Adelfrid. Both had good reason to celebrate. The crowds cheering died away quickly and turned to shouts of alarm.

"Look out," Adelfrid said.

Ardron glanced over his shoulder to see Casteneau bearing down on him with a raised sword. He skipped sideways snatching his own sword from its baldric as he did. Just in time he turned to see Casteneau's raised sword crashing down towards his head. He managed to raise his own sword into a defensive position, but the downward momentum of the blow forced his arm down. He had just enough strength, however, to keep the sword from his head. Casteneau raised his sword again and repeated the forceful downward chop. This time it was parried more easily. When the same chop was tried a third time Casteneau found that Ardron had skipped away to his left, and his sword slashed through fresh air, until the point hit the ground. Ardron swung his own sword horizontally waist high, catching Casteneau across both his downward pointing arms. Then he pulled the sword back towards himself inflicting deep slashes across both of the Norman's arms.

"Put up your swords or by God's Holy Commandments I'll hang the pair of you," Fitzgilbert threatened in a raised voice. In double quick time he had crossed from the dais to confront the waring pair.

Ardron stepped well back and lowered his sword, while Casteneau looked down in disbelief at the quickly spreading red stains of blood on the sleeves of his tunic.

Fitzgilbert summoned the priest to his side with an arm wave. "Take your man and get his wounds dressed," he said. The jeering and cheering crowd did nothing to ease Casteneau's pique as was led away.

"Wager by Battel has proved this man's innocence," Fitzgilbert now addressed his constable, Benet. "Take this man and have his shackles removed. Then you can let him go."

"As for you my Saxon friend you have proved that not only are you deviously clever, but that you can be a capable adversary in a sword fight. I have need of men like you in my sergenti. I pay well and a post is yours if you want it."

"Thank you, Sir John. But I have no desire to become a Norman soldier, and I also have a private mission of my own to complete."

"You should think carefully?" Fitzgilbert said. "The Empress Maude may come to claim her crown any day now, and then there will be war. Shamefully it may be, but in war there are fortunes to be made by shrewd fighting men such as you."

Ardron moved over to where Adelfrid held his scabbard. "If war does come," he said looking over his shoulder. "Then it will be a Norman war, and nothing to do with Saxons. What care we which Norman rules England?"

Fitzgilbert shook his head slowly. "But there you are very much mistaken. For those who do not choose a side then dangers are doubled. Neutrals will find that they have not one, but two enemies. Worse still, there will be no one who has the inclination to protect them."

Ardron slid his sword in the baldric and turned to face Fitzgilbert. "Perhaps," he allowed. "But then, Sir John, you could be wrong. In any case I feel I have to refuse your offer. But I do thank you."

Fitzgilbert shrugged. "I'm sorry too. But if you should change your mind the offer remains open."

***

It was at Welfwulf's request that Ardron spend that night in his shanty dwelling, and not to reject the old man's hospitality, he had agreed. The fare provided was modest, consisting nothing more than mashed rye in milk and stale bread. But it was only typical, and was no more than Ardron expected, in an impoverished Saxon dwelling.

"Eleven years I have worked for that fat priest," Welfwulf said as he bit off a huge chunk of bread. "Everything he asked of me I did, and without complaint. Welfwulf this, Welfwulf that, work harder Welfwulf. Long hours and all for a mere pittance," he went on talking through a full mouth. "While he lived in luxury surrounded by the treasures that were generously donated by the wealthy to God. Donated to God!" he scoffed. "What use has God for gold or silver? Was it not he who made it all?"

"I suppose it was," Ardron non-commitally agreed.

"Could he not make more if he so desired?" The question was rhetorical and not requiring an answer. "No!" Welfwulf went on shaking his head, ruefully. "All those clerics dressed in the finest cloth, gold rings on their fingers, gold chains round their neck. They sit behind great oak tables with the finest meals placed before them, drinking fine wine from silver goblets. It is they, and only they, who benefit from rich donations. And what of these donations? Not just the rich, even the poor donate. Except in the case of the poor it is only grouts, but those grouts are missed more keenly than a wealthy man's gold. Why do it?" Again, it was a rhetorical question. "All are just trying to bribe themselves a place in heaven for when their day comes. And the priests." He scoffed noisily through his teeth. "They take it all, grout or gold they grasp it and use it all for their own living comfort."

"A great deal of what you say old man may be true," Ardron sought to end Welfwulf's radicle rhetoric. "But it is the way of things."

"Aye, it is," Welfwulf said wistfully. "One day the down-trodden will rise."

"Perhaps," Ardron allowed tired of his tirade. "It has been an eventful day and tomorrow I have far to go. So perhaps if you could show me where I can lay my head till morn."

"Of course," Welfwulf said. "Adelfrid show our guest where he can sleep."

Early the next morning the three of them prepared to leave. Welfwulf had reasoned that he would no longer be welcome as the church caretaker, and therefore it was perhaps time for him to move away from Ludgershall. Newbury was his obvious destination since that was where his eldest son lived.

It had rained during the night. But now as they set off the morning sun and clear skies promised a fine day. Welfwulf did not possess a horse, and so they set off travelling directly east at a steady walk, with Ardron leading Rattlebone. The meagre belongings of Welfwulf and Adelfrid were tied up in untidy bundles, which Ardron had loaded across his horse's back. Little over an hour later they arrived at a road junction. The milepost indicated the road north-east to Newbury and the road south-east to Andover. It was the parting of the ways.

As Ardron loosed the two packs from the horse's back Welfwulf once again extolled his everlasting gratitude to Ardron. His gratitude, although completely understandable, nevertheless embarrassed Ardron, and again he tried to make light of the deed. He leaned his arm over Rattlebone's back as he watched Welfwulf and Adelfrid tote their loads onto their backs

"God only knows the amount of debt I owe to you. I would not be alive this day except by your involvement." Welfwulf went on. Then he offered his hand to be shaken. As Ardron took the hand Welfwulf wrapped it in both hands. "May God protect you and those you love," he said as he pressed something into Ardron's hand. Then he turned, adjusted the load onto his back and began to walk after Adelfrid.

Ardron looked down into the palm of his hand and there, clear as a mountain stream and glistening in the morning sun, was a large diamond.

***

The clear skies had gone, and it was raining hard by the time Ardron reached Wherwell. Earlier he had skirted the small settlement of Andover and continued south. But it wasn't raining then, and by now, thoroughly soaked, he regretted that he did not seek some hospitality there. Just ahead of him and nestling in the wooded area he could see the Abbey and the Priory. Encased within the wooden ramparts the priory looked more like a fortification than housing for nuns. Surely the nuns would not refuse him shelter. He approached the wooden gates and dismounted. They were closed and well secured, but close by a bell hung from a wooden bracket. He took the rope and rang the bell several times then waited. Patiently he waited but after a little while and no one had responded he rang the bell again. Almost instantly a small shutter in the gate was slid back and a wrinkle faced nun peered out at him.

"Who rings the bell?"

"I do sister. Ardron of Scorrenstone."

"What do you want?"

"A dry corner somewhere within," Ardron said.

"Go away young man, this priory is home to Benedictine nuns. Men are not allowed in."

"I am sorry sister I did not know. But perhaps you could send me to shelter close by."

She did not reply, instead slid the shutter back leaving Ardron confused. He waited a short while then assumed that he had been rudely dismissed. He was preparing to mount his horse when the shutter was opened again.

"Young man." This time a different nun.

"Yes sister."

"Around the corner to your right there is a side door into the Abbey. You may rest in there for tonight."

The Abbey was expansive, constructed of stone with a tower and a belfry. He slid his pack from Rattlebone and turned him loose to find his own shelter. Then inside the Abbey, he draped his wet effects across the seats to dry. He paid his respects at the altar then removed his wet clothing and wrapped himself in a boar skin cloak. Less than ten miles from Winchester; he should be there early tomorrow morning, he concluded.

He had never been to Winchester, but the story tellers had many times told him of the legend that was the great Saxon King, Alfred. He had made Winchester his stronghold by destroying the Roman constructions and re-designing the town as a fortification. This enabled him first to hold the marauding Danes and then gradually push them all the way back to London. But that was some two hundred and forty years ago, and he wondered just how much of Alfred's influence remained, if any. Tomorrow he might find out.

To pass the time he examined the diamond that Welfwolf had deviously thrust into his hand. Even in the gathering gloom of the abbey, there was still a sparkle to the stone. He turned it several times examining it from different angles and its glister never lessened. Ardron was a complete novice in the world of precious gems and curiosity made him wonder how much this little sparkling bauble was worth. Next, he contemplated if he should drop it in the church collection box. After all it had been stolen from the church and in all conscience it ought to be returned. But then, he agreed with Welfwulf's rhetoric, such donations by the rich were only an attempt to buy a place into heaven. In the final analysis, Ardron decided, valuable donations would not counterbalance any evils performed. God did not benefit from such gifts. He had no need of baubles. That reasoned, he decided to keep the diamond and slipped it back into his purse.

Bored, he got to his feet and began to investigate around the Abbey. It was expansive with stone pillars supporting the high roof. The roof itself made entirely from wood used collar beams with secondary rafters in positions of support. He walked the length of the Abbey towards the altar, where just off to the side a small but stoutly made door caught his attention. The door of thick oak, banded and studded with stout iron strengtheners, was held shut by a heavy iron bolt. Unable to contain his curiosity he, after glancing over his shoulder to be sure he was alone, pulled the bolt back. The door creaked loudly as he pulled it open. Well-worn stone steps descended into cellars and immediately a stale damp smell came up from the darkness. Cautiously he made his way down into the blackness. When his eyes eventually became accustomed to the dark, he found himself in a burial chamber with several tombs hollowed into the very walls. Not a cheerful place to spend time. His curiosity satisfied, he left the dead to their eternal slumbers. After re-shutting and bolting the door he walked back to where he had spread his wet clothing, dusting his hands as he did.

Almost immediately two nuns entered the abbey. Their face-frames and wide collars of white contrasted vividly with their long black habits and wimples. The only recourse to any female decoration was the large crucifixes hanging on long gold chains about their necks. They glided as ghosts down the aisle towards him their sandals treading softly on the chapel floor. Ardron not at all sure what the polite procedure ought to be got to his feet and briefly bowed his head.

"Mother Superior bids we provide you with sustenance. She asks only that you treat this place with the reverence it deserves, and that you be gone tomorrow, early." One of the nuns said. Meanwhile the other laid down the tray on a nearby seat.

"Thank you, sisters," Ardron muttered. "It is my intention to move on early." The nun only nodded and as deftly as they had arrived, the pair left.

He turned his attention to the food. Strips of cheese, a piece of bread and a small jug of milk, the fare was modest, but even so, gratefully received.

***

Winchester was a walled town. Masses of bucolic dwellings thronged both inside and outside its walls. Inside its precincts the modern built Cathedral dominated, but was challenged, to a lesser extent, by the nearby Bishop's Citadel of Wolvesey Castle. Over to the east Winchester Castle was not so grand as either building, but nevertheless, still an imposing structure. Of Alfred's old fortifications little remained. Ardron made his way into a town of short narrow streets between a mixture of stone-built houses and others constructed of plastered wattled walls with straw roofs. The streets were muddied, with the stench of fetid water in the air. As he pondered how he might find Esmond and Swidhurn in this crowded maze, a woman emerged from one of the bucolic houses. She without any undue disinclination, poured a pitcher of slops into the ditch dug as an intended drain alongside the road. Her task complete she paused and stared curiously up at Ardron.

"Mother," Ardron said. "Can you tell me where I might find an iron-worker who could shoe my horse?" In truth there was nothing wrong with the horse's shoe, but she might direct him to Swidhurn, if he had managed to set himself up.

"Onwards onwards," she replied with a wave of her arm. However, it turned out to be the town's ironworker and not what Ardron had hoped. He travelled past and through the town exiting by the southern gate.

Not sure what to do next he reigned in Rattlebone and leaned forward onto the horses neck. Then he heard his name called. Swidhurn perhaps a hundred yards away called again and waved. With a degree of relief he turned the big horse's head and went over to the rough makeshift camp.

Swidhurn greeted him with a huge grin. "We had some doubts that we would ever see you again," he said.

"Well I am here now." Ardron replied.

"You certainly are and what a sight for tired eyes you are. What happened back there?"

"Little of consequence, save to say Adelfrid and his father are alive and fine. By now they should be in Newbury."

Swidhurn indicated that he should sit by the campfire with a wave of his arm. "What news?" Ardron asked. Then changed his mind about sitting by the fire, the day was too warm.

"An iron-worker must have a forge," Swidhurn said seeing his discomfort. Ardron nodded, it was, of course, all in the cause of credibility.

"What news? Well__," Swidhurn went on. "Edyo is here, Esmond has seen her working chores at the Bishop's Citadel, but she hasn't seen us yet.

"Good news!" Ardron said. "What of Hildi?"

"Hildi, we don't know yet. Esmond did not see her. He is out there now watching the castle for any sign."

"What of Fitzhubert?"

"Fitzhubert? It seems he and his Flemings left before we arrived, possibly bound for Oxford."

"Then we don't need to concern ourselves about being recognised. We can give up this charade of a travelling ironworker. But for now we need to establish the whereabouts of Hildi.

"There is a problem," Swidhurn said warily. "Esmond noticed that Edyo has a slaves shackle around her neck. Probably means that Fitzhubert sold the girl into slavery."

"In the Bishop's Citadel? Surely the Bishop is a man of God and would never allow slaves under his roof." Ardron petitioned.

"This man of God," Swidhurn said disdainfully. "Is King Stephen's brother. And, from that which I have learned in the short time I have been here, is something of a despot. A despot who craves power and wealth above all things. Oh yes, I fully believe that he would keep slaves."

Ardron groaned and then sighed. "Then we will have to carry out a rescue,"

"Runaway slaves are hanged when they are caught." Swidhurn pointed out. "Perhaps we should try and buy her freedom."

"It's a dilemma," Ardron agreed. "But if we don't have enough money, or if the Bishop is reluctant to let her go, then it will be much harder to make the rescue. And what of Hildi? If she is a slave too then we have a double problem." He looked up at the sun, it was nearing noon. "When Esmond returns, we will go to the citadel and see what plan we can muster."

The Bishops Citadel of Wolvesey was a complex of solid built buildings. Consisting flint facia over a core of chalk and surrounded on three sides by a similar built wall. The wall's quadrant was completed by the back of the tallest of the buildings. Only by peering through the gate by the gatehouse could the inner precincts be seen.

"It was over there, Esmond said pointing through the gate. "Edyo came out of the building carrying a big basket and she emptied it into one of those barrels. I think it was food slops."

"Why food slops?" Ardron asked.

"Because earlier today I saw two men drive a cart through the gate and take the barrel leaving a fresh one in its place. Then from curiosity I followed them out of the town to a pig pen."

"What part of the day did you see Edyo?" Ardron asked.

"Evening."

"After the main meal," Ardron muttered thoughtfully. "And the slops were picked up in the morning?"

"Yes."

Ardron nodded in approval. "Well done little brother," he said.

"Do you have a plan?" Swidhurn questioned.

"Maybe, but we mustn't hang about here too long in case somebody gets suspicious. Somebody needs to be here this evening to see if Edyo empties the slops every night around the same time."

"I'll do it," Esmond volunteered.

"No I'll do it," Ardron said placing his hand on his brother's shoulder. "You have hung about Wolvesey a lot. Better you keep away for a while." Then he turned to Swidhurn. "Swidhurn I want you to come here tomorrow morning and see if the slops are collected daily." He stared through the gate pensively. "We still need to find out if Hildi is in there," he mumbled.

Later in the evening Ardron returned and waited in the narrow street opposite the main gate, trying to be as inconspicuous as possible while willing Edyo to appear. As he waited a horse drawn cart approached the gate. The cart was well loaded with vegetables. 'It is no different here to anywhere else,' Ardron mused to himself; 'The Saxon has to pay tribute to the Norman masters so that he may use the land that belonged to his ancestors.' But he recognised this cart as a God sent opportune gift. He walked up on the blind side and casually held onto the cart as it was stopped at the gate. Then gave the guard a nonchalant nod acting as if he were part of the delivery, as the man walked around the cart on his inspection. Still holding on he walked in with the cart as it was admitted into the courtyard. Once inside, after a brief glance round to make sure he wasn't observed, he sprinted across to the row of barrels and hid.

Hidden among the rubbish time passed slowly. Two servants did visit the barrels to dump waste, but neither were Edyo and so Ardron stayed hidden. Evening was pressing on and Ardron began to fear that this night Edyo would not be tasked to throw out the slops. When she did come, he almost missed her as he relaxed into cat napping to pass the time. It was only the thump of the basket on the barrel edge that roused him.

"Edyo," he whispered making the young girl leap back in alarm. Fearing that she might give him away he showed himself briefly before slipping back under cover. "It's me, Ardron."

Slowly she approached the barrels again. "Ardron, is that really you?"

"Yes. We have come to take you home."

For a moment, her face lit with excitement then was instantly replaced with anxiety. "You should go," she said.

She must have misunderstood, he thought. "We are here to take you home," he repeated.

"I can't go." She whispered shaking her head.

"Why?"

"I have been made a slave."

"Once away from here and back in Scorrenstone you will be free once more."

"No."

"Why," Ardron waited patiently for her answer.

"Because I have been shamed," she muttered eventually. "I could never face my father or the rest of the villagers."

Ardron understood her meaning. "It's not your fault. All will understand."

She shook her head.

"Do you wish to be a slave for the rest of your life?" Ardron tried a harder approach.

"No!"

"Then let us get you away from here and then we will decide what is to be done."

Edyo thought for a moment then nodded silent agreement.

"Good," Ardron was relieved. "What of Hildi? Is she here?"

"No, she is still with the Flemings."

Ardron groaned, it was a body blow. "Do you know where they went?"

Edyo shook her head.

"Alright," Ardron said. "The cart that collects the waste barrels, does it come every day?

"Not every day, but most."

Ardron was thoughtful a moment. "Watch carefully for it each day. On the day you see the horse sporting a cloth hanging from its collar, make an excuse to come here. Can you do that?"

"I can try," she said.

"Try hard. Leave the rest to me. Now you had better go before somebody gets curious about your delay here."

She picked up her basket and turned to go.

"Be of good cheer Edyo. Soon you will be free." Ardron whispered as he slipped back deep into his hiding space. Now he could cat-nap, that was all there was to do until the darkness was at its deepest.

It was after midnight and the grounds of the castle were silent and deserted when Ardron emerged from his hiding place. In the shadows he carefully stole along the wall until he found a suitable place to climb. Carefully and quietly he climbed up onto the top, then a leap down the other side into a deserted street and he was clear. Now he could breathe a little easier. He was well satisfied with what he had accomplished. When he reached their camp outside the town both Swidhurn and Esmond were sleeping soundly in their blankets. No need to wake them his news would keep until the morning.

***

Two mornings later, and early, Ardron, Esmond and Swidhurn rode into the pig man's compound. They arrived at speed and dismounted in a hurry. Esmond then took charge of the horses while Ardron and Swidhurn burst into the rustic lodge that was the man's home. Taken completely by surprise the astonished pig man stared up at the intruders from a seated position. Then galvanised into action he scrambled to his feet and moved to grab a sword hanging on the wall. But Ardron was quicker and pressed his sword against the man's neck before he could reach it.

"No need for that," Ardron said.

The man's wife now took a hand. From her position kneeling by the fire trough she grabbed at the pitcher at the fireside and hurled hot water at Ardron. He was forced to leap back to avoid being scolded giving the pig man chance to grab his sword. However, before he could wield it into position Swidhurn felled him with a powerful punch to the side of his head. Instantly the young man who had been sitting at the back of the room lunged at Ardron with a knife. He could have easily cut down the youngster with his sword, but instead he leapt clear and hit him at the back of the head with the butt end of the hilt.

"Everybody stand still," Ardron shouted. "Nobody needs to be hurt here today."

It was effective, everybody stood frozen in their positions. To show goodwill Ardron lowered his sword and helped the young man back to his feet. "As long as everyone does as they are told then there is nothing to fear. Two hours from now we will be gone, and no-one will have been hurt." He paused a moment then to the pig man said. "Neither will you be any worse off than you are at this moment. We are not here to rob."

"Then why are you here?" the pig man demanded.

"Sit down, Ardron said indicating the stool from which the man had leapt. "We are here to borrow your cart and make the citadel pig swill collection for you."

The pig man sat on the stool holding the side of his face and glaring at Swidhurn as he did. "Why?" he demanded.

"The why, you need not know." He paused a moment. "I am going to take your cart and I'm going to take this young man with me. While I am away my comrade here," he indicated Swidhurn, "Will remain here to make sure you don't do anything stupid." He waited to allow a moment's thought. "If everybody behaves, and all goes as I expect, I will soon be back with your cart, the swill, and this young man all undamaged." He placed his hand on the youngsters shoulder as a re-assuring gesture. "And then we will be gone." Satisfied that his instructions were clear he squeezed the shoulder of the youngster. "What's your name?" he asked.

"Borden."

"Borden, you go and hitch your horse to the cart. And__," as he moved to go. "You will find another of us outside. He will stay with you to make sure you don't get other ideas."

Leaning against the wall Ardron spotted an upright wooden loom with a half-finished cloth of bright green still attached. It was bright and ideal for the signal purpose. "There is one thing I will take from you," he said to the woman. "That piece of cloth."

Thirty minutes later Ardron and Borden set off for Wolvesey Castle with Borden on the reins. When they reached the gate the guard came to greet them. He stared up at Ardron with some curiosity. "Where's your father, this morning?" he asked in French.

Bordon looked confused.

"Ton Pere, ton Pere," he asked again irritated.

"Ah," Borden understood. Then he made a retching and heaving action.

"The guard understood. "Who's this?" he asked nodding at Ardron.

Again Borden didn't understand. "He wants to know who I am." Ardron said. "I am his uncle," he answered for him in French. The guard stared at him a moment then stood back to allow entry.

Once inside and alongside the waste barrels Ardron went to the horse and hitched the green cloth higher up the horse's collar hoping that Edyo was watching. Borden leapt unto the cart to roll off an empty barrel. "Slowly, slowly," Ardron instructed trying to allow maximum time for Edyo to respond.

Even though they worked slowly the empty barrel was off and the full one loaded, and still there was no sign of Edyo. Ardron fiddled with the horse's tackle prolonging things for as long as he could. He had begun to despair and was already making plans for a repeat trip tomorrow when she appeared coming towards them carrying a wide basket of kitchen waste.

With the cart and horse strategically placed as a screen he guided her to the empty barrel that they had just unloaded. He lifted the lid and indicated for her to get in. Unceremoniously, she was bundled into the barrel, and not wanting to leave any evidence behind Ardron tossed the basket in after her. Despite the situation the kitchen waste made her spit with some distaste. Then with the grinning Borden's help they manhandled the barrel back onto the cart.

"Let's go," Ardron said brusquely, but this time he took the reins, just in case.

Ardron drove the cart with a little more urgency through the town streets, but not as much as would have caused curiosity. Soon they were back at the pig farm and this time much more hurriedly, they mounted their horses, and with Edyo double mounted with Ardron they headed directly south away from Winchester. But as soon as the pig farm was out of sight they swung directly west. Ardron reasoned that if a search for Edyo was begun and the pursuers did find their way to the pig man then he would probably tell all, including the direction they had taken. There was no reason why he wouldn't. His hope was that any mounted pursuit would continue south, perhaps as far as Hamtun. But then for one kitchen slave perhaps they wouldn't even bother.

Nevertheless, anxious to put distance between themselves and Winchester, just in case, Ardron forced the pace. They alternated the horses between an easy canter and then a walk. After an hour at this rate they angled a little more northerly in order to bypass Salisbury.

They made their way across open expanses of plain, and by late afternoon were confronted by the river Avon. Not sure where they would find a bridge or a ford, they followed the river north until they entered a wide valley. Here the river diminished itself by dividing several times and forming a series of shallow brooks. By this time feeling quite secure Ardron decided that it was a good place to stop. There was plentiful lush grass on which the horses could feed, and several good stands of trees to make shelter for a camp. Crossing the Avon here did not present a problem either.

Ardron and Esmond set to work establishing a camp while Swidhurn removed the heavy shackle from Edyo's neck. "There," he said as he tossed it into the brambles, "Now you can consider yourself truly free."

With each passing mile it had been noticeable that Edyo's spirits had improved. She had looked back regularly expecting to see pursuers, but as the distance from Winchester increased and pursuers did not appear, she had become less tense.

As the light began to fade, an abundance of rabbits, completely unafraid and oblivious to humankind, grazed contentedly close by. Having no idea on whose land they were now camped the temptation to poach a couple was irresistible, and Esmond's arrows bagged two. There still remained the plight of Hildi, and as they sat around the fire eating the roasted meat Ardron broached the subject of Edyo's intention.

"Edyo, is it still your intention not to return to Scorrenstone?"

"Of course she wants to return to Scorrenstone," Esmond cut in." Ardron had not mentioned Edyo's dread to the other two.

"I don't know," Edyo replied. Her previous determination wavering.

"Your family will be greatly saddened if you do not." Ardron said.

"What will the rest of the village say of me?"

"They will be happy that you have been returned to where you belong. Blame for what has happened will not be laid at your feet."

She was thoughtfully silent. So Ardron took the initiative. "Then we will see you delivered," he said. "If you should find that things are not to your liking, then, when you are a little older you can leave on your own accord."

That now settled, Ardron delivered his new intentions. "One of us," he said, "Must deliver Edyo back to Scorrenstone whilst the other two continue with the search for Hildi." His comment was greeted in silence.

"I'm not the one going back," Esmond's pronouncement broke the silence.

Ardron ignored him while he selected his words carefully. "Swidhurn, I'm sorry it has to be you." He was genuinely sorry for he would have preferred to keep Swidhurn's strength at his side. "There is no way of knowing just how long this quest will take, and Scorrenstone has need of your iron work skills."

Swidhurn's disappointment was marked but after a thoughtful moment he nodded agreement. "What will you do?" he asked.

"Esmond and I will go to Oxford and try and pick up Fitzhubert's trail from there."

"Where do you think we are?" Swidhurn asked.

"I think we are probably some twenty-five miles from Devizes. Tomorrow if you cross the river and head northly you should soon see sign. We will not cross but will instead head north-east for Newbury and then on to Oxford."

"And if Fitzhubert is not there?" Esmond asked.

Ardron shrugged. "Then we will seek him elsewhere. London perhaps!" he added as an after-thought.

Chapter 3

Ardron strolled briskly down the narrow street, taking care to avoid as much of the street filth as he could. He had not yet seen Esmond since he left him sleeping this morning, but he knew exactly where he would be found. Today there was purpose in his step. For the first time in a month he had hopes that they might be able to gain some direction to their search.

After leaving Swidhurn and Edyo on Salisbury Plain, he and Esmond had journeyed on to Oxford, but once again they had been too late. Fitzhubert's stay had been fleeting and he had soon moved on. Neither was it easy to establish where he had gone, the trail was cold. Acting on a suggestion only, they travelled north and on to Banbury. But, Fitzhubert had not been seen there and so they turned east to Buckingham, with the same result. At this point an acute shortage of funds forced Ardron to sell the diamond. Well aware that he as a humble Saxon had sold a valuable diamond, he had deemed it sound discretion to move on quickly.

Despite being a noble within the king's echelon, Fitzhubert had not been granted estates or castles in England, and because of this he had no particular base. It was, therefore, complete speculation as to where he would turn up next. So, with no particular strategy Ardron had estimated that sooner or later the man would turn up at the king's court. So, he and Esmond moved on to London to wait. But that had been almost two months ago, and with the passing of time Esmond's hopes that he could recover his bride to be, had all but withered and died. Those hopes had been replaced with hopeless disappointment and smouldering anger. Inactivity brought boredom, and boredom only propagated his dark moods. In the earlier days Ardron had tried to combat the frustrations of waiting by using weapon practice with his brother. With the sword Ardron's skill bettered Esmond every time, but nevertheless, Esmond's own skill had benefitted greatly from the practice. However, with the bow the differences between the brothers were much narrower, and Esmond's archery skill often bettered Ardron. But interest in those practice sessions had gradually faded to non-existent as Esmond's depressive moods deepened.

Ardron turned the corner and gingerly picked his way through the mud and debris that was the street to the other side. He glanced up at the crude hanging sign that indicated 'The Badger Sett,' as a beer house. Inside, even though it was mid-afternoon, the light was poor. He stood inside the door for a moment allowing his eyes to become accustomed to the gloom. Eawyn the tavern maid was first to spot him.

"Ardron," she cried hurrying over to where he stood and linked her arm inside his. "What happened to you last night?"

"What do you mean?"

"I was expecting you, but you never came."

"Er, no. I had something important to do," He prevaricated.

"What about tonight?" she asked with a saucy expression. "It'll be worth it."

"Er, yes alright I'll come." He agreed but was not at all sure that he would. In truth he saw her only as an occasional distraction from boredom. "I'm looking for Esmond. Is he here?"

She waved an arm across the room towards a darkened corner. There he saw his brother, head down and arms spread across a table sleeping off the effects of surfeit beer. He started towards him then remembered the girl at his side. "Catch you later," he muttered.

He sat down opposite and attempted to rouse his brother from his drunken stupor. But there was no response. There was nothing to be done except to physically lift him to the outside. He moved round to the other side and lifted Esmond's arm in preparation for the lift, but he was approached by the burly landlord.

"Is it your intention to take this drunken sot away," he asked wiping his hands on his cow-skin apron.

"It is," Ardron replied.

"There is a settlement due." The landlord said brusquely and moved to block Ardron's way.

"How much?"

"Four marks,"

"Four marks?" Ardron queried with surprise.

"Aye, four marks."

Even allowing for his brother's unconscious state he doubted he could have spent four marks on beer. Nevertheless, there was nothing he could do to disprove the claim. "Help me to get him out of the door," he said as he handed over four marks.

"Gladly," the landlord said.

Outside he ducked his head beneath Esmond's arm, and with his right arm wrapped around his torso he half dragged, and half carried Esmond towards the horse trough. Then he flopped him over the water trough and held his head beneath the water. For a moment nothing happened, but then alarm burst through Esmond's befuddled senses as he realised that he was in danger of drowning. Still Ardron held his head beneath the water until that alarm became desperate panic. Only then, did he ease his grip and lifted him spluttering and coughing from the water. But he allowed him only the briefest of respite before ducking him again. This time when he let him up, he dragged him and almost threw him against the wall. Esmond half lay half sat against the wall coughing and spluttering as torrents of water cascaded from his head. When eventually he was able, Esmond cursed his brother long and loud. Considering his state there was little to be gained from informing Esmond of his news, and so he decided it better to get him back to their lodging and allow him to sleep off the alcohol effects.

Their lodgings were no more than the loft in a large stable building, and no more private than a doss-shack. For just a grout or two the stableman rented space in the loft to anybody seeking temporary shelter, and there were always takers. Ardron's immediate problem, however, was to help his brother to climb the ladder. After much heaving and shoving he eventually managed it. Then he found a quiet corner scattered hay around his brother and left him to sleep it off.

The next morning, he woke Esmond with gentle foot prods. He was badly hung over and growled as he rolled awake then sat up.

"You'd better straighten up brother. We have things to do this day." Ardron said, thrusting a crust of bread at him.

"How did I get here?" Esmond mumbled exhaling heavily.

"I carried you."

Esmond took the bread and stared at it half-heartedly trying to decide if he could actually stomach it. Then deciding that he ought to at least try it he bit it hard and ripped a piece off.

Ardron stood and began to strap his sword across his back

"I'm not in the mood for more sword practice," Esmond mumbled.

"No sword practice. Today we try to for an audience with the King's Marshall."

"Why would the King's Marshall see us?" Esmond asked unenthusiastically.

"Because I know him! He is Sir John Fitzgilbert."

"Fitz who?"

"Fitzgilbert. He is the Castellan of Ludgershall. You do remember Ludgershall?"

"I do," Esmond replied tiredly. "That's where you fought the battle of the turnips."

"Yes. If anyone can tell us the whereabouts of Fitzhubert then it must be him. The King's Marshall will know such things."

"And he is here?"

"Yes, he is. Yesterday I saw him ride through the Tower gates. Now get yourself together. I will tend our horses and be back shortly."

With the horses saddled and ready he led them both out from the stalls.

"Good morning to you brother Ardron." He turned to see the stable man approaching. "Are you off somewhere interesting this day?" he went on crunching noisily into an apple.

He wasn't being particularly inquisitive, Ardron knew that. He was simply opening conversation with the intent of receiving due rents.

"Good morning Esol. No, nowhere very exciting." He didn't help Esol broach the subject. He intended to make him ask.

From his pouch Esol pulled out another apple and held it up as an offering to Ardron then tossed it to him. "It's tally day Master Ardron."

"So it is," Ardron replied polishing the apple on his thigh.

"Will you be stopping another week?"

"Er__," Ardron was doubtful. "If the news is good on this day then we might well be moving on tomorrow."

"Oh, I'll be sorry to see you go."

Ardron was not fooled into thinking there was any affection. It was not the leaving that sorrowed him it was the ending of the regular income, modest though it may be.

"Is it back to Storenstun you will be going?" Esol went on only half interested.

"Scorrenstone," Ardron corrected his mispronunciation. "No, I don't think so. At least at this stage I hope not." He tethered both horses to a hitch rail and turned to face Esol. "I'll pay you for tonight, and then on the morrow we'll see."

"Two horse and feed, two men in the loft," Esol sucked though his teeth. "One mark."

Ardron nodded agreement then after feeding the remnants of his apple to Rattlebone, he paid Esol his due. "Can't stay and talk my friend. I have somewhere to be." It mattered not; Esol had his dues and was intent on moving on to his next lodger.

Outside Ardron waited patiently for his brother to arrive. He didn't have to wait too long before he arrived in a less than enthusiastic mood. "Where are we going?" he asked after mounting.

"To the Tower. Where else would the King's Marshal be?"

At the Tower gate they were stopped from entering by the guard. Ardron pleading his cause and was told to wait until someone could be found to hear his request.

"The King's Marshall is very busy," they were told by an administrator who eventually turned up to hear their request. "What is your business?"

"Our business is personal, but if you tell him it is the turnip champion who wishes an audience then I think he will see us." The man looked dubiously askew at Ardron trying to decide if he was genuine. "Tell him," Ardron instructed.

It was over an hour later when the admin man returned with the message that Fitzgilbert would see him that evening in his lodgings.

***

"Well Saxon. What brings you to London?" Fitzgilbert asked waving an arm towards seats the other side of the long table.

Ardron allowed Esmond to sit first. "Sir, I need your help to find someone."

"What makes you think that I can help?" he asked.

"Sir John, the man is one of the king's nobles and perhaps you, as the King's Marshal, will know his whereabouts."

"I see," Fitzgilbert said thoughtfully rubbing his chin. "And perhaps not," he went on. "You may have made a bad choice Saxon. You see, I seem to have lost the king's favour and he tells me nothing. Not even his personal arrangements, and that makes it impossible for me to act as his marshal. I fear I am about to lose the position and much more besides. But we will see. Who is this noble?"

"He is Robert Fitzhubert."

"Fitzhubert?" Fitzgilbert echoed with a hint of surprise. "The Flemish mercenary?"

"The same!" Ardron said.

"Why do you seek that man?"

Ardron then explained his reason and his lack of progress since leaving Ludgershall.

Fitzgilbert summoned one of the lackies standing in the shadowed corner of the room. "Bring wine," he said. "Well my friend," he said with a sigh. "I can tell you that Fitzhubert returned to Flanders some weeks ago. Home administration of his estate was the reason he gave. But rumour is that he was disgruntled that King Stephen had not granted him the estate in England that he thought he deserved."

The news was a bad blow to Ardron; he glanced at Esmond wondering how much of the conversation he understood. His French had been gradually improving up to the point where he could pick out a word or two, but often not enough to follow the detail.

"Tell me," Fitzgilbert went on. "This girl you seek was she taken as Fitzhubert's woman, or one of his knights, or perhaps even worse, just held in his brothel?"

Ardron shook his head. "We just don't know."

The servant arrived with three goblets and began to pour the wine. When he had finished, he began to withdraw.

"Wait," Fitzgilbert stopped him. "Can you describe the girl?" he asked Ardron.

57

Ardron made the description, and when he had finished Fitzgilbert leaned back in his chair and said. "Greville, here is a court servant." He briefly nodded his head in the servant's direction. "Greville, did you see such a girl at court with Fitzhubert?"

"I did, Sir John."

"As a concubine?"

"Yes, Sir."

"Concubine to who?"

"Sir Robert Fitzhubert."

"Fitzhubert! So, we have established that she was actually Fitzhubert's private whore, which, is probably not what you wanted to hear. But at least it means she was treated well enough."

Ardron glanced at Esmond but there was no indication that he had followed what was being said. He placed a sympathetic hand on his brother's shoulder and gave a little shake of the head. In all probability Esmond harboured no hopes that his bride would be returned to him unsullied. Even so to hear it confirmed would still be emotionally crushing. Ardron was going to have to find a gentle way to explain. If one did exist.

Fitzgilbert turned back to Greville. "And when Fitzhubert left for Flanders did he take her with him?"

"No, Sir. She stayed around the court for a few days then she disappeared."

"Thank you, Greville." The servant was dismissed. "Perhaps the girl has made her way back to your village." Fitzgilbert added.

"How would she travel?" Ardron queried.

"And there you have me at a loss," Fitzgilbert replied. "A comely girl or woman would need an escort for protection. She could not, dare not, travel alone."

A silence followed as Ardron tried to assess the probabilities.

"Tomorrow," Fitzgilbert filled the silence, "I will take my leave of the king, and around noon I will be leaving for Marlborough. Before I go, I can make more enquiries." He spread his hands. "I can do no more."

"Thank you, Sir John."

"Now on a different subject," He leaned back and with an arm wave dismissed the servants from the room. When they had gone, he leaned forward over the table. "Have you thought any more about my offer to join my sergenti?"

"I am beholding to you Sir John, but I still have no desire to get involved in any Norman conflict."

"My spies around court," Fitzgilbert went on in a much lower voice, "Inform me that my position is vulnerable. I have lost favour with the king. That band of treacherous advisors which form an exclusive ring around the king have been busy feeding poison into Stephen's ear. They have used my close association with the old king's eldest son, Robert Earl of Gloucester, to feed and fester distrust. I am reliably informed that the king intends to seize my castles and estates at Marlborough and Ludgershall. Tomorrow I return in order to strengthen my defences at both castles. Can you see why I now need good men, like you?"

"You would stand against the king?" Ardron queried.

"I would. Those estates were gifted to me by King Henry for long and loyal service. I am not prepared to see them taken back by a king who is no more than a usurper. With strengthened defences Stephen's men will find it difficult to break us down."

Ardron could appreciate that for Fitzgilbert the situation was dour, and even though he recognised a possible debt, and did hold a deal of sympathy for the Norman, he was still reluctant to be involved. He squirmed a little uncomfortably in his chair. "Perhaps," he said, "If I didn't have my own mission to pursue Sir John, I would stand with you."

Fitzgilbert studied him for a moment then leaned back in his chair. "Of course," he said. "We will speak no more of it."

It was beginning to get late when Ardron and Esmond left. Outside the October night was clear. The large moon was wrapped in a white haze, promising imminent frost. As he prepared to mount, Ardron peered over Rattlebone's withers. Across the street the two sergens, whom he had noticed loitering when he had arrived, had by now made themselves a fire and sat huddled over trying to soak up the heat. They showed not a speck of interest as Ardron and Esmond walked their horses past.

They journeyed unhurriedly, while Ardron related to Esmond the situation as described by Fitzgilbert. But Esmond took the news philosophically showing no emotion. It left Ardron wondering if in fact Esmond had understood more of the discussions than he thought. Or perhaps it was that Esmond no longer had hopes, or even wanted Hildi for his wife.

The road before them narrowed and the pair fell into single file with Esmond at the rear. "What of tomorrow? He asked. It was a question Ardron had been asking himself. They still had no lead and their only hope was a slender one. They relied on Fitzgilbert discovering something in the morning. He half twisted to look back, and as he did, he saw a shadowy figure cross the road behind them. But it was only fleeting, and he paid it no heed. "We will wait until noon tomorrow to see if Sir John discovers anything," he said. "Then perhaps we can make a plan."

***

Ardron waited until mid-morning before saddling the horses. That, he considered, would have given Fitzgilbert ample opportunity to make his enquiries before taking his leave from the king's court. He knew also the Fitzgilbert intended to be on his way back to Marlborough around noon, and so he timed his visit to be at his lodgings somewhere between the two.

He gathered up both reins and began to lead the horses out from their stalls when Esol walked in. He was accompanied by a well-gowned constable and four sergens.

"That's one of em," Esol said pointing at Ardron.

Baffled, Ardron stood his ground and waited for some development. Esol peddled slowly back trying to melt into the background while the five men moved down the stable towards him.

"Saxon," the constable said with some authority, "I am arresting you in the king's name!"

Ardron was taken aback! "On what charge?"

"Treason!"

"Treason? Ardron queried dumbfounded. "On whose authority?"

"By the authority of my Lord, Count Waleron Beaumont."

"And who is he exactly?"

"He is the king's confidante and that is all you need to know." The constable replied then he took a step backwards. "Take him," he ordered the sergens.

Ardron stepped backwards quickly and pulled his sword over his shoulder from its baldric. "Not easily you won't," he warned.

Ardron held his sword at a menacing angle as the four sergens fanned out across the front of him. Trying to appear much more confident than he felt, "Who is going to be first," he challenged. He hoped desperately that one would show bravado and take up the challenge. He did not want all four to come together. To his relief, one did.

He came at Ardron slashing brutally downward three times, making it easy for Ardron to parry. Then he changed tack, bringing his arm across his front and attempting a back slash at Ardron's head. It was easy to duck beneath, and Ardron then thrust his sword into the sergen's exposed midriff. There was a grunt of pain. and with a shocked expression the man dropped his sword and clutched his stomach. He dropped slowly to his knees before spilling forward. Ardron turned to face the other three waving his sword slowly, threatening each one in turn.

"All together now," one of the sergens took charge. And they came at him as one, chopping, swinging and thrusting. He gave ground quickly, struggling to parry the endless onslaught until his back hit against something solid. Two more attacks he parried but the third came swinging in from his left at neck height. He could not get his sword up in time, all he could do was to flinch away from the killer blow. But the swinging sword thudded into a stout wooden upright just behind Ardron's shoulder. He had been lucky. He turned and ran down the stable before turning once again and waving his sword threateningly as the three sergens once again fanned out before him.

Pssh, an arrow whispered through the air before thudding into the chest of one of the sergens. With a gasp and a grimace, he staggered backwards and sat down with a thump. He dropped his sword and instinctively grasped at the arrow shaft before slumping backwards then he began violently twitching in death throws. The sergen nearest to him hesitated and leaned over slightly to look down at him. That was a movement that saved his life as a second arrow skimmed the side of his head.

All eyes turned towards the loft where Esmond pulled another arrow from his sheaf and began to string it to his bow. It was a dominant position and those below vulnerable. The imminent threat was enough, and the sergens took to their heels and ran out of the stable. The constable hesitated just long enough, to issue a threat to Ardron. "You won't get away with this. We know who you are." Then he too retreated hastily from danger.

In the shadows Esol spread his hands in an unarmed gesture and shrugged. He presented no danger, Ardron decided.

Esmond slid down the ladder and looked at Ardron questioningly. "Who were they?" he asked.

"Count Waleron's men."

"What were they trying to do?"

"Arrest us for treason."

"Treason?"

"Aye, treason, brother."

"What___"

"No time for discussion," Ardron cut him off. "On your horse and let's be away from this place quickly."

"What about our belongings?"

"There is no time. Leave them."

Esmond needed no more persuading. They mounted and drove their horses at a gallop through the stable back entrance. For two miles they kept up a gallop then Ardron slowed the pace to a walk allowing the horses a blow.

"What now?" Esmond asked.

"I_ don't know?" Ardron answered in hopelessness. Their last hope of a clue to the whereabouts of Hildi had gone. They could no longer remain in London without putting themselves in jeopardy. And how were they guilty of treason? He wheeled Rattlebone's head over and off the road. "Let's take a breather, he said sliding from the saddle.

"I don't understand those men," Esmond muttered. "How are we guilty of treason?"

Ardron shook his head, I have no answers. Unless__" a thought occurred to him. "In your drunken sessions in the Badger Sett did you by chance take to disparaging the king's name?"

"No, I did not." Esmond replied hotly.

Ardron shook a baffled head.

"How did they even find us?" Esmond thought aloud.

Ardron didn't reply then a thought occurred to him. "They followed us!"

"What?"

"Last night," Ardron went on. "They followed us. I looked back to you and I saw someone in the shadows." He then remembered the two sergens loitering outside Fitzgilbert's lodgings. "Fitzgilbert said that he thought the king was about to seize his estates. Therefore, Waleron must have had him watched, and by our association we are considered part of some plot against the king."

"But we are just humble Saxon's. What could we do against the king?" Esmond said.

"If Fitzgilbert has been arrested, then we could be put under duress to turn king's evidence against him."

"Duress?" Esmond probed

"Torture, then."

"That's a lot of speculation!" Esmond said.

"It is. But it makes sense."

"Alright! But what do we do now?"

Ardron thought for a moment. "I think perhaps we should go back to Scorrenstone. We have no idea where to look for Hildi. She might even be in France for all we know. I hate to admit it brother, but we have failed."

Esmond nodded sadly. "We didn't fail Edyo," he pointed out.

"No, we didn't fail Edyo," he agreed.

There was nothing more to be said and so they both re-mounted and continued west. By late afternoon they had journeyed some twenty-five miles and reached the ferry at Maiden Hythe. The opposite side of the river was thickly wooded, and its dense security would make a good place to make camp for the night.

The river raft was secured and of the ferryman there was no sign. After a few minutes he appeared from the tumbled-down shack a few yards away and waved acknowledgement before disappearing round the side. Ardron assumed the man would be attending soon, and so he busied himself persuading the horses to board the rocking platform that was the raft. With Esmond and the animals safely on board Ardron waited patiently on the quay for the ferryman. It didn't take long before he appeared leading a powerful shire horse.

"Two men two horses, that will be one mark, if you please." Ardron fiddled in his purse and handed over the fare. "My, it's been a busy day," the ferryman went on as he began to harness his horse to the ropes.

The ferry system was a series of ropes across the river, and the horse was haltered to one or the other depending on which way the raft was to be crossed.

"It is profitable to be busy," Ardron humoured the conversation.

"So it is my friend. But this afternoon was non-stop. I was used to ferry Sir John Fitzgilbert's whole caravan across, men, horses and carts."

Ardron interest was immediately roused, "John Fitzgilbert?"

"Aye, took almost two hours to get them all over."

"How long ago?"

The ferryman ducked under the horse and began fastening the traces on that side. "Oh," he paused in thought. "More than two hours since."

Ardron was thoughtful a few moments. If Fitzgilbert were two hours ahead of them then he would have left London early this morn. Therefore, he could not have even been to the king's court but had probably left in haste instead.

"I don't suppose he said where he was going." Ardron ventured.

"No, he didn't. All is ready. You had better get aboard."

Ardron turned away.

"But," the ferryman added. "I did hear one of his sergenti mention Wallingford Castle."

"Wallingford Castle," Ardron paused. "Where's that?

"Fifteen, sixteen miles north west of here. Follow the river he added as an after-thought."

Ardron leapt onto the raft just as the ferry man began to lead the horse to take the strain on the rope.

Fifteen sixteen miles! Ardron glanced to the October sky. Two hours of daylight remained, perhaps a little more. It would be a hard push to reach Wallingford before dark. Better to wait until the morning. Nevertheless, if they pressed on a little, they could perhaps make another five or six miles tonight.

There had been little sleep for the pair. The drifting mist along the river had added to the frost, making it too cold and damp to sleep well. Three times Ardron had got from his inadequate cow-skin blanket to repair the fire. On the last occasion he had given up on sleep and instead had huddled in front of the fire with the cow-skin draped over his head and back. But sitting there alone staring into the flames it had given him time to think. He was not now so sure that to return to Scorrenstone was such a good idea. They had resisted arrest and had probably killed two men of the king's confidante, Waleron. Surely, they were now outlawed. Was it therefore wise to take their troubles back to the unsuspecting village? Certainly, the stableman Esol knew from which village they came, and there was every reason to believe he would pass on that information. Indeed, not to would make him an accessory to the supposed treason charge. Providing of course Esol could pronounce it correctly, he had not done so yet. But then not to return to their home would leave them wandering aimlessly around the country. It was a dilemma.

It was still early when he prodded Esmond to roll out of his blanket. He needed no persuading, probably thankful to be on the move. There was no breakfast, there had been no supper and so to reach Wallingford was now an attractive objective.

As they rode Ardron voiced his concerns about returning to Scorrenstone. He was prepared to argue the point with his brother, but was pleasantly surprised when Esmond muttered quietly. "We can't go back." Then after a few moments silence. "What now?"

Ardron sighed. "We are offered positions amongst Fitzgilbert's sergenti. And for now that would seem to be our best alternative. At least until something changes."

Less than two hours later, and even though the river mist had not completely cleared the impressive building that was Wallingford Castle was visible. The west side with its high stone wall backed up to the river Thames, while its southerly front stole a ditch from the river as a moat. Deep within the castle, but towering above its inner baileys, the stone-built keep was sited upon a steep man-made mote. It dominated completely the whole interior. No less than three inner baileys formed fortifications within fortification.

The drawbridge was down and the gate open allowing access to the outer bailey. Ardron and Esmond were not stopped as they rode through the gate. Inside was a confusion of bucolic shanties, where villagers traded wares and tradesmen practiced their crafts. They threaded their way across to the next inner bailey, and it was at this gate they were stopped by two sergenti guards.

In answer to the guard's challenge Ardron dismounted and indicated Esmond to do the same. "We seek Sir John Fitzgilbert and have reason to believe he is here," he said.

The nearest guard said nothing then after a moment he planted his lance hard into the ground and used it two-handed as a leaning post. With a flick of his head and without speaking he gesticulated to his partner who went inside presumably to fetch a superior.

"State your business," the guard commander demanded.

"We have come from London and we seek Sir John Fitzgilbert. Is he here?"

He got a brusque non-committal, "I will find out." After a curt instruction of 'keep them here' to the guards, he disappeared.

At considerable length, the guard-commander returned accompanied by a smartly dressed noble. "Who are you?" he demanded.

Ardron studied the man a moment. Tall, moving towards middle age with distinguished grey beard. "We are Esmond and Ardron, Saxon's of Scorrenstone. We seek Sir John Fitzgilbert."

"On what business?"

"He has offered us a post in his sergenti, and we are here to accept."

"Then you are for the Empress?"

"Empress?" Ardron queried.

"Aye. The Empress Maude. "You do know that she has landed on the south coast of England?"

Ardron was puzzled. "No," he said.

After studying Ardron for a moment the noble made a slight nod, seemingly, making up his mind. "I am Sir Brien Fitzcount the Castellan here. News reached us yesterday that the Empress Maude has landed in the south of England. She comes to claim her rightful crown."

Ardron heard the news with feelings of dismay. It promised only pending civil war. It would be a power struggle between Norman's and of no real concern to the ordinary Saxon proletariat. His every instinct had been to keep clear of such involvement, but in his new outlawed circumstances he was being dragged in.

"At this time, Fitzcount went on, "she has taken refuge with her stepmother Queen Adeliza in Arundel Castle. She awaits only the rendezvous with her stepbrother Robert, Earl of Gloucester with his army. Your liege, Sir John Fitzgilbert, was declared a traitor by Stephen and fled London yesterday before he could be arrested. This morning early, he left for his castle at Marlborough. He intends to strengthen his defences at Marlborough and Ludgershall and stand against Stephen. He will be in need of good soldiers, and if you can wield that sword half as impressive as it looks, then, he will need you." He paused awaiting Ardron's response, but Ardron said nothing he was still appraising the new situation.

"He has less than two hours start on you. You should be able to catch him easily."

"Thank you, Sir Brien." Ardron said and began to manoeuvre his horse to mount.

"Have you eaten?" Sir Brien asked.

"No Sir, we have not."

He turned to his guard-commander. "See them fed before they leave," he said.

***

65

They rode in thoughtful silence as the landscape changed to vast open expanses of rolling hills and valleys. By mid-afternoon they had neither caught up with Fitzgilbert nor arrived at Marlborough Castle.

"Esmond halted his horse. "Where are we?" he demanded.

Ardron reined in his mount and turned back towards Esmond. "I don't know he admitted." For a little while he had pressed on hoping that every time they breasted a ridge he would see Marlborough, but it had not happened. They had intended a south westerly route from Wallingford but Ardron suspected that they had not slanted enough to the west, and by now he thought they may have come too far south also. "I suppose we had better find somewhere to camp for the night."

Esmond groaned aloud and Ardron sympathised fully with his brother, another cold night beneath the stars was not appealing. However, as they topped the next crest, they came across a small settlement sited on the opposite side of the valley. Could they find some shelter here? They both hoped so. But at the very least they could get themselves a position fix.

They entered the silent hamlet and halted their horses somewhere around the middle. Although there was no one to be seen there were definite signs of occupation. Chicken wandered freely, a horse grazed in a nearby paddock, and evidence of workers was the accumulation of hand tools scattered beneath a lean-too.

"Is there anyone here?" Esmond shouted.

There seemed no response and the brothers glanced at each other wondering what to do next.

"What do you want?" a woman's voice challenged from the shadowy doorway of one of the shanty houses.

Ardron wheeled his horse to face the woman. She was not young nor was she old, but her slight physique, such as he could see, bore testament to the tough life on a Saxon hill farm.

"We come to do you no harm," Ardron said. "We are strangers in the area and have lost our way. Can you tell us the way to Marlborough?" He casually leaned forward in the saddle and patted Rattlebone's neck hoping that a non-threatening action might appease the woman.

"Marlborough?" there was an element of surprise in her voice as she stepped from the shadows. "Newbury is eight miles that way," she said pointing roughly in the direction from which they had come. "Marlborough must be another fifteen sixteen miles beyond that."

Ardron ignored Esmond's muttered curse. "My Lady, we have come far today, and the light already is beginning to fade. Could we, perhaps, find shelter somewhere here?" The suspicion returned to the woman's face. "We can pay!" Ardron added.

She took a few moments to think of a response then she said. "The men folk will soon be returned from Bezinstouk market. You can ask them when they return."

"Thank you," Ardron said. "Is there somewhere we can wait?"

The woman stepped forward. "Over by the paddock," she said pointing.

At the paddock they dismounted then took the liberty to turn their horses loose. They did not unburden the animals they were not sure yet that they were welcome. An hour passed, and by this time getting dark, when the small convoy of four carts rolled into the hamlet. They were laden with clusters of people. Men, women, children, all in high spirits.

Ardron and Esmond got to their feet as the carts neared, but they rolled past without stopping and the only acknowledgement was prolonged curious stares. Even when the carts were halted, people went about their business without even glancing back at the strangers.

"I don't think we are particularly welcome here." Esmond muttered.

Ardron silently agreed, nevertheless, he walked over to where the carts were being unloaded.

"Greetings fellow Saxon's," Ardron said. "Can I speak to the Thegn?"

"We have no Thegn here," one man said as he dragged a heavy sack towards him. "We have a Gebur," he went on pausing to look at Ardron.

Gebur was a family head and to all intents and purposes was still the man Ardron wanted. "Can you point him out to me?"

The man bent around the cart and looked forward. "There," he said pointing at an elder swathed in a thick animal fur wrap. "His name is Artier." The request now settled the man lifted the heavy sack and went about his chore.

There was no warm greeting from the Gebur, instead he stared silently suspicious as Ardron introduced himself and Esmond. Ardron then went on to explain their predicament and express the hope that they would allow them some kind of shelter for the night. It was only when he offered to pay and declared that even the lowest animal shelter would suffice that Artier began to show a little compassion. For further payments, Artier agreed that he would find food for them and fodder for their horses. Then it was to an animal shelter that he eventually ushered them.

Although the shelter was spacious it was crudely built and dilapidated, which afforded very little protection from the outside cold. But it was at least cover and slight protection from the keen wind. They shared the shelter with the farm's horses, oxen and sheep. 'At least there are no pigs in here,' Esmond muttered. Then to make shelter within the shelter, they piled up straw in a corner and settled themselves down into its midst.

It was well after dark when Artier arrived with a pitcher of broth into which a hot stone had been dropped to warm it.

"We don't see many travellers through here," Artier said as he handed out small wooden bowls.

"You would not have seen us except that we got ourselves lost," Esmond replied taking the bowls and handing one on to his brother.

"You were making for Marlborough, I was told."

"We were," Ardron replied.

"Then you are a long way out," Artier scoffed.

"A problem we will rectify tomorrow," Ardron said. Then wishing to change the subject said, "How went the market trading today?"

"It went well," Artier responded. "But it was a strange day."

"How so? Ardron asked dipping the bowl into the broth.

"Well__," Artier paused stroking his grey beard. "The market was rife with rumours."

"Oh, what rumours?" Esmond asked as he took the bowl from Ardron.

"Strange rumours," Artier said with a frown. "Those traders coming from the east spoke of the king at the head of an army marching south."

Ardron was instantly interested. "Is there any truth to the rumours?"

Artier shrugged. "I don't know, but why would anybody invent such a story?"

It was a good point. Ardron decided that in view of the information this morning from Sir Brien then in all probability it was true, and the king would be bound for Arundel. Not only that, it was vital information. Should the king's army arrive at Arundel before The Earl of Gloucester's army then the Empress Maude was in grave danger. He glanced at Esmond, clearly, he too appreciated the situation. Without saying as much he decided that early tomorrow, they would ride, and ride hard for Marlborough, to pass on this information to John Fitzgilbert.

They left before it was properly light without taking leave of their hosts. They passed through the very centre of Newbury, and by mid-morning had reached Marlborough. Marlborough Castle occupied the high ground, with an exceptionally tall mote governing the wooden constructed fortifications of the bailey. Inside there was a hive of industry, Fitzgilbert had lost no time beginning the work of strengthening the castle defences, and Ardron was directed to the stabling area to find Sir John.

"Damnation take the man's very soul," Fitzgilbert cursed when he heard what Ardron had to say. "The situation is grim," he went on. "If the king takes the empress at Arundel then her cause is lost before it's even begun. And many of her sympathisers will find themselves rotting in the Tower. Me included!"

"Will the castle stand against the king?" Ardron asked.

"Arundel will be a hard castle to take if it does," Fitzgilbert said. "Adeliza is the old queen and Maude's step-mother, she would never surrender Maude to Stephen. However, the problem is that her husband William d'Aubigny is the king's man and he most certainly would."

Ardron watched the worry lines on Sir John's face but said nothing. He could appreciate completely the turmoil twisting the man's insides. Suddenly his eyebrows raised as a plan of action crossed his mind.

"This news must be passed to Robert of Gloucester without delay. He must move his army under a forced march to Arundel immediately." He stared hard at Ardron. "You're a west country man, aren't you?"

"I am," Ardron confirmed.

"Will you carry despatches to Earl Gloucester, at Bristol?"

Ardron took a moment to think. He still considered this to be a Norman issue, but having been outlawed by the king he had to choose a side. There was really only one side to choose and that was against the king. He could of course choose neither side, and just remain an outlaw. But then he would be an outlaw to both sides. "I will," he said.

"Good man," Fitzgilbert said, placing his hand upon Ardron's shoulder. "I can have the despatches prepared within the hour. Be ready to leave."

Ardron was about to protest a problem but Fitzgilbert had turned away. No matter he could solve the problem himself. Rattlebone had already carried him more than twenty miles this day and at a decent pace. The horse needed rest, but the urgency of the despatch meant he was not going to get it. Ardron's concern was that he might break the animal delivering it. So, he decided that he would travel as long as the horse held up, and when it started showing signs of distress then he would just have to rest him. But with around forty miles to travel it would be an extreme test of the horse's stamina. He went to look to the animal's welfare while he waited for the despatches.

It was past mid-afternoon when Ardron reached Chippenham and was a little better than halfway to Bristol. He went at an easy trot through the town centre not stopping but attracting curious stares from the townsfolk as he did. He made his way down the hill towards the bridge and had to pay a toll to cross the river. On the other side he decided that Rattlebone had held up well and had earned himself a rest. He slid from the saddle and turned the horse loose to forage in the rich meadow grass.

Ardron chewed on bread and boar meat while he sat and contemplated the position. There were still some twenty or so miles to Bristol, that would mean around another four hours. Even if Earl Robert were to leave with his army tomorrow, he could never hope to be at Arundel before King Stephen. Hells bells, Stephen might be there already, in which case the Empress Maude was as good as Stephen's prisoner. Unless, of course, the castle gates were locked to the king, in which case Stephen would then be obliged to lay siege to the castle. Then, providing that Robert's army were the greater, there could be some hope that the king could be driven away.

But it was all supposition. If William d'Aubigny is loyal to Stephen, then the gates will have been opened and Ardron's forced ride might be a meaningless escapade. Still all he could do was to complete the ride and deliver the message. The rest would be up to the Norman hierarchy.

He found an apple in the bag and took a hefty bite looking round for Rattlebone as he did. The horse was standing in shallows of the river. He watched idly for a moment then a worrying thought occurred to him, could it be that the horse was feeling some heat in his legs? Concerned, he got to his feet and went into the river after him. He led the horse back onto the bank then cautiously felt the animal's hocks and fetlocks, all seemed normal. He pulled him around on the bridle trying to examine his movements. As far as he could see, and to his relief, all looked normal. He took another bite from the apple and allowed Rattlebone the rest. Then he gave the horse an affectionate slap on the rump and the big fellow bucked playfully forward with ears pricked. There is still plenty of energy left there, Ardron concluded.

"Another thirty minutes, boy. Make the most of it," he warned the horse.

It had been dark a long time when Ardron eventually reached Bristol. He had been forced to walk the last three miles leading his tired horse. Crossing the wooden bridge over the river he approached the town gate. It was of course locked and at this hour he expected no more. Still the message he had to deliver was important, and so he shouted long and loud to summon the guard. Eventually a sleepy guard, in a sour mood, responded to his persistence.

"I have urgent despatches for Earl Robert."

The guard didn't question his explanation, instead let him in without issue. No doubt anxious to get back to his slumbers.

"Which way to the castle?" Ardron asked.

"Straight on," the guard responded waving a lazy arm in the rough direction. "Even in the dark you'd have to be blind not to see it," he added sourly.

The castle was awesome, and the darkness did not hide its formidable stature. Its high stone-built bailey spawned a tower at every angle-change in the wall. At the far end of the outer bailey the inner bailey protected a tall mote with an impressive stone-built keep on top. The whole complex was protected on one side by the river Avon and on two sides by the river Frome. A deep man-made moat connected both rivers and protected the remaining side.

Once again Ardron had to rouse a sleepy guard to gain admittance to the outer bailey. The security at the inner bailey was much tighter, and Ardron could not be admitted without an escort. Some twenty minutes had passed before a domiciliary arrived at the gate. He was a man short in stature but wide in girth, and by the nature of his untidy dress, pulled from his bed.

"I have despatches of an urgent nature for the attention of Earl Robert." Ardron explained.

"Let me see," he said.

"No," Ardron was adamant. "Confidential for Earl Robert only."

"I am not letting you in. The earl will be abed by now, so give them to me and I will decide what is to be done."

"What is your name?" Ardron asked.

"Why do you want to know that?"

"Because I am not about to put these despatches into anybody's hand except the earl's. And if there is an unnecessary delay before he reads them, I want to be able point exactly where he should direct his rage."

The domiciliary was not fazed. "If I get him from his bed and these despatches are not important then his rage will be directed at you. Are you prepared for that Saxon?"

"Yes I am."

"Very well," he relented. "Follow me." He led the way into the great hall and bade a guard stay with Ardron and left.

Some twenty minutes passed before he returned trailing behind a taller and much slimmer man. Although Ardron had never before clapped eyes on Robert Earl of Gloucester he knew instantly by the man's bearing who he was.

"I am Robert, Earl of Gloucester," he said with a deal of authority. "You have despatches for me?"

"I do, my Lord."

"From where?"

"From Sir John Fitzgilbert."

Earl Robert held out his hand, "Give them to me."

Ardron handed over the scroll and watched the earl's face carefully. At first there was little reaction, but then he threw his head back and began swearing through gritted teeth. "Find me my constable," he almost shouted to the domiciliary behind him.

"Do you know what's in here?" Earl Robert asked Ardron.

"Yes, Sir. I do."

"When did this news come in?"

"I learned of it late yesterday, and this morning travelled in all haste to Marlborough to inform Sir John Fitzgilbert," Ardron replied.

Earl Robert stroked his grey streaked beard thoughtfully. "Stephen is probably in Arundel right now," he muttered to himself. "Any indication of the strength of his army?" he asked Ardron.

Ardron shook his head.

"Fitzgilbert says I must send an army post-haste," he held up the scroll. "I don't have an army, at least, not one that is yet fully assembled."

Not knowing whether the earl addressed him or was still thinking aloud Ardron remained silent.

"You," Earl Robert addressed the guard. "Find all my knights send them to me."

"Yes my Lord," the guard muttered.

Then as the man moved away. "If they are in bed then get them out." Earl Robert bellowed after him.

Ardron watched as the earl paced up and down in deep thought. Soon the domiciliary returned accompanied with the castle constable.

"Ah Baldwin," Earl Robert said. "How goes our army recruiting?"

"It goes well, my Lord. Every day our numbers swell and by the end of another week we could possibly number around two thousand," Baldwin replied.

"What about tomorrow? How many men could we put in the field tomorrow? Earl Robert asked."

"Tomorrow?" Baldwin's jaw visibly dropped. "Perhaps five hundred. No more."

"Not enough! If we stripped the castle sergenti down to the minimum, how many then?"

Baldwin's confusion was patent. "Er___ another two hundred, perhaps."

Earl Robert sucked through his teeth noisily. "Still not enough." He thought for a moment. "First light tomorrow, or even before, send out messengers and runners to all points. All squires, vassals and fiefs able to hold a weapon are to report to this castle within twenty-four hours. Warn them that they back slide under pain of death. I want a sizable army ready to march within three days."

"Yes, Sir. March where to?"

"To Arundel to rescue the Empress Maude."

Ardron melted into the background as other dignitaries had begun to filter into the Great Hall. The earl sat down and waited patiently until the numbers had swelled then he got to his feet and addressed the assembly, informing them of the developments and his intentions. He swung a pointed finger around the assembly looking for someone. "Ralph," he said.

"Here my Lord," A man of not much more than twenty years stepped forward."

"Ralph, take two-hundred soldiers, of your choosing, and proceed immediately to Arundel Castle as an advanced party. Your task will be to persuade William d'Aubigny to keep his castle gates closed against Stephen. Tell him that I am close behind with a large army of over three-thousand men at arms. And that I shall be most displeased if I find that he has surrendered the empress to Stephen."

"Three thousand men?" Ralph queried.

"Aye. Tell him four if you like."

"My Lord," another knight sought his attention.

"Sir Miles," Earl Robert recognised the speaker. So did Ardron, from their chance meeting in Trowbridge Castle.

"D'Aubigny is not likely to close his gates against the king. He is a Stephen supporter."

"Yes, Sir Miles. That he is, but do not under-estimate the persuasion powers of his wife Queen Adeliza. She will not surrender her stepdaughter readily. And the fact that d'Aubigny believes that we are close with a large army might be enough to persuade him to hold out a little while. He won't want to incur my wrath at the head of a large army."

The meeting descended into small groups discussing their personal arrangements and tactics. Ardron edged forward. Earl Robert had impressed him by his decisive and forthright attitude. Except for the fact that he was born on the wrong side of the blanket this man, the eldest son of King Henry, would have been the undisputed King of England and Duke of Normandy. Ardron decided that this was the man who should be king.

"My Lord," he sought the earl's attention. "May I be dismissed?"

"Of course," Earl Robert replied. Then he summoned a nearby servant. "This man has travelled hard and far today, see that his needs are attended too. And__," as an after-thought, "See also that he is rewarded with five silver pieces."

Ardron stayed in and around Bristol Castle for a couple of days, primarily to allow his exhausted horse time to recover. He planned a much slower trip back, diverting and stopping over a day or two at Scorrenstone before pressing on to Marlborough.

The build-up of Earl Robert's army had been dramatic. Men had arrived in large bands under the leadership of barons, knights and counts, others in small individual clusters. The town of Bristol heaved with fighting men, all in high spirits and spoiling for the fight. The word was that tomorrow the army would be on the move westward to Arundel. Of the empress's fate nothing was known.

It was approaching noon when Ardron walked across the bailey to the stabling area. It was time for him to be on his way, he was eager to be away from all the over-crowded confusion. As he led his charger from the stabling area excited chatter began among the masses. Men scrambled onto the fighting platforms to peer out over the wooden fortification, while others hurried towards the gate. From outside the bailey loud boisterous cheering could be heard. Dignitaries inside the keep, with elevated views, hung from windows and waved banners. Curious, Ardron moved towards the road that led across the bailey expecting perhaps to see a significant knight at the head of more fighting men.

He caught the arm of a sergen hurrying towards the gate. "What causes all the excitement?" he asked.

"It's the Empress Maude. She is here," he said as he squirmed free.

"The empress? Ardron questioned himself. "How can that be?"

The cheers got gradually louder as the party drew nearer until a small armed escort came through the gate. At its head rode a Norman knight, smartly robed in a gown of red and yellow beneath a hauberk. On his head he wore the traditional pointed helmet and over his left arm, a shield of red and yellow squares. He stared dead ahead without acknowledging the cheering crowd. He looked anything but pleased. Neither did the red-robed bishop riding at his side. Immediately behind and flanked on all sides by eight sergenti a woman rode stiff backed and proud. It had to be the Empress Maude, Ardron concluded.

She was a woman in her middle years the flush of youth having passed. Nevertheless, she still retained desirable womanly qualities. Her physique was slight but her demeanour significant. Round-faced, straight nosed with crimped lips that bore only slight traces of a smile. The crowd's adulation she accepted with a degree of arrogance as her right, and therefore had no need to respond.

The escort party was greeted at the foot of the mote steps by the entire community of the castle dignitaries. From the front Earl Robert and his son stepped forward to greet the escort.

"Robert, Earl of Gloucester," the knight said. "I am charged by his Majesty, King Stephen, to deliver this the Empress Maude safely into your care." The words almost choked him.

"Count Waleron," Earl Robert replied. "Consider your duty well performed and with our gratitude." Then he motioned to a group of ladies behind him to move forward and attend the Empress.

Ardron took a renewed and keen interest in the knight. 'So this was Waleron! This was the man whose order for arrest had caused him to be outlawed.

"I want none of your gratitude. This duty was particularly abhorrent to me." Waleron replied.

"Nevertheless, you still have it." Earl Robert replied. "Now it would be extremely discourteous of me not to offer you substance at my table before you depart."

"I will not take bread at your table. Every mouthful would be as bile in my throat and cause me to retch from the pit of my stomach." Waleron snarled.

"As you wish!" Earl Robert then turned to the bishop. "Cousin Henry, Bishop of Winchester. Will you come to my table?

"And the spirit led Jesus into the wilderness to be tempted by the devil. After forty days of fasting the devil charged. 'If you be the son of God, turn these stones into bread and eat.' But Jesus did not yield to the devil." Bishop Henry said loudly as if preaching a sermon.

Earl Robert stared at him a moment nonplussed, then nonchalantly said. "That would be a no then!

He glanced behind him ensuring the empress was at least ascending the mote steps into the keep. Then looking up at the two mounted men he said. "If we have no further business then let me not detain you." In a loud voice for all to hear he went on, "You have my guarantee of safe passage out of the county." Then he made a mock bow and uttered, "Count." Then to his cousin, "Your Grace."

Waleron scowled, then in a loud voice proclaimed. "The dogs of war are released, and many mothers sons will die." He wheeled his horse fiercely and led the small party at a canter through the gate.

Ardron decided to delay his departure by an hour. He anticipated that Waleron and his party would take the road east out of Bristol bound for London. He too needed to travel that road for about fifteen miles. He had no desire to catch up to the group. Whilst there was virtually no danger that Waleron would know who Ardron was exactly, it was, nevertheless, wise policy to keep clear.

He led his horse back to the stables and tethered him to the hitch rail. The arrival of the empress had had a dramatic effect on the general atmosphere. There was a jubilant mood of euphoria and anticipation among the crowd. Here was an army that had just been handed its figurehead, its rallying point, and the very purpose for its existence. And gifted, it seemed, by the very man who had most cause to fear the influence of Empress Maude. Ardron could not begin to comprehend the reasoning behind Stephen's misguided gallantry. Cousin's they were, and perhaps it was the blood ties, but whatever his reasons Stephen had undoubtedly invited open and massive revolt against himself. Civil war was now a certainty.

***

The sun had set, leaving an orange glow in the western sky by the time Ardron reached Scorrenstone. In the gathering gloom he paused on the opposite side of the valley and absorbed the view of the humble settlement that was home. Happy to be home he spurred Rattlebone down the hill to the bridge, galloped across and rode the animal hard up the other side. He reined in the horse and entered the village at a leisurely walk.

By this time many of the villagers had retired to the warmth of their homes, but his arrival did not go unnoticed. As he plodded casually through the village people began to emerge from their homes. Soon a small assembly had gathered, and they began to follow, chattering among themselves as they did. In front of his father's house, he slid from the saddle and turned to face the gathering. He was greeted with smiles and grins, but even so, there were many unspoken questions in their demeanour.

"Ardron, you miserable excuse for a warrior," a voice boomed from the rear, and it was Swidhurn who elbowed his way to the front with a huge grin. "We had begun to think that you had turned Norman. Or that you were dead."

"Neither!" Ardron replied.

"Where's Esmond?" Swidhurn asked looking round with concern.

"He's safe," Ardron just had time to reply as he saw his father emerge from his house.

"Son, it's good to see you." Wolfstan said as he gripped Ardron in a bear-hug. "Are you well?"

"Well enough, father."

"Wolfstan glanced around. "Where is your brother?" he asked.

"He is safe father. He waits for me at Marlborough."

"Marlborough? What is he doing at Marlborough?"

"Tis a long story I have to tell," Ardron said.

"You are alone? You don't have Hildi with you either?"

"No father. I do not." Ardron replied a little ashamed.

"Never mind! Come in rest and eat, then you can tell me all." Wolfstan said as he guided Ardron towards the doorway. Then he turned to address the assembly. "My friends," he said. "In two hours, we will assemble in the meeting house and then perhaps we can learn all."

Ardron had already related the events to his father and Redwald, his elder brother, by the time he sat down in the meeting hall. Now he waited for all the villagers to settle before he was to start again. As he waited, he was approached by Edyo and in close attendance, Cerdic.

"I am happy to see you are well Ardron," she said shyly.

"Sit here," Ardron said sliding along the form to make space for her. "Have you settled back in?"

"I have, and I know that I owe you a great debt," she said quietly.

"Edyo, you owe me nothing. Put the whole episode behind you and carry on with the rest of your life as if it never happened."

"That, I can never do! It was just too horrible. And if you hadn't rescued me, then for me there was worse to come."

"I didn't do it alone Edyo, Swidhurn and Esmond played major parts too." Ardron said placing a sympathetic arm around the youngster. "Don't you spend time thinking of what might have happened because it didn't happen. Instead live each day as it comes, and those nightmares must gradually fade." He looked over her shoulder and with a nod acknowledged a close attending Cerdic.

"How fares Esmond?" Cerdic asked.

"Esmond is well," Ardron gave his assurance.

Then the meeting began. Once again Ardron had to relate the events as they had happened. After that he was bombarded with questions. Where did he think Hildi might be? Was he about to give up the search? What about Fitzhubert, where was he? Was there to be a war? Why did he think that King Stephen let the Empress Maude go? What would be the effects on the Saxon community? How would a war affect the village? Was there danger to the village people if they harboured outlaws? Most of the questions Ardron was unable to answer. But he did assure the community that he was not giving up on Hildi's rescue, that short conversation with Edyo had re-asserted that issue. His problem at this time was that he just did not know where to look.

Later that evening, he talked late into the night with his father and brother. Civil war was inevitable and Ardron feared for the village community. The villagers, as tenants, had been vassals to the Bishop of Salisbury, but the king had stripped him of his estates. However, they still worked the land as tenants but to whom did their obligations now lay?

"We still pay our fief to the de Pinkney brothers at Malmesbury Castle." Wolfstan informed him.

"Aye, but to whom do they homage?"

"We assume that since King Stephen seized all Salisbury's estates, he owns Malmesbury Castle," Redwald replied.

"Yes," said Ardron. "But Stephen is in London and there is a rebel army not more than twenty-five miles from here."

"Ah, I see your point," Wolfstan said. "We have to supply fighting men to defend Malmesbury Castle. And the castle could be vulnerable."

"Perhaps Earl Robert won't come this way. Perhaps he will go direct for London." Redwald suggested.

Ardron nodded agreement. "That is what I hope. This area may then be ignored, at least for a while."

"Perhaps one big battle at London will decide it all." Redwald offered a suggestion.

Ardron screwed up his face and shook his head. "I don't think it can be over quickly. Stephen has a dilemma; he cannot sit and wait for Earl Robert to arrive at the gates of London. He must come out to meet Earl Robert as far from London as possible. That means that he has to pass between Wallingford and Marlborough castles. Both of those castellan's, Fitzgilbert and Fitzcount, stand for Maude. Stephen cannot afford to have both of those behind him, therefore he will have to take one or both castles."

"And while he is occupied doing that, Earl Robert gets ever closer to London." Redwald added.

"Exactly," Ardron agreed.

"And if the castle doesn't fall quickly, then Stephen could find himself sieging one of the castles with the army of Earl Robert descending on him." Redwald grasped the situation.

"I expect that he will have to split his army and try and hold Earl Robert until he has cleared out his rear." Ardron added.

"Stephen seems to have made a very serious mistake letting the empress go," Wolfstan said. "As a hostage she would have been his guarantee that her supporters behave."

"Then again," Redwald added. "If she had been taken hostage, that may have caused her supporters to raise arms against the king, anyway."

Ardron sighed. "Maybe," he agreed. "However, whatever happens is beyond our influence and we must therefore look to the welfare of this village."

They were silent a few moments while each pondered the situation.

"In a war," Ardron broke the silence, "The first casualty is always the rule of law. Bands of soldiers and outlaws look to enhance their own fortunes. They rob and they plunder as if it were a right. And if all our young men are away pressed into service there will be only scant protection for the village. Father I think you should collect all the valuable possessions in the village and secret them away somewhere safe."

"It is a sound suggestion my son," Wolfstan agreed.

"Perhaps," Redwald added, "We should also consider selling surplus stock, turning it to silver which can also be hidden away."

"Now! Ardron, what of your circumstances?" Wolfstan asked. "When war does break-out the king will be far too busy to actively pursue outlaws, and so from that aspect I think you could safely return here. However," he went on. "If you do then you might be recruited to the defence of Malmesbury Castle. Inside its walls and amongst the king's men there is a chance, slim though it may be, that somebody will recognise you."

That was the dilemma for Ardron. "I will give it some thought, Father."

Chapter 4

November 1139

November was a couple of days old by the time Ardron returned to Marlborough Castle. As he rode into the bailey, Fitzgilbert's industry was evident. The fortifications had been strengthened and supplies there were in abundance. Barrels filled with arrows were piled under each wall and spears roughly hewn from stout timber alongside. Sturdy wood shelters had been constructed and were strategically dotted around to provide instant shelter from arrow storms. Over by the blacksmiths shop any number of barrels filled with pitch waited ready to be heated. It seemed Fitzgilbert had prepared his defences well. There was no doubt in Ardron's mind that all supplies would have been thoroughly stocked for Fitzgilbert was a meticulous organiser.

As he dismounted, he was greeted by Benet, the castle constable, "Ardron," he said reaching out and clasping him above the elbow. "It is good to see you."

"Thank you, Benet. Is Sir John here?"

"No, he is at Ludgershall, but I am expecting him any moment. Yesterday I heard news that Stephen's army is reported to be advancing along the Kennet valley. Whether he moves against this castle or Wallingford we don't know yet. Last night I sent out a messenger to Ludgershall to inform Sir John."

It seemed to Ardron's that his own appraisal of the situation had been accurate. "If they are coming here when do you think they will get here?" He asked.

"Before nightfall."

"That's not much time," Ardron commented looking around nervously.

"We are ready," Benet said confidently. "Perhaps another six or seven dozen men would not be unwelcomed. But we have what we have."

Ardron nodded. "Is my brother here?"

"Your brother?" Benet said surprised. "No I thought he would be with you."

Ardron was baffled. "Why would he be with me?"

"Sir John sent a detachment of one hundred men to Earl Robert's army, and your brother went with them."

Ardron muttered a curse. "Why did he send him?"

"He didn't. Your brother volunteered so that he could be re-united with you."

"Riders approaching," a guard called from the lookout position above the gate.

"That'll be Sir John," Benet said. "At least I hope it is." He hurried away to see for himself.

The news about his brother troubled Ardron, Earl Robert would soon lead his army into open conflict, indeed if he hadn't done so already. Although in view of the news about Stephen's army advancing along the Kennett valley, Esmond would be in no less danger right here.

A few moments later John Fitzgilbert rode in through the gates at the head of half-a dozen knights and around forty sergenti. They crossed the bailey at a gallop pulling up at the steps of the mote and dismounted. Their horses were lathered in sweat and were blowing hard, they had been ridden harshly.

"Benet," Fitzgilbert shouted for his constable.

"Here, Sir," Benet called almost running across the bailey. Fitzgilbert did not wait instead led the way up the steps followed by his knights with Benet bringing up the rear.

Ardron watched them disappear into the keep, then with nothing more to see he led Rattlebone to the stabling area. With time on his hands he took to careful grooming of his horse. After seeing the animal fed, he made his way up to the wall and along the palisade. Passing time with other sergens he scanned the horizons for sight of Stephen's army.

The day passed slowly, as did the night, but of the expected army there was no sign. It was late on the second day when Benet came to find him. "Sir John sends for you," he said.

Fitzgilbert along with his knights poured over charts and maps and did not see Ardron enter the private chambers. He waited a little while and then attracted his attention by announcing himself. "Sir John," he said.

"Ah_ Ardron my Saxon friend," Fitzgilbert said. "Come over here," with a wave of his arm. He pushed the charts to one side clearing a space in the middle of the table. "We are here," he said placing a wine glass to mark the spot. "This is Wallingford castle," he placed another wine glass. "We must assume that Stephen is here, laying siege to the castle." This time he marked the spot with several pieces of cutlery. "But we don't know for certain. And that is exactly what we need to know."

Ardron waited, but Fitzgilbert did not expand. "You want me to find out," he said eventually.

"Right! As a Saxon who just happens to stumble into the conflict you would be less suspicious than a Norman. Will you do it?"

Ardron sucked in a deep breath then nodded. "I will do it."

"Good man," Fitzgilbert said. "Don't risk your life any more than you need to. We want to know where Stephen is exactly and the approximate strength of his force. Also, if you can, estimate the capability of the castle defence. Assuming Stephen will not attack us here at Marlborough until he has taken Wallingford, we need to know how Fitzcount's defences are holding."

"When do I leave?"

"Right away."

It was late into the night when Ardron decided that he had gone far enough. He estimated that he had covered around eighteen miles and was perhaps still four or maybe five miles away from Wallingford. He was not anxious to go blindly on and stumble into some unseen hazard. Far better, he decided, to wait until daylight and get a clear view of what was in front of him! He had no experience of being a spy and wrapped in his cow-skin blanket he worried and planned what his best course of action might be. Despite the riot of permutations running through his head he did eventually fall asleep.

He rose early the next morning and had arrived within sight of Wallingford within the hour. He paused atop a small hill and surveyed the scene below him. At the foot of the hill a small brook ran directly across his path, and over to his right was the river Thames. In its meadow were many tents, campfires and men of Stephen's army. The bridge over the river had been destroyed and was now nothing more than random struts of wood protruding above the water. He studied the scene carefully; the castle was less than a mile away and as far as he could tell was virtually intact. He scanned east to west and back again several times but the sight that he was witnessing was far more placid than he had expected. He watched for some time, and the only obvious activity he could see were from the two trebuchets which every few minutes hurled boulders into the castle bailey.

From within a small copse. a little to his right, a small band of horsemen emerged not only surprising him but also his horse. He spooked and pranced. Ardron soon got control and looked to these new arrivals as he soothingly stroked the neck of his horse. They were a bunch of Saxons numbering about a dozen. As they passed close by one of them waved a greeting, perhaps mistaking him as a lookout. Acting on instinct he spurred Rattlebone forward and followed the band, at a safe distance, right into the midst of the camp.

Ardron sat his horse well to the rear of the group as they were first challenged and then talked with a knight, who had emerged from one of the tents. From there they were directed to another part of the camp where they dismounted and began to unload the packs from their horses. Ardron copied their example, except he worked much slower; he needed their lead. When they finished unloading, for the most part, they dispersed among the Norman sergens sitting around campfires.

"Hey Saxon," One of the sergens called to Ardron. "Where are you from?"

"London." Ardron took a chance.

"Here, come and sit here." The sergen shuffled up and made room for him at the fireside. "When did you leave London," he asked.

"Yesterday," Ardron replied as he sat down by the fire.

Another of the sergens picked up a wooden platter and after heaping two spoons-full of porridge onto it, handed it over to Ardron. "Not much happening," Ardron ventured.

"Are you keen to get into it?"

"Not particularly," Ardron replied.

"Is this your first siege," the sergen asked.

"It is," Ardron replied

"You must learn to be patient and value these quiet hours. When the assaults do start then all becomes mayhem and sheer terror."

"We live in hope that those Angevins will eventually surrender." The other sergen added.

"Angevins?" Ardron queried. But surely they are Normans."

"Of course they're Normans, but their empress has married an Angevin, which makes her Angevin too, and in turn her supporters."

Ardron nodded understanding.

"You seem to be remarkably ignorant of the situation, Saxon."

Here was the first hint of danger. "I'm just a simple vassal doing exactly as I'm ordered," Ardron said.

"Who is your liege lord?" the sergen asked.

"Waleran, Count of Meulan," It was the only remote possibility of accuracy.

"Count Waleron? You mean Earl Waleron,"

Ardron was baffled.

"King Stephen made him Earl of Worcester just a couple of days ago."

"Oh did he? I didn't know." Ardron passed it off casually.

"You must be part of his advance party," the sergen concluded.

"Yes," Ardron agreed.

"When do you think he'll get here?"

Another danger point for Ardron. He shrugged and pulled a face without answering.

"We await the arrival of his army then we can really put these Angevins to the sword."

"Isn't this force strong enough," Ardron risked a searching question.

"No, we number less than eight-hundred since Stephen left."

"Isn't the king here?" he pushed his luck.

"The king left yesterday going west."

Ardron fell silent and tucked into his porridge. It seemed as if his assessment that Stephen would have to move west to bar any eastern movement by Earl Robert's army had been correct.

"So we just keep the castle under siege until Waleron turns up with his army." The sergen went on.

After breakfast Ardron wandered the camp freely, but he now discovered that getting into the camp was considerably easier than getting out. He now had information and was anxious to deliver it to Fitzgilbert, but to openly saddle his horse and ride out would almost certainly see him stopped. Then, believed a deserter, he might even be hanged. His best chance would probably be after dark, but even then, he would have to be very careful.

Time passed very slowly, and the only variation in the routine was when an arrow storm was released from the castle attempting to bombard the trebuchets. But they had been positioned perfectly just out of range, and the arrows fell short. It was in late afternoon, as the sun set in the November sky, when Ardron saw a potential opportunity. Groups of horses were being led to the small brook to be watered. Ardron collected Rattlebone and a bunch of four other horses, and he too led them to the brook. There he turned the horses loose in the brook and lay on the bank idly chatting with a group of other horse carers. When the others eventually gathered their horses and went back to collect another bunch, Ardron stayed, but took the opportunity to move away further upstream. Slowly and stealthily he wandered further and further until he considered he was a decent distance away. Acting unhurriedly, so as not to arouse suspicion, he haltered Rattlebone and led him to the other side of the brook. Although he did not know if anybody was actually watching, he took great pains to examine the horse's fetlocks, as if he had discovered a potential lameness. Then he mounted and trotted him slowly around, leaning over watching the horse's gait as he did. Kicking his heels into Rattlebone's ribs he then sent him at a gallop along the brook. Once out of sight of the other horse carers, he turned away from the camp and drove his mount hard. He kept the horse at a gallop for about two miles until he considered he was far enough away to be safe.

Noon the next day he arrived at Marlborough Castle and was admitted immediately into Fitzgilbert's private quarters.

"Do you know from where Waleron is coming?" Fitzgilbert asked after hearing Ardron's report.

"That was a question I dare not ask," Ardron replied. "It would have compromised my own story if I had asked that."

"Yes of course," Fitzgilbert muttered folding his arms and looking down at the charts strewn across the table. "Since he has just been made Earl of Worcester, it is possible that he is in Worcester assembling an army," he said to Benet.

The pair studied the charts a few moments. "But then he could be in London," Benet ventured.

"Yes," Fitzgilbert agreed. "Better for us if he is in Worcester, every day that passes sees us just a little bit more prepared." They were quiet for a few moments while they poured thoughtfully over the charts. Then it seemed as if Fitzgilbert suddenly remembered that Ardron was still present. "Thank you Scorrenstone," he said straightening. "Once again you have done me great service."

For the next three days, Ardron pottered around the bailey. He took his turn acting look-out, and spent his free time making more arrows and sharpening stakes. It was while sitting amongst a group of sergens attaching metal bodkins to arrow shafts when Fitzgilbert came to find him.

"Ardron," he said. "Once more I need to turn to you."

"Anything I can do, Sir John."

"I need to use you as a messenger to Bristol yet again."

Ardron nodded acceptance and waited.

"Our problem is that we don't know very much," Fitzgilbert went on. "We don't know exactly where Waleron is with his army? He could, I suppose, be at Wallingford by now. But if not then, where is he? Also Stephen, we know he went west with an army but where is he now? And our own Earl Robert, what of him? Is he still in Bristol with the empress? Or is he engaged in some conflict? There are so many questions and no answers."

"What do you want of me?" Ardron asked.

"First, I want you to find Earl Robert. Then, to deliver my despatch in which I request that he release my detachment to return here. Another hundred men on these walls would be decidedly useful."

"If he denies your request?" Ardron asked.

"He won't. He knows full well the strategic importance of both Marlborough and Wallingford Castles. If Wallingford should fall then it becomes doubly important that Marlborough stand. He'll release them, I'm sure."

"Will I find Earl Robert in Bristol?"

"Of that I'm not sure. But I have to trust in you to find him, wherever he is."

Ardron nodded understanding. "What else do you want from me?"

"Well," Fitzgilbert drawled. "If during your journey you could, by chance, find out where both Stephen and Waleron are, then that too would be extremely useful." He paused allowing Ardron time for thought. "I need you back here with answers as soon as possible. In fact quicker than that!" He threw in the catch.

"I'll leave within the hour." Ardron said.

He made good time, and just west of the small market town of Calne, he topped a high ridge and he halted his horse, giving it a little breather after the steep climb. The land before him dropped away steeply onto an open plateau with a road cutting a straight swathe away and into the distance. The cloudy day had given way to clear skies with a definite chill in the air, with a probability of frost for the night. The setting sun cast the western skies in a myriad of reds and oranges. But it was not the splendour of nature that captured Ardron's immediate interest. It was the long and orderly column of men that moved slowly along the road towards him that focussed his attention.

Banners there were, but at a distance of about a mile they were unidentifiable. Could this be Waleran and his army? He studied the column and made a rough calculation of its strength. It was not likely to be Waleron, he decided, because if it were then a strength of between three-hundred and four hundred was not much of an army. His instinct was for flight and safety because Fitzgilbert was relying on him to deliver the despatches. But curiosity held him on the ridge top, he could safely wait for just a little longer, he decided.

Fifteen minutes later the column had almost reached the foot of the hill, but still Ardron held his position. There was something familiar about the flag at the head of the column. A white flag with a scattering of red diamonds he had seen before, and although he still might be mistaken, he thought it might be the crest of Miles Fitzwalter. The column reached the foot of the hill and began to ascend towards him. For Ardron it was decision time if he intended to flee it was now or never.

He stayed, and as the column neared, he moved aside off the road to allow the convoy to pass. Miles Fitzwalter was not actually at its head, but he rode in the second row, flanked on either side by a couple of knights.

"Sir Miles," Ardron called and turned his horse to fall in alongside.

The nearest knight drew his sword and quickly moved to bar his way. "Stand-off there peasant," he shouted. "Unless you want your head cleaved open."

Ardron sheered away but called once more. "Sir Miles, I am Ardron of Scorrenstone."

This time Miles recognised him. "Hold," he shouted holding up his hand to halt the column. He leaned forward onto his horse's withers, "Ardron Scorrenstone," he said. "You are a long way from home."

"That I am, Sir."

"What are you doing here?"

"I am bound for Bristol, carrying despatches to Earl Robert of Gloucester from Sir John Fitzgilbert of Marlborough."

"Have you just come from Marlborough?"

"That I have."

"Then I would speak with you." Sir Miles said. "But not here. How far are we from Calne?"

Ardron lifted his arm indicating the direction. "Not more than two miles."

"Then accompany us to Calne. That is our intended over-night stop. I will speak with you there."

Ardron was gripped by indecision. There was some urgency in his mission, and he had intended to get beyond Chippenham this night. Nevertheless, he nodded compliance, tomorrow he should be able to make up the lost time. He stood back off the road and waited as the column moved past on its way to Calne.

"Ardron," his name was called. "Ardron," the call came again. He scanned around and soon spotted a rider breaking rank and driving towards him.

"Esmond," he cried as he recognised his brother. Both brothers leaned forward in their saddles and grasped each other affectionately just above the elbow. The pair chatted excitedly and then fell in at the rear of the column.

For Esmond, the excitement soon passed, and he fell moodily silent and gradually he slowed his horse until the pair were seven or eight yards behind the slow-moving column.

Ardron sensed all was not well with his brother. "What is it?" he asked.

Esmond stared dead ahead stone-faced then after a protracted silence almost whispered. "I fear we are fighting on the wrong side, Ardron."

Ardron halted his horse. "Why do you say that?"

"Why do I say that? If you had seen the savage brutality that I witnessed at Worcester, you would not ask."

"Worcester?" Ardron was confused. "What were you doing at Worcester?"

"I was with Earl Robert's army when we marched on that town." He paused gathering his thoughts. "The town was practically undefended. Most certainly they were taken by surprise and were completely unprepared for any attack. But it made little difference as the earl's army swept into town slaughtering both sergens, and innocent citizens, left right and centre in a frenzy of bloodlust. Then they took to plundering and raping as they rampaged completely out of control across the whole town. After the looting was exhausted came the mindless burning, and the whole town was torched. When we left, I looked back on what remained of Worcester. It looked to me as the fires of hell. Only the cathedral was spared, but that stood in the midst of the raging fires and even God's own hand would have been sorely pressed to save it."

Ardron was shocked. "Earl Robert, what did he do?"

"He did nothing." Ardron was hard pressed to relate these actions to the man he had admired.

"There were prisoners too." Esmond went on. "All roped together and dragged along behind the army in single file."

"What happened to them?"

"I don't know," Esmond said. "They moved only slowly and were soon left behind as we made our way back to Bristol. But the following day the prisoner's guards did arrive back, but there was not a single prisoner with them."

Ardron was silent for a few moments appreciating completely the helpless anguish his brother had experienced. "The country is at war brother, and it will be until, either the Empress Maude is vanquished, or she sits on the throne." He paused for a moment. "In war it is always the weak and the innocent that suffer the most, because they are what they are; the easiest prey."

"Do you condone such brutality?" Esmond replied hotly.

"Oh no. No I don't. But there will be many such crimes until this issue is settled."

"Why does God almighty allow such savagery?"

Ardron shook his head sadly then said. "When man makes war, he takes himself beyond God's realm. Then God and all his saints abandon man to his fate."

Soon after they made camp in Calne Sir Miles had Ardron sought and brought to him.

"Ardron Scorrenstone," Sir Miles said. "Tell me about Marlborough."

Ardron was rather guarded, not wishing to give away Fitzgilbert's strengths and weaknesses.

Sir Miles sensing Ardron's caution held up a hand. "It's alright, he said, "I am commissioned to relieve the siege at Wallingford and will need Fitzgilbert's help. Tell me roughly how many men does he have?"

"Perhaps three-hundred or so," Ardron replied with a shrug. The main reason for my journey to Bristol was to request Earl Robert to return the Marlborough detachment to add to that strength."

"Then I have saved you a long trek," Miles said. "The Marlborough detachment is numbered in this force."

Of course it was. That accounted for his brother's presence among the force. Ardron nodded thoughtfully. "There are still some side-issues that I am tasked to discover for Sir John."

"Like what?"

"The whereabouts of King Stephen!"

"Stephen?" Miles exclaimed. "I can tell you that. On my last information he and his army were at Malmesbury as guest of the de Pinkney brothers. Before that he took Castle Combe from Earl Robert's half-brother, Sir Reginald de Dunstanville." He paused a moment then added with derision. "De Dunstanville, Earl of Cornwall. God take the man for a coward that he is. He fled as Stephen advanced. Never was a castle so easily won. After that flushed with success, Stephen fell upon my own castle at South Cerney. My constable there put up stern resistance and for three days he held out, before being overrun. But overrun he was, and for their heroism Stephen had all the survivors hung."

"All the survivors?" Ardron was astonished.

"All the survivors," Miles confirmed.

Ardron winced. "And you lost your South Cerney Castle?"

"I did," Miles said. "Stephen then installed one of the d'Evereux's as castellan.

"D'Evereux's?" Ardron queried.

"Yes, a titled Saxon family from southern part of Wiltshire who, bizarrely, have sworn for the king."

The news that Stephen was at Malmesbury was also of great concern to Ardron. "My own village of Scorrenstone is tenanted land granted from Malmesbury Castle, and as such the villagers are but vassals to the de Pinkney brothers."

"Then the men old enough to bear arms will probably be drafted into Stephen's cause." Miles finished the thought for him.

That was disturbing news for Ardron. "Where will he go from there?" He asked

Sir Miles shrugged. "I don't know for certain, but my guess would be Trowbridge, to seize the castle of my son-in-law Humphrey De Bohun. After all Devizes Castle is Stephen's and by taking Trowbridge, he will then command a line of castles."

There was silence for a few moments as Sir Miles allowed Ardron time to appraise the information. "Now, he said eventually. "My concern is the siege at Wallingford."

Ardron took a deep breath and re-focussed. "If this is your whole force then you don't have enough men," he said.

"I am hoping that Fitzgilbert can add at least three-hundred to my force." Sir Miles said.

"Perhaps he can by taking men from Ludgershall as well as Marlborough." Ardron said. "But I don't think he will be over-keen to leave himself short of manning." He added dubiously. "What if you should be defeated at Wallingford?"

"That is something I will make sure doesn't happen."

"You know, of course, that the siege force are expecting Earl Waleron's army to re-enforce them."

Sir Miles gave a little chuckle and shook his head. "Then their expectations will be disappointed," he said. "Waleron is on his way to Worcester to see for himself the carnage that Earl Robert has wreaked upon his new earldom."

Ardron raised his eyebrows at this news. "There are around eight-hundred men in the siege force you will need to match it at least, and then I would say that you have a chance."

"Three-hundred men from Fitzgilbert and I will have close to that number. But___," he added with a wry smile, "Don't forget the force that is in the castle with Brien Fitzcount. Added together we should have superior numbers, and if all works out as I plan, we will also have the element of surprise. And that is worth double."

Certainly, to Ardron, it seemed that the lifting of the siege seems a credible possibility. "It might work, Sir Miles," he said optimistically. "And I wish you good luck."

"Will you be with me?" Miles asked.

"If Sir John orders it," Ardron affirmed. "Will there be anything else?"

"No that's all for now."

Ardron got up to leave.

"Oh there is something," Miles cut in. "Did you ever catch up to Fitzhubert?"

"No, Sir. He left the country."

"Well he's back."

Ardron was immediately interested though not sure exactly what his issue with the man was now that he had seemingly abandoned Hildi.

"Yes, Miles went on, "But this time he takes his marks from the empress. It seems he didn't get anything like the reward he was expecting from Stephen. So now he tries his luck on the opposite side."

"And his cousin, William de Ypres? What of him? Has he switched sides also? Ardron asked.

"Oh no. Not that one. He stands at Stephen's shoulder."

***

Wallingford

Miles Fitzwalter had planned his attack well. Under the cover of darkness he had advanced his archers onto the hill overlooking the meadow, and the siege army's camp. Over to the west he had stationed his pedites force in a square formation. At this point, just before dawn, the men in the meadow were completely boxed in but were sublimely unaware. They had the river Thames on their eastern flank and the castle to the north.

Ardron, armed with sword and shield, took his position somewhere in the middle of the pedite formation and waited. They had drilled constantly the previous day, stand shoulder to shoulder, hold the shields high and creep forward slowly as one unit. Should a man fall, another in the second row would step forward to plug the gap.

Even before it was light Miles had his archers unleash their arrows high into the sky to fall as an arrow storm onto the unsuspecting siege army. In disciplined unison storm after storm filled the sky and descended into the panicking sergens below. The deadly arrows thudded indiscriminately all around with many finding human targets. Taken completely by surprise, mayhem broke out as individuals, rudely roused from sleep, acting in self-preservation rushed to find what shelter they could. The deadly onslaught continued unabated. The siege army had become the besieged. It was not long before personal survival became the over-riding importance, and a headlong dash to escape the lethal missiles began. It began and grew in momentum in the only possible escape direction, to the west.

"Here they come," Ardron heard Benet's needless warning from somewhere within the formation, and he lifted his shield. "Stand firm, shoulder to shoulder," Ardron shouted as the fleeing sergens ran towards them in a ragged line. They arrived screaming and shouting in anger, hurling themselves at the front row determinedly bent on revenge. The hand to hand fight became bitter and intense, with the attackers thrusting their swords hopefully through any gaps they could find in the shield wall. There was no skill in this combat, it was sheer brute strength of thrust and slash. The clash of sword on shield and shield on shield mixed with shouts of anger and cries of anguish from the wounded and the dying. Ardron swung and thrust his sword continuously. Although his arms ached and begged for relief, he knew that to lessen his efforts would be fatal. He realised then that all the time he had been fighting he had continued shouting, "Shoulder to shoulder."

"To me. To me," Ardron changed shouted instructions when he realised that gaps were appearing in the ranks, and he was no longer shoulder to shoulder with comrades. The gaps were filled and after a sideways glance he was surprised to see Benet at his side. For him to join the front row then the supply of reserves must be about exhausted he concluded. That was not a good sign. He summoned reserves of energy and doubled his efforts swing, slash, stab. These were not men in front of him, only dangerous hunks of flesh bent on killing him. Flesh appeared before him and flesh disappeared beneath his annihilating sword. Just when he thought that exhaustion would overwhelm him the attack started to abate.

Brien Fitzcount's castle milites had come out from their citadel. These mounted sergens launched an attack into the rear of the attackers. Now the pedite formation began to slowly creep forward pushing their attackers back as the onslaught diminished. There was nothing left for the routed force except personal survival, and individuals began to look to their own safety. Many fled around the end of the military block but did not turn and fight. Instead, they continued to flee west away from the battlefield while others retreated back into the meadow.

To the front of Ardron one knight did stand his ground and shouted for men to stand with him and fight on. But none stood with him and his shouts of encouragement turned to expletives as he cursed the fleeing men for their cowardice. With a sword in one hand and an axe in the other he pressed forward alone with insane bravery felling all before him. He was an enormous figure of a man wielding his weapons with deadly ferociousness. All before him melted away rather than confront this one-man destroyer. With no opposition he moved forward until he confronted Ardron.

Ardron suddenly found himself standing alone with no alternative but to defend himself against this one-man annihilator. Twice the knight brought his axe down on Ardron's shield making him stagger backwards under the force. But he managed to bring his sword up, only to find it easily parried. He danced back a couple of steps to regain his balance, and the knight's swinging axe sped towards his head. Bringing up his sword sharply he managed to parry it, and by luck the axe head being 'T' shaped, locked just above the sword hilt. By leaning back and pulling on his sword Ardron could keep the axe locked as the knight jerked at it a couple of times to free it. Giving up on that temporarily, the knight brought his sword down forcefully three times on Ardron's shield. Leaning back under the onslaught Ardron mustered his strength and yanked at his sword snatching the axe free from the knight's hand. Now, at least, there was only the man's sword to worry about.

The two men squared up to each other until the knight attacked once more, swinging his sword horizontally back and forth, the sheer power forced Ardron to backpedal clumsily. He managed to duck beneath the swinging sword and skipped alongside the knight, dragging his sword across the man's ribs as he passed. But it did no damage. The hauberk's protection was good. The knight then turned and advanced menacingly once more. This time he lunged, but Ardron was quick enough to deflect the lunge with his shield, then sinking to one knee he drove the point of his sword at the knight's mid-riff. With the force of the lunge and the on rush of the man the sword pierced through the hauberk and sunk deep into his belly. With a shocked expression the knight dropped his sword and sank to his knees. Ardron stood upright and with a jerk pulled the sword upwards slicing deeper through the man's inner guts. Then using his foot as a lever against the man's chest, he withdrew his sword. For a moment he examined the sword point. Swidhurn's theory that a sharp point had a better chance of piercing a hauberk than a rounded one, had been proved. The fallen knight, at his feet, clutched his stomach and looked disbelievingly at the blood seeping through his fingers. Slowly he then toppled over onto his shoulder and bent himself into the foetus position as he tried to relieve the pain. As he lay there, he tried several times to reach his sword. Ardron stood back and watched, then he understood what the knight was about. He knew he was dying and wanted to die sword in hand. Ardron picked up the sword and handed it to the dying man. Despite the pain raking his face his eyes showed gratitude as he clutched the sword. Then he began to choke on blood as he tried to speak. This noble knight was dying a slow and agonising death. By Ardron's foot lay the knight's helmet and his axe, and he knew what he should do next. He picked up the axe and after a short pause to steel himself, he swung the axe down with all his strength onto the knight's head. The dull thud and the deep laceration repulsed him. Partially through exhaustion and partly through relief he sank to his knees.

The disciplined formation had broken up and the sergens of Sir Miles chased after the fleeing sergens. Ardron only watched having no desire to go with them. He felt a hand on his shoulder and looked up at Benet.

"That was impressively done," he said nodding towards dead knight. "He would have created havoc if he had not been stopped."

"Who was he?" Ardron asked.

Benet shrugged and went over to the dead knight. After a few moments he knelt down and took a ring from the dead man's finger. After examining it he brought it over to Ardron. "You should have this," he said. "You earned it."

"I can't take that from a dead man." Ardron protested.

"Why not? If you don't then some battle-field scrounger will have it. Besides," Benet went on. "I am sure under the circumstances he would rather you have it than some scavenger."

Ardron took the ring; it was gold. The facia was shaped as a shield and was embossed into quarters with a mullet in the top left quarter. "Do you know this crest?" he asked Benet.

"No," Benet replied shaking his head.

Ardron slid the ring on his finger then held is hand up to exam it. It was a magnificent piece of jewellery in gold, and exceptionally well crafted.

"Come," said Benet, helping Ardron to his feet. "Let's follow the battle." In no particular hurry the pair went after their advancing forces towards the river Thames.

The battle was over only the slaughter of the fleeing stragglers remained. Acting out of fear some of the vanquished ran panicking into the river. In their haste to escape some even neglected to strip out of their hauberks making the swim across impossible for many. Miles, however, had deliberately left a corridor of escape, and those that found it ran south along the riverbank below the hill. But even as the vanquished streamed through the corridor they did not escape the attentions of the archers on the hill. They simply turned to unleash more arrow storms down onto the fleeing sergens.

Ardron had no interest in inflicting retribution upon the routed sergens. The siege was successfully lifted and as far as he was concerned it was over, and there was no sense in needless killing. He looked back over an area that was strewn with bodies of the dead, dying or wounded. This day many men had paid the ultimate price in the struggle for the throne of England. But as he surveyed the scene, he knew that this was only the beginning, and there was more to come. Much more! From the hill overlooking the meadow the archers streamed down intent on scavenging what they could from the dead. The position that they had held had been dominant and therefore their casualties must have been just about non-existent. That was of some relief to Ardron because somewhere among those men was his brother, Esmond. He sheathed his blood-stained sword and went among the prone bodies looking to assist any wounded.

***

Marlborough Castle

"We should go home," Esmond said as they both stood and watched Sir Miles and his men leave through the gates of Marlborough Castle. "These days the king has much more to worry about than the breach we committed in London," he went on. It was true, Ardron silently agreed, the killing of two of Waleron's sergens paled into insignificance compared to the brutality that was being wreaked across the country at this time.

Four days had passed since the successful relieving of the siege at Wallingford, and since then there had been three days of feasting. Firstly, within the precincts of Wallingford Castle, then secondly upon the return to Marlborough. However, the celebrations had been brought to an abrupt halt by the news that Waleron, bent on vengeance for the Worcester outrage, was cutting a violent swathe across Gloucestershire and into Wiltshire. Because Winchcombe was part of Miles Fitzwalter's estate his army had trampled across the town. ruthlessly destroying everything in like for like repayment. At Sudeley he destroyed the historic house that Sir John Sudeley had converted to a castle and obliterated the nearby village. Then acting entirely through spite, he fired Tewksbury Abbey for no better reason than it was Earl Robert's money that funded its development. To add further to Sir Miles woe it was reported that King Stephen now laid siege at Trowbridge Castle, the home of his son-in-law Humphrey de Bohun.

Ardron looked sideways at his brother. "What of Hildi?" he asked.

"Hildi?" Esmond said. "Hildi is gone. Lost to us! We don't even know if she's alive."

Clearly Esmond had given up on his intended bride. In fact, Ardron wondered, would his brother still take her for his bride if she were ever rescued? "And Fitzgilbert?"

"Fitzgilbert? We are not vassal to him, we take his coin as mercenaries and as mercenary's we can withdraw whenever it suits us."

"Not quite," Ardron replied. "We do owe some loyalty. But I take your point and at this stage, with no immediate pending danger to him or his estates, then he might not be too dismayed if we did leave." He thought for a moment as he watched the last of Sir Miles unit disappear through the gate. There was merit in what Esmond had said. "I will speak with Sir John tonight," he said.

Ardron and Esmond left Ludgershall Castle two days later and with Fitzgilbert's reluctant blessing. By mid-afternoon on the same day they were deep into the Royal Forest of Melksham. They were in good spirits; after all they were going home. But realising that they could not possibly make Scorrenstone before dark they began to discuss their options. Making camp within the Forest was not an ideal option, they decided. Forest Law meant that they would need permission from its custodian, Humphrey de-Bohun. As an acquaintance to the man permission could reasonably be expected, but de Bohun was under siege at his Trowbridge Castle. Any challenge by one of his knights then consent   might be difficult to prove. Better, they decided, to press on towards Chippenham and seek shelter there for the night.

Up ahead, beyond the nearby bend, angry shouts disturbed the pacifistic sounds of the forest. Both men glanced at each other but not perturbed, they continued steadily on and towards the sounds of mayhem. They turned a bend onto a long straight stretch of road, and at the other end a lone horseman was beset by a small band of robbers. His horse pranced and turned snorting in terror as the horseman tried desperately to fight off the robbers. Holding the reins in his left hand, his sword in the other, he slashed first one side and then the other attempting to keep the robbers at bay as they, on foot, tried to unhorse him.

Without hesitation Ardron pulled his own sword from its baldric and spurred Rattlebone forward to the man's aid. As he neared, he leaned over to his right and swung his sword catching one of the robbers a lethal swipe below his ribs. As his horse galloped on through Rattlebone's stout shoulders barged another to the floor. Clear for the moment Ardron pulled the animal up sharply and twisted him around savagely. Then he spurred him forward once more, this time intending to trample over the fallen robber. The man on the ground seeing the horse bearing down upon him at a gallop cringed and threw up his arms in a desperate hope of protection. But instead of trampling on the man Rattlebone hurdled over him. An arrow from Esmond's bow whispered through the air and struck another of the robbers in the chest just beneath the collar bone. He went down as if pole axed. Not liking the odds anymore the remaining robbers hesitated then as if by signal ran for the cover of the trees.

Ardron took a moment to look about to ensure the danger had, for the time being, passed. Two of the would-be robbers lay on the ground unmoving, while a third, punctured by Esmond's arrow, lay writhing and clutching at the protruding arrow. Satisfied that no danger was imminent Ardron glanced at the other rider. By the man's clothing it was obvious that he was a noble of some distinction.

"Are you alright, Sir Knight?" he asked.

"Yes I am. And you?" he asked.

"Yes." Ardron said as he dismounted and walked over to the man he had scythed down.

"Is he dead?" the knight asked as he too dismounted.

"Yes. And that one?" Ardron replied nodding towards the other prone figure.

"Him too." The knight replied after pushing him over with his boot.

Esmond meanwhile had ridden up and leapt from his horse close to the wounded robber. But there was still some fight left in the man, and left-handed he struggled to draw a knife from its sheaf. Esmond was too quick for him. As soon as the knife cleared its sheaf, Esmond's foot stamped down on the man's wrist, pinning it to the ground and the knife spun harmlessly away. Then Esmond moved his foot onto the man's chest.

"I will have my arrow back, if you don't mind," he growled, and without mercy unceremoniously yanked it from the man's shoulder.

The man yelled with pain and cursed heartily, but Esmond paid him no attention, instead moved away and began to clean the arrow with grass.

Ardron looked down at the stricken man and watched as he pressed his hand onto the open wound. Blood flowed freely from beneath the man's fingers, even so there was still defiance in the man's eyes as he looked up at Ardron. "You're a Saxon," he said.

"I am," Ardron replied.

"You traitorous son of a whore," he cursed. "I hope the hell fires of damnation swallow you up."

"More likely it will be you who is swallowed up. You were the one bent on robbery and killing." Ardron replied coolly.

"Aye," he agreed. "Driven to it by his kind," he said looking past Ardron.

Ardron turned to see the knight come to his side. "What does he say?" he asked in French.

Clearly this Norman didn't speak English. "He says it is all your fault."

A look of shock crossed his face. "How so?"

"How so?" Ardron passed on the question.

With a look of sheer hatred the man glared at the knight. "His kind," he spat bringing his attention back to Ardron, "Came to our village in force. They asked no questions made no demands instead went about pillaging anything of value including livestock. That which they didn't want they destroyed, burning everything including our food stocks. They left us with nothing. Now we are forced to rob and steal in order to feed our children. We do not set out to kill but if we must then we must. And we try to rob Norman's only."

Ardron was silent a moment. He could relate to the man's predicament completely. It had changed the whole complexion of the incident. Then he translated to the knight what he had said.

"Does he know which force it was?" the knight asked.

The man slowly shook his head after Ardron had translated the question. Now Ardron's sympathies were with the wounded man, and he decided he should do something about his wound. The knight's horse draped a covering cloth over its hind quarters. The cloth of finest silk blazed red with a bright yellow logo of a mythical half man-half horse stretching a bow. Not many in the country could boast such finery to wear, never mind dress their horses in such a manner. Ardron lifted the cloth and tested the silk between his fingers, then looked at the knight. He too was garbed in the finest of materials. He was a man in his early thirties with long, but neatly trimmed, light brown hair and beard. The cloak he wore of blue silk was laced with gold thread and held on his right shoulder by a large clasp of gold. The man flaunted his obvious wealth with a deal of conceit and complete disregard for the poverty of the masses. Such arrogance was bound to prove a powerful magnet to any would-be robber. Resenting such decadence, Ardron took his knife and cut a long strip from the horses covering sheet. He expected the knight to protest but he did not, instead he held the horses head while he did it. Using the silk he began to dress the wound best way he could. When he had finished, he helped the man to his feet.

The knight meanwhile fiddled in his saddle bag and withdrew a leather purse. After peering inside he changed his mind, then pulled the draw strings closing it. Then he walked over to the man and pushed the purse inside his belt. "That should see your village fed through the winter," he said. "And without need to rob again."

Not understanding French the man just looked confused.

There was a definite sound of galloping horses approaching. When they came around the bend and into view it revealed a group of eight Norman sergens led by a knight. The knight slid from his horse as soon as they got close. "Sire," he said with concern. "Is everything alright?"

"Yes Sir William, it is. Thanks to these noble Saxon's here," he replied.

Sire? Ardron was confused. Sire was an address usually preserved for a king, but then sometimes was used a little more freely as term of endearment.

"Yes," he said noting Ardron's confusion. "I am King Stephen. I got separated from my hunting party," he added with a shrug.

Ardron took a half step back and bowed in respect. "King Stephen," he said.

"This is Sir William de Ypres," Stephen introduced the new arrival. Then addressing Sir William the king took charge. "Sir William," he said, "You will see these men well rewarded with silver for I owe them my life."

Sir William bowed acknowledgement.

"This man," Stephen went on referring to the wounded Saxon, "You will see safely escorted back to his village."

While Sir William made the arrangements the king walked with his arms draped over Esmond and Ardron's shoulders. "I would know your names and to where you are bound?" he said.

Ardron gave their names and informed the king that they were homeward bound for the village Scorrenstone.

"Scorrenstone? Where is that?"

"Close to Malmesbury."

"Malmesbury?" The king exclaimed with surprise. "Malmesbury is our destination. I insist that you travel with us."

When a king insists then one does not refuse.

Esmond and Ardron rode at the back of the party as they made their way through the forest. "What have we done?" Esmond asked.

"What have we done, indeed?" Ardron muttered. He was well aware that if they had not intervened then King Stephen just might have been killed, and the bloody struggle for England's crown might be ended. Their intervention had probably saved his life, and that meant the conflict would now continue, and most certainly that would be at a cost of many lives. One life for many! What had they done indeed? Even so, and in all conscience, he could not see how they could have stood by and watched what would have amounted to murder?

Also a burning question for Ardron was the fate of Trowbridge. The last word he had heard was that Trowbridge was under siege from the king. But here was the king on his way to Malmesbury? He dare not, however, ask about Castle Trowbridge's fate. He feared it might spark questions that would be somewhat awkward to answer. Better to lay his curiosity aside for the time being.

Soon they had breasted a long steep hill and looked down over a myriad of tree canopies into the Avon valley. Immediately below them was the village of Lacock with its wooden bridge over the river. From among the trees on this side of the river several thin columns of smoke rose lazily in the still air. A few minutes later they rode into the camp of the king's army.

Ardron had just dismounted when he heard his name called. "Ardron, Ardron of Scorrenstone." He looked about to see a familiar face coming towards him.

"William?" he said, as he recognised the man. "What are you doing here?"

"I could ask you the same thing," he replied as both men grasped greeting arms just above the elbow.

"Esmond," Ardron said looking up at his brother who had yet to dismount. "This is William Grugy, the sergen who taught me to speak French and how to wield a sword."

Esmond nodded acknowledgement as he dismounted.

"What are you doing here," Ardron asked again.

"I am here with my liege-lord Count Hervey de Leone, Earl of Wiltshire, in the cause of the king. And you? How is it that you are here?"

Ardron shrugged. "Quite by accident!" he said. "We are routed back to Scorrenstone when purely by chance we did service to the king. He insisted that we fall in and journey to Malmesbury in his company."

"Come," William said placing his arms over the shoulders of both Ardron and Esmond. "We have much catching up to do." Sitting at a camp fireside they talked jovially as old friends would with much news to relate. For his part Ardron was a little guarded, not wanting to even hint to his old friend that his services so far had been in the cause of Empress Maude. Much water had passed beneath bridges and circumstances changed greatly since their friendship days at Malmesbury. However, much later in the evening Ardron did find an opportunity to innocently ask William about the siege of Trowbridge.

Trowbridge?" William exclaimed. "Trowbridge is still under siege. But the greater part of the force is here. Only a force sufficient to maintain the blockade remained. "Just a matter of time before de Bohun cedes," he added with a shrug. "But it could be a long time. That force is not strong enough to over-run the castle, so it will have to be starvation or disease to make him eventually surrender."

Ardron nodded silent acceptance while glancing at Esmond willing him to remain silent. They both knew that which William didn't. Miles Fitzwalter was on his way to de Bohun's aid. Indeed he might even be at Trowbridge at that moment.

It was well into the evening after they had eaten their fill that they heard their names being paged and were brought to the tent of William de Ypres.

"The king has commanded that I reward you with silver," de Ypres said after he had bade the brothers welcome. "That should make you happy," he said as he tossed a swollen leather purse, to Esmond. "It may be that this country owes you a massive debt of gratitude. With men like you in our ranks then victory most surely will be assured," he went on.

Ardron glanced at Esmond, guardedly. It would never do to inform de Ypres that only recently they had fought at Wallingford against the king's forces.

"Sir William," Ardron said. "We are just two simple Saxon peasants and have no desire to become enmeshed in a conflict that is of little consequence to us."

De Ypres stared at him hard, not pleased with Ardron's response. "Firstly," he said. "I do not believe that you are just a pair of simple peasants. Not with the sword you carry. Nor, with your skill with the bow." The last comment was directed at Esmond. "My Liege has described the way that you conducted yourselves in his rescue, and I believe that you are both seasoned warriors. Secondly, it is your patriotic duty to stand by your king in his time of need whatever your circumstances. Unless of course," he added as an after-thought. "Your sympathies lay with the would-be usurper Maude." He stared hard at Ardron.

He was on the spot and Ardron was not sure how to proceed. He decided to stay close to the truth leaving out incriminating escapades. "It is true, Sir William, that we have become seasoned fighters. That is a skill created from necessity when one day a band of Norman's raided our village and stole away two of our young girls. Esmond and I, and one other, set off to rescue the girls. We followed the leader of that force across the west of England. In Winchester we managed to rescue one girl. Then we went onto London before losing our man who had returned to France. With all trails of the remaining girl then having disappeared we decided to return home. And that is where we are bound."

"Do you have the name of this culprit?"

"Aye, Sir, we do,"

"And he is?"

Ardron hesitated, knowing full well that Fitzhubert was this man's cousin. What the hell? He decided to name and shame. "His name is Fitzhubert!"

"Fitzhubert?" de Ypres surprise was complete. "Why that treacherous vermin is my own cousin and is the very reason we are marching on Malmesbury."

It was Ardron's turn to be surprised. "You're marching on Malmesbury?"

"Aye, we are. Fitzhubert took the castle from the loyal castellan, Walter de Pinkney, after we marched away to Trowbridge."

"Fitzhubert is at Malmesbury?" Ardron questioned.

"Yes he is. But his life can be measured in days, or perhaps even hours. Cousin notwithstanding, I will see him hang from the town gates." de Ypres snarled.

This was valuable news to Ardron. Perhaps, just perhaps, Hildi was there with him. Or if she wasn't Fitzhubert might know where she was. However, would he get a chance to ask the question? He might, if the king's army were successful, and if he could impose on the king for that favour. In view of his recent rescue the king might allow him that favour.

"I will join you in this fight, Sir William. However, my brother will return to Scorrenstone." Ardron said.

Scorrenstone! Where is Scorrenstone," de Ypres asked.

"Close to Malmesbury."

"Close to Malmesbury? Then you must be tenanted to de Pinkney," de Ypres said.

"Yes."

"Then your brother stays too. The de Pinkney brothers are in this camp and as his villeins you are obliged to fight their cause under the privilege of your tenancy."

***

It was mid-afternoon on the following day when the king's army reached Malmesbury. They made camp on its eastern side atop a valley over-looking the river Avon. Ardron sat astride his horse and looked across the valley to the town. Malmesbury was ringed by a stout defensive wall and its gates firmly closed. Above the numerous bucolic houses, the splendid imposing Abbey dominated the view. Close by its side and almost dwarfed in comparison was Malmesbury castle. The castle's stone built keep, atop the mote, thrust upwards and clear above the clutter of dwellings. The wooden bridge over the river had been destroyed. It was a futile gesture, because the river along this stretch would not wet a man's thigh.

Ardron was in dread of this attack because many of the town's people were known to him. How could he continue to live and trade in this district, if during the attack he were forced to confront and possibly kill, some of these people he knew as friends? He looked around at the army behind him now busily making camp. He estimated the force to be around twelve hundred. He knew that there were more than double that number inside the town walls, but many were women, children and elderly, all vulnerable to young strong well-trained sergens. He pondered what Fitzhubert's defence might be. He would need a large force if he were to defend the town walls. Better for him to forfeit the town and mount his defence from inside the castle. Ardron hoped that would be his strategy because that might mean that the weaker of the townsfolk would become irrelevant and therefore ignored by the kings forces. Of course those of fighting age would almost certainly be drafted inside the castle and put to its defence. His own detailed task for tomorrow he already knew. He was to be among the frontal assault force. Esmond, however, would be among the archers. From this hill the archers would be ineffective. They would have to be within the town precincts if they were to rain down their arrows into the castle bailey. Therefore they would not be played until the kings men were inside the town walls

Perhaps there would be no battle, and tomorrow Fitzhubert would surrender to the king. But that was a forlorn hope, Fitzhubert would have to fight. To surrender would mean almost certain execution. For a moment he pondered the vagaries of chance. Despite his earlier resolve to keep out of this Norman war, he had found himself fighting in the cause of Maude at Wallingford, and now it seemed that on the morrow he would be fighting in the opposite cause, that of Stephen. Ardron sighed heavily wishing that he could be anywhere but here.

"It should be quite a fight," William Grugy said. "First we will need to get into the town before we can attack the castle."

"Do you know any of these townspeople?" Ardron asked.

"Hmm__ yes," Grugy drawled. "I met some in my time here."

"How do you feel having to put some of them to the sword?"

De Grugy shrugged, "It is better not to think on that, but to just concentrate on the end objective." There was silence between the two men before Grugy turned his horse and began making his way back to camp. Ardron delayed a little, and then he too turned Rattlebone and made his way to the camp.

It was a clear morning with the keen pinch of frost holding down the temperature when a contingent of forty men approached the main Malmesbury town gate. At its head William de Ypres was flanked on either side by the de Pinkney brothers. Standing on the hill among the king's sergens Ardron watched the exchanges between the horsemen and the men on the town wall. From this distance he could hear nothing of the discussions, but they seemed to be disappointingly protracted, and for a while it seemed as if nothing was about to happen. But then there was movement and cheering broke out in the ranks as the town gates were opened.

For the better part of an hour, the king's men streamed through the gate into the town. In no hurry Ardron held back on the hill and was among the last to enter the town. The mood was jubilant, and the news was that there was to be no battle. Fitzhubert and his forces had abandoned the castle and retreated to the west the previous night. King Stephen now held the castle and had re-instated Walter de Pinkney as castellan.

Greatly relieved Ardron made his way to the Abbey gates and settled down to wait for Esmond to join him. In a soothed frame of mind he relaxed and waited patiently for Esmond to arrive. When he eventually did it was in an agitated state. He blurted out from a distance something about an outrage.

"Calm down," Ardron quietened. But he wouldn't be calmed.

"They are pillaging the town and burning the houses," he shrieked.

Ardron stared at his brother unable to comprehend fully what Esmond was saying. "Pillaging the town? Who is?"

"Stephen's soldiers!"

Ardron turned away and tried to look down the hill, but the view was obstructed. But as he looked, he could now smell the smoke. "Come. The king shall hear of this," he said unable to believe that Stephen would condone such action.

With anger heaving in his chest Ardron strode into the castle bailey and crossed towards the mote. But at the foot of the mote he was stopped by four guards. "I demand to see the king," he stormed.

"Yes you and five-hundred others," one of the guards said. "Now go away," he ordered.

"No I will not go away. I will see the king," Ardron replied hotly.

The guard drew his sword and held it up in front of Ardron's face. "You'll get this blade across your neck if you're still here in one second."

"Oh really?" Ardron replied. He stepped back and drew his own sword. The guard came at him swinging his sword left and right. But Ardron parried both assaults before circling his sword and twisted the guards own sword from his grasp. But that was not an end to it, the other guards joined in. Confronted by three advancing guards Ardron gave ground slowly until Esmond joined the fracas at Ardron's side. Standing shoulder to shoulder the two brothers withstood the three-pronged assault, then began to slowly move forward. The clash of steel on steel rang across the bailey as did the shouts of encouragement from interested spectators. The brothers manoeuvred onto the steps of the mote and gave themselves a height advantage. Continuing to fight off the guards they began slowly to ascend the steps.

"In God's name what goes on here?" an authoritative voice rang out. "Put up your swords immediately."

Instantly the guards obeyed stepping back from the fight. Although Ardron and Esmond stopped fighting, they continued to warily hold their swords pointing forward aggressively.

"Put up those swords I said, or by God I'll see you hung drawn and quartered."

Ardron glanced over his shoulder to see de Ypres at the top of the mote steps. He lowered his sword and placed a hand on Esmond's shoulder indicating that he should too.

"Now pray tell me what you think you are doing?" de Ypres said.

"I would speak with the king on an urgent matter." Ardron said.

"Oh you would, would you?" de Ypres said sarcastically. "What gives you the right to demand an audience with the king? You're none but a lowly Saxon."

Suddenly feeling rather presumptuous Ardron bowed a subservient head. "Sir William, I have news of a disturbing nature to impart."

"What would this disturbing news be?"

"Sergens, they pillage and burn the town," Ardron said waving an arm in the direction of the town.

"You think the king doesn't know that?" de Ypres sarcastically.

Ardron stared at de Ypres. "Surely he doesn't know of it."

"Of course he knows," de Ypres replied. "It is punishment on the townspeople for disloyalty."

"Disloyalty?"

"Yes they opened the gates to Fitzhubert."

"Sir, with due respect. That was probably more to do with the unpopularity of the de Pinkney brothers that any disloyalty to the king."

"Walter de Pinkney was the king's appointed castellan." De Ypres said. "Any arm raised against him is an arm raised against the king." He paused a moment. "Only the fact that you aided the king in his hour of need the other day saves you from arrests." He glared at both brothers. "There's an end to it. Now be off before I change my mind." He turned abruptly and went back inside the keep.

Ardron turned and glanced at Esmond, the outrage on his face was patent. Beyond Esmond Ardron could now see the town in flames with thick black smoke billowing into the air on a lazy breeze.

"There is nothing for us here, brother," Ardron said sadly placing a consoling arm across Esmond's shoulder. "Let us go home." Then taking the bag of silver that had been their reward, he tossed it into the keep after de Ypres.

Chapter 5

Scorrenstone, March 1140

There was excitement in the village on this day, Hengist the pedlar had arrived. His horse had toiled up the steep hill dragging his two wheeled cart into the village while Hengist rang the bell to announce his approach. It had been more than a year since his last visit, and the villagers of Scorrenstone had believed that either he had simply moved to a different area or that some mishap had befallen him.

His attention captured by the bell, Ardron looked across to where the pedlar had parked his cart. "Well well! "Now there's a turn up," he said to Redwald, and nodded in the direction of the pedlar.

"Hengist? Is that Hengist?" Redwald muttered. But it was only a question he asked himself. "I thought he had gone for good." The pair worked to construct an animal pen, but the pedlar's arrival gave them the opportunity to take a pause from their labours. Laying down their tools they strolled over to the pedlar's cart.

"Gather round all you good folk of Scorrenstone I have goods a-plenty for all to trade," Hengist began his sale spiel as soon as he had pulled his cart to a stop. Coin did change hands during his trading but mostly it was goods for goods, trade and barter. He jumped down from his cart and began to unharness his horse. The first to be attracted were the children shouting excitedly and flocking to him as flies to ox dung.

Hengist was not a young man, his straggled mass of grey hair over a heavily gnarled face half hidden beneath a streaked beard, indicated a man of some fifty winters. Heavy overlay of thick fur across his shoulders made him look bigger than he actually was. He exchanged good humoured patter with the children as he led his horse from between the shafts, then with a slap on its rump turned it loose to forage for itself.

"Hengist," Redwald said as he approached. "I thought you long dead for sure."

"Not me, young Thegne," he replied as he climbed back onto his cart and began to roll back the cloth covers off the side. "What of your father Wolfstan, is he dead yet?"

"I am alive and well," Wolfstan answered gruffly, having just arrived to within earshot.

"Ah, Wolfstan old friend," he replied with a huge grin. "I am pleased to hear it." He jumped down and each man grasped the other just above the elbow.

"So you are back to fiddle and swindle my villagers, you old thief."

Hengist feigned a pained expression. "Wolfstan," he appealed. "You well know that I am such a poor trader that I barely scrape a living. I am a poor poor man."

"Ah," Wolfstan said in mock sympathy. "Then as a poor poor man you had better eat with us this night."

"As always, my Thegne, you are a benevolent Christian. And by then I should have found the letter I have to deliver into your hands."

"Letter? What letter?"

"A letter handed to me by a fair-haired young woman in Oxford. She was insistent that it be delivered into your hand."

"Hildi?" Redwald asked.

"Aye," Hengist replied. "That was her name."

"Where is this letter?" Ardron demanded.

Wolfstan laid a calming hand on Ardron's arm. "Hengist, we are most anxious to see this letter. Please find it as soon as you can."

Hengist turned and looked into the chaos of cluttered heaps of trade goods inside his cart. Then after a moment's thought he climbed back onto the cart and began a hunt, muttering directions to himself as he did. "It's here somewhere," he said over his shoulder as he began shifting his wares around.

"When did you come by this letter?" Redwald asked.

Hengist stopped his search and thoughtfully stroked his beard. "What is the month?" he asked.

"March," Wolfstan said.

Hengist shook his head and continued stroking his beard in thought. Then as a thought occurred to him, he raised a triumphant finger skywards. "Candlemass!" he said. "It were straight after Candlemass."

"Candlemass?" Ardron said. "That was at the beginning of February some six weeks hence."

"Aye that be about right." Hengist muttered and went back to his search.

"Why did it take you so long to bring it?" Ardron demanded

"Calm yourself," Wolfstan said. "The man has to make his living as he travels."

Ardron nodded understanding and controlled his impatience.

"Here it be," Hengist said picking up a clay jug and retrieving the letter from within. He glanced at it then rubbed it hard against his ribs a couple of times to smooth out the creases. "And a pretty young maid she was too," Hengist said as he handed over the letter to Wolfstan. Immediately he switched his attention to the clay jug and held it up for the gathered villagers to see. "What'll you give me for this fine clay jug?" He said.

"Ardron," Wolfstan said. "Go and find Swidhurn and Hildi's father and bring them to me." Then as Ardron moved to do his bidding, "Redwald, you come with me."

The small gathering assembled in the village meeting house where Wolfstan informed Hildi's relatives of the received letter. There was deal of anxious excitement on Hildi's father's part and he urged Wolfstan to open it quickly.

First, however, Wolfstan examined the outer carefully. It was neatly folded, and wax sealed with an outline of a knights helmet impressed into the wax. He did not recognise the emblem and he invited opinions, but no-one recognised it. He opened the letter and quickly scanned the contents.

"What does it say?" Hildi's father asked impatiently.

"It doesn't say much," Wolfstan said. "Only that she is in good health and is being treated kindly." He looked up at Hildi's father. "She wants you to be at peace in your mind that she is content."

"Let me see," the old man said. Wolfstan handed over the letter. "What does it mean?"

"We can only take it as it is written," Wolfstan replied with a shrug.

The old man handed it over to his son Swidhurn. "Tell me what it means," he said seeking some re-assurance. Swidhurn read the letter then slowly shook his head. "At least we know that she is alive," was all he could say.

A few minutes later the meeting petered out and broke up. The letter posed more questions than it answered.

"Ardron," Wolfstan said as all began to leave, "Wait with me a while." When they were alone, he handed over the letter. "Tell me what you see" he said.

Ardron examined it. The letter was brief and in decoratively written script with the ornate pen skill of a learned monk. "It's brief, it's in English and it's beautifully written."

"Just so!" Wolfstan said. "Did Hildi have such writing skill before she was abducted? I think not." He answered his own question.

"Do you think that she didn't write it?" Ardron asked.

"I am almost sure she didn't."

"She could have paid someone to write it for her," Ardron said.

"Yes she could have. Wolfstan agreed. "Take a look at the seal. Is that a nobleman's seal?"

Ardron turned the letter over and re-aligned the broken seal. He studied it a moment then nodded agreement. "A knight's helmet, I think it must be," he said. He handed the letter back. "What do you want me to do?" He asked after a moment's pause.

"I want you to go to Oxford and see what you can find out."

"When do you want me to leave?"

"I want you to leave tonight after dark and without a word to anyone. I have no wish to put Hildi's family through any more distress. Let them take comfort in the letter just as it stands."

***

Atop a long sloping hill Ardron reined in Rattlebone and looked down to Oxford a little over a mile away. He leaned forward onto the horse's withers and studied the view. Oxford was a decent size town huddled mostly on the eastern side of the river Thames. A rustic wooden bridge linked both sides of the river allowing some overspill onto the opposite bank. The waters of the river glistened in the weak March sunshine depicting a serene pastoral scene. In the midst of the town Oxford Castle was dominant, chiefly because of the large and impressive tall stone tower built inside the bailey. Ardron thought it perhaps curious that the castle had not been built right alongside the river to use its wide and deep water as an element of protectorate.

There were many questions to be answered not least, would this be where his search for Hildi would end? But where was he to start? Bearing in mind the probable nobleman's seal on the letter then the castle would seem to be the obvious place to start. However, he had no contact in the castle, in fact he did not even know who the castellan might be. "Well big fellow," he muttered to his horse, "There'll be no answers sitting up here." He spurred Rattlebone forward to descend the hill.

Save for the occasional curious stare, he attracted very little attention as he moved through the labyrinth of narrow streets. Eventually, he arrived beneath the castle walls and in an instant, he could see that he had been wrong about its suitable site. A deep-water spur from the Thames ringed the castle completely, and the only way across this moat was via a narrow wooden bridge. At the end of the bridge there was a tall ornate barbican, and no more than a step beyond that, an impressive drawbridge. The walls of the bailey were constructed from gravel cemented by clay, whilst the tower in the west of coral rag-stone. Atop a sixty-foot mote, the castle keep was also constructed coral rag-stone. While no castle can ever be considered impregnable this one looked to be pretty close.

He started across the drawbridge but got no further than the barbican before he was stopped by two guards. Entrance into the castle denied, he turned about and went back into the town streets. His first priority was to see his horse tended, so he wandered aimlessly around until he came across stabling. It was no more than an open barn without ends, but there were stalls aplenty and many empty. At the front, a metalsmith watched Ardron idly as he worked a foot pump encouraging the forge to blaze.

"Is there stabling here?" Ardron asked pulling his horse to stand.

There was no reply from the smith, instead he condescended to jerk his head, indicating that Ardron should make his enquiries inside. Ardron walked his horse inside the stables, but apart from bored horses peering out from their stalls, the place seemed to be deserted. He slid from the saddle and tied Rattlebone's halter around a hitch rail.

"Is there anybody here? He shouted. Nothing! "Hello," he tried again. As he walked further down the barn a man emerged from one of the vacant stalls.

He was a man of senior years wearing a grimy brown smock over a grey shirt that may have once been white. On his head he wore a knitted skull cap with long lugs hanging down both sides of a dirty face.

"Yes," he said sleepily. "What do you want?"

Clearly Ardron had woken him. "Stabling for my horse."

The old man moved to a post and swayed from side to side using the post as a back scratcher. "One mark for a night. Plus a half shilling for fresh bedding and another half for feed," he said.

Ardron nodded agreement.

Then the old man pushed himself away from the post and held out his hand to be paid. "Pick a stall," he said after checking the coins in his hand. "Bedding is over there," he pointed towards a large pile of dry straw. "And feed you will find hanging up in nets back there."

Ardron hesitated a moment, then decided not to take issue. The charge was a mark and a shilling, and he was expected to do the work himself? Never mind, he preferred to attend Rattlebone's welfare personally anyway. He led the big horse down the barn and chose a stall around the middle, estimating that it would be slightly warmer away from the open ends. After liberally scattering straw down for bedding and hanging a net of feed he went to find water for the trough.

"Water?" the old man said looking up from the rope he sat splicing. He pointed down the barn. "You'll find a well out the back."

"And something to put it in?" Ardron queried.

"Should be a pitcher or two down there." No longer interested, he went back to his splicing.

With his horse settled it was time to turn attention to his own welfare. He looked down the barn where the old man still sat splicing and paying Ardron no attention. Although he had not been at all sociable, he was the obvious place to start.

"That's my horse attended, now I have to find somewhere for me to stay." The old man did not even look up seemingly fully engrossed in his task. "Can you tell me where I might find a bed for the night?" Ardron persisted.

The old man laid the rope in his lap. "I might, for a grout or two," he said.

Ardron first reaction was exasperation, and he thought to walk away. But then changed his mind, a couple of grouts was nothing. He fiddled in his purse and dropped two grouts in the old man's lap.

"Now let me see," the old man said. "If thee just wants a bed there's old Grindon's Inn, just round the corner. Now if you wants more in your bed than Grindon's fleas, then there's Mother Baylor's place, she'll find you a whore for a bed partner. Course, thee might finish up with more than fleas." At that he giggled.

"Something in between?" Ardron said not seeing the joke.

The old man sighed and leaned to one side to peer at Ardron's sword, the hilt just visible above his left shoulder. "You could try the sergens barracks in the castle if you be a soldier," he said.

Ardron thought about it. He could just about consider himself a soldier, having fought for the empress at Wallingford and the king at Malmesbury, he could be a soldier for either side. However, before he presented his credentials he would need to know where the castle's castellan sympathy's lay. It would be hazardous to declare for the empress if the castellan were a king's man. "Who is the castellan?"

"That be Sir Robert d'Oyly," the old man informed him.

Ardron had never heard of the man. "And is he for the king or the empress, would you know?"

"Thee wants to know a lot for two grouts," he said. Then after an indifferent shrug. "I don't bother myself with things that don't concern me."

There was nothing more to be gained from the old man Ardron concluded, and so with a brief nod he left. He walked down the narrow street in the direction of the castle still not sure how he was going to make his approach. By chance he found himself outside Grindon's Inn and realised that he was hungry. A mug of ale, a wedge of bread and cheese would not be unwelcome, and perhaps from within he just might learn the empathies of Oxford Castle's castellan.

Even though it was still an hour short of noon the atmosphere inside was boisterous. He found an unoccupied table by the window and sat down. Most of the noise came from a group of young men close to where he sat. Their language was French and so, obviously, they were Normans. He watched fascinated as these young men, with alcohol induced enthusiasm, indulged themselves in a gambling game. Upon the wall hung a pair of cattle horns, a few feet away a rope hung from the ceiling with a ring tied on the end. The object of the game was to swing the rope from a distance and hook the ring around one of the horns.

"Are you here as a customer or just as a spectator?" He hadn't seen the barmaid approach. She was a big buxom woman with a red complexion.

She wiped her hands on a beer stained apron as she waited for Ardron's response.

"Bring me a mug of ale," Ardron replied. "And some bread and cheese if you have it."

"Do you have money?" she asked.

Ardron reached into his belt and pulled out his purse, then tipping it, he allowed a few coins to spill out onto the table. "Will that do?" he challenged.

She only nodded, then waddled away down the room but was soon back with a mug of ale. "No cheese, only mutton," she said as she plonked the mug of ale down on the table.

"That'll be fine," Ardron said. "Who are they?" he asked nodding towards the gamblers.

She glanced briefly in their direction then said with a hint of contempt. "Sergens from the castle."

Ardron nodded, it confirmed what he had already surmised. He took a sip of ale while he thoughtfully watched the sergens. The strength of ale surprised him. The main drink of village Saxons was ale because it was much safer than drinking water. But it was a very weak brew and nothing as compared to the strength of this beer. He decided that he had better contain his intake.

Soon the maid returned with the food and, not too delicately, put a wooden platter in front of him. "That'll be two silvers." she said.

Ardron continued to watch the sergens as he ate. One who had noticed his interest spoke to him. "Do you play?" he asked.

"No," Ardron said. "I've never seen this game before."

"Then come and have a go."

"No," Ardron said, "I don't want to interfere with your game."

"Come on," the sergen insisted. "You're not interfering with anything."

Why not? Ardron questioned himself. "Alright then I will," he said and got to his feet.

"Make way for a novice," the sergen charged his friends.

Good humoured banter passed as Ardron took his position. Twice he swung the ring and twice he missed. But on the third try, more by luck than judgement, the ring hooked over a horn.

"We claim him for our side," a sergen shouted and Ardron found himself drawn into the game.

The company was good, the game was fun and the few shillings it cost to lose was insignificant. Also, he found his mug of ale topped up regularly as the group continually ordered and re-ordered jugs. Not wishing to appear a freeloader he too ordered a jug. Eventually, the game exhausted, they sat at a long table. But the boisterousness did not decrease, in fact quite the opposite, and the group began to noisily sing bawdy songs.

That was a very good song
Sing us another one
Just like the other one
Sing us another one do
To you

Everybody chorused after each little ditty then pointed a finger at the next man to take a turn. Ardron experienced a moment of panic when the fingers pointed at him. His embarrassment was spared when the man sitting next to him put his hand on his shoulder and stood taking his turn.

There was a young man from Valtuka
Who peeped through a hole in a shutter
All he could see
Was a bare lady's knee
And the arse of the knight that was up her

Ardron giggled uncontrollably. He had a mouth full of wool, or so it seemed, because every time he tried to speak, he could not form the words properly. He knew that he was badly inebriated, but he didn't care; he couldn't remember the last time he'd had so much fun. Even the grumpy buxom barmaid began to look attractive to him.

***

Almost awake but trying hard not to be, Ardron didn't feel well. He feared that to become fully conscious would make him feel even worse. Eventually, after twenty minutes or so, he accepted the inevitable and opened his eyes. He found himself in a long but narrow room with lines of small cots down both sides. One or two of the cots were occupied by sleepers, but most were empty. He had no idea where he was.

He rolled over onto his back and was immediately assaulted by a team of minuscule blacksmiths clanging feverishly on their anvils inside his head. He screwed up his face seeking relief but even his eyes hurt when he did. He let out a long involuntary groan. Somebody close by giggled at his discomfort. Turning over onto his shoulder he saw, sitting on the next cot, one of his Grindon's Inn playmates. But he couldn't remember the man's name. "Where am I?" he muttered.

"You're in the castle," he replied.

"In the castle? How did I get here?" Ardron asked struggling to a sitting position. He was then forced to close his eyes as the room began to spin.

"We brought you here,"

"Er," he struggled to remember the man's name.

"Pierre," the man helped him.

"Pierre," Ardron responded. "Why did you bring me here?"

He laughed heartily. "Well the state you were in we could do nothing else, especially after the landlord threw you out into the alley and threatened to knife you."

"Threatened to knife me, Why?"

"He caught you fucking his wife."

"What?" he almost screeched in disbelief. "Who was his wife?"

"That big buxom barmaid."

"Oh no," he groaned in shame as recall came seeping back.

"If we had left you sleeping in the alley then, in all probability, you would have woken naked and skint after the thieves had worked you over."

The man was probably right. Then he remembered his sword. "My sword! Where's my sword?"

"It's safe."

"Where is it?" Ardron demanded.

"You're lying on it," Pierre said.

He lifted the edge of the bedding which was no more than a large sack stuffed with hay. The sword was there, he was relieved to see. "Pierre, I owe you and your friends a great deal of thanks," he said.

"Say no more," Pierre said leaning over to a wooden chest by the side of his cot. He took from it Ardron's purse then tossed it over. "I also took your purse into safe custody."

Ardron caught the purse and croaked through a dry mouth. "Thanks yet again." Briefly he weighed it in his hand. It was considerably lighter than it had been.

"Have you had a visit from the hobgoblin?"

Ardron had no idea what he was talking about. "What hobgoblin?" he croaked.

"The one that takes advantage of a man who has drunk a little too much."

He still had no idea what Pierre was talking about.

"He steals your money, then pisses in your mouth before he leaves!" Pierre enlightened him.

Judging by the weight of the purse and the Godawful taste in his mouth it was possible. "It would seem so," he said.

Pierre got to his feet and walked over to a table in the middle of the room. From a large clay pitcher he poured water into a leather mug. "Where are you from?" he asked offering Ardron the mug.

"A village close to Malmesbury," Ardron replied taking the mug.

"You're a long way from home"

"Yes, I am, Ardron replied taking a mouthful of water and then was forced to screw up his face in discomfort when he swallowed.

Pierre chuckled at his discomfort. "It'll get better, my friend," he said. Then turning serious he looked quizzically at Ardron. "That sword of yours? It's a fine weapon and too fine for a mere peasant. I would say that you are no ordinary Saxon. In fact I would guess that you are perhaps a Saxon warrior. A mercenary, maybe?"

Ardron nodded slowly. "I have hired out my sword for money," he admitted.

"So, what brings you to Oxford?"

"I'm looking for a girl."

"Another one?" Pierre scoffed.

"No," Ardron said slowly shaking his head. "This one is special. She was kidnapped from my village and I am here to find her and take her home."

"Ah__, I see. And you think she may be here."

"Yes, I think she may."

"What is her name?"

"Hildi."

"Hildi?" Pierre was thoughtful for a moment then shaking his head and pulling a face said. "The name means nothing to me. "When was this girl taken?"

"Last summer."

"Last summer?" Pierre was surprised. "Then my Saxon friend I think you are wasting your time."

Ardron stared back without speaking.

"If this girl didn't really want to be here, then she would have made her own way home by this time. I'm sorry to have to tell you this, but after the kidnap the girls will be used and then cast on until no one is interested. After that she will be ignored and able to do as she pleases. The girl you seek would have been back in your village months ago, if she so desired."

There was strong suspicion within Ardron that Pierre spoke sense. "Nevertheless," he said. "Only when I hear it from Hildi's own lips will I give up the quest."

"I have to go. I am on sentry duty in a few minutes," Pierre replied. "When I come back, I'll take you to see Madame Rouselle. She will know the whereabouts of your Hildi. If she is here."

"Madame Rouselle?" Ardron queried.

"Aye Madame Rouselle, she controls all the working girls here. Now, I suggest you go back to sleep, and when you next wake you'll be feeling much better." Ardron looked around the room dubiously. "Don't worry," Pierre went on. "You're in the sergens barrack room and nobody will bother you here."

It sounded like good advice, even so sleep did not come easily after Pierre left. He had needed to find a way into the castle and purely by accident he was in. His first need, however, was to recover from this malaise. After that he could then make enquiries of Hildi. He weaved all sorts of scenarios through his mind until eventually he did fall asleep.

A couple of hours later he awoke again and sat up hesitantly. By this time, well past noon, the barrack room was empty. He swung his legs down to the floor and was then beset by feelings of nausea. Perhaps there was some improvement in his condition, but not that much. He got unsteadily to his feet and went outside. Just a few yards away he spotted a well and was magnetized to it as a dehydrated newt. On the side wall he found a bucket already filled. Not once, but four times he plunged his head inside coming up each time only when he needed air. Then stripping off his clothes, leaving only enough to cover modesty, he tipped the bucket over his head. Only when he heard the giggles did he realise that there were two young girls around the other side.

"Ladies," he acknowledged.

Shyly one of the girls pushed another bucket towards him which he immediately overturned on himself also. The water from deep in the well was cold, very cold. The sudden temperature assault on his body brought inactive senses back to life. He took a deep breath injecting clean air into his lungs and looked around him.

He was inside the stone-built bailey. The tall tower covered all compass points, with the imposing barbican dominating the castle entrance. Behind him the considerable and impressive keep, built on the mote, governed the whole complex. It was a magnificent fortress. Sir Robert d'Oyly must be a wealthy man Ardron concluded. Was he for Maude or Stephen, he wondered? But then it didn't really matter to Ardron, he was now in the castle and needed only to conclude his business. Then he could be on his way. Still dripping wet he gathered up his discarded clothing.

"Ladies," he said with a touch to his eyebrow and made his way back into the sergens barrack room. Inside he found Pierre had returned, and in company of two others. Ardron recognised the new-comers as two other revellers from Grindon's Inn. They all watched Ardron closely with amused expressions looking for signs of his malaise.

He sat on the cot, and then with a rueful expression, looked at the grinning faces and said. "I am beginning to think I just might survive these after-effects."

"Only if you keep away from Grindon's," one of them muttered with a smirk.

"Good," said Pierre when the sniggering had stopped. "Get yourself dressed and we will visit Madame Rouselle."

"What exactly is this woman's role?" Ardron asked as they climbed the steps to the mote.

"She controls the girls."

"The girls?" Ardron queried.

"Aye, the pleasure girls."

"You mean she is the brothel keeper."

Pierre winced. "We don't like to call it that."

"Hildi won't be in there."

"Maybe she will or maybe she won't. Either way Madame Rouselle will know if she is in the castle."

Madame Rouselle was a stout woman who would not see her fiftieth birthday again. Her face heavily painted, was half hidden beneath a large hooded bonnet. She wore a full-length dress of the finest blue silk, cut low, revealing an over exposure of fat cleavage.

"Hildi? Ah yes, the delightful Hildi. She was here," Madame Rouselle said. "She was one of my special girls."

"Special?" Ardron queried.

"Yes, corn-cockle, one of my specials," she said.

"A special," Pierre informed Ardron, "Is a girl kept only for the nobilities of the castle and distinguished visitors."

Ardron had suspected Hildi's fate, but to be now confronted with the harsh facts it was still hard to accept. "Was here? You said was here," he questioned Madame Rouselle.

"Aye, she's gone. Left with William de Roumare more than a month ago."

"William de Roumare? Who is he?" Ardron queried.

"William de Roumare is Lord Bolingbroke of Lincoln," Pierre took the question. "Your girl moves in select company."

"The probability is that she didn't have a choice." Ardron retorted.

"Oh she had a choice alright," Madame Rouselle said. "Roumare was here for a week and he paid me a special commission to keep her onto him only. When he left, he paid me even more to take her with him. But Hildi was an asset to me. I didn't really want to lose her. So I gave her the choice. Stay or go? It took an instant only for her to decide that she wanted to go."

This was not news that Ardron wanted to hear and his face must have shown his disappointment.

"Was she special to you, corn-cockle?" Madame Rouselle asked sympathetically.

But Ardron was deep in thought and slow to answer. "Yes," he muttered. Perhaps it was that Hildi preferred to be a noble's mistress rather than a mattress for all and sundry. That, he decided, made sense, and it would be her situation.

"Never mind," Madame Rouselle said. "Don't lose hope."

Ardron looked at her, not understanding her drift.

"You wouldn't think so now to look at me, but in my prime, I shared King Henry's bed." She went on.

"That was not an exclusive club," Pierre muttered.

She glared at him before carrying on. "Of course he wasn't king then, his brother William was king. But he was the prince, young and handsome with the pick of just about all the women in the land. And he chose me. But as with all men, and with so much available, he soon began to look around for another pretty face to pursue and to conquer. After five or six weeks, I found myself ousted from his bed by a new girl. Tis the same with today's men of rank and wealth. They change their mistresses as regular as their bed sheets. It will surely come to pass that Bolingbroke will tire of your girl, and she will find herself discarded. Then if you are there, you might get her back."

Obviously, she was under the misapprehension that he was seeking Hildi for himself. He thought to explain the situation then immediately changed his mind. He couldn't be bothered. "Thank you. madam," he said and began to fiddle in his purse. But she placed her hand over it and shook her head.

"No need, corn-cockle, you go and get your girl back," she said.

"What do you do now?" Pierre asked when they arrived back in the barrack room.

Ardron shrugged. "Back to Scorrenstone, I suppose. Though the news I have will not be welcome in some quarters."

"You could stay here."

"And do what?"

"Sign up as a mercenary in the service of Sir Robert."

Ardron wasn't interested but was curious about his allegiances. "On whose side?"

"We stand for the Empress Maude." Pierre said.

"Is that your choice?"

Pierre shrugged. "Our politics are decided for us by our superiors."

"You could choose for yourself."

"We could. But then our families in Normandy might suffer. You see we are but vassals living on the Normandy estate of our lord and master."

For the first time Ardron realised that there was not a vast difference between the ordinary Norman sergen serving his master and a Saxon villager. It was only a difference of geography, England or Normandy.

"For a mercenary, such as yourself, then it is money easily earned at the moment." Pierre went on.

"How so?"

"The main thrust of the war is away deep into the west country where the king and his army try to pin down and defeat the armies of Fitzrichard,

Sheriff of Cornwall, and his son-in-law Reginald de Dunstanville Earl of Cornwall, the empresses half-brother."

Ardron remembered that Miles Fitzwalter had been derisive of de Dunstanville for having fled Castle Combe on the king's approach. If this information were true, then it seemed that Miles might have misjudged de Dunstanville.

"For us in this area," Pierre went on. "It means a period of comparative quiet. We are also in a line of castles, Oxford, Wallingford, Marlborough and Ludgershall all sworn to the empress. An attack on one castle will bring the other three down on the attacker." Pierre spread his arms. "Who would be so foolish to try?"

"You make it sound secure," Ardron said. "So why would d'Oyly need mercenaries at this time?" He could see Pierre struggling for an answer. He relieved him of the predicament. "I cannot stay," he said. "For better or for worse I have to pass on this news."

***

It was early the next morning when Ardron took leave of his new friends. He took a south-westerly direction and by noon had passed through the small hamlet of Faringdon. He was not looking forward to imparting the news to Hildi's family, and as a consequence, was in no particular hurry to arrive. North of Cricklade he dawdled allowing his horse to rest and casually graze for more than an hour. Eventually, he continued on his way passing through the village of Essitone nestling beneath the castle of South Cerney and entered a thickly wooded forest. Three or four miles later he emerged onto the open area of a plain. Somewhat disorientated he reined in Rattlebone and studied the sky. The sun was halfway between its zenith and its setting position. At this time of year it set in the south west and that was the direction he needed to go. So the route simply decided he headed towards the sun knowing that by the time it had fully set he would be on familiar territory.

An ugly black plume of smoke drifted lazily into the sky ahead of him, and as he breasted the rise, he looked down to a small Saxon farmstead in the valley bottom. Black smoke gushed from one of the farm building as its thatched roof burned intensely. Ardron took a moment to study the scene, all was not well. A woman ran in fear of her life along the valley bottom chased by a sword wielding man. Beyond that a young man armed with only a staff fought an unequal fight with another sword wielder. "Bandits," he muttered to himself, drew his sword and spurred Rattlebone down the hill at a gallop.

His first target was the man chasing the woman, however, a few seconds before he got there the woman was down, felled by a downward swipe from the bandit's sword. Only in the last seconds did he see Ardron's charge but that was too late. Ardron's sword caught him in a scything motion just below his ribs almost cutting him in half. A few yards away the young man armed with only the staff was in deep trouble as a cross swipe from the bandit's sword cut the staff in half. Angling Rattlebone towards the pair Ardron used his sword as a lance. Aware of Ardron's charge the man turned and set himself into a defensive stance. To no avail, Ardron's sword pierced him cleanly mid-chest lifting him off his feet and carrying him for a stride or two before he dropped beneath Rattlebone's hooves. Once clear, Ardron reined in his horse and looked back. These were not common bandits he had just felled but were Norman sergens.

Wondering just what it was that he had blundered into, he dismounted and walked back towards the young man. He was nothing but a boy of perhaps fifteen or sixteen.

"Look out," the boy shouted before Ardron was close enough to speak.

He turned to see two more Norman sergens moving quickly towards him. Ardron took a defensive stance as both the sergens spread wide apart. It was a good attacking move and placed Ardron at a big disadvantage. If he turned to face one his back would be exposed to the other. Realising fully his predicament he silently cursed himself for not making a better appraisal of the situation. He had seen two attackers and had assumed that was all there was. Too late now to dwell on that, there was nothing he could do at the moment except to back-peddle slowly and wait.

Assistance came from an unexpected quarter when the young Saxon hurled himself onto the back of one of the Norman's. The opportunity would be fleeting and Ardron needed to act quickly. He turned towards the other Norman and attacked with downward strokes left and right. But the Norman was equal to it parrying the attack comfortably. Knowing full well the young man could not distract the other sergen for long, Ardron continued his assault. But the next lunge was diverted away with a circling movement which carried Ardron sword high and wide. Clearly this man was an accomplished swordsman and would not easily be defeated. Ardron moved away deciding that a more patient approach was needed. He stood back and let the Norman come to him. He came with a stabbing thrust which Ardron deflected and turned outside the lunge as the man stumbled past. Turning sharply the Norman came back with forceful downward strokes left and right before bringing in a vicious backhanded horizontal swing. Ardron sunk to one knee allowing the sword to pass just above his head. The momentum of that swing carried the Norman's arm across his front and just for a moment his torso was exposed. Ardron drove his sword into his midriff forcefully. With a grunt of surprise then a look of extreme pain, the man sank to his knees dropping his sword and clutching his wound with both hands.

Ardron turned away quickly to find the other sergen. The youngster had held on grimly for a long as he could but now the sergen had managed to wrestle him off his back. Ardron hurried forward shouting as he did, distracting the man from plunging his sword into the youngster. The Norman turned and faced Ardron holding his sword out defensively in front of him. For a moment both men squared up, and then the sergen's nerve broke. He turned and fled. As he ran past the cart yet another sergen appeared. He took a few moments to appraise the situation then he turned and ran after his colleague.

Looking round quickly Ardron reviewed the situation. Two buildings burned fiercely, and a third with fire just taking hold in its thatch. The immediate danger from the Norman's seemed to be past, at least for the moment. The youngster had run instantly towards the felled woman, whilst another man, close to the animal barn, struggled to get to his feet. Ardron went to his assistance. His right arm was slashed through to the bone above the elbow. Blood ran freely from the gaping wound, dripping liberally from his fingers. By the unnatural angle, the arm was bent Ardron could also tell that it was broken. The first priority, however, was to stop the bleeding.

"No no," the man said as Ardron bent to his aid. "Elflede save Elflede."

"Who?" Ardron was confused.

"Elflede, my daughter, Save my daughter."

"Where?" Ardron asked looking about baffled.

"There," he said pointing to the third burning building. "In there."

If she was indeed in that building, then she needed to get out right away, because the fire in the thatch was spreading quickly.

It was dark inside, and the thickening smoke added to the gloom. At first Ardron could see nothing, but the regular sound of grunting drew him further into the building. At first, he thought he was looking at a pile of rags but as his eyes became accustomed to the light, he realised that a rape was taking place. A man with no care, except for his own gratification, thrust his hips enthusiastically at the young woman beneath him. With each hump he gave off a grunt, the like of which a snorting pig would have been proud. So intent was he on his own fulfilment that he neither saw nor heard Ardron's approach. He sheathed his sword and drew his dagger. Then grabbing the man by the hair, Ardron pulled his head back and laid the knife's edge across the man's throat. The look of surprise turned to terror when he felt the steel begin to cut into his neck. Ardron hauled him off the young woman and onto his knees.

The man held up his hands in surrender. "Don't be too hasty, Sir," he said. "I meant no harm and there is no real harm done."

"No harm?" No harm?" Ardron spat back angrily, pressing his blade edge harder into the neck.

"She's only a Saxon," he petitioned.

"I am a Saxon."

"I'm sorry, I'm sorry," he said. "You can have her if you want her."

"Where are you from?" Ardron demanded.

"I'm from Devizes."

"Devizes?" Ardron was both surprised and puzzled. "You're a long way from home." He dragged the man to his feet. "I intend to take you back and see you hanged in the town square for what has happened here today."

"But Sir, I am only carrying out my Lord's bidding."

"Your Lord's bidding? Which Lord would bid you murder pillage and rape?"

"My Lord, Sir Robert Fitzhubert."

"Fitzhubert?" Ardron was puzzled. Devizes Castle was under the charge of a castellan appointed by Stephen. Had Fitzhubert changed sides again? "Since when has Fitzhubert held appointment at Devizes?" Ardron demanded

"Oh Sir," the man was still terrified, "Two weeks since."

"Two weeks? And how did this come about?" Ardron growled.

The sergen nervously licked his lips and swallowed hard. "By stealth, Sir. We advanced under a cause of friendship and during the night secretly scaled the bailey walls and opened the gates. Once inside we over-ran the incumbents to seize control."

By appealing to those more senior than Fitzhubert, there was still the possibility of retribution for these crimes. "In whose cause does he now hold the castle?"

However, the answer was denied to him when with a vengeful scream, the young woman streaked across the barn and plunged a two-pronged pitchfork into the man's chest. He fell backwards, as a snapped off fencepost, and lay staring at the fork shaft protruding from his chest with shocked horror.

"Now it's my turn," Elflede screamed down at the man. Then using her weight on the shaft she drove the pitchfork right through him. "My turn," she shouted hysterically.

In extreme agony the sergen began to writhe and kick. Then as his body went into its death throes, he began to uncontrollably twitch. Not content with that, the girl continued to hurl abuse at the dying man.

Burning threads of thatch began to drift down from the roof as the fire gained momentum. It was time to get out while they still could. Ardron grabbed Elflede's arm and had to drag her forcibly towards the door, while she continued to hysterically curse the dying man. As they staggered out through the smoke into the fresh air Ardron looked back at the fiercely burning building. Almost immediately, the blazing thatch began to collapse in. They had got out not a second too soon. Elflede was wide eyed and physically shaking but continued to shout hysterically through breaths that came in short gasps. Ardron grabbed her by the shoulders and shook her several times to break her from the hysteria.

"Stop it," he commanded. "Stop it." At first, she looked confused as the hysteria left her, then she gradually began to refocus. There was no time for the luxury of self-pity. "Come, your father needs help," he said, and he led her to where he sat. "Do what you can to control the bleeding," he instructed. But the girl just looked back at him somewhat confused.

"For heaven's sake," Ardron muttered. Then grabbing her he ripped the sleeve from her dress, which he used to make a tourniquet just above the open gash. "Now clean and dress the wound," he instructed when the blood flow had slowed. Now that she had been guided, the girl set about the task. Ardron watched her work for a few moments and regretted speaking to her so harshly. After all, the girl had just been traumatised. "My turn," he muttered as he thought of the pitchfork in the sergen's chest. He permitted himself a wry smile. Then he looked around for the young boy.

He was a few yards away sitting beside the other woman's body. He lifted a tear stained face to Ardron when he neared. "This is my mother," he said. "Why did they have to kill her?" Ardron could only shake his head, there was nothing to say.

"What's your name boy?" Ardron asked.

"Leofric," he muttered cradling his mother's head in his arms. "She was a saintly woman who never harmed anyone," he said and began to rock his mother backwards and forwards as if ushering a baby to sleep. "Find the bastards," he spat venomously looking up to Ardron. "Find the bastards and kill em. Kill em," he shouted.

There was merit in what the boy said. Although perhaps not entirely from a vengeance reason. To allow any of them to report back whence they came, would most certainly bring a horde of avenging sergens down upon this farm. The two that had fled were on foot and could not have got far. Ardron looked for his horse. Rattlebone oblivious to the conflict that had raged around him fed contentedly on grain which had spilled from a sack near the cart. He mounted and spurred the horse in the direction the fleeing sergens had taken.

Soon he was back in the nearby woodland and it didn't take long for him to realise what a difficult task it was going to be to find these men. In mid-March, the undergrowth was still waiting to burst into life, nevertheless, the remnants of last year's growth still held sway. Bracken, though brown and broken, still stood three feet high. Blackened leaves of thick bramble still provided possible cover, and all were carpeted with a thick carpet of rotting leaves. Still, he cast around for an hour before deciding to give up. There was more than twenty-five miles to Devizes and that was a long way to walk. This pair would need horses. So there was a good chance that they would come back later trying to recover their mounts. If they did then he would be waiting for them. He turned Rattlebone and headed back to the farm.

Elflede had the man's arm bound tightly and the blood flow now looked to be controlled. "How does it feel?" Ardron asked.

The man, although ashen faced, managed a flicker of a smile. "I'll be alright," he muttered. "We are heavily in your debt stranger. Heaven knows what would have happened but for you intervention."

Slightly embarrassed Ardron waved a dismissive arm.

"Will you stay the night?" the man asked. "They might come back, and I am in no position to provide any resistance." He pointed at his broken arm to make the point.

"What's your name Ardron asked as he helped the man to his feet?

"Odel," he replied grimacing with pain as he stood.

"I will stay." Ardron confirmed, then he cast around surveying the situation.

There was nothing to be done about the burning buildings except to let them burn themselves out, and they were well on the way to being there. "Is this a barn?" He asked pointing at the building in front of him.

"It is," Odel replied.

To its front not more than twenty-five yards away a drystone wall had been constructed. This was an ideal place to hide, and covertly watch the barn entrance.

"Come," he said addressing the Leofric. "Help me put all the horses in the barn."

That done Ardron helped Leofric to move his mother's body into the barn, and then sat quietly honing his sword as the boy reverently laid her out. Satisfied that he had done the best he could Leofric declared himself finished. Ardron nodded, placed his arm over the youngster's shoulders and sympathetically complimented him on his work. Now there was little else to do until after dark. If the sergens were to come back for their horses, then it would probably be under the cover of darkness.

When they emerged from the barn, the sun was beginning to get low in the sky. There was a distinct chill in the air which under a clear sky threatened another frost before morning. Leofric led Ardron towards the main house. The house was constructed long, narrow and low. The roof thatch, though high at its apex, came down at its eaves to within three feet of the ground. Inside the building had a sunken floor providing extra headroom. For comfort and warmth the floor was lined with animal skins.

122

There was no fire trough, instead there was a large firebox in the middle of the room. The fire in the box danced with happy flames, which was in stark contrast to the mood in the room. Odel sat gloomily in discomfort nursing his broken arm. The girl had taken over the role of her dead mother and worked silently and sullenly mixing dough. Elflede separated the dough into small blocks and laid them on the hot stones on the fire edge to bake into bread-cakes. Then while she waited for the dough to bake, sat back brooding silently on the misfortunes which had fallen upon her and her family. The atmosphere was understandably very sombre.

"Did you tend your mother boy," Odel broke the silence.

"Yes, father, I did."

He nodded satisfaction and the room lapsed back into protracted silence.

"You are villains tied to a Norman Lord, I suppose," Ardron said eventually breaking the silence.

"Yes," Odel replied. "Villains to the castellan of South Cerney."

"Then tomorrow you must go to the castle and report this crime."

Odel nodded. "But I fear it'll do us no good at all."

"Perhaps not," Ardron agreed. "But maybe you could suggest that he consider your losses when your tithe is due. You could get a reduction."

Odel scoffed, and only curled a lip. Meanwhile Elflede scooped up two bread-cakes with a small wooden shovel and held it out to Ardron.

"I will come with you, if it pleases you?" Ardron added as he slid the bread-cakes onto a wooden platter.

"Any support is welcomed," Odel muttered.

"Then it is settled. And we can get that arm of yours reset too," Ardron added. "There will be a Lach in the castle for certain."

The evening protracted with only the very scantiest of conversation. Ardron was thankful when at last the night had closed in, and it was time for him to take post outside to await the return of the two Norman sergens. "I'll be just outside," he said as he prepared to leave.

"Will they be back?" Elflede asked nervously.

Ardron forced a smile. "If they do then I'll be waiting."

"Wait," she said when he reached the doorway. She got to her feet picked up one of the animal skins. "You'll need this," she said holding it out to him.

He nodded gratitude as he took it.

Outside the temperature had dropped considerably. In the clear sky a bright three-quarter moon was encircled inside a silver halo promising a sharp frost. The landscape bathed in this wan moonlight was too bright for Ardron's liking. At this time, however, the moon was low and the shadows it made were long. He found a good position beneath the shadowy side of the drystone wall with a clear view of the barn entrance. He laid his bow at his feet, his sword across his lap and loosed his dagger in its sheaf. All was now prepared, and he settled down to wait.

Soon the cold began to bite into his very bones as he sat huddled wrapped in the animal skin. He longed to move around to stimulate circulation, but he couldn't. If the trap were to work, he must not give away his position. So he summoned every ounce of self-control to ignore the cold. The long minutes turned to endless hours and still the Norman's did not come. Now he began to fear that they would not come at all. Perhaps this pair had obtained horses from somewhere else, and that was a possibility he had not considered. Or even worse, perhaps it was that these raiders were part of a bigger raiding force somewhere close by. If that were so, then tomorrow they could expect a merciless avenging force to fall on the farm. In that case it would be better not to be here when they arrived. As time dragged on extra problems developed. Boredom and tiredness were added to the extreme cold. The moon had become high in the sky shrinking the shadow in which he was hidden to a narrow sliver. Without the cover of the shadow he could not remain in this position, and soon he would have no choice except to move to another position. He was on the horns of a dilemma. If he moved position and it should be that the Norman's were watching, then by giving himself away the hunter would become the hunted. Moving to the inside of the barn now seemed like an attractive idea, at least it would be warmer in there. Still reluctant to move just yet he decided to wait just a little longer.

Then something moved. Someone ran towards the barn, their outline just for a second or two, silhouetted against the dull embers of one of the burned-out buildings. Ardron waited and watched. Soon a second shadow followed, and two men gathered outside the barn. They waited a minute or two before one man opened the barn door a mere chink and slipped inside. The other man waited outside, obviously posted as look-out. Ardron moved slowly to lay his sword at his side and pick up his bow. Carefully he strung an arrow and paused. He waited until the look-out was not looking in his direction then stood quickly. Unhurriedly, he stretched the bow taut took careful aim and let the arrow fly. He heard the dull thud and watched the man stagger back. The arrow had found its mark. He dropped the bow, drew his dagger and ran quickly to the barn. A glance at the fallen man showed his aim had been a good one, even better than he thought. The arrow, protruding from the sergens chest, had pierced the man's heart. He took position against the barn and waited for the other man. A few minutes elapsed before the door opened and he came out leading two horses. Before he had time to understand what had happened Ardron dodged behind the horses and came up quietly behind him. Wrapping his arm around his head he jerked it back and sank his dagger deep into the man's throat. When he let go the man sank to the floor spluttering and gurgling, drowning in his own blood. Task accomplished!

He spent the better part of the next hour collecting the bodies, and by using the horses moved them off the farm into the nearby woodland. Piling them all together he covered the bodies with bracken and leaves. Taking a couple of steps back he surveyed his work. Excepting the one still beneath the smouldering embers the bodies were hidden, and as a temporary measure that would have to do.

These five before him had all died by his hand, and perhaps they had deserved their fate. However, he could not help but ponder how it was that he had become such a proficient killer. Only nine months ago he was a simple peasant going about the everyday business of a hard-working Saxon villager. The killing had begun in London when forced to defend himself against Count Waleron's sergens. Then had continued at Wallingford, heaven knows how many had died beneath his sword in that battle. And of course there was an intervention when he had ridden to the aid of the king. He shook his head ruefully and reflected on what hoax the devil had intended when he had guided Fitzhubert to Scorrenstone that day. But for the kidnapping of Hildi and Edyo he would probably still be an innocent villager. 'On the turn of chance.' He muttered to himself dolefully as he turned away.

Although the fire had fallen to smouldering embers it was still a good deal warmer in the house than outside. He settled down close to the fire his back resting on a support post and glanced around. The two men and the girl were sleeping soundly. He sighed with envy and decided that as soon as he had thawed a little, he too would copy their example. He poked at the ashes in the box to fuel a shower of sparks and tossed on another log. He stared hypnotically into the embers until his eyes grew heavy and closed. But then was jerked awake when his head dropped suddenly onto his chest. He was surprised to see Elflede kneeling at his knee.

"Did they come?" she asked.

"You don't have to worry about them anymore." He replied.

"God be praised." she said. "Truly God sent you to help us in our hour of need." She cuddled close to him and laid her head on his chest.

"God or the Devil?" Ardron replied thinking of his earlier deliberations.

"What?" the girl asked in surprise.

"Never mind," he said.

Contented and no doubt feeling safe she was soon asleep her head in his chest. But for Ardron sleep did not come easy. The girl leaning on him made it difficult for him to get truly comfortable, but he had not the heart to disturb her. Nevertheless, he did manage some short sporadic periods and when he woke, he awoke with a start. Shafts of daylight slanted through the cracks in the wooden shutters. There was much to be done today and already some daylight had passed.

He woke Elflede, roused Odel and shook Leofric awake with his foot. "Come," he said. "We have much to do this day."

Even so, Ardron had to contain his impatience because there were essential chores that needed to be carried out at the start of a farm's new day. Nearly two hours had passed when Leofric declared himself ready.

"Come," Ardron said and led the way at a brisk pace to where he had hidden the Normans bodies. "At an early opportunity," he said. "You must take these bodies deeper into the forest and bury them in an unmarked grave. Do not forget the body still beneath the ashes of that building," he added pointing in the general direction. "And do not be tempted to take any personal trinkets. There must be no clue as to what happened here yesterday. If anyone comes looking for these men then your story will be, they came murdered, robbed, burned then left. Do you understand?"

Leofric looked dubious but nodded.

"But today," Ardron went on. "You must take the horses to Cricklade and sell them. Take whatever you can get. Do not haggle too hard, under no circumstances are you to bring any back." He paused studying the young man for a moment. Could he be relied upon Ardron wondered? But then he could do no more. "Take your sister with you. She will not want to be left here alone," he added.

As they made their way back to the farm, they approached the cart. In the back were several sacks of grain and wool. There were also carcasses of sheep and chicken. "Is that cart yours?" Ardron asked.

"No it belonged to the Normans."

"Then you will need to break it up and burn it." Ardron added. "But for now find a suitable place to hide it."

It was approaching noon when Ardron and Odel reached Essitone. The bucolic buildings of the village straddled either side of a shallow brook with the castle South Cerney beyond in its north. The castle was of modest size, surrounded by a wide ditch with the brook at its front. Having pointed at Odel's broken arm there was not a problem getting past the guard and into the bailey. Inside they were soon directed to the castle Lach.

The room was small and dimly lit. Wood smouldering in a fire basket was responsible for an atmosphere that was heavy with smoke. Shelves lined the walls and were crowded with dozens of small jars. Each jar carefully labelled. The Lach himself, was Saxon. His lined face and long grey hair revealed a man of many years and long experience. He favoured Norman dress and wore a full-length gown gathered in the middle beneath a hefty belt.

He screwed up his face and sucked loudly through his teeth when he inspected Odel's injuries. That did nothing to arouse confidence. "Nasty!"

he muttered and continued to thoughtfully study the arm. "How did it happen?" He eventually asked.

"Norman bandits attacked my farm," Odel answered.

"Norman bandits?" There was mild surprise in his voice, but he wasn't particularly interested. "This is going to hurt," he added as he turned away to assemble his tools.

When all was to his satisfaction, he bade Odel lay down on a long table. After gently probing his broken arm he looked at Ardron and said. "I'm going to need your help." He then indicated that he should take position on the opposite side of the table. "Hold him down," he said as he guided Ardron's hands onto Odel's shoulders. Then he pushed a leather strip into Odel's mouth. "Bite on that and bite hard."

Odel yelled and cursed through clenched teeth as the Lach pulled hard and twisted the broken arm. It took all of Ardron's strength to keep him down as the Lach worked. Not once, not twice, but three attempts before the Lach declared himself satisfied. Although the arm now looked much more aligned the procedure had re-opened the deep laceration, and blood began to flow freely. Unconcerned and unhurried the Lach walked over to the fire and took from it a hot iron. He held it up and inspected the glowing end. Nodding silent satisfaction he brought it to the table. "Take a firm grip," he said to Ardron holding up the iron.

"Oh no," Odel growled spitting out the leather strip, and struggled to get from the table. Unconcerned the Lach then pressed the hot poker onto the wound to cauterise it. The air was filled with an acrid smell of burning flesh while Odel's scream of agony must have reverberated all around the castle. Mercifully, he passed into unconsciousness.

Now with his patient limp the Lach set to work on the wound. He applied a foul-smelling salve before binding over with a fresh dressing. Next, he fastened the arm in a splint before immobilising it by taping it tightly to Odel's side. By the time he had finished Odel had regained consciousness but in a confused state. The Lach helped him to a sitting position and poured him a generous mug of gingered wine, then with a jerk of his head he indicated to Ardron that he wanted to see him outside. After a concerned glance at the ashen-faced Odel, Ardron followed the Lach outside.

"I've done what I can," the Lach said, "But even so he could still lose the arm."

"Lose the arm?" Ardron exclaimed.

"Aye! There is a good chance of gangrene. If the wound starts to fester and stink, then bring him back soonest. The arm would then have to go, or he will die."

Ardron allowed a loud and heavy sigh of dismay.

"The bone should set well enough within three or four weeks, he went on. "But the dressing will need changing regularly." He held up a little jar of salve. "This is my remedy," he said. "Others swear by horse dung, but I prefer this."

"What is it?"

"It is my own personal herbal mixture made basically from lesser centaury. Apply it thickly over the wound until it has sealed itself. If, it seals itself!" he added. "Now, he said after a pause. "That'll be three silvers you owe me."

Ardron was about to respond not I, but changed his mind and fiddled in his purse for three silver coins to pay the Lach. "I am nothing more than a passing stranger who stopped to help this man," he informed him as he handed over the money. "But I will pass on your instructions to his family."

The Lach studied him for a moment with a bemused expression then decided not to get into his reasons. "Give him half an hour, or so. Then you can take him away," he said, pocketing the money.

"Who is the castellan here," Ardron asked.

"Sir Edward d' Evreux," the Lach answered.

Of course he was, Ardron remembered. He had been installed by Stephen after the king had taken the castle from Miles Fitzwalter's sergens

"How do we get to see him?"

"You must find his constable and he will arrange it." Then he was gone swinging the pitcher of gingered wine as he went.

They were kept waiting for more than two hours before they were ushered into the bottom floor of the keep. The sombre grey stone walls added to the gloom in a room that had only two small portals to admit light. The Castellan, Sir Edward de Evreux, sat at the head of a long table with two advisors sitting either side.

Odel's French was not good, however it mattered not, Edward d' Evereux was half Saxon and spoke perfectly good English. Odel described that which had taken place. D' Evereux listened without comment and showed not a jot of surprise.

"My Lord, my wife was killed, my daughter raped, my farm burned, and I was left badly injured," he said pointing to the arm strapped to his side. "But for this young man's intervention then we would probably all have been killed."

For a moment d' Evreux turned his attention to Ardron peering at him hard as if trying to make up his mind, before switching his attention back Odel. "How many were there in this band?" He asked.

"Five maybe seven." Odel replied.

D' Evreux looked quizzically at Ardron. "And you say that this man drove them off?"

"Yes, my lord."

It was clear from the expression on his face that de Evreux had reservations about the accuracy of the story. "That would have to be some achievement," he said. "How did you manage it?" he addressed Ardron.

For the first time Ardron entered the conversation. "My Lord," he said. "I was fortunate. I had surprise on my side and had felled two before they were fully aware that I was there. Two others behaved like cowards and ran away, whilst another was so intent on gratifying himself on the young girl that he was not aware I was even there, until he felt my knife at his throat."

D' Evreux was silent for a few moments considering Ardron's reply. Then seemingly accepting Ardron's explanation nodded slightly and said. "This sort of thing is beginning to happen more and more. Homesteads and small hamlets are easy targets and the purpose of these attacks two-fold. They are launched at estates that take an opposite stand in this war. It enriches the attacker's pockets and deprives the landowner of an income when his vassal's can't pay their dues." His jaw set firm as he considered the situation. "I don't suppose you know from where these men came?"

"According to my friend here," Odel replied pointing his good arm at Ardron. "They came from Devizes."

"How do you know this," de Evreux asked Ardron.

"The man with my knife at his throat said as much and named Sir Robert Fitzhubert as his liege lord."

"Fitzhubert?" de Evreux exclaimed. "Truly a snake with no morals except to further his own ends. You will be avenged," he said to Odel.

"My lord, Ardron interrupted. "My friend here lost a great deal in the attack. May I ask you to consider a reduction when it is time for him to pay his tithe?"

"No need," de Evreux replied curtly. "You will be amply compensated," he said to Odel. "The only way to stamp out these kinds of raids is to retaliate against the aggressor with a ferociousness that costs him dearly. So, Fitzhubert attacks one of my properties, then we will attack three of his. Yes, my Saxon friend, you will be compensated from the bounty we take from Fitzhubert's properties."

"My Lord," Ardron said. "Do I understand that you intend to retaliate by raiding Devizes hamlets?"

He didn't reply. Instead he turned to his advisors and sarcastically sneered. "He's quick witted this one."

Ardron ignored the slight. "But my Lord, it will be innocent peasants that suffer."

"It will. Unfortunately, it is a fact that in war always it is the weak that suffer." He shook his head ruefully. "Regrettable it is, but it is the best and quickest way to stamp out raids of this kind."

"Is there no law, no higher authority to which we could take the case?"

D' Evreux laughed out loud. "Law? There is no law. The country is locked in civil war and there is only anarchy." Then his eyes narrowed as he studied Ardron. "You interest me, Saxon," he said. "You have an air of confidence about you and you saw off a small raiding party single-handed. There is much more to you than you give out. Tell me," he said with a frown. "Are you for King Stephen or for that Angevin She-Wolf?"

"I try to take no side in this Norman war but look out for my own kind."

De Evreux frowned; he did not like the answer. "For a man such as you, a warrior I will wager, neutrality is a dangerous position. You're in the middle with no friends but enemies on both sides."

Ardron nodded agreement. Then to take the heat out of the situation he replied. "I was with the king at Malmesbury when he re-took the castle from Fitzhubert." He neglected to add that he fought against the king's cause at Wallingford.

That satisfied d' Evreux. "I will send my constable to your farm," he said to Odel. "He will assess the damage." Then he went and sat down at the table. They were dismissed.

"My Lord," Ardron said. "I have one more issue."

"What is it?" d' Evreux asked without looking up.

"Three of this man's buildings were destroyed by fire. He will be in need of wood to rebuild."

"Four trees, de Evreux muttered with a dismissive wave of his hand.

"My Lord," Ardron pressed his luck. "They were substantial farm buildings. It will need as many as ten trees to replace them."

"Six," d' Evreux growled exasperated.

Ardron knew he had reached the limit. "Thank you," he said, then bowed through politeness and withdrew.

***

The cold March wind blowing from the north east caused Ardron to shiver slightly. Never mind just a few more minutes and he would be home. He had passed south of Malmesbury using the imposing Abbey as an unmissable landmark. Now approaching Scorrenstone from the east he began once more to rehearse his report. In his mind he had tried several versions seeking a way of making the bad news of his failure a little less odious. Hildi's parents, he knew, would be hugely disappointed. He had decided, therefore, that an edited version of the circumstances would be kindest. He would leave out the fact that Hildi had gone north with William Roumare willingly. It would be charitable to keep her parents in ignorance allowing them to think that she had no say in the matter.

However, his father Wolfstan was Thegne and as such he must be informed of the exact circumstances. It would then be his decision whether to release the information or not. Sighing heavily with melancholy he turned his mind to other things.

Early spring was a busy time in the village. With the winter stocks running down it was now time for the villagers to turn their attention to the new season. There were fields to be ploughed and seed to be sown. Lambs had been born but the sheep herd now needed to be shorn. Women then could spin the wool into yarn and weave yarn into clothing. Soon hay would need to be gathered for animal feed, straw for roofs, padding for furniture, and stuffing for mattress. The bees were becoming active too. The village hives would need attention or there would be no honey as sweetener. This seasonal burden impacted massively into the normal busy routine of a Saxon villager. All this to be achieved against the backdrop of this accursed war! Any moment in time vassals and tenants could be claimed and taken away to fight in their lord's army.

At the valley edge he halted Rattlebone and leaned forward in the saddle taking in the view. Below him a mass of bright yellow celandine thickly lined the banks of the fast-flowing river. The bright green buds on the willows had just broken but had not yet opened to leaf. On the opposite bank there was a hint of primrose. The first of these tiny pale flowers had appeared and made a promise of the mass that was yet to come. Such a pacifistic scene drove away all ugly thoughts of civil war. 'Let the Norman's squabble among themselves and leave alone the common peasant to carry on with his quiet rustic existence,' was Ardron's thought. However, the instant he thought it he knew that it was an impossible prospect. He spurred his horse down the steep bank. The river was not deep, and he saw no reason to circle round to use the bridge.

As he reached the opposite bank and began the steep ascent towards the village, he heard his name called. "Ardron, Ardron," Edyo called as she and Cerdic ran along the riverbank towards him. He halted his horse and waited for them. "Edyo, it's good to see you," he said when she was near.

"They came for me," she said in an agitated state. "They came, but they didn't find me. I ran away and hid."

Her excitable state spooked Rattlebone and he began to shy away. "Who came for you?" Ardron asked digging in his knees and pulling back on the reins to control the horse.

"The Normans. I told you they would."

"You're not making any sense, girl. Control yourself and tell me what happened." Ardron replied as he soothingly patted the horse neck to keep him quiet.

But it was Cerdic who spoke. "Yesterday the Normans came. Edyo thinks they came looking for her."

"They were," Edyo said defiantly

Ardron was sceptical. If these men were indeed looking for Edyo then how did they know where to find her? Nor could he believe that Henry, Bishop of Winchester, would go to so much trouble to recover a minion, a lowly kitchen slave. "What makes you think they were looking for you?

"For what other reason would they have come?" she asked. "They ransacked the village in their search then set fire to the houses."

"Set fire to the houses?" Ardron queried.

"They did," Cerdic confirmed.

For a moment Ardron stared down at the pair as the information sank in. He looked up the hill towards the village but from here in the valley bottom he could not see beyond the ridge. He spun his horse's head, dug his heels into the big horses belly and spurred him at a gallop up the hill.

Evidence of the raid was clear from the moment he entered the village. Almost one side of the main thoroughfare was nothing more than burned timbers. Some stout foundation posts still stood defiant but were charred and blackened. Despondent villagers scavenged amongst the ashes of their homes looking to salvage what they could. An unnatural quietness pervaded as depression laid a heavy blanket over the place. Any villager that did glance towards Ardron paid him only scant attention before refocussing back to the task at hand.

He dismounted and led Rattlebone at a slow walk through the village, absorbing in horror the scenes of utter disaster. Deeper in the village the fire damage was less but was still considerable. He arrived at his father's house and meeting hall, but that too was nothing more than charred remains. A small gathering of villagers stood staring gloomily at the debris, and amongst them he spotted his brother, Redwald. All noticed his approach, but no one spoke.

"What happened?" Ardron asked.

"Normans," Redwald replied.

He already knew that much. "When?" He asked

"Late yesterday."

Clearly this had been one of those raids that d' Evereux had described, or a reprisal for such a raid. It was not as the paranoid Edyo believed a mission to re-capture a kitchen slave. Raid or reprisal it made not a jot of difference to the Scorrenstone villagers; they were victims.

"They rode in at speed and set about pillaging and destroying." Redwald went on his right arm pressing against his ribs. "They ransacked homes looking for valuables. Then they turned their attention to anything that might prove useful and took all they could carry. What they couldn't carry they set fire too. Mindlessly they slaughtered as much livestock as they could find, even though they couldn't carry it away. Even the oxen were put to the sword. It was just purposeless vandalism," Redwald added disconsolately.

"Oh, there was a purpose alright." Ardron muttered. "Anybody hurt?"

"Three killed for trying to protect their homes. Several injured, three seriously." He grimaced as he said it.

The anger was steadily rising in Ardron. Such merciless atrocities carried out upon defenceless people. They should not be allowed to get away with it. There had to be consequences. "Where's father?" he asked.

"Taken!"

"Taken? Why?" Ardron exclaimed.

Redwald sighed heavily. "As they ransacked the meeting hall, they found his register of all the village valuables and their owners that had been secreted away. They beat him trying to force him to tell them where the valuables were hidden. But he wouldn't say, and so they took him with them. No doubt to apply torturous persuasion."

Ardron immediately experienced a pang of guilt. It had been his suggestion that all the valuables in the village should be gathered together and hidden somewhere in secret until such times it was safe to openly possess them. "What did you do?" Ardron demanded accusingly.

"I tried to stop them," Redwald replied lifting his shirt to show blood stained bandages wrapped around his ribs.

Ardron immediately regretted his outburst, he had not noted his brother's stiff movement and grimace of pain when he spoke. "Is there any clue where they might have taken him?" he asked.

Redwald shook his head sadly. "I set Esmond and Swidhurn to follow to find out."

That was good. "I don't suppose we know who these Normans were?" Ardron said.

"Oh yes," Redwald replied. "Twas the same company as came last summer. They came in bold as you like, streaming the Fitzhubert standard of blue and grey."

"Fitzhubert?"

"The same. Protected on both sides by his knights Fitzhubert himself sat astride his horse and watched the mayhem take place."

"As God is my witness, I will see that man burn in hell," Ardron growled angrily

"You will have to find him first," Redwald said.

Ardron nodded agreement. "But you see, I know exactly where to find him."

Chapter 6

March 1140

"You know how to find Fitzhubert?" Redwald queried.

"I do. He is the new castellan of Devizes Castle." Ardron replied.

Redwald sucked noisily through his teeth. "That's not good."

"No it isn't. But maybe we can work some kind of deception."

Redwald wagged a warning finger at his younger brother. "Our priority should be rescue and not vengeance."

"Of course," Ardron replied already deep in thought as the basis of a plan was beginning to form in his mind. Something similar to that which he had left behind at Odel's farm might be the solution. However, there were details to be worked out and he needed a few moments to think it through. "First brother, you must move the village valuables to a new location." Only his father and brother knew that location.

"That is already done," Redwald replied. "As soon as I was patched up enough to be able to move, I moved the chest to a new location."

Ardron nodded approval. His brother was behaving as a Thegne should by putting the interest of the villagers before personal feelings. "I'll be ready to ride within the hour."

"Ready to ride and do what?" Redwald demanded.

"I will bring to you my plan when I have considered the details." Ardron said.

It was a little over an hour later when he rode out this time not mounted on Rattlebone but astride a more modest mare of the village. Neither did he carry his sword. It was important that when he presented himself in front of Fitzhubert, he appeared to be no more than a lowly Scorrenstone villager, and a son, coming to plead the cause of a father.

Ardron kept the mare at a steady clip resting her for a little while at Chippenham, and it was just over four hours after leaving Scorrenstone that he arrived at the foot of the bluff. The town of Devizes was atop the bluff with a long curving escarpment from north through west to south. He dug his heels into the horse's ribs urging her up the long steep hill.

The castle was near the southern edge of the escapement and was further defended by a wide ditch. It was a typical Norman design of mote and bailey but was constructed substantially from stone. Its strategic location and stout construction made it a formidable citadel. Not wishing to delay his approach any longer than was necessary Ardron requested admission into the bailey. Once inside he then sought out the castle constable to request an audience with Sir Robert Fitzhubert.

"State your business," a somewhat disinterested constable said.

Ardron replied in English. "I am from Scorrenstone and__"

"Speak French" the constable interrupted.

Ardron pretended he didn't understand. "I am from Scorrenstone and I am here to plead the case for my father," he said once more in English.

The constable waved his hands in exasperation stopping Ardron once again. "There, sit," he said pointing at a nearby bench. "Interpreter, I need an interpreter." He muttered to himself as he looked around for assistance. "You," he barked at a nearby sergen. "Find the priest and bring him to me." He motioned to Ardron that he must wait, and then walked away.

Ardron settled to wait on the bench, he had decided that it might render a slight advantage if he pretended that he didn't speak French. Things were often said openly when there was a belief that one did not know what was being said. Some thirty minutes had elapsed, and the light was beginning to fade from the March sky when the constable returned, this time accompanied by the priest.

"Good evening my son," the priest said. What is it you want to say to the constable?" He was a man of similar age to Ardron, but his complexion was sallow. Probably spent too much time in the darkened chapel instead of out in the fresh air.

"I am from the village of Scorrenstone and I am here to plead the case of my father, who was taken prisoner by Sir Robert yesterday."

"What was his crime?"

"There was no crime other than he refused to hand over the villagers valuables."

There might have been a trace of sympathy in the priest's expression, but if there was it quickly vanished. "It would have been better that he had done as he was ordered," the priest went on. "After all Sir Robert has the interest at heart of all the people of the country. That is why he supports the empresses claim to the throne. Therefore, he needs funds to promote the struggle and bring this civil war to an early end. And that will be of benefit to all people of England."

Ardron knew that it was such a load of hogwash. Fitzhubert had no one's interest at heart except his own. The priest was only quoting the party line and Ardron wondered how much of that he actually believed. Nevertheless, he took a subservient attitude. "Yes father, you are probably right," he said. "I am here to try and persuade my father to tell Sir Robert where these valuables can be found."

"Do you know where they are hidden?"

"No. My father is the village Thegne and only he knows where they are hidden."

"I see," the priest said. Then he proceeded to tell the constable what had passed between them.

135

The constable listened silently and when the priest had finished, he studied Ardron a moment. "Alright," he said. "Tell him to wait here and I will speak with Sir Robert."

He was kept waiting a long time, and it was dark by the time the constable came to find him. He led the way through the main hall and up steps into the private chambers. Fitzhubert was there along with three of his knights studying charts spread over a long table.

Although it had been several months since Ardron had seen Fitzhubert, and then only a face beneath armour, he recognised him right away. Now as he beheld the man in his relaxed environment, he studied him attentively. Fitzhubert was a man in his mid-thirties not tall but thickset. His black hair was long and curly while his heavy thick beard showed the first hints of grey. He wore a long gown half blue half silver the colour of his personal livery.

Turning his attention away from the charts his deep-set dark eyes stared emotionless at Ardron.

"You have something to tell me Saxon."

Keeping up the pretence of not understanding French, Ardron simply bowed his head and grinned like an idiot.

"Speak up man," Fitzhubert said irritated.

"Sir Robert, this half-wit does not speak French," the constable said.

"Then why have you not provided an interpreter?" Fitzhubert retorted.

"Sir, I have sent for the priest and I had assumed that he would be here before me."

Fitzhubert shook his head exasperated and returned his attention back to the charts.

"I will find the priest, right away, Sir," the constable muttered and hurried from the room.

"Now, Eustace," Fitzhubert addressed one of the knights at the table. "You are sure this map is accurate."

"Near enough," Eustace replied. "Fitzgilbert may have strengthened up his defences a little here and there but it is accurate enough to suit our purposes."

At the mention of Fitzgilbert's name Ardron became attentive, whilst looking around as if in awe of the furnishings in the room.

"Fitzhubert nodded satisfaction. "Then we arrive in the middle of morning mass. While we wait for the service to finish, you will have your men casually take up strategic positions here, here and here." He jabbed the chart forcefully with his finger.

"Aye," one of the other knights spoke. "Then we wait until everyone settles for breakfast. Some will gratefully accept their invitation and sit to eat with them."

"Meanwhile," Fitzhubert went on. "You and I, Quentin, will accept Fitzgilbert's invitation to dine with him in the keep."

"Are you certain that he will invite us into the inner sanctum?" Quentin queried.

"Bound to! Protocol demands it." Fitzhubert replied. "Then when all is relaxed, we spring our trap and overwhelm them. They won't be expecting it. Once we have control, we will give you the signal," he nodded at Eustace. "You will then take charge of the bailey, and the castle will be ours." He stood up straight with a satisfied expression.

The third knight who had remained silent studied Ardron. "Sir Robert," he said with a frown. "Is it wise to speak so in front of this Saxon?"

Ardron, although now alert, continued to gaze round the room. Then as the room fell silent and all eyes fixed upon him, he pretended to suddenly realise that he had become the centre of attention. He flashed a stupid grin and nodded his head a couple of times.

"He's nothing but a simpleton," Fitzhubert said. "And even if he did understand any part of our plan what is he going to do with it? He moves only among ignorant Saxons." They turned their attention back to the chart. It was clear to Ardron, Fitzhubert who had taken this castle through deception now intended to take one of Fitzgilbert's in the same way.

A few moments later the constable returned accompanied by the priest.

"Sir Robert, I do apologize but evensong did stretch on a little," the priest said grovelling.

"Find out what this peasant has to say." Fitzhubert replied exasperated.

"Sir, he told me earlier why he has come. He is here to persuade his father to tell you where his village's valuables are hidden. Then he hopes you will graciously grant his release."

"His Father?" Fitzhubert looked at his constable. "Who is his father?"

"He is the old man from the village Scorrenstone," the constable explained.

"Ah. That stubborn old fool," Fitzhubert said. "What makes him think that he will have more success than our experienced persuader?"

For the first time the priest interpreted for Ardron by asking the question.

"He is our village Thegne," Ardron replied. "And the villagers have decided that they would sooner have their Thegne back than possess a few personal trinkets."

The priest conveyed his answer while Ardron watched carefully. It needed to be convincing, and he was not at all sure that it was.

"Probably doesn't amount to the cost of a barrel of cheap wine anyway." Fitzhubert said dismissively. Then he was thoughtful for a moment. "Very well, he said. "Constable, bring me the dungeon keeper." As the constable hurried from the room he said to the priest. "Tell him he has until the morning to persuade his father. If he fails, then I will hang them both before breakfast."

Ardron was shocked at the man's callous indifference to life. He turned away hiding his feelings. The priest translated, then and only then, could he allow his shock to show.

"Now priest," Fitzhubert went on, "I have a task for you tomorrow."

The priest bowed slightly and replied meekly "I am at your service."

"Tomorrow you are to go with Sir Eustace to Marlborough Castle. Acting as my envoy Sir Eustace will suggest and arrange a formal meeting with John Fitzgilbert, in order to discuss a mutual defence alliance between us. He knows well the arguments to put forward to promote this meeting. You, as a man of the cloth, will be there to assist him in his arguments and to authenticate the sincerity of our intentions."

"I will be pleased to assist in such a worthwhile alliance," the subservient priest replied.

'Devious snake!' Ardron's thoughts were silent. With not an ounce of compunction the man was prepared to even deceive his own priest to his own ends.

The gathering descended into insignificant idle chatter until the constable arrived back accompanied by the shuffling dungeon keeper. The dungeon keeper was a scruffy individual, his face blackened by grime and his clothing worse. He pulled off a scruffy skullcap and made an awkward attempt at a bow. "Your graceness," he said through a sickly grin which revealed crooked and yellowed teeth.

"Take this man," Fitzhubert said pointing at Ardron, "And throw him in the cell with the old Saxon. In the morning thirty minutes before mass bring them both before me." With that he turned abruptly. There were more important matters claiming his attention.

Ardron was led around to the rear of the mote and to a cavern that had been mined into the bowels of the mound. The dungeon keeper lifted a lit lantern from just inside the gate and led the way down stone steps to a dark and dank cellar. At the bottom he held up the lantern. The tunnel end was not more than a dozen yards away. On either side were four heavily barred cells. As he passed each cell the dungeon keeper held the lantern close to the bars and peered in. Shadowy gaunt faces peered back expressionless from the darkness. It was a cell at the end when Ardron recognised his father. He stared back with a forlorn expression, sitting on the floor knees bent and back against the wall.

The gaoler fiddled with keys hanging from his waist, until he found the right one. Then after unlocking the door, he stood aside, and with an elaborate mocking wave invited Ardron to step inside. The gaoler slammed the door behind him and re-locked it chuckling as he did. The shadowy light faded quickly as the gaoler left leaving behind only inky blackness.

"Father!" Ardron said.

"Ardron! Is that you?"

"Yes, it is."

Wolfstan groaned. "How is it that you come to be here?" The dismay in his voice was patent.

Ardron felt his way along the wall towards the sound of his father's voice. "I have come to get you out." He slid down the wall to sit opposite Wolfstan.

Wolfstan was silent a moment then said. "You are locked in here too. So how is this to be achieved?"

"I have a plan. But first, how are you?" He stared hard into the darkness. Oh so gradually his eyes were becoming accustomed to the darkness. He could now vaguely see the outline of his father. His arms were folded across his chest with his hands clamped firmly in his armpits.

"This is a damnable place with unspeakable horrors inflicted upon unfortunates," he replied. "And inflicted with pleasure," he added. Then he held out his hands.

Ardron shuffled across and peered hard at his father's palms. Even in the blackness he could see that the hands were horrifically burned and bloody with charred flesh mingling in the blood. Then Wolfstan turned his hands over to reveal bloody finger ends were once fingernails had been.

"As God is my witness," Ardron growled, "I'll see Fitzhubert in hell for this."

Wolfstan sighed heavily and placed his hands back under his armpits. "I didn't tell them what they wanted to know,"

"Why not?"

"Why not?" Wolfstan echoed with surprise. "I am Thegne. How could I betray my people so easily?"

"But surely you would have known that Redwald would have quickly moved the village valuables?" Ardron replied.

"Redwald? I saw Redwald cut down beneath a Norman sword." Wolfstan said.

"You did. But he lives. He has a large gash across his body and perhaps a broken rib or two, but he is on his feet. None too steady. But well enough to function as Thegne in your absence."

Wolfstan gave a sigh of relief. "This is good news," he said. "And had I known I could have saved myself a lot of pain."

Ardron began to rip the sleeves from his shirt. "Tomorrow Fitzhubert will send for us and you will offer to lead him to the valuables."

"And what happens when he finds that they are not there?"

"Don't worry, Redwald will be waiting," Ardron replied. Using the shirt sleeves as bandages he then began to carefully wrap Wolfstan's hands. "Will you be able to ride a horse with these hands?" He asked.

"There is nothing wrong with my knees," Wolfstan replied.

***

The next morning early, they were brought before Fitzhubert. Pre-occupied holding apart and studying a scroll he ignored the pair when they were led in. Ardron and Wolfstan stood in silence and waited, as did Sir Eustace, the constable and the priest.

Eventually satisfied Fitzhubert nodded rolled up the scroll and said. "That should do. It would convince me." He then dripped hot wax onto the edge and impressed his personal seal. "And it should convince Fitzgilbert," he said with a smirk as he handed it to Sir Eustace.

For the first time he turned his attention to the two Saxon's standing before him. "Well constable. Is there to be a double hanging this morning?" he asked. The constable glanced at the priest and gave a proceeding nod.

"Old man," the priest said in English. "Have you decided hand over your disbursement?"

"Disbursement?" Wolfstan retorted hotly.

Ardron placed a calming hand on his father's arm. "We have decided to lead you to the village assets." He said meekly.

The priest nodded approval and translated to Fitzhubert.

"They lead us nowhere. They tell us exactly where to find their trinkets." Fitzhubert replied.

"Sir," Wolfstan replied after the translation. "It is hidden in woodland. How therefore can I describe a leafy glade in a forest of trees?"

Fitzhubert was thoughtful for a while. "Very well," he said stroking his chin. "We'll play their game for the time being." Then turning to his constable said, "Go find de Gravier and bring him here."

It took a further ten minutes before the constable returned with de Gravier. De Gravier was a young man of tender years, probably having not yet celebrated his twentieth birthday. "Sir Robert," he said tentatively.

"Ah_ Henry my good fellow," Fitzhubert said, "I have a task for you this day."

"At your service," the young man replied with a slight bow.

"I want you to take six sergens and go with these two Saxons. They will lead you to a chest of Saxon silver. Secure it and bring it back here. If they play you false or give you any cause for concern, then hang the pair of them."

"Very good, Sir Robert. Er," he hesitated a moment. "What do I do with them if all is well and I secure the silver?"

Fitzhubert shrugged, exasperated with the detail. "Oh," he said. "Hang them anyway."

Ardron was shocked and again struggled to hide the fact that he had understood what had just been said. The man's viciousness was not hampered by any conscience.

"Put them back in the dungeon until Sir Henry is ready to leave," Fitzhubert instructed the constable. "And Sir Henry," he went on. "Watch them very carefully, I don't trust them."

***

It was early afternoon when the small party reached the bridge just below Scorrenstone. Ardron glanced sideways at his father. It was time for Wolfstan to lead the group. De Gravier rode at the head with Ardron and Wolfstan in the middle.

"Sir Henry," Ardron called. De Gravier twisted round to look back. Seeing no further need to disguise the fact that he spoke French he said. "We are getting close. My father should lead from here." The young knight reined in his horse and halted the column, then wheeling his horse he came back to face Ardron eyeing him suspiciously.

"How far?" he asked.

"Over the bridge we turn and head downstream," Wolfstan said to Ardron after he had translated. "Then we head for that woodland yonder," he added pointing as he did.

"We head for that woodland," Ardron translated to de Gravier.

De Gravier turned and looked to where Wolfstan had pointed. Ardron watched as the young man struggled to make the decision. "OK," he said after a few moments. "You two," he said addressing two sergens. "Load your crossbows and stay close behind these Saxons. Any hint of trouble you will plant your arrow in him," he pointed at Ardron. "And you," he addressed the other sergen, "Plant yours in the old man. "The rest of you," he went on in a raised voice, "Stay alert."

Ardron sighed quietly. Young and inexperienced de Gravier might be, but certainly he was no fool. Ardron and Wolfstan moved to the head of the column and led on. Once over the bridge they led the way along the riverbank before turning away towards the thickly wooded area. Ardron was keenly alert as they entered among the trees. So much now depended on Redwald being in position, but with those loaded crossbows pointing at their backs he prayed that his brother did nothing hasty.

In a small clearing, Wolfstan halted his horse. "We are here," he said. Ardron nodded towards de Gravier indicating that they had arrived. Wolfstan slid from his horse and gave Ardron a hard look. He then walked over towards a thick patch of brambles. "In there," he said. There was no need to translate, it was understood. They stood back while two sergens using their swords hacked back the brambles.

141

Looking around furtively, Ardron appraised the situation. De Gravier still sat astride his horse. Two sergens were digging at the loose earth while two others watched intently. One of the men with the loaded crossbow stood close on Ardron's left, while the other on the other side of Wolfstan. Both were keenly interested in the digger's progress, and not fully focussed on their set task. This would be a good moment for Redwald to strike. He scanned the undergrowth and surrounding trees. Of a set ambush there was not a sign. He cast around once more, absolutely nothing. Redwald should have been here ready, and he was not. Ardron drew a deep breath and silently cursed his brother. Their situation was desperate. Soon the sergens would discover that there were no valuables buried here, and that would have grave consequences for them. Desperate situations call for desperate measures and Ardron began to assess his chances of jumping and overwhelming the bowman next to him. At this moment there was a chance that he could surprise him, but not so the other one. The instant Ardron made a move then the other bowman would snap alert and fire his arrow into Wolfstan. Not an option! He racked his brain desperately trying to find another alternative.

The whisper of an arrow increased then thudded into the chest of the bowman next to Wolfstan. The man looked down at the arrow protruding from his chest with shocked amazement, before staggering back two or three paces then falling to the ground.

Ardron leapt into action knocking the crossbow of the other bowman skywards. The sergen's finger twitched on the trigger, sending its arrow up into the sky before he crumpled beneath Ardron's weight. Seemingly, from out of the very ground, and from the trees the men of Scorrenstone appeared attacking the sergens yelling ferociously as they did. Ardron rolled on the top of the sergen pummelling his fist into the man's face. But the man fought back wriggling his torso forcing himself upwards. The pair rolled over and over first with one on top then the other. Eventually, getting established over the sergen Ardron got his fingers around the man's throat and he began to squeeze. At first the man beneath him struggled to pull away Ardron's hands. Then seemingly he gave up. However, his hand had closed around a large stone and he hit Ardron hard at the side of his head. Stunned and surprised Ardron fell away. Quickly the sergen rolled over and on top of Ardron, pulling a dagger from his belt as he did. Though stunned Ardron was still alert enough to grasp the man's wrist and prevent the dagger being plunged into his chest. But with the weight of the sergens body now pressing down on the dagger its point was slowly inching nearer Ardron's chest. Suddenly, the sergen's head was jerked back, and a knife blade flashed across his neck severing the man's jugular and drenching Ardron in blood spatter. Using his foot Swidhurn then pushed the stricken sergen away from Ardron. With a grin he offered Ardron his hand and hauled him to his feet.

"You looked as if you needed a hand, old friend." he said.

"No, I had him exactly where I wanted him," Ardron replied with a relieved sigh. He glanced down at the dying sergen using both hands trying desperately to stem the blood gushing from his neck. It took mere seconds before the man slipped unconscious and ultimately into death.

"Do not leave one alive," Ardron shouted. It was horrifically merciless, but not one of Fitzhubert's men could be allowed to survive to tell the tale. It was soon over with the Saxon's hacking at the lifeless Norman's ensuring death.

"Ardron," Redwald shouted running towards his brother. "One got away,"

"What?" Ardron looked around in alarm.

"The knight on the horse. He's gone."

"Give me your sword," Ardron demanded of Swidhurn.

"That way. He went that way." Redwald pointed.

Armed with Swidhurn's sword, Ardron ran and leapt onto his horse setting off after de Gravier. As he cleared the wooded area, he could see de Gravier about half a mile ahead. He had already crossed the bridge and rode his mount furiously across the open grassland. This was likely to be a long chase, and so he set the mare beneath him, a steady galloping pace. She was no Rattlebone, and he had to nurse her for stamina, but even though it was the right thing to do he was fearful that at this distance he might lose sight of de Gravier. He thought on that possibility as he rode. He decided, in that event, he might have to press on to Devizes and hope to get there ahead of him.

De Gravier crested a rise and disappeared from sight down the other side. Ardron felt a moment of panic and urged his horse forward at a much-increased rate. When he breasted the hill de Gravier was once more in sight, and so he eased back a little allowing the horse a breather on the gallop. The distance had not decreased, in fact it just might have increased. Even so, Ardron controlled his panic guessing that the horse in front could not sustain that furious gallop. Keeping cool Ardron kept his horse at an easy pace, but when de Gravier once more disappeared from view he again increased the pace. This time, when he was once more in view, the distance had definitely decreased.

De Gravier looked back over his shoulder at his pursuer, and Ardron could sense the man's rising panic because he began to flay his tiring charge. He crested the next rise to see de Gravier angle sharply to his right heading for a wooded area. Ardron knew this particular wood and it was substantial. He spurred his horse into a full gallop, fearful that de Gravier would lose him in the forest.

Less than a minute later he too entered the wood. The narrow track stretched before him taking a sharp turn a hundred yards ahead. He slowed his horse to a walk and proceeded with caution, de Gravier might be hidden and lying in wait. Or, he could have turned off the track at any point. He moved slowly forward peering intently at the forest floor looking for tell-tale sounds of tracks. So far he could see no evidence that de Gravier had turned off. This was not good. Perhaps de Gravier had not even slowed, in which case he could be re-establishing his long lead. He kept searching for a few more minutes then decided that if he intended to turn off then he would have done so before this point. Throwing caution to the winds he spurred his horse forward fearing that de Gravier had probably opened a goodly lead again. The track before him wound and meandered through blind bends. He was chasing an invisible quarry in a direction which he couldn't even be sure was the right one. As he rounded another bend he was confronted by a horse-drawn cart with a gnarled old Saxon aboard.

He dragged his horse to a stop. "Did you see a rider come this way?" he asked.

The old man pulled back on the reins to stop the cart. "Whoa," he growled at his horse. "Aye I did," he said. "Not more than five minutes ago. He demanded that I give him old William, here," he said nodding towards his horse. "In exchange for the one he was riding. I could never let old William go. We've been together so long. Haven't we boy?" The last comment was directed at his horse. "And certainly not to somebody who rides horse to the point of collapse as he does." He picked up a pitchfork from down by his feet and held it out in an aggressive manner. "He wasn't prepared to argue the point when he saw this pointing at him."

"Did he go this way? I have to catch him." Ardron cut in.

"Aye he did," he replied waving his arm in the direction.

Ardron spurred the mare forward

"You'll soon catch him. His horse was staggering. It'll probably drop dead within the next half mile if he continues to ride it." The old man called after him. Ardron pressed on at a fast clip searching expectantly ahead every time he turned a bend.

Riding hard he almost missed the horse lying prone in the long grass by the track side. At first, he thought the animal was dead, but it lifted its head as he passed. Glancing back he thought to put the animal beyond its misery, but it meant that de Gravier was now on foot, so deciding that was his first priority he pressed on. He could perhaps come back later he appeased his conscience. He slowed his horse to a walk. De Gravier, now on foot, would almost certainly seek to hide somewhere in the undergrowth. Although the undergrowth was plentiful, it was barely spring and was still mostly browned and dead bracken. Even so, it was highly possible that he could hide. Carefully he scanned left and right as he moved slowly forward. Then he caught sight of him. Hampered by the knee-high undergrowth de Gravier ran looking back in alarm as he did. Ardron turned his horse in pursuit.

The gap lessened quickly, and de Gravier realising it was no longer possible to outrun his pursuer, drew his sword and turned to face his hunter. Ardron galloped on towards him leaning over sword at the ready. Steel clashed as Ardron swung his sword at de Gravier. Mounted on a galloping horse he had momentum, and it was de Gravier who staggered backwards as Ardron swept past. He turned his horse sharply and came back a second time. This time he did not gallop past, instead held his mount alongside de Gravier and continued to swing his sword downwards several times. The young Norman parried desperately trying to keep the sword from slashing into him. Alarmed by the ring of steel on steel, Ardron's horse shied away giving de Gravier a brief respite. Taking advantage he leapt back four or five paces into the clear. Ardron urged his horse on for a few more yards before leaping off. Now with both men on foot Ardron approached menacingly confident. Full of aggression he launched his attack swinging his sword downwards three times before circling it around and swinging in horizontally. This time Ardron's sword pierced through the defence and opened a severe gash in de Gravier's left side. He staggered backwards then his foot caught in the dead bracken and he fell over backwards. In a flash. Ardron was over the young Norman placing his foot on his sword hand. Realising that now he was at Ardron's mercy, de Gravier looked up in despair.

"Don't kill me," he pleaded.

Ardron hesitated, sword in hand, and looked down at a helpless young man barely out of teenage years. To end his life this way would be little short of murder. After a moment's hesitation he changed his grip on the sword and plunged it into de Gravier's chest. To let him live would put the village and all its villagers in mortal danger. The Norman let out a loud grunt and instinctively grabbed at the sword embedded in his chest. Ardron waited a few moments then withdrew the sword and stepped back. De Gravier rolled over onto his shoulder coughing blood and died.

Retreating a few paces, Ardron slumped down on his haunches and rested his head on the sword's hilt. This reprehensible deed was not of his making he told himself and laid the blame squarely at the feet of Fitzhubert. The circumstances were brought about by that man's insatiable greed and his malevolent treachery. He thought of his latest deceitful scheme to capture Marlborough Castle. Ardron considered Fitzgilbert a friend, therefore, he must be warned.

***

Ardron had reached Silbury and was still some eight miles from Marlborough. He brought Rattlebone to a stop and dismounted, the big horse deserved a rest. They had covered more than twenty miles since he had left Scorrenstone this morning. It had not been a punishing pace. He had kept the horse at an easy loping canter with frequent periods of walking. Nevertheless, it had taken around four hours to reach this point, and four hours continuous is punishing enough for both horse and rider.

He straightened his back and flexed his stiff shoulders, then leaving the horse to graze, climbed part way up the enormous prehistoric mound. This point was a conjunction of three roads. The one he had travelled from Chippenham, the one he had yet to travel to Marlborough and the other south west from Devizes. This was the road the Fitzhubert and his men would most certainly have to travel to get to Marlborough. From his elevated position, he had clear view over the downs and along the Devizes road. It was deserted, and for a moment he wondered if Fitzhubert had perhaps already passed through, but almost instantaneously he dismissed it.

It was only yesterday and no more than thirty hours ago when he and his father had stood before the man as he decided their fate. At that point he was only just about to despatch his envoy to Marlborough Castle to arrange discussions. It was, he concluded, extremely unlikely that the meeting could have been arranged for the same day. Therefore, today was the earliest possibility and that, he thought, unlikely too. Tomorrow, or perhaps even a day or two after, that was the more likely. Nevertheless, the sooner he got to Marlborough and warned Fitzgilbert of the skulduggery afoot the better.

The day was pleasant with the promise of an early spring. The landscape of rolling hills was deserted save for a few sheep contentedly grazing. It belied completely the conflict that raged across the country. The Norman instigated war impacted, particularly on the humble peasant. Deprived of any consideration of rights and subjected entirely to the unregulated self-indulgent desires of their Norman masters, the peasant was forced to suffer all outrages without recourse. Ardron recognised that not all the nobles were shamelessly corrupt. But even among the more moderate, there was very little consideration of the effects that their actions inflicted on the proletariat. Where were God and all his Saints whilst all these atrocities were carried out? He had heard it said, by learned monks, that 'God and all his Saints slept.'

He turned his thoughts back to the events of yesterday. De Gravier and his small detachment had been completely obliterated, and he wondered just how long it would be before a search party would be sent out. All the bodies had been buried in hidden graves and at this very moment their horses would be on their way to Bristol to be sold on the market. No trace of their presence remained around Scorrenstone, and the story put out would be that de Gravier and his men had taken the village valuables and ridden out. It was hoped that the belief would be that they had decided to keep the wealth for themselves and had deserted from Fitzhubert's service. In order to make this story a little more convincing, the men selling the horses in Bristol were to use de Gravier's name freely. Then put out the word that they intended to use the money to buy sea passage back to France. By leaving the Fitzhubert livery on the horses, it was hoped that all this information would somehow eventually filter back to Devizes Castle.

He delayed his journey another thirty minutes before moving on. A little over an hour later he breasted a rise and looked down on the small town of Marlborough. Sprawled haphazardly across the meadows of the river Kennett it provided a pacifistic scene. In its southwest the castle with its wooden bailey and stone keep, built upon a large prehistoric mound, dominated the landscape. The river provided the castle defence in its southern and eastern perimeters.

There was no particular security and Ardron rode through the bailey gate unchallenged. Once inside he sought Benet the castle constable and was directed to the stabling area.

"Ardron Scorrenstone," Benet greeted him with surprise. "What are you doing here?"

"I need to speak with Sir John, urgently." He replied.

"I'm afraid he's not here. He's hunting in Safernoc Forest."

Ardron tutted in exasperation. "When do you expect him back?"

Benet shrugged. "He went yesterday. Probably he will be back tonight."

Nonplussed Ardron stroked his chin, then thought of Fitzhubert. "Is there a meeting arranged with Fitzhubert?"

It was Benet's turn to look puzzled. "There is," he said. "Arranged for tomorrow morning, but how do you know of that?"

"It's a trap, and I need to warn Sir John."

Benet studied him thoughtfully for a moment. "Come," he said and led the way across the bailey into the keep. Once inside the private chambers Benet motioned Ardron to a seat, and then when settled asked him to tell all he knew. When he had finished Benet sucked noisily through clenched teeth and shook his head in amazement. "Sir John was deeply suspicious of Fitzhubert's motives. The man is completely without scruples." He paused a moment. "Did you know that he took Devizes Castle in the name of the Empress Maude, and then sent news to Earl Robert. Much rejoicing and congratulations then took place. However, when the earl sent his eldest son, William, to take charge, the snake locked the gates and drove him away. A message, he then sent, that he intended to keep the castle for himself."

"No I didn't," Ardron said shaking his head. But he was not surprised. The man's avarice for wealth and power overruled all other considerations.

"Even so!" Benet went on. "I don't think Sir John suspected anything as outrageous as this. The nerve of the man!" he added with incredulity. "Sir John will be warned the moment he arrives back." He got to his feet. "You will stay?" He posed it as a question. "Sir John will want to talk to you for certain."

"I'll stay," Ardron agreed.

"Good! Come I'll see you quartered comfortably while we wait."

With nothing more to do until Sir John's return, Ardron turned his attention to his horse. After grooming and feeding he led him to the castle blacksmith to have the animal re-shod. It was during the re-shoeing when a deal of excitement occurred in the bailey. At first, he thought that it might be the return of the hunting party. But it wasn't. Instead, an elegant coach, escorted by eight sergens and a knight, rumbled into the bailey. The coach was substantially built, needing a team of four to pull it. Its decorations, both outer and inner, were frivolous and luxuriant. Ardron had not seen it's like before. Curiously, he watched as the knight leapt down from his horse and took from the driver a set of steps which he placed by the door. Then after opening the door, he held up his hand to assist the lady from the coach.

She was a stunningly lovely woman. Not in the first flush of youth but at the mature point where a woman's physical attributes are at their peak. She wore a full-length dress of velvet, coloured magenta and trimmed at the collar with black lace. Its long open sleeves were also trimmed with black lace, while a matching broad belt pulled the dress in tight round her slim waist. On her head she wore a wimple of white held in place by a silver tiara. Her hair spilled out from beneath the wimple, its colour of shining raven-black contrasted eye-catchingly with the white of the wimple.

"Now there is a woman that a man would happily pay with his life just to lay with her for an hour."

So engrossed was Ardron that he hadn't heard the blacksmith come up behind him. "Yes," he agreed. "Who is she?"

"She is the Lady Rohesa de Vere. Daughter to Sir Aubrey Alberic de Vere, Lord of Hedingham, and Lord High Sheriff of London."

Ardron nodded suitably impressed. "So you would have to say that Lady Rohesa is well connected." He said glancing sideways at the blacksmith.

"Aye you would," he replied. "Even if you were the Saxon Thegne of all the Thegnes, she would have no truck with you." He added with a grin. Then he turned away to return to his forge. Ardron agreed and watched as a flustered Benet suddenly appeared on the scene to welcome the new arrival. Clearly, she had not been expected.

It was late afternoon when the hunting party returned. The small party of around ten, with Sir John Fitzgilbert at its head, rode through the gates in high spirits. Four dead stags and three boars was testimony to the success of the hunt. Ardron watched from a distance, content, at this stage, to remain in the background. Fitzgilbert dismounted and climbed the mote steps, and in no haste, the rest of the party eventually followed. The hunt kill and the horses were abandoned where they stood, left to the sole charge of servants and lackeys.

That jocular mood would soon disappear, Ardron thought, as he watched the hunting party disappear inside the keep. However, it was more than an hour later when Benet came to find him and led him to Fitzgilbert's private chambers.

The chambers were compact but comfortable. Dispersed candles attempted to dispel the gloom of a March evening, not very effectively. The windows each side of the room were draped with heavy velvet curtains and half drawn permitting the last dregs of daylight to infiltrate. The walls were hung with large imposing tapestries, while at the far end a welcoming fire burned in the inglenook fireplace. For personal comfort, the room was furnished with large wooden chairs and a couple of soft bedded loungers. Fitzgilbert's wife, Aline, lounged across one with the Lady Rohesa on the other. Rohesa stared at Ardron dispassionately, no doubt curious about a Saxon's status within these private chambers.

Fitzgilbert stood by the inglenook head bowed lost in thought staring down into the dancing flames. His left arm rested across the thick crossbeam.

"Sir John," Benet said attracting his attention.

"Ah Ardron," he said turning away from the fire. "It is always good to see you, my friend," he greeted warmly walking towards him

"Thank you, Sir John." Ardron replied.

Fitzgilbert placed an arm across his shoulders. "My wife, Aline, of course you know," he said leading him to the nearest lounger.

"Lady Aline," Ardron greeted leaning forward gallantly to kiss her held out fingers.

"The Lady Rohesa, of course you will not know. She is in transit from Bristol back to Hedingham and has graced us with her presence to break her journey."

"Lady Rohesa," Ardron greeted. "I am pleased to meet you."

She held up her hand patronisingly for him to pay homage. He gently took her fingers and lightly kissed her gloved hand. But when he went to let go, she caught his hand. "That ring," she said. Ardron took his hand away and stared down at the ring. It was the ring he had taken from the body of the ferocious knight he had slain on the battlefield at Wallingford. "How did you come by it?" She asked sharply.

Ardron was taken aback by her direct demand.

Seeing his surprise Rohesa tempered her attitude and more meekly said. "It is a very striking design,"

Somewhat embarrassed, Ardron shrugged and was a little reluctant to reveal that he had taken it from a dead man's finger. "It belonged to a gallant knight who fought bravely before dying under my sword on the battlefield of Wallingford."

She stared at him wordlessly.

"A lot of gallant men died at Wallingford on that day," Fitzgilbert interrupted. "Now ladies," he went on, you will have to excuse us we have urgent business to discuss." He led the way to an adjoining room.

This room was much more spartan, laid out purposely to conduct business. Fitzgilbert walked over to the long table and motioned for them both to sit. A tray had been pre-positioned on the table containing a wine decanter and several goblets. "Now," Fitzgilbert said to Ardron as he poured wine into a goblet and handed it to him. "Tell me what you know of this plot and how you came by this information."

***

With blue and silver livery displayed in flags, pennants and in their very clothing Fitzhubert led a considerable force of around a hundred men across the meadow towards the castle. In a party of six men in this exposed position Ardron was feeling very vulnerable. He sat his horse in the back row of Fitzgilbert's welcome party, and not for the first time, he fiddled with helmet attempting a more comfortable position. Dressed as a common sergen it was unlikely that Fitzhubert would recognise him, but nevertheless he did not fully understand the idea that had placed him in the party. It was, he reasoned, a chance that need not be taken. But Sir John had insisted.

He glanced back at the castle gate some hundred yards behind and wished that he were inside instead of here. Fitzgilbert sat his horse upright and defiant seemingly impervious to their vulnerability. Apprehensively, Ardron reached back and eased his sword a little higher in its baldric.

Fitzhubert brought the column to a halt some twenty-five yards away, then accompanied by the two knights, Eustace and Quentin he came forward to face Fitzgilbert.

"Greetings to you Sir John," he greeted when he pulled his horse to a standstill. "I trust this fine day sees you well," he went on.

"Well enough," Fitzgilbert replied tersely.

"Then I am happy, and perhaps that is an omen to a mutually beneficial outcome to our proposed alliance."

Fitzgilbert stared past him to the column of sergens behind him. "With that number of sergens at your back, one could suspect that you come more with an intention of aggression," he said.

"Oh no, not so," Fitzhubert protested with an easy laugh. "This number is in deference to your standing as a well-esteemed knight of the realm. Just a moment," he turned his horse and issued an instruction to Quentin.

The knight nodded turned his horse about and went back to the column. Once there he barked orders to the men. As one they all dismounted and lined the road on both sides.

Fitzhubert waved an arm in their direction. "Sir John. A guard of honour for your inspection," he said.

Ardron was uneasy and hoped Sir John would decline to go amongst the troops, but after a moment's hesitation Fitzgilbert spurred his horse forward. However, he did not fully commit, advancing only a few yards down one side, before he turned his horse and reviewed the other side as he made his way back.

"A fine body of men," he muttered. Then, with a wave of his arm he invited Fitzhubert to enter the castle.

"Have the men mount and lead them in," Fitzhubert said to Sir Eustace.

"No," Fitzgilbert said. "Leave them there at their ease. We can bring then into the bailey to share our breakfast when morning mass has finished."

For a moment Fitzhubert looked uncomfortable, it had put a hitch into his plan. But then probably deciding that it was only a minor setback he spurred his horse forward towards the castle gates. As the small party made their way casually back Ardron followed in the rear. Once inside the gates he peeled off and dismounted, then watched as the party moved across the compound towards the mote. After dismounting, Sir John walked alongside Fitzhubert up the steps and into the keep. As soon as they had all disappeared inside, Ardron turned towards the gatekeeper who waited for his signal. Ardron nodded assent. "Close the gates," he said.

As soon as the gates were closed the castle in-mates who had moved around with a casual malaise snapped to action. Weapons were produced from secreted hideaways and each man took to his post preparing to defend against any attack. Ardron climbed onto the ramparts and looked out at the Fitzhubert force locked outside the castle. Even from this distance he could sense the confusion as the sergens stood staring bemused towards the now secured castle. He removed the uncomfortable helmet and smiled to himself anticipating the satisfaction he would get carrying out his next chore.

"Ah, Ardron my friend," Sir John said when he saw him enter the room.

Fitzgilbert and Benet sat at the long table with Fitzhubert, sandwiched between them. Eustace and Quentin were seated directly opposite, behind them, a row of six pre-posted guards stood at attention.

"All is secure Sir John," Ardron said. Then he watched in quiet satisfaction as recognition spread across Fitzhubert's face. It was quickly followed by puzzlement.

"Very good," Fitzgilbert said. Then he looked at the guard-commander and said. "Arrest them!" The guards strode forward swords drawn and poised ready to strike.

"What treachery is this?" Fitzhubert shouted.

"Treachery indeed," Fitzgilbert countered. "Treachery thwarted by this Saxon," he went on nodding towards Ardron.

"This is an outrage. I have come here today with honest intentions," he protested. "I don't know what this man has told you, but you would take the lies of this__," words failed him for a moment. "Peasant," he spat, "Against mine? I am a man of noble birth and related to royalty in Flanders."

"Yes, you are right." Fitzgilbert said softly. "I would take the word of this peasant against yours. Take them away," he then instructed the guards.

Fitzhubert poured a stream of venomous abuse at Ardron as he was marched out of the room.

Ardron watched him go then turned back to face Fitzgilbert. "What happens now?" he asked.

"Now I send word to Robert Earl of Gloucester. He will be particularly pleased to have this man handed over as a prisoner. This arrest will, in all probability, mean that he gains control of Devizes Castle. Also," he went on, "I will make sure he is made aware of the role that you played in this. Yet again, my friend I, and the cause, are indebted to you. This time I will urge the earl to recognise that officially."

Ardron was not particularly concerned about any official reward. Just the quiet elation in knowing that he was a prime mover in Fitzhubert's downfall was reward aplenty. Nevertheless, he nodded gratitude. "And the Fitzhubert force outside the gate? He asked.

Fitzgilbert shrugged. "I will send word their leaders are my prisoners and order them to disperse. I doubt very much that they will want to launch an attack without the motivation of their superiors. I expect they will mill around for a few hours then gradually filter away."

"Now young man," Fitzhubert went on. "I have a very pleasant duty to offer you."

"Oh," Ardron was surprised. "I had thought to return to Scorrenstone."

Fitzgilbert held up his arms. "Of course that is your prerogative. However, wait until you hear what it is that is requested. It would seem that you have made quite an impression on the Lady Rohesa. She has requested that you guide her escort to the Abbey at Reading."

Ardron was completely taken aback. Rohesa had hardly spared him a glance. Gallantry, however, demanded he indulged the lady's wish. "I will of course be at her service," he said.

"Good. I thought you would," Fitzgilbert said with a smirk. "She intends to leave soon after noon, and to be at the Abbey by nightfall."

***

Ardron leaned forward onto Rattlebone's neck and squinted at the moss-covered milestone. Twelve miles to Reading, he deciphered. Good! Perhaps another two hours would see them at journeys end, he estimated. He gazed back down the road looking for the de Vere coach with its escort. It was not in view. He decided to wait.

A few minutes ago they had passed through the Saxon village of Taceham. Ardron had then ridden on ahead checking that the route was safe. In such lawless times as these, desperation often motivated even the most docile into acts of banditry. The opulent appearance of the coach would in all probability cause resentment, and potential reward might provide temptation. The silent sullen stares of the villagers had made him uncomfortable, and he had ordered the coach increase its speed through the village. Once clear he had breathed a little more easily.

It was almost three hours since they had left Marlborough, and the skies of late March where beginning to grey as the cloud-veiled sun neared its setting. There were, he estimated, still a little more than two hours of daylight left, and that should see them safely at the Reading Monastery and his duty therefore discharged.

He was still a little mystified why the Lady Rohesa had requested his protection. Although at the onset of this journey she had been polite and even attentive, her previous disposition had been indifferent almost to the point of unfriendly. Could it be, he asked himself, that it was the stiff Norman protocol that demanded ladies hide their feelings to the point of complete apathy? In which case, he dared to hope that this delightful vision of loveliness might actually harbour an attraction to him. "Folly," he muttered. "That could never be." She is a rich and sophisticated Lady of Norman aristocracy, while I, am just a humble ignorant village Saxon, he thought on.

A few minutes later and the coach had still not appeared which filled him with sudden alarm. He spurred his horse back down the road at a gallop. Moments later he came to it stationary at the roadside. He rode his horse up to the escort knight.

"Why have you stopped?" he demanded as he dismounted.

"The Lady Rohesa bade us stop, so she could take a little break," he replied.

Ardron glanced around. Rohesa was sitting a few yards away on a fallen tree trunk. The knight was an efficient soldier and had carefully posted men in a discreet defensive circle about her. He relaxed; it was understandable he allowed. The woman had been in the coach three hours and a small break of a few minutes was reasonable. He decided that she could be indulged.

"Ardron," she called and bade him approach. "Sit here," she said patting the tree trunk at her side when he neared.

"My Lady," he responded feeling exalted, and sat at her side. She wore a long gown of dark blue, embroidered on the neck arms and sleeves with gem work. On her head this day the wimple was a delicate pink, Nonetheless, it still contrasted vividly with the black hair that tumbled onto her shoulders. The sweet smell of her perfume heightened Ardron's senses and his stomach churned with excitement. At this close proximity her beauty was even more electrifying, and that served only to remind him of his unsophisticated yokel status. Nevertheless, she smiled at him sweetly convincing him that she took pleasure in his close company.

"Where are you from?" she asked opening conversation.

"I am from a small Saxon village near Malmesbury," he replied.

"I have never been to Malmesbury," she said.

Ardron pulled a wry face. "It's a town pretty much as any other, with the exception of the Abbey.

"I have heard of the Abbey?"

Ardron nodded. "Yes a very grand Abbey," he said.

"So what is this Saxon doing so far from home?" she asked.

"It's a long story, my Lady. And one I wouldn't want to bore you with."

Rohesa accepted his comment then after a silent pause she said. "That sword of yours looks to be a very fine weapon. Is all that knot-work on the hilt silver?"

"It is," Ardron replied.

"May I have a look at it?"

Ardron hesitated a moment then reached over his shoulder and slowly drew the sword. Then he held it across his hands for her to see.

Rohesa held out her hands to receive it. "Let me see," she said.

He hesitated a little more, not sure whether he should pass her the weapon or not. Then deciding that it would be alright he passed it across.

"My, it's heavy," she said. "And is this a battlefield trophy also?"

"A battlefield trophy?" he was surprised and offended. "Certainly not! It was made by our village blacksmith."

"Truly your village must be very fortunate to have such a skilled blacksmith."

"Yes we are. And I am proud to call Swidhurn a special friend."

"Sir Knight," she called to the escort guard. "What is your opinion of this sword?"

The knight walked smartly forward and took the sword from her. After checking the balance we waved and twisted it around. "It's a very fine sword indeed." he said. "The sword of a warrior!"

"Are you a warrior, Ardron?" Rohesa asked.

Ardron was not at all comfortable with the sudden belligerent direction events were turning. "No, I don't consider myself a warrior," He said getting to his feet to recover the sword.

"Neither do I," Rohesa said. "Take him," she instructed the knight.

Ardron then found the point of his own sword pressing against his chest. He tried to step backwards away from the point but found two sergens at his back with drawn swords. Puzzled he looked at the Lady Rohesa but she was already on her feet and moving away without a backward glance. Heavy iron shackles were produced, and his wrist manacled, then looped through a strut at the coach rear.

Chapter 7

Hedingham Hall, April 1140

Ardron was manhandled roughly, and with an unceremonious shove propelled into the centre of the great hall. Standing scruffy and dishevelled he looked around at the sea of unsympathetic faces. The walls were hung with a profusion of banners and shields bearing the de Vere coat-of-arms. The yellow and red quarters with a mullet in the top left corner was identical to the ring he had taken from the knight at the battle of Wallingford.

Four days, or maybe five, Ardron had languished in the dungeons of Hedingham Castle. Kept in permanent darkness he had no concept of passing time. His only calendar had been the daily ration of stale bread and water that was pushed through a small hatch low down on the heavy door. It was still not clear to him why the Lady Rohesa had had him taken prisoner, but within hours of his incarceration, a knight had visited his cell and taken from him the ring. Now as he stood under the de Vere coat of arms surrounded by hostile faces, he could guess that the ring had played a major part in his circumstances.

"Bring the wretch forward," The man seated in a highchair at the far end of the hall demanded. Jabbed in the back with lancers Ardron was prodded forward. The man got to his feet and glared down at Ardron. "I am Sir Aubrey Alberic de Vere, Lord of Hedingham and High Sheriff of London," he pronounced with menace in his voice. He was not a young man probably around fifty, nevertheless, he stood tall and straight. His thick shoulder-length grey hair was supplemented with a heavy grey beard, groomed to fork beneath his chin. "And you, debase reprobate," he growled, "Should tremble before my wrath."

Ardron made no reply and quickly scanned around the onlookers. A gathering of a dozen or so of smartly dressed knights stood either flank of Sir Aubrey's chair. A large number of sergens and other spectators crowded the hall down both sides. As his eyes came slowly back towards Sir Aubrey, he caught sight of Lady Rohesa standing in the corner, her hand rested on the arm of a distinguished looking knight. It was the same knight that had taken away the ring. Ardron stared directly at Rohesa holding the gaze accusingly, but there was no remorse in the return stare.

"Sir Aubrey," Ardron said with a brief subservient bow. "I would know why I have been brought here under these circumstances."

Sir Aubrey sucked in a noisy breath and struggled to control a temper. "Hand me the ring," he muttered holding out a hand behind him without looking back. Between his finger and thumb he held it aloft. "How came you by this ring?" he almost shouted.

Somewhat disadvantaged, Ardron was caught in two minds on how to answer. He assumed the knight he had killed must have been a member of the de Vere family. To confess to his killing, even though the fight in self-defence, would probably go ill for him. He thought to lie and say that he had found it.

"Well?" Sir Aubrey demanded as Ardron delayed his reply.

Ardron straightened his back looked back defiantly then said. "I slew the wearer during the battle of Wallingford."

"You slew the wearer," Sir Aubrey sneered. "How so? By stabbing him in the back, no doubt."

"No Sir. By honourable means in a fair fight of kill or be killed."

"The day has never dawned when you, a mere Saxon peasant, could slay my brother in a fair fight."

"Your brother?"

"Aye my brother, Robert. The best swordsman in Normandy and no doubt in England too."

"I regret Sir, that it was your brother who died, but nonetheless it was a one on one fair fight. "

"Liar," Sir Aubrey's shouted reply cut through all the mutterings of disbelief which rumbled around the hall.

Ardron stared back in silence.

"You, degenerate, are nothing more than a battlefield scavenger picking over the valuables from the dead. The lowest of all that is contemptable and that is how you came by this ring."

"No Sir, Ardron replied shaking his head.

Sir Aubrey ignored the reply. "I intend to have you hung as a public spectacle outside the castle gates at sundown today. And that quick death will fall short of what your type of deserve."

"There was a witness." Ardron cut through the cheers that rang through the room. "I have a witness."

"No doubt you can provide a dozen witnesses and all from the same crowd of lying degenerates," Sir Aubrey said dismissively.

"No Sir, a Norman knight of sound honest reputation. He witnessed the whole fight and it was his suggestion that I should take the ring in order that it did not fall into the hands of some battlefield scavenger"

"Who would that be?" he replied scoffing.

"None other than Sir Benet! The trusted constable of Sir John Fitzgilbert."

Sir Aubrey was visibly taken aback but soon recovered. "I know of no such knight, nor if he even exists."

"He exists," Ardron countered. "Your daughter, Lady Rohesa can testify to that."

He turned to look at his daughter. At first, she made no move then nodded slowly.

Sir Aubrey sighed heavily frustrated at this turn of events. "And if we were to message this knight to come and speak on your behalf, how would that resolve?"

"I am sure he would come," Ardron replied.

Sir Aubrey stroked his beard thoughtfully. "Very well," he eventually said. "But if this turns out to be nothing more than a delaying tactic, then to your hanging, I will add the drawn and quarter." He paused to allow thought. "How say you now? Do you still want me to message this knight?"

"Indeed I do, Sir."

Sir Aubrey showed frustration with gritted teeth. "Very well," he said with a sigh. "Take the prisoner back to the dungeons."

***

By counting the number of times bread and water had been thrust through the small hatch Ardron knew another seven days had elapsed. Several times he had tried to communicate with his gaoler attempting to learn news, but the gaoler was not forthcoming, or perhaps it was that he simply did not know anything. On the eighth day the jangle of keys in the heavy door told him something different was about to happen. The door swung open and the grinning gaoler motioned with his head that Ardron should come.

"What's happening," Ardron asked as he ducked through the door.

"Don't know," the curt reply. "But for you I don't think it's good." Ardron was led between two guards back to the great hall.

Not crowded as before, nevertheless, there were still enough interested spectators around to make Ardron feel uncomfortable. Particularly so when a quick scan did not reveal any of the friendly faces he had hoped to see. He stood waiting in the centre largely ignored. He guessed that this was part of the mind game designed to break down his confidence. It was working, he admitted to himself. Eventually, after walking across to his elevated chair, Sir Aubrey condescended to speak.

"Well Saxon. It seems that your declared witness did not find you important enough to come and speak on your behalf. Or perhaps it is that he simply has nothing to say."

"I cannot believe that" Ardron blurted out. "Did the message relate the importance of the testimony?" Sir Aubrey face set hard and Ardron realised that in his desperation he had posed the question bluntly.

"You question my competence to write, Saxon?" Sir Aubrey was on his feet in anger.

"No Sir. I am sorry." He shook his head bewildered. "I just cannot understand why Benet has not responded."

Sir Aubrey sat down slowly. "Whether you understand or not is of little consequence to me. I see no reason why I should not assume that you are guilty of battlefield scavenging. A truly despicable deed and I intend to carry out the sentence as decided some days ago." He paused allowing the judgment to sink in. "Tomorrow at noon you will be hung drawn and quartered! Take him away!"

"Wait," Ardron shouted as the guards closed in on him. "I claim Wager of Battel."

"Denied," Sir Aubrey said dismissively.

"You would deny me the right to allow God to be the judge of my innocence or guilt?"

"Yes, I would."

"Then you will be damned before God, when you stand before him on your judgement day." Ardron had stepped well over the line of disrespect. But with nothing to lose what did it matter?

"Sir Aubrey," another knight spoke up. Ardron recognised him as the knight who had accompanied Lady Rohesa at the previous assembly.

Sir Aubrey glanced sideways at the knight who spoke. "Sir Geoffrey, you have something to say?" he challenged.

"If it pleases you, Sir?"

"Go ahead," he allowed.

"This man claims that he did defeat your brother in a fair sword fight. No one here will dispute that Sir Robert was a very fine swordsman. Indeed, he was the finest that I have ever seen. On more than one occasion both you and I witnessed him take on three at the same time in arena jousts, and win. In fact, his boast was that he could take on five and win."

Sir Aubrey nodded agreement. "Yes."

"Now," Sir Geoffrey waved an arm towards Ardron. "If this man did beat Sir Robert fairly then he too should be able to defeat three. Therefore, let him prove his skill against three." He paused waiting a reaction to his suggestion. "Either way it should prove an interesting distraction," he added.

Ardron watched Sir Aubrey as he began to smile, clearly gratified by the suggestion. It would provide entertainment, and would also save his soul from eternal damnation, Ardron's chances of surviving the contest were slim, therefore, it would achieve Ardron's death anyway. "Sir Geoffrey Mandeville," he said. "I can always count on you for a solution." He leaned back, his elbow resting on the chair arm. "What say you now, Saxon?" he asked stroking his beard contentedly.

Ardron had no alternative. Die a slow and agonising death by execution or take his chances against three. "Give me my own sword and I accept."

"Your own sword?"

"Yes, Sir Aubrey. "I have my own sword.

"I know of no such sword."

"It was taken from me at the time of my incarceration."

Sir Aubrey sighed, obviously irritated. "We will give you a sword to fight with."

"I prefer my own sword. It is special."

Sir Aubrey briefly closed his eyes then loudly tutted. "If such a sword exists then we will find it and you shall have it. Is that all?" he asked with heavy sarcasm. Ardron with a brief bow nodded content.

***

"Is this your sword?" Sir Aubrey asked from the elevated dais.

Ardron squinted and tried to identify the sword from a distance of about fifteen yards. "It looks like it he replied."

Sir Aubrey hesitated a moment then tossed it into the arena, landing some five yards to Ardron's front. It was no way to treat such a balanced weapon. Ardron moved to pick it up.

"Do not move Saxon," Sir Aubrey said. "The moment you touch that weapon then the contest will begin." Ardron stopped and took a guarded look around.

The arena had been generously squared, at least giving him some room to run around. The perimeter was lined with spectators, some expressions hostile, others simply curious. None it seemed sympathetic. Behind him Sir Geoffrey de Mandeville and two other knights stood ready with swords drawn. All were helmeted, and wore hauberks as armour, while he wore only the rags in which he now stood. Ardron had noted the yellow silks of Lady Rohesa's favour tied around Mandeville's right arm. To Ardron's front, and raised above the arena, there was the small dais which was crowded with the castle dignitaries. Lady Rohesa sat close at her father's side. Ardron stared at her wondering briefly, if perhaps she felt any responsibility for the heavily disadvantaged situation into which she had placed him. She held his stare impassively. Probably not, he decided. He refocused his attention to his plight. His first problem, to arm himself! The three knights would be upon him the moment he bent to pick up the sword. He turned to face them and nodded acknowledgement to each one in turn. Casually he turned away and walked forward stepping over the sword before turning back. Now at least he was facing his opponents.

He delayed his move a long time, preparing himself as he stared at the knights. They stood ready poised to rush in. If he didn't get this next move right, then this contest would be over very quickly. Slowly, he moved two or three steps to the right of the sword. The knights shuffled over to stay directly facing, and that gave him the chance he was hoping for. At a dash he ran left, swooping to pick up the sword as he passed. His dash carried him beyond the knights, and his new position placed them in single file. Only the man on the end was in position to attack. Ardron leapt into attack, swinging the heavy sword downwards. First left then right, all were parried. Without any decrease in intensity, he lifted his sword high spun right round, and brought the weapon in horizontally. The speed took the knight by surprise, and with all of Ardron's weight behind the swing, it crashed into his ribs. The hauberk protected the man from any slash wound, but such was the force that it knocked him sideways. The two knights behind had meanwhile moved into position either side of their comrade. Ardron broke off the attack and once more ran to his left, again placing the knights in single file.

This time it was Mandeville who he attacked. He was a different proposition. He danced back out of range of Ardron's swings, and he thrust his sword hard at Ardron's chest. Although the momentum of his swing had carried his sword down, Ardron was able to bring it back up quickly and divert Mandeville's thrust skywards. Once twice, three times the pair crossed swords until Ardron saw the other two had positioned either side of Mandeville. Again, he broke off contact and ran once more to the left.

"Stand still and fight. You craven bastard." The third knight muttered as he closed in on Ardron. He came in with hefty swinging blows forcing Ardron backwards as he parried. Then the knight lunged forward, the sword point aimed at Ardron's chest. Snapping erect and turning sideways on Ardron allowed the sword to pass across his front, and as the knight stumbled forward, he stuck out a foot, tripping him and sending him sprawling full length. As he began to crawl away to safety, Ardron saw a chance. The man's body was still protected by the hauberk but not so his legs. With all the force he could muster, Ardron brought his sword down hard across the back of the man's legs, then just for good measure, pulled the weapon towards him in a slashing movement. With his Achilles tendons severed right through the man would not even be able to stand. Ardron leapt over him and dashed towards the arena's centre. The odds had now improved. He was also aware of cheering breaking out among the crowd. He was not quite as friendless as he had believed. The neutral in the crowd began to favour the underdog.

He backed away slowly as Mandeville and the other knight cautiously advanced wide apart. He was breathing heavily, and three weeks diet of bread and water began to tell as his strength began to drain. He held out his sword tip, pointing at one and then the other as he continued to cede ground. Soon he would be backed into a corner and that, he didn't want. At the same time he became aware of some crowd disturbance. There were now horsemen in the arena. However, he could not, dare not, shift his concentration. Only when it became obvious that horsemen were bearing down on him did he break concentration to face this new and more immediate threat. But the horsemen, mounted sergens, drove on through placing themselves between Ardron and the two knights. They were not a threat but were instead a shield.

"What's the meaning of this?" He could hear Sir Aubrey's shouted demands.

Not interested in questioning the welcome relief, Ardron sank onto his haunches taking the opportunity to rest and recover. He expected the contest would re-start when these horsemen had been cleared from the arena. But then a group of knights, sporting the royal blue livery of Earl Robert of Gloucester, rode into the arena and brought their mounts to a halt right in front of the dais.

"Sir Robert!" Sir Aubrey exclaimed.

Ardron focussed his attention on the leader of the new-comers, and instantly recognised Robert Earl of Gloucester.

"Stop this contest immediately," Sir Robert demanded. "That man is under my protection."

Sir Aubrey stared at him for a moment then signalled to his constable that they should comply.

Still not quite sure of what had just happened, Ardron remained on his haunches watching and waiting.

"Scorrenstone, what have you got yourself into now?" It was Benet who now approached him and held out his hand. "By all the saints," he went on. "You look dreadful."

"And you my friend look beautiful," Ardron countered with relief as he took the hand.

"You smell worse than you look," Benet said hauling Ardron to his feet.

"You took your own good time getting here," Ardron accused.

"What would be the urgency?" Benet laughed. "You were doing alright," he went on nodding towards the grounded knight being placed on a stretcher. "The message was delayed getting to me," he went on turning serious. "I was with the earl on serious business. The possession of Devizes Castle! But we came post haste as soon as the message was delivered." He fell suddenly silent and stared at Mandeville as he removed his helmet. "My God," he muttered as he recognised the man. "It's a great shame that he wasn't the one you brought down."

"Why?" Ardron puzzled reply

"Come," Benet said ignoring the question. "I have much news to pass on, but for now let's see if we can get you cleaned up."

Less than an hour later Ardron relaxed in a hot tub in the sergens barracks. By the side, a platter of cold chicken dressed with radish and onions. Grand fare for a man just off three weeks bread and water, and Ardron ate wolfishly.

"What happened to put you in this predicament?" Benet asked helping himself to a radish from the platter.

"You may well ask," Ardron responded accusingly. "It was that damned ring you bade me take at Wallingford." He went on to explain the events that had placed him a prisoner, and the accusations that had been laid upon him.

Far from sympathetic Benet only sniggered. "Never mind he said it is all being sorted at this very moment."

"Albeit only just in time." Ardron responded edgily.

"Yes, that was unfortunate, Benet replied with a little more sympathy. "I was detailed to accompany Earl Robert to Devizes and your message was delayed catching up with me."

"As you said," Ardron replied. "Did you take possession of the castle?"

"Erm," Benet hesitated. "No. Not yet."

"Not yet?"

"Soon! It will be soon."

Ardron stared at him waiting an explanation.

"Sir Robert arrived at Marlborough with a small contingent force and took charge of Fitzhubert." Benet started to explain. "Then he rode to Devizes and demanded that the castle be handed over, but the force inside refused. Fitzhubert was given the chance, under pain of death, to persuade those inside to surrender. Ironically, disloyalty begets disloyalty, and so it was proved. They refused and even challenged Sir Robert to carry out the threat. So, he did. Fitzhubert was hung outside the gates in full view."

"Fitzhubert's dead?"

"Aye he is. Died ignominiously kicking against slow strangulation on the end of a rope."

Fitzhubert dead! Ardron should have been elated but he wasn't. In fact, he felt only mild satisfaction. The man had come to the end he deserved. No more would he terrorise and pillage the common populace in pursuit of his personal greed. Ardron reached over and took a chicken leg then stared upwards thoughtfully as he bit into it. "And the castle?" he asked.

"Ah yes, the castle." Benet said. "We left. We had no choice we were too few to do very much. But Sir Robert does not intend it rests there. His intention is to raise a force and lay it under siege. We returned to Marlborough to make plans. It can be only a matter of time before he takes possession."

"What then?"

"What then? It's a good castle and a veritable prize to be in the empress's possession." Benet paused, then after a moment's thought. "I got the notification of your predicament upon my return to Marlborough, so I prepared to leave at once. But Sir Robert insisted that I wait for him because he wanted to personally come to your aid."

"He did? Why?" Ardron asked a little puzzled how he came to be so regarded by a premier Norman noble.

"Sir Robert appreciates fully the vital part that you have played in delivering Fitzhubert into his hands, and also the probable takeover of Devizes Castle in the near future. That is why!"

"Another thing I don't quite understand," Ardron said. "How is it that Earl Robert has such influence over de Vere?"

"How?" Benet paraphrased a little surprised. "He is of course the eldest son of the late king. In effect has the second most claim to the throne behind his half-sister Maude. A much stronger claim than the usurper Stephen, and as such wields great power and influence."

Ardron shook his head, still a little baffled. "I understand that," he said. "But Aubrey de Vere is High Sheriff of London and that is a king's appointment. His brother fought at Wallingford on the side of Stephen. Surely he and the family are in King Stephen's pay."

"One would think so, I agree. But Aubrey de Vere is a very circumspect man. His all-consuming priority is to maintain the de Vere wealth and status. To that end he attempts to rest above it all and maintain a foot in both causes until such times as one side or the other nears victory."

"Can't see how he can get away with that," Ardron replied. "Surely the king demanded his sworn fealty before granting him the sheriff post."

"Oh yes, almost certainly. And he probably made such a vow."

"How then can he honour his oath and still accommodate the lead supporter of the empress?"

Benet laughed out loud. "How indeed? He is able to do that by betrothing his eldest son Aubrey, to Mabel Fitzrobert." Seeing Ardron's confusion, he went on. "Mabel Fitzrobert! The daughter of Earl Robert! So, you see there is to be an alliance and that binds them together."

Ardron shook his head bewildered. "Norman politics," he muttered. "Such intrigues are beyond my comprehension. I am nought but a simple village Saxon."

"Tell me," Benet said after a moment's silence. "What did you do to put Geoffrey de Mandeville in the arena against you?"

Ardron was puzzled. "I didn't do anything. Well other than being in possession of that ring."

Benet shook his head. "That was de Vere's problem not his."

"Then I don't know," Ardron dismissed it.

164

"There must have been something! Something personal! He would not have risked his own life on de Vere's account."

"Perhaps he didn't see it as a risk," Ardron said with a shrug. "Who is he anyway?"

"Who is he? You don't know?"

"Sir Geoffrey de Mandeville, I know that much."

"Sir Geoffrey de Mandeville," Benet explained, "Is the king's confidante and one of the originals that came with Stephen to claim Maude's crown."

"He is here__ and so is Sir Robert," Ardron muttered. "Is there likely to be trouble?"

"While they are both guests of Sir Aubrey I think not. At least I hope not."

Both men were thoughtful for a few moments. "Come hasten yourself," Benet said. "Dignitaries await your presence in Sir Aubrey's private chambers."

Another hour and Ardron and Benet made their way to the private chambers of Sir Aubrey de Vere. De Vere sat casually at ease, in front a blazing fire. Close by his side sat Sir Robert staring somewhat pre-occupied into his wine goblet while swilling the contents around slowly. Opposite a few feet away, Geoffrey Mandeville stood looking stern and detached, almost as if there were a bad smell under his nose. There was a palpable tension in the air; that much was obvious.

"Ah," de Vere said after they were announced. "Come pull up a couple of seats." He indicated that they should join the gathering by the fire. "You are well and recovered?" he asked Ardron with a politeness that was completely different to his previous belligerent conduct. Perhaps it was more to do with the opportune event breaking into the icy atmosphere.

"Yes Sir. I am quite recovered." In truth he still suffered feelings of weakness after his long ordeal, but the reply was the correct response. He turned his attention to the earl. "Sir Robert, I am in your debt for your intervention.

Sir Robert held up his hand in dismissive gesture. "Due to your dedicated action you caused the deliverance of that subversive scoundrel Fitzhubert into my hands, and as a result we also procured Devizes Castle." He glanced at Mandeville as he made the last remark almost sneering.

Mindful of what Benet had told him about the castle situation Ardron was about to seek clarification. However, catching the intended sneer he understood why the false boast.

Sir Robert studied Ardron hard then said. "Haven't we met before?"

"Indeed we have, sir. It was I who got you from your bed to deliver the news that the empress had landed at Arundel."

"Oh yes, recognition dawned."

"And there she should have been seized. Then sent back to that hell-spawn Angevin, Geoffrey, where she belongs," Mandeville muttered.

"That would never have happened," Sir Robert replied hotly. "I had an army assembled and ready to march. That day Stephen showed good sense to avoid a battle that he would surely have lost."

"Gentlemen, gentlemen," de Vere cut in. "Under my hospitality keep it civil. If you, please!"

Both men simmered under silence.

"Young man," de Vere sought his attention, and at the same time steering the conversation onto safer ground. "It seems that I have most grievously misjudged you"

"Yes, you did," Ardron replied testily.

De Vere nodded understandingly. "I could not believe that there was a Saxon in the whole country that could have bested my brother with the broad sword. But I was wrong, as Benet here has testified."

Ardron shrugged. "Your brother was indeed a mighty man with a sword, but I just got lucky. Your brother died a warrior's death."

"Benet told me how you honoured him by handing him his sword as he died." I thank you for that."

Ardron wondered if Benet had also revealed how he dealt the final pain-relieving death blow. "It was no more than he deserved," he said.

"Tell me," Geoffrey Mandeville spoke. If there had been no intervention today do you think you would have won out?"

Ardron shrugged. "Maybe!"

"You think you could have bested me and one other?"

"We'll never know, Sir Geoffrey."

"Would you then say that I was lucky," he persisted.

Ardron shrugged not wishing to be drawn into this antagonism

"Sir Giles was not lucky," Mandeville went on. "And it seems it may be a long time before he can walk again."

"I am, sorry to hear that, Sir Geoffrey. But" Ardron added with a shrug, "I was fighting for my life."

"Indeed," Mandeville allowed.

"You must allow me to make compensation," de Vere interrupted.

"Not necessary," Ardron replied curtly.

"Oh, but it is. The de Vere reputation is at stake."

"What would a village Saxon need? Mandeville spoke again. "A cart full of turnips?"

Ardron glared at the man. He was being deliberately rude and aggressive.

"Have a care, Sir Geoffrey," Sir Robert intervened getting to his feet. "You are close to provoking the man who bested Robert de Vere."

Mandeville bowed his head and waved a floppy submissive hand as capitulation.

"I had thought that forty marks would compensate for my grave misjudgement, young man." De Vere diplomatically moved the topic back and away from the tension.

"I had thought a hundred." Sir Robert interrupted as he sat down again.

"A hundred?" de Vere almost choked on his wine.

A hundred marks was more money than Ardron had ever hoped to own. In fact, so was forty.

De Vere shook his head. "Sir Robert, this is the man who killed my brother. Would you have me reward him so?"

"On a battlefield no one person is immune to death, and each man taking part knows that. It is a chance that all take," Sir Robert countered. There seemed little sympathy in Sir Robert's reply. Perhaps the reason was, Ardron supposed, that Robert de Vere had fought on the side of King Stephen. "Forty marks is adequate compensation," he cut in to defuse the situation.

Whilst de Vere's relief was apparent, Sir Robert looked a little unhappy at Ardron's capitulation.

"I will have my clerk place the money in your hand before you leave," de Vere said.

The conversation fell away for a few seconds before Sir Robert spoke. "Later this evening," he said to Ardron, "I wish to see you in my quarters. And you Benet will you join us?"

The small gathering broke up soon after and probably to the relief of de Vere.

The hour was getting late when eventually one of Sir Robert's servants came to find Ardron and Benet and led them to his quarters. The square chamber, high in the keep, was not large. Its grey stone walls created an impression of gloom, and the lit candles dotted around the room did little to improve the ambiance. However, the vigorous flames dancing and crackling in the fire grate did brighten that immediate area, at least. Sir Robert lounged sideways in a large chair at the fireside, his leg draped over one of the chair arms.

"Come in, come in," he greeted motioning toward two nearby chairs.

"Will that be all, Sir Robert?" the servant sought dismissal.

"Find something to block up those arrow slits," he replied waving a vaguely pointed finger. Two strategically placed arrow slits inbuilt into the walls allowed a cold April wind free access to the chamber. "Then have a guard posted outside my room till morn," he added. "Don't want to be murdered in my bed by that devil's disciple, Mandeville," he muttered turning back towards Ardron and Benet. He paused and looked to the servant making sure he had understood.

"Yes, Sir Robert," the servant said.

"One would think that de Vere, with all his wealth, would have put shutters over those arrow slits for the benefit of his guests," Sir Robert grumbled.

Ardron only smiled. Certainly, the facilities were much superior to humble Saxon dwellings but by no means as warm.

"Now young Saxon, I have heard very good reports of your actions in our cause," Sir Robert said looking hard at Ardron.

"Probably with some exaggeration," Ardron replied in modesty.

"You were at Wallingford with Miles Fitzwalter as he broke the siege, and I am reliably informed that you fought gallantly," Sir Robert said glancing at Benet for confirmation.

Benet nodded agreement.

"You must have fought well. After all you brought down Robert de Vere." Sir Robert went on with a laugh and an affirmative nod. "Prior to that, you undertook a spy mission right into the heart of the usurpers camp." He waited for Ardron's confirmation.

"I did," he agreed.

"And now this latest episode with Fitzhubert," Sir Robert went on. "Not to mention that I now recognise you as the messenger who brought me the news of my sister's plight at Arundel." He continued, nodding approvingly to himself. "One way or another you seem to have contributed greatly to the cause, in fact, I would go as far to say that you may have given more than some of the more auspicious nobles around me."

Ardron shrugged a little and smiled with a touch of embarrassment. He had never set out to actually get involved in this Norman conflict. Yet it seemed that he was continually and unavoidably sucked in. He wondered how it would be viewed if Sir Robert knew also that he had been on the side of the king at Malmesbury, albeit forcibly pressed.

"It would seem that chance continually placed me in those positions, Sir Robert," he said.

"It would seem so," he agreed, then paused a moment before going on. "You should be rewarded' and I have decided to offer you knight service."

"Knight Service?"

"Knight Service," Benet cut in seeing Ardron's confusion. "Is an honour bestowed on a deserving person and includes a socage." He looked at Sir Robert for confirmation on the last point.

Sir Robert puffed out his cheeks thoughtfully, then gave a brief nod. "We will find some land somewhere," he agreed.

"A knight who is not a noble is simply a horse-soldier in a Norman army, or usually referred as a milite," Benet went on. "As such you will, of course, be expected to perform military service as and when required. But then with several hides of land as socage that should be good reward."

Ardron was dubious. Military service to an overlord would almost certainly bring him deeper into the conflict, and despite his past actions, that was something he had tried to avoid. Neither did he know anything about running an estate. He shook his head slowly, "I know how to work a piece of land but to actually manage an estate, I know not the first thing."

"No matter," Sir Robert said with a laugh. "If you know how to work a piece of land then you know a lot more than some socage men." Then turning serious he said. "The normal land tenancy for knight service would be around five hides, but we can look at that a little later."

"Don't worry too much about the management," Benet said. "You can get somebody like me to be constable, and a clerk to work the finance."

"That's right," Sir Robert said. "Most of my knights visit their estates only occasionally. He paused staring at Ardron. "Of course," he went on. "I don't do this purely for your benefit. It is important to me also. I will get a committed knight and a highly skilled fighter. You would be a valuable asset to me personally. Regrettably, it is outside my power to actually make you a noble but once the empress becomes queen, then we can regard the matter again. In the meantime a knight in my service enjoys considerable status and is well paid."

Ardron sighed heavily, "I don't know what to say," he said.

"I understand," Sir Robert said. "You are the second son of a Thegn."

Ardron nodded agreement.

"That is noble Saxon birth! But then as second son you will not become Thegn! Prospects in knight service, however, do open the door to potential advancement into nobility. That, of course, would be subject to loyal service and also dependant on the Empress becoming Queen."

There was no doubt in Ardron's mind that this offer opened the door to tremendous opportunities, but still he delayed. It seemed something of a betrayal to his Saxon birth, also it would bring him deep into the conflict that he saw as a Norman struggle. Up to this point he could honestly tell himself that whoever ended up as monarch, it would make little difference to the Saxon community. But to take this offer would see him siding firmly with the empress and indeed having a personal vested interest in her success. But what if Stephen prevailed? Then it would all turn to ashes in his hands, and not only would the offer be worthless, it could probably be seriously detrimental. A chance for wealth and prestige, or ashes? But then he had very little now. How much worse off could he be? What would his father's advice be? He would urge me to take the offer, he concluded.

"Thank you, Sir Robert. I accept."

"Good," Sir Robert said. Benet sighed with relief at what he too considered to be the correct decision.

"What happens next?" Ardron asked.

"You return to Bristol with me. There are a couple of formalities to be observed, and there will be some training to make you an accomplished milite," Sir Robert said. "I know well that you can a handle a broad sword, but what about a lance?"

"A lance? Never had the occasion to use one," Ardron said.

"As a milite mounted in battle that will be your main weapon. Don't worry," he laughed seeing Ardron's doubt. "You will soon master it I am sure. What about a mace? Have you ever used one of those?"

Ardron shook his head. Already he was beginning to wonder if he had made the right decision.

***

He tightened the cinch beneath Rattlebone's belly then leaned across the horse's withers and waited. Earl Robert stood on the steps of the mote taking his leave from Sir Aubrey de Vere. Yesterday had been a nothing day that had left him bored, waiting while de Vere and Sir Robert conducted business. But this day he was to join the earl's company and make the return journey to Marlborough, and then onwards to Bristol. Once there, he was informed by Benet, he would have to undergo a short ceremony to swear fealty before he could be considered a knight in the earl's employ. However, before that there were two full days of hard riding in front of them.

"Ardron," he heard his name being called. Lady Rohesa hurried toward him. "I had to see you before you go," she said.

"Oh," Ardron replied coldly.

"Yes! I have to confess that I most cruelly misjudged you and I am so sorry."

Ardron shook his head. "It doesn't matter now. It's finished."

"No, I can't let it go like that," she replied. "I have a debt of honour to make it up to you."

"No need," Ardron said. "Your father has already paid me a compensating sum."

"Rohesa," a sharp call came. Both turned to see Geoffrey Mandeville standing a few yards away staring in their direction. Rohesa lifted her hand in a brief acknowledging wave.

She turned her attention back to Ardron. "Still, I fill obliged."

"Don't," Ardron said.

Ignoring his comment, she held out the ring. "I want you to take this," she said.

"No," Ardron said firmly.

"You must. I am sure my uncle would have preferred you to have it."

Ardron still shook his head. "It belongs in your family."

"It does, but it is mine to give away."

"Rohesa," Mandeville called again, this time more impatiently.

Ardron stared at her questioningly. "We are betrothed," she answered his unasked question. "Please take the ring. It is influential in this part of the country and will open many doors."

For a few moments Ardron hesitated still inclined to refuse, but then he relented and reluctantly nodded assent. However, he did not say what was in his mind. He intended to keep well clear of this part of the country in the future if he could.

"Good! Thank you," she said handing over the ring. "Now I must go." She hesitated a moment, "Perhaps we'll meet again."

"Perhaps," Ardron replied.

"Rohesa!" Mandeville was getting annoyed.

"You'd better go," Ardron said.

"Yes," she said holding up her hand for him to kiss her fingers.

The devil inside him made him protract the kiss with an undisguised sensuality just to irritate Mandeville further. He then watched as she hurried across to the scowling man.

Betrothed to Mandeville? Ardron shook his head ruefully, marvelling, as he did, at the cunning measures de Vere was arranging. With a daughter betrothed to a leader in the king's army, and a son betrothed to the daughter of the leader of the Angevins then he would have family connections to those with influences in both armies. Clearly, he could sit out the war and then step forward and congratulate the eventual victor. Thus ensuring the continued wealth and power of the de Vere dynasty.

During the conversation Sir Robert had mounted his horse at the head of the column. After a brief glance back to see that all was ready, he waved the column forward. Ardron, caught out a little, mounted quickly spooking Rattlebone in his haste. The horse reared onto its rear legs then spun round as Ardron gained control. With a grin he looked back at Rohesa standing at Mandeville's side, and gave her a brief wave. She returned the wave guardedly as he joined the column.

Two days later on a bright spring morning they arrived at Marlborough Castle. However, the immediate news took much of the brightness out of the day. It was rumoured that the inmates of Devizes Castle had sent an envoy to King Stephen offering to sell him possession of the castle.

"God damn every living soul inside its walls," Sir Robert fumed when confronted by the news. Ardron retreated into the background while the nobles held a meeting to discuss their next action.

Not privy to any decision made, Ardron could only wait, and as a consequence spent a slow casual day tending his horse and equipment.

Sir Robert was still in a foul mood when they left Marlborough the next day. Although curious about what he intended to do about Devizes Castle,

Ardron stayed clear of the man allowing him to brood, as did his accompanying nobles. By the time they reached Bristol late in the day Sir Robert's mood had improved, and the word that reached Ardron was that the earl intended to raise a siege force and lay it against the castle at Devizes.

The very next day, however, the mood was changed to jubilation when news was received that Miles Fitzwalter and Geoffrey Talbot had, after a prolonged siege, taken back Hereford Castle from the kings supporters. Even more surprising was that this had been achieved while King Stephen had camped and entrenched his army less than twenty miles to the north at Little Hereford. But it was not a popular victory! The townsfolk of Hereford had been outraged against Sir Miles when he desecrated their dead. In order to construct a row of siege engines, he had the graveyard of St Guthlac's church dug up to create a rampart behind which his men could safely work. Then as the exhumed corpses began to fester and smell he had the bodies hurled from the siege engines into the castle.

More good news was to follow a month later. With Sir Robert finalising his plans to lay siege to Devizes Castle, the news was received that the people of Devizes had rebelled violently against the castellan, Count Hervey de Leone, Earl of Wiltshire, the king's son-in-law. Deciding that his position was untenable, Count Hervey soon abandoned the castle. Sir Robert lost no time in despatching two of his sons to take charge of the castle

In the West Country, things were going really well for Empress Maude and her supporters.

Chapter 8

Trowbridge, Summer 1140

"It's not a big estate, in fact I have seen bigger manors," Humphrey de Bohun said.

Ardron studied the chart somewhat dubiously. His eyes followed the line that marked Gloucestershire from Wiltshire and confirmed that the estate was in Gloucestershire, just.

"Norwood Castle is somewhat run down and in need of some maintenance," de Bohun went on.

"How is it manned?" Ardron asked.

"I keep a small detachment there of around twenty sergen and an administrator."

Ardron stepped back and sat, then drummed his fingers on the table thoughtfully. "How many hides? He asked.

"Four!" Then after a short pause added. "Nearly four."

That was less than a service knight should expect but was still more than a simple village Saxon could aspire too. Ardron leaned forward and studied the map again. "This village Myntey," he pointed a finger on the map.

"Is a sizable village and the main income from the estate," de Bohun finished the unasked question.

"There is a small settlement here, Okesey, just outside the castle and Kemble Wick to the north."

Ardron scanned west of the castle and spotted the close proximity of South Cerney Castle, and with it a potential problem. "This castle here is fully manned and the castellan, de Evereux, is in the service of the king."

"Yes," de Bohun confirmed.

"I have previously met de Evereux," Ardron said

"You have?"

"I had occasion to plead the cause of a Saxon robbed by some royalists."

De Bohun nodded without reply.

"He could overrun this castle in a day, if he so desired," Ardron went on.

"Yes, he could," de Bohun confirmed lightly. "But he won't."

"He won't! Why not?"

"Because Edward de Evereux is my cousin, and I pay him a goodwill sum quarterly."

"You pay protection?" Ardron said.

De Bohun winced and shook his head. "No not protection. I see it more as a helping hand."

"A helping hand?" Ardron queried.

"Let me explain," de Bohun said. "Norwood Castle came into the de Bohun family with my mother Matilda de Evereux when she married my father, Humphrey. So you see Edward's father, also called Edward, was my mother's brother. She also had another brother and he called Walter. Walter de Evereux although ailing at this time, is castellan at Salisbury Castle, which is, as you will know is a very desirable and prosperous estate to own. Walter has three descendants, William, Patric and Sybil, all with far better prospects than cousin, Edward. So you can see, of us five cousins he is the poor relation."

Poor relation? Ardron thought. Perhaps he should experience the life of a Saxon peasant before he consider him to be a poor relation. But he stayed silent.

"It is yours for tenancy. If you so wish," de Bohun filled the silent pause.

Ardron looked down and studied the map once more. Opportunity was there for development, and as a castellan, prestige. Also a wealth that only a year ago could not have even been a wild dream. "A quarterly rent?" He asked as confirmation.

"Quarterly rent," de Bohun confirmed.

"A free hand to repair and develop?"

"Of course."

"What of the sergen detachment there?" Ardron asked.

"Their choice! They may return here to Trowbridge or remain at Norwood. In that event they become your vassals and therefore you will have responsibility for their welfare and their pay."

Ardron rubbed his chin thoughtfully. "I will not pay the goodwill sum to your cousin." He straightened up and looked de Bohun squarely in the face.

"I will continue to fund Cousin Edward," he said holding out his hand to shake on the deal.

Ardron hesitated for a moment then took his hand.

***

Although bathed in the warm sunshine of an August morning, Norwood Castle, at first sight, was not imposing. Its bailey on the western side of the mote was not particularly large, nor had it survived the ravages of the elements. The wooden palisade walls had leaned in places and completely collapsed in others. Inside the bailey there were several smaller buildings, workshops, stabling and living quarters but these too were in obvious need of repair. Pleasingly the mote was steep; however, the smaller palisade on the top that wrapped the keep had also suffered a lack of maintenance. The living quarters themselves comprised nothing more elaborate than a basic two-story building and constructed of wood also.

Ardron and Esmond rode through the gate unchallenged. People inside, few as they were, paid the new arrivals little or no attention, instead went about their own business.

"Not much of a welcome for the new castellan," Esmond remarked.

He was right, Ardron silently agreed. There was much to be achieved here and not least security. They dismounted at the bottom of the mote and climbed the steps to the upper keep. The room was spacious and airy, decorated by many wall tapestries that had seen far better days. For furniture it relied upon two long narrow tables down the middle surrounded by an assortment of benches and stools. At one of the tables three sergens sprawled, their attention focussed on playing cards. In the middle of the table a flagon of wine added to their cosiness. All eyes turned towards the new arrivals with a measure of unwelcoming curiosity.

"Who is in charge here?" Ardron demanded.

"What's it to you?" the grey bearded sergen asked.

"What's it to me?" Ardron paraphrased with anger cutting the edge of his temper. "I am the new castellan here. On your feet when you talk to me." Unaccustomed as he was to the status of rank, he needed to stamp his authority here at the very onset.

"Oh! Forgive me Sir," grey beard said getting to his feet and motioning the others to stand also.

"I say again. Who is in charge here?"

"Sir, we have two milites here, Luc and Jarcot," greybeard replied.

"Which of them is in charge?"

Greybeard shrugged and looked to his comrades for support but received only blank stares.

This was worse than he thought. No one seemed to know who exactly was in authority. "What is your name?" he asked.

"Dardot,"

"Well then Dardot. Where can I find this pair?"

Dardot looked uneasy. "Jarcot is up there," he said pointing at the ramp that led to the next floor.

"And Luc?"

"He shook his head and pulled a face. "I don't know." he said.

Exasperated, Ardron turned, and motioning to Esmond to follow, made his way to the ramp.

The top floor was divided into three rooms and acted as the castellan's private quarters. The second room they looked in was the bedroom. Even though nearing midday the shutters were still closed darkening the room. In the gloom the shapes of two sleeping bodies reposed on the bed.

Angrily, Ardron marched over to the shutters and one by one threw them open allowing sunlight to pour into the room.

Roughly awakened from their sleep the pair began to stir. "What the___," the man muttered while the girl just looked bleary eyed.

"Out," Ardron shouted. The fury in his voice stung the girl into action. She leapt from the bed quickly, gathered up her clothes and holding them to hide her nakedness, ran from the room.

Sitting up the man mouthed a stream of obscenities in Ardron's direction. "Who the hell do you think you are?" He demanded.

"Are you Jarcot?"

"Who are you," he replied ignoring the question.

"Can you read?" Ardron demanded.

"Of course I can read."

"Then read this," Ardron said thrusting the parchment that declared him Castellan of Norwood under his nose. "I ask again. Are you Jarcot?"

He scanned the appointment silently then realising his vulnerable position sullenly muttered. "I'm Jarcot."

"Get out," Ardron said tersely. "And have the whole compliment of sergens standing too in the bailey in twenty minutes."

"Go easy," Esmond warned after Jarcot left. "You are likely to finish up without any sergens at all if you carry on like this."

"From what I have seen so far, would that be so bad?" Ardron retorted. But Esmond was right he admitted to himself, it would not do if they were all to leave for Trowbridge."

Thirty minutes later Ardron took a position near the foot of the steps looking down on the assembled sergens. A quick count totalled no more than two dozen.

"Is this it?" he asked Jarcot.

Jarcot turned and scanned round, "Pretty much," he replied. "Luc and four others are out,"

"Doing what?" Ardron demanded.

Jarcot shrugged, "Castle business, I suppose."

"You suppose? You don't know?"

If it were the truth, and not just an easy answer, then it seemed at that least somebody in the castle was doing what they should. He took a deep breath and glanced at Esmond. If he was going to make a success of this, he needed to establish his authority at the onset, and in no uncertain terms. He was unsure of how these Norman sergens would react being subservient to a Saxon, but then he decided that it was a problem for them to handle.

"For those who do not yet know who I am, I say, I am Ardron of Scorrenstone and the son of a Saxon Thegn. I was made a knight in knight's service by Robert Earl of Gloucester himself. This rank was awarded to me for services previously rendered in the cause of Empress Maude. Your patron Sir Humphrey de Bohun has made me the castellan of this castle, and I intend that neither of them will have cause to regret my appointment. To this end I intend that there will be changes made.

Firstly, the maintenance state of this castle is a disgrace. We could not hold off a flock of sheep. A programme of repairs will be drawn up as soon as I have carried out a detailed inspection. All will be expected to work, no exceptions. Discipline will be tightened. Security does not exist, and so there will be a return to guard duties. You are sergens therefore there will be combat training. If we are called to battle, I don't want to see any man disadvantaged for the lack of training.

If none of this appeals to you however, you do have a choice. Until midnight tonight you are still vassals of Sir Humphrey de Bohun. As such you have the right to stay in his service. For those who wish it they may leave for Trowbridge. Those who are still here come the morning will swear fealty to me and serve." He paused and looked around at the impassive faces not having the slightest clue of how many would leave, or indeed, if he would actually have any sergens tomorrow.

"Do I have a clerk," he asked.

"Here, sir," a diminutive man replied.

"Gather your books and bring them to me," Ardron said. Then looking at Jarcot said. "Dismiss the men."

Ardron was no accountant; in fact, he struggled to follow what the clerk was showing him. The clerk, a man called Louis, seemed to have an efficient system of bookkeeping, and Ardron had little option at this stage except to trust the man. He had, for accountant purposes, divided the whole estate in three, and staggered the quarterly rentals due. This ensured that coffers of money and goods were brought to the castle each month throughout the year. Of much more interest to Ardron at this time were the number of villeins he could muster for the work.

"Villeins?" Louis responded. "A few spread around. Perhaps six dozen, all obliged to donate one day's work per week if so required."

"They will be required," Ardron said, already aware that he was beginning to behave as a Norman master over the Saxon community. "And timber?" he went on. "I am going to need timber for repairs."

"No problem, Sir. You have jurisdiction over a good section of Braydon Forest to the south of Myntey. You can take your timber from there."

Ardron gave a satisfied nod, he could supplement his sergens with extra labourers from the villages and obtain the wood material from the forest, but he still needed money to employ and pay tradesmen. "How much money do I have to use?" he asked.

"Hmm! Some, maybe. Not a lot and I advise frugality." It was a typical accountant response.

Their conversation was interrupted by Esmond walking in. "Thought you would want to know. The rest of your compliment has just arrived," he said.

Ardron walked over to the door and watched the small party arrive. Four horsemen ahead of a two wheeled cart. Jarcot approached and spoke to the leader as he dismounted. The man listened intently then looked up towards Ardron. After nodding understanding he turned away and focused his attention on the cart unload. The reason for their absence from the castle became apparent when two dead fallow deer and several pheasants were unloaded. Whether the party had gone hunting out of necessity or for simple pleasure Ardron had no way of knowing at this stage. Either way the bounty they brought would most certainly be useful. He turned his attention back to the accountant.

"How do I get extra money?" he asked.

"You can always increase the tenancy of your vassals. Ardron sucked in a noisy breath somewhat reluctant to take that option. Louis studied him for a moment then said. "There might be another option."

Ardron nodded and waited.

"Sir Humphrey de Bohun."

"Sir Humphrey? Ardron queried.

"Yes. You are tenant here," Louis explained. "The castle therefore still belongs to Sir Humphrey. You could make a case that you are making the repairs for his benefit, therefore, he ought to make some recompense for the cost."

That was an idea that did appeal to Ardron. Unless the situation altered, then at some point, when Ardron relinquished his tenancy the castle would revert back to de Bohun. The idea definitely had merit.

Louis was first to notice Luc standing in the doorway waiting for permission to enter. "Sir," he said nodding towards the door.

Ardron followed his gaze and then with a casual arm wave beckoned Luc into the chamber.

"Sir, I am Luc," he said as he entered. "I am at your service."

"Take a seat," Ardron said. "We are looking at ways to raise finance to improve the castle structure and to make the whole complex more efficient."

Luc moved across and sat alongside Louis. "I am not sure what use I can be," he said with a dubious shake of his head.

"Tell me about the sergens," Ardron said leaning back and studying the man opposite. Luc was a young man, perhaps in his mid-twenties with close cropped hair and a thin manicured beard. Vain enough to bother about his appearance, Ardron hoped this was a sign that the man possessed a high degree of personal pride.

"The men?" Luc blew thoughtfully. "I suppose they compere pretty closely to any other bunch of sergens. They are in service either because they are beholding to their master or simply because of money. Most here are from the de Bohun estate in Normandy and as such are vassals to Sir Humphrey." He paused a moment. "The question is, if they swear fealty to you in the morning, what of their obligation to Sir Humphrey? Bearing in mind that their families still live and work on the de Bohun estate?"

Ardron nodded understanding the predicament. "Just as long as their families continue to pay that which is due to the estate, they will continue to live there."

"And the sergens that stay here?" Luc asked.

"Those that swear fealty to me will be in my employ and not Sir Humphrey's. They will be paid by me."

Luc nodded seemingly satisfied. "They are not a bad compliment of men. Things may have become somewhat apathetic here because we have been in something of a backwater without any real leadership guidance."

Ardron nodded sympathetically. "I will make allowances. But even so," he warned, "Things will be changed." He was determined that his new-found wealth would not be dependent on the tenuous goodwill arrangement between de Bohun and de Evereux. Particularly so since he was now firmly allied to the empress's cause while de Evereux to the king's.

***

Norwood Castle, December 1140

Into December and things had changed dramatically in Norwood Castle. The palisades had been repaired, the accommodation buildings and workshops likewise, and the whole complex now looked formidably efficient. Guards were posted on the gate and, although inside the bailey there were lots of coming and going, no one entered without being challenged. There were regular training sessions, not only for the sergens, but also for the Saxon villeins obliged to serve on demand. He had made Luc his castle constable, and he had served admirably. Bound by the terms of his knight service to Earl Robert, Ardron had been forced to spend a good deal of time at his Bristol stronghold, but his absence from Norwood had not proved a handicap to progress. Luc along with Esmond had continued the work with enthusiasm and diligence.

On the estate there were also changes about to be put into practice. North-west of the castle Ardron had divided the open land into small parcels of around three acres. These plots were offered to rent for any proletariat with ambition. Nor was it restricted to one plot per family. If a man had sufficient ambition, and could convince Ardron of his ability, then two or three of these plots were available to turn into small farms. By opening up extra land for rent to potential farmers and cottars, then extra income and supplies would be generated into the castle coffers. In addition by opening the offer broadly, he hoped to poach more residents from nearby Cirencester and Malmesbury and thus increase his estate population. With it, also, his potential fighting force. Ardron was well pleased with the progress so far made.

"Will you be back for Christmas?" Esmond asked as he watched his brother assembling clothing and personal belongings into a travel sack.

Ardron shrugged. "Maybe," he replied vaguely. He had been invited to attend the empress's Christmas celebrations at Earl Robert's castle. He knew it was not so much an invitation but more in the nature of a summons. In truth he had found it hard to relate to Maude. Although he was not privileged enough to move within her circle of confidantes, her frosty temperament and her intractable disposition reached out beyond that inner circle. It was common knowledge that her personal servants lived in dread of her unpredictable nature.

"I would much prefer to spend Christmas at Scorrenstone instead of here," Esmond said.

Ardron nodded understanding. "Then you should go. If I am not back, then Luc can preside."

"Sir!" A servant begged his attention.

"Yes?"

"Jarcot requests your attention with some urgency." The servant said. "He waits for you in the hall."

"I will be there presently." Ardron replied. Then turning his attention back to his brother asked. "When will you leave for Scorrenstone?"

"I had thought that the twenty-second would be the very latest I should leave."

Ardron nodded. "The celebrations are planned five days hence on the twentieth and twenty-first. I ought to be back a day or two after." He held up a Norman robe for a quick examination. He much preferred to dress as a Saxon, but when he attended these Norman gatherings then he was obliged to dress as a Norman. Satisfied the robe was suitable he folded it and placed it inside the travel sack. "Come," he said. "Let us see what is so urgent that Jarcot summons us."

"Sir," Jarcot blurted out as soon as he saw Ardron. "Edward de Evereux approaches with a compliment of horse sergenti."

Ardron was immediately alert. "How many?"

Jarcot lifted his arms in a bewildered gesture. "Five dozen or more, I am told."

Five dozen was not an invasion force, nevertheless, it was a substantial number to bring on a casual visit and it smacked more of a substantial protection force. De Evereux surprise visit seemed like a man intent on a confrontational meeting.

"Have the gates closed," he instructed. "I would learn the purpose of this visit before I allow admittance."

Jarcot hurried away to have the order carried out.

With the bailey closed Ardron climbed onto the palisade above the gate and looked down upon de Evereux and his sergenti as they approached the gate. "Greetings to you Sir Edward."

"What greeting is this faced with a closed gate?" the indignant reply.

"Why does a neighbour come calling with a substantial force of armed sergenti?" Ardron replied.

"The visit is social," de Evereux said. "For the sake of future relationship I would learn of your sympathies and intentions."

"Then Sir Edward you may enter with pleasure, but only with a party of five."

This provoked some discussion among the knights at the head of the column. "Do I have your word of safe conduct?" De Evereux asked."

"Of course!" Ardron replied then a further discussion developed.

"He doesn't trust you," Esmond remarked.

"Clearly," Ardron muttered.

"Would you be prepared to come out and hold a discussion outside your stronghold?" de Evereux said after a few moments.

"No," Ardron's reply was curt.

"Clearly you don't trust him." This time it was Luc who muttered.

"He wants a meeting, not I." Ardron's reply was again curt as he watched the anxious discussions taking place.

There was some head shaking and some nervousness among de Evereux's knights, but it seemed that a decision had been made, albeit dubiously. "Very well I accept," de Evereux finally agreed.

Ardron said nothing instead got down from the palisade and organised a guard of honour which had a double purpose. Not just to tribute his guest but also to be on hand in case more than the agreed number tried to force an entry through the gate.

Standing on the steps of the mote Ardron waited as Sir Edward rode into the bailey at the head of a party of six knights. He smiled inwardly at de Everex's defiance. By adding the extra two to the agreed number he had registered a point that indicated a little non-compliance. Ardron was not about to allow him even that meaningless point. But for now he invited the visitors to dismount while Luc organised grooms to tend their horses.

In no particular hurry to approach de Evereux stood and took a long unhurried look around the inner bailey. Then when he was ready, he approached Ardron on the steps.

"Welcome to Castle Norwood, Sir Edward," Ardron said.

De Evereux response was a brief nod and another telling scan around the bailey. "There has been much strengthening to the castle defences." The way it was said was almost a complaint.

"There has," Ardron replied as a matter of fact. "Come join me please in my private chambers." Then seemingly as an after-thought, "You may bring two of your knights." Cleverly he took back that tiny bit of initiative from de Evereux.

Ardron was gratified to see that a table had been laid with light refreshments and wine. He invited his guests to sit while Esmond and Luc remained standing by the door like a pair of sentries.

"I knew that there was much more to you on that day you brought that distressed farmer to my castle," de Evereux said almost accusingly.

"Things were no more than was declared at the time," Ardron replied.

"A Saxon peasant driving off a raiding party single handed?" De Evereux sneered sarcastically.

There was no point Ardron could see in labouring the point. "But that is not what brings you here today," he said.

"No it isn't," de Evereux agreed. Ardron waited. "For some time now I have been receiving reports. Disturbing reports," he added.

"Of?" Ardron asked.

"Of castle improvements and intense sergen training. Villeins brought in armed and trained. One would have to think that some sort of aggression was being planned."

"Primarily self-defence preparation. For who knows what demands might be placed upon us in the future. Therefore, it is much better to be prepared." Ardron replied.

"And in so doing you have upset the balance of power in this locality," de Evereux countered. "With such a threat close at hand I have likewise to step up my defences."

"You have to do what you must, Sir Edward." Ardron replied easily. "But far from upsetting the balance of power I have merely evened it up. Less than six months ago this castle was practically defenceless and completely subservient to your whim. Not so now."

De Evereux leaned forward across the table. "Be very wary Saxon in the event of any attack I can count on powerful allies." he growled.

Ardron poured a little wine into a goblet and pushed it across the table towards de Evereux. "I can assure you Sir Edward that at this time I have no plans to attack your estate."

De Evereux ignored the wine. "And in the future?"

Ardron shrugged, "Who can say what is in the future."

De Evereux picked up the wine goblet and leaned back. "For you," he said, "It would be a grave mistake to make any such attack. I have enough close allies to crush you."

"No doubt you are referring to your Uncle, Walter Lord of Salisbury, and his sons. Your cousins!"

"Yes, I am referring to my cousins, William and Patric at Salisbury, and the de Pinkney brothers at Malmesbury and even the king himself. I am loyal to the crown and I am sure that given the excuse to crush an Angevin rebel like you he wouldn't hesitate.

"And what of your other cousin? Ardron countered." Humphrey de Bohun, will he stand by and let Norwood fall to you? Then there, is of course, Miles Fitzwalter. How he would love the opportunity to regain his South Cerney castle. So it would seem that any escalation of conflict would bring all manner of complications! Drink your wine my dear Baron and let us agree to a truce, albeit an uneasy one."

Sir Edward scowled. "It may also be a temporary one," he said.

Unsurprisingly, because of the charged atmosphere, the meeting broke up almost instantly. Acting out the social graces Ardron accompanied Sir Edward and his party to their horses.

"That could mean trouble," Esmond muttered as they watched them ride through the gate.

"Maybe not," Ardron said. "While Sir Humphrey continues to pay goodwill it should compensate the man and make the task of overcoming Norwood not worth the risk."

"Ah," said Esmond. "But what if Sir Humphrey decides that Norwood is no longer as vulnerable as it was, and doesn't then feel the need to continue paying Sir Edward goodwill?"

"In that case, there could be trouble." Ardron said turning away to climb the steps.

***

The celebrations at Bristol Castle were spectacularly lavish. The great hall was highly decorated with an abundance of holly, mistletoe and coned branches of conifer. Red and blue streamers of the finest silk hung from overhead beams contrasting vividly with the greenery. The great hollowed Christmas log smouldered at the far end of the hall, its slow burning embers, scented by frankincense, infused the air. The long tables that had been overloaded with an immoral amount of artistically decorated food were now being cleared away. The amount left over would have fed the poor of Bristol for more than a week. Ardron stood deep among the hall bystanders and watched in silent disgust as the servants cleared away the mountain of uneaten food. Three untouched stuffed and displayed peacocks laying in beds of fruit, were carried away so carefully that it took two men to carry each platter. Now the entertainment started as a multitude of jugglers and acrobats ran in and took to the floor while the musicians began to get themselves organised.

"My aunt knows well how to spend my father's money," the woman next to him whispered. He turned to look at the young woman. Barely the height of his shoulder she was dressed in a long gown of blue made from silk. Across her shoulders a cape of deep red contrasted with a white wimple which was held in place with a narrow head rail of gold.

"My Lady," Ardron, acknowledged, but diplomatically passed no comment.

"I am Lady Mabel de Vere. My husband is Aubrey de Vere Earl of Oxford." Ardron nodded politely. "My sister-in-law exalts your bravery."

He was confused.

"Lady Rohesa de Vere."

"Lady Rohesa! Oh_, then you must be," he hesitated a moment realising who she was.

"Yes I am the daughter of Earl Robert and the Empress is my aunt."

"Oh_," Ardron said "My lady may I congratulate you on your recent wedding?" With that wedding de Vere had got his alliance.

"Thank you," she said.

"I revere your father," Ardron remarked diplomatically.

"You don't say as much for my aunt," Lady Mabel laughed.

"I don't really know the empress." he said.

"Not many do," she replied. "She is aloof to all except her most inner circle.

Ardron could appreciate that last remark. Maude had made no attempt to socialise, indeed her only contact with the vast multitude of her guests had been earlier in the day. Each person had been announced and permitted to approach, bow low and kiss the hem of her dress in a show of fealty. In turn, she muttered little more than a trite welcome.

"Where are you from?" the empress had asked Ardron.

"I am from Norwood Castle, your Majesty."

She turned and for more information looked to Earl Robert standing at her side. "Norwood Castle is on the Gloucester Wiltshire border," he informed her. No longer interested in him Ardron had bowed and subserviently backed away.

"But there is one who does know her better than most." Lady Mabel went on nodding towards Sir Brien Fitzcount. Then she laughed at Ardron's puzzled look. "No! Not romantically. He is more like a favourite uncle," she said. "It was he, who at the king's bidding, took her when she was but nine years old to Germany to marry the Holy Roman Emperor Henry. It was Sir Brien who went to Germany and brought her home when her husband died eleven years later. And of course it was Brien again who just a year later took her to Anjou to marry Geoffrey. That too was at the king's bidding."

Ardron glanced over to where Maude sat upright and regal. Little wonder the woman is aloof, he thought, her father King Henry bartered her about like a horse. "What did you mean she has no money?" Ardron queried.

"Oh she does have some money. She receives regular funds from her husband Geoffrey. He lives in hopes that her war is successful. If she becomes queen, he can see himself as king. However, it is common knowledge that they do not get on, so the funds he sends are somewhat limited. She can't really afford to lay on a celebration such as this one. So my father pays."

"Geoffrey is a Plantagenet is he not?" Ardron asked.

"He is."

"So if Maude were to win this struggle, we could have a Plantagenet King on the throne of England?"

"Yes," she said guardedly. "But it wouldn't be Geoffrey. Aunt Maude would see to that," she said with some derision. "Her son Henry, however, I would have to say definitely!"

In that case the Norman dynasty would end after only three generations, Ardron considered. But if Stephen were to prevail then it would be his son Eustace who would become king, and the Norman dynasty would continue.

Ardron felt a hand on his shoulder. "Lady Mabel," Humphrey de Bohun said leaning forward to kiss her fingers. "I need to take this young man away with me. Please forgive me."

He passed polite pleasantries as he led Ardron along the back of the hall and behind the dais to where a small cluster of nobles had gathered. Earl Robert, John Fitzgilbert and Miles Fitzwalter he recognised but not the other two.

It was Fitzgilbert who saw him first. "Ah, Ardron my friend," he said guiding him into the circle. "We have just learned some very interesting news. I'll let Earl Robert explain. But first let me introduce you to Sir Baldwin de Reviers and Sir William de Keynes."

Ardron had heard of de Reviers; his exploits in the far west, in Maude's cause, were legendary. Surprisingly, to Ardron, his physical statue did not match his acclaimed exploits. He was shorter than Ardron by a full head and shoulders. Scars about his face, however, did bare testimony to personal conflicts at least. De Keynes on the other hand was quite the opposite. He was taller than Ardron, barrel chested and thick round the girth.

"Today we have learned that my cousin, King Stephen has made yet another blunder," Earl Robert started to explain. "Fearing that Lord of Bolinbroke, William Roumare, might declare support for the empress he attempted to buy his loyalty by making him the new Earl of Lincoln. However, he refused Roumare's request that with the title Lincoln Castle should follow. Instead he left the castle in possession of his friend William de Aubigny." Earl Robert paused a moment before going on. "Earlier today we learned the Roumare aided by his half-brother Ranulf Earl of Chester did, by cunning, seize, the castle."

"This is good news indeed," Fitzwalter interrupted.

"Only if we can secure the support of Roumare," de Reviers corrected.

"That is true," Earl Robert continued. "The Empresses cousin Henry, son of the Scottish King, is Lord of Doncaster and Earl of Huntingdon, if we can secure Lincoln in the empress's favour then we can establish a large footprint across that north eastern area." He paused a moment and stared at Ardron. "So what we propose to do," he went on. "Is to send an envoy to William Roumare and persuade him to declare for Maude. With this recent defiance of the king he will never be more ready."

Ardron nodded agreement although he could not yet see why they sought to involve him.

"Roumare's half-brother," he went on, "Is my son-in-law, married to my daughter Maud. While the wife of Roumare is the Lady Hawise and she is sister to Sir Baldwin here." He placed his hand on de Reivers shoulder. "You will appreciate strong family connections here." He paused allowing Ardron time to absorb the situation. "For myself I cannot be the envoy. So who then better to send in my place than Sir Baldwin?"

A pregnant pause developed. "Yes I can see that" Ardron filled the void. "But how does that concern me?"

"I am coming to that," Earl Robert said. "Roumare's grandmother was Saxon, his mother, Lucy, therefore is half Saxon. So you can see he too has Saxon blood in his veins. We think you should accompany Sir Baldwin as part of the envoy."

Ardron was silent a moment. He could not see how he could exert much influence on Roumare's decision. However, a surge of excitement coursed his veins. There was a personal motivating factor. Last heard Hildi was mistress to William Roumare. If she were still, then perhaps there would be a chance to speak to here and maybe return her to Scorrenstone.

"I am at your service, Sir Robert," he said. "However, in truth, I cannot see how I could have very much influence on William Roumare's decision."

"Perhaps not," Earl Robert replied. "Then again just some such small influence might just tip the balance. In any case it could do no harm to the negotiations."

"Then I agree," Ardron said with a slight shrug. "When do we leave?"

"After Christmas celebrations, but before the new year," de Reivers said.

***

Stamford, 1141

It was the last day of the year and the light was beginning to fade when the small band of twelve came down the slope towards the wooden bridge over the river Welland. On the opposite bank the ground rose steeply towards the town that was Stamford. Surrounded by stone walls, built by the Romans centuries before, Stamford looked more like a fortress town. Perched on the edge of the hill just west of the town a mote and bailey castle dominated the meadows below. Baldwin de Reviers held up his hand halting the column a distance from the bridge. Their intention was to pass through the town on their way north, but today they had covered more than thirty miles and their need now was a place for an overnight stop.

Ardron leaned forward onto Rattlebone's withers. "Who is the castellan?" he asked.

Baldwin sighed heavily and shook his head. "I don't know," he said.

"Then you don't know his sympathies either?"

There was no reply just a shake of his head.

Ardron took a deep breath and sighed heavily. "Then wait here he said I will find out." It made sense since dressed as a Saxon he was the only one that did not look Norman.

The bridge was not manned. He crossed and spurred his horse up the steep hill to the town gate. The gate was still open and manned only by a single guard who sat looking bored and disinterested by the portcullis.

Giving a friendly wave Ardron brought the horse to a halt. "We have travelled far today, my friend," he said. "We seek a resting place for the night."

The guard got slowly to his feet and peered across the valley to where Baldwin and his small band waited. "More of the kings army?" he queried.

"More of the king's army?" Ardron was puzzled.

"Yes. king's army," the guard replied a little exasperated.

He had no idea what the guard meant. "Yes," he said taking a chance.

The guard nodded. "You are a day behind."

Ardron was even more puzzled. "The king came through here yesterday with an army?" he sought confirmation. "Which way did he go?"

His suspicions aroused the guard studied him warily, Ardron had to say something quickly. "We thought we were ahead of him," he improvised hastily.

"No you're behind," the guard said. Then with an indicating jerk of his head said, "He went north early this morning."

This was not good news. It looked pretty certain that the King was on his way to Lincoln to retake the castle.

"How many are you?" the guard asked.

"A dozen!"

"Then you should be able to get shelter at the castle, Sir Gilliam is a loyal patriot to King Stephen."

"Thank you," Ardron said wheeling his horse around. Then as a casual afterthought he leaned back and said. "How strong is our king's army?"

"Over a thousand and perhaps half as many again," he replied.

Around fifteen hundred men was not a particular large force. Perhaps Stephen did not anticipate much resistance or maybe he hoped or planned to re-enforce along the way. Either way it was not good news. He allowed Rattlebone to make his own pace down the hill and over the bridge. Sir Baldwin was not going to be happy.

Baldwin was dismayed when he heard what Ardron had to say. "We are too late," he groaned. "If he left early this morning," he mused peering ahead and thinking aloud, "Then he will be in Newark tonight and in Lincoln before noon tomorrow." He rubbed his chin thoughtfully. "We couldn't overtake him if we rode all night." This time, he did address Ardron.

Ardron did not reply. This part of the country was as a foreign land to him. He knew not how far Newark was or indeed Lincoln. "What do we do?" he asked eventually.

Baldwin shook his head, bewildered.

"Will Roumare stand? Or will he flee?" Ardron asked.

"My God if he stands," Baldwin was once again thinking aloud. "We might still hold Lincoln Castle." He had arrived at a decision. "What do we do?" he answered Ardron. "We return to Bristol at all speed and inform Earl Robert. "Perhaps we can raise an army of our own and may yet salvage the situation." He pulled his mounts head around and indicated the turn-about.

Ardron hesitated and stared disconsolately up the hill towards the town. His hopes of perhaps finding Hildi were once more dashed. For a moment he considered ignoring de Reivers and pressing on to Lincoln alone. But he couldn't do that, not now. He was in knight's service to Earl Robert and taking his coin. With a sigh he pulled Rattlebone about and followed the troop away from Stamford.

It took three days hard riding to return to Bristol, but had they known they need not have bothered. Ranulf, Earl of Chester, had arrived the day before to plead help from his father-in-law. Being warned of the king's advancing army, Ranulf had fled Lincoln and rode hard for Bristol to beg Earl Robert's help. As if the prize of Lincoln Castle was not enough incentive, he as added insurance, left his wife Maud, Robert's daughter, at the besieged castle. Earl Robert had already begun preparations to raise an army.

***

January 1141

Two weeks later Ardron at the head of a band of three dozen joined Earl Robert's army assembling in Gloucester. The number so far assembled was around fifteen hundred men. However, Ranulf, Earl of Chester, had left to assemble extra forces from his Welsh allies with the arrangement to rendezvous on the roman Fosse way just south of Ledecestre.

After his return from Stamford, Ardron had gone immediately to Norwood to raise his own contributing force and to make arrangements for his absence. He had decided to take around half of his sergens as the professional element and had then supplemented that number with carefully selected Saxon villeins. Hearing of Ardron's intentions Swidhurn had almost pleaded that he be allowed to join the force, after all Hildi was his sister. At first Ardron tried to dissuade him because it was possible that Hildi was no longer with Roumare. But the blacksmith had been adamant.

For his perceived absence Ardron had installed Esmond as temporary castellan of Norwood. By now Esmond had developed a passable knowledge of the French language, therefore, combined with his native tongue he should have no communication difficulties. However, Ardron did have some concern about Edward de Evreux. The man had been disturbed by the growing strength of Norwood and was self-declared for the king. If he discovered that Ardron was away in the cause of the empress and Norwood's forces were temporarily depleted, he might see an opportunity. He had briefed Esmond to be guarded and to increase security by using remaining estate villeins to boost the castle force. It would be of no profit if he were to return after this campaign to discover that he had lost his castle.

It was mid-January when Earl Robert's army left Gloucester for Lincoln. Travelling conditions were not good, persistent rain added to the normal winter's mud, made for slow progress. Nevertheless, they reached the rendezvous point in eight days and found Ranulf already camped waiting with more than a thousand men.

"God's piles, "Luc cursed as they rode into the camp." They're all Welsh men."

Ardron looked sideways at the man riding alongside. "Something wrong with that?" he queried. So long as they fought alongside and fought well, he didn't care what their nationality.

"They are fierce undisciplined rabble who would probably fight for nothing if there was the opportunity to sink a blade into a Norman." Luc replied. "Any Norman!" He added.

Ardron examined the Welsh men more closely as he rode through the camp. There was no welcome cheering, no enthusiasm and no smiling faces. Expressionless silence was the only greeting. Ardron was left to wonder what promises had been made to encourage their support in this fight. Clearly these men had no particular interest in either causes for the English crown. The possibility of soldier's loot, in victory, was their probable motivation.

Today it had not rained, but even so the ground around the camp was sodden and muddied, made worse by a thousand pairs of trampling feet. Now with the additional fifteen hundred men it would very soon become a quagmire. It had been a punishing trek, and if rumour was correct, there was to be a day's rest. Despite the underfoot conditions Ardron thought it a welcome respite. He led his small band a few yards away from the camp to find ground that was a little drier. He selected a site upstream of the River Soar. Not only did it put needed water close to hand but by going upstream the water was cleaner.

Swidhurn took it upon himself to unload the pack horses and to tend the animals, while Luc organised the erecting of a makeshift shelter. Seeing all was progressing, without his intervention, Ardron made his way back to the main camp to receive instruction from command.

Occupying the highest point, in the shelter of a thin copse, a large tent had been erected and banners flew the yellow livery of Earl Chester, but Ardron was turned away when he tried to approach. A little nonplussed, he wandered on through the maze of campfires and impassive faces until he began to see faces more familiar. Eventually, he saw one that he did know. Miles Fitzwalter stood hand resting on sword hilt silently watching men struggling to erect a large tent.

"Sir Miles," Ardron said quietly as he came up behind him.

Miles did not acknowledge him, instead uttered curses. "God damn Chester's eyes for the selfish bastard that he is," he said. "He got here before us and shamelessly took all the prime campsites, leaving the Commander-in-Chief, and us to struggle in the mud."

Ardron did not reply. It was true that the early arrivals had made their camps along the hillside ignoring the riverside meadows below, but he could not blame them for that. Had the situation been reversed then they would have done as well. He glanced across the assembly of Earl Robert's men. A sorry looking bunch they were. So mud spattered were they that it probably made little difference anyway, he concluded.

"Do we have any orders?" he asked.

Miles turned his attention away from the men erecting the tent. "Not at this time," he said. "But all commanders are to assemble here at sunset. If we ever get this tent up!" He muttered turning back to watch the strugglers.

Just before sunset Ardron returned, and the tent was up. Long, wide and double peaked, it slanted away from the top canopy creating maximum floor space inside. Along its top edges small triangular flags of blue flapped in the breeze. In case there were any doubts, the two peaks flew the blue livery of Robert Earl of Gloucester. Although it was roomy inside it was not sufficient to hold all the commanders that assembled. Ardron joined the mass standing outside waiting. A few minutes later those within began to file out. Fitzwalter, Fitzcount, de Keynes and de Reviers he recognised but the other three he did not. Last to emerge was Earl Robert and impromptu cheering broke out as he did.

"My friends," he said holding up his hands to quieten the cheers. "We are assembled here with a force big enough, strong enough and courageous enough to do battle and defeat Stephen at Lincoln. And that, with God's help, is exactly what we will do. Ranulf Earl of Chester has brought with him allies from the welsh marshes. Let me introduce Madog ap Maradudd, King of Powys."

Madog stood impassive with arms folded accepting as a right the resounding cheers that erupted mostly from his own supporters. His thick black hair, greased with animal fat, hung onto his shoulders and was held tidy by a tight headband around his head. He wore a heavy fleece of sheepskin dyed black and fastened tight about his waist with a broad leather belt.

Earl Robert held up his hand once more to quieten the cheers. "And here we have Prince Cadwaladr, brother of King Owain of Gwynedd," he said indicating the other welsh man.

Cadwaladr stepped forward demonstratively acknowledging the cheers that came his way. The deliberate enthusiasm of his followers was intended to better the Madog accolade, and they succeeded. Ardron studied Cadwaladr, his rough dishevelled appearance smacked of many things but to Ardron not a royal prince. His wild unkempt hair was dark and long, as was his full beard. His clothing was simple homespun, with a tartan cape of sorts slung across his shoulder and held in place by a large silver brooch. His muscular arms were bare from his shoulder, as were his legs from the knee down. Ardron decided that it was better to have both in their ranks rather than against.

"At this time," Earl Robert spoke again. "We are but sixty miles from Lincoln and I intend to be at its walls within four days from now. That means there is to be another early start tomorrow."

"Sir Robert!" one of the knights sought his attention. "We have travelled long and hard to reach here this day. Might one day be granted for rest and maintenance?"

Sir Robert glared at the man. "It might not," he said firmly. "Sooner or later Stephen is bound to get word that an army approaches. I intend to be upon him before he has time to make defensive preparations." He paused a few moments. "We move off before the sun is fully risen."

With only questions aimed at Earl Robert, that seemingly, to Ardron, were almost irrelevant, he lost interest, peeled away and made his way back to his troop. His men were looking forward to a day's rest, he knew, but there were not going to get it.

Not only was the makeshift shelter now erected, a pair of campfires, more akin to bonfires were blazing heartily. Always there were two campfires within his troop. Natural segregation occurred. Normans at one, Saxons at the other. This segregation was not malicious in any way and due to the language differences. Ardron was left to contemplate what miscommunication difficulties might occur during the coming battle now that the third language of Welsh was added.

He eased himself to sit in the Saxon circle at Swidhurn's side. Almost opposite two chickens were being plucked. He thought better than to ask from where they had come. An army on the march must, to a large extent, live off the land. It was the unfortunates that those who lived in its path were the losers. Swidhurn, nursing a large clay pot on his knee, nodded a greeting as Ardron settled in. He offered up the pot to Ardron.

"What is it?" he asked.

"It's a very fine brew of mead," Swidhurn replied.

Ardron lifted the pot onto his upper arm, tipped it and took a couple of long gulps. He agreed that it was very agreeable, before passing it to the next man and indicating, at the same time, that it should be passed right round.

"Sir," someone close by sought his attention. "What is Lincoln like?" he asked.

"I have never been so I cannot give you a first-hand description," he replied. "I can only tell you as I have been told." He paused a moment gathering his thoughts. "It's a sizeable city atop a steep ridge, I am told. It has a cathedral and a castle close by. It was in ancient times a Roman city and as is common to all large Roman cities it is contained within a wall." He paused and then said with a shrug, "More than that I cannot tell you."

"Have you ever been in a battle?" another asked.

He thought of Wallingford and then of Malmesbury. But he couldn't really claim Malmesbury as a battle. There was no point hiding his inexperience. "Only one," he said.

"What was it like?" he persisted.

Terrifying he thought to say, but on no account could he say that. However, the question deserved a truthful answer. He took a deep breath. "All is mayhem and confusion and you have no idea what is happening across the battlefield. All that really concerns you is the man before you. He is bent on killing you. In order to live he has to, and you must do likewise. As fast as you knock em down another will take his place. And you must keep doing this as many times as it takes in order to survive. You will need to be strong and resolute. So I recommend that you work to improve your strength and practice armed defence daily. You were all picked on your abilities. You are selected the best among my villeins and so you will not lack in skill."

By the time he had finished the pot had worked its way back to Swidhurn. He reached over and took it from him, it was still half full. He got to his feet and turned it upside down allowing the contents to splash onto the ground. "There is no rest day tomorrow," he said. "We leave tomorrow before the sun is up. Get some rest." Nobody spoke as he moved away, but he could sense the resentment.

The circle of Norman sergens were a little more boisterous and much more at ease than their Saxon colleagues. Ardron stood back and watched for a few moments. They too had acquired alcohol but in their case flagons of wine.

He decided to let his constable break the bad news. "Luc," he said. "Gather up those wine flagons and empty them in the river." Luc's expression was one of surprise. "We move out tomorrow before sun up and I would have every man sober."

It was the morning of the fifth day and the first day of February when Earl Robert's army approached Lincoln. They came from the south west and for the last half mile had tramped across water-logged meadow. When they neared the bank of the Fossedyke the reason for the swamped land became apparent. The dyke had flooded and overflowed its southern bank while the dyke waters flowed with an intensity that was daunting. The head of the column halted to study the fast-flowing waters while those just behind fanned out either side to stare disconsolately at the racing current. The opposite bank being a little higher had contained the water; just. The expanse of common land over on that side, although wet and heavy, was not water-logged. Therefore, it could provide a tolerable camp site.

However, a company of around two score of King Stephens sergens did patrol that side, and with belief of security, they jeered, and cat called at the impeded army.

Ardron, mounted on Rattlebone, brought his troop splashing through a foot of water to the dyke's edge, and stared at the rushing waters before him. He sighed with disappointment, it seemed they had progressed at forced march only to be thwarted by a flooded dyke. Any delay no matter how small only gave Stephen extra time to prepare his defences. Earl Robert had worked on the assumption that Stephen would have received word of his approaching army two days ago. Now this further delay only worked in Stephen's favour.

"What now?" Swidhurn asked the question that Ardron was asking himself.

"Perhaps there is another crossing somewhere," Ardron muttered staring forlornly at the fast- flowing water. He peered upstream only to see what appeared to be a distant lake. That would be no crossing place.

The Fossedyke, built by the Romans centuries before, was maintained as a navigation connection linking the river Witham, just east of Lincoln, to the river Trent some seven or eight miles in the west. But on this day, it served another purpose and that of a defensive barrier.

Ardron watched as some men waded carefully to the dyke's edge and prodded the water with long branches unsuccessfully trying to gauge the depth. After that they tossed in those branches to gauge the ferocity of the current. They didn't like what they saw as the branches were quickly swept away

The jeering from the sergens on the other side stopped suddenly, and to a man, they wheeled their horses and began galloping back towards the city walls. Something had happened! Ardron glanced downstream and to his amazed admiration Earl Robert, astride his horse, had plunged into the swollen dyke setting the example for all to follow. And follow they did. Ardron turned towards his own troop. "Come," he said. "The man leads by example and we can surely follow."

Chapter 9

Lincoln, February 1141

Ardron drove Rattlebone to the edge of the dyke and plunged in. Immediately he was gripped by the ice-cold waters making him gasp in shock. The horse beneath him began to kick against the waters keeping its head high. The fast-flowing current began to carry them downstream, but even so the big horse was making progress across. The point of alarm for Ardron came at about the halfway point when Rattlebone floundered and sank beneath the surface. Fearing that they both might drown he kicked himself from the saddle, and when he did the horse recovered to head the surface. Freed of Ardron's weight the horse began to swim once more towards the opposite bank with Ardron now clutching Rattlebone's tail. Their ordeal did not end when they reached the other side, the steep revetment made it difficult to clamber out of the water. He received welcome assistance when Dardot leaned forward and grabbed Rattlebone's bridle and began to heave the big horse upwards. At first Rattlebone struggled to get a grip with his front legs, but eventually he scrambled onto the bank knocking Dardot over as he did. With a huge grin the veteran sergen crawled forward and hauled Ardron out of the water too.

"Shis," Dardot uttered. "That sure shrivels a man's balls," he said grinning through his thick grey beard.

Ardron could only nod as he choked away the water from his lungs. Then he had to clench his teeth hard to stop them involuntarily chattering. He looked both ways along the dyke, to see it full of horses and men either bobbing in the water or scrambling up onto the bank. He looked to his own and was relieved to eventually find that all had made it across. Next, he turned his attention to their horses. A good horse beneath a man would be an essential asset in the coming battle. Most looked distressed with ice cold water draining from their coats and some shivering.

"That's not good," Swidhurn muttered.

Ardron nodded agreement. "Mount your horses," he ordered. Then when all had mounted, he led his troop at the gallop across the common. The gallop had a double purpose. Mainly it was to get the blood once more circulating in both men and horse, but it also gave him the chance to take a closer look at the city that was Lincoln. At the far end of the common Ardron held up his hand and brought the troop to a halt.

Lincoln was atop a high and steep ridge, which ran up from the south east to curve away directly north. At the point of the curve was the castle, its extra tall keep protruding high above the stone-built bailey. Its dominant position on the edge of the ridge subjugated everything below. Close behind and dwarfing the castle in comparison was the impressive cathedral. Clustered around these domination points and spilling down the hillside were the towns-people's dwellings. Some houses were of stone construction, but most were typical Saxon. Wattled willow, plastered with mud and straw for walls, and thatched straw for roofs. The whole complex was encased within secure stone walls. To the south of the city, just without the wall, the river Witham ran into a large lake which leached out at a western corner into the Fossedyke.

Directly above them, standing along the top edge of the ridge, clusters of the king's sergens stood motionless, staring down across the West Common watching Earl Robert's army crossing the Fossedyke. Ardron turned and looked back to review what they were watching. He estimated that by now around half of the Angevin army had crossed, leaving him to ponder why it was that they had been allowed to make that crossing unhindered. Could it be that their arrival had been a complete surprise? That was unlikely he decided. Perhaps it was that Stephen and his advisors had not expected them to cross the boggy land and the flooded Fossedyke and had deployed elsewhere. Whatever the reason, he decided that it was good fortune for Earl Robert. With only a few men across the dyke at that point they had been very vulnerable. Now with each man that set foot on this side the army got stronger. He wheeled his horse and led the gallop back to the Fossedyke. The next task was to gather kindle and burning materials. Large bonfires would enable men to dry not only themselves but also all their equipment.

By late afternoon, the whole army had crossed onto the common. Blazing bonfires burned almost everywhere, and now that they were warm and dry the men of the earl's army were in a much better mood. Word had been spread that tomorrow Earl Robert planned to launch his attack, and so as men sat around their fires in good humour, they looked to their weapons and equipment. Commanders meanwhile were summoned to attend the war counsel.

"Tomorrow with stout brave men and God's help I intend to bring Stephen the usurper to heel." Sir Robert said. "This battle might just bring about an end to this accursed war. We have travelled too long and too far to fail. It will not be easy, but we do have the advantage of numbers perhaps by as many as a thousand men." He paused to look around the assembly. An advantage of one thousand men was probably an exaggeration, Ardron thought, however, he kept that thought to himself.

"This is how I intend to deploy," Sir Robert went on. "We will form up conventionally with a centre and two wings. Brien Fitzcount and William de Keynes," he said addressing both men. "You will form up with your forces on the right and you will be fronted by our welsh allies, Madog ap

Maradudd and Cadwaladr." He glanced around at each man and received accepting nods. "Ranulf, Earl Chester," he went on. "You and your forces will form the centre." He paused, noting the satisfaction in Chester's expression. "Miles Fitzwalter and Baldwin de Reivers," he went on, "you will take up the left with me. This left wing will be the vanguard of the attack."

"Earl Robert," Earl Chester interrupted. "I, as the one much aggrieved by Stephen, should be the one in the vanguard to launch the attack."

Earl Robert shook his head. "You are not as much aggrieved by Stephen than Baldwin and Miles, both who have lost estates to him. And even these two nobles are not as aggrieved as the Empress Maude. She lost that which was hers by right, the crown of England. As her representative in this battle it is I who will strike the first blow at this crown thief." Chester's face betrayed his displeasure, but he, nevertheless, nodded acceptance. Earl Robert paused and glanced around. "Any questions?" he asked.

"Where will we form up?" someone asked.

"We will form up across the common facing the ridge."

"And Stephen?" he asked again.

"His siege army are camped on the top of the ridge north west of the castle. I expect him to line up along the top of the ridge."

"He has the terrain advantage!"

"He does," Earl Robert agreed. "We have the advantage of numbers and we have right on our side. We will not fail because of a little hill."

Ardron sucked in a breath. The ridge was not a little hill, it was a steep incline rising some four hundred feet. A simple walk would be taxing but to ascend while fighting will be daunting.

"What if Stephen takes refuge behind the wall and fights from within?" someone asked.

"He has to come and face us," Sir Robert replied. "If he doesn't then we will over-run his siege camp."

"He might be prepared to lose that base," the questioner persisted.

"He might," Earl Robert agreed. "But I know my cousin. He will face up tomorrow. His pride will not let him do otherwise."

"Sir Robert." A voice from the back demanded his attention. "A delegation from the city approaches under a white flag."

The Earl moved through the assembly to stand and wait for the delegation. Ardron who had been towards the back during the briefing now found himself at the front as the assembly did an about-turn. The small party of six horsemen approached beneath a white flag and a holy cross held high upon an oak pole. Earl Waleron at the head Ardron recognised. Alongside, mitred and robed in the finest velvet, which was threaded and decorated with gold, the Bishop of Lincoln.

"Your grace," Earl Robert acknowledged the bishop with a brief bow of the head. "And Earl Waleron," he added as chivalry demanded.

"Why have you brought an army to this place?" Waleron demanded.

"Why have you thought to lay siege to this castle?" Earl Robert asked.

"That is the kings business and of no concern to you." Waleron replied heatedly.

"That would depend entirely on whether or not you recognise Stephen as King."

Waleron scowled bad temperedly. "It is upon this issue that all of the ills of the country have been inflicted."

"Those ills I will see brought to an end when I bring the usurper to justice." Earl Robert replied quietly.

Waleron was outraged "Be gone from this place," he shouted for all to hear. "Only death awaits those who stay. King Stephen is God's anointed King. And God will not fail to punish, most severely, those who defy his holy ordinance."

"If that is what you are here to say then I say it is you who should be gone and this very instant." Earl Robert replied his temper beginning to rise.

"Earl Robert," the softer voiced bishop sought his attention. "I carry greetings from King Stephen who enquires of your health."

"Bishop Alexander. You may tell my cousin that I am in rude health." The earl replied regaining his composure.

"That is good. By the graciousness of his majesty I have a request to impart,"

"Which is?"

The bishop glanced sideways at Waleron who sat staring ahead impassively, no longer interested in the negotiations. "Tomorrow is the Feast of Purification." The bishop went on. "The king desires that no one should die on such a holy day. He requests that any conflict be delayed by one day."

"Request denied," Earl Robert said quietly. "I intend to attack tomorrow."

"I told you that it would be a waste of everybody's time," Waleron snapped.

The bishop took a deep breath and sighed. "I hope you will respect the sanctity of the Cathedral."

"Of course," The earl confirmed.

With nothing left to say the small delegation turned their horses and made their way back to the city. "And with that last remark," a voice said close at Ardron side, "The bishop does ensure his own safety." He turned to see Miles Fitzwalter at his side nodding knowingly.

February 2nd, 1141.

Although there was no frost this morning there was that early morning chill that is typical February. Ardron sat motionless mounted on Rattlebone staring across the common towards the ridge, while the horse beneath him fidgeted nervously. He was kitted in a full body hauberk complete with metal helmet. His right hand held a lance pointing skywards, while his left arm looped through the strap of a large metal shield. Being in knight's service to Robert Earl of Gloucester, he and his troop had formed up on the left which was to be the vanguard when the battle began.

Luc was on his immediate right and Jarcot on the left. As the only three milites in his particular troop they were attached part of the cavalry, whilst the rest of his men were dispersed amongst the other pedites. Therefore they would fight on foot. Earl Robert's whole army had taken up their positions across the common early, and at this time had been set for the better part of an hour.

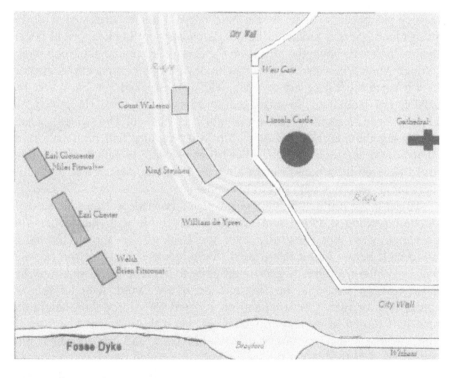

Just as Ardron had begun to wonder if perhaps the king did not intend to commit to an open battle, his army started to file out the west gate. In unhurried and orderly fashion, they filed out from the security of the city walls. First came the king's cavalry, drilled and disciplined. They came three abreast at measured speed, with banners streaming in the morning breeze. They rode along the edge of the ridge for a short distance before dividing in half and taking up two positions wide apart. They were followed by the mass of pedites, not so drilled but nevertheless organised, marching almost casually to their places. Mostly they began filling the centre between the two detachments of cavalry while the rest began taking positions behind both sets of horsemen. The King's own standard was set firmly in the centre section.

Miles Fitzwalter, sitting at the head of Earl Robert's cavalry some three or four yards in front of Ardron, kept looking back impatiently as he waited for the word to advance. "God's breath," he shouted back his patience exhausted. "Why must we wait until they are set?" To Sir Miles, chivalry came a poor second to winning. As if stung by his challenge Earl Robert ordered his cavalry to advance.

At a casual walk they set off towards the ridge which soon turned to a gentle canter. Close to the foot of the ridge the canter turned into a full gallop. With lancers now lowered and pugnacious yells from the riders the cavalry stormed up the hill. But the hill was steep and only halfway up the momentum began to fade, as the hard-pressed horses struggled with the steep climb. At that moment, the king's cavalry on Stephen's right began their own charge down the hill. With the downward momentum they swept through Miles Fitzwalter's cavalry with devastating consequences. Ardron took a lance hit full square on his shield which rocked him back over his saddle, but somehow, he managed to recover his seat. He pulled his horse's head around to look downhill at the jubilant kings' riders continuing their charge. Many of Sir Miles cavalry had been unhorsed, some would never get up again, but Miles was still mounted, and he now urged his men to turn and charge after the king's horsemen. The downhill momentum was now with Fitzwalter's men.

Towards the hill bottom the two cavalries clashed. Ardron rode straight through seeking a target and scored a direct hit with his lance. The horseman was shot forcefully over the back of his mount turning a somersault before he hit the ground. As he glanced back Ardron saw the unhorsed man was already getting groggily to his feet. He tossed away his lance reached over his shoulder and drew his sword, then he spurred Rattlebone forward. Confused and unprepared for Ardron's onslaught the man half turned away and cringed from the strike that was about to hit him. Ardron's sword slashed across his back and ribs sending him sprawling. Whether or not the sword had cut through the chainmail he did not know, nor had he time to look, before another sword wielding rider was upon him. Above head-height their swords clashed two, three times ringing like bells as they did. Ardron tried an aggressive thrust to the man's mid-rift unsuccessfully. It was not easy fighting on horse-back, sword in one hand shield on the other arm, and trying to control a confused horse with his legs. He kicked Rattlebone forward three or four yards, then turned him about savagely to come back with more momentum at his assailant. The two horses collided with Rattlebone's size being the decider. The other horse staggered, and his back legs buckled. As the knight struggled to stay mounted, he was left exposed, and Ardron swung his sword horizontally scything across his chest and knocking him backwards. Grabbing desperately at the reins trying to stay mounted the knight succeeded only in pulling his horse's head high. High at the front, and down at the back the animal had no chance of righting itself. It went over and down.

The two cavalries were now fighting at close quarters. Therefore, useless lances were discarded. Ardron moved up the hill a few yards and found another target. They rode at each other hard and clashed shields head-on, each attempting to unhorse the other. They both turned back and rode at each other clashing shields again. This time, Ardron tried to bring his sword over but found only the top edge of the other man's shield. However, it did have the effect of knocking the other knight's shield lower, and Ardron seeing an opening swung his sword backhanded and horizontal, slashing across an exposed face. Although some of the slash was thwarted by the helmet nose guard, one side of the face was deeply lacerated. But the knight seemed not to be aware that blood streamed from his facial wound, and he came at Ardron with renewed vigour. Both men pulled their horse around to ride at each other clashing swords just once as they passed. The same manoeuvre was repeated with exactly the same result. As they turned a third time and rode at each other Ardron dropped his sword at the last moment and pierced the other knight's throat. At the same time, he ducked beneath the other man's wild swing. As he pulled Rattlebone up, he glanced back to see the other knight slumping over his horse's neck, before sliding from the saddle. The horse now free of control, galloped away from the madness and mayhem as fast as it possibly could.

Ardron pushed on up the hill a little more. They were now near halfway and definitely making progress. But there was now a new element in the fight, he seemed to be surrounded by foot soldiers.

Although astride a horse with height advantage, the sheer number of pedites seemed like angry bees swarming from a disturbed nest. He slashed down frantically, first one side then the other seeking no particular target, just intent on keeping them back. He realised that in these circumstances he could not protect his horse. A simple sword thrust into its belly would bring it down, and him with it. Growling and shouting he thrust the big horse forward, clearing a path ahead with a swinging sword. When he found a few yards of space, he swung over a leg and slid quickly from the saddle. Rattlebone was lathered in foaming sweat, and his big eyes rolling in terror. Ardron slapped him on the rump muttering, "Off you go big boy," as he did. The horse needed no persuading, it set off at a panicked gallop down the hill. Instantly, Ardron regretted his decision as he turned to see a mounted knight galloping towards him with a lance levelled directly at him.

He crouched and waited for the gap to close. At the last possible moment, he leapt to his right, placing himself on the shield side of the horse. The lancer tried to adjust his thrust, but the angle meant it was across the front of his horse. He galloped on through and reined in his mount. Once more he lined up on Ardron. Again, Ardron crouched and waited, but this time the lancer fully expecting him to move in the same direction swerved his mount at the last moment. Ardron's move to the right was not enough, as the lancer's late veer brought the point directly on him. Only a late despairing dive saved him from being skewered. He rolled over and got back to his feet. Something drastic had to change, otherwise he would not survive. He had no alternative he decided, he had to bring the horse down. Once more he set himself, feet slightly apart and holding his sword before him in a two-handed grip. But help came unexpectedly. As the lancer turned once more and lined up on him, another lancer came charging down the hill. Not seen until it was too late, the new arrival buried his lance point into the side of Ardron's attacker. Their horses then collided stumbling over each other. As the animals fell, they rolled down the slope burying their riders beneath flailing hooves.

But there was no time for concern for his rescuer, because Ardron was immediately attacked by a sword wielder, yelling like a maniac. Three times he brought his sword down from high aimed at crashing through Ardron's defences. Three times he was equal to the attack as he parried each blow, giving ground as he did. He was equal to the task, equal that was until his heels stumbled against a lifeless body lying prone on the ground, and he fell backwards. Stunned, he lay there a moment and watched his attacker with a triumphant expression close in for the kill. He could do nothing except bring up his sword. Then he watched in disbelief, as the attacker in his rushed enthusiasm to finish him off, impaled himself on the end of the raised sword. He gasped loudly and looked astonished as his own weight, bearing down on the sword, drove the tip through his hauberk and deep into his stomach. He fell groaning and sprawled on top of Ardron. For a few moments Ardron lay there staring up at the grey skies thankful that God in his heaven had protected him. It crossed his mind that he could just lay here and feign death until the fighting was over. He had, after all, fought well and done his share. But he thought of the lancer over yonder, who had come to his rescue, perhaps beneath the horses he needed help. He kicked his legs free of the body lying over him and crawled clear.

When he got to his feet he looked to where those horses had piled up. The patch was clear except for a lifeless body with a broken lance protruding from its side.

He took a moment to look around him and could see that the momentum was with the Angevins as they advanced up hill. Hardly able to believe the evidence of his own eyes he took another moment to confirm that which he thought was happening. There was no mistake, the king's men were actually retreating back up the hill. It looked as if Earl Robert's left wing had triumphed, and in a little more than half-an-hour.

From his position high on the ridge he had a clear view right over the battlefield. His optimism shrank, clearly, the battle was not yet over. The two centres had clashed, and it seemed held the ground from which they had started. While over on the far right the king's men had overrun the Welsh and were biting deep into Brien Fitzcount and William de Keynes forces. Both armies had advanced significantly on their left, which in effect meant that the armies had swivelled.

At that moment he watched a large number detached from the centre, attacking the advancing king's force. Earl Chester, it seemed, had deemed it more important to move to aid the Angevin right than to hold the centre. It was not a move without merit, as now the beleaguered king's force stuttered and turned to face the new threat.

Not sure what to do next Ardron began to climb the hill to join the rest of Fitzwalter's force. After only a few strides Fitzwalter himself came down the slope. Seemingly, in no particular hurry he allowed his mount to pick its way carefully downwards. After a few yards he stopped then he called for all to gather around him.

"We have chased away these rabbits," he said. "They will not stop running until they reach the Humber. But there, my brave sergens," he went on pointing down the hill. "Is the king and his nobles. Five guineas to the man who brings me his crown." He paused and circling his sword triumphantly cried. "Let us re-join the battle." Then he spurred his horse down the hill leading the charge towards the king's centre.

Ardron joined the downward charge, recognising as he did the shrewdness of this move. It re-affirmed to him why it was that Earl Robert rated Miles Fitzwalter as his leading general. By attacking the king's centre from the side, he would be relieving the pressure on the Angevin centre which had been weakened by Earl Chester's move to aid the far right.

Even before Ardron had reached the new fight, loud cheering had broken out from over the other side. Faced by the Earl Chester's detached force the men of the king's left had turned and were fleeing ignominiously from the battlefield. The king and his close gathering were now left isolated and besieged from three sides. The end was inevitable, and victory assured.

But still the king's men fought on bravely. However, it was now meaningless. Ardron pushed into the fray crossing swords with many but not intent on killing. He waited and hoped that common sense would prevail and eventually they would throw down their swords in surrender. But still they fought on defending stoutly, a hopeless cause.

Then somewhere right in the midst Ardron saw King Stephen. Axe in hand, helmet lost at some point in the battle, he faced up to a half-circle of eight. He swung that axe wildly before him without any specific target, intent only in keeping the pack at bay. The pack meanwhile stood clear just taking the opportunity to poke swords at him when the axe blade flashed in the opposite direction. To Ardron it was reminiscent of a badger baiting. The king's strength owed much to adrenalin, and clearly when exhaustion eventually overcame adrenalin, then the pack would dive in like starving wolves on an exhausted deer. Close by his foot Ardron saw a good-sized rock. He glanced at the king and back at the rock assessing his chances. Then picking it up he moved in stealthily behind Stephen and waited an opportunity. When it came, he swung the rock with all the force he could muster at the back of the king's head. Stephen slumped forward onto his hands and knees. With yelps of glee the pack moved in for the kill. Ardron was quicker, and with sword in hand he leapt over Stephen. The first strike descending onto the king's undefended back was intercepted by Ardron's upward swinging sword. He continued the upward curve sending the other sword spinning somewhere skywards. Then he continued the arc downwards, deflecting into the ground another sword thrust intended to stab the king. The pack flinched back, confused by one of their own defending the king. But not for long, they soon faced up menacingly. knowing full well, that to kill the king they had first to overcome this knight. Ardron stood sword half raised in a two-handed grip and waited.

"Stand-off there! Stand-off I say!" A voice demanded.

Ardron did not lower his guard but did risk a glance to his left.

William de Keynes dismounted from his horse and strode purposefully towards Ardron. For a moment he stared at him hard but did not speak, instead he turned his attention to the downed king. By this time Stephen had raised himself groggily to his knees. De Keynes gripped the hood of his hauberk and pulled it back clear of his head. "King Stephen," he muttered. Then using the hood, he hauled the exhausted king unceremoniously to his feet. "The King," he shouted. "I have the King." Then half dragging Stephen he marched away shouting "Come see! The King! I have the King."

Ardron watched de Keynes go, gathering in his wake a following of the curious and the triumphant. However, still to Ardron's front were most of those who had assailed the king. They stared at him accusingly, his action had robbed them of the ultimate prize reward. He decided a strategic withdrawal was prudent.

He wandered away and found a place a few yards up from the bottom of the ridge and sat down. Although hither and thither some small pockets fought on, the battle was in effect over. Bodies of men and horses littered the common and hillside. Some did move, but some would never move again. In reflective mood he sighed and removed his helmet. Men sang and boasted about the glory of battle, but they were the survivors, and no opinion could ever be heard from those who fell. There was no glory in battle it was simply gory with hell added.

An assembling crowd of men moved across the common towards the Fossedyke heading for Earl Robert's tent. He was just too far away to actually see for certain, but he guessed it was the prisoner, King Stephen, being taken before the earl. He wondered what would become of him. Usually a thief is hung no matter how trivial his crime. In this instance Stephen was guilty of the ultimate theft, the throne of England! However, he could not believe that Earl Robert would sanction his execution, they were after all cousins, as was of course the empress. However, he could not say as much for her. What little he knew of Maude he had found her inflexible and ruthless. Whatever; this victory had opened the way for her to take her rightful place as Queen Matilda of England. The war, it seemed, was over, and a measure of peace could now be enjoyed.

But then perhaps it wasn't quite over, he argued with himself. There would be those who would fight on regardless, at least for a little while. Then he realised that while any chance remained of gaining Stephen's freedom the die-hards of his cause would never give in. In that instant he understood that Stephen had become even more of a problem. To keep him a prisoner indefinitely would keep the flame of hope burning amongst his supporters. To exile him back to Blois would not be the answer either. He would simply bide his time gather support raise an army and return. The only other alternative was his execution, but that would certainly cause frenzied anger and start an uprising. Even when the anger had waned, there was still his son Eustace. Allegiances would switch to him in attempts to put him on the throne. He now recognised that this battle had proved nothing. The war could not be over, and depressingly, it never would.

Already the scavengers were on the battlefield beginning to pick over the dead, robbing them of any valuables. If his experiences at Malmesbury were any sort of guide, then very soon it would be the city itself that would be ruthlessly plundered. What unspeakable horrors were in store for the defenceless citizens of Lincoln? Instead of jubilation from a battle won, his mood deepened and the sooner he left this place then the better it would be, he decided. At his earliest opportunity he would assemble his troop then, with Earl Robert's permission, return to Norwood. But it now occurred to him that he didn't even know if he still had a troop. He looked back over his shoulder towards the castle, nor had he established if Hildi was within. First things first, he should look to his men.

Having made his way back across the common he arrived at the place where his troop had bivouacked the night before. Only five men were present, and they all from his Saxon villeins. They were in a sombre mood sitting before a fire that was still in its infancy. He made his way round each man shaking hands and conferred upon them his pleasure that they had survived. When he reached the last man however, the reason for their solemn mood became apparent. A little distant behind were two bodies already sewn up in canvas. Two fatal casualties so far, he expected that there would be more.

"Who were they?" He asked.

"Wilfrid and Octatha," the question was answered by a man who he knew as Beldwine.

Ardron nodded sadly not knowing what to say. "Their families will be looked after," he promised. "Where are my sergens?" he then asked and received only a sullen shrug. He looked out across the battlefield the scavengers had moved in in force. It was distasteful practice to him, but it was the way of things and victorious sergens would have their bonus rewards. His own sergens were no better or indeed no worse than all the others and that, he anticipated, was where they would now be. There was nothing much he could do here at the moment. Perhaps his time would be better spent in the castle looking for any sign of Hildi. "Those that return are to stay here," he said to Beldwine but loud enough for all to hear. Then after a moment's hesitation, he left to make his way back across the common.

On foot he ascended the ridge just below the castle. The substantial city wall at this point served as part of the castle bailey, with the exceptionally high keep protruding menacingly above that. He reached the ridge top and took a moment to look back. From this height the figures down below on the common were as miniatures moving about in almost slow motion. This position should have been dominant for Stephen's forces. That left him to wonder how such a strategic advantage could have resulted in a humiliating rout. It could have been only that the king's men had not been sufficiently committed to his cause. Both of his flanks had capitulated ignominiously easily, leaving the king at the centre hopelessly outnumbered and surrounded.

He progressed along the wall and entered Lincoln City through the west gate. Inside all was havoc as its citizens, loaded with hastily gathered possessions, rushed to escape an anticipated despoiling. But that despoiling had already begun as the first of the victorious Angevins swaggered through the streets hardheartedly snatching, from the defenceless, even those meagre possessions.

Ardron found the main gate into the castle, just off the Cathedral quarter. He wasn't challenged when he entered. Indeed the atmosphere inside was one of welcome and extreme jubilation, as would be expected from inmates that had been under siege for more than a month. He wandered across the crowded bailey rubbing shoulders with happy and somewhat drunken sergens. There seemed to be no-one of sense from whom he could make enquiries, and from his position down in the midst of the crowd, no way to see very much. He looked about and decided that he should get on the bailey wall where he could at least look down into the crowd. When he reached the foot of the mote loud cheering broke. He looked up the steps to see a Norman noble attended by an escort of adherents emerge from inside the keep. The man ventured no further than a couple of steps down from where he accepted the crowd adulation with egoistic hand waves.

"Who's that?" Ardron asked the man at his side.

"Who's that?" he replied looking curiously at Ardron. "Who are you?" he demanded aggressively.

"I am a knight in service to Earl Robert," he replied.

The man's face relaxed into a huge smile and, enthusiastically, he grabbed Ardron's hand shaking it vigorously. "Welcome my friend. Welcome."

"Who is it?" Ardron asked again.

"That my friend is Sir William de Roumare Earl of Lincoln. Lord of Bolingbroke."

Ardron looked with interest at Roumare. Of medium build and wearing a patterned robe of yellow with a cloak of dark red draped across his shoulders, he depicted a figure of some substance. His head was covered by the hood of a hauberk polished black for effect. Only his face was visible with a full, neatly trimmed, beard. However, the generous streaks of grey in that beard aged him to around his mid-forties. Belted and clasped at his side, a sword with a highly decorated scabbard of silver. With such an ostentatious facade Ardron could appreciate how it would have turned the head of a simple Saxon girl like Hildi. Particularly so if she was pinioned into a life of prostitution to survive.

"And the woman at his side?" Ardron asked

"That beauty, my friend," the man replied. "Is his wife, the Lady Hawise."

Ardron nodded, gave the man a brief smile and pushed on ahead. He made his way up the side of the mote and onto the Roman wall. The wall was impressively substantial with a walkway along this stretch that was as wide as two men lying head to toe. From this height he had a birds-eye view across the multitude of merry makers below. There could have been as many as three hundred jubilant revellers milling about the bailey, and it would have been somewhat hazardous for a woman to venture in amongst them. Hildi would not be down there, he concluded. How to find her? Where to look? But yet he didn't even know if she were still in Lincoln. It then occurred to him that it was unlikely that she would be in the castle. For certain a man would not keep his mistress where he kept his wife.

Feeling a little stupid for not thinking of that before, he turned away and looked out over the wall at the panoramic view. Except for the town houses built on the steep hillside the view across the surrounding flat lands was uninterrupted and seemingly endless. Below the castle, but still within the city walls, the pillaging of Lincoln had begun. Scattered fires had started, which among dwellings with thatched and straw roofs would spread alarmingly quickly. Distant shouting and screams he could hear as the merciless wreaked havoc on the townspeople. Just beyond the city wall was the bridge over the Witham, and he could see a crowd, in blind panic, trying to escape over the river. But the bridge was narrow, and the mob in its desperation, were causing a life-threatening crush into the bottleneck. Others avoided the bridge and tried to cross the river in boats, but these too became swamped and soon over-turned. This was the ugly consequence of defeat, and there was not a shred of mercy from the victorious. He hoped fervently that Hildi was not down there among the mayhem. Surely, he thought, if Roumare did think anything of her he would have taken steps to ensure her safety.

Behind him cheering broke out once more and he turned to see Robert Earl of Gloucester ride in triumph through the castle gates. He rode sedately at the head of a select entourage smiling and acknowledging the accolades with reserved dignity. Just two ranks behind, encased between a pair of guards, was the subjugated, and humiliated, King Stephen. To Ardron reminiscent of a young colt separated from its mother for the first time, nervous and bewildered. The entourage was proudly swathed in an excess of royal blue banners, the distinguishing colours of Earl Robert. Intended, no doubt, to add further degradation on the captive king. The new arrivals dismounted at the base of the mote then the dignitaries in the party climbed the steps and disappeared into the castle's private quarters.

Ardron's dilemma was as before. Where and how to find Hildi? There was one person who would know for definite, but he could hardly approach Roumare and ask him directly. But perhaps his castle constable might be approachable, and just might have that information. He decided that he should try to get himself admitted into the castle private quarters. From there he would have a better chance of discovering something.

"Ran-ulf Ran-ulf Ran-ulf," the crowd began to chant as Ardron made his way down from the wall. Ranulf Earl Chester rode into the bailey at some speed. Only briefly acknowledging the crowd, he jumped from his horse at the foot of the mote and ran up the steps two at a time.

Briefly, Ardron wondered about his haste, but decided it was of no concern to him. As he approached the two sergens guarding the entrance to the castle private quarters Baldwin de Reivers came out.

"Ah," he said seeing Ardron. "Take a dozen men and go to the cathedral. It seems there is a mob trying to break in. Sir Robert wishes that the sanctity of the cathedral be preserved, and those men driven away."

Ardron looked down at the revellers in the bailey below and wondered from where he would get a dozen reliable men. Before he could ask, however, Ranulf, Earl Chester pushed between them his face betraying bad humour as he descended the steps. Ardron watched him mount his horse, snatch its head around and head out of the castle. He looked questioningly at de Reivers.

De Reivers shrugged and pulled a face. "He thinks Stephen should be hanged here and now," he said. "Because Earl Robert refused to even consider it, he now leaves to vent his anger on the people of Lincoln."

Nodding understanding, Ardron then asked. "Where do you recommend that I get a dozen sober and reliable men?"

"Hmm," de Reivers said with a frown and a glance at the rabble below. "I see what you mean. Hold here." He then went back inside. Just three or four minutes later he re-emerged with four sergens. "That's all that could be mustered," he said.

"Five? Five against a mob?" Ardron said.

"You," de Reivers said addressing one of the doorway guards. "Go with him. Now it's six."

Ardron gave him a hard look.

"Well, do your best." he said with a shrug. "I'll try to gather more and relieve you as soon as I can."

The cathedral was but a short walk from the castle across the Cathedral quarter, and even before they got there Ardron could see a mob of perhaps thirty at the main door. "Draw your swords," he instructed as they approached. A pile of brush wood had been piled against the door and lit in an attempt to burn their way in.

"Stand back there," he shouted. But only those nearest heard him and their reactions was no more than curious stares. "Stand back," he shouted again holding his sword high as he began to push his way into the mob. The accompanying sergens closed in tightly behind him, cursing and swearing at the now surprised mob.

"There is gold in there, lots of gold." One man said confronting Ardron. "And women too."

Ardron pushed him roughly to one side. By now they were right in the midst, and at this point very vulnerable. Nothing to be done now, except push their way on to the front and bluster as they did. Sword held threateningly in his right hand and roughly shoving a side all who barred his way with his other, he made it through into the cathedral vestibule. Beneath the shelter of the vestibule they fanned out across its mouth and faced the mob.

"Disperse," Ardron shouted. "In the name of Sir Robert Earl of Gloucester, I order you to disperse."

However, some did not heed and rushed forward clashing with the defenders. But it was more akin to an inn brawl than was particularly dangerous. The rush was held with shoulders and shoves without the need for bloodshed. The crowd hesitated, then cringed back in a half circle milling about before them. Slowly at first, but gradually gaining momentum, the crowd began to drift away, disappearing down the narrow road called Steep Hill, seeking easier targets. Ardron then turned his attention to the burning brush stacked against the cathedral door. They had just about succeeded in dragging it all away to burn harmlessly in the quadrangle in front of the building, when a fleeing man stopped to warn them that some had broken into the cathedral down the side of the building.

With a groan Ardron took one man and moved around the north side to investigate. As they approached the west transept, they discovered the door that had been breached. The heavy wooden door hung askew, hanging on just one substantial hinge. The curved entrance was small and exposed a dark corridor within. One hand on the door and sword in the other Ardron leaned forward peering into the darkness. In the gloom a shadowy figure moved towards him. He raised his sword and called for the figure to stop. It did stop, but only momentarily, then after a hesitation retreated back into the darkness. Ardron straightened up and glanced back at the other sergen. "Stay here," he said. Ducking into the narrow corridor, he moved slowly through the darkness towards angry voices somewhere up ahead. At the end of the corridor he was confronted by a closed door. The raised voices came from within. Straightening himself up, he took a firm grip of his sword, leaned back then he gave the door a robust kick. It flew open with suddenness and left him looking into one of the cathedral's vestries. In an instant he took in the scene before him.

Immediately before him a sergen sword in hand stood ready to attack. Behind that man a bishop's cape lay on the floor, onto which an array of silver sacraments had been tossed. The other side of the cape stood three more sergens. To his left, lying on the floor with his back propped against the wall, was a young priest. His face was heavily bloodied, evidence of a severe beating, however, his spirit was undaunted, as he screamed for the wrath of God to descend on the pillagers.

The swordsmen lunged into the attack, but it was clumsy and Ardron easily deflected the lunge. As the man stumbled forward, he drove his fist into his unprotected face sending him staggering and falling, with a clatter, among the sacraments. Ardron held out his sword to threaten the rest waiting to see which would attack next. One man reached to his scabbard gripping the sword's hilt. Ardron turned his sword point to focus on him with a threatening look. The man after hesitation changed his mind and allowed his hand to drop clear. The three then stood staring back sheepishly.

"Get out," Ardron growled.

"There is enough for everybody," one ventured.

"Get out," Ardron shouted.

Slowly they began to move nervously towards him. Still with sword at the ready, Ardron moved sideways to allow them through the door. The last to go was the man lying amongst the silver. He grabbed at a candlestick as he got to his feet, intent on taking at least some reward for his trouble. But he found Ardron's sword at his throat. Grudgingly, he stared at Ardron for a moment then without a word being spoken he dropped the candlestick back onto the cape and followed the others.

"God bless you my son," the priest said as Ardron helped him to his feet.

"Are there anymore?" Ardron asked.

"I think not," he replied wiping away blood from his nose

"We should get you some attention," Ardron said

"I'll be alright," the priest made light of his injuries.

"Nevertheless?"

The priest nodded agreement. "Come," he said then led the way through to the nave'.

The nave' was spacious long and wide with an awe-inspiring grandiose. The ceiling, high above, was curved and decoratively ribbed. Stone pillars masoned to the highest standard lined each side of the nave' supporting not only the roof but also entresols on either side. But Ardron was completely unprepared for the sight which struck him first. A multitude of people were crowded into the nave, all seeking a safe haven from whatever the battle outcome. The vast majority were women and children, all who had placed their trust in God's protection, and that the conscience of rampaging men would respect the holy building. Some sat, some lay and some just stared hopeless into space. Some, on their knees with heads bowed, lined the rail in front of the high altar in earnest prayer.

"Jesus and all that is holy," gasped Ardron. "How many do you have here?"

The priest shrugged and spread his hands. "How many do you see?"

"Four hundred?" Ardron guessed.

"I would say as much," the priest replied and then carried on talking. But Ardron was no longer listening, his attention had centred upon a young woman kneeling in fervent prayer. Her elbows rested on the rail while her hands joined in prayer provided a prop for her bowed head. Her interlocked fingers fiddled nervously with a dangling crucifix.

"Father. What happened to you?" Ardron's attention was snatched back to see that the questioner was a monk.

Before the priest could make light of his reply Ardron cut in. "Yes," he said. "He needs attention." Gently he guided the priest towards the monk and the priest allowed himself to be led away. Slowly Ardron then walked over to stand before the kneeling woman.

"Hildi, he said softly in English.

She looked up questioningly.

"It's me, Ardron."

"Ardron?" She replied bemused. She stared at him searching her memory trying to relate the Saxon villager she once knew, to this Norman knight standing before her. "What are you doing here?" she asked eventually.

"Looking for you."

"Looking for me?" she echoed.

"Yes, we never stopped," he replied. "Come," he indicated that they should move away from those who prayed. Although the nave' was crowded they did manage to find a quiet space behind one of the pillars.

"I have come to take you home," Ardron said.

"Take me home? Home to Scorrenstone? No," she said slowly shaking her head.

"Why not?"

"Look at me," she said. She wore a long gown of fine silk hanging into loose folds. Its dark green colour shimmered blue with her every movement. A white wimple of satin covered her head and hung over her shoulders held in place by a snood of silver. She tossed back the wide sleeves of her dress and held up her hands to reveal rings of gold on her fingers. "What do you see?"

To Ardron Hildi had always been a desirable and attractive girl but standing here before him those expensive adornments turned her into a stunningly beautiful young woman. He didn't know how to answer the question.

"Do you think I could go back to wearing homespun wool and working long days in the fields?" she asked.

"Where does all this finery come from?" he asked.

"From my devotee, William Roumare."

"William Roumare Earl of Lincoln and all other titles," he sneered. "You warm his bed."

"I do, she snapped back defiantly."

"Hildi, it's not real," he appealed. "It's not going to last."

"You don't know that."

Ardron rubbed his fingers over his brow wondering how to proceed next. "He has a wife. The Lady Hawise and he will never leave her. She has noble blood running through her veins and commands riches of her own. That is too much for Roumare to walk away from. You can't compete with that."

"I love him, and he loves me," she retorted.

"Maybe," he sighed. "But without the security of marriage you are vulnerable. Sooner or later maybe next week, maybe next year, maybe even longer, his head will be turned by another and you will find yourself cast aside."

"Perhaps," she allowed. "But as long as he wants me, I will stay."

He tried a different tract. "What about Esmond?" he asked.

"Esmond?" her attitude softened. "Esmond will always have a special place in my heart." She paused to conjure up memories. "He was my first love." She said softly. "How is he?"

"He is well," Ardron said. "At this moment he is acting castellan at my castle."

"You have a castle?" she uttered in surprise.

"I do. Norwood on the Wiltshire Gloucester border!"

"How?" She asked.

"It's a long story," he said. "It was awarded to me by Sir Humphrey de Bohun on the order of Sir Robert Earl of Gloucester, for services rendered."

"You have come here with Gloucester to aid William?" she muttered.

"I have come with Earl Robert because he asked me too, and I accepted because I hold the man in high regard." He paused then added. "I wouldn't have lifted a finger to aid Roumare."

"He is a good man," she muttered.

Ardron scoffed. "A good man? Have you any idea what is happening outside this building?" he didn't wait for her reply. "Lincoln is being brutally pillaged. Its people being burned from their homes, robbed, raped and murdered. Roumare is Earl of Lincoln and these are his people, yet he sits celebrating in the castle."

"But is it his sergens or is it Earl Gloucester's army that rampage across Lincoln?" she replied hotly.

She had a point. "Mostly Gloucester's," he admitted. "But Roumare does not protest, indeed his own half-brother Earl Chester leads a mob of his own."

"Ranulf?" she said. "Ranulf is an evil man and nothing like William. You can't lay this at William's feet, it's not his fault."

"Not his fault?" He said his voiced raised a little. "Not satisfied to be made Earl of Lincoln, did he not seize the castle for his own payment?" He shook his head and sucked through his teeth in exasperation. "This whole mess can be laid at his feet."

"You are wrong," Hildi sprang to his defence. "It was most probably Ranulf's doing."

"Is the older brother guided by the younger brother?" he asked.

"Excuse me Sir," someone interrupted. Ardron turned to see the monk just over his shoulder. "Bishop Alexander wants to see you." he said.

Ardron nodded, "I'll be there presently."

"Sir," the monk replied. "The Bishop means now."

"I'll be there presently," Ardron repeated firmly.

The monk nodded subserviently and retreated four or five yards to stand waiting.

It was a timely interruption and gave the pair a moment for tempers to cool. Ardron tried another tract. "Your brother is here. He will want to see you." He said it then realised that he didn't even know if Swidhurn had actually survived the battle.

"Swidhurn is here?" Hildi said with surprise.

"He is!"

"I won't see him," she said.

"You must. He did not come to fight in this battle. His sole objective was to come for you, and he has endured much to be here. He will not leave without at least seeing you."

She nodded acceptance. "I will be here until William sends for me."

He paused, there was nothing more to say at this point. "Perhaps I will see you again before I go, and perhaps you will have changed your mind."

"I won't," she said holding up her hand for him to kiss her fingers. He paused there was no doubting that she had learned the refinements of a Norman lady. Then taking her hand loosely he lightly kissed her fingers.

"Lead on," he said to the waiting monk. The monk folded his arms inside his sleeves and wordlessly led the way towards the holy area. Level with the altar he turned down a stone vaulted passageway and into the Bishop's chamber. He knocked lightly on the door then cocked an ear to hear a response from within. Satisfied that permission had been granted he opened the door. "Your grace," he said then stood aside to allow Ardron to pass. He then stood in silent modesty just inside the door. After a moment's hesitation Ardron walked slowly forward and up to the desk.

The chamber was spacious with a stained-glass window at the far end. The room was liberally furnished with superior hand carved furniture made from the finest oak. Ornaments of the highest quality made from precious metals adorned the furniture profusely, in effect gilding the lily. Almost dwarfed behind a huge desk, Bishop Alexander sat head down quill in hand. He wore a cassock of red velvet with a silk skull cap of matching colour, and a wide purple sash across his shoulder. A large pectoral cross hung from a large gold chain about his neck. He continued to look down ignoring Ardron.

"Your grace," Ardron said and waited. He looked about at the ostentatiousness of his surroundings and it offended him. This Bishop, supposedly a man of God, surrounded himself unashamedly in such luxury. A man of such wealth who would still, without conscience, take grouts from his impoverished congregation. He now wished he had allowed those robbing sergens to make off with those few silver trinkets. They would not have been missed.

"Ah, Sir Knight," the Bishop now deemed to address Ardron as he laid down his quill and scattered a fine coating of sand over the paper. "We are, I am told, indebted to you for preventing theft from this house of God."

"It was my duty," Ardron replied.

"Quite so! It is also your duty to protect this cathedral I assume."

"It is."

The Bishop nodded with satisfaction. "Good," he said. "How many men do you have?"

"Five!"

"Five?" he responded in horror. "Five is not enough. You must go and get more, at least fifty."

"I was given that which was available at the time." Ardron said. "More will come, eventually."

"I should have been given priority," he blustered. "Don't you know what I protect here?" he spread his arms. "There may be as many as four-hundred souls out there." He paused waiting a reaction. When none came, he retorted indignantly, "Earl Gloucester shall hear of this."

Ardron wondered if it really was the souls that concerned him. Or was it perhaps the treasures, or maybe his own person. "You must excuse me your grace," he was unsympathetic. "You will appreciate that I am a little short-handed."

"Yes, yes. Be about your duty. I will draft an urgent note to be delivered to Earl Robert himself."

Less than an hour later Ardron was relieved by Baldwin de Reviers own son at the head of two dozen men. Whether the relief force was the initiative of de Reivers senior or prompted by a note from the bishop he didn't know. Nor did he care. He still had things that he needed to attend to. Not least the recovery of his horse.

It had been a long day and was wearing down towards late afternoon when Ardron arrived back at his troop bivouac. He stood and surveyed the line of sewn up canvas and could see that the death toll had risen to four.

"We have two wounded," Swidhurn said as he moved up behind him.

"Swidhurn!" he exclaimed. "I am so pleased to see you."

"I don't want to be involved in many more of these arguments," Swidhurn said nodding his head back towards the battlefield. "It's dangerous! A man could get hurt," he added with a grin.

"You have a point," Ardron agreed. "I have some news for you, but I'll tell you all about that later." He decided to wait until they could sit together and discus the Hildi situation. He glanced across their camp. Today there was only the one campfire and not the normal two. The problems of language had been set aside, for now all were joined in unity as comrades in arms.

"Show me the wounded," he said.

"The first he attended was Dardot. He had a severely injured shoulder smashed by a wielded axe. His hauberk had achieved some protection against its cutting edge but not against the fury which the blow had been delivered. Dardot sat ashen face obviously in pain with his arm strapped tightly to his side.

"Have you seen a lach?" Ardron asked.

"A lach," he muttered. "There are so few of them, and they are as busy as a one-armed juggler dancing in hot embers," he sneered. "I was told that my injuries were not as urgent as some and, therefore, I was to go back tomorrow."

"Make sure this man gets plenty of wine." Ardron instructed Jarcot who stood close by. It was the only pain easer available. Jarcot unfolded his arms and held up a jug to show that he already had that covered.

The second casualty was more serious. One of the Saxon villeins had a severe wound in his side from a spear or a lance. Ardron leaned over and lifted the pile of blood-soaked padding covering the wound. It was not good. He glanced at the two attenders by the man's side and received sad head shakes.

"Bind him tightly with clean cloths," Ardron said. "If the blood seeps through add more cloths on top and bind him again. If the blood flow can be stopped, he will have a good chance." He said it but didn't really believe it himself.

He made his way slowly round the campfire greeting each survivor. Not many had escaped unharmed, but all wounds were minor and could be self-treated. He counted thirty fit survivors, two severely wounded and four dead. Despite their losses the men were in good humour, no doubt relieved by their own personal survival and a conviction that this battle had ended the civil war. With a jerked head movement, he indicated to Luc that he should follow him a stride or two away from the campfire.

"Tomorrow, he said, "I intend to take my leave from Earl Robert and leave this place. The town of Newark is close, and there we should be able to find a lach with time to tend our wounded."

Luc nodded agreement. "There is nothing left for us here," he said staring across a meadow littered with campfires and the sounds of revelling men. "I'm sure our men will be happy to be homeward bound."

Ardron nodded "Now I must be about finding my horse," he said

Luc raised his arm pointing towards the west. "You will find all the loose horses gathered and penned over that way."

He had no trouble finding the pen. Indeed he could hardly miss it. More than a hundred horses were contained in a tight area. He had more trouble finding the men detailed to look after them. Eventually, he found them a few yards away beneath a small copse of trees sitting cross-legged absorbed in a game of stones. More intent on the pot of silver, for which they gambled, they paid Ardron little attention. "Go help yourself," one of them said dismissively with a wave of his hand.

For twenty minutes, or more, Ardron searched through the horses without finding Rattlebone. He just was not there. So, he returned to the keepers to report that his horse was not among them.

"Just pick one. Any one you like," was the exasperated reply.

In that instant he knew that under these circumstances someone would have already laid claim to Rattlebone. He tried once more to question the gamblers, but soon realised it was a useless exercise. Positioned as they were, yards away from the horse-pen, they would not know what had been taken and, pre-occupied with gambling away their booty would not care.

He made his way back to the campsite wondering what he could do to find the horse. Dejectedly he squeezed into the circle around the fire and with a brief nod accepted the wine jug offered.

"Did you find your horse?" Luc asked.

"No. I think someone might have claimed him." He sighed heavily then added. "Stole him." He took a long pull on the wine jug while the translation went around the fire.

"Sir," it was Beldwine who sought his attention. "I have seen your horse corralled yonder." He pointed vaguely to the east.

"Where?" Ardron demanded.

"Campsite over there."

"Show me." Ardron said.

Beldwine led the way along the Fossedyke, until they neared the lake that was Brayford waters, and it was one of the larger camps that they now approached. Clearly, with much drunkenness and reckless horse play the sergens in the camp were in exceptionally high spirits. From its perimeter

Ardron paused and watched a tug-o-war competition taking place across a blazing fire trench. The losers would be in for a painful roasting.

"This way," Beldwine said impatiently, pointing towards an enclosure constructed roughly from brushwood. Arnold leaned on the fence and although there were as many as eight or nine dozen horses in the enclosure, he spotted Rattlebone almost instantly. He put two fingers in his mouth and whistled. The big horse stood still, and then with ears pricked looked in his direction. He whistled again, this time Rattlebone began to walk towards him. Ardron scrambled over the brushwood to greet the animal, then after giving him a welcome pat on the neck led him towards the cross rails that served as a gate.

"What do you think you are doing?" Ardron was challenged as he led the horse out.

"I am reclaiming my horse," he answered as he replaced the rails. He looked up to see a drawn sword pointing at his chest in the hand of a sergen clad in helmet and a hauberk. Obviously, he was posted to guard the horses. "No, you won't," he said. "William," he then called. "We have a horse-thief here."

"There is a horse-thief about here somewhere, but it is not I," Ardron replied.

From the darkness a second guard emerged and for a moment appraised the scene. "A horse thief with an eye for a horse," he said. "I do believe that is Sir Albert's mount."

Ardron shook his head. "No, he's mine. He got loose on the battlefield today and I am here to claim him back."

The guard studied Ardron for a few moments trying to decide what to do. Then deciding that the dispute was above his station he said to the other guard, "Go and find Sir Albert, let him sort it out."

It took a few minutes before the guard returned accompanied by Sir Albert. Even before he got close Ardron could see something familiar about the man, and the tunic of red and yellow squares only confirmed his suspicions. It was Sir Albert Casteneau. This was not good.

"Who is the thief that tries to steal my horse?" he boomed.

"The horse is mine." Ardron said.

For a moment Casteneau studied Ardron then recognition dawned upon him. "Well well," he said. "Strike me blind if it's not the turnip coward." He leaned forward his face only inches away from Ardron. "Be off with you before I cut you in half."

"I will not leave without my horse."

"Your horse? The animal is mine." Casteneau raised his voice. Then as a thought occurred to him, he began to grin. "Will you be prepared to fight for him? Except this time like a man and not with turnips?"

"I am at your service."

"To the death," Casteneau said.

"As you wish," Ardron replied easily.

Both men retired a few yards apart with Casteneau flashing his sword vigorously left and right with downward sweeps.

"Sir," is the horse worth risking your life for?" Beldwine muttered seemingly intimidated by Casteneau show of strength.

"He is. But that's not the real reason. There is some history here," he said, and handed over the horse's reins. Slowly, he drew his sword and turned to face Casteneau. He then worked his shoulders to loosen up before stepping forward, sword raised in a firm two-handed grip.

Casteneau came forward at the rush, bringing his sword down to clash across Ardron's. Then he tried left and right. Ardron was equal to the attack and successfully blocked. He then launched an attack of his own, pressing forward with horizontal swings, but Casteneau was a match to both. The clashing of steel rang out like bells and began to draw curious spectators. Casteneau then launched a frenzied attack, leaping forward several times on his front foot whilst swinging his sword left and right, forcing Ardron back until he stumbled against the brushwood fence. A fleeting expression of elation crossed Casteneau's face as he brought his sword crashing down in a death swipe. But Ardron had rolled away and the Norman's sword chopped through the brushwood only. He turned to see Ardron standing a couple of yards away guardedly waiting. Casteneau this time tried a low lunge which Ardron, with a downward facing sword, deflected away. Then as Casteneau overbalanced slightly, he let one hand off the sword and slammed a clenched fist into his face. Startled the Norman staggered back and paused. Then he drew his hand across his nose and inspected his fingers. The fingers were bloodied. Then with his face betraying furious temper he launched a violent assault. Ardron gave ground rapidly as he fended off the barrage of blows. Then as Casteneau lunged he snapped up straight and dodged sideways deflected the lunge harmlessly past. He then spun right round swinging his sword at Casteneau's unprotected back. But from somewhere, Casteneau brought back his sword just in time to block the slash. Both men turned and faced up once more. This time it was Ardron who swung his blade across the front, and as he expected, the swing was blocked. But that was only a feint, because he pulled his sword back in a backhanded swing aiming at Casteneau's head. However, Casteneau saw it coming, and although he ducked beneath the swing it did catch him a glancing blow, once more drawing blood. With a growl like a wounded bear he lunged at Ardron and both men locked swords at the hilts. Pressed together with only the upraised sword hilts separating their faces they pushed hard against each other. Casteneau was breathing heavy. From this Ardron took encouragement, he felt that he was beginning to get on top. He broke the deadlock and danced back four or five paces. But one of the spectators deliberately stuck out a tripping foot sending Ardron stumbling backwards.

He fell, full length but raised himself quickly onto an elbow. Casteneau charged in for the kill. Although Ardron managed to raise his sword it was now only one-handed. He managed to intercept the descending blows, but they crashed down with such force that he was in danger of wounding himself with his own sword. Casteneau stood above him feet apart perfectly balanced to continue raining down the blows until Ardron could no longer sustain any defence. He saw just one chance and he took it. He brought his right leg up and aimed a kick into Casteneau's crotch. The kick was only partially successful, but nevertheless, it was enough to make the Norman jump back. Ardron rolled away quickly and sprang to his feet. Now it was Ardron's turn to be furious. He leapt forward swinging his sword left and right continuously in rapid succession, and it was Casteneau who stumbled backwards defending himself as best he could from the onslaught. The Norman gave ground rapidly until his back came up suddenly against the trunk of a tree. Startled, he allowed his grip to loosen on his sword, and a forceful sideways slash from Ardron sent it spinning away. He leaned forward his sword horizontal and pressed against Casteneau's throat.

"Hold up there," An authoritative voice shouted.

But breathing hard through sheer anger Ardron thought to sink his sword into Casteneau's throat anyway.

"Hold up there, I say." The voice repeated. "Under the pain of death do not deal the killer blow."

Terror was in Casteneau's eyes as Ardron fought to control the urge to lean forward on his sword. Gradually, his anger began to subside, and without reducing the control he held over Casteneau's life, or death, he glanced round to see who it was that spoke.

"Put up your sword," Sir Brien Fitzcount said quietly.

Still Ardron hesitated.

"Put up your sword," Sir Brien repeated.

Ardron took a deep breath, stared into Casteneau's terrified eyes then stepped back and lowered his sword.

"Someone tell me what this is all about," Sir Brien said.

"He's a horse thief. A common horse thief," Casteneau accused.

Sir Brien stared at Ardron. "I'm no horse thief. The horse is mine." Ardron said.

"All this is over a horse?" Sir Brien queried. "Bring the horse to me."

Beldwine led the animal forward.

Sir Brien took a slow walk around the animal studying its conformation. "I'll settle this argument," he said and drew his sword. "I'll bury my sword in its belly. This way no-one gets it and the argument settled."

Ardron leapt in between him and the horse and raised his sword. "No Sir Brien. You will not," he said.

Sir Brien stepped back shocked. "Lower your sword at once," he said.

"Not while it's your intention to slaughter my horse," Ardron retorted.

"You realise that I could have you hanged for this!"

Ardron realised fully the consequences of his actions, but yet he could not stand by and see Rattlebone destroyed.

"What say you?" Sir Brien asked Casteneau. "Should I order him hung?"

Casteneau glanced at Ardron with a smirk curling the edge of his lips. "You should, Sir Brien," he said, nodding slowly.

"Mark you though," Sir Brien said. "It will not gain you the horse. I will still bring it down with a sword thrust in the belly." He paused and waited for his words to sink in. "What say you now?"

"I still say hang him," Casteneau said without hesitation.

"Even though you don't gain the horse?"

Casteneau nodded agreement.

Sir Brien waited a moment then sheaved his sword. "The horse is yours," he said to Ardron. "Take him away."

Relieved, Ardron nodded his gratitude and put up his sword. With the hostility he could sense all around him, he decided that it would be better to leave this place as soon as he was able. He gathered the reins from Beldwine and with a head jerk indicated that they should go.

"Just a minute," Sir Brien said. Ardron waited while the man came over. "Tell me Ardron of Norwood," he said as he stroked Rattlebone's nose. "Would you really have crossed swords with me?"

"That, Sir Brien, is something I will leave for you to decide," Ardron replied.

***

The morning was wearing on, the camp struck and all loitered around just waiting for Ardron to give the word. He peered across the west common waiting impatiently for Swidhurn to appear. He would not wait much longer, he decided. It was fourteen miles to Newark and for the sake of his wounded he wanted to be there before nightfall.

Earlier this morning he had gone to the castle and had obtained Earl Robert's permission to leave Lincoln and journey home. Swidhurn meanwhile had gone on to the cathedral to talk with his sister, promising that he would re-join the troop within the hour. But that was two hours ago and Swidhurn still had not arrived back.

"There he is." Luc said pointing away toward the top of the ridge. There was a rider atop the ridge but, still more than a mile away, Ardron could not be sure. The rider descended the ridge then set off at a canter in their direction. Ardron was now sure that it was Swidhurn and he was not surprised to see him alone. Obviously, he had been every bit as unsuccessful, as he himself had been at trying to persuade Hildi to come with them.

"Mount up," he instructed his troop. Before he himself mounted, however, he looked to the two wounded lying on hastily constructed litters that would be dragged along behind horses. "It will be a bit uncomfortable," he warned both men. "But we will go slowly and try to make it as smooth as possible."

He mounted and began leading the troop along the Fossedyke towards Brayford water. Just a couple of hundred yards, or so, Swidhurn had caught up and he fell in alongside Ardron.

"You had no luck with Hildi then?" Ardron said.

"No, she is adamant that she intends to stay." Swidhurn replied.

"You did your best," Ardron said with a shrug.

"Not quite," Swidhurn said. "I haven't given up yet."

Quizzically, Ardron glanced sideways at the blacksmith.

"I intend to stay, in case she should change her mind,"

"That might take a very long time." Ardron said.

"I know," Swidhurn replied.

"How will you live?" Ardron asked.

"I'm a blacksmith," he said. "And a good one. There must be an opportunity in a city this size for a master smithy."

Ardron looked across the ridge at the houses on the hillside, many still smoking from yesterday's ravages, there would be work for Swidhurn of that he had no doubt.

"I had thought," Swidhurn went on, "To try and get work within the castle bailey. That way I can stay in touch with Hildi's comings and goings."

It was a good plan. "You will need money for tools and equipment," Ardron said.

"That I will," he paused. "I had thought__."

"Of course," Ardron said anticipating the comment.

By now they were near the Witham Bridge, the scene of so much pandemonium yesterday. He pulled his horse to one side and with a wave of his arm indicated that the column move on and cross the bridge.

"Are you sure this is what you want to do?" he asked.

"It's what I have to do," Swidhurn replied.

Ardron nodded then leaned over to fiddle in his saddle bag. He pulled out a purse of coins and thoughtfully weighed it in his hand. "Then my friend," he said. "May God look favourable on your plan." He tossed over the purse. "It is Earl Robert's intention to take the king back to Bristol and there to imprison him. I don't know just how much longer he will stay in Lincoln, but you should beg for an audience with him. If you do get an audience, then mention my name, and tell him I would be indebted if he could use his influence to get you a position as blacksmith inside the bailey." He shrugged. "I don't know if I have a great deal of influence with the earl, but it couldn't hurt."

Swidhurn nodded his gratitude. Then for a few moments they wordlessly looked at each other. There was so much to be said, but words were not necessary. "God speed your journey home," Swidhurn muttered. Then he wheeled his horse's head and rode up the hill to the southern gate.

Ardron watched him go, "God's blessings, my old friend." he said as Swidhurn disappeared through the city gate.

Chapter 10

Norwood. April 1141

Ardron carefully weighted the quiot in his right hand then held it up to his face while he studied the pin ten yards away. Judging the distance to the best of his abilities he took a half step forward and prepared a looping lob to hit the pin.

"Look," Fique behind him said sharply. "He waggles his arse like a cat hunting a mouse." Ardron smiled to himself, the comment was designed to disrupt his concentration. It was a successful ploy, the quiot landed well short of the pin to the delight of those on the opposite team standing behind him.

Ardron took a moment to stare at the quiot lying in the sand three feet away from the pin before turning and glaring playfully at Fique, the sergen who had sledged him. With a huge grin and fists held shoulder high Fique swayed his torso in triumph. Shaking his head ruefully Ardron re-joined his own team and received consoling sympathy. The next man to throw a quiot moved forward and took his position on the mark.

More than two months had elapsed since the battle of Lincoln. Ardron and his troop had made a slow and casual return to Norwood. They had delayed in Newark for the better part of a week, waiting for Dardot to become fit enough to make the journey. The gravely wounded villein had also survived. However, it would be several weeks before he would be strong enough to make the long trek. That had been too much of a wait for most of his impatient colleagues. Ardron had, therefore, decided to pander to the majority and start homeward. Before he left, however, he paid the local lach for continued treatment and left behind one of the man's friends to safeguard his welfare.

Since their return home the prevailing mood had been one of jubilation. King Stephen had been deposed and was held in Bristol Castle by Robert Earl of Gloucester. The empress had already begun negotiations to take her rightful place as Queen Matilda of England. Many of Stephen's supporters had re-assessed their altered situation and had chosen humiliating discretion over complete ruination. They had changed allegiances swearing fealty to the empress. There were no battles left to fight, and peaceful prosperity seemed assured for the foreseeable future. Due to the new situation it was a relaxed and happy atmosphere that pervaded not only in the castle but also around the surrounding estate.

Ardron's attention was distracted when he saw Esmond ride into the bailey at a pace. He dismounted almost before his horse had come to a halt and strode purposefully towards Ardron.

"What is it?" Ardron asked.

"Sir Humphrey de Bohun is but a mile behind me, coming this way to make a visit on you."

"Shall I stop the game?" Luc asked having come up quietly behind Ardron.

"No no." Ardron said. "Let them play it out. It can be no more than a social visit. But have the servants notified they are to prepare for guests this night."

Only a few minutes later, at the head of a dozen accompanying sergens, de Bohun rode into the castle bailey. For a few moments he sat his horse and looked around the castle compound with interest.

"Welcome Sir Humphrey," Ardron said as he strode forward to greet the man.

De Bohun re-focused his attention and replied with a brief nod as he slid down from his horse. "There have been some major changes around here," he said.

"I hope they meet with your approval," Ardron replied.

"Most certainly! I have never seen the place looking better," he replied. "Perhaps I should consider raising your quarterly," he added with a grin.

"My home is your home," Ardron said waving his arm and standing aside inviting de Bohun to walk up the mote steps to the keep. In the keep a pile of oat cakes, a jug of wine and an assembly of goblets had already been laid out on the table.

"Can I offer you refreshments?" Ardron offered.

"That would be cordial," de Bohun said as he unclipped the hook and allowed the heavy cloak to slip from his back. Before it dropped too far, he dragged it around his front and then tossed it on the table.

"What News?" Ardron asked as he poured the wine.

"A lot," de Bohun replied making himself comfortable on the bench at the table. "But first, how do you fare after Lincoln?"

Ardron nodded as he seated himself opposite. "I lost four men and two wounded. Both still in recovery." He shrugged. "All things considered not too bad I suppose."

"A bloody business," de Bohun sympathised. "Still the outcome was a triumph." He lifted the goblet. "To Empress Maude," he said.

"Queen Matilda," Ardron corrected.

"Of course," de Bohun agreed. "Did you know that she went to Winchester to talk with Henry, Bishop of Winchester?"

"No I didn't," Ardron replied shaking his head.

"Yes, she and Earl Robert went to see the good bishop." Ardron detected a hint of sarcasm in the last remark. "The man's ethics were bought fairly easily. He was offered the post of chief accountancy in England of all gifts of bishoprics and abbacies. In return he would receive Maude into the holy church as the Lady of England, hand over the royal crown, the keys to the treasury and use his influence to persuade other bishops to accept Maude as Queen."

"This man, the brother to Stephen, and one of the original conspirators in the seizing of the empress's crown, could switch loyalty so easily?" Ardron said with incredulity.

"Aye! He did. He swore fealty that very day."

Ardron shook his head bewildered. "How does he appease his own conscience with that?"

De Bohun grinned. "He said, that while he does love his mortal brother, he should place the cause of the immortal father ahead of all other considerations."

"An easy get out," Ardron retorted. "And with financial reward to ease the pain."

"Indeed," De Bohun agreed. He stared into the goblet and swilled the wine around its bottom. "Empress Maude stayed a couple of days at Trowbridge on her way back to Bristol." He paused. "Did you know she intends to march into London at the head of a triumphant parade very soon?"

Ardron shook his head. "I have not left the estate since my return, and news doesn't reach this backwater easily."

"This brings me to the purpose of my visit," said De Bohun. He emptied his goblet and leaned forward. "I am charged by Earl of Gloucester to extend an invitation to you to ride in that parade."

Ardron was surprised. "That is an honour indeed. But why me?"

"The invitation is extended to all the nobles and Milite Commanders who supported the empress in her cause, and to all those who fought in the battle of Lincoln. Especially, to those who fought at the battle of Lincoln."

It was not so much an invitation as a demand, Ardron knew. Nevertheless, it was indeed an honour to be included in the event. "When will this parade be?"

"The exact date is yet not decided, but I expect it to be late May or early June," de Bohun replied.

"I would be pleased to attend," he said as he topped up de Bohun's goblet.

"Include, as many sergens and villeins as you can possibly spare." De Bohun added. "The bigger the parade the more impressive it will be."

'Also the more intimidating,' Ardron thought without saying.

The assembly will be at Oxford Castle" de Bohun went on. "From there the march will be on to Wallingford, where Empress Maude will be waiting. After that, the triumphant march into London, followed quickly by a coronation."

Ardron nodded thoughtfully. "I will have to leave an effective defence force behind for the castle's protection, but I will take as many as I can." Ardron said.

"Protection against who?" de Bohun queried.

"Your cousin, Edward de Evreux. He visited a little while ago and made vague threats because he perceived the castle improvements as a potential threat."

De Bohun laughed out loud. "You really are out of touch," he said. You have nothing to fear from the de Evreux's. Accepting their cause lost, they have defected to support the empress. That means not only Edward of South Cerney, but William and Patric of Salisbury too. Strange how principles evaporate when faced with ruination," he added with a smirk.

"Indeed," Ardron agreed.

***

London. Early June 1141

The March of Triumph into London had been a success. Empress Maude rode at its head, accompanied by Robert Earl of Gloucester. More than a thousand nobles, knights and sergens made up the procession in orderly ranks three abreast. A myriad of flags were held proudly aloft and fluttered in the April breeze. Each man was helmeted and garbed in ceremonial hauberks; their horses draped in the colours of their particular noble patron. The nobles themselves, held up their shields proudly bearing their personal emblems, and boasting their triumphant association with their Liege Lady. The crowd lined the route and tossed flower heads in the path of the victorious empress as the procession wound its way slowly towards Westminster.

Ardron, as a knight in the service of Earl Robert, was near to the procession head, in the midst of the earl's large company of men. He had brought with him a contingency of just twelve from Norwood, including his brother Esmond. He had not pressed those who preferred to remain behind.

As they progressed through the narrow streets it did not escape Ardron's notice that in amongst the crowd was a fair sprinkling of sergens. He suspected that their purpose might be to encourage the crowd's enthusiasm. He had silently held some reservations about the London populace. They had warmly welcomed Stephen as king, but how would they now actually receive his vanquisher? But all seemed as it should be, nevertheless, he decided to reserve judgement.

That was over two weeks ago and since then Ardron had practically been in limbo. So much so that he was seeking an audience with Earl Robert hoping that he could be excused back to Norwood. However, the earl was extremely busy with the empress's affairs, and that made it difficult to see him. His best chance, he had decided, was probably to approach Fitzgilbert. In his role of Marshal, he was responsible for all arrangements within the royal court. Therefore, was in position to arrange a meeting with Sir Robert.

Standing outside the great hall of Westminster he could see Sir John Fitzgilbert, but at that moment he was pre-occupied with a gathering of London's wealthier merchants. Ardron stood back watched and waited while Fitzgilbert issued instructions of protocol. Eventually satisfied that his instructions had been understood Fitzgilbert stepped back, then after a moment's hesitation, walked towards the great imposing oak doors. Ardron took his chance and moved to intercept him.

"Sir John," he said.

"Ah, Ardron Scorrenstone." Fitzgilbert recognised him.

"Ardron of Norwood, he corrected.

"Of course," Fitzgilbert allowed. "I had heard of your advancement. And you have my congratulations, I am sure it is well deserved."

Sir John," Ardron went straight to the point. "I have a small matter that I wish to lay before Earl Robert. However, I have great difficulty actually getting past his army of advisors. I wonder if you could perhaps use your influence to get me an audience."

"I could try. What is the issue you wish to raise?"

"Oh. It's not an issue. It is a small private matter of little importance."

Sir John nodded. "I will do what I can," he said.

They had reached the entrance doors to the great hall, and as if by magic the doors swung slowly open allowing them to enter. Ardron peeled off to move down the side and take a place amongst the other knights that lined both sides of the hall. Fitzgilbert meanwhile walked down the centre towards the throne upon which Empress Maude was seated.

Ardron found a suitable place amongst the others, then took stock of his surroundings. He was in the great hall of Westminster where Empress Maude was about to hold court. Although there were perhaps as many as two hundred people within, its great size and height miniaturised the crowd, making it look sparsely attended. The empress was at the far end seated upon a throne raised on a dais. Her half-brother Earl Gloucester stood attentively at her side. Standing a little over to the side and at the foot of the dais was Bishop Henry, looking impressively splendid in his ceremonial robes. Also in close attendance was Sir Brien Fitzcount, his hand resting on his sword hilt, and looking somewhat pensive and ill at ease. Ardron wondered if the man had some notion of what was about to unfold and did not entirely approve. But he dismissed it instantly as nothing more than whimsical speculation. He continued to scan around casually, recognising here and there some familiar faces. But then he spotted a face that he did not expect to see. Geoffrey de Mandeville stared back at him expressionless for a few moments before with the briefest of nods he acknowledged Ardron. His presence at Maude's court could only mean that he too had sworn fealty to the empress. Yet another of Stephen's original band of conspirators, who had through expedience changed loyalties, Ardron reflected. It was less about loyalty and more about personal gain, he concluded.

Fitzgilbert meanwhile approached the empress then after bowing low spoke to her. Ardron was too far away to hear what was said but after a brief exchange of words the empress nodded assent to whatever it was that had been said. Fitzgilbert then backed away slowly until he was clear, then he turned and walked back through the doors. A few moments later he returned, this time leading the merchants towards the throne. Ardron could see plainly the apprehension upon their faces. They shuffled forward as naughty children coming to receive punishment from an angry parent. One by one the merchants approached the dais, bowed low, and laid gifts at Maude's feet. Then still bowing backed away slowly. Maude received them impassively without speaking, only nodding slightly.

"Merchants of London," she said after she had watched the last of them back away. "You have welcomed my cousin Stephen into your city and served him well, contributing generously to his campaign. However, in aiding the usurper you have cast yourselves as aiding and abetting treason, and for this you must pay reparations." The merchants glanced furtively at each other with nervous anxiety. "You will forfeit the sums as decreed," she went on. Then she nodded towards a clerk who stood close by.

The dapper little man stepped forward, opened a large accounts book, and after clearing his throat, began reading out names and the sums apportioned against each man. The sums were not inconsequential, ranging from three hundred to five-hundred marks, which drew gasps of surprise from the merchants. Eventually, his task complete, the clerk looked up, and snapped the book closed. Then, after acknowledging Maude, with a bow he withdrew into the background.

"Your Imperial Majesty," one of the bravest of the merchants stepped forward and addressed the empress. "Our coffers have been emptied by the war, and we cannot at this time pay these huge sums. We beg your indulgence that you grant us time to pay these dues."

"Your coffers were emptied in the cause of Stephen, not mine," The empress replied curtly. "Therefore, do not expect sympathy from me.

Nevertheless, I will give you some time." She paused a moment. "You have fourteen days."

Ardron thought the merchant was about to choke. "Your Imperial Majesty," he pleaded. "We need more than fourteen days."

"In fourteen days," the empress replied. "If the reparations are not paid then assets will be seized." With a dismissive wave of her hand the matter was closed. Fitzgilbert then stepped forward and ushered the disgruntled merchants from the hall.

The next matter at hand was presented by Bishop Henry himself, and concerned his nephew Prince Eustace, son of Stephen. "Your Imperial Majesty," he said. "In the case of the young Prince Eustace might I be allowed to send him to the family estates in Boulogne?"

Maude's face set firm, "You will not," she said defiantly. "I will keep him close and under my supervision, where he will not be allowed to create any mischief."

"But in Boulogne he will be safe." The bishop petitioned.

"In Boulogne he will be beyond my control, and in likeness of his father before him, could build himself a power base and eventually launch an attack on my realm.

"But cousin," Bishop Henry still protested. "He is but a boy."

"A boy can be a figurehead to ambitious men," she replied brusquely. "The matter is closed."

The bishop grudgingly nodded acceptance. "May I now bring up the circumstances of Queen Matilda, Stephen's wife?"

The empress said nothing, instead sat very still and stared impassively at the bishop.

After a moment's hesitation Bishop Henry went on. "Currently she has taken refuge in Guildford Castle with her children around her. May I beg you look sympathetically upon her circumstances and guarantee her safety?"

Maude was silent for a few moments then eventually said. "While she stays within the castle precincts and does not try to interfere in royal affairs then I will allow her to stay there in safety. However, any attempt to re-kindle or re-establish the old order will be seen as treason, and the penalty for treason is hanging. Man or woman makes no difference." She warned. "And you may make my position on that perfectly clear to your sister-in-law, my dear bishop."

The bishop nodded assent, bowed deeply and stepped back half-a-dozen paces.

"I have an announcement," Maude declared. "My good uncle, David, King of Scotland, has served my cause loyally and effectively from the very onset. Indeed his efforts were so effective that Stephen was forced to make considerable concessions, ceding to him the administrations districts of Carlisle, Northumberland, Doncaster and Huntingdon. Therefore, as a well-earned reward I intend to grant his request that he be allowed to place his own Chancellor in position as the Bishop of Northumberland."

To Ardron the significance of that announcement was lost. However, the initial greeting of complete silence spoke volumes. The first to re-act was Bishop Henry as a gasp of 'no' escaped his open mouth. Even Earl Robert looked on speechlessly astonished.

"You can't do that," Bishop Henry now protested.

"I can and I have," the empress replied firmly.

"You must allow the church to select its own bishops," Bishop Henry protested.

"Must I?" She replied feigning shock.

Henry remembered his station and gained some self-control. "Your Imperial Majesty," he appealed more evenly. "The monks of Durham will never accept a Scottish Chancellor for their appointed bishop."

"They will. And they will get used to it because I am of mind that it will happen."

"Your Majesty," Henry persisted. "For certain there will be protests from the senior ecclesiastical of the church."

"Let them protest," she replied dismissively.

Earl Robert leaned forward and spoke quietly into her ear. She took a deep breath and let out an exasperated sigh. "It will happen," she said as she stood up. "That will be all for today," she announced bad humouredly.

Sir Brien stepped forward and gallantly offered his hand to assist the empress down the dais steps. She took the hand nodding her gratitude as she did. Then unhurried, but regally, she walked down the centre of the hall. On both sides, all present, bowed paying homage as she passed.

"And they said that no woman would be strong enough to rule England," the man standing behind Ardron muttered.

***

Two days later, Ardron was led into Earl Robert's chamber by his personal clerk. The earl was alone and seated at a large desk. His hand cradled his forehead as he looked down studying documents spread out before him.

"Sir Ardron," he said as he leaned back in his chair and pushed the documents away. Then using his fingers he slowly massaged tired eyes. Ardron had a sudden moment of guilt. Clearly the earl was burdened with matters of state, and his own personal request for dismissal would be trivia in comparison. "Will you take a goblet of wine," he asked.

"Sir Robert, I don't wish to burden you with my trivia. Perhaps I could come back at a more convenient time." Ardron said.

"Nonsense," Earl Robert replied as he stood. "You are here now, and a diversion is not unwelcome." He walked over to a small table by the window and picked up the wine decanter. "Wine?" he asked again.

Ardron nodded. "Thank you," he said.

"What can I do for you?" he asked as he poured.

"Sir, I seem to be serving no useful purpose here and I seek your permission to return to Norwood."

The earl stopped pouring and stared at Ardron. "I'd rather you stayed, Sir knight," he said.

It was not lost on Ardron the last 'sir knight' remark served as a reminder that he was in his knight's service. "If that is your wish Sir Robert, then I will of course stay."

Earl Robert turned his attention back to pouring wine. "Those I can trust, I mean really trust, are not so many. And you, Sir, are one that I know I can." He picked up the goblet and handed it to Ardron. "My God," he went on. "At least half of those who do pledge fealty to Empress Maude do so with their fingers crossed behind their backs, I swear." He waved Ardron towards a seat by the window. "The sooner the empress has her Coronation the better it will be for all concerned. But I'm afraid my sister grows impatient and is becoming ever more demanding, which does nothing to smooth the negotiations." He swilled the wine around the goblet and stood staring out of the window lost in thought. "Who can blame her? Not I," he went on thinking aloud. "When Stephen rode into London, he received his Coronation within four days. It is moving towards a month since we arrived in London, and yet we have not even been able to establish a date. I swear these bishops do drag their heels deliberately. And none more so than cousin, Henry." He took a long gulp from the goblet. "It suits him not, to see a speedy end to these arrangements," he went on. "We need him to influence the other bishops, and he knows well that once the plans are made and the Coronation goes ahead his importance to us will all but evaporate. So, the longer he can protract these negotiations then the longer he remains central and the more concessions he can demand. Christ on the cross!" he swore venomously. "I wouldn't turn my back to that man if he lay dead in his coffin."

Ardron did not know how to respond. Although he could sympathise with Earl Robert these were problems of state and far above his station. He shook his head slowly in empathy but passed no comment.

"Do you know," Robert went on. "I found out only yesterday that some of Stephen's, so called loyal barons, actually offered to support Theobald if he laid claim to his younger brother's crown?" He shook his head ruefully. "However, he laughed them out of his court, asking why he would want to partake in such madness. But undeterred those same barons then approached Geoffrey of Anjou, Maude's own husband. Geoffrey of

Anjou," he repeated shaking his head with a high degree of incredulity, "One of the reasons given for supporting Stephen's usurp, was because if Maude were queen then her husband, Geoffrey, would automatically become king. And that they did not want. Oh no! But now suddenly it has become more desirable than having Maude as autonomous queen. Are they mad?" He paused a moment perhaps realising he had been babbling and unburdening himself somewhat inappropriately. "Sensibly," he said grinning at Ardron, "He too turned it down." He emptied his wine goblet. "However, none of this is your burden," he went on as he picked up the wine decanter. He held it up as an offer to refill Ardron's goblet. Ardron shook his head, he was not particularly enamoured of spiced wine.

"It would seem that your main problem is one of inactivity," he said as he re-filled his own goblet.

Ardron nodded agreement. "Then I will find something for you to do. Will that make you feel better?"

"Yes Sir, it would."

"Then I think I have a task for you," the earl said, taking a seat the opposite side of the window. "Where are you lodged," he asked.

"Westminster," Ardron answered.

Earl Robert bit his lower lip thoughtfully and stared ahead at nothing in particular. "Then I would you move into London," he said. "Discard those Norman clothes and don the Saxon style of dress. I want you to walk among the common populace of London and to be my eyes and ears. I hear so many rumours and I need to be able to distinguish the genuine from the fanciful." He paused and studied Ardron. "Can you do that?" he asked.

"I can," Ardron said dubiously. I'm not sure what it is you ask me to discover."

"The truth, Robert said emphatically. "Those close to me tell me that the ordinary peasant on the streets of London supports the empress's claim to the crown. But I suspect they tell me that because they think that is what I want to hear. What I want from you is to melt into the community and to find the consensus of opinion then report back to me. Mayhap, you might also discover if there are those in higher authority who plot against the empress. I suspect there are."

Ardron nodded agreement. "I can do that!"

"Good!" Earl Robert said getting to his feet. "Erm__," he drawled as another thought came to him. "There will be no need for you to keep your men about you. Just keep as you see fit and dismiss the rest back to your estate. If you so wish."

***

"Have you seen my brother? Ardron asked the inn keeper.

The inn keeper, a small but portly man, stared at him. "He wandered out straight after breakfast, but I didn't see which way he went," he said with minimal interest. "Have you tried the stables," he suggested.

It was a sound suggestion, if he had left the inn then in all probability his horse wouldn't be there either. He crossed the cobbled yard to the stable building cocking an eye to the weather as he did. It still needed a couple of hours till noon, but the sky was blue and the clouds few. The promise was of another fine day. A decent day to attend an open-air theatre, he concluded. He found Esmond in the stable tending the horses. "Very dutiful of you brother," he said.

Esmond looked up from his labour and leaned across Rattlebone's withers. "We should take a day and ride out," he said. These horses are in need of exercise."

Ardron nodded agreement, then took a handful of oats and fed them to the grey mare that was Esmond's horse. "You are of course right, he agreed.

It had been over a week now since they had moved out of Westminster and into the precincts of London to start the role as spies for Earl Gloucester. Having no particular need for his sergens he had dismissed them all to return to Norwood. However, and because Esmond was a Saxon, he stayed behind to assist and to be company. They had frequented inns, visited markets and listened to street corner speakers in their attempts to gauge the feelings of the London populace. So far Ardron's findings had not been as he would have liked. There were obvious feelings of discontent among the proletariats, mainly because the wealthy merchants, unhappy about the reparations they were forced to pay, had looked to recuperate their losses by increasing prices. At the same time they cut their work forces and reduced pay. As a consequence, there were large price hikes on goods sold on the street market, and at the same time less money available to spend. The common man on the streets probably cared little who actually ruled England, but when the situation began to affect their living standard then it was natural that they would look for someone to blame. The merchant traders neatly side-stepped the issue by pointing the finger of blame at Empress Maude. This facet of discontentment Ardron had relayed back to Earl Robert, but although he had shown concern, so far, he had failed to address the problem. However, it was still early days and there had been hardly enough time for Robert to correct the situation.

"Right you maybe brother," Ardron said. "But not today, perhaps tomorrow."

Esmond looked at him quizzically without speaking.

"This afternoon we will be entertained by the Bagshot players."

"Bagshot players?"

"Yes, a group of travelling actors who perform plays and sketches,"

"Why do we need to be there?" Esmond asked.

Ardron took a breath and thought a moment. "I have heard that the play they currently perform is amusing, but at the same time it's politically controversial." With a shrug he said. "It might be informative in assessing the populace sympathies."

"I think that we have a pretty good idea where the majority of sympathies lay, "Esmond replied.

Ardron nodded agreement. "Nevertheless, I think we should go and have a look."

Four hours later the pair made their way into the open amphitheatre and moved as close to the front as they could get. They seated themselves on a wooden plank, which served as a bench seat. The area filled up rapidly as more and more people gathered to be entertained.

The play began with a solitary member of the players addressing the audience as he recited the prologue and set the scene. Ardron was slightly uncomfortable when the scene was set inside Maude's royal court, and he became even more uncomfortable as the play progressed.

Maude had been cast as a witch, desperately seeking the crown, which was physically passed between bishops quickly and secretly behind backs. Another actor representing Bishop Henry, proffered an endless stream of frivolous and ridiculous excuses to the empress to delay the coronation date. After each successful excuse, he would return to the gathering of bishops and be awarded a bag of coins. Often the play was interrupted by a band of sergens pointlessly marching across the stage. This pretence represented the Earl Gloucester, demonstratively parading a powerful but impotent force of arms. Another scene portrayed the empress and her husband, Geoffrey Plantagenet in a domestic scene each trying unsuccessfully to poison the other, or to plunge knives into each-others back. All through the play one actor spent the entire time ignored and imprisoned in a small animal cage, throwing out begging arms to all who passed. The obvious representation was the incarcerated King Stephen. Action behind that cage represented William de Ypres taking advantage of the king's absence to shamelessly flirt with Stephen's wife, Matilda.

When the parody ended the whole cast paraded across the stage, and their performance was enthusiastically received by the audience, who clapped, whistled and cheered. Ardron sat thoughtfully motionless. Whilst the production was undoubtedly amusing, it did hold up the new order to ridicule. But what it was that Ardron found disturbing, was that although the version was ludicrously over-exaggerated there was a fragment of truth in each facet. To a disgruntled populace, it was exactly what they wanted to see and hear. It suggested gross incompetence and could only harden opinion against the Angevin cause.

He shuffled out amongst the crowd deep in thought. Whilst the production held no real threat to Maude's position, it did foster resentment among the common people, and in an atmosphere of uncertainty and tension it might in the final analysis tip the balance. He decided not to burden Earl Robert with this trivia, but instead lay his thoughts before Fitzgilbert. In his position as Marshal, Fitzgilbert would be in position to move the Bagshot players on, and away from London if he so desired.

***

Westminster 24th June, Midsummer's Day.

Within the Royal Palace of Westminster Ardron waited impatiently outside the royal chambers. The news he had to relay was important, but still he was required to wait. Eventually, Fitzgilbert came out and gave him the nod as a warning that his audience was imminent. Ardron moved to the door to stand beside Fitzgilbert, but still they waited.

"The Archbishop will be out soon," Fitzgilbert said sensing his impatience.

Eventually Theobald la Bec, Archbishop of Canterbury, came out and after a moment's hesitation came over to where they stood. He was a man of middle years with a sallow complexion. He wore a black cassock buttoned the full length with buttons of gold. A broad red sash about his waist matched the full-length cape draped over his shoulders. He fiddled nervously with a large pectoral cross hanging from his neck on a long gold chain.

"You understand my position, don't you, Marshal?" he appealed.

"Oh I understand your position alright," Fitzgilbert replied sarcastically.

"Good, I knew you would," the archbishop replied missing the sarcasm completely. "The empress makes my position very difficult," he went on. "She is not an easy sovereign to serve."

"On the contrary, it's very simple," Fitzgilbert replied. "Do as she demands."

"Ah, would that I could," the archbishop said. "But I am bound by God's laws above those of a ruler."

"Sometime, you will have to show me exactly where it is written in the bible, that a sovereign cannot be crowned except by the permission of the previous monarch. Who by the way is usually deceased?" Fitzgilbert countered.

The Archbishop stared hard at him perhaps realising for the first time that there was no sympathy to be gained from the Marshal. "Usually deceased is right. But in this case not. Before God I swore an oath to King Stephen and I cannot break that oath without his permission."

"Which, of course, we know will never be granted, Fitzgilbert said."

"I will seek guidance from his Holiness in Rome."

"Of course," Fitzgilbert knowingly replied.

The archbishop nodded and held out his hand for Fitzgilbert to kiss the ring.

"You will excuse me your Excellency, but I have much to do before the feast begins tonight," he said ignoring the hand.

"What was that about?" Ardron asked, looking back to where the bewildered archbishop still stood.

"His latest Coronation delay excuse," Fitzgilbert said. "He has sworn fealty to Stephen; therefore, he cannot perform the Coronation service without betraying that fealty. Unless he can get permission from Stephen himself." He shook his head in bewilderment. "The excuses these bishops give to delay the Coronation sometimes beggars belief. It is almost as if they work their delays waiting for some sort of divine intervention that will change everything and restore the status back to as previous." He sighed heavily. "God forgive me, but it would have been better had Stephen not survived Lincoln."

Ardron felt a jolt in the pit of his stomach. But for his actions on that day Stephen may not have survived that battle. He bit his lip and said nothing.

Fitzgilbert pushed open the big door. "Wait here until I announce you," he said.

When admission was granted Ardron walked into the large chamber. Empress Maude, Lady of the English, sat at the head of the table. Robert Earl of Gloucester and Sir Brien Fitzcount, Lord of Wallingford were seated either side. Also seated at the table, Miles Fitzwalter, Earl of Hereford, Robert Fitzedith, Baron of Okehampton, who Ardron knew, was also another half-brother to Maude. But most astonishing to Ardron was that Geoffrey de Mandeville, Earl of Essex also rated a seat at this gathered echelon, of the Angevin cause.

Among such high-ranking nobility Ardron could not help but be a little apprehensive. "Your Imperial Majesty," he said acknowledging the empress with a bow.

The slightest of nods acknowledged his respect.

"Sir Ardron," it was Earl Robert who addressed him. "You have some important news to tell us?"

"I do, Sir." He replied feeling more comfortable addressing the earl. "I have it on reliable authority that Queen Matilda."

"Ex Queen Matilda," the empress corrected him.

Ardron acknowledged the correction and started again. "I have it on reliable authority that ex Queen Matilda, aided by William de Ypres and his Flemings, ravage the countryside to the south east. And, at this very moment advance towards London itself." The impact he expected did not happen.

Earl Robert nodded acceptance. "Well done, my Saxon friend. But you only confirm that which we already know."

Ardron realised that his news was not so important after all.

"As we speak," Robert went on. "Messengers are on their way to inform Matilda that if she dares approach London then her husband's life will be forfeit."

"And if she does advance on London?" Sir Miles posed the question.

"Then be assured Stephen will be executed," Maude decreed.

"And after that?" Sir Miles persisted.

Maude looked confused by the question.

"After that," Sir Miles went on. "She will fall on London with all her might, seeking revenge and looking to put her son Eustace on the throne."

"Then we will stand and repulse her attack," de Mandeville said.

"Where will we stand?" Miles countered. "Here, in this Palace?"

"Why not?" de Mandeville countered.

"Because it is undefendable," Sir Brien added.

"Then we should move into London and occupy the Tower," the empress said.

"What of the people of London?" Sir Miles asked.

"What of them?" Maude demanded.

"He means," Earl Robert broke in. "Will they be for us or against us? If they stand with us, then moving into the tower is a good suggestion. However, should they favour Matilda then we would find ourselves under siege in the tower and within a hostile city."

"How will they stand," Fitzedith asked.

Earl Robert shrugged and shook his head. "How will they stand?" he asked Ardron.

Ardron hesitated, he was on the spot. He knew that the empress wanted to hear that they would stand with her, but in his heart, he knew they were more likely to favour Matilda.

"Come man, speak up." Earl Robert insisted impatiently.

"I think that they will welcome Matilda," he replied quietly.

"What does he know?" de Mandeville scoffed.

"I trust his judgement," Earl Robert replied.

"Then what do we do?" Maude demanded.

"We wait," Robert replied. "We wait to see Matilda's response to the execution warning. If she holds off, then we will press on with our own plans ignoring her threat, until after the Coronation. But as a precaution, we ready ourselves for a speedy move to occupy the tower, should the need arise. Whether we do actually occupy the tower will depend on Matilda's actions, and the attitude of the London populace." He took a deep breath. "In the meantime we should go ahead with this evening's celebrations. It will be a welcome diversion."

***

The evening feast was as lavish as it was immoral. Ardron looked on disapprovingly at the massive amount of fare overfilling the long tables. And yet still more was brought forth from the kitchen in a continuous and seemingly endless conveyance. The magnitude already amassed would have fed a hundred famished and undernourished families of England for half a year, he thought. But then, he allowed, if the upper echelon of the England's aristocracy could not indulge themselves in this amount of avarice then who could?

Herb dumplings floated in bowls of vegetable broth, with still steaming bread decorating the platter. Meat terrain with chicken, beef, and pork-plaited pies were complimented by generous slices of hog roast. Hocks of mutton lay on beds of mint, while the traditional boar's heads, decorated with fruit, were placed strategically around the tables. In between these heads, artistically ornamented cock pheasants added contrast, and somehow, cooked without even singeing their vivid coloured plumage. Wine, mead and cider flowed freely, too freely, and soon became slopped around carelessly in alcohol stimulated inanity. Even when everyone had eaten more than their fill the food continued to come.

After the feast, the dancing began with an octet of musicians delivering a lively and popular selection of dance music. Ardron feeling a little out of his depth, stood back and watched, trying as he did, to evaporate into the background. Ring dances or chain dances it made no difference to him, he could do neither, nor had any inclination to try.

"You're not dancing, Sir Ardron!" a woman's voice said.

He recognised the woman at his side, "Lady Rohesa," he acknowledged. "No I don't dance," he then replied.

"Really?" she said. "When you wield a sword you do."

Ardron smiled but made no comment. Instead took the opportunity to study her closely. Her obvious beauty had impressed him on previous associations, but here at this moment she looked even more stunning than he could remember. Her captivating loveliness held his undivided attention, and it took a moment or two for him to suddenly realise that he was staring at her rudely. Recovering quickly, he sought to cover his embarrassment. "I imagine that you like to dance," he said somewhat inanely

"Yes I do, and it is my poor fortune that you don't." she replied.

His heart leapt, and for the briefest moment he thought to volunteer to give it a try, but instantly decided against it, fearing that he would only make a fool of himself. He ought to have known that she would be here.

As the wife of de Mandeville it was her duty. "I must offer my belated congratulations on your wedding of some months ago." He proffered.

"Thank you," she replied.

"Sir Geoffrey is indeed a fortunate man." He added.

"Thank you again," she said holding up her hand to show off the very broad gold wedding ring.

"Very impressive," Ardron muttered.

"I see that you still wear the de Vere ring I gave you," she said.

He held up his hand, fingers spread and fiddled with the ring nervously. "Yes, I do. How could I not, after such a generous gesture?"

"I hope it goes someway to righting the wrong I did you," she said.

"If that misjudgement makes us friend's milady, then I see it only as a very fortunate mishap for me."

"Gallantly said, sir knight," she said teasingly.

The conversation lulled a moment or two before she asked. "Tell me is it the Saxon custom to ring the church bells on the evening of midsummer?"

Ardron was confused by the question. "Church bells?" he queried.

"Yes church bells. Can you not hear them?"

"No!" he answered.

She cocked an ear. "No," she agreed. "In here the music drowns them out. "Come," she said taking his hand and leading him through a pair of open glass doors. Out on a long narrow balcony, overlooking the River Thames, away from the noises of merrymaking, the church bells of London could be clearly heard. Ardron looked down the river towards the city and shook a confused head. "This day is also the Nativity of John the Baptist. Perhaps that is what the church celebrates," he suggested.

"Look," Rohesa said pointing north towards the city. "They have fires also," she said slipping her arm inside his.

It was true, fires were scattered around in several places within the city walls. That was puzzling and a little disturbing. "Probably celebratory bonfires, he suggested though not himself convinced.

He boldly covered her hand resting on his arm with his own hand, and she made no attempt to remove it.

"Rohesa!" a voice demanded her attention. "Come." They turned to see de Mandeville standing in the doorway. "Come," he demanded again. "Quickly!"

She glanced up at Ardron, who nodded that she should comply. He watched her obediently go to her husband, and then to disappear into the hall. For a moment, de Mandeville stood staring hard at Ardron, then he too turned away and followed his wife. Ardron watched the doorway for a few moments wondering if there was any chance that she might re-appear. That was just folly he rebuked himself and shifted his gaze back towards the city. The church bells and fires were puzzling, and a little concern began to creep uncomfortably into his thoughts. After a couple of minutes, with no obvious answers, he made his way back to join the festivities.

Inside there was a subtle change in the atmosphere. The music still played, people continued to dance. The loud, fuelled by a surfeit of alcohol, continued to behave noisily but some others had changed priorities. One or two were discretely leaving the party, including de Mandeville with Rohesa. At the top end of the hall, among the nobles surrounding the empress, serious discussions were taking place. Ardron scanned around attentively looking for indicators.

"Sir Ardron Norwood," a servant addressed him. "I have been looking for you."

He glanced at the servant and placed a friendly hand on his shoulder. "You have found me," he said, while he continued to study the changing atmosphere in the room.

"Your brother waits without the hall, and would speak with you most urgently," he said.

"My brother?" He said bringing his full attention to the servant.

"Yes, Sir."

"Then lead the way."

Just outside the door he found Esmond waiting shuffling his feet impatiently as he approached. Curiously, however, Luc, his castle constable, was standing alongside.

"What are you doing here? Why aren't you at Norwood?" Ardron demanded of Luc.

Luc only waved impatiently towards Esmond, indicating that his news was the priority.

"The people of London are on the rampage." Esmond blurted out. "They gather in hordes and incited by a few are rioting. They prepare to march on Westminster."

"They wouldn't dare," Ardron muttered.

"They would and they are. It is said that by tomorrow Matilda, at the head of an army led by de Ypres, will be in London and the people have already opened the gates to welcome her."

Ardron was astonished. "The rioting must be put down and the gates closed," he said.

"Put down," Esmond said. "You don't understand it's the whole populace. Two thousand, three, maybe four thousand. Even women wield makeshift weapons."

Ardron was in a dilemma. He still owed allegiance to Earl Robert. "It is my duty to stand with Earl Robert," he said. "I must report and see what he intends."

"Make way, make way," someone demanded loudly and Ardron was pushed aside as the empress surrounded by an entourage of her closest nobles, including Earl Robert, marched briskly through.

"See," Esmond exclaimed, as the entourage passed on. "Even the empress has to flee for her very life."

John Fitzgilbert brought up the rear of the entourage and Ardron stepped forward to block his path. "Sir John," he said. "What is the situation?"

"The situation would seem to be, that we are about to be overrun by London's loyal citizens," he replied disdainfully.

"What are we to do?"

"What are we to do," he paraphrased. "We withdraw to Wallingford. What else?" then he stepped round Ardron and followed the entourage

Ardron by now had grasped how grave the situation was. "Crucify me upside down," he cursed. "All my personal belongings are in our lodgings in London."

"Then you have lost them," Luc said. You can't go into London dressed like a Norman noble."

Ardron sighed heavily, Luc was right.

"What do you need? Esmond asked. "I mean what do you need that is worth risking your life for?"

He was right, Ardron agreed. "Nothing, he said dubiously. "Regrettably, I will lose my sword," he added with a shrug.

"I grabbed that before I came," Esmond said.

"You did?" Ardron was pleasantly surprised. "Then let us get to our horses and leave this place."

"Where are we bound?" Esmond asked.

"Wallingford Castle of course," Ardron said.

"Perhaps you will want to go on much further," Luc said. "I left Norwood to deliver sad news." He paused a moment choosing his words. "Regretfully, I have to tell you that your father, Wolfstan, has died."

Ardron was stunned. "How? When?"

"It seems that he was struck down by some malaise which left him virtually paralysed and unable to speak." Luc replied. "He died three days after that. The when? Probably nine or ten days since."

The news was devastating to Ardron, he had thought there were still decades of life in his father.

"Come," Esmond demanded urgently and jolted him from his shock. "There will be time to mourn once clear of London."

They rode west at an easy canter until they reached the West Gate and the bridge over the river Brent. Then about eight miles from London they allowed the horses to slow to a walk. It was getting late and with Wallingford still more than twenty miles away they decided to stop and continue in the morning. But it seemed all the inns along the road had no rooms available. Even stable areas had been let as shelter, such was the exodus of the Angevins from London. But it was a fine summer evening and the trio decided to rough camp on the banks of the river.

The mood was sombre. To Ardron the news and the events were a double dose of cruel adversity.

By this time, his father's funeral would have taken place, and he felt an enormous amount of guilt that he had not even been in attendance. Redwald, his brother, would now be appointed Thegn of Scorrenstone, and perhaps his swearing in ceremony had already taken place also. If so, he had missed that too.

"What will happen now?" Esmond asked quietly breaking the silence. Both men stared at him without replying. "I mean about Empress Maude's Coronation."

"Simple. There will not be one." Ardron testily replied.

It was true, Maude's Coronation was as far away as it had ever been. She could not for the foreseeable future return to London, therefore, could not be anointed queen. But even more depressing to Ardron was that a war that had seemingly ended was now about to re-erupt and prolong the hardships and misery of the ordinary people as it did. He laid a large portion of the blame for that at the feet of reneging bishops. If they had performed the Coronation half as speedily as they had for Stephen, then Maude would now be queen. All the defaulters would have had to fall in line and accept her as monarch. His thoughts turned next to King Stephen imprisoned at Bristol castle. Would Maude really carry out her threat and execute him? If she did then for certain Queen Matilda would attempt to have Stephen's son, Eustace, crowned King of England as a natural progression. Tomorrow, Matilda would be welcomed into London, and in the ideal position to pursue that path, if necessary. Ardron then realised that at this time the only way Maude could stop Eustace's elevation to king was to keep Stephen alive. Therefore, she could not execute Stephen. The depressing consequences were that the bitter conflict would protract on and on, with no foreseeable conclusion, and with the promise only of more widespread anarchy.

Dispirited and dejected, he felt that he needed to escape from the hostilities and the treacherous double dealing of self-promoting zealots. Under the circumstances, he decided, that Earl Robert would have to forgive him temporary desertion to attend to personal matters.

"We don't go to Wallingford tomorrow," he announced. "Instead we travel to Scorrenstone."

Chapter 11

Winchester. July 1141

On this last day of July, the sky was blue, and the absence of a breeze promised a day that would be equally as hot as it had been yesterday. The column of around a thousand men snaked in ragged lines along the winding road for the better part of half-a-mile. At its head, Empress Maude rode sandwiched between Robert Earl of Gloucester and Brien Fitzcount. Just behind, held aloft, her standard of white and grey over-stamped with the red heraldic lion, hung limp in the still morning. Without warning the flag bearer suddenly broke rank and galloped a little way ahead yelling, 'God save the Lady of the English,' as he tried to flutter her flag into life. He then pulled over to the side of the road allowing the column head once more to catch up. Maude half smiled and nodded brief appreciation at the man's enthusiasm.

Ardron's position in the column was a little way back towards the middle. This day his mount was an unfurnished and somewhat fractious grey filly. She was a Rattlebone offspring, who had a huge frame into which she would eventually grow. Rattlebone, he had left behind at Scorrenstone to perform more stallion duties for the village benefit. Leaning back in the saddle he took a look behind. Seemingly growing smaller with each stride, the town of Andover was gradually disappearing into the distance. Sometime around mid-afternoon, he estimated, they would reach their destination of Winchester. The events that would then follow were uncertain and entirely in the hands of Earl Robert's battle skills and the divinity. He glanced round at his own small compliment of sergens that was his contribution to the force. The faces were impassive each man, no doubt, quietly considering the potential dangers of the coming battle. Only Jarcot seemed unconcerned as he sang a bawdy ditty about a less than virtuous miller's daughter. Ardron smiled inwardly, wondering if he really was as nonchalant as he seemed.

After the debacle that was the retreat from London Ardron had returned to Scorrenstone. Although the visit was underlined with sadness at his father's passing it had, nevertheless, been an agreeable interlude. A much-needed respite away from the tribulations of the civil war. He had delayed more than a week before his conscience demanded his return to Norwood. Redwald, now Thegne, had asked him to turn his back on the Norman war and stay in the village to become his main aide. But Ardron's pledge of fealty to Earl Robert bound him to that duty. However, he had recommended that Esmond take up that role, pointing out that the youngest brother was now proficient in the French language, and that his experience as deputy castellan made him highly suitable. Those arrangements in place, he returned to Norwood, feeling the ache of leaving Esmond behind. Over the past months Esmond had made himself an invaluable aide.

Soon after his return to Norwood he received a 'call to arms' from Earl Robert, and that he was to report to the assembly at Oxford Castle. There he learned that immediately on the arrival of Queen Matilda and William de Ypres in London, Bishop Henry had on that very same day, recanted his vow of fealty to Maude, and swore the same to Matilda. Then wishing to recover his episcopal wealth of Winchester, Henry had personally led a force laying siege to Maude's garrisoned sergens in Winchester Castle. Not only outraged by the man's appalling treachery, but also not prepared to lose control of Winchester, Earl Robert had immediately assembled a force and now marched to relieve the siege.

At the village of Wherwell the column was halted to rest and water the horses. Ardron took the opportunity to wander away from the main body towards the Abbey and the Priory where he had sheltered, from the inclement weather, on his first visit to Winchester. Half hidden amongst the trees alongside the river Test, the scene appeared absurdly pacifistic untouched by civil war. Taking a few quiet moments, he settled down on the riverbank to enjoy the tranquillity. Absent-mindedly he tossed stones into the slow-flowing river and watched the ripples spread.

"Have a care that you don't wake the cockatrice." Benet said and settled down at his side.

"The cockatrice?" Ardron queried after recovering from his surprise.

"Aye the cockatrice." He stared at Ardron. "You don't know about the cockatrice" he asked.

Ardron shook his head.

"Well well! It's a creature of Saxon legend. Are you sure that you haven't heard of it?"

"Never!"

"Here is I, a Norman, telling a Saxon about a Saxon legend." Benet took a breath. "Supposedly it is a serpent with two legs and the head of a cockerel. Legend is that it supposedly dwells in the rivers around these parts." He paused a moment.

> "I'll dispersing wind of misery,
> A cockatrice thou has hatched unto the world,
> Whose unavoided eye is murderous."

He recited with a grin. "To look a cockatrice in the eye means certain death. Supposedly!"

"Then I had better not toss any more stones in the river," Ardron replied.

"Not if you believe it," Benet said with a laugh.

***

It was, in fact, early evening by the time they reached Winchester. On learning that the Angevin force was closing in the bishop's men abandoned the siege of Winchester Castle and took refuge in the Bishop's Citadel of Wolvesey. In effect the siege-force were now themselves the besieged.

The empress rode through the castle gates to boisterous cheering from the relieved sergens within. The Castellan, William Pont du l'Arche, flustered around the empress leading her and two of her maids into the keep, presumably to prepared quarters. Earl Robert meanwhile lost no time in arranging a war counsel while the rank and file, including Ardron, hung around both inside and outside the bailey awaiting developments. Less than an hour later it was Fitzgilbert that emerged, and he signalled to Ardron that he should accompany him. Under a white flag Fitzgilbert led Ardron and his small compliment of sergens right up to the main gates of the citadel and waited.

Eventually, the Wolvesey Castellan joined the small band of men standing on the ramparts above the closed gate.

"Who comes here beneath a white flag?" he called down.

"And Jesus wept," Fitzgilbert muttered to Ardron. "He knows exactly who I am." He took a deep breath. "I do. John Fitzgilbert, Marshal of the horse in the court of Empress Matilda," he called back.

"What do you want, John Fitzgilbert."

"I wonder how many guesses he would need," he muttered again to Ardron. "I bring greetings and a message from Sir Robert Earl of Gloucester to be delivered to his grace Bishop Henry."

"Bishop Henry is not here. He left for London earlier this afternoon. You may deliver your message to me."

"So, the rabbit has run away." Fitzgilbert said to Ardron. "Should have been expected." He turned his attention back to the man on the ramparts. "We require that you surrender Wolvesey forthwith, and with all honour and without cost of lives. A free passage away from Winchester will be guaranteed to all."

A short discussion then took place on the ramparts before the castellan replied. "We are under obligation to stand within and to defend, with force if necessary."

"You have until after mass tomorrow morning to reconsider." Fitzgilbert replied. "I urge you to see sense and consider your position carefully. After all, if your leader won't stand with you to defend his own

246

interests, then why should you? Is such a cowardly man worth dying for?" Fitzgilbert hesitated a few moments then when no reply came, he called. "Until mass tomorrow." He then wheeled his horse to lead the withdrawal.

All the time Fitzgilbert was delivering the ultimatum Ardron had studied the citadel. Its location used the city wall as its back with the river Itchen beneath. The wall constructed of stone, possibly three feet thick, continued around the other three sides and raised some twenty-five feet giving the inmates on the wall considerable height advantage. In three corners large square towers rose an additional twenty-five feet providing further significant height advantage. Wolvesey, Ardron concluded, was intimidatingly formidable and would not be taken without considerable cost of life. He wheeled his horse and followed Fitzgilbert.

"Do you think they will surrender?" He asked.

Fitzgilbert glanced at him sceptically. "Would you?" He replied.

Ardron glanced back over his shoulder at the redoubtable fortification. There was no need to answer.

"Prepare for a long siege," Fitzgilbert went on. "Starvation or disease will be the only thing that will force them out."

As they began to move through the streets, a steady stream of townsfolk had already begun to abandon their homes. Anticipating an imminent attack, they were seeking safety further away from the Citadel. The narrow streets were heavily congested as a slow-moving tide of human privation shuffled along. Belongings and personal chattels were piled onto horses, mules and a myriad of carts, or simply humped across human shoulders. Women were not entirely excused these donkey duties, and additionally shepherded bewildered young children. Noisy bellowing cattle were driven amongst all this confusion adding considerably to the havoc.

"Make way, make way," Fitzgilbert shouted bad-temperedly. Growling and cursing he forced a gangway down the very middle of the shuffling throng. "At least," he said glancing back at Ardron. "Those empty houses will make good cover for our siege force."

Once back inside the castle Fitzgilbert lost no time making his way into the keep to make his report. Ardron meanwhile shuffled away to join his own troop. Although the Normans and Saxons were assembled in the same place there was still that division within the troop that two languages cause. First, he spoke in French to the Norman section and reported the situation, there were no comments. They were seasoned sergens and as professionals they knew what to expect. He then turned his attention to his Saxon villeins wondering, as he did, how much they had understood of his French, if anything. Questioning eyes stared at him expectantly.

"There will be a siege. Almost certainly," he said, "And just as certainly it will be a long one." He took a breath and waited for the groans to die away.

Eventually it was Bedwine who spoke. "Sir, it is a bad time for us Saxons to get involved in a long siege."

"There is never a good time for a long siege," Ardron retorted.

"Yes Sir," Beldwine persisted. "But for us Saxon villagers, August and September is harvesting time. If we don't gather in the harvest, we will have no supplies for winter food. Nor will we have the fief to donate."

"I understand your problems completely," Ardron replied with a shrug. "I too am a Saxon," he reminded him bridling his pique. "The villagers who have stayed behind will have to work a little harder to cover absences." He paused a moment. "Our immediate loyalty is to Earl Gloucester and the Empress." He said it, but as he did, he guessed with a degree of certainty, that probably these Saxon's cared not more than a turnip about the empress's ambitions. "Nevertheless," he went on, moderating his attitude a little. "I will try to arrange some relief, if the siege does protract on." Soon after that he left leaving them all to discuss the situation free from his ears.

Less than two hours later Ardron received his orders to join the siege force at the Citadel face. He lost no time in taking up the position and actually seconded three now abandoned homes fairly close to the Citadel wall. Not only did these homes provide his troop with shelter but also desirable cover. He split his force in half with one shift stood too on watch, while the other at rest but on standby. As day turned to night there was nothing left to do now except to wait for the Wolvesey inmates to capitulate or for the deadline to pass.

**

2nd August 1141

Ardron paused a moment in the narrow street, hitched the sack a little higher across his back and looked towards Wolvesey Castle. The setting sun illuminated the grey walls, while the casting of long dark shadows made for sharp contrast. From one of its towers a red and yellow flag, depicting half man half horse, fluttered insolently in the evening breeze. The Citadel defenders had run up this standard, the flag of King Stephen, yesterday in open defiance to Earl Gloucester's surrender ultimatum. Earl Robert's re-action had been to launch several arrow storms over the walls and into the bailey. This tactic he had repeated several times since, all at random. Its effectiveness, although at the onset could have been telling by this time had, in all probability, reduced considerably. The defenders would have lost no time in building many hides into which they could safely shelter. In retaliation they had launched arrow storms of their own at the attackers. But, with the houses and narrow streets providing effective cover, that had proved to be futile. Still, all this to-ing and fro-ing of arrows kept the fletcher's busy, Ardron concluded, as he turned and ducked in through the house door.

In contrast to the bright summer evening the inside was murky, and it took a few seconds for his eyes to adjust. In the corner four men passed the time in a game of chuck-a-lok, while others had draped themselves across hastily constructed bundles of animal fur and skins trying to sleep. In the middle three others huddled just staring boredly into a bubbling cauldron of broth. Dardot was first to see Ardron and acknowledged him with a lazy salute.

"Bread cakes," Ardron said as he swung the sack down on to the rough-hewn table.

"Grubs up," Dardot shouted and aimed a soft kick at the nearest sleeper.

Ardron tipped the sack spilling out the bread cakes then proceeded to divide the bread into three separate piles. "These go to the other two houses," he instructed indicating two piles.

Dardot kicked again at the sleeper this time getting a response as a bleary-eyed Fique sat up looking somewhat confused. "Get yourself on your feet," he said. "Take those breads to the other two houses," he went on pointing at the piles on the table.

Fique rubbed his eyes and looked somewhat bewildered as he mentally grappled with the instruction. Eventually the instructions made its way through his cerebral fog and he got to his feet. By this time Ardron had put the two piles back and held out the sack. "Watch out for arrows. Keep close to walls for cover," he advised as Fique took the sack.

With the prospect of food relieving the boredom the room began to stir and men shuffled towards the bubbling cauldron. After giving the broth a vigorous stir Dardot began slopping it into wooden bowls and handing out. Each man helped himself to a bread cake and shuffled off to a convenient corner to eat. Conversation was all-but non-existent as each man concentrated more on his bowl of broth.

"What news?" Dardot asked as he offered Ardron a bowl of broth.

Ardron shook his head impassively. "No change." he muttered as he took the bowl. Nor was there likely to be for many long days, he added in thought only.

Dardot's reaction, a simple shrug. The reply had been that which he had expected. "I suppose there are worse places than Winchester to spend the summer," he muttered mostly to himself. Picking up a bread cake he broke it in half and took huge bite. Within seconds he had spit it out and with a deal of venom. "Then again," he said. "If this is a sample of the local food then perhaps not."

"What's wrong with it?" asked Ardron has he sniffed the bread.

"Break it open and take a bite out of the middle."

He broke the bread open but had no need to take a bite, he could easily see that the middle was nothing more than wet dough. It had not been thoroughly baked. The probability was that the demand was such that the bread did not spend enough time in the ovens to ensure it was baked right through. Ardron said nothing but shuffled away to find himself space to settle. Choosing a place close behind the door he unhooked the baldric and allowed it, and his sword to slip from his back. After laying it down carefully he settled with his back resting against the wall and legs outstretched. Then picking up the bowl he took a sip of broth before glancing around the silent room. The atmosphere was as muted as a scolded congregation under a priest's Sunday sermon tongue lashing. Each man seemingly lost in private thoughts making the most of the modest fare. Ardron sighed quietly. Morale was not high, and at this very early stage a little unsettling since there would be many siege weeks to come. He sipped the broth and picked fastidiously at the edges of the bread cake, ignoring its unbaked centre. Soon giving in, he laid the bowl and bread aside and rubbed at tired eyes. Being a Saxon of village stock himself, he could easily sympathise with the concerns of the Saxon element in his force. The annual harvest was imminent, and it was personally of much more importance to them than the empress's aspirations.

He leaned back and closed his eyes allowing his thoughts to stray to Scorrenstone. It had been a hot summer and he imagined that the crops in the village fields would be at an advanced stage, almost ready for the harvest. He allowed himself to sink into sleep and dreamed of happier days before the struggle for England's crown had begun.

His sleep was fitful in wild nonsensical confusion, beginning with pastoral calm of lazy village days, then progressing into macabre complications. The community food store was completely empty, and all hands toiled mightily to see it re-stocked. However, it mattered not how hard they worked the barn remained empty. The situation became fraught when the fief was demanded but there was nothing to pay with. In retaliation, and from simple malice, the Norman collection party then set fire to the store. Standing in the middle attempting to fight the fire, the steadily increasing smoke rasped Ardron's throat and stung his eyes, but he could not, would not, give in.

"Sir," someone demanded shaking his shoulder. Ardron opened his eyes with a start and stared up at Beldwine. "Sir, we must go. We cannot stay," he insisted.

Struggling to control his befuddled brain, Ardron stared up questioningly at the Saxon. "What?" he muttered bad-humouredly. But all around the room men were on their feet and hastily gathering their belongings.

"Sir, there is fire. We must go." Beldwine said.

"Fire?" Ardron repeated inanely associating it to his dream.

"Yes Sir, fire all around and spreading quickly." Ardron snapped alert and jumped to his feet. "Come Sir, see."

Ardron grabbed his sword and baldric, then followed Beldwine outside. Thick smoke eddied lazily down the narrow streets and drifted upwards into the sky forming columns of grey, before disappearing into the black of the night sky. Flames there were, many naked flames burning fiercely. Great tongues of fire leapt into the sky as blazing buildings collapsed noisily in showers of sparks. The straw roofs of the houses provided the perfect fuel for an inferno. A quick look round revealed the fires were well spread with some in infancy and some well aflame, the obvious danger was to become surrounded and then entrapped. An arrow thudded a mere couple of yards away. On the hard-packed ground, that was the street, it failed to stick. Instead it skidded along the ground and then it lay there with the cotton wadding wrapped around its shank burning intensely. Momentarily struggling to understand Ardron glanced towards the sky from whence it came. Two more arrows, trailing sparks and flame in the night sky, arced over the town to descend somewhere amongst the houses. Flaming arrows were being launched from within Wolvesey Castle. It made sense to Ardron, absolute sense! Burning the houses close to the castle would push the siege force back from beneath its walls. It would also eradicate the buildings that had provided obliging cover. The castellan had also chosen the moment well. The fresh wind that blew across Winchester blew away from the castle and carried the flames towards the town. Ardron realised immediately that there was no point trying to fight the fires here. The castle archers could ignite fires at a rate much faster than they could possibly hope to put out.

"Pull back," he shouted his instructions. "Pull back out of arrow range." That would, he decided, be the point to fight the fires."

At a spot around three-hundred yards he paused. An archer with a strong arm and a good bow could reach this point but, Ardron estimated, he probably would not bother. With many fires burning fiercely and a fresh wind blowing it would spread onwards quickly enough. "This will do for now." He said it but at this moment he had no idea what they should do next.

He looked back towards the castle. Tongues of leaping flames bit into the orange glow that was the sky. Wisps of burning debris drifted on the wind. Dry timbers cracked noisily, devoured readily by the flames that quickly turned it into blackened char. The houses bunched in narrow streets, were as grist to the mill to rampant flames, as it leapt the narrow spaces unchecked. Desperation and chaos were endemic, without the slightest resemblance of strategy. People either fled in undignified haste away from the flames or ran towards it on some madcap idea of rescue or salvage. Those whose homes were not yet burning, either hastily gathered belongings to join the exodus, or made preparation to protect their homes. Those that chose to stay, worked in small groups trying to damp down their own houses using foul water from the gutters. But the gutters were not deep, and the water scooped amounted to a mere slop in a bucket.

"What now?" Jarcot asked.

Ardron looked to his men, a mere handful and several not with them. He could only hope that those missing had the good sense to escape the burning area. Hope was all he could do for he was not about to return into the inferno to seek men who might or might not be in there.

"What now indeed," he replied at something of a loss. "We help wherever we can," he answered with a shrug.

"We should knock down rows of these houses to form a fire break," Dardot suggested.

"Oh yes," Jarcot almost sneered. "Do you think these people will stand by while we do that?" he said nodding towards people frantically dowsing their homes with water.

Ardron silently agreed with Jarcot. Even if the houses were knocked down, the debris would still remain and be tinder for the fire. There was not enough time to clear it all away.

"We help people save their homes where we can," he said nodding towards the desperate house owners. "When it becomes hopeless, then we retreat further back and start again." It was a vague instruction, much more akin to a suggestion, but at the time the best he could do.

"You heard him," Jarcot came to his support. "Find someone to help and get on with it," he barked.

Stung by Jarcot's rebuke, the men reacted and moved away, but not clearly directed, did so with a degree of confusion.

"When this is over, we will re-group in the Cathedral grounds," Ardron called after them.

"If indeed the Cathedral survives," Dardot muttered.

He had a point, but Ardron made no comment. "Water, we must find water," he said instead.

"Over there," Jarcot shouted and indicated a man a few yards away frantically working a water pump.

"Yes," Ardron agreed.

At the pump while one man pumped furiously people fought each other to fill their containers. Pushing and shoving they grappled to thrust their buckets under the gushing water. The result was that more water was being lost than saved.

"Stop," Ardron shouted but to no avail. He indicated to Jarcot and Dardot that they should move in with drawn swords to affect some order.

The two men moved forward swords in one hand and grabbing collars with the other, they unceremoniously hauled people away. "Form an orderly queue," Ardron ordered now that he had their attention. Then more sympathetically added "It will be quicker."

For a few moments, the people stood back intimidated and not sure what was happening. Then almost as one they reacted rushing forward quickly to get towards the queue front. Despite much pushing some sort of queue was established. and a semblance of order was achieved. Even so, Ardron could see that the improvement was practically negligible and would have very little effect on checking the advancing flames. Each man when his bucket was full of water ran off to a different place, intent only on protecting his own particular dwelling, and understandably so. He looked back towards the fire, it was advancing quickly. and it would be upon them within perhaps thirty minutes or less. Ideally it was a row of houses along the front of the fire's path that needed to be dowsed down. But amongst all this panic he was powerless to direct the people to abandon their own personal interests and work for the good of all.

"It's not going to work," he muttered to Jarcot.

"No," Jarcot agreed. "Perhaps we should look to ourselves and abandon Winchester to its fate," he added gloomily.

His comment did have merit, but still he was reluctant to accept it. He let out a heavy sigh through puffed cheeks, "We'll stay here for now and maintain order at the pump," he said. The three of them stood sentry at the pump ensuring that the situation did not go back to the free-for-all, while they watched the blaze relentlessly getting nearer.

A few minutes later, Fitzgilbert appeared at the head of a couple of dozen sergens. "Ah Scorrenstone," he said when he saw Ardron. "What are you doing?"

"We are making sure the water flows from this pump without letting it degenerate into the mass brawl that it was," he replied. There was no response from Fitzgilbert. Ardron wasn't even sure that he had even heard him. Instead the man, lost in his own thoughts, stared ponderously towards the roaring flames.

"Do you have a plan?" he asked not turning his attention away from inferno.

Ardron shook his head. "No, Sir John. I do not."

Fitzgilbert turned his attention away from the fire and stared at him quizzically..

"Other than to stay here and continue to supervise the use of this pump," he added in response to Fitzgilbert's gaze.

The Norman nodded slightly, then turned and looked once again towards the approaching fire. "Were you in there?" he asked.

"We were."

"But you got out! And all your men, did they get out too?"

"Ardron gave a shrug. "I can't be sure, but I hope so.""

"Anybody trapped in the middle of that__ well." Fitzgilbert didn't finish. He had no need to. After a moment's pause, he snapped from his contemplative mood into the effectual character that had made him a Royal Marshal. "We are moving to the river," he said decisively, "We'll use the water to try to cut across the fire from the side."

Ardron nodded. It was as good a plan as any. "Good luck, Sir John," he said.

"Aye we'll need it. Do you want to join us?" he replied.

"Er, no," Ardron said after a moment's thought. "I think we might serve better staying here."

"Mayhap," Fitzgilbert said. "God's mercy be with us all." He went on placing his hand on Ardron's shoulder. "We'll all need it tonight."

"We will," Ardron agreed.

The ranks of the fire-fighters swelled rapidly as the townsfolk began to mass and rally round against the common peril. It was in nobody's interest that the fire be allowed to engulf the whole of Winchester. Problems were many, and not least getting water to the flames. Nothing was spared, all fluids were fair game, including publican's stocks of ale and the dyers barrels of urine. Mostly, however, the flames were fought with shovels and wet cloths, attempting to beat the flames into submission, or soil thrown at the fire in smothering attempts. But the fires, burning intensely, continued to devour all before it, overcoming the fire-fighters puny attempts. Working in small independent groups without any co-ordination they were continually forced back giving way reluctantly to the flame's avarice. Resolutely determined, they fell back a few yards to reform and start the struggle over again. A defence line of sorts was eventually achieved, all-be-it a crooked and ragged one. Even then the outcome hung in the balance for a time as the flames reached out to the unburned buildings. Hardly discernible at first, the fires advance was slowed, then eventually arrested. The fire-fighters began to inch forward slowly snuffing out the flames and started to edge into the smouldering and scorched area.

At the pump, the water being lifted from the depths began to slow considerably until each push of the handle coughed only meagre amounts. Ardron decided that staying on at this pump to supervise water distribution no longer performed any purpose. Reluctantly, he decided that they should find an alternative task. He glanced at Dardot and shook his head. "Leave it," he said softly.

Dardot nodded acknowledgement. "OK. What now?" he asked with a sigh.

"What now," Ardron paraphrased with a shrug. "We join Fitzgilbert down by the river." It was more a suggestion than any positive order.

"Look there," Jarcot said pointing towards the fire. Several yards away a man and a woman struggled to stifle the burning roof of their house. The man, atop a ladder, wobbled perilously as he continually over-reached trying to beat the flames into submission with a wet cloth. His wife at the bottom of the ladder struggled to keep the ladder steady.

Although the flames burned intensely, the fire was still in its infancy, and there was a chance the fire could be controlled. However, the roof was, as most Winchester houses were, dry straw and it wouldn't take long for the fire to take an uncontainable hold. Quick action was needed.

Ardron said nothing, he had no need. Instead he led the rush to their assistance. Within seconds he had himself taken the man's position at the ladder top. Using a wide hay-rake he reached across the roof and broke away bundles of blazing straw, tossing them behind him to the ground. Dardot and Jarcot immediately pounced on the bundles beating the flames to submission with shovels. But the flames in the straw roof spread rapidly, running before Ardron and from his position all he could do was chase. He needed to get ahead of the flames, which would mean surrendering at least half of the roof to its fate. Nevertheless, half of a roof was a better price to pay than a whole roof and probably the whole house too. He slid down the ladder and tried to move it, but the man held it firm, and even tried to go back up the ladder himself. Handicapped with the hay-rake in one hand he tried one-handed to wrestle the ladder away from the man.

"No no," the man pleaded holding on tenaciously supposing Ardron had given in.

There was no time for Ardron to explain his intentions. "Let go," he demanded but the man was determined not to lose the ladder. "Damn you," Ardron cursed. "Get him off me," he appealed to Dardot.

For a moment Dardot looked bemused but then decided that Ardron knew what he was doing and moved to help. He threw an arm around the man's neck and unceremoniously dragged him away before swinging him roughly to the floor.

Ardron moved the ladder further along the side of the house to a point that he judged to be ten or twelve feet ahead of the fire. Atop the ladder he worked furiously hauling unburned straw off the roof. The cracking of newly ignited straw warned him that the flames were getting closer, however, it was the increasing heat that concerned him more, causing him to double his efforts. Eventually, as the fire neared, the heat became intense and he was forced to give way. He had managed to establish a narrow firebreak and as he came down the ladder, he hoped it would be enough.

When the first chinks of light began to dawn in the eastern sky the flames were close to being under control. As the light strengthened, it revealed scenes of utter devastation. Where there had been myriads of bucolic dwellings only hours before, now only leaning props of charred wood, standing on a bed of blackened ash remained. Sporadic fires still flickered in places but gone was the intensity replaced by slow smouldering and seemingly apologetic flames. Not quite all had been consumed by the inferno, hither and thither, and by some divine miracle, parts of dwellings had survived. A wall, part of a wall, or a building corner still stood defiant but ravaged and covered with soot. From the embers, grey black smoke floated and drifted away skywards on what was, by now, a gentle morning breeze. There was no doubting, however, that the fire had achieved the desired intention. The whole area of the castle approaches had been levelled. No doubt the castellan was well pleased by the night's work.

Ardron glanced at Jarcot and Dardot their faces, blackened by soot and smoke, betrayed their exhaustion. It had been a gruelling night with no respite. Using his sleeve, he wiped away a rivulet a sweat. The acrid smell of smoke upon his clothing was strong enough to taste. He sat down next to the pair, his back resting against the town stocks.

"At least we managed to save this," Dardot said sardonically, as he patted the top stave of the stocks, but his dry humour received no response.

For the next few moments, the three sat in silence. Ardron wondered about the other members of his small contingency. How many, if any, were injured. Indeed, how many, if any, had not survived. The arrangements were to re-assemble in the cathedral grounds and he suddenly became anxious to find out. To the north-west, elevated above the modest dwellings, he could see the cathedral's short square tower untouched by the fire.

"We should make our way to the cathedral," he said.

"Aye we should," Dardot agreed, but it was Jarcot who made the first move hauling himself tiredly to his feet.

They arrived at the cathedral to find around half of the Norwood contingency already there. After tired greetings were passed, they settled down amongst the ruins of the Old Saxon Minster to wait. Some talked excitedly, exchanging experiences of the nights exploits but most were content to sprawl across the old tombstones and doze. Over the next hour the number gradually increased until only three were missing. However, these particular three had been seen and so were reported as safe, therefore, it only remained to wait. With each new arrival Ardron's spirit's had been lifted, and now it seemed that there were to be no serious casualties. He was now able to relax, contentedly he settled down.

"How could someone be so callous," Beldwine complained angrily. "Those people have lost everything. Their homes, their lively-hood and probably some of them, their lives." He went on addressing no one in-particular but addressing all. "Henry Blois, a bishop? A man of God? And he did that to his people." He waved his arm in the direction of the fire ravaged area. "Those people are his congregation." He added with incredulity. "For Christ sake," he spat an angry curse.

Ardron seated with his back resting against an ancient weathered shrine looked up at the angry Saxon. "Beldwine," he said quietly. "The bishop is not in the castle. He is probably in London by now."

Momentarily stung by the revelation, Beldwine soon recovered. "Some God-awful bastard is responsible! Whoever that be, should be hung, drawn and quartered." Then feeling even that punishment would be inadequate, "twice!" he added, which caused a few sniggers.

"Be calm Beldwine," Ardron said quietly, understanding the Saxon's extreme pique. He was just too tired to explain the shrewd strategy in the castellan's actions. The humane cost to the common people would not have entered into his reckoning at all. In this bitter struggle for the English crown the ordinary masses just did not matter. Beldwine stared at him a moment then turned and silently shuffled away but spitting in disgust as he did.

By this time, the sun had cleared the horizon shortening the long shadows and giving the promise of another warm day. Ardron wondered how much longer he should wait for the missing men to arrive. But it was not unpleasant resting here, everybody was tired. They deserved a rest. He decided therefore, he would wait for as long as it took. He closed his eyes and allowed a shallow sleep to pass over him. The drone of voices faded into the background and, although he could hear all being said, he allowed his sub-consciousness to ignore it. It was mere minutes only when an angry voice cut through his doze, startling him awake.

"You should not be here," the angry voice demanded. "Who is in charge?"

"I am," Ardron said getting groggily to his feet.

"An angry monk turned his attention to Ardron. "This is a sacred place. Get your men away from here."

Ardron glanced around at the scattered ruins of the old minister and an ancient graveyard that looked in desperate need of attention. "What's sacred about this place?" he asked.

Surprise registered across the monk's face. "There, right there," he said in a raised voice and pointed at the weathered shrine where, only seconds before, Ardron had used as a prop for his back. "That is the original grave of St Swithun."

The sandstone shrine he pointed at had not stood the elements too well. Any script carved in the stone had long since faded to unreadable. Ardron was puzzled. "Original grave?" he queried.

"Yes, original grave."

"There is more than one?"

The monk was exasperated. "No. St Swithun's mortal remains are resting beneath the altar in the cathedral."

"Then what is sacred about this place?"

"Sighing heavily the monk glared at Ardron. "This was the Saint's first resting place. When his remains were moved from here, he was so angry that he caused it to rain for forty days."

"Perhaps we should have dug the old man up last night. We could have done with some." Dardot mocked.

The monk glared at Dardot. "Show some respect you vulgar hog," he spat angrily.

"Am I correct in believing that this is just an empty grave?" Ardron asked.

"Yes, yes. Now get this rabble away from here," the annoyed reply.

"Look at this rabble," Ardron replied coldly. They are exhausted because they spent the night fighting the fires. During the whole time I did not see you, or any of your kind, lending a hand."

"We made prayer to the almighty!" the monk indignantly replied.

"Of course you did." Ardron almost sneered. "Much easier than fighting blazing fires." He eyed the monk coldly. "Well brother monk, since St Swithun's remains are not in that grave, then I don't see this as a sacred site. But be assured that we will move on. However, it will not be until I am satisfied that my men are rested enough. Now putting it politely! Go forth," he raised an arm towards the cathedral, "and piss as you go."

The monk expression showed his outrage. "The Abbot shall hear of this," he spluttered.

***

Mid-August 1141

Cautiously, Ardron emerged from the thick copse and looked down to the River Itchen in the bottom of the shallow valley. Over the river, the small hamlet of Abbas nestled on the northern side. A modest Norman built church presided over a small collection of humble Saxon dwellings. Even though he was expecting to see it, the scene just west of the village horrified Ardron. The army of Stephen's queen, Matilda, with its supreme commander William de Ypres had bivouacked in the meadow. The hour was still early, but not so early that an army on the march wouldn't be up and about preparing to move. However, although there was some activity it appeared almost casual, as those that were about, tended menial chores.

Two days ago, there had been reports that a substantial army had already left London and was advancing on Winchester. Last night, however, the latest reports were that Matilda's army was now camped only five miles to the north east of the city. Those reports had also estimated the army to be around five-thousand strong. That was alarming!

This morning, before the sun had risen, Ardron had set off to judge for himself the accuracy of that estimate. Although he was not encouraged by what he now saw, and even though there was probably less than a quarter of the entire strength visible, he concluded that it was an exaggeration. He made a wild calculation that the number was probably a little over two thousand. But even that number would give de Ypres's force superiority in numbers.

The grey filly beneath him gave out a loud whinny and pranced restlessly. "Quieten down girl," he demanded squeezing his legs tight around the horse's ribs to keep control. When she had settled, he looked around nervously to see if his location had been compromised. Two-hundred yards away he saw the reason for her restlessness. Another small band of around ten horsemen had emerged from the copse, and also surveyed the riverside scene. At the head he recognised Robert Earl Gloucester, Brien Fitzcount and Reginald de Dunstanville Earl Cornwall. It would seem that like him they too had come to assess the threat for themselves.

He turned his attention back to the scene below and judged by the unhurried behaviour that, for today at least, this army was not about to advance on Winchester. However, that was, doubtlessly, only a temporary situation and an attack would for certes come and come soon. What would Earl Robert's strategy be he wondered? Perhaps he would try and defend the city from within its walls. But that would be difficult. The walls were long and the Angevin force would be stretched very thin to cover its entire length. Then there was, of course, Wolvesey Castle still in the hands of Bishop Henry's forces. That was virtually an open gate into Winchester for any attackers. Perhaps Gloucester would abandon the city to its fate and withdraw into Winchester Castle. In effect that would place the Angevins under siege with the enemy under the castle walls. Would Earl Robert then be obliged to burn the houses just as the Wolvesey castellan had? Neither alternative seemed to be a choice plan.

Ardron then surmised that, despite being outnumbered, it was probable that Earl Robert would, at some point, have to leave the city boundaries and enter into open battle, just as King Stephen had done at Lincoln. And well he knew how that had ended! Whatever alternative Robert chose it was not a future to look forward to. He thought to ride across to the other party to proffer his respects but then decided not. They were deeply engrossed and with a great deal to discuss. Instead he wheeled his horse's head and made his way back the way he had come.

Less than half-an-hour later he rode into the Norwood contingency camp located just outside the city wall. For the most part his men were up and about. Expectant questioning faces stared at him as he rode in. Wordlessly, he rode past into the horse pound and dismounted. A young Saxon posted on groom duties approached and took the filly's reins.

"See that she is well fed and groomed," Ardron instructed, patting the horse's neck affectionately. Then for good measure he slapped her on the rump as she was led away. He watched her go for a moment before turning and making his way back into the heart of the camp.

Someone thrust a bread cake in his hand as he settled into a vacant slot around the campfire.

"The news is bad, isn't it? Dardot suggested.

Ardron pulled a wry face. "Could be a lot worse," he replied taking a mug of ale that was being handed to him. He looked around at the anxious faces, some sitting most standing, and estimated that the whole compliment was there. And why wouldn't they be? The news meant a life and death situation.

He took a deep breath. "De Ypres's army is camped five miles away at Abbas," he confirmed. He looked for reactions. The faces all stared back impassively without comment, no-one was surprised. "The good news is that their strength has been greatly exaggerated." He paused a moment. "I can say with certainty that they have nothing like five thousand men at arms." In all probability that was true, but the truth was that he could not actually be certain. "They showed no signs of breaking camp, so I don't expect de Ypres to march on Winchester today" he added. "However, tomorrow might be different." He took a pull on the mug of ale. "So," he went on. "Today we must break camp and move to within the city walls." He waited a few moments for reactions. Getting none, he repeated it all in English for the benefit of those Saxon's who did not speak French.

Soon after the men had finished breakfast, they began to pull down their camp. "Where do you suggest we re-site the camp?" Jarcot asked.

It was a question that Ardron had considered on his way back from Abbas. He knew that Earl Robert had evicted the monks from the cathedral offices and had made it his command centre. The cathedral grounds, he decided, would be a good place to be. Being close to the nerve centre might have some advantages and not least being in position to see and hear developments as they occurred.

"I think we should set up camp in the corner of the cathedral grounds," he replied.

Jarcot half flinched and stared back with amused surprise. "What about that furious monk?"

"Since Earl Robert took over the cathedral offices, that furious monk has become irrelevant, and so to a lesser extent, has his Abbot," he replied.

260

By early evening they had established themselves in the south-east corner of the grounds looking across the scorched earth towards Wolvesey Castle. It seemed that Ardron's notion would turn out to be a good one, because in that very afternoon he was in position to witness the deployment of messengers. Four riders were despatched to seek armed support from Miles Fitzwalter of Gloucester, Geoffrey de Mandeville of Essex, Ranulf Earl of Chester and Aubrey de Vere Earl of Oxford. Ardron watched the riders leave estimating, optimistically, that if each of them turned up with only two hundred-and-fifty men at arms then the Angevins would at least have parity with Matilda's royalist army. That night he retired to his bed with much improved hopes.

Early the next morning he was awakened by Dardot. "Sir," he said. "Somethings afoot."

Still sleepy Ardron rolled off his bunk and rubbed at tired eyes. "What's happening?" he mumbled

"De Ypres deploys his forces across the northern city walls."

That was as expected, Ardron thought, reaching for his boots. Glancing through the tent doorway he could see by the half-light that a new day had barely begun. "Roust the men," he instructed as he began cross gartering his laces. Dardot nodded and left to do his bidding. He paused a moment thoughtfully staring after the veteran. He doubted that de Ypres would launch straight into an attack. There would, he guessed, be blustering, threats and negotiations first. He reached for the pitcher of water at his bedside and lifting the clay pot to his mouth took a long drink, then leaned forward thinking of the possible day's events. Then with head bowed, he poured the rest of the water over the back of his head. He shook vigorously to clear the water surplus, and now felt much more alert. Still not certain whether or not an attack was imminent, he decided to pull on his hauberk just in case. After that he drew his sword from its baldric and inspected its fine edge. Satisfied all was well, he thrust the sword back and hitched the baldric over his shoulder fastening the buckle on his chest.

As he made his way to the north wall, it seemed as if the whole city was awake. Animated people bustled around, perhaps on the verge of panic, but having little idea what they should do. As he neared the wall, the bustling crowd thickened and the reason, he could see, was that the north gate was still open. People seeking sanctuary within the city walls shuffled along choking the narrow-tunnelled entrance. Despite bullying shouts from the gate guards to move quicker, they trundled forward, slowly dragging hastily gathered belongings with them. Ardron forcefully elbowed his way across the lumbering throng making his way towards the steps that led up to the walkways behind the parapets. The walkways were crowded, and not just with sergens, as many concerned civilians peered anxiously outwards. It was the first time Ardron had been on the defending end of a siege, and he wondered if these scenes of chaos were normal. He supposed they were.

Elbowing his way to the front, he looked out over the parapet and across the flat ground that fronted the city. De Ypres it seemed had split his forces. One to the north-west had taken up position straddling the Andover road and was busy getting established. Over to the north-east the larger of the two forces was already well installed along the riverbank, over-spilling across the Abbas Worthy road. Ardron paid a silent compliment to Earl Robert for getting his messengers out so speedily yesterday. All roads north were now effectively sealed. The very fact that de Ypres had split his forces led Ardron to believe that an attack was not immediately imminent. At least, not any conventional attack that he could think of! More likely he was locking the Winchester occupants in. The force to the north-west was positioned to, not only bar the road north, but also to dominate the west side of the city. The force to the north-east achieved exactly the same down the other side. That just left the road south which led down to the coast and the major port town of Hamtun twelve miles away. He could not believe de Ypres would deliberately leave the back door open, and the logic was that he wouldn't. Unless__, a thought occurred to him, he was giving the Angevin forces the opportunity to abandon the city and flee south. Ardron's decided that he ought to find out.

He descended the steps and made his way across the city. The chaos had not lessened; indeed it had increased. He eventually reached the southern wall to find its walkways were also thronged with people curious, angry or just plain nervous. He found a place along the parapet and looked out over the bucolic buildings without the town wall. Beyond he saw that which he expected. De Ypres's forces had positioned themselves across the Hamtun road, in effect cutting another possible supply line. Any thoughts that de Ypres might be inviting the Angevins to withdraw were groundless. He was bent on uncompromising conquest.

Ardron sucked through clenched teeth as he now thoughtfully pondered the situation. Laying siege to a town the size of Winchester would be so much more difficult than sieging a castle. It was bigger, and therefore, required many more men to surround its perimeter. Extended and stretched there was bound to be holes in the blockade. Small parties of four or five might steal through. But to what advantage? He questioned himself. At this time, he had no answer, but it was something worth bearing in mind as a possibility. However, on the other side of the coin, the extended length of the town wall posed exactly the same problems for the defenders. The walls could be breached by small raiding parties, and that could mean bitter hand to hand skirmishes in the streets. There were just too many questions and at this time just no answers. He descended from the wall and made his way back to the cathedral. As he walked along its front Earl

Robert and Brien Fitzcount emerged from the south transept. They strode with purpose in their step appearing to be in some haste.

"Ah, Norwood!" Earl Robert said spotting Ardron moving towards him. "Take ten of your best sergens, fully kitted, and accompany Sir Brien."

"My Lord," Ardron acknowledged although not understanding why.

"We are to meet with de Ypres under a white flag," Sir Brien said sensing his confusion.

"At once," Ardron agreed.

"Assemble here in five minutes," Earl Robert instructed.

In less than five minutes Ardron stood too with ten fully kitted sergens. All were Normans he preferred to muster professionals for this task.

"Good luck," Earl Robert said addressing Sir Brien, then stood back to allow the troop to pass.

They exited through the north gate in orderly fashion three abreast. Sir Brien in the front rank, Ardron on his right and Jarcot his left. They advanced at an unhurried casual pace across the open ground to the small contingent waiting patiently beneath a white flag. Seven or eight yards from the waiting party, Sir Brien held up his hand halting the troop. Without instructions the following sergens fanned out line abreast behind the leading trio facing de Ypres's group. In their midst William de Ypres mounted on a fine bay charger sat with an attitude of nonchalance and massive confidence. It had been almost two years, at the sacking of Malmesbury, when Ardron had last seen the man but he recognised him instantly.

"Good day to you Sir Brien," de Ypres said. A curt nod was the only reply. "I had expected that it would be Earl Robert who would come to meet me."

"Earl Robert has other important duties to attend." Sir Brien retorted. It was an intended slight, but if it rankled de Ypres, he didn't show it. Instead he silently studied the three men before him. His gaze lingered upon Ardron a little longer than the others and with a deal of curiosity.

"You Sir," he said to Ardron. "Don't I know you?"

This was not a good time for the revelation that he had stood with the king at Malmesbury albeit under pressed circumstances. Not sure what to say Ardron gave a vague shrug hoping that the question would pass

"Who are you?" de Ypres pressed.

"I am Ardron. castellan of Norwood!" It did not enlighten de Ypres, which was deliberately intended.

"Enough of these trivialities," Sir Brien cut in saving Ardron's embarrassment. "What is it you want?"

De Ypres continued to study Ardron a moment then dismissed the matter as unimportant. "What do I want? Well Lord Brien I am here on behalf of Queen Matilda to offer you terms of surrender."

"Surrender?" Sir Brien replied with mock surprise. "Then you are wasting everybody's time."

"I think not," de Ypres said leaning forward and patting his horse's neck casually. "You are at this moment locked in the city with all roads in or out of Winchester blocked. Nothing can pass without we let it."

Sir Brien shrugged. "Neither can you get in. You don't have enough of an army."

"I don't need to get in. We just stay here until either starvation or disease drives you out. There are a lot of people in there to be fed," he added with a nod towards the city. "It's only a matter of time."

"We have enough supplies to last for months." Sir Brien countered.

"Really!" de Ypres replied unconvinced. "I suspect not. A month from now, maybe six weeks, the price of a dead rat will be out of reach of all but the wealthy."

Ardron now understood why he had allowed the mass of people outside the walls to enter the city unchecked. Each one was another mouth to feed.

"Why put yourselves through all that?" De Ypres went on. "Surrender now and everyone will be spared. Sergens will be allowed to march away completely unhindered. The nobility, of course, will be expected to pay forfeit to the queen."

"Ransom you mean," Brien interrupted. "Castles land and estates all forfeit."

"Surely you would not expect treason to go completely unpunished," de Ypres replied mockingly.

"The point of where treason actually lies, is the issue upon which this war is fought."

De Ypres nodded begrudged agreement.

"And the empress?" Sir Brien asked.

"Ah yes the empress! She will of course be treated with the chivalry that her status demands. She will be allowed to return to her loving husband Geoffrey Plantagenet in Anjou, eventually."

Sir Brien paused a few moments then went onto the offensive. "Now let me offer you our terms," he said. "I advise you to break your camps and return whence you came. If you do that then I promise that we will not pursue you."

"Forgive me, Lord Brien but your bargaining position seems to be very week." De Ypres paused, "But I'm curious! If we don't what would be the consequence?"

"The consequence might be that you find yourself trapped between two armies."

"Ah yes, the messengers," de Ypres said dispassionately. He leaned back in his saddle and signalled two riders to come forward. Each turned their horses and circled the gathering. Then riding at a gallop through the space between both groups each rider emptied a sack. Two severed heads bounced along the ground. One head rolled at the feet of Ardron's horse. The filly shied violently and tried to bolt, but Ardron held her firm, fighting to control the bucking and prancing. It took a few seconds, but he did eventually restore the horse to calm.

"There are your messengers," de Ypres said studying Sir Brien. There was no doubt that the latest event had rocked Sir Brien, but he soon recovered his composure. "At least," de Ypres went on pointing at one of the heads. "That one did manage to deliver your message before he lost his head." He paused for effect, "Yes he did. He delivered it to Sir Geoffrey de Mandeville." He allowed the confusion to sink in. "Sir Geoffrey is over there," he waved his arm in the direction of the camp straddling the Abbas Worthy road. "He and his army ride with Queen Matilda."

The news must have been a body blow to Sir Brien, but if it was, he did not show it. "You have but two here. We sent out eight messengers," It was a blatant exaggeration but bluff and bluster was all that he had left. "As regards Mandeville," he went on. "Allies like him soon become a liability. It takes only a gentle breeze for that man's loyalties to bend."

"That maybe so, but his wife, as you well know, is the Lady Rohesa. That will mean Aubrey de Vere of Oxford will be reluctant to take sides in this instance. He would do nothing that might place his sister's welfare in jeopardy. So, if he is one of your anticipated allies then I fear that won't materialise either. And of course, since de Vere is Earl of Oxford, he has influence over Robert d'Orly, Oxford's castellan, I doubt that Sir Robert would wish to sour his relations with his senior." He allowed himself a smug smile. "Honestly," he went on. "At this moment, I can't think of many that might come to your aid. Baldwin de Reviers, maybe! Oh, that's right, I have just remembered he's in France. Earl Ranulf of Chester? No, he's such a self-centred man and there is absolutely nothing in this for him. His brother, William Roumare? Not a chance" He got what he wanted at Lincoln. He is satisfied. Oh, there is of course Empress Maude's uncle King David of Scotland. But I'm afraid you'll be eating your own turds before he could get here. That just leaves Miles of Gloucester. Thanks for the warning we'll watch out for him."

"We have nothing more to discuss," Sir Brien snapped. "If you think you can intimidate us then you are badly informed. "We will be standing in Winchester long after you have given up and skulked away in disarray." He signalled with a brief wave that the discussion was over and that they were returning inside the city walls.

"The offer remains open for three days only," de Ypres raised his voice as the Angevin party turned to withdraw.

Ardron glanced back as they rode at a casual pace back to the city. De Ypres's faction still held their ground watching them go. The man appeared much too confident for Ardron's comfort, and it seemed that he had good cause. He appeared to hold all the advantages.

***

September 13ᵗʰ, 1141

Ardron stood back and watched in thoughtful silence as Dardot added nettle leaves to the weak mixture that was to pass for broth. Chopped up turnips and wild horseradish consisted the basic ingredients and anything remotely edible was added.

Four weeks Winchester had been under siege, and already food shortages were acute. Despite urges from her Generals, Maude had insisted that the town's people of Winchester should continue to receive provisions. Fitzgilbert had been particularly vociferous, pointing out that if the food were restricted to the fighting force only, then the supplies would last three months and even beyond Christmas. But the empress's argument was that if the military were fed while the people starved that would breed intense resentment and lead to trouble. There was, she said, enough acrimony outside the city walls and the last thing needed was insurrection from within.

The expected re-enforcements had been a disappointment too. Miles Fitzwalter at the head of three-hundred men had arrived within ten days, but so far, he was the only responder. The remaining messenger had gone on to Ranulf Earl of Chester. But Chester had, so far, failed to arrive and the suspicion was that de Ypres had predicted his, no response, accurately.

"Sir," Jarcot interrupted his thoughts. "Sir John Fitzgilbert summons you to the castle keep."

Ardron nodded acknowledgement but for a few more seconds continued to watch Dardot's attempts to concoct something nutritious from what was little more than water. Shaking his head ruefully, he turned away and made his way to the castle. He supposed that the summons meant another night raid. Random raids with random strength at random targets had been the strategy for the past month. The objectives were to kill and destroy creating fear into the besieging force in the hope that their resolve would be weakened. Whilst the destruction achieved on these raids were deemed a success, it seemed as if there had been very little weakening of resolve.

He made his way across the bailey, passing the lengthy column of townsfolk queuing to receive their daily ration of supplies, and climbed the mote steps entering the keep. Inside, the keep was busy with sergens and servants. The servants put together meagre bundles of rations while the sergens looked to their weapons.

He climbed the stone steps to the first chamber where several other group commanders idled passing time in small talk while they waited to be summoned. Today there were many more than was normal, this was unusual. Something bigger than a usual night raid was planned! Benet was first to spot Ardron and from across the chamber he waved him forward.

"Are you well, my friend?" he enquired as he indicated that Ardron should pass through into the second chamber.

"What's happening?" Ardron asked.

"Sir John will explain all," he replied falling in behind and directing Ardron to continue on. They passed through into the inner-most chamber, where Earl Robert, Brien Fitzcount, Miles Fitzwalter, Reginald de Dunstanville, William Pont du l'Arche and John Fitzgilbert leaned over a table studying charts. Seated at the far end, and looking very sombre, Empress Maude herself presided over the meeting. Their arrival went unnoticed for a few moments as the castle war counsel continued deep in earnest conversation. It took a loud cough from Benet to gain their attention.

"Ah, Scorrenstone," Fitzgilbert was the one to respond. He still called him Scorrenstone despite his new role as castellan of Norwood

"Imperial Majesty," Ardron acknowledged the empress with a bow.

Meanwhile, Fitzgilbert had turned his attention to Reginald de Dunstanville standing at his side. The Earl of Cornwall craned his neck to peer at Ardron, then acknowledged Fitzgilbert's comment with a nod. Selecting one of the charts he rolled it quickly before handing it to Fitzgilbert. Then after a muttered comment to the empress he and Fitzgilbert came towards Ardron and Benet.

"This is Ardron of Scorrenstone Castellan of Norwood." Fitzgilbert placed emphasise on is. From that Ardron could guess that there he had been the subject of some discussion. "He's a good man to have on your side in a battle!" Fitzgilbert added

Earl Cornwall held out his hand to be shaken. "This is Sir Reginald de Dunstanville, Earl of Cornwall and half-brother to Empress Maude." Fitzgilbert informed Ardron.

"It is an honour, Sir," Ardron responded taking the hand. The man before him, not much older than he was himself, looked at Ardron with dark penetrating eyes. His beard was trimmed short and thin following the line of his jaw with a neat moustache that curled upwards at the ends.

"I have heard good things about you," he said. "Not only from Sir John, but from both Sir Brien and my brother, Earl Robert."

"I do what I can," Ardron replied modestly.

Earl Reginald glanced at Fitzgilbert then after a moment's hesitation said. "What we are about to discuss calls for the utmost secrecy. You cannot mention it to anyone outside this room."

Ardron nodded understanding. "You can rely on me," he said

"Good," Reginald replied assured. Then he moved to Ardron's side placed an arm across his shoulders and guided him towards a flight of stone steps. Fitzgilbert led the way with Benet bringing up the rear.

The top rooms of the keep were the private quarters of the castle dignitaries. This room was suitably well-appointed with decorative and comfortable furniture with large tapestries hanging on the walls. In the privacy of an inner-most chamber Reginald could now relax a little, and he led the way to a long table. "We intend to withdraw from Winchester," he said

Ardron's surprise was evident, and his feelings at the news were mixed. The withdrawal meant a defeat, a capitulation and following the debacle of London was another stunning blow to the empress's ambitions. But on the plus side, it did mean a possible escape from starvation which gnawed a little deeper each day.

"Today we have a huge and dangerous assignment in which Sir John, here, has especially requested that you join him." Reginald went on.

"Sir Reginald," Ardron replied. "Whilst I am flattered that Sir John regards my abilities highly, I must point out that I am in knight's service to Earl Robert. It might first need his approval."

Earl Reginald nodded agreement. "Then be assured that my brother is content to allow you to join Sir John."

"Then I am at your service, my Lord."

"Good," Earl Reginald nodded acceptance. ""Sir John will outline all the details. But remember utmost secrecy!"

"As ever."

Satisfied, Reginald leaned back slightly. "Now I must return to the war counsel," he said. "Sir John," he glanced at Fitzgilbert. He waited only a moment for Fitzgilbert to nod concurrence and then he smartly left.

"Right my friend," Fitzgilbert said after he had watched the earl leave. "Come, I'll show you the plan." He unrolled the chart on the table. After he had weighted the corners, he took a long breath and looked at Ardron. "We are to create a diversion," he said leaning over the chart. "Winchester," he jabbed a finger on the map then ran his finger over the chart stopping at Wherwell. "We will occupy Wherwell Priory and turn it into a fortification. Then wait to be attacked."

"Wherwell Priory?" Ardron was surprised.

"Yes. It's a stout stone-built building and shouldn't be too difficult to defend for a short time."

"What if we are not attacked?" Ardron queried.

"We will be!" Fitzgilbert replied confidently. "De Ypres will see it as an attempt to break the blockade and that, he will not let happen. Nor would he be comfortable with a strong force in his rear. Yes, he will attack."

"What will our strength be?"

"What is the strength of your contingent?" Fitzgilbert asked

"Two dozen. No more."

Fitzgilbert nodded. "Then we should be in excess of two-hundred."

"Will that be enough?"

"Yes, I think so. We only have to hold out ten hours, or so." He paused a few moments allowing Ardron to study the chart. "We leave at dawn and need to be in place early tomorrow morning."

"Why don't we leave under the cover of darkness?" Ardron asked. "We would be in place sooner and have more time to mount barricades."

"Fair question," Fitzgilbert replied. "But you see we want de Ypres to know that we have occupied the Priory and to concentrate on dislodging us. We are the tethered goat waiting for the wolves." He leaned over the chart. "While de Ypres concentrates on attacking us, Miles Fitzwalter will lead a force from the west gate and attack the siege force on the Salisbury Road. Once he has created a breach, he is to hold it open for the empress, accompanied by a small force led by Brien Fitzcount and Earl Reginald. They will ride hard for Stockbridge." He traced the route with his finger. "Once across the river Test, they will swing north heading for the safety of Ludgershall Castle. One hour after she has left, then Earl Robert will lead the rest of the force out of Winchester along the same route, also making for Ludgershall. When they have had sufficient time to clear the bridge at Stockbridge then we too can withdraw to Ludgershall."

Ardron was silent for a few moments while he thought on the plan. It seemed sound and it had a good chance of succeeding. "What of Winchester?" he queried.

"Winchester will bleed!" Fitzgilbert replied solemnly. "What is more we are counting on it. We expect that as soon as the town is undefended the siege force will fall on Winchester to rob, ransack and rape. While they are busy doing that Earl Robert's force makes good its escape."

Ardron's disappointment was huge. He shut his eyes momentarily in despair. Once again it was the commoners who would bleed and suffer. But wasn't it always so? It was the way of things. He leaned forward staring silently at the chart without actually seeing anything. How many innocents would die tomorrow? How many daughters raped and how the poor, that did survive, would be even poorer after the pillaging.

"You are sworn to secrecy on this plan," Fitzgilbert said. "You can't even tell your sergens the actual objective. As far as they are concerned, we go to Wherwell attempting to break the blockade."

Ardron stared at him. His men it seemed where not allowed to understand the reason why they might die tomorrow.

"If word leaks out," Fitzgilbert went on. "Then de Ypres will surely ignore us and move instead to intercept Empress Maude on the road to Stockbridge. What a glittering prize that would be for him to carry back to Matilda."

Nodding understanding Ardron looked once again at the chart. Wherwell lay eight miles to the north-west. Stockbridge seven miles to the west, and only five miles south of Wherwell. It was a triangle much too tight for comfort. "I will prepare my troop," he said.

Chapter 12

The sun had risen on a typical September morn, a chill in the air with a thin autumn mist, when Fitzgilbert led a force of two hundred from the north gate. Faced with such a strong force the blockade on the Andover road offered only weak resistance then melted away. That had been an hour previous, and since then progressing at a steady canter, they had made good headway. As they now passed through the hamlet Cilbodentune they were less than a mile from Wherwell.

"At least there'll be food at Wherwell," Jarcot said cheerfully.

"No doubt," Ardron replied non-committal.

Jarcot leaned back in his saddle. "Did you hear that men? We eat something better than Dardot's nettles tonight."

"What's wrong with my nettle broth?" Dardot countered feigning offence.

Ardron said nothing. If all worked out as planned, then this night they should be on their way to Ludgershall. At least those that survived would.

Ardron spurred his horse to gallop up alongside Fitzgilbert. "Sir John," he said. "We have made good time."

"We have," he agreed. "Just ahead we descend down to the river Test, and the bridge. Just beyond that is the Priory."

"When do you intend to inform the rank and file of our purpose here?" Ardron asked the question that he had come to ask.

"When we reach our destination then there will be no earthly reason why they can't be told."

Ardron had no chance to comment because the air was filled with the whisper of flighted arrows that descended with thuds all around. Instant panic and mayhem erupted as some arrows found marks in men and horses. Confusion reigned as horses reared, men shouted and cursed not understanding from where the arrows had come. Confusion worsened when only seconds later another storm of arrows fell with the same results. This time it was clear that the arrows were being fired from the trees on the high ground to their right. Seeking to escape from this deadly cascade, many turned their horses away and galloped down the hill. But then rising from the thick bracken, or from behind almost every tree, men appeared with long pikes and lancers. There was no time to issue orders, no time to rally and no time to even think. Instantaneously it became the situation, each man for himself.

The inexperienced filly beneath Ardron bucked and reared in panic. He managed to hang on and stay in the saddle as he fought to bring the horse back under control. He had almost achieved control when one of the arrows pierced his hauberk and struck into his thigh. He gasped with pain and, instinctively, reached down to squeeze his leg attempting to ease the pain. The young horse momentarily free of control now took off bolting in blind panic. She ran the way she faced, barging through the massed panic back the way they had come. For fully half-a-mile she ran at full throttle with Ardron hopelessly pulling on the reins trying to slow the horse. It wasn't until she began to tire that Ardron began to regain control, and he gradually managed to reduce the horse to a walk. Then, eventually stopping, she stood, blowing hard while frothing at the mouth and lathered in sweat.

Now that she was standing, he took the opportunity to examine the arrow in his leg. The chain mail of the hauberk had reduced the thrust of the arrowhead, and it had not penetrated the flesh too deeply. Deep enough, however. He grabbed the shaft with both hands gritted his teeth and yanked the arrow out. Pain was brutal but fleeting, and immediately he felt better with the arrow gone, however, the wound now bled profusely. Dismounting he cut a strip from the saddle blanket and wrapped it around his leg. Steeling himself he pulled the knot tight over the wound stemming the blood and sucking a noisy breath against the pain as he did. He now turned his attention to the horse. Apart from the obvious signs of distress she appeared unarmed. He patted her neck and walked her round a couple of times then spoke quietly to her. "I'm afraid we have to go back my beauty," he said. Re-mounted and still talking to her he urged her into a relaxed canter back towards Wherwell.

As he rode through the point of the ambush the devastating effects were evident, dead sergens and dead horses littered the roadway. In the forest either side of the road sounds of clashing steel warned Ardron that fighting still went on. He rode on through hoping to find Fitzgilbert's main force, perhaps rallying somewhere up ahead. He descended the steep hill and crossed the bridge onto the open meadow. There was still no sign of a rallying force, instead small scattered groups fought in deadly conflict. Just the other side of the meadow, nestled among the trees, he could see the Priory. Fitzgilbert, he knew, was a tenacious man and he presumed that, despite the rout of his force, he would still attempt to occupy the Priory. He spurred his horse at a gallop across the meadow. Someone called his name.

Looking around he pulled back on the reins. To his right, with his back to a farm building, Benet along with a young squire faced up to five. The five wore the black and green livery of de Ypres Flemings. The Flemings had fanned out to the front of Benet and the squire. The pair slowly backed away holding their swords out to their front. Ardron pulled his horse around and set off at a gallop towards them. With sword outstretched, he bore down on the Flemings. As he neared, he leaned over in the saddle and swung his sword at the nearest man. Not seeing Ardron until the last moment, the man had no time to defend himself. Ardron's sword sliced across his neck. Whether the sword cut through the hauberk there was no telling, but the man went down pole-axed, at the very least with a broken neck. He reined in the horse and tried to turn, but the horse was once again fractious. Ardron decided that he could fight better on foot.

He jumped from the saddle and, limping heavily, hastened towards Benet's aid. Before he got there Benet took advantage of the Flemings hesitation and launched a ferocious attack at the nearest man. His sword crashed down on the man four times, five times. The Fleming parried desperately giving ground and stumbling backwards as he did. Eventually, he fell sprawling on his back. With a two-handed grip, Benet drove his sword downwards into the man's mid-rift with such force that it pierced the Fleming's hauberk. But Benet's back was exposed and another of the Flemings charged up behind him quickly. Ardron could see the danger but could do no more than shout a warning. It was not enough, and the Fleming's sword drove into Benet's back pushing him forward to stumble over the stricken man at his feet. Then standing with two feet spread the Fleming drove his sword into Benet as he rolled over to look up at his new assailant. Just to make sure that the sword had penetrated, the Fleming used his shoulder to press down on the sword. By now Ardron was upon him and growling aloud with sheer anger he launched a ferocious assault on the Fleming. He, like the other Fleming, could do nothing except parry while giving ground. He was no match for Ardron's sheer strength, increased by insane fury. Eventually, he fell backwards also, and Ardron mercilessly drove his sword not once but twice into the prone figure. "Die you bastard," he growled as he twisted his sword for good measure. The Fleming let out a high-pitched squeal, just as a woman would do.

Breathing heavily, Ardron stared down at the man as he went into convulsions of death. Only now did he notice the individualised helmet the man wore. Polished metal decorated atop with the head of a squawking cockerel. Suddenly remembering the other two Flemings he turned about quickly. But there was no danger. They had decided that the odds of two on two were not to their liking and they fled.

"You. What's your name?" Ardron demanded from the squire.

"Jacques," the boy replied. He was a boy of tender years, a mere teenager.

"Watch over me," he instructed as he went to Benet's aid.

Benet had curled himself into the foetus position attempting to ease his pain. Ardron gently turned him to examine his wound. It was not good, blood oozed freely from the stomach wound.

"Damned cockatrice," Benet muttered. Ardron shook his head not understanding and pressed down hard on the wound attempting to stem the blood flow. "It was the damned cockatrice," he said again curling a lip. Ardron was not sure whether that was a grin or a grimace. Blood then began trickling from Benet's mouth and he began to choke on his own blood. Ardron hauled him to a sitting position hoping it would assist with his breathing. Benet's eyes rolled upwards, and his head slumped back leaving eyes staring skywards unseeing as he died.

"Benet," Ardron demanded shaking his friend willing a response, but none came. He let him fall back gently. 'Cockatrice?' what did he mean? Then he remembered the individualised helmet. The cockerel! He took a deep breath to control his anger and stomped across to the slain Fleming. He ripped the helmet from the man's head and in fury hurled it as far as he could. In pointless spite he kicked the dead body, before ripping back the hood of the hauberk. Carefully manicured tresses tumbled forward over a youthful face. Ardron stared astonished at the lifeless body. It looked like a woman. It was a woman! What the hell was a woman doing on a battlefield? For a few moments he stared down dumbfounded at the lifeless body.

"Sir," it was Jacques who roused him.

"Get my horse," he instructed while he knelt and searched the body for some identity. He found none, which left him a little puzzled. What to do? She must be somebody's ward. 'Oh hell,' he chided himself 'Why bother? She was the enemy and he would not have been so concerned had it been a man.' He half turned and looked back to Benet's lifeless body. He should be more concerned about his friend. He wondered what he could do for him. If he survived the day, and if the opportunity allowed, he decided, he would come back for him and ensure that he received a knight's funeral.

The squire came up with the horse. Ardron took the reins and positioned the horse to mount. "Where is your liege lord?" he asked.

"Dead sir! Cut down by two Flemings with axes."

"Ah_," Ardron muttered sympathetically. He grimaced as the wounded leg cost him pain when he mounted. "Do you know where John Fitzgilbert is?"

"No Sir. I do not," the squire answered.

"Never mind," Ardron said. "I can guess." He offered his arm to the youngster and pulled him up onto the horse behind him.

The gates of the Priory were wide open and Ardron drove his horse through at a full gallop. In the courtyard all was mayhem. Men brawled for their very lives. Clashes of steel on steel mingled with shouts of anger and curses as men fought desperate hand-to-hand combat to the death. In front of the abbey Ardron saw what was left of Fitzgilbert's greatly depleted force fighting ferociously beneath his red and amber banner. He drove his horse on through clearing a path to the very steps of the abbey. He pulled the horse to a stop just a little too savagely, causing the animal to rear then fall. He rolled clear, jumping to his feet, sword at the ready. "Stay close," he shouted at the squire as he hauled him to his feet. Immediately, he was set upon by two Flemings. He was quick enough to parry both artless swipes, before aiming a head slash at the nearest man. However, he managed only a resounding metallic ring on his shield. Fitzgilbert's men overwhelmed by numbers, were giving ground being forced up the abbey steps. At the top they began to pour through the door into the abbey. There was now a danger of Ardron finishing on the wrong side, as the door was being forced shut. He pushed the squire ahead of him and through the rapidly narrowing gap. A quick glance over his shoulder at the baying Flemings, and he was the last man through the door.

"Barricade the door." Fitzgilbert's instruction was needless. Men had already begun piling benches at its front. That finished, they took advantage of the unexpected respite and slumped in silence across the pews, panting heavily. There was very little fight left in them. They were completely exhausted.

"What now?" somebody asked.

"We are safe for now," Fitzgilbert said. "They can't get in."

"And we can't get out."

"Don't worry. We only have to wait, and we will get out." Fitzgilbert replied. That seemed enormously optimistic to Ardron, but he kept his opinion to himself.

It was at this point that Fitzgilbert announced the Angevin intention to retreat from Winchester. It provoked no reaction! It must have seemed somewhat irrelevant in their current situation. "Don't you see," he went on. "De Ypres was waiting for us. He knew we were coming!" He paused for effect. "If he knew that, then he knows the rest of the plan." There was still no reaction but Ardron was beginning to understand his reasoning. It was to be a race to the bridge at Stockbridge.

"At this very moment," Fitzgilbert's explanation went on. "The empress should be well on her way to Stockbridge. Compared to us she is a much bigger prize for de Ypres. If he can get to the bridge before the empress, then he can cut off her retreat. Stockbridge is five miles south of here and every minute he delays lessens his chances and increases the empress's chances of escape." He paused enjoying the rising spirits among the sergens. "He will leave soon," he added confidently.

Ardron tried to work out the possible programme and assess the chances of the empress crossing the river before de Ypres could get there.

He rated her chances fairly good, but then he suddenly thought of Earl Robert and the main force following behind. He was particularly vulnerable. If the river crossing was denied to him, he would be trapped and caught in the open with de Mandeville in pursuit. He would have to turn and fight. It all seemed just too depressing.

He examined the faces around him looking for members of his own troop. Some just lounged from sheer exhaustion while others looked to comrades who had suffered wounds. Although there were perhaps thirty in all there was not one of his own troop. He could do nothing except pray that all had escaped but given the circumstances that seemed to be a forlorn hope. Close to where he sat was the pulpit from which the clergy delivered his sermon. Draped across the winged brass figure of the Holy Ghost was an ornately decorated sash of silk. Just what he needed! He dragged it down and used it as an additional bandage on his wounded leg.

"You didn't escape unscathed, Scorrenstone."

He looked up at Fitzgilbert. "It's nothing," he said turning his attention back to securing the make-shift bandage.

"Can you climb steps?"

"Sir John, I can climb a greased pole if need be."

Fitzgilbert smiled. "Good. Come with me." He led the way to the base of the bell tower. "We need to know what's happening outside and we should get a good view from up there."

Ardron ducked past the bell ropes and peered up to the belfry. The stone tower was square with wooden steps clinging to the wall and ascending steeply in a series of levelled landings. Without waiting for Ardron, Fitzgilbert began the ascent. Due to the pain in his leg and that the steps were little more than the width of a ladder' rung, Ardron found the climb taxing. Nevertheless, he reached the top on the heels of Fitzgilbert. The wind was fresher at this height and whined between the pillars like a distant wailing wolf. Edging forward cautiously, they peered over the parapet at the activity below. But the unmistakable impression was the lack of activity. Groups of men stood around in clusters as if waiting for the abbey doors to re-open. Ardron looked at Fitzgilbert wondering if he had perhaps miscalculated the situation. Perhaps de Ypres didn't know the Angevin plans. Maybe it was just chance that he had discovered Fitzgilbert's force moving north.

"How was it possible for de Ypres to discover the evacuation plan," he asked.

Fitzgilbert shrugged. "Spies maybe. Or perhaps there is a traitor in our midst. I can't be sure."

There was still no urgency from the surrounding force below. Ardron was dubious. "They're in no hurry down there. Perhaps de Ypres doesn't know all the plan." He suggested.

"Perhaps," Fitzgilbert's non-committal answer did nothing to raise Ardron's spirits.

As they watched two men entered the courtyard leading a horse which dragged a litter behind. On the litter was a body. Ardron immediately recognised the helmet placed carefully on the chest of the dead sergen. The men led the horse right up to de Ypres himself.

"What have we here?" Fitzgilbert muttered.

De Ypres lifted the cloth covering the face of the body then turned and glared at the two men. Immediately, both men fell to their knees subservient before him. They were too far away to hear what was said but clearly de Ypres was not at all pleased.

"It's a woman," Ardron answered Fitzgilbert's query.

"How do you know?"

"Because I killed her."

"You killed a woman?"

"I did. God forgive me. But she had just killed Benet."

There was no mistaking the shock on Fitzgilbert's face. "Benet is dead?" He repeated with a deal of incredulity.

"I regret Sir, but it's true."

Fitzgilbert turned away and looked out into the distance while he absorbed the news. After a few moments he re-adjusted his focus to the scene below. By now the two men had been dragged from their feet and were being frog-marched away.

"Do you know who she was?" Fitzgilbert asked.

"No!"

No matter," he said. "Whoever she was she meant something to de Ypres. I suspect those men were charged with her safety and they failed in their duty. I wouldn't give a rotten apple that they live another hour."

This new event had lit fury in de Ypres's belly. Beside himself with rage, he moved among his men shouting and gesturing stirring them to instant action. Fearing his wrath men now moved with speed and purpose. Soon they began to pile sheaves of straw in front of the main door and in other strategic places about the abbey.

"God's mercy," Fitzgilbert muttered. "De Ypres intends to burn the abbey, and us with it."

"By all the saints," Ardron muttered, "You're right." He stood and leaned over the parapet to get a better view. There was no doubting the Flemings intentions. As soon as there was enough dry straw piled it was set alight, then they moved along to another vulnerable spot to start another fire. He sank back beneath the parapet and looked at Fitzgilbert in despair.

Fitzgilbert shook his head. "They will move on very soon," he said. "They have too," he added. Ardron wondered if the last remark was more to convince himself.

From the height at the top of the bell tower they had the prime view over the whole Priory complex below. Now they could see burning arrows being loosed onto the abbey roof. They were fired at random and in hopeful speculation that some would strike and find tinder to burn. No doubt some would. The situation was dire

Ardron looked down the inside of the bell-tower, this was not a good place to be. If the wooden steps were to catch fire, they would find themselves trapped at the top with no way down. "We can't stay here, Sir John," he said.

"No," he agreed. "You go down. I'll follow in a minute."

Ardron needed no persuading and he started down. With his foot on the top step he waited and looked at Fitzgilbert. He was still pre-occupied staring over the parapet at the activity below. "Sir John," he said firmly. "We must go now."

"Yes Yes," he said tetchily. "Go, I'll be right behind you."

When Ardron reached the bottom, he looked up to see Fitzgilbert had also started down. He watched and waited a moment before turning to enter the nave. Inside the nave was just beginning to fill with smoke, it was now obvious to the sergens trapped within what was happening outside. Their face revealed confusion and desperation. "What to do?" one of them asked Ardron. He nodded calmly, but that calmness masked real feelings. "Sir John will be here in a moment," he replied.

"Sir John?" they demanded as soon as Fitzgilbert arrived.

Fitzgilbert held up his hands in a calming motion. "Stay calm," he said. "They will leave soon, and we will walk out of here." Ardron didn't share his optimism, and from their expression neither did most of the sergens. But it was a measure of the man's influence that none questioned his authority. "Cut down those altar cloths," Fitzgilbert went on pointing down the nave. "Cut then into strips to make masks to cover your faces against the smoke."

Men moved to carry out his bidding, but their task was interrupted by the sound of shattering glass. The stained-glass windows were being deliberately smashed in what seemed to be mindless and pointless vandalism by the Flemings. However, a few moments later the reason became obvious when burning torches were tossed into the abbey, adding potential to the already rapidly spreading fire. Now the priority became the quenching of those burning torches, but it was proving impossible to keep up with the numbers that were thrown through the windows.

"Sir John," one of the sergens sought his urgent attention. "Four of the men left through the transept door to surrender." Fitzgilbert uttered a stream of curses that would have made the devil blush. "It served them nought," the sergen went on. "They went out with arms aloft but were immediately set upon by the Flemings with swords and axes. They were mercilessly chopped to pieces."

"There can be no surrender," Fitzgilbert shouted. "By God I will personally chop up any man that tries."

Now the smoke was becoming thick. Eyes red and bloodshot streamed, and despite the rags wrapped around mouths and noses there was much coughing and choking. Up above the dry and ancient timbers of the wooden roof were, by now, well alight and with the collar beams being rapidly eaten by flames the burning timbers were in danger on imminent collapse.

"What a choice," someone voiced a thought. "Be chopped into pieces or burned alive by the flames."

"Are you mad?" someone replied. "The smoke will kill you long before the fire."

"Maybe not," Ardron said remembering his last visit to this abbey and the door that led to the crypt. "Jacques," he said, "come with me." Half running half stumbling, he led the way up the nave as quickly as he could. With visibility no more than four paces he had trouble actually locating the door. When he did, and to his relief, he found it still was not locked. He slid back the heavy bolt and pulled the heavy door open. He remembered well the same damp stench that greeted him from the bowels of the crypt. But that mouldy smell was as fresh air compared to that in the rest of the abbey. "This will be our refuge," he said to Jacques. "Stay by the door I'll send up the men."

The smoke was even thicker as he made his way back down the nave. Undoubtedly, they were very few minutes from death by smoke inhalation. At first, he had trouble making himself understood. "Up to the altar and into the crypt," he shouted pushing and pulling each man in the direction. Not at first understanding, their re-action was slow. Gradually each man began to follow his direction. Perhaps still not fully understanding, they made their way up the nave more in hope of salvation than confidence.

"Where is Sir John?" Ardron caught hold of the last man's arm.

"Up there," he replied with a vague wave of an arm.

Half blinded by eyes that stung, he stumbled in the direction he had indicated and eventually found Fitzgilbert atop a pile of tables trying to peer through one of the broken windows. "Sir John, come I have found safe refuge." He shouted.

Fitzgilbert looked back, "They should have left by now," he said as he started to descend. Just as he reached the bottom, he suddenly collapsed to his knees let out an agonising scream and clutched his face with both hands.

"What is it?" Ardron demanded. But he received no reply as Fitzgilbert began clawing at his face. He went to help, but as he reached out something scalding hot dripped onto his arm causing him to gasp with pain. On his arm bubbling like acid, molten lead. Instinctively he attempted to relieve the searing pain by vigorously rubbing it off. All around him it was raining molten lead as the flashings on the abbey roof melted. They needed to be away from beneath this lead shower and quickly. Unceremoniously, he hauled Fitzgilbert to his feet and stumbling through the smoke he, half dragged half carried, him to the crypt door where Jacques still stood waiting with the door just ajar. He shoved Fitzgilbert roughly through the door.

"Shut it," he coughed when inside. "And seal its edges," he added as he began to help Fitzgilbert down the steps. He made his way, half dragging Fitzgilbert, down the long narrow crypt to the end. At the end, above head height not more than two hands width but longer than a tall man, was a barred grill. It was an unexpected gratuity. It provided an invaluable supply of fresh air, and the men standing on whatever they had found pressed their faces against it gulping in clean air.

"God's piles," he cursed loudly. "Get away from there. Do you want to tell the Flemings we still live and where we are?" He helped Fitzgilbert to a sitting position, back resting against the wall then turned to face the sergens. Reluctantly, they had accepted his demand and slowly began to move back. "Sit on the ground beneath the grill, he instructed, "And be quiet." There was a definite surliness about their attitude, but they did as he ordered. He waited a moment until satisfied all was settled then he turned his attention to Fitzgilbert.

Gently he moved Fitzgilbert's hands away from his face. Then a gasp of horror almost escaped his lips, but just in time, only just, he managed to smother it. One side of the man's face was no more than raw flesh blackened by fire and slowly oozing blood. Where once there had been an eye, only charred white pus remained.

"How bad is it?" Fitzgilbert muttered.

"It's not good, Sir John," Ardron replied. "You are not going to be as popular with the ladies as you were," he tried to make light of the injury. "But then, you are not going to die either," he added. The wound was in urgent need of cooling, but here in the crypt there was no water. The most he could do at this time would be bandages. He unwound some of the silk sash that bound his own leg wound and cut a piece off. It was an awkward bind, but he managed to cover one half of Fitzgilbert's head covering the burned side of his face.

"It's up to you," Fitzgilbert said catching his arm as Ardron straightened. "Get these men back to Ludgershall."

Ardron nodded. "I'll get them to safety," he reassured. He said it, but he was nowhere near as confident as he sounded.

"Sir," Jacques said. "Your arm needs attention."

"Yes," he replied as a matter of fact. He hadn't forgotten it, the throbbing pain would not let him, but at last he now had time to give it some attention.

There was nothing left to do now except wait. Wait for the Flemings to leave and the fire, raging above their heads, to burn itself out.

Settling down in the gloom he tried to work out the possible sequence of events yet to be played. By this time, he estimated, that the empresses escort party would be close to Stockbridge and perhaps even beyond. If de Ypres left now or indeed had left a few minutes ago he would be too late arriving to cut off her retreat. In which case, she would be safely at Ludgershall Castle before dark. However, Earl Gloucester and the main body of Angevins could not yet be at Stockbridge. If de Ypres was still at the Priory, he was five miles from Stockbridge, but still he could be there well within half-an-hour. He doubted Earl Robert was that close. The likelihood was that de Ypres could occupy the bridge and block the earl's retreat, which would leave the Angevins caught out in the open with de Mandeville's army bearing down on them. It was a depressing summation.

It was a long afternoon with regular rumbling and thundering sounds of collapsing timbers above their heads. Smoke there was, leaching into the crypt but not enough to cause anything worse than coughs and sore eyes. The underground chamber did get extremely hot at one point as the ground above their heads became buried in burning debris and hot ash. But as it got near the point of unbearable, it levelled out, and then very slowly began to cool.

Much later, nearing sunset, Ardron decided they ought to make some sort of effort to escape this horror. He climbed up on one of the boxes and peered out from the grill. Save for the lazy drift of smoke wisps he could see no movement and nothing that was cause for concern. He bade all inside be silent while he listened intently for any evidence of the Fleming sergens. All seem quiet. It was time to move.

The first problem encountered was the crypt door, it was jammed. Eventually with several shoulder barges it opened just a fraction.

"Jacques," Ardron called the young squire. With his wispiness of youth, he was easily the thinnest. "Do you think you could squeeze through there?" he asked pointing at the barely open gap.

The youngster nodded readily, "I'll give it a try."

"Good," Ardron approved. "If you get through then before you do anything, have a stealthy look around to make sure there are no posted sentries. If there are then come back in. However, if you are alone see if you can move some of the debris to free this door." The squire nodded eagerly and started to push into the narrow gap. Ardron caught his arm before he went further. "Work quietly," he warned.

At first it didn't look as if Jacques was going to get through, but then he wriggled right into the gap, but was stuck. Fearing the boy's ribs would break Ardron ordered two burly men to push hard on the door hoping to achieve just another inch of movement. It must have been achieved, because Jacques slipped through as a pip squeezed from a lemon and was gone. Now there was nothing they could do except wait. They were reliant upon him completely.

Anxious to be out of the crypt some men started to mutter with impatience as seconds went to minutes and the minutes protracted. "Relax," Ardron tried to quell their impatience. "He will be making sure that all the Flemings have gone." But Ardron too began to wonder when fifteen minutes became twenty, and still Jacques did not arrive. At last there was sound of movement the other side of the door, "Sir Ardron," Jacques called.

"Yes,"

"The door is blocked by fallen timbers," Jacques informed him.

"Can you clear some of it?

"With an axe I could."

"Can you find an axe?"

"I have been looking but haven't found one."

That was a hitch. "Alright, Ardron said. "Have all de Ypres's men gone?"

"Yes. The place is deserted."

"Are the nuns still in the Priory?"

"I don't know."

"Make your way to the Priory. If the nuns are there, see if you can get an axe from them." Ardron suggested.

"Will they have an axe?"

"Not a battle-axe, but they have to chop their wood with something."

Another twenty minutes passed before Jacques returned. "Sir Ardron," he said.

"Yes."

"I have a saw,"

"Good. Now go to work."

It took another half hour before Jacques had cleared away enough debris to half-open the door. Half-open was enough and each man squeezed through. Outside the sun was setting, and in the mellowing light low angle shadows were cast across the remnants of the abbey. The walls and pillars, made from stone, still stood but were blackened by soot. Collapsed timbers slanted haphazardly across that which had been the nave. These timbers blackened and charred, still smouldered letting off a blue haze of smoke, while at times an evening breeze fanned some embers back to glow and spark. Remarkably, a few of the roof rafters and collar beams still held place having survived the fire and added, significantly, to the now skeletal appearance of the abbey.

Ardron helping Fitzgilbert led the way, picking his route carefully, across the hot white ash and out from the precinct of the fire ravaged building. Once clear he took a moment to look back sadly at the ruins which only eight hours before had been the imposing Wherwell Abbey. "God will punish de Ypres for this," someone said. 'Perhaps,' Ardron thought, but one thing for certes was that by his grace they had survived a raging inferno. Now it seemed appropriate to make good their escape and leave this immediate area in case the Flemings were to come back.

He counted two dozen men in the party. All, save himself and Jacques, were sergens of Fitzgilbert. Four, including Fitzgilbert himself, carried significant wounds and could not make the eight miles journey to Ludgershall on foot. From somewhere he needed to acquire horses. After a battle there is often one or two running free. "You four," he addressed four men standing surveying the ruins. "Search around to see if you can find horses."

While he waited for the horse-searchers to return he made the rounds inspecting the wounded. The injuries were so severe that if horses were not found then they would have to be carried on stretchers to Ludgershall. More-over his injured leg was painful enough to make an eight-mile walk seem daunting.

With the availability of water, he was now able to administer cooling to the make-shift bandages covering Fitzgilbert's face. He allowed the water to trickle over the bandages then after allowing time to soak he repeated.

"Does that bring any relief?" he asked.

Although his burns were horrific and must have been agonising the man was still lucid. "Some," he muttered pushing himself up to a sitting position his back resting against a tree. "Help me to my feet," he said, "I need to address the men." Ardron helped him to his feet and to totter over to confront his men.

"Gather round and listen to what I have to say," he said. "We need to get back to the safety of Ludgershall Castle. But as you can see, I am greatly indisposed. Therefore, I cede command to Sir Ardron." He gestured towards Ardron standing at his side. "I have every confidence that he will deliver us all safely. From this point on, he will make all the decisions, and you will accept him has your commander. Obey his instructions as if they were issued by me." He paused a moment then he carried on with a little more empathy. "This has been a bad day for us all, losing many friends and comrades. We can only hope that our comrades to the south have fared better and that our losses and sufferings have not been for nought." He paused waiting for reactions, receiving none he gave a satisfied nod. Then he offered up a brief prayer. "God look down with mercy on us thy enfeebled servants. And deliver us from the hands of our enemies." He gestured to Ardron that he had finished and wished to return to the tree. "God will have precious little to do with it," he muttered quietly. "It's all down to you, Saxon."

Some thirty minutes later the four horse-searchers returned having found three horses. It was not as many as Ardron had hoped, but still it would have to do. Now the priority was to leave the vicinity of the Priory in case the Flemings should return. He had a litter hastily constructed that could be dragged behind one of the horses. This would accommodate the most severely wounded man, the other three, including Fitzgilbert, he judged fit enough to ride.

"We head west," he charged when all was prepared.

"Sir, Andover is three miles north and from there we could get more horses," someone suggested.

"We go west," Ardron brooked no argument. Although Andover was close, his intention was to give it a wide berth fearing that it might be occupied by Matilda's forces.

After little more than a mile they reached the shallow river, Anton, just outside the village Clatford. Considering that there was enough distance from the Priory to be safe, he called a halt. "We camp here for the night," he directed. "Definitely no fires," he added. Perhaps they were not that safe, he mused.

It took a little time for the men to settle but when they did most sat talking quietly while others sprawled out to sleep. Satisfied all was well, he took one of the horses and, after assuring Fitzgilbert that he would be back soon, he rode out.

By using the farm building as a reference point, he soon found the body of Benet. However, the battle-field scavengers had got there ahead of him and had picked ruthlessly over his possessions. Anything that might possibly yield a profit had been taken, its triviality mattered not a jot. "God take those parasites for what they are. The scum of the earth," he muttered.

Inside the farm building he found an old horse blanket. It was not particularly clean, but it would have to do. He wrapped Benet's near naked body and hoisted it across the horse's withers. This would be an additional load upon their meagre horse stock. Briefly, he wondered if perhaps they should have gone to Andover to obtain extra horses. 'No!' it was a dangerous gamble that need not be taken. Besides, he felt sure that Fitzgilbert would not mind sharing his saddle with his dead constable.

It was not late when he returned, nevertheless only Fitzgilbert remained awake. He watched in silence as Ardron reverently eased the body from the horse's back and laid it out close by.

"What have you there?" he asked but Ardron suspected that he already knew the answer.

"Tis Benet," he replied. "I could not leave such a man to be disposed into a mass communal grave unheralded and unrecognised by uncaring men of labour."

Fitzgilbert nodded his approval. "You are right," he said. "He deserves a warrior's funeral and I will see that he gets one." Discernibly his speech was becoming slurred and halting as his facial injuries began to stiffen

Ardron settled down to sit at his side. "I am afraid, Sir John, he will have to ride double with you to Ludgershall." He said as he gingerly straightened out his injured leg

"I have no objections," Fitzgilbert slurred

It had been a cold night, typical of September, and the heavy overcast clouds promised only rain for this the new day. With no breakfast to organise there was no reason why the onward journey to Ludgershall should be delayed. They crossed the river and continued west until they reached a road which was little more than track. Here they turned north heading for the hamlet Turkilleston, and by this time it had started to rain heavily, adding irritating discomfort to the trek. Soon clothing became soaked and heavy whilst the road underfoot turned to mud. Ardron was suffering additional discomfort as his wounded leg repaid him with increasing pain with every step, until he could do little more than drag it.

On the edge of Turkilleston, they came across a small Saxon farm and here Ardron called a temporary halt. Not bothering to seek out the villein of the farm, he indicated they should take refuge in a nearby animal shelter. Thankfully, the men crowded into the small area and then stood shaking clothing to drain off rainwater.

"How far are we from Ludgershall?" Jacques asked.

"Four miles." One of Fitzgilbert's men answered for Ardron. Silently, Ardron was grateful for the interjection because in truth he had only a vague idea. He sat down heavily squeezing his aching leg as he did. Carefully he lifted the edge of the make-shift bandages looked in and, as he expected, he could see that the wound continued to bleed. 'Four miles,' he thought. 'At their current rate of progress another hour and half.' The thoughts of yet another hour and half were daunting.

"Jacques," he said. "When the rain eases see if you can cut me a stout piece of wood that I can use as a crutch."

"I'll go now," he replied keenly.

"No," Ardron replied sharply. "When the rain eases," he added quietly.

It was the better part of an hour before the rain eased, and then eventually stopped. Ardron delayed the onward march a little, giving Jacques time to find a pole for a make-shift crutch. Few minutes later he returned this time with the farm villein.

"Sir," he addressed Ardron. "This man has a cart he is willing to lend."

Ardron looked up at the Saxon peasant with a warm glow of relief flooding through him. "Good man," he muttered.

The villein stared at Fitzgilbert clearly recognising him despite his head swathed in bandages. "Sir, he said in English addressing him. "I have a horse and a cart I can place at your disposal."

"What does he say?" Fitzgilbert muttered. Suffering greatly from his facial burns, he was only half interested.

Ardron made the translation then took over the conversation. The peasant was, of course, a villein landholder to Fitzgilbert and was offering his service to his liege lord by offering to drive the cart and ferry the wounded to Ludgershall. Thirty minutes later with the wounded loaded aboard the cart, including Ardron, the party set off for Ludgershall.

A little over an hour later it was a sorry bunch of stragglers that arrived at Ludgershall Castle. The centre of attention, naturally enough, was fixed upon Fitzgilbert and he was helped up the mote and into the keep attended by a worried Lady Aline and the castle lac. Now with his task complete, and a little surplus to requirements Ardron continued to sit in the cart absent-mindedly massaging his wounded leg. Later when the lac was less occupied, he would get his injury attended.

"Have a care there," he called bad temperedly to two men who had unceremoniously dragged Benet's body from the horse allowing it to fall on the ground. "That is your esteemed constable."

Both men looked at Ardron then somewhat sheepishly loaded the corpse onto a stretcher more reverently. Mission achieved and tension now released he realised that having not eaten since he had left Winchester early yesterday, he was hungry. As he made the effort to get down from the cart Jacques moved to assist but, subbornly independent, he shunned the squire's helping hand. "Come boy," he said when he had steadied himself. "Let us find the kitchen."

The mutton was cold the bread warm, and whilst he sat eating, he learned what an unmitigating disaster the retreat from Winchester had been. Empress Maude and her small entourage had made it safely to Ludgershall and had, on this very morning, left for Devizes. However, that was the only good news. De Ypres had raced to Stockbridge and occupied the bridge, effectively cutting off Earl Gloucester's retreat. With no alternative, Earl Robert turned back towards Winchester, however, he found himself faced against Matilda's main force led by de Mandeville. Out in the open and outnumbered with de Mandeville to his front and de Ypres's Flemings in his rear Earl Robert's force was cut to pieces. The rumour now was that Earl Robert and William Pont du l'Arche were taken prisoners and the remnants of the army scattered. Of Miles Fitzwalter, there was no news and was, therefore, posted missing, feared dead. The news was sickening and the loss of her main General, Earl Robert, meant that the ambition of the empress to be Queen of England now looked even less likely. She did, however, still hold King Stephen captive at Bristol and that to all intents and purposes was the only card she now held.

One week later, with his wounded leg on the mend, Ardron took his leave from Fitzgilbert and left Ludgershall for his Norwood estate. He was accompanied by Jacques. The young squire had almost pleaded to be allowed to go with him and serve as his personal squire. As they exited the gate, he looked back to see Fitzgilbert, his face still swathed in bandages, atop the mote watching him go. He raised an arm in salute which Sir John acknowledged. The Fitzgilbert injuries were horrific, he was hideously disfigured for life. One whole side of his face was contorted by burn scars and in differing shades of red. Where an eye should have been there remained only an empty socket without even an eyelid, which was such a repulsive sight that when the bandages were eventually discarded it would have to be permanently covered by a large black patch. After such an ordeal Ardron wondered if the Fitzgilbert indomitable spirit could ever be the same. Couldn't be! He sadly concluded, as he spurred his horse to a canter.

It was early evening by the time they reached Trowbridge and Ardron decided to take a liberty and impose on Sir Humphrey de Bohun at his castle for an overnight rest. His entreat was well received, and he was invited to stay and to casually dine in Sir Humphrey's inner sanctum. He received a huge surprise when he entered the chamber. Miles Fitzwalter lounged in front of the fire, wine goblet in hand and feet raised upon a footstool.

"Sir Miles," he said with surprise in his tone. "I am pleased to see you hale and hearty. I had heard reports that you were missing feared dead."

"Well as you can see, dead. I am not." He replied coldly.

"It is a sight that gladdens my heart." Ardron replied as he took a seat opposite. "The retreat from Winchester did not go well!" He said quietly when settled.

"It went disastrously wrong," he retorted. "Caught between two forces outnumbered and exposed we were ruthlessly put to the sword. Many good men died on that field. Those that did survive and were not captured fled for their very lives." He paused staring at Ardron. "I can see the question in your eyes, Saxon," he accused. "Yes, I too fled ignominiously. I threw off my finery and dressed as a humble sergen to make an escape."

"Sir, you escaped. No escape under those circumstances could be considered ignominious." Ardron replied.

"You were with Fitzgilbert at Wherwell?"

"Yes, I was," Ardron confirmed.

"What happened?" he demanded. "You were supposed to fortify the Priory and engage de Ypres, thereby gaining us enough time to clear the bridge at Stockbridge."

Ardron nodded. "That was the plan."

"You didn't hold out very long," he accused.

"Sir, Ardron replied. "We were never able to fortify the Priory. They knew we were coming and were waiting in ambush before we even got to Wherwell. We were surprised, cut down and scattered far and wide. In the end less than three dozen of us made it to the abbey. There was no refuge there either. De Ypres put the abbey to the torch with us locked inside. We only survived by sealing ourselves in the crypt and waited for the fire to burn itself out."

By his expression it was clear that all this was news to Miles as he stroked his beard thoughtfully. "And Fitzgilbert?"

"He survived. But he is terribly disfigured losing an eye and is horrendously scarred about his face."

"How could they know?" de Bohun asked.

"Spies," Miles almost spat. "They must have had someone very close to our inner circle, because our plans were guarded and not well known." He turned his attention back to Ardron. "If de Ypres did know our plans then I would say that he made a serious error. He ought to have ignored Fitzgilbert and allowed him to tend the roses in the Priory if he so desired. He should instead have hurried direct to Stockbridge and laid his trap for the empress's party to walk into. Maude would then have been his prisoner." He shook his head slightly bewildered and with a slight smile said. "I will bet a tidy coin that Matilda is not at all happy with her general today."

"Perhaps he thought he could take both Fitzgilbert and still be in time to capture the empress," De Bohun offered.

"Clearly," Miles agreed. "He allowed his dislike of Fitzgilbert to cloud his judgement. I believe that he may have missed a golden chance to actually win the war."

The room was silent while the other two considered that last remark. "Where is Empress Maude now?" Miles asked.

"She left Ludgershall for Devizes a week ago," Ardron replied. "As far as I am aware, she is still there."

"We must go tomorrow," de Bohun said to Miles. "She will be in need of a general, and you are the only man able to replace Earl Robert.

Miles shook his head slowly. "No, I think she will take the counsel of her half-brother Reginald de Dunstanville before mine. But yes, Humphrey, you are right we should go to Devizes and present ourselves at her command."

"What will you do?" de Bohun asked Ardron.

He shrugged non-committal. "I will return to Norwood, attend my affairs and wait for instructions.

Chapter 13

Bristol Castle, Christmas 1141

So!" William de Evereux said somewhat light heartedly. "I suppose you know that we have all been excommunicated."

"Yes cousin," Edward de Evereux replied surly. "Makes me wonder if we were a little too hasty switching sides."

Ardron said nothing but studied both the de Evereux cousins suspiciously. Could it be that they were considering reneging their fealty and reverting back to Stephen's cause? He understood they were referring to the Bishops Church Council in London that had excommunicated all that supported Empress Maude's cause.

"They were only responding to Stephen's demands," de Bohun replied softly.

"Ridiculous," William retorted. "It means of course that they have excommunicated about half of the country," he went on shaking his head ruefully.

"If you put it like that," de Bohun said. "You'd be right. But I believe it only refers to those of rank and status."

"Like us," Edward replied.

"Like us," de Bohun confirmed. "But here we are celebrating the Feast of St Stephen just the same. What say you Ardron?" he asked.

Ardron shrugged. "In truth, I am afraid that I attach little importance to what some faceless and distant bishop has to say or do. Most of them are little more than self-serving hypocrites. I would have thought that it was their charge from God that they welcome as many Christian into his house as possible, and not to disbar the many." His acidic comments were greeted with a startled silence. The uncomfortable pause was ended by a fanfare of trumpets heralding the entrance of the Empress Maude.

She walked at the head of a small procession, moving slowly down the middle of the reception hall. Guests, lined on both sides, paid respectful homage as she passed. To Ardron she looked distinctly drained and tired, perhaps showing the strains of all the recent setbacks. However, the man on her right, whose arm she held, looked entirely to the contrary. Earl Robert showed no ill effects from the eleven weeks he had been held prisoner by Stephen's Queen Matilda. Indeed, it looked as if he had thrived. Obviously, he had been well treated and perhaps it was, that released from the stresses and strains of furthering Maude's cause, he had benefitted greatly from the respite. It was now two weeks since the prisoner exchange, King Stephen for Earl Robert, and this was his first official appearance. Following close behind the pair was Brien Fitzcount accompanied by Reginald de Dunstanville. In the rear John Fitzgilbert, sporting a rakish black eye patch, was accompanied by Miles Fitzwalter and William Pont du l'Arche. He too had been Matilda's prisoner.

When she reached the dais, at the far end, she turned to face the congregation and waited for the warm reception to fade. When it did, she paused a few moments for effect, then warmly welcomed everybody to the banquet.

"God save the Lady of the English," some enthusiast shouted from the back, and the applause started again. After a few moments Maude held up her hands to quieten the cheers.

"Thank you," she said. "It warms my heart to be surrounded by my most ardent and loyal supporters." She paused to gather her thoughts before going on. "We have had a year that saw us at Westminster and actually on the throne of England. Only the formality of a coronation ceremony separating us from being the legitimate ruler that my father decreed. Alas, those London Bishops did play me false. Insisting that protocol demanded all rites be satisfied before a coronation could take place. Endless tiresome and trivial formalities placed barriers between me and that ceremony." She waited a moment. "And yet, today we have learned that four days ago Stephen and Matilda held a fresh Coronation to re-affirm their legitimacy to rule, arranged by those same bishops. This less than two weeks after his release from captivity!"

Low mutters of astonishment rumbled around the hall. Ardron could easily understand the outrage that Maude must be feeling. A coronation that could not be arranged for the empress in eight weeks, had been achieved for Stephen in as many days.

Maude waited for the muttering to cease before going on. "Therefore, my conclusion has to be that it matters not what I achieve, or what pinnacle I attain, there will always be resentment from the barons, bishops and even the common people, against a woman becoming absolute ruler. Against me, becoming ruler," she added pointedly. "We achieved so much earlier this year only to lose it all in the latter part, and we find ourselves in precisely the same position that we were at this time last year. However, this does not mean the fight is over. Stephen may call himself the legitimate king, and yet he can only boast complete autonomy over less than half of England. We control the West Country, reaching as far east as Wallingford. In the north, my good uncle King David and my esteemed cousins, control the north reaching as far south as Doncaster. Our good ally, Ranulf Earl of Chester, reaches well into the West Midlands. Oh no!" She purred, "Stephen cannot consider himself secure yet."

The last remark was greeted with enthusiastic applause. "We reached the top of the mountain only to find ourselves back at its foot. But take heart, my friends, we start the climb over again," she said. "But this time when we reach the top there will be a major difference. It will not be I who will rule. I intend to place my son on the throne and crown him Henry II, the first Plantagenet King of England. He being male will, without doubt, have a claim much more palatable to the establishment than mine."

At first the announcement was greeted by shocked silence, but soon a ripple of applause began which gradually increased to a tumultuous ovation. For a while Maude basked in the approval. This was a major shift to the main objective, and Ardron could appreciate what it must have cost the egotistical empress in pride. Her eldest son was not yet nine years old, and she was admitting that his chances of becoming ruler were better than her own. At least through his formative years she would be the power behind the throne, and if that were to come about then she would at least have achieved part of her aspiration. But even that was dependant on him actually becoming king and becoming king while still an inexperienced adolescence. Standing in the way of that ambition, of course, was Stephen himself and his son Eustace.

Without more ado she turned and walked towards the large double doors that were the entrance to the great hall. As if by magic those doors swung slowly open and sedately, she led the way into the banqueting area.

Once again, the Christmas banquet at Bristol Castle was spectacularly lavish. There was an over-indulgence of elaborately decorated food. There was no mistaking the artistry of the kitchen staff, nor the pretentious desire to boast extraordinary wealth. It left Ardron pondering Lady Mabel's comment from last year, regarding the empress's desire to freely spend Earl Robert's money. When the dining was eventually ended, then the jugglers and acrobats took over the floor entertainment while food excess and the dining tables were hastily cleared.

Feeling somewhat surplus at the moment Ardron took a slow and casual glance around the great hall. He could see many faces that were familiar and just as many that were not. Up by the smouldering Christmas log, he spotted John Fitzgilbert seemingly in casual conversation with Reginald Earl Dunstanville. and a third person who he did not know. Slowly he eased his way through the throng towards the group.

"Ah Scorrenstone," Fitzgilbert greeted as he neared. With an arm across his shoulders he welcomed Ardron into the company. "Sir Reginald you know," he said. "And this is Sir Robert d'Oyly the new High Sherriff of Oxford and Castellan of Oxford Castle," he introduced the third member of the group. "Ardron here," he added for the benefit of d'Oyly. "Was our saviour at Wherwell."

Ardron studied the man before him with interest, having once spent a night in the barrack rooms of his castle. D'Oyly was a tall man well into his thirties with dark eyes and a seemingly stern expression. Those dark eyes considered Ardron for a moment, then he said. "If that is true then I am privileged to make your acquaintance." He held out his hand to be shaken.

"Something of an exaggeration," Ardron responded modestly taking the man's hand. "We found safe refuge, waited until the danger was past and then stole away to safety as quickly as we could."

D'Oyly caught hold of Ardron's fingers as he released his grip from the handshake. Then turned his hand to look at the ring Ardron wore. "You have a de Vere ring," he exclaimed.

"Yes," Ardron agreed twisting it nervously on his finger.

"May I ask how came you by it"

There was no demand in the question seemingly only curiosity. Nevertheless, Ardron was immediately guarded. "Why do you ask?"

"Curiosity only," d'Oyly replied off-handed. "Aubrey de Vere is a good friend and ally of mine."

Ardron decided there was no reason not to answer his curiosity. In fact it would be suspicious not to. Nevertheless, he decided that he would not divulge the whole story and wouldn't mention the de Vere he killed on the battlefield at Wallingford. "It was given to me by Lady Rohesa."

"Oh," it was a phrased as a question

Ardron twisted the ring uneasily around his finger while he gathered his thoughts. "Yes," he said. "She believed that she had grievously misjudged me, and as a token of recompense, offered me this ring." He held out his hand and spread his fingers. "I accepted the gift to show I held no resentment."

D'Oyly accepted the explanation with a simple nod. "It seems, the Lady Rohesa makes a habit of grievous misjudgements of late," he replied with a strong hint of a sneer.

"He refers," I think," Earl Reginald cut in, sensing Ardron's confusion. "To her choice of husband."

"Geoffrey de Mandeville?" Ardron involuntary questioned.

"Quite so," d'Oyly confirmed. "I'm afraid she moored her boat to a piece of floating flotsam with that one, and who knows where that will drift." He took a deep breath. "Made life a little complicated for her brother Aubrey too," he added.

Ardron could easily understand the awkwardness of the situation for Aubrey de Vere. He was married to Lady Mabel which made him son-in-law to Earl Robert. At the same time his sister was married to Geoffrey de Mandeville and he was now, after a third change, back firmly in the royalist camp.

"How is Lady Rohesa?" Ardron asked trying to change the conversation direction slightly.

"D'Oyly shrugged "Perhaps you should ask Sir Brien Fitzcount. She is, I believe, at this time his guest at Wallingford Castle." He scanned around the hall momentarily presumably looking for Sir Brien.

"Is de Mandeville with her?" Earl Reginald asked bemused.

"Wouldn't have thought so," d'Oyly replied. "Fitzcount wouldn't show hospitality to that man under any circumstances."

"So where is de Mandeville?" Fitzgilbert posed the question.

Earl Reginald scanned around the room. "Sir Brien," he called and raised his arm to attract attention after spotting Sir Brien not too far away.

Sir Brien acknowledged the earl and made his excuses to the small band he had been in conversation with before slowly coming over to join the group.

"Do you have the Lady Rohesa de Mandeville staying with you?" the earl asked.

"Yes!"

"But not Geoffrey de Mandeville!"

"No. She is alone. She intends to spend the Christmas period at Wallingford."

"Without de Mandeville?" This time it was Fitzgilbert who spoke.

"Seemingly so! She had come straight from the coronation ceremony leaving de Mandeville to join in the celebrations at Westminster." He paused while Earl Reginald and Fitzgilbert exchanged knowing looks. "Interestingly," Sir Brien went on. "She did pass comment on how drawn and frail Stephen looked, and looking greatly exhausted, he barely made it to the end of the ceremony."

"That is interesting," Earl Reginald agreed.

It was interesting to Ardron too, but from a different perspective.

***

Trowbridge, June 1142

They had reached the bank of the river Biss when Ardron called a temporary halt. On the opposite side the ground rose upwards towards Trowbridge Castle. Without dismounting he allowed Rattlebone to wander into the shallow water to drink, Luc and Jacques, his squire, followed his example. Leaning forward slightly in the saddle Ardron patted the cash sack yet again just to ensure it was still there. It was the middle of the year and his quarterly fief owed to Sir Humphrey de Bohun was due.

The earlier part of this year had been abnormally quiet with only low-key skirmishes between the warring sides. The low rate of active aggression had lulled Ardron into hopes that this war was beginning to lose intensity, and just might dwindle away. If that did happen then perhaps the two sides would sit down and negotiate a peaceful settlement of sorts. It was his hope, but not really his expectation.

By all reports the king had been very ill, and at one time rumours had circulated announcing his death. However, the rumours were soon proved false. In the meantime, taking advantage of this lull Earl Robert had built unauthorised castles at Cirencester and Bampton to strengthen the Angevin grip on the West Country. It was probable that these actions had proved to be provocative, and Ardron's frail hopes of peace were to become wrecked.

Stephen it seemed, fully recovered, once again picked up the gauntlet of war and at the head of a considerable force marched into the west. His first objective was to destroy the newly finished mote and bailey castle as Bampton. Then continuing west he did precisely the same at Cirencester. With Stephen rampant in the area, Ardron expected him to turn his attention to the nearby castles of South Cerney and Norwood. He had ramped up the defences considerably at Norwood, preparing for an attack that he feared he would not be able to hold. However, unexpectedly, Stephen by-passed both castles and instead moved to Malmesbury, where he rested his forces a few days before going south.

Inside Trowbridge Castle the bailey was, unexpectedly, an intense hive of activity. Some two dozen knights fully armed and dressed in hauberks assembled around their horses busying themselves in last minute preparations to leave. Further down the bailey, horses were being harnessed into a row of ready loaded carts. Ardron, surprised by the heightened hustle and bustle, glanced round enquiringly at Luc. He too at a loss, returned a baffled shrug. They crossed the bailey slowly and dismounted at the mote.

"Something's happening." Luc said as he handed the reins to the young squire.

"It would seem so," Ardron replied surveying the activity. After a few moments he turned his attention back to his horse and unhooked the cash sack from the saddle.

"Will we be here very long?" Jacques asked, as he took the reins of Ardron's horse.

"Two hours. Not more," Ardron replied glancing back once more to the scene of industry.

"Sir Ardron!" It was Roger de Aumale, de Bohun's constable, who greeted them. "Is Sir Humphrey expecting you?"

"Not exactly," Ardron replied. "He knows of course that we would be coming but not precisely when."

"Follow me I will see you refreshed and let Sir Humphrey know you are here."

"My young squire?"

The constable glanced over at Jacques leading the horses away towards the stabling area. "I won't forget him," he promised.

"It's busy here today! Is something afoot?" Ardron asked.

The constable paused halfway up the mote and looked over the busy compound. "Yes there is," he said. "But I will let Sir Humphrey inform you of the developments."

Inside the keep they were shown to one of Sir Humphrey's private chambers. Even though the day outside was bright the inside was dim, lit only by arrow slits on the walls. They settled to wait in front of an unlit fireplace. After a little while, two servants arrived and silently placed a tray of fruit on the table and a jug of wine.

"I would say that my Lord de Bohun intends some kind of expedition," Luc said as he went over to the table and began pouring the wine.

"And you would be right." It was de Bohun himself who spoke as he walked briskly into the room. "Are you here to join us?" He too was dressed in his hauberk

"I am here to pay my quarterly lease," Ardron said getting to his feet.

"Oh," de Bohun looked disappointed. "Have you not been summoned by Earl Robert?"

"No Sir, I have not."

He looked puzzled. "But you are in knights service to the earl?"

"Yes Sir Humphrey, I am. But I have not been detailed to any campaign."

"Hmm," de Bohun grunted. "But still he would be pleased to see you join him, of that I have no doubts."

"What precisely is the objective?" Ardron asked.

"I am obliged to rendezvous with my Lord, Earl Robert at Wareham. From there we set sail for France then journey onwards to Anjou."

"Anjou?" Ardron was surprised. "May I ask what business Earl Robert has in Anjou?"

De Bohun frowned a moment then said. "I don't suppose I am giving away any secrets, but the campaign is in need of funds and sergens. Earl Robert travels to Anjou to negotiate with Count Geoffrey Plantagenet who has both funds and a large army."

Ardron was puzzled. "I was under the impression that the empress had resolved that under no circumstances would she tolerate her husband's involvement."

"And that impression was correct," de Bohun confirmed. "But circumstances change. Our need is great and so, unfortunately, a little pride needs to be set aside. Besides, the objections before were, that should the empress prevail Geoffrey would have expectation of becoming the king. That is why she brooked no interference from him, and to keep him out of it completely. But now the circumstances have changed. The empresses new objective is to place Prince Henry on the throne. Which, should she succeed, would make Geoffrey the king's father only."

"Will that make him more co-operative?" Ardron asked.

De Bohun shrugged. "Perhaps," he said unconvincingly. "However, the earl has to try." He was silent a moment. "So will you join us?" he asked.

Ardron was tempted, he had never been to France. In fact he had never left England. Almost instantly, however, he decided that his own interests would be better served at Norwood.

His fighting force had been effectively reduced as a result of Wherwell. He had committed only a token force of around thirty, but less than half of these had made it back to Norwood. French sergens and Saxon villeins in about equal numbers had been posted missing, presumed dead. The most significant to Ardron had been Dardot, who he assumed to be lying in a mass grave somewhere near Wherwell. Jarcot had also been missing, but eventually had returned after a long absence. However, he returned missing a right arm. As a fighting man he was now of little use, but Ardron retained him as a trainer.

Unlike the Norman aristocracy, he held no estates in France from which he could recruit French replacements. His replacements had to be recruited from his Saxon villeins. They were simple Saxon villagers and needed to be intensely trained. At the very onset, as Norwood Castellan, he had decreed that all villeins of fighting age be required to report once per month for combat training. However, he considered that to be the minimum standard, and essential for their personal survival. But to have an effective fighting force, he needed to have a nucleus of battle-hardened professionals. At this time, as a result of Lincoln and Wherwell, that nucleus was a little shallow. He concluded that his time would be better served over-seeing the training

"Sir Humphrey," he said. "I am not forgetting that it was you who first gave me lessons in sword skill. Valuable lessons they were too, and because of that, I see myself as forever in your debt. If I thought I could be of particular value I would not hesitate to join you."

De Bohun stared at him hard, making him feel a little uncomfortable. Then after a moment's thought, he waved a dismissive hand. "Perhaps it was that Earl Robert decided that you should be granted a respite, particularly so after Wherwell. But regarding those lessons! Well twas nothing. You have a rare talent, and I only gave you pointers. Judging from your current reputation, I doubt very much that I could best you today."

Ardron smiled a little relieved and nodded accepting the compliment.

"I must beg your indulgence," de Bohun said. "I am to leave soon, and I still have things to do. So I must take my leave. However, please feel free to dally as long as you wish." He waved his hand towards the refreshment tray on the table. "Please help yourselves." He paused a moment then turned to leave.

"Sir Humphrey," Ardron said, then held up the cash sack. "The quarterly lease."

"Of course," de Bohun said. "I'll send my clerk."

Ardron nodded. "God grant you a safe journey and a satisfactory outcome," he said.

***

Norwood, December 1142

It had been a successful day's hunt. When the snow lies thick on the ground no animal can move without leaving a trail and is, therefore, easy to track. Ardron cast a surveying eye over the catch. He was satisfied. All at Norwood castle would eat meat for at least another week. But now it was mid-afternoon and the dullness that is December was beginning to deepen. It was time to make their way back, particularly so since the severe frost that had persisted unrelenting for the past three weeks was beginning once more to increase its icy grip.

More than an hour later and the light fading fast the hunting party arrived back at Norwood. With the extreme cold biting right through the leather skin protection into a man's very bones, the castle was indeed a welcome sight. At the foot of the mote Ardron was greeted by Jarcot who held the reins while he dismounted.

"A successful hunt," Jarcot muttered.

At first Ardron did not reply, he was concentrating solely on controlling wobbling frozen legs. "Very good," he eventually stuttered. Even his jaw seemed to have a problem forming words.

"There is someone here to see you," Jarcot said.

"Oh!" Ardron queried. "Who would that be?"

"It is your Saxon friend who you left at Lincoln."

"Swidhurn?" Ardron was surprised.

Jarcot nodded. "He arrived this morning and has been waiting all day."

"Where is he now?"

"I showed him into your chamber. He waits for you there." Jarcot replied as he handed the horses reins to squire Jacques.

Ardron momentarily turned his attention to Jacques. "Groom him well and see that he is well fed," he instructed slapping the horse rump as it was led away.

Inside the chamber it was appreciably warmer with a large welcoming fire blazing in the inglenook. Swidhurn was close to that fire slumped in a large wooden seat, deep in sleep. Ardron went to the table in the middle of the room where a wine flagon and hot bread had been laid out awaiting his return. He poured two chalice of wine and went over to where Swidhurn slept. He studied his sleeping friend a moment as he placed one goblet on the inglenook shelf.

It was almost two years since Ardron had seen Swidhurn, and it seemed to him that his friend had aged more than that. Hints of grey mingled in the long hair that hung over his ears and was repeated in his beard. He leaned forward and gently shook him. Swidhurn snapped awake immediately and was then overtaken by confusion as he struggled to recall his surroundings.

"Swidhurn," Ardron said and held out the goblet. It's good to see you."

"Ardron," he muttered taking the goblet and started to get to his feet.

"Sit, sit," Ardron said placing his hand on his shoulder. "This is a pleasant surprise," he added, then moved to the fire holding his arms forward to the flames soaking in the warmth. "By God, the winter is raw out there."

"Aye it is, Swidhurn readily agreed.

"Have you come far today?"

Swidhurn nodded. "I left Oxford yesterday, camped somewhere near Farringdon, then journeyed here this morning."

"You camped out last night?" Ardron queried with incredulity.

"Aye I did."

"Tis a wonder you didn't die from exposure."

Swidhurn only nodded.

"What were you doing in Oxford?"

"I went to get Hildi. But I found the castle under siege and was unable to get in."

"That's common knowledge," Ardron scoffed. "For some weeks now the king's sergens occupy the town and have put the castle under siege."

"Not common knowledge to me it wasn't." Swidhurn complained. "Not until I got close, anyway."

Ardron was puzzled. "What is Hildi doing at Oxford?"

"She was sent there by Roumare."

That added to Ardron's confusion. "William Roumare, Earl Lincoln?"

"Yes, the same."

Ardron turned his back to the fire to warm his rear and to face Swidhurn. "Why?" He asked.

Swidhurn took a deep breath. "Perhaps I had better start from the beginning." He took a long drink while he gathered his thoughts. "For a long time Hildi stayed at Lincoln Castle as hand maid to Roumare. And that was good, because I had established myself as a blacksmith in the castle bailey so I could be nearby. Then a couple of months ago Roumare moved the Lady Hawise, his wife, to Lincoln, So, understandably, Hildi as his mistress could not stay. She was moved to Castle Bolingbroke a few miles east of Lincoln. At first, I didn't know she had gone, but when I discovered the change I, at my first opportunity, travelled those few miles to visit her. She seemed to be in good spirits, although a little disappointed that Roumare had moved her. Nevertheless, she accepted the situation. She wasn't too upset; her new location was still a comfortable position with all privileges. I returned to Lincoln re-assured of her well-being." He paused sighing heavily, then stood with arm resting on the inglenook and peered into the flames.

"Here I was at fault. I was blind and too complacent," he went on. "Roumare had another favour, and I did not pay any heed. I had noticed Roumare spending a lot of time with a pretty young coquette from his court, but I did not realise the significance until it suddenly hit me across the face, like being swiped with a wet herring. He had another mistress! Hildi had not been moved to appease the Lady Hawise, she had been moved to make way for her replacement. At my first opportunity I made my way to Bolingbroke, only to be told the Hildi had been sent back to the Oxford whore house, whence she came. The very next day I gathered my belongings and left for Oxford. That was some nine or ten days ago."

"You're telling me that for more than a week you have travelled more than a hundred miles through the very teeth of this bitter winter." Ardron asked with astonishment.

Swidhurn straightened and made hard eye contact with Ardron. "I need your help!" he said.

"And you have it," Ardron replied. Though, at this time, he was not sure what exactly he could do. "What can I do?"

"You're a known knight, if you present at the Oxford castle gate, they will let you in." Swidhurn replied. "Once inside we can find my sister then take her out."

Ardron was thoughtful a moment it sounded simple. Much too simple. "You want me to march up to the castle gate at Oxford and demand admittance.

"Us," Swidhurn corrected. "And yes, that's about the sum of it."

Ardron shook his head slowly. "It's just not that simple. Firstly, do you think the siege sergens will just let us through?"

It was Swidhurn's turn to shake his head. "No, not likely. But under the cover of darkness we might be able to sneak through. Then it would be up to you to convince the gate guards to let us in."

"OK," Ardron said dubiously. "And if we do get in, and we do find Hildi, and if we should get out and clear safely, what then? I mean what would you do with Hildi? I doubt very much she would want to return to Scorrenstone."

Swidhurn did not reply instead stared hard at Ardron. Then as if by telepathy Ardron realised what he was thinking. "You want to bring her here to Norwood." Ardron sighed. "It could work," he said. He was thoughtful a few moments not sure how to proceed with the next problem. "However," he went on. "There is an added complication. I don't suppose you know that trapped inside Oxford Castle is Empress Maude herself. And for those laying siege it means it would be more than their very lives are worth to let her escape. Which of course means those guards will be extra vigilant."

"I didn't know," Swidhurn replied. "Makes no difference to me. I am still determined to get Hildi out."

Ardron made a resigned sigh. "I thought as much. I don't suppose I could persuade you to wait a little while."

"To what point?"

"The empress trapped inside a siege is not a situation that can be allowed to continue, and sooner or later Earl Robert will have to mount a relief army to rescue her."

"When will that be?

Ardron stroked his beard. "Can't be sure! As I understand the situation at this time, the earl is in Dorset sieging the castle at Wareham. He means to get it back. That might take a few more weeks yet."

"Could be months," Swidhurn countered.

"Could be months," Ardron reluctantly agreed.

Swidhurn made a face.

"You're going to go back with or without me, aren't you?" Ardron concluded. Then after a thoughtful pause he said with a sigh. "We leave tomorrow."

It was early afternoon the next day, with nine inches snow underfoot and a chill wind that freezes blood, when they breasted the rise that looked down on the farm that belonged to the Saxon, Odel.

"We will rest here for a couple of hours," Ardron said.

"Do you know these people?" Swidhurn asked.

"I do. I had occasion to lend aid several months ago. He will welcome and feed us," Ardron replied.

"How far are we from Oxford?"

"Three hours. Not more,"

"Shouldn't we yet press on?"

Ardron shook his head. "The horses need rest. We need rest. But most of all we all need a little respite from this biting cold." Without waiting for any reply he spurred Rattlebone down the hill, the spare third horse following behind on a long halter. As they neared the farm a young man emerged from the barn and stood watching the approaching strangers suspiciously.

"Hello Leofric," Ardron said when close enough.

The youngster stared at him more closely until recognition spread across his face. "Sir Ardron," he said with happiness. "You are welcome," he grinned. "I'll tell father you are here," he could hardly contain his excitement as he bounded towards the bucolic farmhouse. A few moments later he re-appeared with Odel.

"Step down, please" Odel invited them to dismount. "Leofric, take their horses to the barn and see them fed," he instructed. Then without waiting for his son to react he waved an arm towards the house. "Come," he said, "We have food and warmth inside, and you are most welcome to share."

More than three hours later, fed and well rested, Ardron decided that it was time to brave the cruel elements and continue on. Even so he could not help an unspoken reluctance to abandon the agreeable warmth of the farmhouse, but needs must. The light had faded by the time they started their onward travel. Under a clear sky a silver aura had wrapped around the near full moon and promised yet more frost this night.

Less than three hours later and still almost three hours remaining before midnight they arrived at a point south west of Oxford and here, they paused. Throughout the journey Ardron had, in his mind, played over and over the possible scenarios that they would have to overcome to get into the castle. From his previous visit he was aware that the castle was ringed by a moat which was a spur from the nearby Thames. The main way across that moat was by a single bridge which ended halfway across. It needed the drawbridge to be lowered to complete the crossing. That wasn't a possibility! The inmates would under no circumstances lower it and even if they did then the royalists outside could not miss the clanking sounds of a drawbridge being lowered. No! There would have to be an alternative. He had thought long and hard trying to remember if there was a secondary gate. He thought that there must be, but he just didn't know. And even if there was then there still remained the problem of entry. Persuading the castle inmates to let them in would take some convincing. The more he pondered the more convinced he became that this was an ill-advised enterprise. But they were here now. He wondered that even at this late stage Swidhurn might be persuaded to abandon this foolhardy enterprise. That wasn't likely, he decided. Swidhurn's absolute resolve was clear.

"Do you have a plan?" Swidhurn asked.

Ardron scoffed. "A plan? No I do not."

"So, what do we do?"

Ardron sighed. "I guess we get as close as we dare then tether the horses. Then we'll creep forward on foot to discover the exact situation. We might then be able to make a plan."

In fact the situation was more relaxed than Ardron imagined. Completely unchallenged they were able to ride their horses' right into the town itself. The streets were full of Stephen's sergens and all seemingly in high spirits. With a newfound confidence Ardron led the way through the narrow streets to the same stable where he had stabled his horse the last time he was in Oxford. The open-ended barn was manned by the same grumpy old man. Nor did it look as if he had even changed his clothing in the intervening time. He wore the same grimy smock over a dirty shirt and the same knitted skull cap on his head. And as it was before, Ardron handed over the marks demanded then they were obliged to bed and feed their animals themselves.

With the horses settled they made their way, feigning a casual air, towards the castle itself. It was as they neared the bridge that the relaxed air evaporated. A group of sentinels slouched and huddled close around a burning brazier. Their focus changed when they noted Swidhurn and Ardron moving towards them. After glaring at the pair for few moments two reluctantly deserted their place at the fireside and with swords drawn approached aggressively.

"State your business," the taller one demanded. The man stood over the ground at more than six-foot-six and probably the tallest man Ardron had ever seen. Neither was he skinny being thickset. He was a giant of a man.

"We're strangers in town and it was curiosity that brought us here just to look," Swidhurn muttered almost apologetically.

"That sort of curiosity is likely to get you killed," the giant growled shaking his sword threateningly.

"Thank you," Ardron said glancing beyond the giant at the frozen moat. "We'll make our way back right away." He turned slowly taking the opportunity to look along the length of the moat as he did. The darkness on the opposite side of the castle was scattered with campfires. Understandably so, in these sub-zero temperatures men needed to keep warm or die from exposure.

"We bid you a good night," Ardron said pleasantly over his shoulder as they walked away. "What did you see? He muttered to Swidhurn when they were out of hearing range.

Swidhurn took a quick glance back over his shoulder. "Men reluctant to leave the warmth of their fire."

"What else?"

Swidhurn hesitated then said dubiously, "More campfires back towards the town?"

"Yes and most likely men huddled around those too. But what about the moat? Ardron asked.

Swidhurn was thoughtful for a moment "It was frozen?" he said.

"Exactly! How thick do you think that ice is?"

"You're not thinking to walk across?" Swidhurn uttered as he followed Ardron's thoughts.

"It's a possibility," Ardron replied. "With those sergens reluctant to leave their fireside we could well cross unseen."

"Assuming, of course, the ice holds our weight." Swidhurn said.

"Assuming the ice holds my weight," Ardron paraphrased making the small correction. "Even if the ice is thick enough, I can't very well walk up to the main gate and knock to be let in. Those guards on the bridge would see me for certes. We need to find another lesser gate."

"A postern gate!" Swidhurn muttered.

"Aye a postern gate."

Out of site of the sergens on the bridge the pair now ducked off the road and moved down to the moat. They moved stealthily with ears and eyes straining for the possible proximity of patrolling sergens, but they saw none. The moat along this stretch was wide at least thirty long paces and on the opposite side touched the castle wall. After a few minutes they encountered a brook feeding into the moat from the north. This too was frozen over.

"This will be a good test piece," Ardron whispered and stepped cautiously onto the ice. He stood for a few moments waiting for the ice to crack, but it held. With a little more confidence he moved slowly on. It took no more than a dozen paces to reach the other side. He stepped onto the bank on the other side. He looked back at his snow trodden footprints and was a little more optimistic that the ice on the moat would be as thick. He waved Swidhurn over to join him.

"Promising," Swidhurn muttered when he too had crossed.

"Yes, but this is only a brook," Ardron replied. The moat is a spur from the river. It flows around the castle and then back into the river. It will be deeper and therefore the ice thinner, particularly so in the middle." Swidhurn stared at him enquiringly without making comment. "We won't know until we try," Ardron added.

They pressed on turning east along the northern wall of the castle. Here the town wall became part of the castle butting up to the mote and the keep. It was just beyond where they found what they sought, a small secondary gate.

"A postern gate," Swidhurn muttered with relief.

"Aye it is. And look the remnants of a bridge." Ardron whispered. Protruding from the moat four or five stout posts that had once been supports for a narrow bridge. Whether the bridge had been destroyed by the defenders or the attackers mattered not but those posts gave Ardron improved hopes of a safe crossing. "If I can get from post to post I should have a better chance of making it across," he murmured."

Swidhurn nodded agreement. "I'll go first," he said.

"No," Ardron replied firmly. "You stay here."

Swidhurn was taken aback and about to protest but Ardron cut him off. "Somebody has to stay outside the castle. Because I have a much better chance of being let in, the person staying outside has to be you. If I make it across and if they let me in, then I need you to be waiting with the horses' tomorrow night when I come out with Hildi." Then after a moment's pause added, "If, I come out with Hildi."

Thoughtful a moment Swidhurn eventually nodded agreement. That settled Ardron turned his attention to the moat and planned his route across from post to post. "Here goes," he muttered more to himself. "If I get across, and if they let me in, then meet me by that brook around this time tomorrow," he charged Swidhurn. Then he stepped tentatively onto the frozen moat.

The ice held. He stood quite still listening for the sound of cracking, but none came. So he began, in slow time, to move tentatively forward one step at a time towards the first post. That objective secured he planned his move to the next post and this one towards the middle of the moat. If the ice was going to give way, then it would give way there in the middle where the ice was probably thinnest. He made it there too without mishap. Nevertheless, he wrapped his arms thankfully around the post hugging it in gratitude. Before he moved on, he glanced back towards Swidhurn hoping for some encouragement, but he could not see him. Returning his attention to the task before him he set off for the next and last post. When he neared the opposite bank his nerve wavered, and he made an uncontrolled dash for safety. On the opposite side he looked back over the moat and realised that he had worried needlessly. The ice was thick and had comfortably borne his weight.

The postern gate was set within a shallow arched vestibule with heavy double doors that looked more akin to substantial church doors. Ardron was thankful to be in the shadows of the vestibule out of sight from across the moat. It now only remained to convince those within the castle to admit him. Wrapping his hand into a fist he thumped vigorously on the doors. There was no response! It took several thumps before he eventually got a reaction from within.

"Whose there?" A half-interested enquiry.

"I am Sir Ardron of Norwood in service to the Earl of Gloucester." He replied.

There was a long pause. "What is your business at this hour?"

"I want entry,"

Then silence. That silence protracted for a long time until Ardron was convinced that he had been ignored, so he banged on the door again. Still there was no response. "Hello," he called banging vigorously on the door yet again.

"Who is it wanting entry?" this time a different voice.

"Ardron of Norwood," he repeated.

"State your business!"

This was hardly the time to enter into a protracted conversation to explain his reasons. Straight to the top, he decided. "I would speak with Sir Robert d'Oyly," he said.

Once again, another delay before the voice asked. "Are you alone?"

"Yes I am," Ardron confirmed.

"Step away from the door and clear of the castle."

Ardron did as was ordered and waited. After what seemed an age, he became aware of movement above on the ramparts where two men stared down at him. He spread his arms to indicate that he held no weapon, but the men above were in no hurry and took time to carefully survey the situation. Eventually seemingly satisfied that it was not a trick the two men disappeared. Soon there were sounds of bolts being released and barricading bars being removed. The door was then opened just enough to allow Ardron to slip through. He was now inside. However, he found himself on the end of five sword tips.

No-one spoke. No-one moved, least of all Ardron. He waited in silence for something to happen. Eventually from his right a taller man dressed in a hauberk moved alongside and lifted a lantern to light Ardron's face. He leaned forward his face mere inches away as he belligerently studied Ardron close up. Ardron held the man's gaze defiantly

"I am the constable of this castle," he said eventually. "Who are you and what is your business with Sir Robert?"

"I am Ardron of Norwood and my business with Sir Robert is of a private nature." He slid the de Vere ring from his finger. "Give him this and it will verify my identity."

The constable lowered the lantern and studied the ring for a few moments. "Sir Robert will be abed by this time," he said taking the ring. "I will only disturb him if the business is urgent." Then he lifted the lantern back to light Ardron's face.

Ardron sighed. The business was not so urgent. "Do not disturb him. My business can wait until the morning," he said.

The constable stared at him suspiciously obviously wondering why he had run the gauntlet of a siege force to gain entry if the business was not urgent.

"If you can just find me a bed for the night and report my arrival to Sir Robert in the morning I would be in your debt, constable." Ardron sought to appease the man.

His mind made up the constable straightened and nodded. "Hand over your sword," he demanded. Ardron hesitated a moment and thought to protest but decided it would serve him nought. He reluctantly unbuckled his baldric and handed over the weapon. "Put him in one of the cells," the constable ordered over his shoulder. Then addressing Ardron he said, "I will report your arrival in the morning. With this," he added holding up the de Vere ring.

It was an uncomfortable and cold night in the cell for Ardron. The damp atmosphere added to the biting cold making sleep impossible. Indeed it was only as he relieved himself into the bucket that he realised just how cold it was. That bucket was frozen solid. Nor was the constable in any hurry to release him, and it was not until morning mass had finished before he came.

"Sir Robert will see you," he announced disinterestedly as he fiddled with the locks and bolts.

"Does he know who I am?" Ardron asked.

The constable shook his head. "No," he replied curtly and stood waiting by the open door. Ardron stepped out of the cell and found himself flanked by two armed sergens. The constable was taking no chances. "Follow me," he said and led the way.

As they crossed the bailey patent evidence of long privation was everywhere. Whether due to fires caused from burning arrows or wantonly ripped to pieces for fire fuel, that which had been workshops or living quarters now remained only skeletal foundations. They passed a group of hollow-eyed men huddled around a brazier. They stared disinterested at the small party as they passed. Ardron was shocked to notice that the fire was being kept alight by burning arrow shafts. If men were burning their arrows to keep warm, then there could be little fight left in them. He looked towards the constable expecting him to deliver a severe rebuke, but he chose to ignore it. Immediately after morning mass comes the ritual of breakfast, but there was no sign of breakfast this day, nor, it seemed, was there any expectation from the men. The food supplies, Ardron guessed, must be completely exhausted.

The keep inside was bereft of furniture. The walls of the great hall, upon which had once hung majestic tapestries, were now bare grey walls and as cold as any gravestone in the depth of winter. Probably more fire fuel. This castle was defeated and surrender, it seemed, so very close.

Ardron was led into Sir Robert d'Oyly's private chamber and announced. This chamber was warmer with a fire burning in the inglenook. Even so the room was sparsely furnished with only a single table and half a dozen seats. But what it was that took Ardron by surprise was the presence of Empress Maude sitting close to the fire. He took a half step back and bowed, "Your Majesty," he acknowledged.

"I know you?" Question or a statement from Sir Robert.

"You do, Sir. We met last Christmas at Bristol Castle." Ardron replied.

Still a little unsure Sir Robert studied him more closely. "This ring," he said picking it up from the bench, "Is a de 'Vere ring. How is it that it is in your possession?"

He had asked the exact same question almost a year ago. "It was given to me by the Lady Rohesa as recompense for a wrong she thought she had done me." Ardron replied patiently.

"Ah__, Now I remember," Sir Robert acknowledged. "You were the hero of Wherwell?"

"Can anyone be a hero in the face of such a catastrophic defeat?" Ardron modestly played down the compliment then glanced nervously at the empress fearing he might have caused offence.

"Sit," Sir Robert indicated a place at the table. Then turning to the constable said. "You may dismiss the guards." He took a seat opposite and indicated to his constable that he too should sit.

"Do you bring news from the outside?" Sir Robert asked.

"No Sir I do not."

D'Oyly looked at him quizzically "You do not bring news from Sir Brien Fitzcount?"

"Sir Brien? No I'm afraid not."

"We had hoped that he would be mounting a rescue from Wallingford."

Ardron shook his head bewildered. "I am afraid, Sir, that I just don't know."

"What of my brother Earl Gloucester?" The empress asked.

"I had heard that he had returned from France with your son Prince Henry at his side." Ardron said.

"My son! Henry?" Maude said surprised. "He is none but a child." There was a pause. "Where is Gloucester now?" she asked.

"I am not sure," Ardron replied. "Last that I heard he was at Wareham trying to raise the siege of Wareham Castle."

"Not much prospects of a rescue from there either," Sir Robert said gloomily. Then after a long pause he turned to Ardron and said "Now, tell me. "How did you get in?"

"Under the cover of darkness I stole through the king's perimeter guards, crossed the frozen moat and banged on the postern gate to be let in."

"You crossed the frozen moat?" The empress queried.

"I did your majesty!"

"It held your weight without problem?" Sir Robert sought clarification.

"It did!"

"How did you get past the king's men?"

"In weather as cruel as this they don't move far from their fire braziers and their fires highlight their positions. It requires only to steal past in the darkness between their positions." Ardron said.

Sir Robert was thoughtful a moment. "Alright," he said. "Why?"

"Why?"

"Yes why. If you do not bring news, then why did you take such a chance to get in?"

Ardron gathered his thoughts. "There is someone within this castle that I want to take out."

"Oh really?" Sir Robert responded.

"It is a girl who was kidnapped from the village of Scorrenstone and I am here to take her home."

"We don't have any kidnapped girls here," Sir Robert retorted clearly irked.

"I am sure you don't, Sir Robert," Ardron appeased. "She was kidnapped over three years ago by Fitzhubert and after being passed around for a while she was taken by Sir William Roumare from here to Lincoln as his mistress. Recently he grew tired of her and returned her back to here. I believe she is still here."

"Still here? Where?"

"Probably in your castle brothel."

"You would take this risk for a whore?"

"I would. That which fate has dealt her is not her fault."

Sir Robert gave a little sigh. "What's the girl's name?

"Hildi,"

"Do you know of such a girl?" Sir Robert asked the constable.

"No," he replied. "But I'll make enquiries."

"Do so, if you please."

The conversation lulled while the constable left the room. Then after a while Sir Robert asked. "How did you intend to get out?"

"Exactly the same way I came in. I have an accomplice on the outside who will be waiting for me at midnight with horses.

Sir Robert turned and looked at the empress, then as if getting silent permission said. "We might permit you to leave under certain conditions."

Ardron was taken aback. He had never considered the possibility that once in the castle he might not be permitted to leave. "Conditions?" he asked.

Empress Maude got up from the fireside and came to sit at the table. Ardron stood out of politeness while she sat.

"You have been a steadfast and faithful knight to my brother and to my cause," she said. "And still we would ask further service of you."

Ardron nodded compliance. "I am at your service my lady."

"Good," she said. "The condition is that you take me and my maid out with you tonight and deliver us safely to Wallingford."

Ardron was stunned. The responsibility was frighteningly awesome. If he failed to sneak through the royalist siege line and the empress were to be captured, then he would be regarded as the man that had delivered the figure head of the Angevin cause directly into the king's hands. All would be lost. And yet in conscience he could not refuse her command because her situation within these walls was desperate. The castle was within days of complete capitulation, perhaps even within hours.

"It would be my honour, your majesty," he heard himself say.

"We are in your gratitude," Maude said with a huge smile. Then sighing heavily with relief she addressed Sir Robert. "What time will we leave?" Sir Robert indicated with an arm wave towards Ardron that it was his decision.

"An hour before midnight, majesty." Ardron said.

"Very well. I have much to do before then," she said in high spirits.

"Please, my lady. We cannot carry any baggage," Ardron said fearing that the empress intended to pack.

"Of course not," she replied as she left. Both men stood in silence and watched her leave.

"You have raised her spirits," Sir Robert said quietly staring after her. "I have not seen her so cheerful in many days." Then, bringing himself to address the present situation, he asked. "Is there anything I can do to help? Perhaps a small contingent of sergens?"

"Definitely not," Ardron replied. "The smaller our number the better our chances. However, with a party of five we will be short two horses."

"Ah__ There my friend I regret that I cannot help you. We slaughtered all our livestock for meat many weeks ago."

"Then we'll have to manage," Ardron said glumly.

Sir Robert nodded sympathetically then added in a lower tone. "Twould be better we mention to no-one that the empress attempts an escape tonight. There could be treacherous ears even within my own castle,"

The suggestion was sound and Ardron nodded agreement.

"Come," Sir Robert then said. "Let us see if my constable has managed to find this village girl of yours."

Madame Rouselle's bordello was now very different from that time when he had made that brief visit almost two years ago. Gone were the luxurious fine quality soft-furnishing and the mellow touches of feminine features. Ravaged by the needs of those locked inside a siege the place had degenerated to the basic and perhaps even beyond. In the reception area where once there had been bespoke furniture and an excess of superior furnishings there remained only basic wooden benches. In all probability, these benches too were in danger from firewood scavengers. Curtains and drapes were there none. The artisan hand-woven mats that had re-dressed the harsh stone floor had also disappeared leaving the place more akin to a large prison cell.

Except for the constable who sat on one of the benches staring down at his feet with an air of tedium the room was empty. Almost tiredly the man got to his feet when they entered. "It seems, Sir Robert," he said. "There is a girl here called Hildi who came from Lincoln some weeks ago."

D'Oyly glanced at Ardron for his re-action. Ardron said nothing instead gave a brief satisfied nod. "Where is she now?" Sir Robert asked.

"Madame Rouselle has gone to find her. It seems she is in bed," the constable replied.

"In bed at this hour?" Ardron queried.

The constable nodded. "Under the circumstances, is there a better place to keep warm?"

Under the circumstances there wasn't. "Point taken," Ardron said.

They waited in silence until Madame Rouselle bustled into the room, her already ample frame exaggerated by additional layers of clothing. "Milord," she muttered when she saw Sir Robert, then made a vague bob that passed for a curtsy.

"Madame," Sir Robert acknowledged. "Where is the girl?"

"She is coming," Rouselle replied staring at Ardron. "I know you?" she said her brow furrowed in concentration. Ardron nodded without attempting to enlighten her. "Oh yes," she said as she remembered. "You came once before looking for my Hildi!"

Without looking Ardron could feel Sir Robert's eyes drilling into him with curiosity? He had neglected to mention that, although not intentionally. But then he had not considered it to be relevant to the present circumstances.

"Yes that was almost three years ago now," he said dismissively seeking to end that line.

She looked slightly aghast. "As long ago as that?" Then she turned her attention to Sir Robert. "Milord may I ask why you want to see this girl?"

"This knight intends to take her out of here tonight."

"Take her out! How?" Her surprise was clear.

"He has a plan," Sir Robert replied dismissively.

"I don't suppose you could take me as well, corn-cockle," she queried Ardron.

"Not possible," he replied curtly.

"Oh well," she said with a sigh. "It was worth the asking."

"Ardron, what are you doing here?" They hadn't noticed Hildi enter the room. She stood just inside the door cloaked in a heavy blanket which she clutched two-handed just under her neck.

"He has come to take you away, corn-cockle," Madame Rouselle answered for him.

"Take me away? To where?" she asked.

"Anywhere you want." Ardron replied.

"I won't go back to Scorrenstone," she said firmly.

"You don't have to," Ardron agreed.

"This is the girl, I suppose," Sir Robert cut in.

"It is!"

"Good," he said satisfied. "Then I will leave you here to explain." Looking at Madame Rouselle he then instructed. "Have this girl brought to my quarters two hours before midnight." With that directive he turned to leave indicating to the constable with a flick of his head that he should follow.

"Why have you come?" Hildi asked after the pair had left.

"You don't need to ask that," Ardron replied.

"But I sent you away before."

"You did, but your circumstances are very different now," he pointed out.

She nodded silent agreement. "How do you intend to get out?"

He glanced at Madame Rouselle not wanting to give too much away. "Your brother waits outside with horses and under the cover of darkness we intend to slip through the cordon of sentries."

"Swidhurn is here?"

"He is."

She nodded thoughtfully then asked. "Where will I go?"

"Well, you could come to Norwood castle."

"And do what?"

Ardron had not thought that far ahead. He shrugged and lifted his arms somewhat at a loss. "I suppose," he said. "You could take over the running of the domestic arrangements. I am sure my constable would be pleased to shed those responsibilities."

She nodded thoughtfully. "I have done those duties in Lincoln."

"Then are we agreed?" Ardron asked.

"Where exactly is Norwood?

"North of Malmesbury and a little south-east of Cirencester." He doubted that had enlightened her a great deal.

She was silent a few moments then her mind made up said, with a sigh. "Alright I agree. Then after a short pause. "I suppose that I had better go and pack a few things."

"No! Ardron said. "Not possible. You can only leave with the clothes you wear."

"She looked shocked. "But I have an extensive and very expensive wardrobe."

He didn't doubt it. As mistress to William Roumare, Lord of Bolingbroke and Earl of Lincoln she would have been pampered. "Nevertheless," he said, "You will have to leave it all behind."

"There is of course the question of compensation," Madame Rouselle interrupted.

"Compensation?" Ardron queried.

"Yes, corn-cockle, I am losing one of my treasured girls."

Ardron stared at her. She was bargaining from a weak position and the truth was she had no idea just how weak her position was. He was the potential saviour of the empress and a compensation claim from a seedy brothel Madame would not even be allowed into the equation. "There will be no compensation," he said.

"There has to be" she exclaimed indignant.

Ardron sighed. "You can compensate yourself from the wardrobe that Hildi leaves behind."

"Not enough. I will be appealing to Sir Robert."

"Feel free to do so, corn-cockle," Ardron replied sarcastically. "In the meantime," he went on talking to Hildi. "If the good lady here doesn't want your wardrobe then I suggest you tear up all the dresses and burn them. At least you will get warm as they burn." He piled on the pressure.

"Don't you dare do any such thing," Madame Rouselle retorted.

The day passed slowly for Ardron. There was not a familiar face within the castle walls that he might pass the time with, and others of equal status seemed to be busy with their own areas of responsibility. Most of those that were not on duty were much more inclined to find places to sleep. With the imposed starvation diet then energy levels were low, also, a man asleep did not brood upon his hunger. Ardron managed a little sleep himself during the afternoon. That, however, was interrupted by a prolonged bombardment of missiles bombing into the castle from the royalist trebuchet. The missiles, consisting rocks and pieces of rusty iron, peppered the castle precincts indiscriminately causing much more inconvenience than any real damage. Still, Ardron mused, its probable purpose was to harass and to degrade morale and to that end there was perhaps some success.

As the day began to diminish towards dusk Ardron climbed onto the western battlements and studied the positions of the campfires mapping out in his mind possible routes between. The landscape before him was covered with a thick mantle of snow which would not only make the underfoot conditions energy-sapping and foot numbingly cold, but would also provide a backdrop against which anything dark would contrast. He looked to the skies looking for the moon. Its pallor was just visible in the gathering gloom and at its half-full stage. That was not bad, but then not too good either. He prayed that tonight there would be thick cloud cover obliterating any of the moon's silver glow. He felt keenly the awesome responsibility that was being placed upon him. If he failed to smuggle the empress safely through the cordon, then her quest for the English crown on behalf of her son was at an end. Additionally, all her loyal followers would find themselves without the figurehead of their cause and completely at the mercy of King Stephen's whim. He tarried a long time on the battlements alone with his sombre thoughts and watched the sun's glow, diffused behind thick cloud, disappear beneath the horizon.

The sun had disappeared completely and only the merest hint of sky soreness remained when the nearest thing to a meal was trundled out. It consisted a mug of hot broth, no more. However, to be calling it a broth was indeed flattering, it was more akin to onion flavoured hot water. There was little doubt in Ardron's mind the castle was indeed at the very point of capitulation and at this moment in time the whole of the Angevin ambitions hinged entirely upon Empress Maude's escape.

The early evening was just as monotonous as the long tedious afternoon had been. The time was worn away by playing checkers in Robert d'Oyly chambers. Ardron could neither concentrate his mind nor his interest on the succession of games. Eventually he reached the point where he simply could not face another game. He moved to the fireside and using a whetstone methodically honed his sword edge while staring unseeing into a smouldering fire. In his mind he rehearsed his plan over and over again. But he knew that there were just too many variable possibilities to form a precise action and he would have to react to events as they occurred. Nevertheless, he still had the basic idea that he would follow until some differing event altered it for him.

Rousing himself from his musings he glanced around the silent chamber. Shadows claimed every corner of a room lit dimly by candlelight. Judging by the frugal number of candles in use, Ardron guessed that here too there were acute shortages. In the middle of the room Sir Robert, sitting opposite his castle constable, leaned over the checkerboard contemplating his next move. Beyond that sitting apart and almost apologetic Hildi sat quietly demure waiting patiently for instructions. For a moment, their eyes met across the room and Ardron gave her a brief re-assuring nod. She had dressed sensibly donning man's clothing, even down to cross gartering around her legs. Although her attire had raised eyebrows when she had arrived nothing was said. However, Ardron approved completely it showed sound judgement as far as he were concerned, and he made the point with an approving comment.

There could not be more than an hour-and-half to midnight when he decided that was probably close enough to get started. But so far, the empress had not yet made an appearance. He wondered how it could be diplomatically hinted that she should stand too. He thought it but he knew that nobody would dare suggest that she hurry up. But once outside the walls he would be in charge and empress or not she would have to do exactly as he bid her. And he knew also that would have to be established before they even set off. In his mind he rehearsed the different ways he might issue that instruction without seeming over presumptuous.

It was only a few minutes later when Empress Maude swept into the room. She came in on breeze of energy and good humour. For a few moments everyone in the room just stared at her. She wore a full-length gown, complete with substantial hood, made entirely from white bedsheets.

"What_?" Sir Robert muttered. Then recovering from his surprise asked. "What the hell are you wearing?"

Ardron got to his feet in admiration when he realised the purpose of the gown. "Your Majesty," he croaked, "You are inspired."

"Do you like it?" she asked pulling the hood over her head.

"Do I like it?" He could only paraphrase. "If you were to lie down in the snow, I am sure I would trip over you before I saw you."

She smiled pleased by his comment then stood aside to allow her lady-in-waiting to pass. She too wore a white bedsheet gown and held two more in her arms. "Cecily," she said, "Hand out the gowns."

The maid moved forward and handed one to Hildi and the other to Ardron.

Ardron shook it out held it up and briefly examined it. It would do. However, he could not wear it over his sword. It might come to pass that he would need his weapon. Nevertheless, with a little adjustment he could still make it work. He pulled the gown over his head and allowed it to drop full length to the floor. There were no sleeves just slits through which to pass his arms. He stood a moment with arms outstretched in a brief inspection. It was by no means tailor measured but then to serve its intended purpose it did not need to be. He picked up his sword and sheathed it into the baldric, then hauled it onto his back fastening the buckle across his chest in the usual way. Perhaps it did compromise the gowns camouflage qualities a little but not enough to be troubling. So far satisfied, he tried the hood looping it over his head. Its surplus material flopped to almost cover his face. He was happy! The gown was good and would not only provide effective concealment but might also deliver a little extra screening against the harsh cold.

He looked around the room. The women fiddled frivolously with their gowns attempting to improve its fashion. All of which was completely irrelevant Ardron thought. Notwithstanding this needless triviality there was, he decided, no reason why they should not begin the escape. "We should prepare to leave," He said with authority.

"Yes," Sir Robert agreed with a heavy sigh. "There's nothing to be gained by delaying longer." He added.

Ardron nodded agreement. It was time for him to be autocratic and lay out some instructions. "When we get outside the gate there will be no talking," he instructed. "Sound travels a long way on a still night. And keep your eyes on me," he added. "I will give all the instructions, and these will mostly be hand signals. I will have no truck with conflicting suggestions," he said eyeing Maude deliberately. He paused a moment allowing for comment. None came. "If God is with us, we will get through," he said. "If not!" he said shrugging philosophically without finishing the sentence.

"Do you have a plan?" Sir Robert asked.

"Vaguely!" Ardron said. "Once outside and across the moat we will, hopefully, link up with my outside contact. Then we will head west through the siege lines. Once clear, if we get clear, then we will mount the horses and swing south. When Oxford is well behind us, we will turn back east to find the river. After that we will follow the Thames all the way to Wallingford."

Sir Robert nodded without comment.

"What can go wrong?" Ardron queried cynically.

"When do you expect to reach Wallingford?" Sir Robert asked. "If you reach Wallingford," he added taking Ardron's lead.

Ardron let out a loud sigh. "Midday tomorrow, perhaps." He suggested tentatively.

Sir Robert nodded thoughtfully. "Then midday tomorrow I will negotiate terms of surrender. Perhaps I can get favourable terms if Stephen still thinks you are here," he went on addressing Empress Maude.

She nodded agreement.

For a few moments, the room was silent, then; "Let's get started." Ardron said quietly.

Chapter 14

Oxford, December 1142

"Good luck," Robert d'Oyly whispered around the edge of the closing door. Then the door shut with a heavy thump and was followed by the sounds of bolts and bars dropping into place securing it tightly closed. Standing deep in the shadows of the vestibule with three women in his charge Ardron suddenly felt enormously exposed being on the outside of the postern gate. He stared at the fastened door for a moment considering whether he should bang on the door and plead for re-entry. No! It was too late for that, there was no alternative except for him to make good on his promise or die in the attempt.

He glanced at the three women standing quietly watching him expectantly. His confident re-assuring nod belied the real emotions he was now feeling. The fate of the Angevin cause at this moment depended upon him succeeding in leading Empress Maude through King Stephen's siege lines. He felt the full weight of that responsibility. He moved to the mouth of the vestibule and peered out at a landscape under a deep mantle of snow. The half-moon was not excessively bright, but the pallid light it cast on the blanket of virgin snow was mirrored by millions of minute frost crystals serving to magnify its wan light. This next move was fraught with danger. If anyone were watching the postern gate then they would, for certes, see them emerge from the vestibule. He would, he decided, make this first move alone. He turned and with hand gestures he bade the women wait. Then after a moment's hesitation he stepped out from beneath the vestibule.

An icy wind cut across his front as he stood motionless scanning around for any sign of movement on the other side of the moat. Seeing none, he cautiously made the dozen steps down to the water's edge. Sometime during the day there had been another light sprinkle of snow. The footprints he had left behind last night were now mostly covered, but although nothing more than shallow indents they were still clearly visible. Those indents clearly marked the route across the moat. He glanced back at the vestibule just to satisfy himself that the three women had stayed hidden in its depth. All was well.

Using the same three bridge posts as guides he made his way over treading in each indent precisely. When he reached the other side he immediately stooped to a crouch, his eyes pierced the night while his ears strained for sight or sounds of danger. Nothing___ all was good. It was time to bring the others across. He re-traced his steps back over the moat to the vestibule.

Trying to appear a little more confident than he actually felt he led the way back to the moat. Once there he, with hand gestures, indicated that the three women should crouch down in the snow using their camouflage gowns to good effect. Yet another hasty scan around showed no obvious dangers. It was time to be pressing on. He tapped Hildi on the shoulders and led her to the moat's edge. He pointed at the footprints in the snow, and then indicated the three posts that should be her bridge across. He used his fingers as one, two and three as he pointed at each post in turn.

"Do you understand?" he whispered. Hildi nodded. Then with an encouraging smile he motioned for her to start to cross.

Nervously, she stepped onto the ice and began to slowly make her way to the first post. Her progress was painfully slow and tried Ardron's patience, as she took an interminable long time. Eventually, she made it to the second post, which was enough progress to satisfy Ardron. He then indicated that the maid, Cecily, should follow issuing precisely the same instructions in exactly the same way. She made it to the second post a little quicker than Hildi. So now it was the Empresses turn. This time feeling keenly the significance of his protégé, he waited only until she reached the first post before he set off after her. He felt the need to stay close in case something went wrong.

Safely on the other side they reformed quickly. Taking a moment to glance back Ardron was concerned to see the tell-tale footprints in the snow. It looked as if a small company had crossed the moat, if seen that would be certain to arouse curiosity. There was nothing he could do about it. It was best that they press on quickly.

The next obstacle was the brook, but had they arrived at the actual confluence of brook into moat. He had veered off course slightly. Irritated about the delay, slight though it was, he took a northerly course away from the moat alongside the brook, until he reached the point that he thought was last night's crossing place. It mattered not whether it was, or wasn't, here they would cross and hopefully find Swidhurn. He crossed the narrow stream first and cast around the shadowy night for any sign of Swidhurn, but in the night's dim light he could see nothing. Anxiety was beginning to take hold. Was he in the wrong place? Perhaps it was that something had prevented Swidhurn making the rendezvous! He was beginning to worry, if he wasn't here or couldn't be found then the whole scheme was in serious jeopardy. They needed horses to make good their escape. He forced all the disquiet to the back of his mind and signalled to the others to cross.

"What now?" the Empress whispered when they were all on the other side.

What now indeed? With or without horses they would have to press on, there was no alternative. Trying to appear more assured than he actually felt, he indicated with an arm wave that they should continue west. After only a few paces he detected some movement from a small copse just ahead. He signalled for everybody to crouch down and at the same time drew his sword.

"By God, I almost didn't see you," Swidhurn muttered as he drew close.

Ardron couldn't help a heavy sigh of relief. "Swidhurn," he said. "What a sight for a lost soul."

Swidhurn stared at the small party clearly unable to understand why there were twice as many souls as he was expecting.

"This is Empress Maude," Ardron said quietly. "And her maid servant, Cecily."

"Empress Maude?" Swidhurn uttered in surprise, then sunk obediently onto one knee. "At your service, your Majesty," he said.

"Stand up man," The empress demanded. "There is no protocol here at this time."

He got timidly to his feet, in the presence of such royalty very unsure of himself.

"Swidhurn!" It was Hildi that eased his unease.

"It is good to see you sister," he responded taking her into a brotherly hug.

"Time for this later," Ardron cut in. "Horses, we need horses."

Swidhurn re-focussed. "I have them tethered half-a-mile hence." Then after a pause. "There is only three! I didn't know we needed more." he added apologetically.

"Never mind," Ardron cut in. "Lead on, carefully."

Their first serious obstacle came after just a few yards. To their left and right huge campfires lit up the night, with just a narrow passage of shadow in between. Swidhurn in the lead went to ground indicated that all should do the same. Ardron crawled forward to review the situation.

"We can make it across, if we go quietly and carefully," Swidhurn whispered.

Ardron was fretful and racked his brain for alternatives. "Is there no other way?"

"No," Swidhurn was adamant. "I came through here so we can go back."

"But you were only one. We are five." Ardron replied.

Swidhurn nodded agreement. "It is the only way," he said staring questioningly at Ardron.

He was thoughtful for a few seconds. "Alright," he reluctantly decided.

"I will take Hildi across first then I will come back," Swidhurn said.

Ardron slipped off his camouflage sheet and handed it to Swidhurn. "This may help."

The pair set off crouched low and walking slowly until they neared the midway point. Here they went to their knees and began to crawl. They passed the halfway point and was then lost in the darkness out of Ardron's view. He strained his ears for any sound of a challenge, or an alarm being raised, but apart from sounds of high spirits from those campfires all was quiet. Seconds dragged to minutes and the minutes increased, still there was no sign of Swidhurn's return. Doubts crept into Ardron's mind. Had something gone wrong? What if Swidhurn did not return? He was over the other side with his sister and the horses. His personal objective was now achieved, so what if he just stole away? Silently cursing himself for such shabby thoughts he, immediately, dismissed them from his mind. Swidhurn was a loyal friend, he would never do such a thing! Or would he? Still more minutes passed, and those dark thoughts returned before he saw him crouching low running back towards them.

"I began to think that you were not coming back," Ardron muttered.

"What?" Swidhurn's surprised question. "Oh, I see," he went on. "Had to get Hildi hidden away," he said thrusting the white sheet camouflage into Ardron's hands. Ardron looked down at it confused for a moment. Swidhurn was still clad in the one Ardron had given him. "It's Hildi's," Swidhurn explained.

"Let's get this crossing finished," Ardron said.

"I will take Cecily across," Swidhurn replied. "Give us a few yards start and then follow with the empress."

Ardron nodded agreement. Then he watched the pair set off as he pulled on the white sheet. Just as before, Swidhurn started off by crouching low and walking slowly towards the middle. Around halfway, again he dropped to his knees signalling the maid to do the same. Slowly they crawled forward until disappearing from Ardron's sight.

"We must do the same," he said quietly to the empress, not sure how she would react to an undignified crawl. However, to his relief she simply nodded compliance. Taking Swidhurn's example they set off crouching low. However, before they had neared halfway voices alerted Ardron to someone's approach. He sank to the ground indicating Maude to do the same.

Silhouetted against the distant fire glow, the shadowy figures of two sergens walked casually towards them, chatting in good humour as they did. On they came until Ardron feared that they must walk right over them. However, less than five yards away they stopped, adjusted their clothing and began to urinate. One began to sing as he did.

'One thing that I know,
Piss holes in the snow,
Do leave a golden glow,
And if__.'

A sudden gust of wind lifted Ardron's camouflage sheet and made it flap. He grabbed hold of the cloth quickly and pulled it in tight.

The sergen stopped singing and listened. "Did you hear something?" He asked his companion.

"Only you pissing like the nag you ride," his companion answered.

Both men sniggered and soon began to re-adjust their clothing. Then in no particular hurry they turned and began to return to the comfort and warmth of the campfire. Ardron watched them go and could not help a heavy sigh of relief. He heard the empress give a little chuckle as he did. They then completed the rest of the crossing without further incident and linked up with Swidhurn.

"Where's Hildi?" Ardron queried noticing her absence.

"On a bit yet," Swidhurn replied waving his arm to indicate the direction.

Three-hundred yards further, and they came to a Saxon homestead. The central bucolic building lay in a shallow valley and was flanked by three roughly constructed animal sheds. "We must cross the farmyard," Swidhurn muttered to Ardron. "But cautiously," he added. "Sergens use that house as sleeping quarters."

Ardron was uneasy. "We should go around," he suggested.

Swidhurn shook his head and pointed across the valley. "The horses are tethered in that copse."

They could still go around, Ardron contemplated. If they gave the homestead a wide birth, then they could still come upon the copse except from the other side. However, it would be a long way around and, in so doing there was no telling what other hazards they might encounter. But that copse was so temptingly close. "Is Hildi over there?" He asked.

"She is."

That meant that Swidhurn had made the crossing at least three times. Ardron nodded thoughtfully. "Lead on," he said.

Swidhurn nodded. "Wait here for my signal," he said then turned and set off running down the slope. Down the hill he ran, stumbling sliding and floundering in the deep snow, until he reached the nearest animal shelter. Using it as cover he signalled that someone else should now follow.

"Go ahead, my Lady" Ardron quietly bade Cecily. She hesitated somewhat unsure. "It'll be alright," he re-assured. "If you do see anything not right, drop down into the snow and cover yourself with the sheet." He smiled and waved an inviting arm towards where Swidhurn waited. Cecily hesitated another moment before setting off. She made her way down the hill slower and more deliberate than Swidhurn, but she eventually made it and without incident. Turning to the empress he nodded reassuringly, aping more confidence than he actually felt. With the weight of responsibility bearing down heavily on him he felt the need to keep her close. "We will go together, my Lady." He said. "I will lead." She nodded compliance. "Stay close," he instructed then set off down the hill.

The snow was much deeper on the side of this hill, and the lower they got the deeper it got. But apart from several stumbles they made the cover of the animal shelter without incident. Ardron looked back up the hill staring uneasily at the mess of footprints they had left behind. The sooner they cleared the area the better it would be, he determined.

"Almost there," Swidhurn whispered. "Up the hill and into that copse."

Ardron leaned forward and peered around the corner. The farmyard was deserted, and as still as a graveyard would be on a night such as this. Except for a faint fire-light glow escaping from the cracks in the window shutters, one would believe the house was deserted. Just for a moment he imagined the scene inside the building and envied how cosy and warm it would be. He curled his toes and lifted his heels trying to create circulation through feet that seemed like frozen lead stumps. Refocussing, he turned away and nodded at Swidhurn indicating that it was safe to go on.

"Come," Swidhurn said to Cecily. "Let's go." The pair set off hurrying across the yard and then began ascending the incline on the other side. Their progress through the snow slowed as the hill became steeper, but with Swidhurn pulling and pushing Cecily they reached the top without incident and disappeared into the copse.

"Good," Ardron muttered to himself before turning back towards Maude. He glanced back down the yard to the house. All was quiet. "When you're ready, my Lady." he said.

She nodded acceptance. "Let's go," she said and pushed past Ardron as she set off. Apart from being a little slippery, crossing the yard was easy because the snow was well trodden and compacted. However, scrambling up the incline where the snow was much deeper was a lot more taxing and became harder the higher they got. Taking a chance on being over familiar Ardron pulled the empress's arm over his shoulder and wrapped his own around her waist, half dragging and half lifting her through the last few yards. Once they had made it into the copse he allowed Maude to sink to the ground slipping slowly from his grasp, while he himself bent over breathless, hands resting on knees.

"Well done," Swidhurn said quietly.

Blowing hard, Ardron looked up at the other three who stood quietly watching. He half turned and looked back down the hill before straightening up. Still nothing moved in the farm below, all was going well. However, there was no time to delay, they needed to put distance between themselves and Oxford. He turned his attention to the horses.

"Hildi you ride double with your brother," he instructed. "Your Majesty you take my charger, Rattlebone, and Lady Cecily you will ride double with me." Just as eager to escape the area, as he, it took no time for all to get mounted. After a quick glance around ensuring all was well Ardron led off heading west.

Progress was slow, as mounted double, the horses struggled to get their feet out of the deep snow. Often, they resorted to four-legged bunny-hops to get from deep drifts. Even though concerned about the animals stamina, Ardron pushed on for the better part of an hour before calling a halt. He slid quickly from the saddle then helped Cecily down. He glanced back at the others. There was no need to order a dismount, all followed his example, giving the horses a much-needed breather.

"How far do you think we've come?" Ardron asked.

Swidhurn shook his head, "Two miles? Maybe!"

Ardron agreed, but two miles was probably enough. "We'll give the horses ten minutes then we will swing south."

"South?" Swidhurn queried. "We should continue west. Every yard away from Oxford is another yard of safety," he appealed.

Nodding sympathetically, Ardron agreed with his conclusion. "Nevertheless, south it will be," he said. "I am tasked to deliver the Empress to Sir Brien Fitzcount at Wallingford Castle." For a moment he thought Swidhurn was about to argue, but after a moments consideration he nodded a reluctant agreement.

"How far is Wallingford from here?" He asked.

"From Oxford. ten or so miles," Ardron answered. "But we are west of Oxford and we'll have to make a wide circle around the town."

Swidhurn nodded slowly. "Fourteen, fifteen miles?" He suggested.

"I'd say," Ardron allowed.

"It's going to be tough for the horses." Swidhurn muttered looking glumly at the animals.

"Yes," Ardron agreed. "For the next few miles the women ride, we walk."

Just a few minutes later they set off again heading south, passing west of Oxford. With the two men on foot leading the horses their progress was no quicker. For another hour Ardron kept the southerly course until he considered, that by that time, they had cleared well clear of Oxford. He then deliberately turned east and kept going until he reached the river. The river was a welcome sight to Ardron, and for the first time he was beginning to feel more than just optimistic about their chances of success. He called another halt.

"Have you any idea where we are?" Empress Maude asked as he helped her to dismount.

"Yes, my Lady," Ardron replied. "We are two or three miles south of Oxford on the banks of the Thames."

"I can see that," she retorted. "But where do we go from here?"

"We follow the river, my Lady. And it will take us all the way down to Wallingford."

"How far do you think that is?" Swidhurn joined the conversation.

Ardron shrugged, "six miles maybe seven."

"At this rate, another three hours?" Swidhurn estimated.

"Could be," Ardron concurred.

"Unless we freeze to death first," Swidhurn muttered.

"Unless we freeze to death first," Ardron repeated as he gathered the horse reins and led the animals to the river to drink.

The horses did drink, but somewhat unenthusiastically. Probably due to the icy temperature of the waters. As he waited Ardron squatted down on his haunches and peered across the dark water with Swidhurn's last comment ringing in his ears. Truly it was desperately cold, and that cold was the biggest danger now. His own fingers were nothing more than frozen stubs which could be hammered between two rocks without feeling. If anything, his feet fared even worse, they had gone from painfully numb to painful throbbing. He doubted very much that he could actually walk six or seven miles, and he assumed that Swidhurn would be having the very same problems. When they resumed, he decided, they would have to ride for a while. He looked to the darkened sky in the east it needed at least another four hours to sunrise and with the sun the temperature would rise. Not by much, but then even a couple of degrees might help. He considered whether they should stop here build a fire and rest then press on at sun-up. Almost instantly he dismissed it, they were still too close to Oxford to be comfortable, and in any case how could he find dry kindling in these conditions. For now, they would just have to press on, there was no alternative. He stood up and one by one checked the horses for condition. They were bearing up, it seemed.

Over an hour later Ardron realised that he had made a miscalculation. The river although flowing south, meandered east and west wildly adding more miles to the distance. Another hour, with the river now heading westerly and the horses once more struggling beneath double rider weights, he knew that they would soon be forced to make another stop. But just a little further along the river they came to a small hamlet. He reined to a halt and leaned forward peering into the darkness trying to decide whether it was a fortunate or unfortunate happenstance.

"This must be Abingdon," Maude said drawing alongside.

"Abingdon?"

"Yes," she replied. "There is an Abbey here where my father, King Henry, studied as a young man."

Still unsure of the town's favours he was still dubious. "Will they be favourable to our cause, my Lady?" he asked.

"At the worse the monks in the Abbey will be neutral. At the best they will be sympathetic to the daughter of a previous student of such eminence."

Ardron was thoughtful. Here was potential opportunity for badly needed rest, warmth, food and perhaps even the possibility to obtain a couple more horses. The benefits seemed huge, and the potential for treachery slight, but nevertheless, still present. The plight of the distressed horses influenced his decision, he doubted they could last the time and distance to Wallingford.

"How far are we from Oxford?" he asked.

"Six miles perhaps seven. Not more." Maude replied.

That was discouraging. With the circuitous route they had taken he estimated they could have travelled ten or more. Still six miles was not bad. Particularly so if the siege army did not know that the empress had escaped the castle.

"We make for the Abbey!" he decided.

By staying in the meadow, they arrived at the road which led to the abbey. Even in the darkness the abbey was an impressive sight with a series of tall gable ended buildings. Two large square towers poked up into the night sky, while clustered beneath, clung many smaller buildings all behind impressive stone arches. The gatehouse spanned the road and at this early hour was firmly closed. Ardron dismounted and using the hilt end of his sword rapped on the heavy oak doors. It took several raps before he received a response.

"Who seeks entry at this hour?" The voice spoke English

"Cold and weary travellers," Ardron replied.

"The gate will be opened at sun-up. Come back then."

"Let us in now," Ardron demanded. "We have travelled far, and the winter's cold has suffered us to frost chilled bones." There was no response.

Maude then dismounted and stepped forward. "What is the problem?" she demanded.

"He seems unwilling to let us in," Ardron said.

"Open this door in my name. I am Empress Maude, daughter to King Henry de Beauclerc, King of England." She demanded in French with authority. "And I am the lawful Queen." Still there was a long pause before there were sounds of bars and bolts being withdrawn.

A pale face peered around the edge of the door and studied the small party. "All the monks are at vigils, and will be for at least the next hour," he said responding in French.

"We are in urgent need of shelter." Ardron said. The pale face continued silently to study the group. "Shelter will only be temporary; we intend to journey on after a short rest." Ardron added.

"Are you indeed Empress Maude?" Pale face asked fixing his gaze on Maude.

"Be assured I am," Maude responded firmly.

He hesitated a moment longer before stepping back and opening the door wide. The monk, pale faced with black hair and beard was of slight stature and clad in a full- length black habit.

"The Abbot will be informed of your arrival, your Majesty." He said making a servile bow.

"Black monks." Ardron heard Swidhurn mutter. They were indeed black monks of the Benedictine order, but Ardron made no response to Swidhurn's mutter. Instead he expressed gratitude for the monk's benevolence.

"Follow me," the monk instructed.

When all had dismounted, he led the way walking briskly across the compound to the cloisters. He waited here while the horses were tethered before continuing on through the cloisters and into a long gallery. Although away from the freezing temperatures outside, it was only marginally warmer inside. Using the flame from the lantern the monk lit a candle. He then set the candle back down back on the table. "Wait here," he charged then left.

In the gloom the far end of the gallery was out of sight, even so it was obviously very long. It was Swidhurn who found more candles on other tables and he lit a half-a-dozen. Ardron took one and through curiosity advanced down the gallery some way. Fully a hundred feet in length and thirty feet in width the gallery was stone built with an impressive architectural wooden roof. Curved collar beams were supported by secondary rafters, which in turn were held up by two rows of stout oak pillars. Single rows of rough-hewn benches and tables lined the walls on both sides. It was, he concluded used as a dining hall.

"Perhaps we can buy some food," Maude suggested as she casually took a seat at one of the tables.

Feeling his own hunger Ardron thought it a good suggestion. However, he appreciated that his hunger could not possibly compere to that of the three women who had, under siege, survived on practically nothing for weeks. "We will ask," he agreed as he unbuckled his baldric and placed it on a table. Then seeing no further use for the white camouflage sheets that they still wore he discarded that also. Following his example, the others did likewise.

It seemed an age before the monk returned, although in fact it was probably no more than twenty minutes. This time he was accompanied by another monk but not the abbot. This monk much older, lined of face, and clean shaven with grey hair. "I am brother Ignacious," he said, "And you are welcome here." He paused studying Maude, perhaps trying to establish for certain whether or not she was the empress. "The abbot sends his apologies your Majesty," he went on, deciding that she was. "He is currently leading the *lectio divina* and will attend you as soon as he is able."

Ardron heard Swidhurn snatch a breath. Feeling that he was about to protest he put his hand on his arm. "The abbot feels he pays homage to a higher authority," he muttered. "Brother Ignacious," he said louder. "Could we trouble you for food? We would be grateful for simple fair!" He paused a moment. "We can pay," he added.

"As our guests you will be provided with food as a common courtesy." Ignacious said with a pious smile. "Payment is not necessary. However, if you wish to contribute to our hospital fund then all donations are welcome."

"Thank you, good brother," Ardron replied. "There is yet one other favour we have to ask of you."

Ignacious waited.

"Our horses are in need of feed and shelter also."

"Stabling is over the other side of the courtyard," he replied. "Brother Francis, here, will show you where."

Outside Ardron gathered in the reins of the horses and followed brother Francis across the courtyard. The stables were not large, but then Benedictine monks did not need a stable full of horses. Just a couple to pull carts and maybe another for ploughing, would probably suit their requirements.

Just inside the double doors brother Francis lifted down a lantern and using the flame from the one he carried, he lit that also. "Boy. Where are you boy," he called. On getting no response he called again this time a little more impatiently. Eventually, a young boy did emerge from the gloom out of one of the stalls, but obviously only half awake. "Sleeping in, you lazy toad," the monk scolded. The boy looked sheepish having been caught still sleeping, although the hour was not yet five o'clock. He was of tender years, perhaps ten or eleven, not more, and had a dishevelled appearance none too clean. "Tend these horses and look lively, urchin," brother Francis charged. "Or you will feel the swish of bamboo across your shoulders."

Ardron handed over the reins to the youngster. "Put them somewhere warm, feed them well and there will be a couple of marks for you," he said. "You may loosen the cinches but don't remove the saddles," he added."

"Yes, Sir Knight," the lad answered eagerly, and led the horses down the stable into the gloom.

"Doesn't he have a name?" Ardron asked.

"Good gracious, no. he is just an urchin. He won't have a name until he is old enough to take holy orders. Then it is the abbot who will give him a name."

"Does he want to be a Benedictine monk?"

"What choice does he have?" brother Francis replied. "He arrived here a starving beggar and received the benevolence of the abbot to be taken into train as a monk. Here he will stay until he is old enough to begin training or__." He paused a moment. "If he is of mind, he can go back to being a street beggar."

"What of his parents? His family?" Ardron queried.

"He has none."

Ardron watched the boy leading the horses into the shadows, dwarfed by the size of Rattlebone, and felt sympathy for him. But then, at this time in England there were so many like him. At least this lad had shelter and regular meals, albeit in an austere environment. He turned his attention to his next problem. "We are five travellers with only three horses. We need to buy two more horses to complete our journey."

Brother Francis pulled a dubious face. "We don't have many horses, and we need the horses we do have. I doubt very much that any could be spared."

"We can pay a very good price," Ardron said. "An excellent price," he emphasised.

The monk sighed. "I have little to do with the stable. You will need to speak to Brother Jacob."

"Where will I find him?"

"Brother Jacob will be at *lectio divina* for the next hour, but after that he will be here in the stable tending his duties."

With nothing more to do or say Ardron made his way back to the long gallery. Brother Francis meanwhile had peeled away to further his duties, whatever they may be. Arriving back Ardron found that during his absence the food had arrived and was set down on one of the tables.

"Hope you don't mind. We started without you," Swidhurn said through a mouthful of bread.

Ardron nodded without speaking and walked over to the black cauldron and peered in. Even though he had not eaten since leaving Odel's farm some thirty-six hours previous the white lumpy fluid looked particularly unappetising. "Gruel," he muttered to himself. Nevertheless, he ladled a dollop onto one of the wooden plates, helped himself to a wedge of bread and sat down alongside Swidhurn. He took a large bite of bread and looked across at the other table where the three women tucked greedily into the gruel as if it were a veritable feast. But then they were three-quarters starved! The gruel became even more unappetising to him when he discovered that it was cold. Nevertheless, he started to eat it, though somewhat fastidiously.

"How far do you think we are from Wallingford?" Swidhurn asked.

Ardron shrugged. "Six miles? Maybe eight."

"A little over an hour, good going. More than two if the going is slow?"

"I would say so," Ardron agreed.

"How long do you intend to stay here?"

"Not very long. Just enough time to see the horses fed and rested."

"Two hours?" Swidhurn suggested.

Ardron nodded.

After only a few mouthfuls of the unappetising cold gruel, he decided that he had had enough, and he pushed the wooden platter away from him. However, he wasn't the first to finish. The women, who had fed, with avarice, suddenly found that stomachs that were unused to plenty could not cope with gluttony, and they too had slid away their platters, although somewhat reluctantly.

"Ladies," Ardron addressed. "We are going to be here for a little while, so I suggest you make yourselves comfortable and take your ease."

"We should move on," Maude insisted.

"Yes, my Lady. As soon as the horses are rested!" Ardron patronised. "And" he added, "I am trying to negotiate the purchase of two more horses, but the monk I need to talk to is, at this time, at prayer and unavailable." Maude was placated and gave a brief understanding nod.

It had been a long and arduous trip through the night up to this point, and soon tiredness crept up on the small party. Cecily, after first making sure her mistress was as comfortable as could be, stretched out along a harsh wooden bench, then settled down herself on another close by.

Swidhurn slumped half lying, half sitting, on another bench, with his sister leaning on him heavily. Ardron was the only one awake, deciding it was his duty to keep a watch. However, he too felt exhaustion and although sitting upright he slipped into a shallow doze. A doze that was interrupted regularly when his plunging head jerked him awake, but only then for him to drift off again with precisely the same results. He had no idea how long he had been in this state, but he suddenly snapped alert when nearby voices drifted into his stupor.

Four monks had entered the gallery and busied themselves laying mugs and platters in preparation for breakfast. They talked amongst themselves quietly as they did. Across the room Cecily was already alert and Maude was beginning to stir. But close by Swidhurn and Hildi slept on. There was no perceivable danger and so Ardron could see no reason to wake the pair. He got up and approached the monks.

"Has prayer ended?" he asked.

"For the time being," one replied setting down a pile of wooden platters on a table.

"For the time being?"

"Yes. There will be morning mass in another hour," the monk said."

Of course. There was ever morning mass before breakfast. Ardron could not help but wonder how these Benedictines managed to achieve anything between prayers. However, one thing was certain, if he wanted to catch brother Jacob, he had better seek him out straight away. "I will be over in the stables," he said to Cecily. She was the only one fully alert. "Stay here, don't move," he instructed.

The hour was close to seven, and in the east the darkness beginning to weaken, but not the freezing temperature. Ardron found brother Jacob sitting at what passed for a desk in a stable. He was not surprised to see Ardron.

"You must be the knight that my stable lad told me about," he said leaning back in his seat.

Ardron nodded conformation. "Is all well with our horses?" He asked.

The monk turned and looked back down the stable to where the urchin worked mucking out the boxes. "Yes," he said hesitantly.

Obviously, he hadn't concerned himself too much, having left it all to the boy. Ardron let it go.

"We have three horses, but we are five. So, we really need to purchase two more," he said.

Brother Jacob got to his feet shaking his head. "I'm afraid, good Sir," he said. "We don't have any to sell. We have only five and all either pull carts or pull ploughs. We need them all."

Ardron was thoughtful a few moments. "Good brother," he said. "I am guardian escort to her Majesty the Empress Maude. She is here in the abbey," he went on nodding towards the great hall.

"Yes, I know," Jacob replied. "Nevertheless, it would prove a future hardship to let two animals go."

"Our journey onward is especially important, and therefore our need great. We can pay a very big price for two horses." He paused a moment to allow him some thought. "A price from which you could replace them three times over." he added.

"Ah, but you see my friend, these horses are like old friends to us,"

Was he genuine or was he bargaining for an even better price? Ardron wasn't sure. He was sure, however, that their need was almost desperate.

"All right," he said. "I will pay you three times their worth and__," he went on. "Two or three days hence I will be coming back this way and I will return your horses."

"You want to hire them?" Jacob queried.

"No. I will buy them and when I bring them back you may keep the money. That my friend, is a dazzling deal indeed for you."

"Hmm. How do I know that you will bring them back?"

"You have my word," Ardron said exasperated. And if I don't you still have made a huge profit, he added in thought only. But the monk still wavered. "Do you recognise this ring?" Ardron asked slipping the de Vere ring from his finger.

Jacob looked at it. "I do. It is the crest of Sir Aubrey de Vere Earl of Oxford."

Ardron handed it to him. "It is something of a treasure to me. So, if I place it in your care you will then have a guarantee of my return."

The monk took the ring and studied it closely in silence while he thought. Then he began to slowly nod his head. "You'll bring the animals back?"

"Yes."

"And we can keep the money?"

"Yes."

"Sir Knight, then you have a bargain."

"Good," Ardron muttered. It would be a costly bargain but compared to what might be at stake an acceptable one. He took out his purse and for a few moments they haggled the price. Jacob was always going to win and Ardron, with a need that was desperate, was at a definite disadvantage. He was made to pay dearly for two horses. Feeling somewhat bilked, he began to count out the marks. He stood back then and watched the monk gather up the coins gleefully. "Have the horses made ready, he demanded. "We will be leaving presently."

He was further miffed when he returned to the long gallery to find Swidhurn and Hildi waiting alone. "Where is the empress?" he questioned.

"She has gone to see the Reverend Abbot," Swidhurn replied flatly.

Ardron stared at him hard. "I told everybody to stay here."

Swidhurn shrugged. "The abbot sent a monk to find her and she left with him. What could I do? She is the empress. I'm just a Saxon peasant."

Ardron sighed and nodded frustrated agreement. "Prepare, we will be leaving shortly," he said. Then he looked around. The four monks had finished breakfast preparations, and now sat on the other side of the gallery, talking quietly. He walked towards them their conversation fading as they watched him approach. "Good brothers," he said. "Could one of you take me to the Abbott's office?"

"Surely," the nearest one responded getting to his feet. He led the way down the long gallery climbing a twisting stone staircase in the eastern corner. Two large chambers on the next floor each contained three ante rooms, but it was to the single chamber at the west end to where he led Ardron. In front of the large oak door he paused. Then after knocking he pressed his ear against the door listening for a response. He must have got it. for almost immediately he grabbed the heavy handle and opened the door.

"Reverend Abbot I beg your indulgence. But this knight insisted I bring him to you." The monk said.

"Ah! Sir Ardron," It was the empress who responded first. "This is the knight I told you about," she went on addressing the abbot.

Unlike the rest of the Abbey this room was markedly less austere. It was tastefully furnished with impressive hand-carved furniture. The abbot sat behind a spacious desk seemingly dwarfed by the substantial personal library covering the entire wall behind him. Large Imposing tapestries hung either side of the door through which he had just entered. Much more pleasant to Ardron, however, was the pleasing warmth of the room made so by a blazing fire in the inglenook.

"Good Knight, come in," the abbot welcomed Ardron.

"Thank you Reverend," Ardron said still taking stock of the surroundings.

"It would seem that you have accomplished a very daring and dangerous deed," the abbot said. "The light of God shone on your endeavours and he saw you safely through."

Ardron brought his attention to bear. "Perhaps," he allowed. "However, the deed is not yet fully accomplished."

"Ah young man. Do not fret for within these walls all are safe."

Ardron nodded dubiously. "Maybe," he said. "But then I would not trust the kings generals not to storm this abbey if they knew that my Lady was within."

"They wouldn't dare," the abbot said heatedly. "They would incur the wrath of God, the Pope and the church if they did."

Ardron did not reply. He did not see that as much of a deterrent as the abbot. "Nevertheless," he said moments later. "We should journey on and without more delay," He turned towards Maude. "All is ready my Lady. At your earliest convenience."

"Very well, Sir Ardron," she said getting slowly to her feet. "We will take our leave of you good abbot. And we tender our thanks for your generosity."

"As you wish," the abbot replied. "Which way will you go?"

"We go south west," Ardron cut in. "To Marlborough and the security of Sir John Fitzgilbert's castle. He could feel the empress staring at him, but to his relief she said nothing.

"Then go with my blessings," the abbot said getting to his feet and muttering something in Latin, while he waved his arm in the sign of the cross.

"Why did you say that?" Maude asked once they were outside the room.

"If the kings' men should find their way here, then it would do us no harm if the good abbot unwittingly misdirects them in the wrong direction." He replied.

"He wouldn't give us away." The empress countered.

"Perhaps not," Ardron said. "But then being a holy man, he might find it difficult to lie. Whatever," he shrugged, "Under the circumstances it is wise to keep our intentions to ourselves."

Maude nodded agreement.

Less than twenty minutes later they left Abingdon Abbey. They crossed the river to its east side and took the road to Wallingford. The winter sun though bright was weak and watery but did give hopes of perhaps some degree of thaw. A thaw, no matter how slight was welcome, because underfoot conditions on the Wallingford road were as hard packed snow, covered by a crust of ice. With such hazardous underfoot conditions progress was cautious and slow. Even so, Ardron estimated that all being well they should reach Brien Fitzcount's castle within two hours. To be able to hand over his responsibility for the empress's security into a fortified environment with a considerable armed force to defend her would be an enormous relief. But until then they were still dangerously vulnerable. Therefore, with still eight or nine miles to safety, he dared not lower his vigilance yet.

An hour later they came to the Saxon town of Dorchester. Ardron, perhaps anxious to reach safety, did not bother to skirt the town. Instead they rode confidently on through its very centre. Few residents braved the cold and those that did paid very little attention. Things were going smoothly and Ardron began to relax, just a little.

Minutes later they reached atop a small rise and looked down upon a small hamlet nestled at the river side.

"Ardron," Cecily called. "I think my horse is lame."

He did not look back but closed his eyes in exasperation and groaned inwardly. Why could things not go smoothly?

"Sir Ardron," Cecily called again.

He reined back on Rattlebone and halted the group. With a sigh he then slipped tiredly out of the saddle. "Where is the problem?" he asked.

"Front left, I think," Cecily replied.

"Right, I'll take a look," he said and helped her down.

Swidhurn appeared at his side and took hold of the mare's reins while Ardron lifted its leg. The horse's shoe was loose, and held on, barely, by a single nail causing the shoe to wobble and spin.

"Swidhurn," Ardron said pointing at the loose shoe. Swidhurn nodded understanding. The two men swopped positions. Using the back edge of his dagger Swidhurn prised the shoe off and tossed it aside, then he patted the mare's neck.

"How far do we have to go?" He asked.

"Two miles," it was Maude who answered. "That is Shillingford down there," she pointed at the hamlet.

"Two miles? Swidhurn said. "Then she'll be fine."

Ardron closed his eyes momentarily with relief. 'Thank God for small mercies.' he thought.

Without more delay the group moved on to Shillingford. Unlike Dorchester the empress's arrival here caused more excitement. A group of men standing by the ferry recognised Maude. Instantly, they removed their hats from respect then began to clap and cheer. Their reaction provoked curiosity from other villagers, and soon the narrow road was lined with cheering well wishes. Soon a small cavalcade began to form behind. Some followed on foot, others rode horses or mules.

Ardron leaned back in the saddle and looked to the rear wondering if he should be concerned. He caught Swidhurn's eye who grinned widely. It was turning out to be an additional escort, and could be nothing other than a good thing, he decided.

What a welcome sight the formidable stone walls of Wallingford Castle were to Ardron when eventually it came into view. The imposing bailey entrance, guarded by two intimidating towers, was itself defended at its front by a false curtain wall. Word had spread on ahead, so by the time they arrived, men spilled out from the curtain wall gate, to see for themselves if this really could be Empress Maude. Ardron pulled over to the side, allowing Maude to take the head, where she could lead through the castle gates in triumph. There was an air of incredulity that the empress had somehow escaped from the besieged Oxford Castle. But the cheers on the approaches were as nothing to that which greeted Maude as she rode into the castle bailey. Well-wishers surged forward surrounding the horses and in effect cut off the empress from the rest of the group.

Brien Fitzcount waited at the foot of the mote to greet her. When she neared his sergens moved forward to push the crowds back clearing the way for her to approach. Ardron was too far back to hear what was said but when Maude dismounted, Sir Brien moved forward and with easy familiarity hugged her. Then he led the way up the mote steps to the keep, with Cecily following close behind. Ardron still mounted watched them disappear inside the keep.

"What now?" Swidhurn asked.

What now indeed! Ardron shrugged slightly. "We attend the horses," was all he could think to say. Inside the stabling area, they had not even finished unsaddling when the castle constable came to find them. "Sir Brien wishes you attend him in his private quarters," he said. Then he led the way into the keep, up steps and through into the private quarters of Brien Fitzcount.

"Ah my good friends," Brien greeted getting to his feet and crossing the room in their direction. "It was not my intention to ignore you. Indeed, I thought that you had followed. When I realised that you had been left behind I, at once, sent my constable to find you and bring you here." With his arm he invited them towards the inglenook and a blazing fire. Maude and Cecily had already taken up prime position at the very front, almost close enough to be toasted. Between the pair and perhaps not as close to the fire as the others sat another younger woman. But Ardron had eyes only for the woman that sat at the edge. The Lady Rohesa flashed him a huge smile, and because of that smile his heart skipped a beat. Suddenly, he was so glad that she was here to witness his accomplishment.

"We owe you so much," Sir Brien went on. "How you managed to escape a besieged castle and pass through Stephens forces is remarkable." He shook a bemused head. "The very stuff legends are made of."

Ardron smiled trying to hide embarrassment. "Had it not been for her Majesty's idea of white camouflage, I doubt very much we would have succeeded," he said, thinking of the moment when one of Stephens men had got close enough to almost urinate on them.

"Nevertheless," it was Maude who spoke. "We would not have made it without you and your friend's help."

"I am at your service, my Lady," Ardron muttered.

The young woman got to her feet. "Welcome to my husband's castle she said.

"My wife Matilda," Brien Fitzcount introduced. "And the Lady Rohesa de Mandeville. But" he went on, "I think you have met."

"Indeed, Sir Brien. We have." Ardron replied. "It is a great pleasure to see you my Lady," he said addressing Rohesa. "Thank you for your hospitality Lady Matilda," he forced his attention away and back to the hosts wife.

"Come, come. Sit by the fire," Brien invited with another arm wave. "Hot food is being prepared, and no doubt having travelled through the night you will be looking forward to a good rest. As we speak rest chambers are being prepared. And tonight, there will be a celebration in honour of our empress's deliverance." He shook his head once more. "I still can hardly believe that you are here and managed such a daring escape. God!" He exclaimed. "How I would love to be able to see Stephen's face when he takes the castle's surrender in triumph, only to find that the golden prize is not there."

***

It was only a small chamber in one of the towers. But it mattered not to Ardron. There was a four-poster bed, bread and wine upon a small table and a fire in the grate. At this moment he needed nothing more. He laid his baldric and sword on the table and slipped from his chain mail. Having not slept since the night before last. and only then fitfully in that cold and damp cell, the bed looked especially inviting. He stripped of his remaining clothes and clambered up on the bed. He could not suppress a yawn as he drew the drapes closed to shut out the daylight. Tired as he was, sleep did not come easily, his mind played out that which has still to be accomplished.

In that state of shallow sleep, he thought he heard the chamber door squeak open. He was immediately alert listening intently. There was a definite quiet rustling. Without doubt there was someone else in the room. Perhaps it was a servant about his or her duties? Or perhaps not! He thought of his sword on the table and wondered if he should leap into action and make a bid for it. No! He was not likely to be the first there. Better wait, but to be ready.

The rustling sounds continued for a little while, but since there was no further development, he began to believe that there was probably no threat. He reached out to pull back the drapes, but he didn't succeed. They were suddenly jerked back. To his astonishment Lady Rohesa stood before him wearing nothing but a saucy look. For several seconds she stood there while he salaciously ogled every detail of her naked body. Then without a word she pulled back the bed covers and slipped into bed at his side.

"Rohesa," he said. "What are you doing?"

"Do you really need to ask?" she replied.

"No," he said after a moment's hesitation.

Feeling somewhat exalted above all men he moved close to her allowing his fingers to caress her body softly and slowly. At the same time, he allowed his lips to brush lightly across her cheek seeking her mouth. His lips found hers and she responded to a soft gentle kiss. He lifted away staring down on her with feelings of desire rising from his very fibre. This time they kissed with urgent passion. Now, in no hurry he explored her body contours with gentle touches. Soon he felt her excitement begin to grow, but he continued to touch and tease the erogenous areas deliberately prolonging his foreplay. Eventually, after several minutes and sensing her impatience, he rolled onto her and made his penetration pushing himself deep inside. For a few seconds he savoured the moment with not the slightest movement. Beneath him was the most desirable woman he knew, and she surrendered to his carnal desire! Slowly and gently he began to rock. It didn't take long before she began to pant and groan, and then he felt the convulsions shudder fiercely through her body. He lay perfectly still waiting for her spasms to cease and her settled return. Having succeeded in achieving her climax, it was now his turn. This time, he was not so gentle thrusting at her repeatedly aggressive until his senses too began swim and he also exploded into his own orgasm. For a short while, and still coupled, they lay in the afterglow.

"That was fantastic," Rohesa eventually muttered.

"Yes, it was," he agreed. His ardour, however, was not yet satisfied and he began once more to rock slowly.

"Again?" she muttered with surprised pleasure.

"Again," he replied.

This time with their urgent needs satisfied their love making was more casual, more restrained, and it lasted longer. When she eventually went into another orgasm her moans and shudders triggered him too and they climaxed together. For a while after they just lay unmoving, their salacious desires now satisfied.

"Wow," Rohesa said at last. "That was even better."

Ardron rolled away feeling secretly smug about his performance. But at the same time, enormously privileged that he had been allowed to possess such a sophisticated beauty as Rohesa. He lay on his back staring up at the drapes atop the four-poster bed completely dumbfounded by this unexpected honour. Rohesa, meanwhile, moved close and rested her head on his chest.

For a while they lay in silence, but it was not an awkward silence. Instead it was a silence of tranquil contentment. But it left Ardron to ponder. What had just happened and where would it go from here? Where could it go from here? She was married! Married to Geoffrey de Mandeville!

"Rohesa," he tried to form the question but didn't know what to ask.

"Yes?"

"Er," he hesitated. "What are we doing?"

She raised her head to look at him. "We?" she paused. "You mean what am I doing here?"

It sounded harsh and not what he meant at all. "No. I mean where do we go from here?"

"Where do we go?" she paraphrased. "We don't go anywhere my gallant knight. I am wife to Geoffrey de Mandeville."

"You can't be a happy wife," he replied, "Otherwise you wouldn't be here."

"No. I'm not," she admitted. "Nevertheless, I am his wife."

"You could come with me back to Norwood castle."

She laughed at his naivety. "No," she said. "You just don't take de Mandeville's possessions. I am his trophy wife, and he would most certainly muster his army, roll over your estate burning pillaging and eventually raze your castle to the ground. And for you, he would find a most unpleasant way to kill." She paused. "And what about me? What about my reputation? Would you have me exposed for an adulterous tart?"

No! He would not. At this time there was no way forward, she was right. "Why did you marry him?" he demanded a little piqued.

"Not completely my choice," she said. "It was an attractive alliance between my father and Geoffrey. For my father, it was an opportunist avenue to the king through Geoffrey. For Geoffrey it was an entrance to the de Vere family status. I suppose at the time I was not too unhappy about the arrangement, However, I very soon learned that de Mandeville does nothing if it does not show de Mandeville financial reward, or at least some prestige."

"Where is he now?" Ardron asked.

"Somewhere over in the Fenlands protecting that flank for Stephen against the rebellious Nigel, Bishop of Ely."

"That sounds to me as if he is serving without reward," Ardron ventured.

"Oh no. Rohesa countered. Stephen had to make him Earl of Essex and gift him Saffron Walden Castle as his base."

"He is an earl now?" Ardron was surprised, considering how readily the man switched his allegiance to Maude after Stephen was captured at Lincoln.

"He is."

They fell into silence her head upon his chest his arm draped around her shoulders. Eventually she lifted his hand and said accusingly. "You aren't wearing the ring I gave you,"

"No. But I know where it is. I had to leave it with the monks at Abingdon Abbey as a guarantee that I would return their horses." But don't fret. I fully intend to recover it, because to me it is a treasured possession."

"Good," she muttered then after a few moments. "I should go."

"Not yet," Ardron said pushing her gently onto her back. His intention clear.

"You're insatiable," she giggled in fabricated protest. Nevertheless, she spread her legs.

Chapter 15

He was young, this boy before him. Early teens perhaps. He was a Saxon, his face dirty, sweat streaked with dried blood in his scalp.

"When did this happen?" Ardron asked.

"This morning early. They came from the south-west, burst in on us wielding swords and axes. We were brutalised then they pillaged anything and everything of value. Not satisfied with what they could easily take they tortured my father to reveal where our meagre valuables were hidden."

They talked in English with Louis, Ardron's accountant, translating for the benefit of the Normans present. "How?" Luc asked.

"They stretched him," the young man replied after translation. "They tied his hands and feet, then tied a rope around a tree attached to his feet. The other end was fast to a horse saddle, then under whips, urged the horse forward."

Louis translated and Luc made a face and winced.

"How is he? Your father?" Ardron asked.

The young man shrugged. "Broken arms, broken shoulders, I think."

"Did they burn and vandalise?"

The young Saxon shook his head. "They vandalised but did not burn."

"Normans or Saxons?"

"Saxons for sure," he replied.

It made sense. England at this time was virtually lawless and getting worse every day. The ordinary populace were soft targets. Normans tended to raid into estates where the castellan held a different loyalty to their own. These raids had a dual purpose. Not just to enrich themselves but also to deprive the castellan of an income when the victims could not pay their fief. That which they could not take they destroyed leaving only devastation behind. Saxon raiders, however, had a different agenda. They looked to rob, not just to enrich but also to survive. Many of these bandits had probably been victims themselves and then, deprived of means to live or feed families, had themselves turned into outlaws bent on stealing. Even so they should not be allowed to get away with it.

"What is your name?

"Abrecan, Sir?"

"How many were these raiders?"

"Six, eight. I'm not sure, the Saxon replied.

Ardron nodded thoughtfully. Outlying farms and hamlet were the usual targets for small robber forces. Villages were well populated and could count on numbers defence. It would, therefore, need a strong attack force to attack and devastate a village. A force something like that which Fitzherbert had led on his own village of Scorrenstone years before. For a few moments, his thoughts recalled the chaos and the terror of that day. Blinking away the thoughts he refocussed his attention.

"What sort of things did they take, other than personal valuables?"

Abrecan thought a moment. "Some livestock, equipment, tools anything and everything."

"Livestock?" This gave Ardron some hope. "What sort of livestock?"

"Our horse, a small heard of cows, chickens and our oxen."

"How many cows?"

"Four."

Four, plus one ox, might just be enough to slow them down. "How did they carry all this away?" Ardron queried.

"They came prepared with a horse drawn cart," Abrecan said.

"Which direction did they go?"

"South-west. The way they came."

"Where is your farm, Abrecan?"

"A mile or so west of here."

"Can you lead us there?"

"Yes, Sir,"

Ardron nodded thoughtfully. "We are going to do something about this." It might well be that the bandits had already made good their escape. However, they were using a cart which meant they would have to use a road, or track, which narrowed down their escape routes. They were driving livestock which would slow them down. Perhaps there was a chance of finding them, or perhaps not, nevertheless, he intended to try.

"Luc. Select six of your best sergens and have them ready to leave immediately. The constable moved to go. "Luc," Ardron called stopping him before he left. "Add in two of Jarcot's trainee Saxons." It would do no harm for two villein Saxons to witness that their lord was at least prepared to come to their aid.

"Sir," Jacques, his squire, sought his attention. "May I come with you?"

Ardron shook his head. "No," he said. Two novices on the trip was enough. "But you can saddle my horse, "and," as an afterthought. "Find a mount for our young Saxon here."

Less than half a mile south of the farm, in Braydon Forest, the road split. One continued south-west to the village of Crudwell, while the other slanted due south towards Hankerton. Without any obvious evidence which way the raiders had gone, or indeed if they had even come this way,

Ardron had no choice but to split his force. Luc took four men and went south while he, with the remainder, went towards Crudwell.

On the fringe of the village he halted. He had crossed from his own estate almost a mile back and this village was under the fief of Malmesbury and the de Pinkney brothers. Even so, he was determined to continue. He studied the village. Bucolic Saxon houses lined either aside of a narrow brook, with a simple footbridge linking both sides. The surrounding fields were set to arable crops, though looking somewhat backward due to the current drought. Residents there were, scattered about the village and fields, busily going about their duties. It looked idyllically peaceful and quiet.

He spurred Rattlebone forward and proceeded into the village slowly with reverence. The last thing he needed was conflict with the Crudwell villagers. Half-a-dozen residents emerged to stand and watch in suspicious silence as they rode past. A few yards and they came upon the village blacksmith workshop. At its front Ardron halted and waited. Eventually, the blacksmith emerged and stood staring up at him curiously. He was a heavy muscular man his face blackened by smoke, as were the clothes he wore.

"Good day to you, smithy," Ardron said pleasantly.

The man said nothing but continued to stare. Eventually, he responded with a brief nod.

Due to his uncommunicative attitude Ardron decided that there was no purpose in small talk, better he get straight to the point. "Could you perhaps tell us if a group of men have ridden through the village earlier? They would have a cart with them and would have been driving a small group of animals." The smithy continued to look back expressionless without speaking.

Ardron sighed, understanding what was needed. He pulled up his hauberk and fiddled about in his purse. Placing one mark on his thumb he flicked it in the direction of the smithy who caught it deftly.

He glanced at the coin in his hand then said, pointedly. "Not today, Sir Ardron. Least-wise none that I have seen."

At least the man knew who he was, but whether that was a good thing or not he wasn't sure. With nothing more to be gained he nodded acceptance and wheeled his horse about. "Thank you," he called over his shoulder as he urged his horse back the way they had come.

"They must have taken the road to Hankerton," he said to Abrecan. "Now we need at all haste to catch up with Luc."

"We don't have to go all the way back," Abrecan said. "We can follow the Swill across country," he said, indicating the shallow brook which ran through the village. "It passes just north of Hankerton."

A mile down the Swill they reached the Hankerton road. Here they paused and dismounted a few minutes to rest the horses. Ardron estimated that at this point, he was probably back onto his own estate, although in this thickly forested area he couldn't be absolutely sure. It mattered not, because to reach Hankerton he would have to turn south and that would take him back onto the Malmesbury domain.

"Sir," one of the sergens uttered a warning, drawing his sword as he did. A rider came from the south approaching at the gallop. "It's alright," he said lowering his sword when the rider neared. "It's Roland."

The sergen, Roland, rode right up to the party before hauling back savagely on the reins to halt his horse. "That's the luck of the devil," he said with a grin. "Sir we have found them." He addressed Ardron. "Luc sent me post haste to find you. But I did not expect to find you so soon."

"Step down a moment," Ardron said taking hold of the horse's bridle. He waited until Roland had dismounted then said. "Now, report."

"Sir, we came across the robbers camped down by a brook just off the road, a mile or so from the village. We stole forward and from higher ground were able to watch unobserved. Luc then sent me off to find you and lead you to their camp."

"They are the same bandits?"

"Surely Sir. Four cows and an oxen graze on the meadow nearby."

"And their number?"

"I counted seven."

Ardron was content, it had to be them. But he needed to be sure. "Abrecan," he summoned the peasant Saxon. "Will you recognise these men again if you see them?"

"Surely, Sir."

"Good! Mount up men," he instructed. Then to Roland. "Lead on."

It took only a few minutes before Roland turned off the road and led them along a valley bottom into a wooded copse. Here they found Luc and three others concealed deep in the undergrowth.

Luc stood and greeted Ardron. "Good to see you, Sir," he said holding onto Rattlebone's reins. "The raiders are camped just over that hill." He said, pointing away to the higher ground. They are in a shallow dell by a brook. Maurice du Prevuer is up there watching their movements. And," he added with a smirk, "They are oblivious to our presence."

"That's good. That's very good," Ardron said dismounting. "Show me!"

Luc led the way up the hill with Ardron accompanied by Abrecan following. Just below the brow they slowed and crept forward cautiously. They joined Maurice to lay on the stomachs and peer down into the dell at the raiders campsite.

A few feet from a fast-flowing brook, Ardron counted seven men. Two lay fully reposed, three sat around a campfire, while another, knee deep in the brook, washed. The seventh man was on the cart among their contraband. Their horses grazed free in the meadow, along with the cows and oxen. The whole scene was one of tranquil pacification. Fully confident that they had got clean away they hadn't even bothered to post a look-out.

"Are they the men" Ardron asked.

Abrecan took a moment to be sure. "Definitely," he said.

"Good," Ardron said wriggling away below the hill's brow.

Back in the copse Ardron gathered his force. "We are ten they are seven," he said. "We are professionals they are a rabble. We have the element of surprise on our side. All the advantages are with us, so if we act swift and decisive, they won't know what has hit them." He glanced around all the faces were impassive and seemingly unconcerned. That was good. "We are going to charge down that slope right into their midst. Cut them down if we have to, but I fully expect them to panic and scatter like chickens. We must then round them up, make sure none get away. First, however, I want to see if we can reduce their numbers still further. Luc," he turned to his constable. "Select your best two bowmen. Just before we charge, we will fire off three or four arrows. If we can make a kill, or two, that will not only reduce their number further, but will add to the panic." He paused and glanced around. "Any questions?" None came. "Good," he said. "Mount up and we will advance to the top of the hill. Abrecan, you are to stay here." He instructed firmly.

Just below the brow, he halted the column and advanced to the crest with the two bowmen. Astride Rattlebone, he looked down into the raiders camp. Nothing had changed, except the man in the brook now sat on the bank drying his feet. "Choose your targets bowmen, and fire when you're ready."

The first arrow was on its way when the man sitting at the campfire leaned forward. That action saved his life. The arrow passed mere inches over him and thudded into the ground a few feet away. Startled into action the man sitting opposite jumped to his feet. He wasn't so lucky. The next arrow struck him low down in his gut, sending him staggering before falling backwards. Two more arrows were on the way when Ardron signalled the charge.

Swords drawn they went at a full gallop down the hill. Ardron was right, the robbers below wholly surprised and completely unprepared, did the only thing they could, run. Into the camp they poured then split off each chasing a panicked fugitive. Ardron leaning over with sword in hand chasing down one man trying to cross the brook. As he neared, he lifted his sword high out of harm's way and used his foot instead to push the man over. He went sprawling full length into the water. Turning Rattlebone sharply, he came back at the man, this time sword at the ready. Realising there was no escape the man offered no fight, and slowly got to his feet in surrender. Ardron hauled his horse to a halt, then marshalled the fugitive back to the campsite.

Gradually one by one the outlaws were rounded up and returned to the site. Huddled together Ardron made the count. Five, plus the one lying flat with an arrow in his stomach, that made six. One missing.

"One got away," Luc informed him.

"No, he didn't," Maurice shouted, riding in at walking pace his sword prodding the last outlaw ahead of him.

"Good!" Ardron was satisfied. "These men will draw straws," he instructed. "Hang the one who draws the shortest." Then he spurred his horse over to where the arrowed man lay. He had been dragged over to a tree, his back resting against the trunk. Both hands wrapped around the arrow pressing his stomach firmly, attempting to relieve the pain. Blood ran freely through his fingers. Hopeless despair of death was in his eyes as he slowly raised his head and looked up. Ardron dismounted and looked to Roland for the answer to the unasked question. The sergen shook his head without emotion, the man would be dead soon. He turned away, and leading Rattlebone walked back to the main group.

"Sir. They refuse to draw straws." Luc informed him.

"Hang any man that refuses," he said loud and clear in English, to be sure they understood.

Sullenly and reluctantly each man then drew a straw.

It was a tall young man with wild unkempt hair, and a black beard to match, who was the unfortunate. He didn't accept easily. It took three to hold him down while his hands were tied behind his back. All the time he struggled and swore vociferously, hurling curses at Ardron. Eventually, tied he was hauled to his feet and dragged off to the selected tree where a rope had been hung over a stout bough. With the noose around his neck, and the free end attached to a horse's saddle, they awaited only Ardron's word to proceed. The remaining outlaws shuffled their feet uncomfortably, preferring not to protest too much, probably fearing their own vulnerability. However, there was an exception.

Anger blazed in the man's eyes. "He has a wife and children," he bellowed.

Ardron studied him a moment and guessed that this was probably the leader of the pack. "As did the people you have robbed," he replied quietly.

"For God's sake man," he continued to protest. "Think of his family?"

"What's your name?" Ardron asked.

343

He stared back trying to decide whether to give it or not. "Will," he eventually said

"Then Will, are you volunteering to take his place?"

He did not reply, instead turned his head and spit with disgust before staring back defiantly.

"I thought not," Ardron said quietly. Then to his waiting men. "Proceed."

Roland astride the horse urged the animal forward dragging the rope and lifting the man twelve feet in the air. On the end of the rope he kicked and twisted violently, trying to relieve the tightening noose, but it only tightened more. Slowly the life was being strangled out of him, and he began to emit gurgling sounds. His struggling gradually reduced, until with bulging eyes and a hanging tongue his struggles ceased altogether. Then his lifeless body continued to swing and spin slowly on the end of the rope.

An uneasy silence descended, some men stared at the lifeless corpse, others deliberately looked away, Only the sounds of bird songs cut into the late evening. Nature was unconcerned with the drama just unfolded, putting into perspective the value of human life in the general order of things.

"It is done," Ardron broke the silence. "Luc, strip these thieves of all their possession. Then put two to digging a grave," he instructed. "Make it big enough for two," he added looking towards the wounded man.

Assisted by Maurice, Luc searched each man in turn, occasionally they stopped to admire an object before tossing it into a pile at Ardron's feet. Valuable or not, each and every possession was added to the pile. When it came to Will, he resisted struggling hard to avoid being searched. It took a long wrestle and several meaty blows from both Luc and Maurice before they were able to contain him. The pair then held him down while Ardron made the search. The reason for his wild struggles became apparent when a hefty purse full of coin was pulled from his pocket.

"Let him up," Ardron instructed. He weighted the purse in his hand before peering in. "You've been busy," he accused. Using the back of his hand Will wiped blood from his nose without replying. His scowl and look of loathing said it all.

"Mayhap we hung the wrong man," Maurice suggested.

"Aye mayhap," Ardron agreed. Then he crooked a finger at Abrecan. "Find your possessions. Load them on that cart and take it home. The Saxon villeins will help drive your livestock."

Abrecan needed no further persuasion and set about the task quickly. Thirty minutes later, after expressing everlasting gratitude, Abrecan was gone, driving the cart himself and leaving the villeins to drive the livestock. By this time, the grave was dug. Wide enough for two, but not very deep. Still it would suffice.

Ardron turned his attention back to the robbers. "Remove their footwear," he ordered. When they all stood barefooted, staring back apprehensively fearing Ardron's next order he addressed them. "You men may thank the saints that look down upon you, because I am going to show you more mercy than you deserve. You will have two minutes start ahead of my archers to flee. After that, you become target practice. Any of you that do survive, will spread the word that all contemplating raids onto my estate can be sure that I will have them hunted down and hung without mercy." He pointed at the lifeless corpse still dangling on the end of the rope. "As was he." He paused, "Your two minutes have begun."

It took no more than three seconds for the robbers to realise their only chance was now to run. All took off, except Will who stood defiantly staring at Ardron.

"What of him," he asked nodding at the arrowed man.

"Take him with you, if you wish," Ardron said nonchalantly.

"He will die, if I move him!"

"Yes," Ardron agreed.

He scowled back with loathing in his eyes. "Grey Wolf shall hear of this,"

"By all things on this earth, who is Grey Wolf?" Ardron queried unconcerned.

"Grey Wolf is our leader. And to you he is the worst enemy you could have."

Ardron nodded indifferently. "You have just wasted half-a-minute."

"Do I send the archers after them?" Luc asked, moving to his side while watching the robbers running at full speed towards the village.

"No don't bother. Let then go and spread the word." He turned his attention to the corpse. "Have that cut down and put into the grave."

"What about him," Luc asked nodding at the dying robber.

"He goes in there too, when he is dead." Luc nodded silent agreement. However, to Ardron his body language seemed to be one of disappointment or disproval. "You don't approve of my actions?"

"No." he replied curtly.

"I had to hang one. It needed a hard example of the probable penalties for raiding into Northwood."

"I don't disapprove of that." Luc replied. "You should have hung the lot."

Ardron was taken aback.

"You have let enemies live. Enemies that may well be bent on revenge," he added.

Ardron watched him go and silently conceded that he might have a point. However, those men were Saxons and although, without doubt, some were blackguards, others were, probably, nothing more than simple peasants forced into the outlaw world through depravation caused by this war.

***

Norwood

The red-hot metal rod snorted angrily as Ardron plunged it into the water tub. He felt a rivulet of sweat trickle down his bare chest and another drip from the end of his nose. Glancing up, he was just in time to see a secret smile of amusement cross Swidhurn's face. Outside it was a hot day in late June, but much hotter in Swidhurn's blacksmith workshop. Nevertheless, Ardron was prepared to put up with discomforts in order to achieve experiences across a wide range of trade skills. This week he had decided that it would be Swidhurn who would tutor him in the skills of black smithy.

Swidhurn had taken up the position of castle blacksmith at Norwood. It was an easy decision for him to make because his sister, Hildi, had settled in at Norwood, and had assumed the role of organising all domestic arrangements. At first Ardron had been chary about those arrangements fearing his constable, Luc, would see it as an erosion of his responsibilities. But he need not have been concerned. Luc seemed not only genuinely pleased to be rid of that part of his obligations, but also to enjoy Hildi's company.

"Sir," a voice demanded his attention.

Jarcot stood in the doorway. "What is it, Jarcot?"

"Sir, you have visitors approaching," he said.

"Who is it? Do you know?"

"They fly the blue standard of Edward de Evereux."

"De Evereux?" Ardron uttered surprise. "How far away?"

"Ten minutes, not more."

Ardron nodded acceptance. "How many in the party?"

"Escort of eight, maybe ten."

"Alright!" Ardron said. "Allow them admittance into the bailey, and have a clean robe laid out for me in my quarters immediately." He picked up a nearby pail and after dipping it into the water barrel he tipped it over his head dowsing himself completely. "Swidhurn," he said shaking surplus water from his hair. "I'm afraid I have to go, castle business." Swidhurn acknowledged with a silent nod.

A few minutes later, having made a hasty change to appear, at least, presentable. Ardron descended the mote steps just as Edward de Evereux rode into the bailey at the head of his escorting knights.

"Welcome, Sir Edward," he said when the cabal halted before him. "Please step down," he invited.

Curious about this unexpected and unusual visit he searched de Evereux's face for clues. Relations between both castles had not been exactly cordial, but neither were they particularly hostile. Detached toleration would be a good description.

"Greetings to you, neighbour," de Evereux muttered on dismounting, his expression and demeanour betraying nothing except friendliness.

"Will you join me in my chambers," Ardron invited.

He nodded agreement. Ardron stood aside allowing him to lead up the steps. "Luc," he said over his shoulder, see the needs of those knights are attended. If you, please."

Ardron was pleased to see that Hildi, anticipating his wishes, had already laid out a flagon of water, another of wine and rock cakes. He invited his guest to sit, and he settled on the opposite side of the table. He held up the wine and the water allowing de Evereux to choose.

"This is most unusual Sir Edward," Ardron said. "To what do I owe this pleasure?" He asked as he poured the wine.

"An invitation and a request," de Evereux replied. He paused changing the subject, "I could not help but see that your villeins and cottars have served you well this year. Unlike most, your tenants have an abundance of crops."

"Yes," Ardron agreed. "Our villeins have worked extra hard and, as you say, unlike most, this year have good crops in the fields." He paused. "But you haven't come here today to discuss crops."

"No! I have an invitation, a proposition. Which may prove financially profitable to you."

Ardron eyed him suspiciously. "Oh."

"You know of course that King Stephen has seized Wilton Abbey and is currently building up a considerable force. Probably preparing to attack Salisbury Castle."

"I know he is at Wilton, but his objective could just as easily be Wareham Castle."

"It could," de Evereux agreed, "But it is more likely to be Salisbury. Two days hence, I intend to take a force of around one-hundred and fifty to bolster the castle's strength,"

Ardron was thoughtful. Edward de Evereux was not known for actually getting involved in battles for either side.

"They are my relatives you see," he added.

"Of course," Ardron said now understanding. "William, Patrick and Sybil are all cousins of yours."

De Evereux nodded agreement.

"So how does that sit with your conscience, taking arms against the king? After all you were once a supporter."

"Yes," de Evereux agreed. "But that was before." He took a long drink on the wine. "If a considerable force could be assembled as the castle's defence, it may well act as a deterrent to Stephen and cause him to look elsewhere."

"Thus, avoiding conflict with the king." Ardron finished for him. He was no fool. Although having switched sides to support the empress, if he never raised his sword against the king then there would, perhaps, be chance of reconciliation if things were to go badly for the Angevins.

"So__," he went on. "Where do I come in?" he asked, but he already knew the answer.

De Evereux fidgeted nervously. "If you were to join us, with perhaps another hundred and fifty it would almost certainly dissuade the king from attacking Salisbury."

Ardron had doubts that he could actually raise one-hundred and fifty men from his estate. However, he thought it better that he did not inform de Evereux of that. Instead he replied. "What makes you think that I would be interested in joining such an enterprise?"

"Money! We could pay you, and your men, a considerable mercenary's wage.

"I don't go to war for money."

"Security then. You don't want the threat of the king at Salisbury."

"Salisbury is forty miles from here. So, I don't see it as much of a threat."

"Well__, your exploits in furthering the cause of Empress Maude are well known. This would be another opportunity for you to thwart Stephen."

"I am in knight's service to Robert, Earl of Gloucester he is my master, and your own cousin, Humphrey de Bohun, is my patron. That is from where I receive my instructions. I do not seek conflict as a pastime, nor for financial reward. Therefore, my dear baron, I feel I must decline your invitation"

The disappointment on de Evereux's face was evident. Ardron did not care. He didn't entirely trust the de Evereuxs. If the king did advance on Salisbury and the de Evereux clan were to decide to throw open their gates and re-join Stephen's cause, that would leave him isolated. That would, almost certainly, result in him and his sergens as prisoners of the king.

Ardron reached over and re-charged de Evereux's tumbler. "Drink your wine Sir Edward," he said.

"Now if that was the invitation, then what is the request?"

"It is a small matter. A matter of courtesy only," he replied.

"Nevertheless, ask."

De Evereux swilled the wine round the bottom of the tumbler. "It was simply to ask permission to bring my sergenti across your estate on our way to Salisbury, instead of going around."

"When will this be?"

"Two days from now."

Ardron nodded. "You have my permission to cross, providing you take nothing and leave behind only your tracks," he said. "And I wish you every success on your venture," he added.

Just a week later in early July, Ardron received news of a great Earl Robert victory at Wilton. Gloucester's force had advanced on Wilton Abbey almost undiscovered by King Stephen's forces. Then faced with imminent defeat Stephen had fled east, leaving William Martel to fight a rear-guard action. That rear-guard soon crumpled and was quickly overcome. However, the delay achieved was sufficient to give Stephen an unassailable lead on his flight to the safety of Winchester.

A further week and Ardron received an invitation to Devizes Castle to celebrate Earl Gloucester's victory.

***

Devizes Castle, July 1143

Ardron stared thoughtfully into the pewter goblet then swilled the remnants around the base. Lifting it to his mouth he gulped down the wine. For a moment he remembered how the gingered wine had burned his throat when first he had tasted it four years ago. There were no such discomforts anymore. Gingered red wine was very much to his taste these days. He reached across for the decanter and topped up his goblet. "Was it really necessary to burn down the Abbey?" He asked.

For a moment Miles Fitzwalter stared at him. "Of course," he replied with a hint of surprise.

"I doubt very much the homeless nuns would agree with you." Ardron said.

Miles sighed, slightly exasperated, that he had to explain tactics to a lesser soldier than he. "If we had left it then there would have been nothing to prevent Stephen returning to re-fortify it."

Ardron held up the decanter offering to re-fill Miles goblet. "And what of the common people of Wilton, they were brutalised and robbed."

"Ah, regrettable," Miles agreed. "But," he added with a sigh, "Victorious sergens must have their reward."

Nothing changed. It mattered not who fought in the battle nor who won, it was ever the poor populace who became the victims. He topped up Miles goblet and looked down the dim candle-lit room.

The banquet hall in Devizes castle was long and wide with the ceiling high. Nevertheless, the crowd of revellers present were sufficient in numbers to make the hall seem crowded. To his surprise he had found that, for this victory feast, he had been elevated to a seat at the top table, albeit on the end and many feet away from the royal echelon. Even so, when the feast had begun Empress Maude had leaned forward caught his eye and lifted her gold goblet towards him, in a sign of recognition. Young Prince Henry, sitting immediately on her left, had through curiosity, leaned forward to see who it was his mother had just acknowledged. It was the first time Ardron had seen the young prince and although the boy was probably not yet even into adolescence, he seemed to be remarkably composed, not over-awed by the occasion at all.

Ardron's attention strayed back again to a knight seated at the opposite end of the top table. He did not recognise him, but by his clothing and demeanour he could tell that he was a man of wealth and position. Clearly, however, he was not enjoying the current merriment. His face was set to a stony expression and he ignored completely the scrumptious range of courses that had been laid before him. He was, however, indulging himself significantly on the wine.

Finally, he could not contain his curiosity. "Who is yonder knight?"

"That, my dear Saxon," Miles replied. "Is Sir William Martell."

"William Martell? The man who covered Stephen's retreat from Wilton?"

"The same!" He is being held for ransom."

Ardron could now understand the man's sour expression and his detached manner.

"Because he is the king's man," Miles went on, "Is no reason why we shouldn't be chivalrous."

"No, Ardron muttered agreement. "Will the king pay the ransom?"

Miles shrugged. "He did sacrifice himself for his liege, and if Stephen has a conscience, then he will feel obligated." Ardron said nothing but decided to reserve judgement.

With the celebratory feast coming to an end the entertainers were released into the space between tables. Jugglers meandered around tossing balls and batons, while acrobats vaulted and somersaulted. Skilled they were, but for all the interest they generated they might not have bothered. Servants hurried to clear away the surplus, while the castle dogs were released to scavenge for table scraps. The guests now began to fidget, rising to move away from the tables and adding to the muddle. Ardron leaned back where he sat, goblet in hand, to watch the confusion.

A dog nuzzled at his elbow, causing him to lift it with surprise. Its sad eyes looked up appealing. Ardron smiled to himself, leaned forward and snatched a ham bone from his plate just before a servant claimed it. For a few seconds he teased the dog, before with a pat on its head he let it take it. The dog laid down with the bone trapped between its front paws and contentedly gnawed at the bone. Ardron watched the dog thoughtfully, aware that any poor Saxon family would be just as content with that bone.

"Sir," A servant sought his attention from his blind side. Ardron switched his attention to the timid fellow. "A rider has arrived from your estate with an urgent message. Your estate has suffered a series of attacks."

Ardron stared at him a moment. "Where is this messenger," he asked.

"He waits outside in the bailey," he replied.

"Show me the way," Ardron replied rising from the table.

Out in the bailey, he found Louis, his castle accountant, waiting. He greeted Ardron with a stiff bow. "Sir, I am the bearer of bad news."

"What is it?"

Louis held out a written message. "Our estate was attacked yesterday in three different places, all co-ordinated to happen at the same time around midday."

Ardron took the message, giving Louis a hard look as he did, trying to decide the seriousness of the account. "All were outlying farms. One in the north and two others east and west." Louis went on as Ardron broke the seal and opened the message.

The message was in Luc's hand. Ardron felt the fury rise in him as he read. It was just as Louis had said, except there was much more horror added to the raids. It was reported that, in all cases, isolated farmsteads were targeted, livestock driven off, crops destroyed, valuables and non-valuables taken. But the additional horror was that, in all cases, the villeins had been made to draw straws and the unfortunates with the shortest straw were hanged. One instance was a boy of ten.

Obviously, it was reprisals for his previous actions. For a few moments he was angry with himself realising that he should have hung the whole band and hid their bodies just as he had done at the farm of Odel some three years ago. He had been too lenient, influenced by the fact that those men were Saxon's, and had allowed that, the current war circumstances may have forced them into the way of outlaws. Because of this compassion three innocents had paid with their lives, one a mere boy. The departing words of the outspoken outlaw 'Grey Wolf shall hear of this,' roared through his mind

"Can you find this man a bed for tonight?" he asked the manservant.

"Yes, Sir."

"We will leave for Norwood first thing in the morning," he said to Louis. Then grim-faced he turned abruptly and stomped back into the Banqueting Hall muttering 'Grey Wolf' as he did.

Inside he scanned the guests seeking William de' Evereux, but he could not see him. He began to push through the throng of revellers. Eventually, he saw Sir William, seated well back taking little or no interest in the floor entertainment. Standing at his side and seemingly equally disinterested, his brother Patric, his sister Sybil and, Cousin Edward. Ardron squeezed and elbowed his way towards the quartet.

"Sir William. I would talk to you in your capacity as Sheriff of Wiltshire," he said, somewhat more brusquely than he actually intended. Taken by surprise, William de' Evereux, looked up sharply. Ardron had not seen William since the gathering at Bristol Castle some seventeen months previous. What he now saw shocked him. Gone was the ruddy complexion and robust physique, replaced by a sallow haggard look and considerable weight loss.

"What do you want?" Patric demanded.

Ardron felt somewhat embarrassed by his brusque attitude. After all, it wasn't William de' Evereux's fault that Grey Wolf had singled him out to attack. "I would know if you have had any reports of an outlaw calling himself Grey Wolf," he replied a good deal less terse.

There was hostility in the Patric stare. "You bring up outlaw business here, now, during celebrations. This is not the time nor the place. And besides can you not see that my brother is ailing?"

"I can indeed see that William is not well. I wish you a speedy recovery," he went on addressing William. He then turned his attention back to Patric, "I apologise for the time and place but I'm afraid that this timing is not of my choice. It seems that I have become the target of a personal vendetta by this outlaw. My estate of Northwood has suffered three attacks in a day."

"Then deal with it," Patric replied curtly.

"There have been some reports of this outlaw." It was Sybil who now intervened with a more conciliatory intervention.

"There have," William agreed speaking for the first time. "Three or maybe four. All in the northern part of the county. It would seem," he went on, "That he has established quite a following among the Saxon peasants."

"Not all the Saxon peasants," Ardron defended.

"Not all." William allowed. "Just the disgruntled."

"God knows there are plenty of them," Patric muttered.

Ardron let the remark pass. He did not want to get into an argument over the common Saxon's plight. "My estate is in the north of the county," he said. "So, it is likely that this Grey Wolf is based somewhere in north Wiltshire."

"Or in southern Gloucestershire," Patric cut in.

"Or in southern Gloucestershire," Ardron agreed without looking in his direction. "Are there any clues in those reports?" He addressed William.

"None that I could see," William said. Clearly with the problem being a distance from his Salisbury Estate, he wasn't too concerned. "Speak with Humphrey de Bohun," he added.

The conversation was abruptly cut when Robert Earl Gloucester accompanied by Prince Henry joined them. "Gentlemen," he said. "May I present his Royal Highness Prince Henry." One by one Earl Robert introduced the young prince to each man cordially. When he came to Ardron he introduced him as Ardron of Norwood and added, "A Saxon who has contributed greatly to the Empress's cause."

"I know of you, Sir." The young prince said straight away in English.

"I am flattered, my prince," Ardron replied.

"You were highly influential in my mother's escape from Oxford Castle."

"Just doing my duty."

"A duty much appreciated," he replied. "When I am king there will be no Saxons in this country. Nor will there be Normans. We will all be English," he declared.

"Hasten that day, your highness," Ardron said.

"Thank you, gentlemen," Earl Robert said. "But we must move on."

"Gentlemen," Prince Henry said as he made to leave.

Ardron watched them move away, marvelling at the sophistication of the young prince, who was not yet eleven. Even more impressive to him was that he had taken the trouble to learn English. Something that most of the noble lords had not done. However, he could not help but ponder what exactly were the chances of him actually becoming king. Stephen was king and he had a son, Eustace, and it was he who was next in line. It would take the removal of Stephen, something that at this stage looked a remote possibility, then Eustace. Eustace would not relinquish the crown easily. Depressingly, the likelihood seemed fixed that the war would go on, even into the next generation.

"How can I speak with Sir Humphrey? he is in France." Ardron returned to the previous topic.

"He is indeed," It was Edward de Evereux who answered. "He is still in negotiations with Geoffrey Plantagenet trying to persuade him to lend support to his wife and son."

"Then how can I speak to him?" He asked again. "Moreover, being in France what then would he know?"

"Probably not a lot," William replied. "It was his constable, de Aumale, who reported raids on the Trowbridge estate. It so happened that he gathered sergens and set off in pursuit of the outlaws. Unfortunately, deep in Melksham Forest, they rode blindly into an ambush, and suffered casualties as well as humiliation."

"Then it will be de Aumale with whom I need to talk."

"Quite so." Patric cut in. "Now if there is nothing else?"

There was nothing further to be gained, Ardron decided. Factually there had been nothing gained. Clearly the de' Evereuxs preferred not to be involved.

It was early afternoon on the next day when Ardron and Louis rode into Norwood. It had not been a pleasant journey from Devizes. Heavy rain, although welcomed in the current drought, had done nothing to improve Ardron's dark mood. Nor was he pleased when there was neither Luc nor Jarcot in attendance to greet him.

"They left mid-morning in something of a hurry," Maurice du Prevuer informed him. "Something about live-stock wandering loose around Minety."

"Why would that concern us?" Ardron challenged.

Maurice shrugged non-committal. "Rumours around the bailey are that most of it was that which was stolen a couple of days ago." Ardron frowned somewhat puzzled. Better it would be he wait for Luc and Jarcot's return to learn the full situation.

Inside his private chambers he began to remove wet clothing. A hauberk is not only cold when wet but also heavy, and he struggled to get it off. That accomplished he sat down and began unlacing his boots when Hildi entered. Surprised and a little embarrassed to find him undressing she hastily apologised and instantly began to back out of the chamber.

"It's alright Hildi, he said. "Come in."

"Sir," she said. "Welcome home. Can I get you anything?"

Ardron thought a moment. "Yes, Bring me some wine and a little cheese, maybe with an oatcake."

"Right away, Sir."

"Hildi," Ardron said. "I have told you. You don't have to call me sir."

"No, Sir."

Ardron shook his head ruefully.

"While you were away you had a visitor," she said.

"Oh! Who was that?"

"It was your brother."

"Redwald?"

"No, your younger brother Esmond."

"Esmond? Did you see him?"

"Yes."

"Hmm." Ardron said pensively, remembering that the pair were once betrothed. "How did that go?"

Hildi hesitated.

"Awkward," Ardron suggested an answer for her.

"Awkward," she agreed. "It seems," she said, "He is to be wed."

"Did he tell you that?"

"No," she said shaking her head. "He told Swidhurn."

"How do you feel about that?" Ardron asked.

"I hope he will be happy," she replied dispassionately. "I will bring you your food," she conveniently dismissed herself.

He watched her go wondering if she was as unconcerned about it as she seemed. Then he realised that he didn't know who it was his brother was to marry, or even when. He would have to speak with Swidhurn as soon as he could.

It was late into the afternoon before Luc and Jarcot returned. There was no answer to the mystery only more question. It was, as had been rumoured, livestock from the recent raids were found just wandering loose.

"It makes no sense," Luc had said. "The animals are not from just one of the raids, but from all three."

"Perhaps," Ardron suggested. "They feared the consequences of pursuit and abandoned the animals because they slowed down their getaway."

Luc shook his head. "Then why did they rendezvous, herd all the animals together then ride off and leave them?"

He had a point. Ardron gave a bewildered shrug. "They must have had a reason," he said dismissively. He decided that it was a mystery unlikely to be discovered, therefore, not worth pondering. "Where are the animals now?"

"They are penned down at Minety," Jarcot answered. "Messengers have been sent to the victims farms telling them where to find their livestock."

Satisfied, Ardron nodded approval. "We need to discover who this Grey Wolf character is, and where he and his outlaw band can be found."

"We do," Luc agreed.

***

Scorrenstone August 1143

Ardron, riding alone, approached the village from the east. Breasting the steep edge of the narrow valley he paused and surveyed the pacifistic scene. The river Avon, flanked on both sides by dense willow, still meandered timelessly along the valley bottom, while cattle grazed contentedly on the rich sward along the valley sides. Seemingly, Scorrenstone village life was timeless. It was four years since the Fitzhubert raid had propelled him personally along a course of events that had drastically altered his life. Although for him everything was changed, the rural scene before him had not. Despite all the conflict raging through the west country this village, at least, appeared untouched. The same bucolic houses lined the far side of the valley and the fields surrounding grew precisely the same crops. After indulging in a few nostalgic moments, he urged Rattlebone forward. Almost as if the animal too remembered a former life in the village, he reared slightly before setting off just short of a canter down the hill.

Ardron was greeted warmly with grins and arm waves as he rode through the village centre to Redwald's house. As he dismounted Acha, his sister-in-law, emerged from within. Her face registered surprise but it was quickly replaced with a beaming smile. Then after greeting him with an appropriate hug she stood back and surveyed him critically

"My you're a real Norman now," she said referring to his Norman style dress.

Ardron glanced down slightly embarrassed, then dismissed the comment with an enquiry about her health.

"Will you come in?" she invited.

"Is Redwald within?"

"No, he is over in the western pastures," she replied.

He nodded. "Then I will find him, and we'll catch up later, Acha," he said.

On foot, and leading Rattlebone, he walked on through the village and out towards the west pastures. These pastures, he knew, had always been left to grow providing winter hay for animal fodder. However, as he neared it was obviously not as it should be. It looked as if some of it had been partially ploughed and extremely badly at that. Standing at the field's edge he saw his brother with several others surveying the field glumly. There was no particular greeting as he neared, all watching him approach silently impartial.

"Hello brother," Ardron greeted Redwald.

"Hello Ardron," Redwald replied so casually that it would almost seem as if he had seen him only hours before. "What brings you here?"

"Esmond's wedding news," Ardron replied. "I know Edyo is to be his bride. And wasn't that a surprise?"

"Not to us," Redwald said.

Ardron conceded with a hand wave. "I don't, however, know when the event is to be. So I thought I had better find out." Redwald nodded understandingly without comment. "What happened here?" Ardron asked.

"Boars," Redwald replied. "They come at night ripping up the meadow foraging for roots and insects. And we aren't allowed to cull them." He sighed heavily. "Norman law!" He added contemptuously, staring at Ardron making him feel uneasy. Almost as if he were silently accusing him of being part of the Norman establishment, but then he might have a point, Ardron silently conceded.

"We'll mount a night watch to scare them away," Redwald said turning his attention to the others. "That will, at least, prevent the field getting any worse. But I'm afraid the damage is done, and we're only salvaging what we can from this crop." He shrugged. "Nothing more we can do." He turned to walk away. "Come brother," he said placing an arm across Ardron's shoulders. "Let us find Esmond."

They had dined royally on a rabbit stew well prepared by Acha, and now in the afterglow well repasted, the three brothers sat outside supping beer and enjoying a balmy evening. Ardron had learned the wedding event was to happen on the day of the autumn equinox. This could combine conveniently with the September harvest supper celebrations on that same evening. Although Esmond did not need his second brother's approval, nonetheless, he had it in abundance from Ardron. He was particularly pleased that Edyo had, seemingly, managed put behind her the ordeal of her previous kidnap. However, on previous visits he had noted that it was Cerdic who had paid Edyo closest attention. He had more than half expected that it would be he, who won her hand. But so far during this visit he had not even seen Cerdic. This he found strange because Esmond and Cerdic were inseparable friends.

Unable to contain his curiosity. "I haven't seen Cerdic," he casually remarked.

"Cerdic?" Redwald responded. "No, Cerdic went for combat training at Malmesbury Castle and didn't return. Instead, he stayed on as one of de Pinkney's sergens."

"When was this?"

Redwald shrugged. "Four, five weeks ago."

"Why would he do such a thing?" Ardron asked staring hard at Esmond.

Esmond held his stare knowing full well the question Ardron was really asking.

"Who knows." Redwald replied. "Perhaps it was the money," he added with a shrug.

The trio fell silent allowing the topic to fade.

Now in the conversation lull Ardron broached the second reason for his visit. "Have you heard of an outlaw operating in the area calling himself Grey Wolf?" he asked softly.

"Grey Wolf!" Redwald paraphrased glancing at Esmond. "Yes, we have heard stories," he said nodding knowingly as he did.

"What have you heard?"

"It would seem that he has established quite a following," Esmond cut in. "He has influence and has used it to join together small outlaw bands into one large group."

"Have you had any trouble with these outlaws?" Ardron asked.

"No, we haven't." Redwald said. "From what I have heard his band only attacks easy targets, such as isolated farms and homesteads. This village is sizeable and would perhaps prove too difficult for him." The conversation paused. "Have you had trouble?" Redwald asked.

"I have," Ardron replied with a sigh nodding as he did. "He, or some his group have attacked three homesteads on Norwood, and at each hanged a person. One a mere boy of ten."

"That's brutal," Esmond said sucking in through his teeth. "Not heard of him doing anything like that before."

"I think it may have been as reprisal against me," Ardron said.

"Reprisal?" Redwald queried.

"Yes! I tracked down a band of his raiders and hung one to set an example. Then I let the rest go, hoping that they would spread the word of the consequences of raiding the Norwood estate. But I badly under-estimated the viciousness of the man. He returned the message three-fold."

"It would seem so," Redwald agreed.

"I intend to find the man and bring him to justice."

Redwald leaned forward and picked up the beer pitcher. "You won't find that easy," he said." He is a Saxon and not all Saxons see him as a bad man. While you___."

"While I," Ardron took up the point, "Am seen as part of the Norman community."

"Exactly," Redwald agreed, and began topping up mugs.

"I know that." Ardron said. "That is why I need your help. I need Esmond's help!" he went on glancing at his young brother.

"Oh?" there was suspicion in Redwald's reply. "And how can that be?"

"Do you remember," Ardron went on addressing Esmond. "When you went on ahead of me to Winchester with Swidhurn?" He didn't wait for an answer, he was sure that he did. "Swidhurn set up as a travelling smithy while you mingled casually amongst the people seeking information about Edyo and Hildi."

"Of course," Esmond replied.

"Well, I wondered, if perhaps, you would again, along with Swidhurn, do exactly the same. Wander amongst the Saxon community as smithy and assistant, whilst trying to gain information of the whereabouts of this Grey Wolf. Or at least where I ought to be looking."

"You would place your brother in jeopardy? Redwald challenged. "And only weeks away from his wedding nuptials?"

"No. I wouldn't want him to place himself in any danger," Ardron countered. "He need only listen to gossip and as soon as he gets any sort of lead, send to me a message and I will take it from there."

"But he has many arrangements to prepare for his wedding." Redwald still opposed. "Not to mention the pending start of the summer harvest."

"I'll do it." Esmond cut in. Then after a pause. "With your permission brother."

Redwald scowled, took a long pull from the beer mug then was thoughtful. "You will be back in the village before the end of August," he growled reluctant consent.

***

Trowbridge, August 1143

Humphrey de Bohun's constable, de' Aumale, had greeted Ardron cordially in his patron's absence. Perhaps, it was that he had expected Ardron had come to pay his fief early. If he was disappointed, then he didn't show it, as he played amicable host. Busily, he ordered the servants to find refreshments before he gave Ardron his full attention.

"Now, Grey Wolf," he said with a sigh as he sat opposite Ardron. "I know of the man. Of course I do. He caused me great embarrassment."

Ardron studied the man before him. De' Aumale belied his senior years. Perhaps it was, that because he did not grow a man's beard, he did not exhibit greying and that might make him appear younger. Without commenting Ardron nodding briefly and in so doing avoided adding to de' Aumale's discomfort. He knew full well, however, that he referred to his ambush episode.

"We took two raids west of here." De Aumale went on. "The first on a small family farm in the hamlet of Eckweek. A family of simple villeins were robbed of what meagre possessions they owned and left completely terrorised. The second raid, pillaged and ransacked the church at Stoche, stripping the place of all the silver sacraments, and even taking the wall tapestries. Can you believe that?" He paused before adding with a growl. "The Godless heathens, what could they profit from wall tapestries?" He sighed before going on. "I gathered together a party of a dozen good sergens and set off after them. We tracked them south-west from Stoche, and thought we were closing in. But they had deliberately slowed, making sure that we followed. Then in the forest just north of Frome we rode into a carefully prepared ambush. Although we were tracking a small party of no more than half-a-dozen, there must have been another two dozen or so lying in wait. Taken by surprise, we were cut down and forced into a hasty and ignominious retreat to count our dead and wounded."

"How did they know you would follow?" Ardron asked.

"Pretty good question that," he sniffed. "It would seem that they are well led by this leader who calls himself Grey Wolf."

"Any idea where they were heading?"

"We were tracking then south-west is as much as I can tell you," de' Aumale replied.

Ardron sighed silently, that didn't really tell him much.

"Still," de' Aumale went on. "We shouldn't be troubled again."

"Why not?"

"Because I have agreed to pay his demands,"

Puzzled, Ardron stared at him.

"We received a message fastened to an arrow fired into the bailey. If I decide to pay a quarterly sum, then Grey Wolf will make sure that the de Bohun estate is not raided again."

"You agreed to that?"

"I did." He shuffled a little uneasily in his seat. "When Sir Humphrey returns then he may decide otherwise. But as his constable, and responsible for guarding his interests during his absence, I decided it was the best action to take." He stared defiantly at Ardron before adding. "At least at this moment in time."

Ardron leaned back in his chair. Under the circumstances he could not blame the man for taking the easy way out, but he feared it set a dangerous precedent.

**

August 1143

The hunt had been a successful one, and they had continued far too long into the evening. Their over-indulgence had meant an overnight stay in the forest. Now as Ardron led the hunting party back to Norwood, the early morning September mist had rolled away. A stark unfiltered sun was beginning its climb towards its zenith, promising yet another day of frazzling temperatures. The long summer had been hot. Too hot! The evidence of that was obvious as they passed through villages and hamlets. The crops in the fields, on which the people depended to survive, were scorched, withered or practically non-existent. It was going to be a long hard winter for the populace, with a real possibility of famine.

It was early in the afternoon when they neared the open plain afront of Norwood Castle. Ardron's squire, Jacques, spurred his horse on past the hunt party and pressed on, at the gallop, to warn the castle of his master's approach. As he rode through the castle gates Ardron was greeted warmly by a gathering of smiling faces and waving hands. At the foot of the mote Jarcot held Rattlebone's reins as Ardron dismounted. He took the time to pat the horse's neck before issuing instructions for the animal to be well treated. It was a needless instruction; everyone knew his fondness for the big horse.

"Your blacksmith has returned," Jarcot said.

"Swidhurn?"

"Aye Swidhurn."

360

"And my brother Esmond?"

Jarcot shook his head. "Only Swidhurn," he replied.

Ardron hesitated a moment. Six weeks had passed since Swidhurn and Esmond had set of on their mission to discover what they could of the outlaw Grey Wolf. "Have Swidhurn brought to me in my chamber," he instructed.

"No need," Jarcot replied. "He is already there, waiting for you."

Ardron said nothing, only nodding acceptance. "The hunt was good," he needlessly informed him. "Have the kills attended." He took a moment to stroke the horse's nose and was tempted to groom the animal himself but decided more pressing issues awaited him in his chamber.

Inside, the chamber was darker than outside but not any cooler. Luc, Swidhurn, and his sister Hildi, awaited him and all stood in respect as he entered.

"Relax," he muttered with a dismissing hand wave as he walked over to the shelf containing the wine decanter.

Luc stayed on his feet as the others re-settled. "Sir, the hunt was good?" he asked.

"Rewarding," Ardron replied selecting a wooden goblet. After a brief inspection to establish its cleanliness he poured himself a wine from the decanter.

"Swidhurn waits to make his report," Luc added unnecessarily. "And there are despatches from Earl Gloucester."

"Despatches from Gloucester?" He queried as he made his way to sit on the settle.

"Arrived yesterday."

"It is good to see you Swidhurn." Ardron acknowledged his friend. "Your mission went well?"

Swidhurn shrugged non-committal. "Hard to say", he said.

"And my brother, Esmond?"

"Returned to Scorrenstone fearing his Thegne's wrath. He was over-due a couple of weeks."

Ardron only nodded. Redwald was the village Thegne in every sense of the word, even a brother would not get special consideration.

"What did you learn?" Ardron asked.

Again, Swidhurn shook his head dubiously. "The man, Grey Wolf, has a great deal of support amongst the common people and not many are willing to give out information to strangers. Indeed, we were regarded with a great deal of suspicion. So we were obliged to tread warily. We travelled far and wide from Safernoc Forest in the east, almost to Bath itself in the West. Then as far south as West Under the Plain. His support is strong. Through fear or regard I am not sure." He shook his head. "There is a definite reluctance to give out information."

"Didn't you learn anything?"

"We learned that he has united a number of outlaw bands, and now commands a considerable force. He is well organised and attacks soft targets. Easy picking objectives, such as outlying farms or homesteads and churches. He targets a lot of churches. One priest did confide in us that it seems the man despises the clergy. Sees them as parasites, living comfortable off the backs of lowly peasants."

Ardron frowned at that comment it seemed as if he had heard that somewhere before. "Anything else?" he asked.

Swidhurn hesitated. "I would say," he went on tentatively. "His support seemed to be particularly strong around the Castle Combe area."

"Do you think he has his base there?" Ardron asked.

Swidhurn pulled a face and sucked noisily through his teeth. "Maybe," he said. "But then I have a theory. I think that he may have established more than one base."

"Makes sense," Luc ventured. "A good tactic. Mobility would make him hard to find."

"Yes, it would," Ardron agreed. "However, I think Sir Reginald Dunstanville owns the Castle at Combe and he would surely root out this Grey Wolf."

"Perhaps he does," Swidhurn ventured. "But the castle stands derelict and has, since the king burned it to the ground four years ago."

"Yes of course," Ardron replied nodding his head. Hildi held up the wine decanter in front of him. "Anything else?" he asked holding up the goblet for Hildi to refill

"Only that this Grey Wolf has a son acting as his lieutenant. He is reputed ruthless and cruel, more feared than Grey Wolf himself."

"Does this son have a name?"

"Adelfrid," Swidhurn answered staring hard at Ardron.

"Adelfrid?" Ardron sought his memories. "Don't we know an Adelfrid? "We do."

"Adelfrid," Ardron remembered, "He was the son of Welfwulf the old man I defended in a Wager of Battel."

"Yes," Swidhurn agreed.

"No," Ardron concluded. "Can't be the same." But the thought continued to nag on. "What of these despatches, he asked Luc deftly changing the subject.

Luc fetched the rolled parchment from a nearby table and handed it to Ardron.

"I am summoned to Bristol Castle this week," he announced as he read on down. "My God," he muttered aloud. "The king has arrested Geoffrey de Mandeville and imprisoned him in the Tower of London."

That news was greeted with silence until Luc ventured to ask. "What for?"

"I don't know," Ardron said.

"De Mandeville is one of the king's longest serving supporter. He has been with him from the very onset." Luc added.

"Longest maybe," Ardron said. "But perhaps not one of his loyalist. Remember how he changed sides to support Maude when she defeated Stephen at Lincoln. Then swapped back again to side with Matilda at Winchester."

"Yes," Luc agreed with a nod. "Perhaps he has been found double dealing again."

"Maybe," Ardron muttered but his thoughts had turned to the Lady Rohesa. Where was she?

***

Scorrenstone, September.

The Weodfodthegn muttered his appeal to the Gods to look favourably upon the wedding pair, then requested from Frige, the mother of Gods, to bless the pair with fertility.

Ardron stood behind the marrying couple between Redwald and Durwin, the bride's father. It was a position he would have expected Cerdic as the groom's special friend to occupy. But Cerdic was yet again absent.

He watched with interest as the Weodfodthegn performed the rites of this ancient Saxon religion. How Redwald had managed to secure the services of a Weofodthegn he could only guess, but it had been Durwin's condition that his daughter be married to Saxon tradition. Later today the pair would stand together in the village church and wed under an orthodox Christian ceremony. But for now, in the slightly chilly air of an autumn morning, they stood on the banks of the river Avon and made their vows.

His mutterings and gestures finished the Weodfodthegn signalled to Durwin to make the exchange of swords. Durwin stepped forward and with a newly forged sword lying flat across his arms offered it to Esmond. Esmond bowed his head slightly in acknowledgement and took the sword. Taking the sword symbolically pledged, to a father, the protection of his daughter. Then unsheathing his own ancestral sword, Esmond passed it to Durwin. Traditionally, Durwin would now keep this sword until Edyo's first-born son was of age to receive his father's ancestral sword. A nod then from the Weodfodthegn signalled the ceremony's end.

Clapping and cheering now broke out amongst the gathering of well-wishers. Slowly the group began to break up and make their way casually back up the hill where light refreshments awaited. After the afternoon church ceremony, the main celebrations would begin. Celebrating, not only the wedding, but also a traditional thanksgiving on this day the day of the autumn equinox.

Side by side Ardron and Redwald made their way up the hill. "You should stop for the thanksgiving supper." Redwald almost demanded.

"Alas, brother I know I should, but I am overdue my Lord's summons to his castle in Bristol. I must leave straight after the church service." Ardron was uncomfortable. It was perhaps pressure by Redwald to affect a Thegne's jurisdiction over a subordinate.

The pair stepped aside to make way for the elaborately garlanded cart trundling up the hill containing the wedded pair. A wide grin flashed from Esmond towards Ardron indicated that his younger brother was a happy man. Smiling, with an acknowledging wave, he watched the cart pass, reasoning as it did that Edyo also seemed happy and, seemingly had put behind her the horrors of her kidnap four years ago.

"One day," Redwald went on. "Your loyalties between your Saxon roots and your Norman friends will be tested. Of that I have no doubts."

"You may be right," Ardron replied. "But at this time, I owe my position and my wealth to the Norman's. But be assured, my Thegne, I still work to the best of my abilities to look after the welfare of any Saxons that I can."

Redwald said nothing for a couple of strides then quoted from Mathews gospel. "No man can serve two masters, for either he will hate one and love the other. Or will be devoted to one and despise the other."

Ardron nodded. "I serve all, the best way I can, giving priority to where I am needed the most." he shrugged. "That's all I can do. Would you have me return to the village and serve as your assistant?"

"Brother," Redwald replied indifferently. "You must do as your conscience dictates."

"Aye. I must," Ardron muttered. The pair walked on in silence for a few strides then Ardron said. "The Norman's are here to stay. They are never going to go away and, so, whether we like it or not we must accept their way of life. We make it easier for ourselves if we accept that."

"You are right." Redwald allowed with a nod. "But whose colours do you serve? The king or the empress? Get it wrong and the consequences will be severe. Perhaps there is merit in the argument for you to return here. Wait to see who prevails then swear your fealty to the victor."

"I am afraid I am well past that point, brother." Ardron said with a sigh. "For better or worse, it is well known that I am associated to the cause of the Empress Maude."

Chapter 16

Bristol Castle, September 1143

Word had been received the day before yesterday that Sherborne Castle had, as ordered by the king, surrendered possession the Reginald de Dunstanville. Now Gloucester's part of the arrangement was to return William Martel safely back to London.

"How is it that you were detailed for the escort duty?" Miles Fitzwalter asked.

"Perhaps it was that Earl Robert felt that I deserved the honour," Ardron diplomatically replied as he tightened the cinch around the horse's belly.

Miles laughed out loud. "Truly, my friend, you practice well the art of discretion."

Ardron straightened up and glanced down the party of five dozen escorting sergens. All were busy with their last-minute preparations. "I am sure I know not what you mean, Sir Miles," he said.

Miles sniggered knowingly and placed a hand on Ardron's shoulder. "Good luck, my friend," he said. Then he turned and walked away glancing back only once.

Ardron watched him go, knowing full well at what it was he hinted. His summons to Bristol Castle had been for this purpose entirely. The task had been presented to him as a specific honour. However, his suspicion was, that should Stephen turn false to his word and consider seizing the escort commander, then Ardron as that commander, and a Saxon, would be of little ransom value in the Angevin echelon order. He patted Rattlebone down the neck and handed the reins to his squire, Jacques. He now waited only the release of William Martel into his official care.

Anxious to get started he glanced skywards, trying to estimate the time. His plan, to reach Chippenham before nightfall and rest there, before moving on to John Fitzgilbert's Marlborough Castle the next day. From there it would be to Brien Fitzcount at Wallingford Castle before delivering William Martel to the king at Westminster on the fourth day.

After what seemed an age to an impatient man, Earl Robert eventually emerged from the keep with his prisoner. For a few seconds, the pair talked before Earl Robert offered his hand to be shaken. Martel declined to take it. With a brief shrug, Earl Robert indicated with a dismissing arm swing that he was free to join the escort party.

"Sir William," Ardron acknowledged as he directed Martel's attention towards the horse selected for him. "I intend to be in Chippenham before night fall and to deliver you to your king at Westminster four days hence."

Martel gave no indication that he had even heard Ardron, instead brusquely said. "Let us be away from this place soonest, Sir Knight."

"Ardron, Sir William. My name is Ardron."

"Order you men mounted, Sir Knight," he replied tersely, as he mounted.

Ardron nodded and sighed inwardly. With Martel's belligerent attitude it promised to be a long journey.

When mounted Ardron looked back along the column. All was ready. He glanced towards the keep and to Earl Robert. A brief nod signalled that he had permission to leave. "Forward," he shouted and dug his heels into Rattlebone's ribs spurring the big horse forward.

***

Westminster, 1143

It was early afternoon when they were ushered into the Great Hall of Westminster. It was more than two years since Ardron had stood in this place at the court of the Empress Maude. Little had changed. The Great Hall was lined on both sides by throngs of knights and merchants, all standing quietly obediently waiting and watching. At the far end was the throne, this time, however, it was Stephen and not Maude who sat. On either side, stood the close aides of the king including William de Ypres and Bishop Henry.

Following behind William Martel, and between two of Stephens personal guards, Ardron walked straight down the centre aisle towards the throne.

"Sir William," the king said getting to his feet. "We are glad to see you restored to your freedom and once more within our ranks."

Martel went down on one knee in homage to his king. "Your Majesty," he said. "I am in your debt for my restoration."

Stephen left the dais and placed a welcoming hand on Martel's shoulder, then offered his hand giving him permission to rise. "Are you well my faithful knight?" he asked.

"Well enough, my liege." Martel replied as he got to his feet.

"I know well of my cousin's hospitality," Stephen said moving back to sit on the throne.

"Thanks to your speedy generosity, Sire, my incarceration was only brief compared to that which you had to endure."

Stephen nodded agreement. "Maybe so," he said. "Nevertheless, we shall organise a feast to celebrate your return. Stand here at my right hand, my friend." He indicated a place close to the throne. Then for the first time he studied Ardron. "Who is this?" he asked.

"Sire," Ardron went down on one knee. "I am Ardron of Norwood. Knight in service to Earl Gloucester and tasked with the safe delivery of Sir William."

"Well, Sir Knight you have discharged your duty." Stephen said peering hard at Ardron. "Sir Knight," he said, "We have met before."

"We have, your Majesty. One day some four years ago in the Royal Forest of Melksham."

"I remember." Stephen said. "You and your friend came to my assistance when I was beset by robbers."

"I am flattered, Sir that you remember." He decided against adding that he had also come to his aid on the battlefield of Lincoln.

Stephen paused a moment. "How does it come to pass that I now see you serving in Cousin Maude's cause?"

"Accidents of circumstances had me furthering her cause and following rewards have placed me indebted to my Lord Robert, Earl Gloucester."

"And how say you now?" Stephen asked. "Do you consider her claim to the throne more legitimate than mine?"

Ardron was well aware of the potential danger in the reply. The whole room was silent waiting with intense interest on his reply. He bowed his head and said nothing, taking valuable thinking time.

"Well, Sir Knight?" It was de Ypres who pressed for an answer.

He decided to speak daringly. "Your Majesty," he said. "I am a simple Saxon and know not all the legal intricacies of royal claims. But I have served the empress to the best of my abilities and have been rewarded. Because of that she has my sworn fealty. My word is my bond." He added defiantly staring hard at the king's brother, Bishop Henry, who had not been as steadfast.

"I know this man also," de Ypres said to the king while fixing Ardron with a glare. "He stood at Fitzcount side beneath a white flag at Winchester without."

"I did," Ardron replied unflinching. "I was also inside the Abbey that you callously burned at Wherwell."

De Ypres laughed aloud. "Well you feared better than that hell spawned Fitzgilbert," he sneered. "You still have both eyes."

"Enough," the king cut in. "Sir Ardron you will stay here at our pleasure."

Not sure whether he was to be a prisoner or not Ardron pressed his luck. "Sire, if it pleases you, I have discharged my duty and have pressing business back at my Norwood estate."

"It pleases me for you to stay," Stephen demanded. "Now stand aside, I too have pressing business here today." Ardron got to his feet bowed briefly, then moved over to the side fearing that he had just become the king's prisoner.

"Bring in de Mandeville," the king ordered.

Dirty and unkempt, and blinking in the bright light de Mandeville was pushed and prodded up the aisle between two guards. Momentarily, he stood before the king before being forced to his knees. The state of de Mandeville shocked Ardron. Although he had no regard for this man, who switched sides more often than a miser counts his money, he was shamefully degraded.

"You are not looking well my good Earl of Essex," The king mocked him. "Did you not relish being a guest in one of your own dungeons?"

"I would know for what reason I have been held prisoner in London's Tower," de Mandeville demanded.

"Do you really have no idea?"

De Mandeville slowly shook his head.

"For some time, I have been irritated by your continuous double dealings, the under-hand ways you have been taking advantage of your position. Not to mention how you cheat me of my due fiefs. But you did well and truly, overstepped the mark when you took our daughter-in-law, Constance, hostage."

"I deny it." De Mandeville replied hotly. "I imposed only a long hospitality on Princess Constance. More-over to protect her from the brutality of her own husband, your tyrannical son, Prince Eustace."

"What goes on between my son and his wife should be of no concern of yours." Stephen replied hotly.

"Perhaps you should curb his excesses," de Mandeville muttered.

"Hold your tongue," de Ypres shouted angrily, stepping forward with his hand on his sword hilt.

An uneasy silence descended while everybody waited for Stephens response. After a few moments, the king leaned his elbow on the armrest and rubbed his chin thoughtfully. "You are luckier than you deserve," he said quietly. "I was prepared to leave you in the Tower until you rotted. But many of your fellow barons have pleaded your cause for clemency." He paused before going on. "You can have your freedom at a price."

De Mandeville permitted himself a brief smirk. He knew fine well that Stephen needed the support of those barons and that had forced his hand. "What is this price? he asked.

"You will surrender onto me the Tower of London, your Castles at Pleshy and Saffron Walden."

De Mandeville's jaw visible dropped open. "You would take everything and leave me with nothing," he exclaimed.

"That is the price," Stephen said with a shrug.

"Your Majesty," de Mandeville appealed. "I was one of your first supporters. I journeyed at your side from France to London when we knew not if we were to be welcomed or crushed."

"True! But since then you have sought to enrich yourself at every opportunity even to the extent of switching sides when it suited." He paused for effect. "The price remains."

"What of my wife Rohesa. You cannot be so heartless to see her dishomed?"

"The Lady Rohesa is of de Vere stock, a family of wealth. She will not be cast out." He leaned back. "I would have your decision."

De Mandeville glared back silently. As far as Ardron could see there was no decision to make. Accept and give up all, or rot in the tower.

"I accept," de Mandeville reluctantly muttered.

Stephen nodded to the guards, who stepped forward and unceremoniously hauled de Mandeville to his feet, half dragging him away. He looked back towards Stephen with intense anger blazing in his eyes.

***

Three weeks had passed since de Mandeville's humiliation and although Ardron found himself held, at the kings pleasure, he had not been imprisoned. He was instead under virtual house arrest within his allocated lodging. Obliged, to report daily to the king's court at Westminster his attendance was enforced by two sergens posted by de Ypres who accompanied him each morning. However, mostly ignored by the king and his close advisor's he, nevertheless, felt confident that with a little guile he would be able to escape. His own escorting sergens he had dismissed to return to Bristol, keeping only Jacques, his squire. It would be easier for two to escape than to leave London with an escort of six dozen. For the time being, however, he was content to bide his time and wait for that opportunity.

Whilst he was mostly confined in his lodgings, his squire Jacques was not. It fell on the young squire to exercise the horses every morning in the meadows of the river Fleet. Acting on further instructions from Ardron he had, whilst carrying out chores, become his eyes and ears on what was happening within London's streets. It was somewhat disappointing to Ardron that these reports seemed to describe mostly contentment from the London populace. People went about their business of making enough of a living to survive. Seemingly, there was little interest among the lowly of who was England's monarch. So long as they were left in peace to continue their own existence they did not really care. Ardron could not help but consider those less fortunate, outside the capital's confines, who were by an accident of geography living under constant threat that conflict would be their visitor.

As with previous court sessions, this morning dragged on with a seemingly endless procession of merchants presenting Stephen with all manner of trade goods before seeking his favour with some deal advantageous to themselves. Dragged on that was, until the court usher interrupted proceedings talking quietly with the king.

"Show them in right away," Stephen instructed.

Ardron watched with interest as a baron and a Benedictine monk were shown into the great hall. The usher then formally announced, 'Sir William de Chesney, Castellan of Oxford,' and 'Abbot Daniel of Ramsey Abbey. It was William de Chesney who mostly captured Ardron's interest. This was the man, appointed by the king, to take over the castle from the deposed Robert, d'Orly. Both bent a knee before the king and waited permission to rise.

"What news? Sir William," The king asked.

"Grave news, Sire." Then with a purposeful hand gesture he diverted attention to the abbot.

"Your Majesty," the abbot began. "I have to report that God-less Geoffrey de Mandeville did, descend on Ramsey Abbey, along with a band of hell-spawn outlaws and murderers, then did, with fire and sword, despoiled the abbey. Any who showed dissent were mercilessly and cruelly slaughtered. Those that did survive were driven away. Now these disciples from hell occupy the abbey for their own purposes."

The king leaned forward in his seat then glanced sideways to de Ypres clearly concerned. "When did this happen?" he demanded.

"Two days ago." The abbot replied.

De Ypres leaned forward, anger across his face clear. "I knew it was a mistake to allow that bastard his freedom," he muttered.

It was not lost on Ardron that de Ypres, being so secure in his position, he could casually criticised the king.

"Clear the court," Stephen instructed the usher.

Ardron shuffled out amongst the leaving crowd, thoughtfully. Clearly de Mandeville had declared an intention of rebellion and revenge. He wondered just how much the news would be welcomed amongst the Angevin's. He doubted they would want to receive such an unreliable and treacherous snake as an ally. However, it did open up the possibility of another front on Stephens eastern flank.

He decided that now was the time that he should leave and carry the news west.

The next morning, he instructed Jacques that if he were summoned to court this day, he was to exercise both horses as normal, except it was to be only gentle exercise and much later than normal. He did not want the horses to be tired. Around midday, or shortly after, he wanted Jacques to be ready mounted and waiting for him over the Ludgate bridge.

His plan simplicity itself. He would, as was expected of him, be at Westminster for the court session. Then at the midday recess, he intended to stroll seemingly aimlessly towards the west. His shadowers, not suspicious because he was afoot, would undoubtedly follow. When he reached the Ludgate, he then intended to make his dash for freedom. Quickly through the gate over the bridge and away on the waiting horses. The plan, however, did need Jacques to be waiting and, more importantly, for those followers to be on foot. If they were mounted, then it would probably not work, and it would be better to await another time. All this, of course depended on there being a court session this day.

He was collected for attendance at court later that morning, and he took his place amongst the throng of onlookers. The session dragged on, with seemingly endless number of trivial disputes. At one point the king tired of the banal, left the court, leaving his brother, Bishop Henry, to settle the issues. Around noon the king returned, but after only a few minutes, called a halt to proceedings to re-convene after a two-hour break.

As he shuffled out with the throng Ardron was spotted by his two escorts and they fell in just a couple of paces behind him. As he left the building Ardron acknowledged the pair with a cheery wave and, with a sarcastic slant, informed them that he intended to stroll along the riverbank. Seemingly aimlessly casual, he meandered slowly along the Thames, deliberately lingering several times just watching the waters flow. His two keepers meanwhile, followed in closer attendance, making no attempt to indulge in any sort of cordial contact. From a stall trader he purchased a bread cake, and for a few minutes, he wasted time leaning against a tree nibbling the fare. Hoping he had been convincing enough about his lethargy, he then continued casually along the riverbank as if enjoying the October sunshine of an autumn day. When he reached the point where the river Fleet flowed into the Thames, he turned along its bank heading towards Ludgate.

As if by divine providence a cart hauler had had a mishap at the gate. His horse had spooked and reared, and in so doing jerked the cart sideways, tipping it onto its side. With the cart on its side and the horse lying prone the contents of turnips, cabbages and apples were strewn across the ground partially blocking the gateway. Much to the annoyance of the gate guards, who in bad humour, shouted, growled and cursed the hapless carter. However, sympathetic bystanders went to the man's aid, first righting the two-wheeled cart and hauling the horse back to its feet. Then in good humour they began tossing the contents back in the cart. Ardron saw here a golden opportunity and he joined in the fun, setting himself the task of soothing the horse and holding its headgear whilst the cart was re-loaded. When the cart was re-stacked, minus a few pilfered items, he continued to control the horse while the carter climbed back on his cart. Then using the excuse of a skittish horse, he kept hold of the bridle and led the animal through the gate and outside the city wall. Glancing behind he could see his two markers standing in the gateway watching, probably expecting him to come back. But he continued to lead the horse on and over the bridge. When on the other side he released the horse's bridle and stood clear. With a cheery wave at the carter he watched the cart trundle on down the road. Glancing over the bridge to the river below he saw Jacques was in position mounted and ready waiting.

"Jacques," he called.

The young squire found him, and responded instantly, driving up the riverbank to the bridge leading Rattlebone on a long halter. Ardron climbed up into the saddle received his precious sword from his squire, then with a backwards look to the two followers gave a departing wave. It was that easy!

By early evening, and getting dark, they had crossed the Royal Forest of Windsor and arrived at its western edge. Being a distance of around thirty miles from London, Ardron decided that they were safe enough, so he decided to stop and rest. It would undoubtedly be a cold and hungry night spent in the forest, but with a decent fire they could, to a large extent, keep the cold away.

Within a thicket they came across a sheltering rocky overhang, providing an ideal place for a night refuge. 'This will do.' Ardron had declared. They turned the horses loose to forage for themselves, while they gathered dry brushwood for a fire. Ardron then set to kindle a fire into life while Jacques foraged around seeking blackberries.

With flames soon dancing and wood crackling, they settled down to wait out the night. Darkness closed in rapidly and as it did the temperature dropped. Soon a three-quarter large moon breasted the horizon but as it rose higher a misty glow developed around its edge, warning an impending frost.

"Sir," Jacques said. "How much longer do you think this war will go on?"

Ardron had no answer. "Do you grow weary, boy?"

Jacques hesitated, "Yes Sir," he replied quietly.

"As do we all." Ardron said nodding knowingly. In the firelight he studied the fresh-faced youngster. "How old are you boy?"

"This summer, If God spares me, I will be fifteen."

"Fifteen!" he nodded thoughtfully. "If God spares you to a long life, then you might even live to see this war end."

"Do you think God even knows there is a war going on down here?

Ardron shook his head ruefully. "I don't know," he replied. "I wonder if he even cares."

The pair fell silent while Ardron poked needlessly at the fire.

"Can the empress win?" Jacques asked nervously.

He needn't have worried about his questioning loyalty because it was a question Ardron had pondered himself. Ardron sighed. "She had it won after Lincoln," he answered. "But the people of London decided that they didn't want a woman as England's ruler." He shrugged resignedly. His additional thoughts he kept to himself. Perhaps, he thought, if Maude had been a little more conciliatory, a little more charitable towards the populace then they may not have thrown open the gates to Stephen's queen, Matilda, and her army. "Water under the bridge," he muttered to himself with a sigh. "Can she recover and win?" he returned to the question. "Yes, I suppose she can." He answered. "She, perhaps, has a better chance now that she sees England's crown not for herself but for her son Prince Henry. Certainly, he, as a male, has a better chance of being accepted. But it will take the defeat or even the death of Stephen. Even then there is his son Eustace who will undoubtedly rally enough support to make a claim for himself." He shook his head ruefully. "There is no quick or easy solution. This war will go on for a long time yet."

Jacques stared thoughtfully into the flames without speaking.

"Throw some more wood on the fire, young sir" Ardron instructed. "Then get your head down and sleep."

The slight frost had made for uncomfortable sleeping, and as a consequence they were about their business early this morn. Jacques had completed the saddling of his mare and led her round to where Ardron was tightening the cinch on Rattlebone's belly.

"Sir," he almost whispered.

"I see them," Ardron muttered and continued his task. "Mount your horse," he added.

Satisfied on the tightness of the cinch he turned to face the four men who had emerged stealthily from the undergrowth and now stood mere feet away watching. They were armed menacingly. "Is there something I can do for you?" He challenged.

They were dressed in ragged smocks, belted around the waist. Grimy sheepskins draped their shoulders, seemingly adding bulk to their size. Their leggings were cross gartered with simple chewed leather footwear. Obviously, Saxons. Rough beards and wild unkempt hair added to their intimidating appearance.

"That's a fine-looking horse," the man leaning nonchalantly on a long bow suggested. "He'd fetch a good few marks at a market," he added.

Ardron didn't answer. Thumbs pressed inside his belt, he studied the men before him. The bowman apart, the others all held hand weapons. A long-handled battle-axe, a mace chain with the iron ball missing from the end, and a roughly constructed club by the last man. "The horse will not be going to a market," he said quietly."

"Then we'll settle for your purse," the bowman said.

"No, you won't," Ardron replied defiantly.

"Then, you Norman bastard, we'll take it all."

"Ride," Ardron instructed Jacques, taking the time to turn and slap the rump of his mare, then he drew his sword and faced the four men.

It was the man with the battle-axe who attacked first. Axe raised over his right shoulder he charged forward growling as he did. Ardron stepped back and at the last moment he swerved to his right. As the axe descended, he used his sword to divert it. The axe passed close by, but harmlessly past his left side. He came again this time more cautiously, then swinging the axe horizontally he aimed at Ardron's head. Ardron ducked and felt the draft only inches above his head. The momentum of that swing exposed the axe-man's right side for an instant. An instant was all Ardron needed. Straightening up, he thrust his sword forcefully into the man's ribs. Penetration was only partial, but enough to make the man gasp and stagger sideways. Pressing home his score, Ardron leapt forward and with all his strength brought his sword down on the back of the man's exposed head. Just for good measure, he pulled the sword back towards him, extending the laceration wider and deeper. He wouldn't be getting up in a hurry.

He turned quickly and just in time to see the chain swinging towards his head. Instinctively, he flinched and put up his left arm for protection. It was only partially successful. The chain curled around his arm and lashed him across his back. The instant stinging pain forced him to straighten involuntarily and throw his head back with a grunt. But the two-handed grip the man held had spun him temporarily off balance and he stumbled sideways with a stuttering step. Half-turned and off balance he was vulnerable. Ardron seized the opportunity, and cursing the man loudly, plunged his blade into the man's kidneys area. The would-be robber jolted upright, his mouth dropping open in pain, before he leapt away trying to unimpale himself. Ardron withdrew his sword and let him go. No longer interested in continuing his attack, the robber dropped the chain and sank to his knees. He leaned sideways trying to press a hand against his back wound. Then he slumped forward and writhed on the ground trying to find a position to ease his pain.

Ardron turned quickly, looking for the next attack, and saw the archer with arrow strung and bow drawn aimed straight at him. Panic was beginning to rise when in from the side, with his horse galloping flat out, Jacques rode straight over the archer sending him tumbling and rolling under the horse hooves. No time to be relieved, Ardron turned looking for the last man. That man held Rattlebone's halter, trying to lead him away, but the big horse was having none of it. He plunged and reared and struggled against the halter. Ardron moved to confront the man. He let the halter go and turned holding the club up threateningly. For a moment, the pair faced each other, before the outlaw decided that a small club against a broad sword was unequal. He tossed the club, stepped backward and held up his hands in surrender. Then turning quickly, he took to his heels and ran. Twisting back Ardron saw the archer getting to his feet groggily, only to be run down by the horse yet again as Jacques came galloping back the other way. Ardron permitted himself a wry smile, the boy had done well. Perhaps even saved his life.

Just for a moment he thought to walk among the injured would-be-thieves in gloating triumph, but then decided not. Instead he swung onto the back of Rattlebone, wincing as he did against the back pain. Taking just a moment, he glanced across at the writhing outlaws. "Not a Norman bastard," he muttered. "A Saxon bastard." Then set off at a casual canter after Jacques.

***

It was early afternoon by the time they reached Marlborough Castle. It was a welcome sight to Ardron because the pain across his shoulders had been getting steadily worse, and by the way his shirt kept sticking to his back, he knew there was some bleeding. As usual the bailey inside was a hive of activity and when they reached the foot of the mote, Jacques had to help Ardron dismount. It was the Lady Aline who was first to greet him, summoning servants quickly when she recognised his difficulties. However, pridefully, he shunned their help. Holding himself erect, he walked stiffly up the steps and into the keep.

"Jesus Holy Christ," Fitzgilbert exclaimed when Ardron was shown into his private chamber. "What happened to you?"

"Forest outlaws," Ardron muttered.

Fitzgilbert cocked his head slightly to focus better, with his only good eye, and indicated a seat by the inglenook. "Here, sit here, Scorrenstone," he said." He still referred to Ardron as Scorrenstone, even though now recognised as Norwood. "Find the lach and bring him here," he went on ordering a servant.

Less than an hour later Ardron had been treated. There were some bleeding lacerations though not bad enough to require stitching. However, the bruising was severe, and would get worse over the next couple of days before getting better, the lach concluded. Then sitting at the table with food and wine laid before him, Ardron found himself more relaxed than he had been at any time since starting this mission.

"You seemed to have been away a long time," Fitzgilbert said adjusting his black eye patch to a more comfortable position. "Did you dally to enjoy the delights of London?"

Ardron scoffed. "Detained at the king's pleasure."

Fitzgilbert smiled and nodded knowingly. "Were you imprisoned?"

"No. Fortunately! More like an open arrest."

"But you escaped."

"I did. Yesterday."

"How goes the war for the usurper? Any insight?" Fitzgilbert topped up Ardron's wine chalice.

"Something interesting," Ardron replied, swilling the wine around the chalice. He then proceeded to relate the rebellion of de Mandeville.

Fitzgilbert showed no surprise. "I have heard such rumours about open rebellion in the fens. "You have now confirmed it." He almost beamed." It's likely to be a big problem for Stephen. Most certainly, I wouldn't want to go in there after him. You can hide an army in those marshes."

"Do you think Earl Gloucester would want to know?" Ardron asked.

Fitzgilbert nodded, "He will! Now that it is confirmed I'll get a messenger out today."

Ardron nodded silent agreement. At least the responsibility for passing on that information had now been passed to someone else. "Is there any other news I have missed," he asked.

Fitzgilbert was thoughtful a moment. "Had Humphrey de Bohun returned from France before you went to London?"

"No. He was still in France last I heard."

"He's been back in Trowbridge for two or three weeks by now."

"Ah!" Ardron commented. "And his mission, was that successful?"

Fitzgilbert scoffed. "I'd say not. After keeping him hanging around for endless weeks Geoffrey Plantagenet finally announced his verdict. And that was, that he would not be donating a single mark nor a single sergen towards his wife's cause in England."

Ardron shook his head bewildered. "And that was it?"

"He did undertake to carry out some raids into Norman estates in France." Fitzgilbert paused. "One can readily see that those raids would do more to enhance his own fortune and be just about as much use, to Maude, as a beaker of piss to a wool dyer."

Ardron sighed heavily and understood how much of a disappointment that would be to the Angevin cause. "One would have thought that they would share the common goal for their son, Prince Henry."

"One would," Fitzgilbert agreed. "But he's a vindictive devil is Geoffrey Plantagenet. Meanwhile, my friend," Fitzgilbert changed the subject. "You must accept my hospitality and relax and recover here at your leisure."

"Gracious of you Sir John and I accept with gratitude. Just for a day or two until I feel well enough to travel."

***

October 1143

In the event it was five days later when he rode back into the bailey of Norwood Castle. He was greeted by Luc who, clearly, was pleased to see his patron.

"My Lord, I am mightily pleased to see you," he said. "We had heard that you were held prisoner by the king."

"Prisoner? No! Detained? Yes! He replied as he dismounted. "Anything I should know?" He asked as he passed Rattlebone's reins to Jacques.

"Only one matter requires your soonest attention," Luc replied. "But it will wait until you are refreshed." Ardron nodded then made his way up the mote and into the keep.

Later in the evening as he sat by a blazing inglenook fire he related to Luc, Jarcot and Swidhurn his experiences in London.

Luc shook his head in rueful sympathy over the woodland attack by the outlaws. Then rubbing fingers across his brow almost sheepishly said. "That brings me to the matter that I have to report."

Ardron reached for the decanter topped up his chalice before passing it on. "Is it good or bad news?" He asked.

Luc took the decanter from Swidhurn, then pausing before toping up his own chalice, said. "I'm not sure. Little more than a week ago we had a visit from a monk of sorts."

"Off sorts?" Ardron queried.

"Aye of sorts. As it turned out, I don't believe he was a monk." Luc replied.

Ardron glanced at Jarcot, who nodded agreement.

"He said he was sent to deliver a message." Luc went on.

"A message?" Ardron interrupted again.

"From Grey Wolf," Luc said.

Ardron sighed heavily and felt the gloom settle in his stomach. "Go on," he said preparing himself for harsh news.

"At first he asked to see you. But when I eventually convinced him that you were not here, he gave the message to me."

"The message was?"

"That Grey Wolf would protect this estate against any further outlaw raids for a consideration."

"The consideration was?" Ardron asked.

"One hundred marks paid quarterly."

Ardron crossed his arms and allowed his head to fall onto his chest. He should have expected it. That was, after all, the exact proposition placed before Francis d'Aumale de Bohun's castle constable.

"What did you do?" he asked leaning back.

"My first reaction was to kick his holy arse all the way across the bailey. But I didn't. I assumed he was nothing more than a messenger. It was a dilemma. Because at that point I believed that you were the king's prisoner. Jarcot and I got our heads together and wondered if we could use this to our advantage."

"In what way?"

"We thought that we might be able to discover the outlaws camp." It was Jarcot who answered the question."

"Yes," Luc continued. "We decided to pay him the money and offer to provide him with an escort for his safety." But he saw through that and declined the escort offer. Nevertheless, I gave him a hundred marks, then when he left Jarcot and I set out to follow."

An idea not without merit, Ardron thought. "Was you successful?" he asked.

"No," Luc drawled. "For eight or nine miles we followed. But not knowing where he was heading, we were obliged to keep him in sight, mostly. But if we could see him then, probably, he could see us, and so it turned out.

Somewhere to the west of Chippenham, he stopped to make camp for the night. He made a fire, a bed and looked to be settled for the night. Jarcot and I took turn about to watch his camp. He bedded down, but when his fire eventually died away, there was only pitch darkness and very hard to see. When the dawn broke all seemed to be as it was. We could see the brown of his habit amongst his blanket, and it looked for all the world that he still slept. After a while, because there was no activity, we decided that all may not be as it seemed. We abandoned the follow plan, and went into his camp, believing that we would, at least, recover the hundred marks. But he was gone, leaving his monks habit draped amongst his bedding to fool us, and under cover of darkness had stolen away." He paused. "I'm sorry sir but I have cost you one hundred marks," He added apologetically.

"Luc," Ardron responded. "When I'm away you have complete autonomy over the castle affairs. It was a good plan that didn't succeed." He spread his arms resignedly. "At least we won't have to worry about outlaw raids for the next three months." He shook his head in reluctant admiration for this outlaw Grey Wolf. "Have to admit," he went on. "It really is a clever scheme. If he can get enough payments then he doesn't even have to act as an outlaw, just sit back and prosper. And," he added with a drawl. "I suppose he could even claim that he protects against outlaws." He chuckled at the prospect.

"Now," he said getting to his feet to take a chart from the shelf. "Let's see if we can figure out where that man was possibly heading."

***

Malmesbury, March 1144

The morning was bright and the heavy mist that had begun the day had, with the rising of the sun, almost cleared. Only the residual remained in the valley below the town where the dampness of the river Avon held on to the last dregs of the haze. Ardron stood on the opposite side of the valley gazing across to the hillside town wrapped around its castle and imposing Abbey.

"I have been here before," he muttered to himself as he recalled his enforced recruit into king Stephen's cause.

"You have?" Humphrey de Bohun queried.

He hadn't intended the comment over-heard, and under the circumstances he had no wish to expand the remark. He answered de Bohun's query with a dismissing shrug. "It's a long story," he said.

This siege was in its comparative infancy, being little more than two weeks since the Angevin force, commanded by Sir Roger Fitzmiles eldest son of Miles Fitzwalter, had advanced on this island of royalist, in the heart of the Angevin held west country. Earl Robert had decided that with the king in Lincolnshire chasing the elusive Geoffrey de Mandeville around the fens, the time for an assault was perfect. This force was not sufficiently strong enough to mount an all-out attack on Malmesbury. But it was sufficient to mount an effective siege of the town. A siege that would announce an intention to eventually seize the castle and town, perhaps also, weakening resolve, whilst giving Earl Robert time to raise a more significant force.

Behind him an escort force was preparing once again to approach the town under a white flag to yet again offer surrender terms. Several times Roger Fitzmiles had approached the town gates and waited under that flag to offer terms. But so far had received only ridicule and abuse from the sergens manning the wall. He had been ignored completely by the castellan, Walter de Pinkney. This day it was Philip Fitzrobert, Earl Robert's son, who was detailed to approach the town gate beneath the white flag. Satisfied all was in order Fitzrobert led the casual descent to the river and the town main gate.

"Why does he even bother?" de Bohun said.

Ardron only shrugged without answering. Ardron's opinion was that Fitzmiles, a man still in his early twenties, did not yet have the battle expertise nor the charisma of his father. The unfortunate death of Sir Miles during a hunting accident on Christmas Eve was a significant set-back to the Angevin cause. Since his death it was his son Roger, who had stepped up to take his place as Earl Gloucester's close confidante.

"What is your opinion of that young man," de Bohun asked nodding in the direction of Philip the earl's son.

"I don't really have one," Ardron replied. In truth he knew very little about the man, barely out of teenage years. "Why do you ask?"

De Bohun wrinkled his nose and made a face. "Well___," he drawled. "Our gracious earl seems to be loading more and more responsibility on a man that has yet to prove himself under battle conditions."

"He is castellan of Cricklade isn't he?" Ardron ventured.

"He is," de Bohun agreed. "And also, the newly built Tetbury Castle too."

"Privilege of being son of the Supreme Commander, I suppose." Ardron said.

"I suppose," de Bohun agreed.

The party had reached the main gate and waited patiently for some reaction. Out of earshot from the watchers on the hill, there was no way of knowing if negotiations were taking place. But guessing, from the inactivity and the restlessness of the escorting sergens, it did appear as if the response was exactly as of previous attempts. Bored waiting for something to happen Ardron excused himself and made his way back to his troops camp. For this siege he had contributed a total of three dozen. Two dozen of professional sergens and a dozen of competent villeins. Because this siege was actually taking place close to Norwood he would, he estimated, be able to rotate those standing too, as and when he saw fit.

Maurice du Prevuer had by this time rekindled a fire from yesterday's ashes and had laid out dough on warming stones. It would be the better part of another hour before they would be ready for eating.

"Any progress," he enquired looking at Ardron.

"Not that I could see," Ardron replied squatting down by his side.

There was an extended silence between the two before Maurice spoke. "We are likely to be here a long time," he said gloomily.

"Oh yes," Ardron replied. "I can't see anything happening until Earl Robert arrives with a larger force."

"You don't think we could mount a successful attack."

"Well Fitzmiles could mount an attack but I think the outcome would be in balance. Better to exercise caution and wait until we have superior numbers."

"When do you think Earl Robert will arrive?"

Ardron shrugged, "A month__. Maybe!"

Maurice was thoughtful and absentmindedly poked at the fire. "At least," he said. "We are less than an hour away from Norwood."

Ardron nodded agreement without a reply.

"They're back," Luc declared walking into the camp.

"No progress?"

"No progress!" he affirmed Ardron's summing up.

"But I suspect Roger Fitzmiles's patience is wearing thin.

"Oh?"

"Aye, When Fitzrobert reported no response once more, Fitzmiles showed definite pique. He muttered to himself and kicked the water bucket, as he stomped back into his tent."

Ardron nodded without speaking. He hoped that Fitzmiles didn't lose patience and attempt something foolish.

It was later that day when he was sent for and accompanied by the young Fitzrobert, was shown into Fitzmiles's tent. Already inside was de Bohun and another of old King Henry's bastard sons, Robert Fitzedith, Earl of Okehampton,

"Ah! Ardron of Norwood," Fitzmiles greeted. "I understand that you are a local man."

"Yes Sir," Ardron replied.

"Do you know the people of Malmesbury?"

"There was a time that I counted some of them as friends."

"But not now?"

Ardron shrugged. "Many things have changed."

"Indeed," Fitzmiles said. "But even so what do you think the reaction of the towns people if we attack the town?"

Ardron stared back not sure how to reply to a question that seemed obvious.

"What I mean is," Fitzmiles went on. "I have no quarrel with the common people. It is the castle I want to get close to. If I ignore them, and issue the orders to our sergens that anyone caught pillaging will be severely punished, will the populace stand aside?"

Thoughtfully Ardron stroked his beard. "Very possibly," he said. "Not all, however, some are loyal to the castellan and some are his villeins. Some may well be prepared to fight, but if they are not attacked then they might well stay neutral. Others, women, children, old and feeble will no doubt seek refuge and hide."

"Good that is the answer I had hoped for.

"Do you intend to attack?" Ardron asked.

"I do!"

Ardron was dubious. He wanted to suggest that an attack should be delayed until the arrival of Earl Robert with a large force, but he held his counsel, and instead asked. "How do you intend to let the townsfolk know that you intend them no harm?"

"You have local Saxon's in your camp?"

"I do."

"Then you will task them to secrete themselves into the town and spread the word before the attack." The reply was brusque without hint of suggestion. Instead it was a decision made and the topic closed. Roger Fitzmiles then outlined his plan at length and detailed each man to an allotted assignment.

Two days later, Ardron lined up alongside Fitzedith, afront a twelve dozen or so men, over the brow of Blicks Hill in the north. He glanced over his shoulder at the force. All were on foot, and at this moment in various stages of relaxation. Some stood, most sat, some even reposed. Mostly, however, faces betrayed some nervous tension. There was no singing no chanting. This attack was to be a surprise.

Fitzmiles's plan was simplicity, itself and Ardron had, begrudgingly, conceded it had a good chance of success. Both the Angevin and Royalist sides were estimated to be just about equally balanced. Balanced that was, providing the ordinary Saxon populace of Malmesbury did not side with de Pinkney's sergenti. The whole success of his plan hinged on that.

A strong and determined attack was to be made at the town's main gate in its east. The assault force, supported by archers, would advance behind a wall of shields. Every time it came under fire from arrow storms, a complete three rank cover of shields would be thrown efficiently into position. When the advance was close enough to the towns palisade, then the full assault would be unleashed. A reserve force would then be thrown in as added strength to the attack. However, this was not the main point of attack. Once the incumbents within the palisade were convinced this was the main assault, it was anticipated that sergenti from other areas would be sucked into defending the east gate. Then, and only then, when the north perimeter was so weakened Fitzedith would launch his attack. If the north wall was successfully breached, then the defenders in the east would find themselves out-flanked.

"Have you seen action before?" Fitzedith asked.

"Yes Sir, I have."

"Oh! Where?"

"Wallingford," Ardron replied. Then added "Lincoln and Winchester."

"Good God," Fitzedith muttered in surprise. "You are more experienced than I." Then he chuckled. "Should it be that it were you, who command this attack and not I."

"No Sir," Ardron said. "You are an earl with royal blood. I am but a Saxon in knights service to Earl Robert."

"Truly sir," Fitzedith said. "I hope my half-brother values you as he should."

Even below the brow of the hill, they could hear the commotion taking place in the valley beyond. "And so, it begins," Fitzedith said.

To Ardron it seemed an age after that before a solitary figure appeared at the hill crest and gave the signal for Fitzedith's force to attack. The foot soldiers ran over the hill and with blood thirsty yells descended the other side to attack the northern palisade. Most ran waving swords and axes, some with lances while a few carried makeshift ladders. The wall was exactly has had been hoped, lightly defended. It took only a few minutes before the first breach was made. After that breaches appeared almost everywhere, as the defenders began to abandon the palisade and retreat back into the tangle of town dwellings.

"Time for us to join the attack," Fitzedith said.

Ardron silently approved. He didn't like sitting back in safety whilst his own troops went to battle. "Yes," he agreed. "Never ask a man to do that which you are not prepared to do yourself."

Inside, the town streets were all confusion. The defenders on the east wall realising attackers had gained access behind them, had for the most part, abandoned the palisade and were bent on achieving the security of the castle before the gates were closed. Ardron turned a corner into a narrow street and was confronted by two fleeing sergens. Without hesitation the nearest man launched into a sword attack. The attack was a clumsy wild swing coming down from shoulder height. Ardron leaned hard left and at the same time brought up his sword to deflect the haymaker away to the right. Bringing his sword back in a forearm swing he sliced into the man's neck. As the man slumped to his knees, pressing his hands to his wounded neck, Ardron turned to face the other. But his sword was already in the air in a horizontal swing and it hit Ardron with considerable force on the upper left arm. He felt the blade whack in hard, but his hauberk held preventing actual penetration. Shrugging off the blow, he stood threateningly poised, his outstretched sword slowly to-ing and fro-ing in front of the sergen. Under pressure the sergen tried to, viciously, knock it away. The swords clashed but the momentum took his sword away while Ardron, with a quick twist of the wrist, had his sword back in position right in front of the sergens face. In panic the man staggered backwards, stumbled then fell. He hit the ground hard, knocking off his helmet as he did. He could then do nothing as Ardron moved over him closing in for the kill. With his sword point at the man's throat he hesitated.

"Cerdic," he muttered in recognition.

At the same time, the sergen taking advantage of Ardron's hesitation, jabbed his sword forcibly upwards finding its way under Ardron's hauberk. The point stabbed into his left side below the ribs. Ardron gasp with pain and involuntarily stepped back. Recovering, quickly, he jumped forward and slammed down on the up-pointing sword, knocking it from Cerdic's grasp. With his sword once again at Cerdic's throat he struggled to hold his temper.

On his back and using his elbows Cerdic tried to crawl away from the sword point. At that instant he recognised Ardron.

"Ardron!" he muttered in surprise.

Barely in control of his temper, Ardron grabbed the youngster's clothing and hauled him to his feet.

"Ardron. I didn't know. I didn't know," Cerdic protested.

His temper cooling, Ardron pushed Cerdic away unceremoniously and pressed his left hand hard to the wound. After a few moments he lifted his hand to examine the wound. The hand was soaked, he was bleeding profusely. Suddenly he felt sick and slumped to his knees.

"What can I do?" Cerdic shouted in panic as he took a step towards him. He got no further; he was felled by a blow from behind.

"You bastard," Beldwine, shouted and was about to plunge his sword into Cerdic's back.

"No. No, Ardron shouted. "Spare him."

Beldwine looked confused but stayed his hand.

"He is my prisoner," Ardron said.

"Sir, you are wounded?"

"I am, Get me some help."

Beldwine hesitated a moment before he turned and shouted, "Roland, Roland."

The sergen must have been close because he was there within seconds.

"He is bad wounded," Beldwine informed him

For a moment Roland stared down at Ardron as if unable to understand the situation.

"Get me back to camp," Ardron said.

The pair hauled him to his feet and placed his arms over their shoulders.

"What about him?" Roland asked nodding at the groggy Cerdic.

"Cerdic," Ardron instructed. "Follow."

"No. No." Ardron shouted in panicking pain as they moved off. Lifting his left arm so high was not only much more painful, it also increased the blood flow. So, it was left to Beldwine to half carry half drag Ardron, while Roland moved a couple of steps ahead to protect.

Their progress was slow, but eventually Ardron was laid on a cot in his tent, while all those who had already returned from the fight buzzed around, concerned as mother hens. Gingerly, his hauberk was removed to reveal the wound. No wider than a sword blade width, but deep penetration. Beldwine pressed cloths on the wound attempting to stem the blood flow.

"Someone go and find a lach," Maurice ordered.

It took almost half-an hour before Roland returned with a woman, only just beyond her teen years.

"She's a lach?" Maurice queried.

"No," Roland replied. "She's a lach's daughter and helper," he shrugged. "Best I could do." He offered as an excuse.

Luc blustered into the tent having just heard of the situation. "Someone report," he demanded taking immediate charge. Having been quickly appraised of the situation, he, looking down at Ardron with a brief smile and re-assuring voice said. "Don't worry, Sir! We'll soon get you comfortable." Ardron could only nod feeling as if his welfare was, at this stage, beyond his control.

"Girl," Luc said pointed at Ardron. "Tend him."

The girl was very young, and just to add to the confusion, she was a Saxon who could speak very little French. It was left to Beldwine to translate.

But words were not necessary, because she could see exactly that which was expected of her. She sat beside Ardron and moved his hands which pressed the cloth against the wound. Then she peered at the injury. After a few seconds she gave Ardron an indifferent look, replaced the cloth and stood up.

"Well?" Luc demanded impatiently.

"I can stitch the wound," she said to Beldwine. "But if it continues to bleed internally, he could die." She paused. "Also, I have seen these types of wounds fester and begin to stink. If that happens then he will die." For a few moments Bedwine stared dubiously at the young girl.

"Well!" Luc demanded again.

After the translation Luc jabbed a finger in her chest aggressively. "Tell her if he dies, she dies too." He said threateningly. Then after Bedwine had translated he turned towards Cerdic. "Tell him that goes for him too."

"Clear the room," the girl said in French, indicated that she did understand some French.

"Clear the room," Luc repeated. "You and you," he pointed at Bedwine and Roland. "Stand guard outside to make sure she doesn't leave. Him," he said pointing at Cerdic. "Put in chains."

"Luc," Ardron said.

"Yes sir,"

"How went the battle?"

"The battle was won. Roger Fitzmiles holds the town and now lays siege to the castle."

"Casualties?"

"Light. From our troop we have two others wounded. None dead."

Ardron heaved a satisfied sigh." Good," he said.

"Wait," the girl stopped Luc leaving. "Heat this in a fire," she said as she handed him an iron. "Bring it back when its red hot. Red hot," she emphasised.

Luc stared dubiously at the iron, not understanding.

Ardron remembered how the lach had used a hot iron to cauterise Odel's wounded arm. Vividly he recalled the man's scream under that hot iron and knew what the girl intended. It filled him with dread. Nevertheless, he translated for Luc and gave, reluctant, assent with a slow nod.

Luc hesitated just a moment longer, then after taking the iron and giving a warning glance at the girl he ducked out.

Ardron watched the girl as she busied herself taking things from her pouch making her preparations. "What's your name," he asked.

"Kendra," she replied.

"Well Kendra. Have you done this before?"

"Something similar," she replied.

"And your success rate?"

She sucked noisily. "Oo, not good." But the twinkle in her eye indicated that she teased. "You're Saxon," she said as she sat down by his side.

"I am Ardron of Norwood. Once of the village of Scorrenstone."

"I have heard of you," she said removing the cloth and began cleaning the wound.

Fifteen minutes later Luc returned with the iron glowing red at its tip.

"Wait." she said in French as he prepared to leave. Then added in English," I need your help." Luc didn't understand and glanced at Ardron for help.

"She needs your help," Ardron translated.

Luc looked anything but comfortable but turned back. Kendra positioned him behind Ardron. "Take his shoulders and hold him down," she instructed placing his hands on Ardron shoulders. Luc nodded understanding what she wanted him to do, despite the language change.

"This will hurt a little," she said positioning herself by Ardron's side and holding up the hot iron.

"This will hurt a lot," Ardron countered.

"Better you bite down on this," she said offering Ardron a thick strip of leather. "I will count to five and then I'll cauterise." She paused." Ready?"

Ardron bit down on the leather strip and prepared.

"One. Two." Then without warning she pressed the hot iron against the wound. Ardron gasped with the pain, smelled the scorching flesh and couldn't repress a grimacing yell.

It was two hours later when he regained consciousness, and at that instant was not sure where he was. He lifted his head to look around. Kendra sat at the foot of his cot passing the time sewing.

"Oh, you're awake," the girl muttered laying down her work.

He tried to sit up and was immediately stung viciously by his wound.

"Lay back," she instructed.

"How did it go?" he asked.

"Time will tell," she replied. "You're cleaned and stitched. Now you have to keep the wound clean and to rest a lot.

He grunted and laid back, waiting for the pain to subside. But it didn't, not by much. Instead it felt uncomfortably hot and throbbed mercilessly.

"I'll give you something for the pain," she said.

He watched as she took what appeared to be dry fungi from her pouch. Using a pestle, she ground down the fungi, then added a generous amount of green powder. She tipped it all into a goblet, added water and stirred vigorously. "Drink," she said.

Ardron was not sure if the pain was perhaps more desirable than the foul taste. Nevertheless, he drank it all. Within minutes things began to change. He watched fascinated as the tent covers began to sway gently, as long grass in a strong wind. At the end of his legs, his feet seemingly grew enormous, while the girl appeared to keep falling backwards with only the blink of his eye bringing her back upright. The hallucinations became gradually stronger as horrific gargoyles glared at him from the folds in the tent canvas. Ardron began to shout attempting to scare them back from whence they came. But they simply ignored him. Suddenly Kendra was there, cradling his head to her bosom protecting him from the hallucinations. He was soothed as a small child would be with a mother's cuddling protection. But Kendra was not his mother and now urges of desire began to envelop him.

The sun was about to set and the shadows lengthening when Kendra emerged from the tent.

"Where do you think you are going?" Beldwine challenged.

"I'm going home," she said.

"Not until we are sure that our patron will not die." Beldwine said.

"He's not going to die," she said meaningfully. "Believe me. He's not going to die."

"Wait," Beldwine instructed and ducked into the tent.

"Sir," he addressed Ardron. "The girl wants to go home."

Ardron nodded approval. "Let her go," he said.

For a week, the wound laid Ardron low, with crushing boredom for company. There had been a visit by a Lach who after inspecting Ardron's wound had declared himself satisfied with his daughter's work. Then he held out his hand for payment revealing the real reason for his visit.

Now on his feet at last, albeit a little tentatively, he decided that he should return to Norwood. Fitzmiles had the castle well locked down and had begun constructing siege engines atop Blicks Hill. To keep just the castle under assault and sealed did not require a large force. Nevertheless, he decided that he should leave behind a token force at least. This smaller force of around a dozen he had placed under Luc's command and attached them to de Bohun's stronger troop. Then after taking his leave from Fitzmiles, he left for Norwood. Because he didn't want to jar at his wound, he rode submissively in the back of a cart instead of the head of the column mounted on his charger. In the cart also was the still shackled Cerdic.

"When we get to Norwood," Ardron said to Cerdic. "I will have you set free to go where you want. Except back to Malmesbury," he added.

"I am truly sorry Ardron," he replied, apologising yet again.

"You didn't know." Ardron dismissed the apology with a wave of his arm. "Where will you go?" he asked after a short pause.

Cerdic shrugged. "I don't know," he said.

"Why not return to Scorrenstone?"

"I could never go back there," he replied looking wistfully back down the road.

"Because of Edyo?" Cerdic looked back at him sharply. "You weren't at Esmond's wedding. Your best friend's wedding!"

Cerdic slowly nodded. "I wish them both only the best, but I just couldn't stay there and watch."

"You could have," Ardron contradicted. "You would have eventually found another and then it wouldn't have mattered."

He stared back at Ardron without replying. The look said it all. Ardron sighed heavily. "If you wish," he went on. "You may stay at Norwood and train as one of my sergens."

"Ardron that is truly gracious of you," Cerdic said staring back at him wide eyed. "I mean, under the circumstances"

"We'll speak no more of the circumstances," he replied with a wry smile. "But you had better get used to calling me sir." Then added, "Unless we are alone."

Even at the gentle pace it took less than an hour to reach Norwood. Word had been sent on ahead warning of his return and he was somewhat embarrassed to be greeted with clapping and smiling faces as he was helped down from the cart.

"All is prepared Sir," Louis greeted him. "The Lady Hildi has prepared your bedroom and there are refreshments laid out in your private quarters.

Ardron nodded appreciation. He was two steps up towards the keep when he remembered Cerdic still sitting in the cart. "Jarcot, where's Jarcot," he said.

"Here Sir," the reply was immediate.

"Remove the shackles from that young man." He said pointing at Cerdic. "You are tasked to train him and train him well. He is the newest Norwood sergen."

Chapter 17

Norwood Castle, April 1144

Every Morning, early, a servant blustered into his bed chamber bringing him hot water to attend his ablutions. As had recently become a habit, Ardron did not immediately rise. Instead he indulged himself and lazed in bed, revelling in that state between waking and sleeping.

More than two weeks had passed since his return, and each day that passed gradually improved his condition. The wound had effectively closed leaving a sore gash amid stretched and burn-scarred skin. His movements were still restricted, reminding him so every time he moved just a little too quickly or twisted hurriedly. Effectively being an invalid gave him the excuse to be indolent and allow others to take up the effort required to run the estate. Maurice du Prevuer had proved an able deputy in Luc's absence, and since he had no previous experience as castle constable it was even more pleasing. Fique, meanwhile, had taken on the responsibility of keeping the castle supplied with meat, by leading a regular hunt. Whilst Hildi continued to run the kitchens and any social arrangements. Even Louis, his clerk needed no input from him. All-in-all, Ardron silently acknowledged, that his role was not perhaps as necessary as he had always believed.

He rolled onto his back and opened his eyes. A wide shaft of sunlight slanted across the bottom half of the chamber, indicating that outside there was a bright spring morning. This day, he decided, that perhaps he should begin to consider rotating his small detachment under de Bohun's command. It was a task that he felt that he should do personally. This meant, of course, that he would have to lead the replacements to Malmesbury and relieve the incumbents. Was he yet fit to ride the six or so miles? He mused a while on the answer before deciding that perhaps it would be better to wait just a couple more days.

He still received updates on the Malmesbury siege, and at this stage it seemed to have settled into the usual period of inactivity. The attackers couldn't get in, the defenders couldn't get out. Fitzmiles still launched regular bombardments from his trebuchet on Blicks Hill, and regular arrow storms into the castle. The castle would then reply with arrow storms of its own, in all probability returning the same arrows. It was, expectedly, going to take time. Earl Robert had kept his army in readiness at Bristol, probably deciding that there was little to be gained by advancing on Malmesbury. Fitzmiles was achieving all that could be achieved at this time.

After stretching and yawning, he did eventually climb from his bed and shuffle across to the only window in the room. Not much wider than a narrow rectangular slit, the view it afforded was restricted but, nevertheless, he could look to the south across the flat expanse surrounding the castle. Beyond that, the forest fringe had begun to sprout vivid greenery of spring growth. As he watched a lone rider emerged from the trees and rode casually in the castle direction. For a few moments Ardron watched uninterestedly as the rider neared. The brown habit and wide brimmed hat the man wore marked him as a monk.

"Monk!" he muttered to himself. The possibility of this monk's business sparked him to more earnest action. He washed hastily and dressed quickly. Taking enough time to girdle his sword he was satisfied that he looked suitably officious. Taking a moment to look from the window confirmed the monk had disappeared from view. He hastened down the steps into the reception room.

"Sir," Jacques found him. "There is a monk below in the bailey. He requests to see you."

Ardron nodded without speaking and led the way from the motte down into the bailey.

"You wished to see me?" he asked sharply.

"Good morning to you Sir. I trust you are in rude health and are as one with God and nature on such a lovely spring morn."

"Well enough," Ardron replied curtly.

Not exactly a young man this monk. Even under his wide brimmed hat Ardron could see a ruddy complexion, and such a complexion was not normally associated with men who spend long hours in-doors and at prayer. "Is there something I can do for you, brother?"

The monk removed his hat and held it against his chest. "If it pleases you, good sir. I am here to collect your gracious quarterly contribution to aid the poor and unfortunates."

Ardron gave a wry smile at the polite way the man presented Grey Wolf's quarterly demand. "Oh, I see." He said. He knew this day would eventually come and they had put their heads together to come up with a pre-conceived plan. It remained now only to get it started. "Take this monk's horse to our blacksmith," Ardron said to Jacques. "Tell him to see it well-tended fed and watered." He watched while Jacques gathered the reins and led the animal away. "Brother monk, he said. "I have to find my clerk. Meanwhile, if you would be good enough to follow me, I will see you attended." He led the way into the reception room and left him seated there while he left to seek out his clerk. Except he had no intentions of seeking Louis at this point, instead he looked for Jarcot. He found him in the stable already leading out his horse to be saddled. Ardron nodded approval.

"Luc's not here," he needlessly informed Ardron.

"No," Ardron agreed. "You'll have to take Fique."

Handicapped by only having one arm Jarcot struggled to tighten the cinch round the horse's belly. Ardron took the cinch from him and completed the task, but not without some discomfort when he made the last tightening pull on the cinch. "Take the Saxon, Cerdic too," he said straightening and patting the horse's neck.

"Cerdic?" Jarcot queried, disproval in his voice.

"Aye Cerdic. It might prove useful to have a local Saxon along." Pausing only a moment to gauge Jarcot's reaction he added. "Leave as soon as you can. I'll delay this monk as long as I can to give you a start." He emphasised on the word monk, indicating that he too did not believe this was really a monk.

He found Swidhurn in his shop already cutting little notches in the shoes of the monk's horse, then waited and watched while he completed the task.

"Will this work?" Swidhurn asked dubiously.

Ardron winced. "Perhaps the weather could have been kinder."

"Yes," Swidhurn agreed. "I would have a much better chance of following these tracks had it been much softer underfoot." He led the horse down the workshop deliberately leading the animal through a mud patch. The hoof prints with notches cut in the shoes were readily identifiable. "All I can do is try my best," he said.

Ardron nodded. "Don't be tempted to keep this man in view. If you lose the tracks, then so be it. But if he suspects he is being followed, then he'll take steps to lose his follower and probably will not go to Grey Wolf's camp."

"I understand," Swidhurn said. "We still have the other plan."

"Yes. Jarcot is preparing to leave now."

"We are banking a lot on the hope that this man will take the same route as last time."

Ardron shrugged. "It's the best chance we have."

Jarcot and his small party were to go direct to the place where they lost track of the monk on the last occasion. There they were to wait in the hope that he passed through again. The success of the plan relied heavily on some good fortune. However, it was doing something and there was, as it happens, little to lose.

Delaying his return for as long as he dared Ardron did eventually return to the waiting monk. "I regret to inform you, brother, that my clerk is it this time attending morning mass." He shrugged and held out his arms in resignation. "Perhaps," he added, "You would want to attend morning mass also."

Just for an instant the monk was taken by surprise. Almost immediately, however, he recovered and shaking his head with a smile said. "Thank you, Sir. But I have already made morning salutations to my God."

"Perhaps, as a special favour, you would do us the honour of leading prayers in our mass?" Ardron was persistent.

"No, I wouldn't want to trouble you."

"It would be no trouble. In fact, I insist." Ardron said.

Unmistakably uncomfortable, the monk realised the vulnerability of his situation and contrived a forced grin then made his confession. "Sir," he said. "I have to confess that I am not really a monk."

"You don't say," Ardron drawled sarcastically then drew his sword from its baldric.

Now visibly alarmed. "What are you going to do?" he asked.

"What am I going to do?" Ardron paraphrased as he picked up a whetstone. "I am going to sharpen my sword." He then sat down on the bench opposite, raised the sword between his legs and began to slowly hone its edge. "So why the monk façade?" he asked.

The man shrugged. "These days the forests are full of outlaws and robbers. And who is going to try and rob a penniless monk?"

Nodding reluctantly Ardron agreed the idea did have merit. "Sensible scheme I suppose, whose idea was that?" he asked.

"I suppose it was our leader," he replied.

"Grey Wolf?"

"Yes, Grey Wolf."

"Who is Grey Wolf," Ardron asked but he did not expect an answer.

"No one knows his true identity for certain," he replied. "Leastways I don't."

"How do you contact him?" Ardron was persistent.

"There are ways. But forgive me Sir, but I can't talk on that."

"Why not? There is only you and me here in this room."

He shook his head. "Anyone who reveals information, no matter how slight, is likely to suffer the pains of lingering death."

Ardron nodded acceptance, there was little to be gained by continuing, besides, he didn't want to raise the man's suspicions, so he allowed the conversation to dry up. Save for the scrape of stone on steal, an uneasy silence protracted, but not for too long. Soon servants began bustling in preparing the area for breakfast.

"Ah! Morning mass must be almost at its end," Ardron said getting to his feet. "You will of course stay for breakfast." He left the room without waiting for a response. It was important to delay the man as long as possible giving Jarcot and Fique the best start he could.

The communal breakfast further aided Ardron delay tactics by almost another hour. Even after that when the man had been paid and was preparing to leave Ardron still found another reason to put off his departure. "It seems," he explained. "My blacksmith didn't quite understand my instructions when I told him to see your horse tended and fed. After feeding, he unsaddled the animal and turned him out in the paddock." He raised his arms and let them flop in a show of mild exasperation. "I will have the animal brought in and re-saddled." He said it, knowing full well that the horse was still tethered in the stable fully saddled. Nevertheless, it bought Jarcot another half-an-hour.

Eventually the delay excuses exhausted the man was ready to depart, and as Ardron watched him leave, in less than good humour, he had given Jarcot and his party almost an hour-and-half start. He calculated that should amount to six or seven miles. Ought to be enough!

**

Less than two days later and very much to Ardron's surprise, Luc rode into the bailey at the head of the Norwood detachment. Ardron stood at the foot of the mote watched and waited with mounting curiosity.

"What are you doing here?" he questioned.

"Sir," Luc replied, "The siege is ended."

"Ended? How?"

"The king left Suindune this morning at the head of a large army marching on Malmesbury to relieve the siege."

"The king? I thought he was pre-occupied in the marshes of Anglia." Ardron said.

"As did we all."

Ardron was nonplussed, there were so many questions. "Where is Fitzmiles?"

Luc jerked a thumb over his shoulder. "Somewhere close behind us. He'll be here soon."

"He's coming here?"

"He is," Luc replied

Ardron's nod was confused. "See to your men, Luc," he said. "Then report to me in my chambers."

Less than thirty minutes later Luc accompanied by Maurice de Prevuer came to Ardron's chambers. To Ardron, he looked a little jaded and very obviously low in spirits. Nodding towards the chairs he bade them sit while Hildi moved around topping up goblets with wine. The brief secret smile she flashed to Luc was not lost on Ardron. Nor was Luc's silent pleased response.

"Now," Ardron said softly, "Report."

Luc took a sip from the goblet and gathered his thoughts. "For some days there had been rumours of a large royalist army moving west. Roger Fitzmiles sent out riders to scout the truth. Those rumours were confirmed as true when the force was confirmed having reached Suindune. What was most surprising though was that King Stephen was at its head. Even then, Sir Roger wasn't completely convinced that Malmesbury was the destination. Not convinced that is, until this morning when that army left Suindune and continued westward passing through the hamlet of Purton. Then, less than ten miles from Malmesbury it was clear that Malmesbury was the destination. If, in fact, there was ever any doubt," he added

"Sir," Jacques stood timidly in the doorway.

"What is it?" Ardron asked.

"Sir Roger Fitzmiles approaches at the head of a reduced force."

"Thank you, Jacques. I will be there presently."

"Reduced force?" he queried Luc.

Luc nodded. "Sir Humphrey de Bohun fled south for the security of Trowbridge, while Sir Philip Fitzrobert went north to Tetbury. Fitzmiles and Fitzedith were left with their combined forces of about three hundred."

Ardron nodded. "Stay. Take your ease while I go and greet our guest." He said.

Fitzmiles rode through the bailey gate at the head of a small band of knights with his livery of red yellow and white fluttering proudly in the afternoon breeze.

"Sir Roger Fitzmiles, Earl of Hereford." One of the knights needlessly announced when the party came to a halt.

"Welcome, Sir Roger," Ardron greeted. "And to you Sir Robert," he added spotting Fitzedith, Earl of Okehampton in the party.

"Thank you Norwood and I am pleased to see you recovered from your wounds," Sir Roger said. Then after a pause added. "I would impose on your hospitality for a few hours if you please, Sir.

"My house is your house, Sir Roger."

"We are twelve," he replied jerking his head backwards. "The rank and file numbers less than three hundred, and with your permission they will camp without your gates."

"You have it," Ardron said.

"Can you feed them?"

"Indeed! Please gentlemen, step down and enter my quarters. I will have refreshments brought to the main chamber."

Less than an hour later with the twelve wined and fed Ardron moved to the matter which he had been impatient to raise. "What happens next, Sir Roger?"

"The siege has failed." He replied with a sigh. "So, I will return to Bristol and place my forces at Earl Robert's disposal and await his decision. Almost certainly he will want to march against the usurper."

Ardron nodded agreement. "So where is the king now?"

"By now he'll be in Malmesbury."

"Yes," Ardron agreed. "Then what?"

"Then what?" Fitzmiles asked nonplussed.

"He means," Fitzedith interrupted. "What will the king do next?"

"Precisely," Ardron agreed. "With a large army at his disposal in the middle of Angevin territory he is not likely to sit and wait to see what Earl Robert will do. Nor is he likely to suddenly consider mission accomplished and return to London. He is going to attempt to increase his footprint in this area." He paused a moment then added. "This castle, my castle, is the nearest, therefore, a likely target."

"Will you stand?" Fitzmiles asked.

"Aye. I'll stand. But under attack from a force with vastly superior numbers I don't know for how long."

Fitzmiles nodded without replying.

"After Norwood," Ardron went on. He would probably press on to South Cerney, and Edward d'Evereux."

"Will he stand?"

Ardron shrugged non-committal. He doubted that very much. In fact, he expected that d'Evereux would throw open his gates and swear for the king.

"Whilst I agree with what Norwood says about Stephen increasing his footprint in the area, I rather think he is more likely to go South," Fitzedith said.

"South?" Fitzmiles queried.

"Aye. South, on to Devizes Castle. If he could capture Empress Maude what a glittering prize that would be. And for us the war would then be virtually lost."

"A glittering prize indeed," Fitzmiles said. "But Devizes Castle is formidable and would not be overcome quickly. Then with Trowbridge Castle close by in the west and Ludgershall in the east it would not only be a lengthy undertaking but a risky one. No, I don't think he has the time nor the army strength to take Devizes."

Luc, who had stayed silent in the background listening suddenly stepped forward. "There is a very attractive consolation prize available to the king, and probably quickly achievable," he said.

Both Fitzmiles and Fitzedith regarded him sceptically, ready to willingly dismiss this remark from a mere senior sergen.

"This is Luc, my castle constable," Ardron introduced. "Go ahead Luc, have your say."

Luc moved to the table and unrolled the map, found his mark then jabbed his finger three or four times on the spot.

"Tetbury?" Fitzedith queried.

"Tetbury?" Fitzmiles repeated. Then as the relevance occurred to him said. "My God, the man is right. Don't you see?" he responded to Fitzedith puzzled look. "Phillip Fitzrobert, the earl's own son is at Tetbury and the castle not overly defended. If the king could capture Fitzrobert, he could make Earl Robert dance to his tune."

"Christ! Crucify me upside down," Fitzedith swore. "We must make all haste to re-enforce the castle at Tetbury."

Ardron silently proud of his constable placed a congratulating hand upon Luc's shoulder.

"Tomorrow, first thing" Fitzedith suggested. "You take an escort party, making all haste, to Bristol to report to my half-brother. Impress upon him to move his army to Tetbury with urgency. Meanwhile I will take our forces to Tetbury to bolster its defences."

"Agreed!" Fitzmiles said. Then to Ardron. "How many men can you spare?"

"None!"

"None?"

"None. I will need everyman I can find in case the king does come this way."

Fitzmiles stared at him a moment before eventually nodding silent agreement.

Before breakfast, the next morning Fitzmiles, along with an escort of around a dozen, left for Bristol. With Tetbury being only seven miles to the west, Fitzedith was not in so much of a hurry. He stayed for morning mass and then breakfast. It was nearing noon when he and his sergens eventually rode away to Tetbury.

Ardron, meanwhile, did not lose a minute. He, along with Luc, inspected the castle defences and looked to strengthen any potential weaknesses. There was still the chance that Stephen would spread east from Malmesbury, and he wanted to be sure that he was as ready as he could possibly be. After making a list of improvements he set to planning an order of priority. He was still comprising that order when Hildi interrupted him, announcing that her brother Swidhurn had just returned.

"Is he alone?" he asked.

"He is," Hildi replied.

That was not so good. It surely meant that he had not linked up with Jarcot. "Have him attend me," he instructed.

A few minutes later Swidhurn came to him and for a moment stood in the doorway. Then moving into the room without speaking he spread his arms in a gesture of despondency. "I did what I could," he said eventually excusing himself with a shaking head.

"Twas always a long shot." Ardron sympathised. "Come sit and tell me what happened." He held up the wine decanter.

Swidhurn shook his head and reached instead for the jug of beer. "It was not hard to pick up the monks trail soon after I left here, but it got progressively harder until it just about petered out." He paused pouring beer into a goblet. "Generally, he seemed to be heading south and so I continued slowly in that direction." He held the goblet in front of him ready to drink. "Then," he went on. "Little more than a mile or so east of Scorrenstone I found trail again, still heading south. But by this time the evening was closing in. So I marked the spot and decided to go into Scorrenstone for the night and pick up the trail again in the morning." He used the pause to take a long greedy drink, leaving beer froth on his moustache. "That was a mistake," he said. "The next morning, I found the spot, but it looked as if an army had ridden over and obliterated everything."

"Ah," Ardron said. "Heading south?"

"Yes."

"That, I imagine, would have been Sir Humphrey's troops retreating from Malmesbury." Ardron said. "The king brought a force and relieved Malmesbury," he added.

"I had heard that!" Swidhurn said. "Anyway!" he continued. "I didn't give up but continued on hoping to find the trail again. I got as far as Combe Castle before I gave up." He paused. "I tried! I did cast left and right as I journeyed but there was nary a sign. It was hopeless."

Ardron nodded agreement. "I know you did your best, my friend," he placated. "If you couldn't do it, then nobody could." He added with a shrug. "Let us hope that Jarcot has a little more luck."

There was a pause before Swidhurn altering the subject said brightly. "I bring you some good news from Scorrenstone. Your brother's wife, Edyo, is with child__. You're about to become an uncle again."

Another two days passed before Jarcot returned with his company of two. Ardron greeted them cheerfully, he had this very day learned that King Stephen had advanced on Tetbury. Which meant that, for the time being, at least, Castle Norwood was not in danger of attack.

"We lost him," Jarcot said before he had actually dismounted. "However, it is not all bad we do have some ideas." He added when he had dismounted.

"Good," Ardron responded. "See to your horses and your comfort, then report to me in my chambers."

"He came through exactly where we expected," Jarcot said as he began his report. "We stood off a safe distance and followed. For more than a mile we kept him in sight. Then at a small hamlet in a valley bottom we think he spotted us. So, we dropped back a distance and the last we actually saw of him was when he rode into a shallow river. Your Saxon friend here," he nodded towards Cerdic, "Identified the river as Bybrook. With him now being out of sight we too rode the Bybrook, scouring the banks on both sides for sign. Then because of those marked horseshoes, we eventually picked up his trail where he came out, a good mile downstream. From there we hazarded a guess that he had continued in the same direction and had climbed a steep hill. Atop was a Saxon village, and we enquired there if a lone monk had passed that way. But we were greeted with suspicion and their denials were emphatic. Too emphatic!" He paused a moment. "But we weren't about to give up that easily. So, we enquired if we could perhaps buy some food purely as an excuse to dally. And this is where Cerdic proved his worth. The villagers thought we were all Norman, but they didn't know that Cerdic was a Saxon." He nodded towards Cerdic to pick up the report.

"On the pretence of watering my horse, I wandered to the village well where several of the village women were gathered," Cerdic said. "As women do, they chatted amongst themselves. At first, they went silent when I approached. But when I spoke the few words that I know in French, they assumed that I didn't speak English. They continued to talk amongst themselves trying to guess from where I had come. Eventually, one of them got up the courage to ask. But I pretended that I didn't understand. So, I just pointed at the sun, smiled and talked gobble-de-gook, hoping none of them guessed that wasn't French. One of the women concluded that I was a halfwit and said as much. But never-mind, it paid a dividend when another of the women informed the others that we were looking for the monk that had passed through earlier that afternoon. We were on the right track, and so I informed Jarcot."

Taking the nod as his cue, Jarcot continued the report. "After leaving the village we continued south until we came to a wide deep valley. But from that point there was just no way of knowing which way that monk had gone. So, it was at this point we gave up. However, from our high vantage point we could see Bath in the distance." He fell silent a few moments as Ardron nodded acceptance of the failed operation. "But we do have a theory!" Jarcot went on.

"Oh!" Ardron waited.

"Could it possibly be that this Grey Wolf operates out of Bath?"

Ardron creased his brow dubiously. Outlaws operating from a town? Most unusual.

"After all. "Not all thieves live in the forest." Jarcot went on. "Some, live in castles!" Noting the smile from Ardron, Jarcot continued. "He could be posing as a legitimate merchant trading his contraband through the markets. What better place?" he paused for effect. "After all, his identity is not well known. He could be anybody," he suggested.

The theory did have possibilities. It was true Grey Wolf's identity was unknown. Therefore, he could not have been outlawed officially. Ardron was still dubious, nevertheless, he nodded possible acceptance. "We will have to follow through on that theory," he said.

***

May 1144

In the early morning sunshine, and just below the hamlet of Boks, Ardron leaned forward and peered thoughtfully into the clear waters of the river Bybrook. He had, he felt, just wasted three days in a fruitless search. Still, he conceded, the attempt had to be made, then he re-aligned his thoughts to the task at hand. He plunged the wooden platters, still stained with debris of last night's roasted rabbit, into the water and, using the flat of his hand, cleaned best he could. After a rough wipe in the grass he made his way back to the camp. Maurice busied himself routinely checking the horses hooves while Fique tied belongings behind saddles.

He looked over his shoulder at Ardron. "Looks set fair," he said nodding skywards. "We should sleep comfortably in Norwood tonight."

Ardron glanced skywards and nodded agreement without replying.

"All my life I have heard stories of the Roman town of Bath and now I have seen it." Maurice joined the conversation straightening up a moment. "You can keep it," he added scornfully. "Apart from a few Roman ruins it is not a lot different to many other towns around."

"Where is Jarcot?" Ardron asked.

Fique grinned. "He's down there in the trees. I guess last night's rabbit didn't agree with him."

"Couldn't possibly be anything to do with the cook," Maurice offered with a smirk.

"Definitely not," Fique countered quickly, feigning offence.

Ardron patted Rattlebone's neck ignoring the banter while he surveyed the surrounding hills. They were in the bottom of a steep valley just east of Bath. From here it mattered not north south or east it would be a long taxing climb. East to Chippenham, he decided their route, then north. Fique was right they should sleep comfortably in Norwood tonight. To his right Jarcot emerged from the thicket muttering some uncomplimentary remarks about Fique's cooking abilities.

Maurice moved alongside leading his mount. "What did we achieve after a couple of days in Bath?"

"Nothing," Ardron replied with a rueful head shake. They had found absolutely nothing that could conclusively confirm or deny that Grey Wolf operated out of the town. They had wandered the markets looking for anything that looked suspiciously like contraband. The inns and taverns they had frequented, watching and asking casual unobtrusive questions. They had discovered nothing. "We had to give it a try," he added.

"Yes," Maurice agreed. "But it could still be a possibility," he ventured.

"It could," Ardron allowed. But still he believed it most unlikely though did not say as much. "Are we ready?" he asked glancing round. Then he mounted atop Rattlebone and without waiting for confirmation said. "Move out."

It was a steep and protracted climb towards the top of the valley. Still a way off the top and still in the thickly wooded area they reached a well-trodden track with a rough-hewn direction sign 'Quarry.'

"Quarry?" Jarcot muttered curiously.

"I have heard of this quarry," Ardron said uncertainly. "I think it must be the place from where they quarried the stone to build Malmesbury Abbey."

"Malmesbury Abbey? Fique muttered sceptically. "That's a long way to haul stone."

"Aye it is," Ardron agreed. "Nevertheless."

"How long ago was that?" Jarcot cut in.

Ardron sucked in a breath thoughtfully. "Three hundred years ago, more."

"Those tracks are not three-hundred years old." Jarcot said nodding down at the deeply rutted road.

"No! they are not," Ardron agreed. "Shall we take a look?" He didn't wait for an answer, instead wheeled his horse's head to turn down the road. A hundred yards down the track he changed his mind and halted. "I am not sure this is a good idea," he said. "We have no idea what we are getting into."

"I was thinking exactly the same," Maurice agreed.

"We'll continue. But we'll climb up the hill through the trees." Ardron said indicating the direction with a nod of his head. "If we can get above the quarry, we could perhaps look down and see what the situation is from there." No one disagreed. The climb, however, was particularly steep. It meant dismounting and scrambling up the hill, pulling their horses on a long halter. When he thought they were high enough, Ardron turned along the hillside, until they arrived at a small clearing and they were, indeed, above the quarry.

Standing on the cliff precipice they surveyed the scene in the quarry below. Dwellings there were, of mud and wattle, scattered haphazardly. On the opposite face two expansive yawning holes in the rock face

400

indicated tunnel entrances to underground mines. Afront of those, an enclosure contained both horses and cattle all grazing quietly. Chickens foraged at liberty where they would, and beyond all that, at the far end a natural lake providing water. Habitation was further evident, because a small group of men and women lazed, in casual placidity, in the morning sun. Sitting with their backs towards them they hadn't seen Ardron and his companions looking down from above. Clearly a group of Saxons had taken up settlement in the quarry. Maybe legitimately, or perhaps not.

"Get down," Jarcot demanded with urgency as he dropped quickly to his knees.

In that instance, Ardron just stood confused, looking down at his sergen. Jarcot tugged at his clothing hauling him down. With the four men now on their knees, Jarcot pointed away to their right and the entrance to the quarry.

"Look there," he said. The narrow entrance to the quarry had been stoutly barricaded by a high row of palisade with a substantial entrance gate. This barricade was guarded by three sentries. "What settlement barricades themselves in and posts guards?" he added.

He was right, something was amiss, Ardron silently agreed. "Have they seen us?" He asked.

"I don't think so." Jarcot replied.

The four men were silent for a moment before Fique spoke. "Could it be we have found Grey Wolf's camp?" he posed the question.

"Maybe we have," Ardron granted.

"If that is so, then we had better slip away from here before we are seen," Maurice suggested.

Ardron nodded agreement. However, he crawled forward on his belly to peer down the sheer face of the cliffs. Two more well-worn tracks led directly beneath, suggesting that there were probably two more mine entrances on this side of the quarry. For a few moments more, he studied the scene below, seeking more evidence of an outlaws hide out. Seeing nothing more, he crawled back and indicated that they should move back into the cover of the trees.

Under cover and now on their feet Ardron appraised the situation. "It could be an outlaw's hideaway camp," he agreed. "However," he added. "Strategically it's a failure." He paused a moment before going on. "It would be the devil of a job to breach that barricade but if a siege is laid those insides could not get out. Then if attackers were to take up position up here with arrow storms, they could wreak havoc on the defenders below."

"So, you have some doubts about it being Grey Wolf's camp." Maurice tended.

Reluctantly, Ardron nodded.

"Unless!" Jarcot ventured. "There is another way out."

Ardron was thoughtful a moment. "Unless there is another way out," he muttered more to himself. "Jarcot come with me."

The pair crawled forward once more to the precipice and peered down the cliff face. "See those well-worn tracks," Ardron said. "Do you think they lead to a couple of mine entrances?"

Jarcot was thoughtful a moment. "Why else would tracks like that lead to a sheer rock face?"

He was right, Ardron nodded, then studied the scene a little longer. "That is at least four tunnel entrances," he said. "Anyone of them could possibly have another entrance and that could be their emergency escape." He sighed heavily "Let's go," he said. "I've seen enough."

Back in the tree line Ardron related his findings and theory to the others. No one spoke for a few seconds until Maurice raised the question.

"On whose estate does this quarry lay?" he asked.

It was a good question, and relevant, leaving Ardron very thoughtful. "It might be part of Sir Humphrey de Bohun's estate." He offered thoughtfully.

"Do you think he knows that there is a settlement in the quarry?" Maurice asked.

Ardron shrugged. "I don't know but we need to find out," he replied.

"If this is Grey Wolf's hide-out," Fique butted in. "We need to move out of the area before we are discovered." No one disagreed.

An hour later, and on the high ground just north of Chippenham they paused a while to rest the horses. Still yet a fair distance across the flat land before them, they could see a substantial column of men on horse and foot, snaking slowly towards them.

"It's an army of some sort," Fique had needlessly informed everyone.

"Aye, tis," Jarcot agreed. "But whose army?"

"Could it be the king having left Tetbury?" Fique responded.

Ardron leaned forward onto Rattlebone's withers and stared hard into the distance, but the column was just too far way to identify the livery. The last information he had was that Stephen had laid siege to Tetbury Castle and that Earl Robert was amassing an army to go to its relief. Had that relief now taken place and was this Stephen's army in retreat? If so, retreating to where? He could have with-drawn back to nearby Malmesbury. More logically east to Suindune then eventually London. But this column was moving south.

"It could be anybody," he said with a shrug. "We will wait here until we know," he added. Then he began to dismount. "We can easily move away if we need to."

The others, almost reluctantly, followed his example and dismounted.

With the exception of Maurice, they all then settled to wait, reclining casually in the midday sun. Maurice, however, had taken the self-imposed duty of sentry and perched himself on the thick trunk of a fallen tree, watching the slowly advancing army.

"It's not the king's standard," he called out twenty minutes later.

"It's not?" Ardron queried.

"No. The king's standard is mostly red; this one is blue."

Ardron moved over to where Maurice sat and studied the still distant column. "You're right," he confirmed. "I do believe its Humphrey de Bohun's livery," he said peering hard towards the procession. "We'll go down and meet him," he said turning away. "Mount up," he ordered the still reclined Fique and Jarcot.

At the bottom of the hill, and the advancing column still half-a-mile away, they were confronted by an advance guard of eight riders. "Move away," the leader demanded.

"It is I, Ardron of Norwood. Friend and fief to Sir Humphrey," Ardron responded.

"It is indeed," another rider interceded as he recognised Ardron.

"I would speak a few moments with Sir Humphrey."

The leader accepted the explanation. "You three move away," he said nodding towards Ardron's companions. "And you, Sir Ardron, wait here."

Ardron nodded consent for his companions to move back a little way up the hill.

"You," the leader picked out one of his riders. "Go back and inform Sir Humphrey. See if he will speak with this knight."

"Ardron. What are you doing here?" de Bohun asked when the column eventually reached him.

"I am on my way back to Norwood, But I would request a few minutes of your time."

De Bohun leaned backwards towards his constable, Francis d' Aumale. "We will rest here a while," he instructed.

"You are out in force today," Ardron said as they settled at the roadside.

"Yes, we are on our way back to Trowbridge after relieving the Tetbury siege."

"Tetbury has been relieved?"

"Yes, but a hollow victory indeed."

Ardron shook his head in confusion. "What happened?"

"We joined Earl Robert's army south of Malmesbury and marched on Tetbury. But" he added with a sigh, "When we reached Tetbury, we found that instead of standing to fight, the king had fled north the previous day." He shook a rueful head. "It seems he has no stomach for a decisive battle anymore."

"Why would he," Ardron said. "He might lose, and t'would be Lincoln all over again. But" Ardron added, "Why flee north? Surely east and back to Suindune was a safer alternative."

"You would have thought so," de Bohun agreed. "He takes advice from de Ypres," he added with a shrug. "Who knows what their plans are. I have doubts that even they have a clear plan."

Ardron was not so dismissive. He knew de Ypres to be a shrewd planner, but he said nothing.

There was a pause in the conversation before de Bohun asked. "What was it that you wanted to speak with me?"

"Yes," Ardron drawled, not sure how to begin. "Your estate, Sir Humphrey, extends well to the north of Melksham."

"It does!"

"As far as Bath?"

" Good Lord, no"

"Where then, may I ask, is the boundary?"

"There is a small river called Bybrook, which feeds into the Avon. That is my northern boundary." He paused and fixed Ardron with a stare. "Why do you ask?"

"Bear with me a few moments more, Sir Humphrey." Ardron replied. "Do you own a disused quarry atop the valley overlooking the Bybrook?

De Bohun shrugged. "Francis," he summoned his constable.

The constable's response was immediate. "Yes, Sir."

"Do we have a disused quarry in the north of our estate?"

"Indeed, we do Sir," he replied. "A potential valuable asset."

"Potential?" de Bohun queried.

"Disused at this time, Sir. But there is high quality stone to be mined when the opportunity arises."

"Does that answer your question?" de Bohun asked Ardron.

"One more question. Just to be sure." Where exactly is this quarry?" Ardron addressed de Aumale.

"Just beyond the hamlet Cosseham, and high above the settlement of Boks."

That was, for Ardron, confirmation. He nodded thoughtfully. "I am afraid I have to tell you, that quarry is not disused. There is a substantial settlement there."

"The devil, you say," de Bohun responded. "Living there on my land and not paying any fief." He stared accusingly at his constable.

"I will have it checked out immediately," de Aumale said.

"Not so fast," Ardron interrupted. "The quarry has been fortified, and I believe outlaws use it for their hideaway. Perhaps even by Grey Wolf himself. So, I would advise some stealth."

There was a pause then de Aumale said. "I'll find out."

De Bohun nodded agreement. "Thank you, Francis!" he said and watched him walk away. "He'll find out," he muttered. "He's a good constable."

They were further interrupted when a servant arrived bringing a platter of bread and cheese with a jug of ale. "Are you quite recovered from your wounds," de Bohun asked changing the subject as he offered up the platter in Ardron's direction. For the better part of the next hour, the time was spent in pleasant cordial exchanges. Eventually, Ardron made his excuses and moved on. De Bohun's force trundled on its way to Trowbridge.

Ten days after that, news reached Ardron at Norwood. King Stephen had descended upon Winchcombe with exceptional savagery. His army attacked and overcame the castle reducing it to rubble. Then his army turned upon the town, pillaging and slaughtering mercilessly, leaving behind a town in flames. The only conceivable reason for such viciousness seemed to be spiteful revenge upon Hugh Bigod, the castellan. He at the very onset of Stephen's usurp, had been a major supporter. However, yielding to a considerable bribe, he had recently reneged, and joined the Angevin ranks.

***

Devizes Castle (Midsummer's Day), June 1144

The midsummer feast had been impressive. And now as the tables were cleared of debris food the centre area was given over to entertainment. Empress Maude sat at the head with the young prince to her right. Sitting ramrod straight next to him Robert Earl Gloucester viewed the performing jugglers with bored indifference. Clearly his thoughts were elsewhere.

Ardron had lost his place at the top table but even so his placing had been close enough to suggest he had not lost the empress's favour to any great degree. The great hall at this point was mostly confusion as servants scurried about clearing hastily while guest shuffled around finding themselves comfortable spots. Ardron scanned across the confusion seeking the Lady Rohesa. Seated in their respected positions their eyes had met across the dining benches. She had acknowledged him with a nod and smile, while he lifted his chalice in salute. Eventually, he spotted her across the other side of the confusion gently holding the elbow of a distinguished knight and surrounded by a small cluster of young admirers. He smiled to himself and began to weave his way through in her direction. However, he got only as far as halfway before he was stopped by Humphrey de Bohun.

Ah Ardron," he said. "How do you enjoy these celebrations?"

405

He glanced over his shoulder at Rohesa less than twenty paces away a little piqued that he had been stopped. "I find them highly impressive and much to my liking," he replied.

"On that other matter, regarding the illegals in the Boks quarry, we must get together and talk and very soon," de Bohun went on. "But not tonight."

Ardron nodded agreement. "Yes," he agreed and thought to move on but de Bohun was not finished.

"Have you heard the news?"

"News?"

"John Fitzgilbert's newly intended?"

John Fitzgilbert is getting married again?" Ardron queried.

"Aye. He is! And to the delectable Sybil de Evereux, my cousin."

"Sybil de Evereux? What happens to the Lady Aline his current wife?"

"Ah! Now that is the clever part, and all carefully arranged. Arranged by none other than Earl Robert himself." He paused for effect. "He arranged for Fitzgilbert's marriage to be annulled and intends to wed off the Lady Aline to Stephen de Gay."

"Stephen de Gay?" Ardron exclaimed. "That man must be into his late sixties."

"I suppose," de Bohun agreed.

"How did Patric de Evereux ever agree to his sister's choice of husband?" Ardron asked. "His dislike for Fitzgilbert is well known."

"Well," de Bohun went on. "He offered Patric the title, Earl of Salisbury, if he agreed. Which of course he couldn't refuse. So, this alliance cleverly achieves a truce between Fitzgilbert and Patric de Evereux. It also locks Patric into the Angevin cause."

"And Sybil? How does she feel about this marriage?" He asked, thinking of the daunting facial disfigurement of Sir John.

De Bohun shrugged. "She agrees. "And why wouldn't she? Considering the enormous influence of Sir John, and of course his huge wealth, she will become a lady of prominence."

Ardron shook a bewildered head in awe of how this Norman autocracy established alliances with marriage beds. "When is all this to happen?" he asked.

"Very, very soon."

"I will be sure to congratulate Sir John." Ardron said glancing around to see if he could see him.

"Now Ardron I regret I must leave you and attend my lady wife," de Bohun said. "We will get together soon regarding the other matter."

Ardron nodded acceptance, secretly relieved that he was now free to seek out Rohesa. She had moved only a few feet from where he had seen her last and now attended by two. Slowly and politely he elbowed his way in her direction. Unseen by her he came up behind her.

"Good evening, my Lady," he said softly.

"Ardron," she said feigning surprise. "I did think you were ignoring me,"

"Ignoring you? How would that be at all possible?" he replied.

"Well these good gentlemen did pay me much attention while you were inattentive," she chided as she referred to the two men in front of her.

"Good evening to you, Sir," Ardron said as he recognised Ranulf Earl of Chester.

"We have met?" Ranulf stared at Ardron quizzically.

"We have, Sir. We both fought with your father-in-law at Lincoln."

"Ah Lincoln," he said wistfully. "That should have been the end of the war. But here we are, still a long way from victory. And__," he added. "I swear the rewards do get less."

Ardron glossed over the comment with a wry smile and acknowledged the other man, "And a good evening to you too Sir Philip." He recognised Philip Fitzrobert youngest son of Earl Robert.

"Good evening to you too, er" Philip hesitated.

"Ardron, Ardron of Norwood."

"Of course," he replied remembering. "I trust your wounds have healed," he added proving that he did remember.

"All is well Sir Philip," he said with a nod. "My Lady," he now addressed Rohesa. "Will you permit me, to steal you away from these distinguished gentlemen for a few minutes?"

She paused a hesitating moment. "Gentlemen," she then said.

"Please excuse us," Ardron added as he offered his arm.

She took his arm and allowed him to lead down the great hall to a vacant window recess.

"I have not seen you these past eighteen months," he said. "I hoped that you hadn't forgotten me," Ardron said.

"Of course, I haven't forgotten you, Sir Alwyn," she teased.

Ardron smiled at the intended tease. "I have hungered for every tiny piece of gossip of your whereabouts. I was at the king's court that day to witness your husband's fall from grace and the metered punishment. I was concerned for you welfare."

"Without speaking she took his hand. "The ring you wear," she said. "Whose livery is that?"

"It's yours, of course."

"Yes, even though I am wife to the disgraced Geoffrey de Mandeville I am, nevertheless, still a de Vere. And the de Vere name still carries influence even with the king. I was allowed to stay on at Saffron Waldron Castle as a permanent and honoured guest. However, it was not a satisfactory arrangement for me. After being mistress of all things domestic, I became nothing more than a resident. I soon tired of that and since I was only some dozen miles from the family castle at Hedingham, I soon moved back there.

"And since then?" Ardron asked.

"I pass my time in all things feminine, travel and visit a great deal," she said with a shrug.

Ardron was silent moment. "Rohesa," he said quietly. "That day at Wallingford lives permanently at the fore-front of my memory. I felt exalted above all men." He paused. "Did it mean as much to you?"

She giggled and took his hand. "It was very nice," she said.

"Very nice? Is that all?"

"Don't be so serious," she said. "I am still wife to Geoffrey de Mandeville. Even if he is outlawed, I am still shackled."

Ardron was hugely disappointed.

"You hoped that we could do it again!" she said.

He stared into her face hoping to see sign that she teased him but saw only sympathy. "I had hopes," he said disappointedly.

She laughed aloud. "Who knows what lies in the future," she said. Then added a consoling smile said. "But I will say there has been no one else. Can you not be satisfied with that?"

Ardron took a deep breath and sighed. "No," he said.

"Ah," she said sympathetically.

The pause was interrupted by the same man upon whose arm Rohesa hand had rested earlier. "Lady Rohesa," he said. "You promised to dance the next carole with me."

She looked around the hall and recognised a carole being played. "So, I did, my Lord" she said getting to her feet.

"Sir Ardron, she said. "May I introduce Sir Payn de Beauchamp, Lord of Bedford."

"A pleasure to meet you Sir," Ardron said getting to his feet. The man before him, similar age to Ardron, tall straight and, save for a thin shadow of a beard, clean shaven

Payn de Beauchamp looked at Rohesa questioningly. "Is this the same Ardron that rescued the empress from Oxford."

"It is," she confirmed.

"On such deeds are legends made. I am indeed pleased to make your acquaintance," he said.

Ardron shrugged slightly embarrassed. "We have to deal within the circumstances in which we find ourselves," he replied.

"You are too modest my friend," de Beauchamp replied.

"The carole, my Lord." Rohesa reminded him.

"Indeed," de Beauchamp acknowledged. "I hope we will get other opportunities to talk," he said as he began to move away.

"It would be my pleasure," Ardron muttered in reply as he watched Rohesa being led by de Beauchamp's to the dance floor.

He sat back into the seat, heavily. It seemed that he didn't mean as much to the Lady as she did to him, 'You win, or you lose.' he consoled himself. 'Looks like I lost this time.'

Minutes later he approached John Fitzgilbert. "Sir," he said." I hear that hearty congratulations are in order due to your forthcoming marriage." He looked across the room to the handsome young woman that was Sybil de Evereux. "May I say that you are indeed a lucky man."

Fitzgilbert cocked his head to study Ardron with his good eye, then turned to gaze across the room also. "Thank you, Scorrenstone," he said. "Truly, under the circumstances, I agree with you. I am a lucky man."

Soon after that with the attraction of the festivities now greatly reduced, he began to consider what would be an appropriate time to leave. "Sir," a servant interrupted his contemplations. "I have a note for you."

"Thank you," he said woodenly as he took the note. Scanning the hall, he looked for Rohesa, but could not see her. Nor could he see de Beauchamp. Gloomily. he resolved, just a few more minutes then he would leave. He turned his attention to the note.

> *Travellers Rest*
> *Without the northern wall*
> *Rohesa*

Travellers Rest

Something behind him moved and invaded his sleep. Opening his eyes with a degree of alarm he was confronted by a stone wall within easy touching distance. Ardron lifted his head in confusion trying to establish his situation. A little higher was a small window, through which there were the first hints of weakening darkness. He rolled onto his back and found himself watched by Rohesa, her head resting on an elbow supported hand. He breathed a sigh of relief as he now remembered his location.

"Rohesa," he muttered still a little dazed.

"Gallant, sir knight," she responded. "For discretion sake you will have to go soon."

"Yes," he agreed drowsily.

"Do you still feel exalted above all men?" She teased.

"Even more so," he said rolling to face her. "Would that I could take you for my very own."

"Ah," she said. "While Geoffrey lives, I remain his wife and chained in limbo."

"Hmm," he agreed.

"Perhaps something fatal will fall upon him whilst he plunders the fens." Rohesa said.

"Not likely," Ardron replied, "He has the luck of the devil."

"Nevertheless, if the devil were to dessert him and he was to die then I would be free to remarry." She shrugged and sighed, "I am a mere woman and I can only pray that it does happen." She paused. Is that a mortal sin?" she asked.

"I suppose it is."

"Even so. I cannot help but desire it." There was a long pause. "You could kill him," she suggested.

"What?" Ardron stared at her hard.

"You could kill him," she said again. "After all you bested my uncle with the sword. He was considered to be one of the best swordsmen in France. Geoffrey de Mandeville would not be as formidable as was my uncle."

"Are you serious?" Ardron asked with incredulity.

"Hmm," she replied casually.

"You want me to cross the country with the specific objective of killing a man?"

"Why not? We would be free to marry after that."

"That is premeditated murder."

"Who would blame you? Not the king, he would be delighted. Nor any of the Angevin royalty. They would applaud it as poetic-justice for his treachery. Not the church! They would be able to recover Ramsey Abbey. The populace of the fens would be relieved. They would be rid of a plundering tyrant. So_, who will care?"

"It's just not possible," Ardron said. "He is surrounded by an army."

"Except when he goes hunting," she said. "He takes only four or five with him."

"You've really thought this through, haven't you?"

She nodded. "In my quieter moments I cannot help but consider my situation, and I look for possible ways out of my predicament. Geoffrey's death seems to be the only alternative. I really don't want to be his estranged wife waiting for him to die of age." She laid her head on his chest. "You could kill him for me," she said. "For us," she added."

Ardron was astonished. "Do you really mean it?" was all he could mutter.

"She lifted her head and looked him in his face. "Of course not," she said with snigger. "But we can still daydream of what could be." She looked to the tiny window and at the strengthening daylight. "Come my gallant knight," she said seductively. "Do for me once more, then you must go."

Chapter 18

Cosseham, October 1144

Ardron stood gazing down the hill watching Maurice de Prevuer riding up towards him at an easy canter. He did not appear to be in any particular hurry, and so Ardron could guess that the news he would bring was not that what he wanted to hear.

"Anything?" Ardron asked as soon as he was within earshot.

"Nothing," he replied as he reined in and dismounted.

"How far did you go?"

Maurice shrugged. "Two miles or so."

"Christ on the cross," Ardron cursed. "What treachery is this?"

There was a hopeless expression and a non-committal shrug before Maurice said. "It is a bit misty this morning, perhaps they were there somewhere but just out of view."

Ardron gazed down the hill. It was a cold October morning with a very heavy due, and although there was an autumn mist, visibility was still good. There was no doubt in Ardron's mind de Bohun was not coming.

The arranged plan had been to rendezvous at Cosseham last night and then at first light make a surprise attack on the quarry stronghold before the dwellers were awake. Now, it was moving towards mid-morning and of de Bohun there was nary a sign. Ardron along with his small attack force was alone. He stomped back to camp, with Maurice behind leading his horse. His force of Norman sergens and Saxon villeins gazed expectantly at him as they lazed ready just waiting for the word.

"Any news?" Luc asked.

"No news. It would seem that we are on our own." Ardron replied bitterly, as he squatted on the edge of the circle.

There was a pause before Luc spoke again. "What do you intend to do?"

Ardron sucked noisily through his teeth and shook his head without replying.

"We should withdraw," Luc offered. "It's not our land and it's not our fight. And_" he went on. "By now we will have lost the advantage of surprise. Those outlaws will know we are here."

Ardron stroked his beard thoughtfully, Luc had a point. But yet here they were, and just about half-a-mile way was Grey Wolf and his camp of outlaws. De Bohun's constable, de Aumale, had established that, with a degree of certainty. It was upon this information that de Bohun had put together this plan inviting Ardron to join him in eliminating this scourge of the area. Now it seemed that he had not turned up to his own party.

Luc was right, by now the outlaws would know they were there but if, as he suggested, they withdrew then by tomorrow Grey Wolf and his followers would be gone. Gone to? Who would know where? The whole process of search and destroy would have to start all over again.

"We carry on the attack," he said getting to his feet. "We may be short on the numbers we expected, but each one of you is a trained and blooded warrior. A bunch of outlaws will be no match for us." There was a ripple of cheering from some, while others looked a little less keen. "Are you with me on this?" he asked.

"We are." The reply, agreeing nods.

Ardron needed more enthusiasm. "Are you with me?" he demanded more earnestly.

They were on their feet now. "We'll follow you through the fires of hell," Pique roared leading the cheering.

"Then to your horses." Ardron was satisfied.

A mere hundred yards away from the quarry barricade but just out of sight, Ardron paused the column and glanced back to see if all were ready. Grim expectant faces stared back as he drew his sword. All followed his example. "We will go in hard and storm the barricade. Hopefully, they will crumble under the onslaught." He said to no one in particular but for all to hear.

He spurred his charger, Rattlebone, forward and led the gallop around the bend and the charge at the barricade. To his surprise the gates along the palisades were wide open. Somewhat nonplussed he, nevertheless, led an unhindered gallop through and into the very heart of the quarry. Had they achieved the element of surprise? It seemed so. But as the gallop came to a halt there were, no shouts of alarm, no expected panic, in fact there was no sign of life as the raiders pitched about in confusion. Some dismounted and stormed into the crude dwellings, only to emerge moments later alone and bewildered. The place seemed deserted. Had the outlaws fled during the night?

"Sir, Sir." Someone sought his attention urgently. Ardron glanced around and found Beldwine pointing back towards the barricade. The gates were being closed and from seemingly out of the very ground armed defenders began to man the barriers.

"It's a trap," Ardron muttered. "It's a trap," he shouted a warning just as arrows began to thud into the ground all around. It was Luc who pointed up towards the cliff top where archers stood releasing arrows into the sky to fall among Ardron's men. The urgent need was to find shelter from this deadly rain of arrows. The mine caves could provide that refuge. He spurred Rattlebone along the line shouting. "Into the caverns, into the caverns." His men needed no persuasion and fled in all haste into the dark mouths of the mine entrances. Ardron was amongst the last into the cavern. He looked back expecting to see casualties. He was somewhat relieved to see the only casualty seemed to be a single horse on its side, its legs still kicking in death-throws.

Although the cavern was wide and high at its entrance, within a few yards it funnelled down to low and narrow, forcing all to dismount. He walked back and looked out across the quarry. So long as his men stayed a few feet inside the caves they were safe from the archers on the opposite cliff.

"We are safe for now," Ardron said to Luc who joined him at the entrance. "They can't get in."

"No," Luc agreed. "But we can't get out, either."

Ardron nodded wordless agreement. He silently cursed himself for his stupidity. He had led his men right into a carefully prepared trap. Clearly, he should have heeded Luc's advice and withdrawn from the whole action when de Bohun failed to appear. Too late for recriminations now.

"We should be in the caves on the cliff side." Luc went on. "Directly beneath them, those archers wouldn't be able to fire down on us."

"No," Ardron disagreed. "On this side we are on the downside of the hill. Behind us it falls away sharply. There is a better chance of finding another way out on this side." His brain was already starting to look for solutions. "Fique," he called.

"Sir," the reply was immediate."

"Take two men and explore back there." He pointed into the darkness. "Find another way out."

"Sir," Fique accepted compliance. Then hesitated. "It's as black as a Moors arse back there," he said.

"Take a few minutes in the dark, and your eyes will adjust."

Still he hesitated. "Could get lost," he said.

"Don't," Ardron replied. He turned to Luc. "If he doesn't find another way out then we will have to wait for night fall. Under the cover of darkness we'll then have to fight our way out," he said. "In the mean-time look to any casualties."

Leaving two men to watch from the mine entrance he wandered back deeper into the mine and found a suitable place to settle. At this time of the year it would be suitably dark sometime after six, and since it was only mid-morning now, there would be a long monotonous wait. Even that was fraught with perils. In the darkness they would have some cover from the archers on the cliff top. However, to launch an attack against a defended barricade would almost certainly mean casualties. No way of avoiding that. Another alternative would be to surrender. That was not a palatable alternative. He did not consider himself important enough to command much of a ransom from his superiors, which meant, in all probability, he would have to fund his own ransom, and that would probably cost him everything. He desperately needed Fique to find another way out. It then occurred to him, if another way out did exist, then these outlaws would know of it. In which case, it would surely be manned to prevent escape. The whole situation was depressing, and not for the first time he silently berated himself for the situation in which he had led his men. Temporary relief from these gloomy thoughts did eventually come in the guise of short catnaps.

"Sir," It was Cerdic who roused him. He looked up bleary eyed and just for a moment confused. "You need to see this." Cerdic went on.

Trying to appear much more alert than he really was, Ardron jumped to his feet. "What is it?" he mumbled.

"Come," Cerdic said and led the way back to the cave entrance.

At the entrance Cerdic pointed towards the cliff top. "There is fighting up there," he said.

Ardron followed the direction to where he pointed. Men on the top crossed swords. "By God you're right," he uttered, and realisation hit home. "Rouse the men," he said excitedly. "It must be de Bohun."

Minutes later he led the charge from the cave down the quarry towards the barricade. Even more to his relief as they neared, he could see that the barricade was under attack from the outside. The defenders had re-positioned to the inside, but now with this new onslaught they found themselves attacked from both sides. It was over in a very few minutes the defenders threw down their swords and surrendered.

As the vanquished were rounded up to be marched down the quarry, de Aumale rode up to Ardron with a huge grin. "Mission accomplished, I believe," he said.

"You were late," Ardron responded angrily.

"Late? Not at all," he said. "Just in time," he added as he pulled his horse's head about and glanced up to the cliff top. "You take responsibility for the prisoners. I must look to Sir Humphrey."

Ardron reined back pulling Rattlebone to stand. There was no doubt that de Bohun's timely intervention had saved him from total embarrassment, and possibly even his neck, but he could not repress angry feelings that he had been cleverly, and unwittingly, used.

Thirty minutes later de Bohun himself rode into the quarry at the head of a procession leading the vanquished archers as prisoners. He pulled to one side, leaving the procession to herd the sauntering prisoners down the quarry.

"Norwood." He said greeting Ardron cheerfully. "A successful campaign I would say. Wouldn't you?"

Ardron bit his lip and controlled his temper. "Why were you late?" he asked softly.

"Late? Ah yes. Some confusion over the dates. I have to own." He said.

"That is just so much horse shit," Ardron countered angrily. "You used me as a decoy." he accused. "You allowed me to blunder in, in order to spring their trap. Then when we were bottled up, and all were looking inwards, it was safe for you to make your attack from behind."

"Perish the thought," de Bohun replied. "What were your casualties?" he asked.

"Four wounded."

"Fatally?"

Ardron shrugged. "Perhaps one," he said.

"One possible fatality! Then casualties were light. The outlaws are all apprehended. Therefore, I would say the attack was a resounding success." He said nonchalantly. "Come my friend," he went on. "Let us see if we have one, Grey Wolf, amongst our prisoners."

He had a point Ardron conceded, only slightly appeased. He then, without comment, spurred his horse deeper into the quarry.

At the far end beside the lake the outlaws had been rounded up, herded together and seated under guard on the ground. Ardron walked Rattlebone slowly across the front scanning the prisoners carefully, looking for any slight sign of a possible leader, or even a familiar face. Clearly all before him were Saxon, and not all were men. Some were women and some were children. Here before him was a whole community of Saxons and living entirely on outlaw gains. Ardron being himself Saxon, could feel some relation to their circumstances. Even so, he harboured no sympathy to these people who lived on the misery of those they robbed. Mostly their demeanour was sullen and depressed, but here and there was some defiance left with hostile stares. His horse had made only a few strides before Ardron recognised a familiar face. He reined back and pointed at the man.

"That man there," he said. "Get him to his feet." Two sergens stepped in and physically hauled the man to his feet, No doubt about it! This was the man who called himself Will and had challenged Ardron fifteen months ago when he had caught up with the raiders and had took to hang one of their number. His presence here today confirmed in Ardron's mind, that this was indeed the camp of the outlaw calling himself Grey Wolf.

"I know you," he said. You are a member of Grey Wolf's robber band." Will only stared back expressionless. "Point him out," he demanded.

But the man continued to stare back expressionless. His defiance earned him a solid thump between the shoulder blades with a sword hilt by one of the sergens. Ardron briefly waved an appeasing hand at the sergen, stopping more violence. He hadn't really expected that the man would have given up his leader, particularly so in front of all the other outlaws. Ardron continued slowly along the line. Towards the end of the line he reined in his horse sharply, and just for a moment sat there staring unseeing ahead. 'Of course,' he muttered, and turned the horse sharply to go back a few paces.

"That man there," he said pointing at a slight figure, head bowed looking down. His mass of long grey hair tumbled down around his head and almost covered his face. "Bring him to me."

The man was unceremoniously dragged to his feet and frog marched up to Ardron still holding his head down. Ardron nodded to one of the sergens who grabbed a handful of long hair and roughly hauled his head back. Despite the changes, and although Ardron had not seen this man for more than five years, he recognised him.

"Welfwulf!" he exclaimed.

"Hello, Sir Ardron. You look to have prospered," Welfwulf said casually.

"You know this man," de Bohun queried.

"I do. I once fought a wager of battel on his behalf."

De Bohun surprised expression was evident.

Ardron looked down on Welfwulf, now sixty, if he was day. The hair that had been dark, although still wildly unkempt, was now the colour of polished silver. As too was the large beard that covered the lower part of his face.

"Grey Wolf? You are Grey Wolf!" Ardron said.

"Who me?" Welfwulf laughed out loud. "You do me too much credit, sir. You know me I am a non but a petty thief. Always was, and always will be. And you well know it, having once benefitted from my theft."

"What does he mean?" de Bohun asked.

"He once unloaded a diamond onto me," Ardron was dismissive. "Nevertheless," he went on quickly turning back to Welfwulf. "I believe you are the outlaw known as Grey Wolf."

Welfwulf wordlessly shook his head with a casual smile.

Glancing across the captives, Ardron sensed a restless change of atmosphere. There were less bowed heads and much more interest. He was thoughtful a moment. Perhaps he could spark some reaction among outlaws and confirm that which he thought. "Beldwine," he called.

"Sir," The reply was instant.

"Speaking in English, so that all understood, he said loud and clear. "I once saved this man's life; therefore, I now have the right to take it. Get two men to help, find a good length of rope, then." He pointed at a nearby tree. "Take this man over to that tree and hang him." This caused an immediate aggressive reaction from the captives. Many got to their feet shouting 'traitor' and 'shame' in protests.' Such was the hostility that

416

Ardron could see the situation was on the verge of a riot. More bloodshed he didn't want. Nevertheless, the communal attitude had confirmed that which he suspected. Welfwulf was Grey Wolf. He waited a few moments surveying the outraged mob before eventually, holding up an appeasing hand. "Beldwine," he said. "Forget that order." Half turning his horse to face de Bohun he said. "Without doubt, Sir Humphry, there stands the outlaw Grey Wolf."

"Clap that man in irons," de Bohun instructed his constable de Aumale. The mood of the captives remained hostile, and some began to hurl stones. "The devil take their arses," Ardron heard de Bohun swear. Then he ordered his sergenti to stand-to and make ready. The sergenti drew their swords while his archers armed their bows and stood poised.

For a few moments, the outcome was in the balance. But the sight of armed sergens just waiting for the order to attack eventually brought the crowd to order, and although clearly resentful, some degree of calm was restored. De Bohun waited for the mood to calm a little more before issuing his next order. "The women and children may go," he said. It was a good move, not only did it reduce the size of the crowd before him, it also made an appeasing concession. Except for a belligerent few, the women and children began to shuffle away, albeit deliberately slowly.

When it had suitable thinned Ardron pushed his horse forward. "Welfwulf had a son called Adelfrid." He said. "I would see if he is among these outlaws."

"Go ahead," de Bohun replied. Ardron circled the outlaws slowly, scanning carefully as he did, but if Adelfrid was there he did not recognise him. Shaking his head glumly he arrived back at de Bohun's side.

"Destroy the camp," de Bohun then said loudly. "Let not one stick of wood remain uncharred."

Ardron and de Bohun moved a safe distance and watched from horse-back while the order was enthusiastically carried out. Ardron gave an assenting nod for his own men to assist. To the rank and file, it was bonus day.

"What will you do with the prisoners?" Ardron asked.

"I will march then down to Earl Salisbury," he replied. "After all, not only does my cousin now out-rank me, he is the High Sheriff of Wiltshire."

"What will he do?"

De Bohun shrugged, "If I know Patric, he will hang the leaders in public and the rest he'll either keep or sell as slaves. Tis the usual penalties for outlaws." He paused a moment. "I would appreciate some assistance in the manning of that march down to Salisbury, if you feel obliged." He added.

"Of course," Ardron agreed.

"A nest of thieves cleared out," He added smugly. "A good day's work, my friend. Add that to the other good news of yesterday and. Well!" he left the rest unsaid, his smile said it all.

"The other good news?" Ardron queried.

"Geoffrey de Mandeville," he reminded him.

Ardron shook a bewildered head.

"Oh! you haven't heard?"

"No," Ardron replied.

"He received his just deserves at last. He was killed last month by a stray arrow when he attacked Burwell."

"De Mandeville is dead?"

"He is!" Then went on ruefully. "Unfortunately, it is, perhaps, also good news for the king. But__ Oh well."

Ardron was no longer listening his mind was racing with the possibilities. Was he really killed by a stray arrow or had someone performed a service to Rohesa? Rohesa's burning desire had been satisfied. She was free. Now free to remarry. His hopes began to soar.

"The Lady Rohesa?" he asked.

"Lady Rohesa?" he responded. "No need to worry about that one. Someone did her a huge favour and she lost no time in announcing her betrothal to Lord Bedford."

Ardron was stunned. "Lord Bedford?" he muttered.

"Aye. Payn de Beauchamp, Lord Bedford."

"I see," he muttered. But he didn't, not really.

He now realised that she had tried to manipulate him with false inuendo. 'Free to marry,' he thought derisively. She had not actually said to whom she would be free to marry. Now, he wondered if she had used the same suggestion on someone else. It was just possible, that someone had succeeded.

"Was it really a stray arrow or one well aimed?" he asked.

De Bohun shrugged. "Don't know," he said. "Guess it doesn't matter. Does it?"

"I suppose not," Ardron allowed.

"Sir," Fique standing by his horse sought his attention. "We did find another way out of that mine," he said. "But we wouldn't have been able to get the horses out that way."

Ardron nodded, only.

Fique looked across the quarry where the make-shift houses were beginning to belch smoke as they were set alight. "Doesn't matter now though," he said.

"No. But thank you anyway." Ardron said.

***

"Sir," Luc said, attracting his attention.

Ardron leaned back in his chair and pushed away the papers before him. "Luc," he said, "Come in."

"Despatches just in," Luc said and handed over the roll.

Ardron examined the wax seal. "It's from Sir Humphrey," he said recognising the seal. He got up and walked over to the window before breaking the seal. Opening the roll, he scanned the brief message. "It is an invitation to allocate six good men to aid the transport of outlaws down to Salisbury Castle," he said. Briefly he wondered if the invitation was really optional or a demand. It mattered not, to allocate six was no hardship, indeed some might even welcome the distraction. He turned back to return to the table, Luc still hovered.

"Was there anything else," he asked.

"Yes, Sir. A personal matter."

Ardron nodded and waved towards a vacant seat as he sat. "Take a seat," he said. Noticing Hildi hovering in the doorway, he said. "Hildi, can you have a flagon of wine brought up with a couple of goblets?" She nodded without speaking and then disappeared. "What can I do for you?" he asked.

Luc hesitated a moment before replying. "I have a desire to return home, back to Normandy."

Ardron nodded resignedly. 'Why not he thought? "You are well overdue a holiday," he said.

"Sir," Luc said. "You don't understand. I wish to return and stay indefinitely."

Ardron was taken aback and temporarily speechless.

"I have a small holding in Normandy which my father manages in my absence. But the years begin to creep up on him. Its time I returned to run my own affairs," Luc went on.

"Oh, I see." Ardron's reply was dejected. "I would be most reluctant to lose my constable. You are my right arm."

Luc nodded, "Sorry," he said. "My motivation reduces a little more each day because I grow very weary of this endless war."

"As do we all!" Ardron agreed.

"I have no desire to see you in difficulties," Luc went on. But if you could see your way to letting me go, it is my opinion that Maurice de Prevuer would make an excellent replacement."

Ardron nodded agreement. "Yes, I think perhaps he could make an adequate replacement. But he is not you." He paused a moment. "Is there anything I can do to make you change your mind."

"Only if you see my leaving as a serious problem for you personally."

Luc had just given him a golden opportunity to reject his request. A simple 'I can't do without you' and the subject was at an end. He stared at his constable across the table. He had served well and loyally, and his resignation would hurt, and hurt a lot, but he couldn't bring himself to reward excellent service with such selfishness. "You really want to go?"

"Yes, Sir."

Ardron rubbed his brow, tiredly, as Hildi returned bringing the wine flagon herself.

"There is more," Luc added. Ardron looked up. "I would take Hildi with me."

"My God," Ardron muttered. It was the worst kept secret in the castle that the pair often shared a bed. "Not only do I lose an irreplaceable constable, but you would take my housekeeper with you."

"Sir."

Ardron sniggered ruefully. "Very well," he said. "But there will have to be a period of adjustment."

Luc nodded agreement. "Autumn is ending, and winter begins," he said, "This is a quiet period on a farm, and since there is little to be done until the snows of January have passed, I thought that early February would be ideal. If that is convenient?"

"Notice of almost three months. That is more than fair." Ardron replied.

Luc grinned and placed a familiar arm around Hildi's hips as she stood by his seat. "Then it is agreed?"

"It is, Ardron concurred. "Of course," he warned. "You will have to clear the other matter with Swidhurn, Hildi's brother," he said looking up at Hildi's smiling face."

"We know that." Luc went on. "However, there is another problem."

"Oh."

"Yes. My smallholding is on Sir Humphrey de Bohun's estate which means when I take up the option, I will become a villein to Sir Humphrey." He paused allowing a moment for thought. "If it should be that as his villein he calls me back to arms then I would likely finish up serving at Trowbridge Castle. If that were to be the case, I would sooner stay at Norwood."

"I see," Ardron said stroking his beard thoughtfully as he blindly studied the desktop before him. "OK he said after a few seconds. I will draw up release papers which I will sign then ask Sir Humphrey to counter sign. That ought to see your resignation made a little more permanent."

"Will he agree?" Luc asked.

Ardron shrugged and made a wry face. "I think so," he said.

***

Trowbridge Castle

It was just a week later when Ardron arrived at Trowbridge Castle accompanied by Luc and five other Norman sergens. As they rode into the bailey it was immediately obvious that the prisoners were ready to start their march to Salisbury. They were chained together and tethered to a stout post. Before dismounting, Ardron took a few moments to looked over the sitting rabble. A sorrier looking bunch would have been hard to imagine. They were silent, subdued and very obviously resentful.

"Is that all of them?" Roland queried. "That's not all of them," he answered his own question.

Ardron agreed but passed no comment. Seated haphazardly as they were, they were not readily countable, but even so, it was patently obvious that their number was not much more than a score.

As he dismounted, he was greeted by Francis d'Aumale. "Welcome Sir Ardron," he said. "Sir Humphrey awaits you in his private quarters."

De Bohun had seated himself at the fireside and had stretched his legs forward to warm his feet. He was not alone. "Ah Ardron," he greeted. "Come in and take a seat here, where it's warm." He indicated with a casual arm wave at a space between the two men.

The other man got to his feet and turned to face Ardron. His pale face was lined with age, and his grey hair cropped short. However, it was still long enough, to be curled decoratively over his ears. With a carefully manicured moustache and a neatly trimmed beard at the end of his chin, Ardron guessed he was a vain man who attempted to disguise his senior years.

"Have you met Sir William de Peverel High Sheriff of Nottingham?" de Bohun asked.

Although Ardron had seen de Peverel at formal gatherings he had never been formally introduced. "No Sir. I have not had that pleasure."

"The pleasure is mine," de Peverel said. "Your exploits in the service of the empress are legendary."

Ardron shrugged modestly. "Only doing my duty sir."

"Come. Sit," de Bohun indicated the place in front of the fire. "Sir William is in route to Bristol, to advise Earl Robert on the construction of a soon to be built castle at Faringdon."

"Oh," Ardron was immediately interested. A castle at Faringdon right in the middle of the Thames valley would be strategically important, particularly so since the fall of Oxford.

"The Castle at Nottingham, built by my father," de Peverel explained. "Is of a particular formidable construction. And the earl feels it will be desirous to have many of those same features."

"Yes_," Ardron agreed. "Bearing in mind its forward position, I can see how such a castle would need to be formidable."

"Are you here to escort the prisoners down to Salisbury?" de Bohun asked.

"I have brought six sergens to place at your disposal, but I won't be travelling. I am here primarily to talk to you on a private matter." Ardron replied.

"A private matter?"

"Yes."

"Then we will talk about that later," de Bohun decided. The conversation then lulled and Ardron took the opportunity to enquire about the rest of the prisoners.

"The rest of the prisoners?" de Bohun said. "A few I set free, feeling they were either just camp followers or small fry. The bigger majority I took as slaves. I kept some for myself, but most were placed out into villages or farms where they could still benefit me, albeit indirectly. Didn't see any reason why I should have made a present of some three dozen slaves to cousin Patric." He paused a moment before adding sarcastically, "Earl of Salisbury,"

Ardron smiled. "I get the distinct impression you don't really approve of his appointment."

"You'd be right," he replied. "Trade off your sister for a title!"

"I don't suppose John Fitzgilbert complains too much." Ardron responded.

"Indeed not," de Bohun agreed. "Cousin Sybil is a veritable prize indeed."

"How long will it take?" de Peverel asked.

Both men looked at him a little confused.

"The march to Salisbury," de Peverel explained his question.

"Ah," de Bohun responded. "Well it's a little more than thirty miles from here. So, it should take two days comfortably. But_," he added. "These prisoners will definitely not be in any hurry to face their punishment so I would expect they drag their feet considerably. Three days probably, perhaps four."

"Their punishment?" Ardron asked. "What do you suppose that will be?"

"Patric? Oh, he'll hang em for sure."

Ardron stared into the fire without comment. They were after all outlaws. The very word meant outside the law, which meant there would be no rights and no protection.

"Sir!" Francis de Aumale entered the chamber and sought de Bohun's attention. "The prisoner who calls himself Welfwulf asked if Sir Ardron would see him."

"Did he say why?" Ardron asked.

De Aumale shrugged and shook his head.

"Probably wants you to champion him when he pleads Wager of Battel. Again_!" De Bohun said. Then roared with laughter at the suggestion. Ardron saw no humour. De Aumale and de Peverel just looked confused.

Welfwulf sat in the corner of the small cage his legs spread before him on the floor, his head slumped onto his chest in shallow sleep. For a few moments Ardron studied him quietly. He found it hard to believe that this slight old man had elevated himself into the infamous outlaw Grey Wolf. After a few moments he picked up a broken arrow shaft from the ground and ran it across the cage bars waking the old man.

"Ardron," he muttered then corrected himself. "Sir Ardron."

"Welfwulf," he acknowledged, settling down on a wooden box. "You wanted to see me?"

"I did."

"Well, here I am."

The old man nodded and adjusted to a more comfortable sitting position. "You have done well for yourself since that day at Ludgershall five years ago. From a mere Saxon peasant, you have risen to a be a Norman knight with a castle and an estate. And a highly esteemed Norman knight at that."

"Have you requested me here to discuss my status, or was there something specific you wanted to talk to me about?"

Welfwulf pursed his lips while he thought a moment. "Tis said that if you save a man's life then you have a responsibility for that life," he said.

"I have heard it said, but I place little credence to it." Ardron replied.

"Nor I, truth be said," Welfwulf said.

"Then what do you want?"

Welfwulf got to his feet looked down his cage. "I have my own separate space here," he said. "Three strides that way and one and a half across. Doesn't compare to your estate though does it?"

"Is there a point to this," Ardron was becoming impatient.

"Yes." Do you know that we had reached a point where we no longer had to rob anyone? In fact, we no longer had to resort to any outlaw activities. We could survive quite comfortably on the contributions received from the rich gentry, like yourself. A sort of tax in reverse."

"You mean extortion," Ardron corrected. "That is outlaw activity."

"Technically," Welfwulf allowed. "But you could afford it."

"Four-hundred marks a year is not petty money. That could buy a big herd of sheep."

"A hundred head?"

"I suppose," Ardron agreed.

"And yet, you and your staff never missed a meal after you paid. Just how many sheep could a Saxon peasant buy in a year?"

"You can't justify your actions like that. The people you brutalised were the very people you now claim sympathy for." Ardron retorted.

"Yes. We had to be brutal in order to make it much more desirable for the estate owners to pay the contribution than to keep getting attacked."

"You hanged three of my villeins. You can't get more brutal than that." Ardron replied angrily.

Ah__. Regrettable," Welfwulf said nodding sadly. "That was not of my doing. The triple raid was on my instructions in order to demonstrate your vulnerability but that was all. Twas one man in the raiding party who persuaded the rest that revenge hangings would be fitting vengeance." He paused a moment. "After all it was you who started it, by hanging one of ours and killing another.

Ardron stared at him. How had he suddenly reasoned that it was his fault.

"Even so, when I learned what they had done the man was suitable chastened, and all your livestock returned," Welfwulf went on.

"Suitable chastened? Ardron sneered angrily. "One of those hung was a boy of ten. How do you justify that? The boy screamed in terror as he was dragged away while his father fought and pleaded to be allowed to take his place."

Welfwulf looked down sadly unable to look into Ardron's face. "A father will do all he must to protect his children," he said softly, "I know that the leader of that raiding party never intended that a boy of such tender years should have been hung."

There was a protracted silence between the two men. "I have something to ask of you," Welfwulf said quietly.

At that moment Ardron was not particularly disposed favourably towards him, but still he asked. "What is that?"

"At this moment, my life expectancy can be measured in days, perhaps only hours. So as a dying man I wish to put right a wrong."

"I'm listening!"

"Do you remember my son, Adelfrid?"

"Yes, I do. He must be a young man by now or at least close to it," Ardron replied

"He is a young man. Nineteen years old." Welfwulf agreed. "Since that day at Ludgershall I have dragged him around with me. He has known nothing except the life of an outlaw. Quite early on his elder brother pleaded with him to stay at Newbury and help to work the farm. It was the right thing to do and I knew it. But, selfishly, I didn't want to be alone and so insisted that he come with me instead. Now entirely because of my selfishness he is a wanted outlaw, and probably under the sentence of death if he is caught."

"If he is caught?" Ardron queried.

"Yes,"

"Then he's not among these prisoners."

Welfwulf was guarded. "No," he said eventually. "I have no right to ask," he went on. "But if you could find him and tell him it is my dying wish that he gives up the outlaw life and return to his brother in Newbury. A farmer he is to be."

Ardron studied him thoughtfully.

"A father will do all he must to protect his children," Welfwulf muttered.

"Indeed," Ardron agreed. In that next moment he realised that in all probability it was Adelfrid who had led the triple raid upon his Norwood estate. Therefore, it was, perhaps, his idea to hang three in reprisals. "How do I find him?" he asked, though not sure what is own reasons for finding the young man were.

"First you must promise me that you will send him to Newbury and not have him arrested."

Ardron hesitated. "I can't do that," he said shaking his head.

"Please," Welfwulf pleaded.

"I will think on this. I will let you know my decision in the morning, before you leave for Salisbury," he replied.

During the evening Ardron broached the subject of Luc's independence and had managed to secure a loose promise from de Bohun that he would not, except in the most extreme circumstances, recall Luc to arms. Having secured that agreement, he was then able to turn his thoughts to the problem of Welfwulf's son, Adelfrid.

He was undecided whether he should make the promise to Welfwulf and give the young man the opportunity to mend his ways and return inside the law. Or, whether he should be sought and brought to account for his crimes. He was after all, probably guilty of a triple hanging. Lying abed in one of the guest chambers inside the Trowbridge Castle, he agonised long into the night before he did eventually fall asleep.

Still undecided the next morning, he resolved to make the promise in order to discover how to find Adelfrid. Once he had the youngster in custody, he would make the decision on his fate. It was not the honourable thing to make such a promise to a condemned man but, the actual decision could be made after capture and interrogation.

First, he gave the good news to Luc and could not help a pang of disappointment as he beheld his constable's extreme delight. But then, why wouldn't he be delighted? He would be withdrawing completely from the chaotic anarchy that was England, to begin a more tranquil life of a farmer. And a huge bonus would be that the woman he loved would be with him. Just for a moment he thought of Rohesa and felt the sting of disappointment.

Dismissing those thoughts, he wandered along the line of prisoners who were all seated upon the ground and each chained to another. The convoy of human flotsam was being prepared to leave. He found Welfwulf still caged, but now the cage had been lifted onto a cart to be pulled by a horse pair. For a moment he stood back, wondering, even now, if he could make a promise that he wasn't sure he would be able to keep. Even so, he decided to make that promise, then decide when the circumstances were examined more closely whether or not it could be honoured.

Welfwulf stood waiting, peering at him in silence his hands clutching the bars either side of his face. Ardron hesitated a moment before climbing up onto the cart to face him.

"Very well, Welfwulf," he said. "I will make that promise to find Adelfrid and deliver him to his elder brother."

Welfwulf stared back studying him hard. "How do I know you will keep that promise?" he asked.

Ardron shrugged. "You don't." The silence stretched while Welfwulf decided. "Alright," Ardron said after a few moments and prepared to leave.

"Wait!" Welfwulf said. "I have to trust you. But my curse will descend on you if you play me false."

Ardron sighed with indifference. "I have been cursed before," he replied apathetically. "Are you going to trust me or not?"

Welfwulf shoulders slumped visibly and he sighed heavily. "Adelfrid deserves another chance," he muttered, probably to convince himself. His decision made he nodded. "He has a passion for a young Saxon wench and that's where most of his time is spent."

"This girl's name?"

Still Welfwulf hesitated. "Edwina," he said eventually.

"Edwina. And where can this girl be found?" Ardron asked.

"Boks," Welfwulf muttered inaudibly.

"Where?" Ardron demanded.

"Boks," Welfwulf replied louder.

"Of course!" Ardron said. Boks, he knew, was little more than half-a mile from the quarry. "I will find her," Then he turned to climb down from the cart.

"Sir Ardron, I am trusting you to keep your word as an esteemed knight," Welfwulf almost pleaded

Ardron hesitated a moment one leg already on the cartwheel. He looked at the old man a moment then nodded without replying before climbing down.

***

Mid December 1144

Just two days ago there had been a light sprinkling of snow, but now a gentle thaw had set in leaving only fringes of snow in the shaded areas. Ardron had decided it was past the time when he should attempt to find Adelfrid.

Early afternoon by the river Bybrook, in the valley below Cosseham, he called a halt deciding this was the ideal place to make camp. He glanced skywards at a drab grey December sky. Even with cloud cover there would, he anticipated, be a cold night to come.

"It will be cold night tonight." he warned. "Find plenty of firewood." He waited while his small troop of two dozen began, not too enthusiastically, to dismount. "Not you Cerdic. I have a special task for you." He led the way back up the steep side to the top of the hill and looked down at the landscape falling steeply away before him. "There," he said pointing at the small village of Boks at the foot of the hill.

"You are to go there and ask for the village Thegn. When he identifies himself, you will say that you have a message to be delivered personally to Edwina. When the maid is identified then mark her well in your memory and deliver this message. The outlaw Adelfrid is to bring himself to Norwood Castle where he will be informed, by me, Sir Ardron, of the last wishes that his father left for his future." He paused. "Have you got that?"

"Yes Sir."

"Any questions?"

"Yes. What if Adelfrid himself is there?"

"Then deliver the message to him directly and mark him to memory." Cerdic nodded assent. "Take Pique with you as escort." Ardron added.

Back at the campsite, preparations were well under way to settle in for the remains of the day, with a cold night to follow. He slipped the reins allowing Rattlebone to walk into the shallow river to take a drink. The horse's drink was shallow for the waters must have been close to freezing. Once back on the bank, he dismounted, and began to loosen the tack. From almost nowhere his squire appeared taking Rattlebone's head. He glanced up and muttered, "Jacques," acknowledging the youngster.

His tack clear he humped the saddle and equipment across his shoulder. "Feed him then turn him loose," he instructed, standing back allowing Jacques to lead the animal away. He turned towards the camp, for a moment he hesitated while deciding which of the two fires to choose. It made little difference, both were in their infancy and struggling to get a hold. In the end he chose the nearest

Almost two hours later Cerdic returned, by which time those campfires were significantly better. Nevertheless, Cerdic hoisted the thick sheepskin higher across his shoulders and pulled down on the leather skull cap as he seated himself next to Ardron. "Message delivered successfully, Sir," he said.

Ardron nodded satisfied. "To who?" He asked.

"Well," Cerdic drawled. "The village didn't have a Thegn, so I had to speak with one of the elders called Rothgar. He wanted me to give him the message, but I had to insist that I speak to Edwina personally. Eventually, they brought forward a young girl, a good-looking young girl," he added. "Then I was able to deliver your message."

"What did you say?"

"Exactly what you told me. That Adelfrid was to come to Norwood to learn the last wishes of his father concerning his own future."

Ardron nodded satisfied. "Adelfrid was not there?"

"If he was, he didn't make himself known," Cerdic replied.

"You would know this girl again?

"Oh yes," Cerdic replied. "With hair as red as the setting sun she is unmistakable."

"Good! You have done well."

A few minutes later, seeing him sitting alone, Maurice de Prevuer came and sat at his side. First, he blew into cupped hands then held them up towards the fire. "Could be a frost," he suggested.

Ardron glanced skywards at the heavy cloud laden sky. "Only if those clouds clear," he replied.

De Prevuer agreed with a nod then broached the real reason why he had joined him. "You have a plan? Sir."

"A plan? When did I last have a plan?" Ardron taunted. "Of course I have a plan," he relented with a brief smile." De Prevuer waited. "Tomorrow morning, we ride into Boks and seize Adelfrid, if he is there. If he is not, then we take his girl Edwina, as a hostage and demand an exchange, him for her."

"And if he is not enamoured enough with the girl to offer himself up?" de Prevuer asked.

"Then we just have to hope that the villagers of Boks think enough of the girl to take matters into their own hands and deliver him to us."

"Is there likely to be trouble?"

"I hope trouble can be avoided, but you never really know."

De Prevuer nodded. "I will prepare the men, just in case," he said.

It was around mid-morning when Ardron led his troop into Boks village. They rode in with imperious arrogance. The village lay above the river, sheltered in a dell and nestling at the foot of two hills. Although not entirely deserted, Boks was mostly inactive, only a handful of villagers actually braved the cold to go about their business. The arrival of two dozen mounted Normans, however, sparked curiosity, and people began to emerge slowly from bucolic homes. Others, a little more wary, preferred the security of their dwellings, remaining inside peering out. Nearby, however, two men were working to repair an old cart. Tools still in hand, they stopped and stared with a deal of suspicion at the new arrivals.

"I am Ardron of Norwood." Ardron announced himself. "I would speak with Rothgar."

Using the mallet in his hand one of the men wordlessly pointed the way further into the village. With a brief understanding nod, Ardron spurred Rattlebone on at a sedate walk and led the way deeper into the village. It was not lost to him that some of the villagers fell in behind and followed. He glanced over his shoulder, somewhat warily, hoping it was not a sign of potential trouble. At what he thought might be the centre he stopped and very soon a reception of sorts began to gather.

"I would speak with Rothgar" he said.

A man pushed himself forward through the assembling villagers. "I am Rothgar," he said. He was tall, this man, probably in his middle years with a mass of unkempt grey hair and beard to match. "Is there something you seek here?". He spoke with authority.

Ardron introduced himself again. "Yes, there is something I seek. The outlaw known as Adelfrid."

"Someone was here yesterday seeking him," Rothgar replied.

Lifting an arm, Ardron waved in Cerdic's direction. "Yes, it was this man. He was sent by me."

"Then I'll tell you what I told him. Adelfrid is not here."

Ardron nodded and quickly scanned around the villagers hoping to see a face that he might recognise as Adelfrid. Unsuccessfully! He did, however, notice the young girl with red hair and guessed this would be Edwina.

"Perhaps he is not here," Ardron said. "However, I would wager that you do know where he is."

Rothgar stared back and shrugged. "I don't," he replied defiantly. "He left here some days ago and went to Salisbury.

"Salisbury?"

"Aye Salisbury. His father was taken there to be hanged."

Ardron nodded understanding. "He will be back," he said confidently. "When he does return, you tell him that he is to report to me at Norwood Castle."

"Why would he do that?" Rothgar asked sarcastically.

"Because he knows me, and I have a message for him from his father. A message that could, if acted on, bring him back under the law's protection."

"Then give me the message and I will tell him myself." Rothgar said.

"No," Ardron replied. "There are other questions to be answered first."

Rothgar scoffed. "Then what incentives would there be for him to surrender himself to you?"

Ardron stared at him a moment, then leaned back and spoke in French to de Prevuer and Pique. "Seize the girl with the red hair," he said.

Immediately, the pair drove their horse forward in among the villagers taking them by surprise. But when they confronted the girl, a young man, also with red hair, leapt forward staff in hand raised at a threatening height. Instantly, Ardron drew his sword and drove his own horse forward.

"Stand-off there," he shouted. "No-one need be hurt here today." He turned back towards Rothgar. "I will take this girl as a hostage. She will not be harmed and will be well treated. Within one hour of Adelfrid presenting himself at Norwood the girl will be on her way back here. That I promise you."

Anger blazed in Rothgar's eyes. "And if Adelfrid decides that he will not present himself at Norwood?"

"I think he will. But if he doesn't then I suggest that you bring him. Forcibly if needs must." He turned his attention to the young red-haired man who still held the staff in a threatening position. "You sir," he said. "What is your name?

He stared back deciding whether or not to give it. "Harold," He eventually said.

What is your relationship with this girl?"

"She is my sister," he growled.

"I thought as much. If you wish, you may come with her to chaperone her safety."

The young man stared back defiant for a few moments then lowered the staff. "I will come," he said.

"Good," Ardron said. "Can you find a horse?"

Harold looked to Rothgar. After a moment's thought, Rothgar eventually nodded permission.

***

Devizes, Christmas Eve

It was very late by the time Ardron arrived at Devizes. He had missed the evening mass and celebrations at Devizes Castle, deliberately so. Atop the hill but still outside the town wall he, along with his squire Jacques, arrived at the Travellers Rest Inn. Leaving Jacques in the stables to attend the horses he made his way into the inn. Save for a handful of well inebriated die-hards sitting in the corner, probably by now talking scribble, any Christmas revellers had long since gone.

The well-rounded inn keeper greeted Ardron affably confirming that he had a room saved for him and another for his squire. "If you can wait a few minutes, Sir, I'll have a fire lit in the room and a warm stone placed in your bed," he said. Ardron nodded ascent, helped himself to a leather bottle of wine, two goblets then made his way over to the fading fire.

The invitation to attend the Christmas celebrations was, he well knew, more of a command than invitation. He had decided to comply but to cut the time spent there to be as short as was appropriate. To this end, he intended to miss the eve celebrations and attend the main ceremonies the next day only. His disinterest, he told himself, was war weariness. Seemingly no progress had been made over recent months, indeed the situation seemed to have settled down to an inactive stalemate. The probable explanation was that King Stephen had concentrated his interest to clearing out the remaining rebels in the east of England after de Mandeville's demise. Also, he expected that Lady Rohesa would be at the celebrations with her new husband, Lord Bedford, and that was a situation that he would rather avoid if he could. But avoidance was unlikely. Well! he decided with a mental shrug, such a meeting might prove more awkward for her than it would for him.

He dragged his seat closer to the fire and poured a little wine into the wooden goblet. Taking no notice of the raucous laughter over in the corner, he took a long drink. For a moment he savoured the spicy sting as the ginger in the wine tingled on his tongue. Then using the poker, at his feet, he stabbed at the embers in the inglenook sparking temporary life into the fire.

"Throw an extra log on, Sir. If you wish." The inn keeper called across the room. Without turning Ardron's acknowledgement was a lazy indifferent arm wave. But he didn't bother.

Minutes later he was joined by his squire. "All is tended Sir," he reported.

"Have a drink," Ardron invited the youngster holding up the leather bottle, and at the same time indicated he should sit in the chair opposite.

"Thank you, Sir. But I don't really have a taste for gingered wine." He replied apologetically as he sat.

Ardron nodded understandingly. "Inn keeper," he called looking back. "Have you a little cider for my squire?"

"Coming up," he responded.

Sounds of happy voices and jollity at the entrance door attracted Ardron's attention. Instinctively he turned to watch as a small group of revellers entered noisily. Their high-spirited jubilation even eclipsed the noisy throng in the corner. Expansively dressed and over-exuberant they were instantly identifiable as part of the upper echelon of Norman society, doubtless merrymakers from the castle celebrations. Ardron's heart took an extra beat when he recognised among the revellers Payn de Beauchamp, Lord Bedford, and there, right behind him, Rohesa. Instantly, he turned to face the fire and leaned forward attempting to make himself as inconspicuous as possible. He knew that eventually a face to face meeting with her was inevitable, but anticipating that would come tomorrow he hadn't, at this time, steeled himself ready.

The inn keeper was trying valiantly to announce above noise that their rooms were warmed ready. Eventually, his message began getting through and the revellers began, still noisily, taking their leave from each other. Now, with a little more time, the inn keeper delivered the cider to Jacques. Rohesa standing quietly at her husband's side watched him, and probably for the first time, noticed the pair sat by the fire. Something must have been recognisable, and through curiosity she left her husband's side and slowly moved wider to get a better look.

"Ardron?" she said surprise in her voice.

Ardron, like a youngster caught stealing apples, straightened up reluctantly. "Hello Rohesa," he said getting to his feet.

She wore a full-length dress of burgundy with an amber chamise beneath. The white silk wimple on her head was held in place by a wide expensive looking gold band. With bangles of gold on her wrist, and rings of gold on her fingers, her whole appearance was not only eye-catching stunning, but deliberately boasted ostentatiousness. "I looked for you at the castle tonight, but you weren't there," she said.

"No! I'll be there tomorrow."

"Rohesa," de Beauchamp called his wife. "Come along we are going up now," he said.

"You go ahead Payn, I'll join you in a few moments," she replied.

De Beauchamp hesitated a moment, then decided to allow it. "Just a few moments," he warned as he left.

"Your Ladyship," Jacques who had stood when Ardron did, now offered his chair.

"Thank you," she said as she sat.

"Sir," Jacques now addressed Ardron. "If you don't need me anymore then I'll retire also."

"You may go," Ardron allowed, pleased at the squire's tact.

Ardron sat down opposite. "I understand that congratulations are in order on your recent marriage."

"Thank you," she replied.

There was a silence between them before Ardron spoke. "For you, it was a very fortunate chance arrow that killed de Mandeville."

"Indeed," she agreed.

"If indeed it was a chance arrow." He added sarcastically.

"What do you mean?"

Ardron sighed heavily. "The last time we__," he hesitated a moment before rephrasing, "Met. You talked about the possibility of Geoffrey being killed by my hand."

"Oh that," she scoffed. "That wasn't at all serious."

"Nevertheless, it worked out perfectly for you," he said.

"Yes, it did," she agreed. "But then the sort of life that Geoffrey lived, I suppose, it was inevitable that he would come to an early and inglorious end."

"I suppose," Ardron allowed staring into the fire's embers. "You didn't wait very long after his demise, did you? Betrothed in a few days, married within a month. Not even a decent time allowed for mourning." He added accusingly.

"Mourning? Why would I mourn?"

"Appearances sake?" he suggested.

"What care I for false grief?" she said. "Everyone who knows me, would have known it was hypercritical."

"Maybe." He conceded with a nod. "But you didn't even wait to see if other alternatives presented themselves."

She was quiet for a few moments. "You had hopes?" she said.

"Of course, I had hopes," he said angrily.

There was raucous laughter from the revellers over in the corner almost as if they mocked him. He glanced over to see one of them with hands behind his back trying to drink from his goblet using only his teeth to lift it.

Rohesa shook her head sadly. "It could never have worked," she said. "I am a de Vere and used to the very best of all things. Expensive living, expensive jewellery, expensive clothes and pampered to extreme. Look at me!" she said holding out her arms. "If I had married you, I would have bankrupted you within a year. I couldn't do that to you. I care too much about you to do that." She paused a moment. "Payn on the other hand is a wealthy and generous man. He can indulge me in all things. And__," she added. He is Lord Bedford and as his wife I have the title too."

"Lady Bedford." Ardron mocked.

"Indeed," she said. But__," she added going on sympathetically, "We can still enjoy our little trysts whenever the opportunity arises."

Ardron stared at her. "You would make a cuckolder of me?"

"Why not? In truth you are a better lover then he and, if it were not for the circumstances of wealth, then it is with you I would prefer to be."

"Are you serious?"

"I am," she said firmly. "So, you see, you are really no worse off than you were before. You will still enjoy my special favours," she added leaning forward and placing a consoling hand on his knee.

Ardron set his face grimly, twisted the de Vere ring on his finger before slipping it off. Lifting her hand, he placed the ring in her palm.

More raucous laughter from over in the corner, and this time, for some unaccountable reason, one of their group had up ended his beer mug over his own head. This was too much for the inn keeper who now started to demand that they all leave.

For a few moments Rohesa stared down at the ring then asked. "What does this mean?"

"You should give it to your husband," he said. She stared back at him. "Now you should go, he is waiting for you," he said, then turned back to stare into the fire embers.

"You don't mean it," she said.

"I do."

She stood to go, "Take the ring back, we can still have what we had before."

He glanced up at her and saw the tears that filled her eyes. She meant it, that much was obvious. Then he realised that it had always been her plan to take the best of both situations.

"I will keep it close to me," she said with a voice that quivered. "When you want it back you need only ask." She stayed looking down on him, waiting for his response.

Ardron didn't look up. Instead he picked up the poker and began to disturb the hot ashes in the fire.

She waited and waited for Ardron to react, but silent he stayed. Realising that his mind was set and therefore the conversation ended, she turned slowly and sadly walked away.

By this time, the inn keeper had the rowdy revellers outside the door, and as he slid the heavy bolts into place one of the maids walked around the tavern snuffing out the candles. When all were extinguished except the candelabra on the inglenook above Ardron's head, she hesitated.

"What about that one?" Ardron heard her ask the innkeeper.

"Leave it," the innkeeper replied.

"What about him? She then asked.

"We'll leave him too."

***

Devizes Castle, Christmas Day

Once again it had been a lavish feast. They had dined on an array of meat and fish dishes, wild boar, venison, mutton, salmon and pike. There was the usual exotic presentation of swan and peacock finished off with sweet and savoury tarts. Now laid before him Ardron looked down on a roast apple stuffed with dried grapes and honey.

"It costs an enormous amount to continually patrol my western border against the marauding Welsh." Ranulf Earl of Chester bemoaned. "I am forced yet again to increase the fiefs on my villeins. And heaven above knows, it is plenty high enough already." He shook his head ruefully. "We need more rewards from our leaders." He looked accusingly up the room towards the royalty at the top table.

Ardron shrugged non-committal. "I am told that money and resources are tight," he replied. Truthfully, he had little sympathy for the man who he estimated to be wealthy enough to bear the costs personally, without loading extra burdens on his villeins.

"I doubt the truth of that," Ranulf retorted.

Ardron set his jaw firmly without replying, and wondered how, and who, had made the seating arrangements that had placed him next to Earl Chester. His place at the top table it seems he had lost, but only just. He was still close enough to consider himself well regarded.

"Take your situation for instance," Ranulf went on. "You were at Lincoln. You were at Winchester. Your rescue of the Empress from Oxford Castle is legendary. Yet here you are in knight's service to my father-in-law and the castellan of a modest estate only. Seems like poor reward to me, you could have expected better."

"I am content," Ardron replied with a shrug as he cut a slice from the apple.

"Content?" Ranulf poked a finger pointing across the room at Patric de Evereux. "How can you be content when that man there is granted an earldom for simply trading his sister to Fitzgilbert? Funds were found to finance that deal," he said making the point. "Did you know that he was at Lincoln, both him and his brother William?"

Ardron frowned. "No, I didn't," he said.

"No, you wouldn't," Ranulf said. "He was for King Stephen that day, but he soon retreated back to Wiltshire when the battle turned. Yet my father-in-law now grants him a title. But it is a title that is likely to disappear if the king should win the war. So, if Earl Salisbury wants to stay Earl Salisbury, he will have to commit fully to Empress Maude's cause. So, in that respect, it was a good deal for the cause, a good deal for him and a good deal for Fitzgilbert." He paused and smirked "Not so for the wench, I fancy," he went on. "Can you imagine how she feels waking up every morning to see Cyclops and his disfigured face close by?"

"I was at Wherwell with him when he got that disfigured face," Ardron replied quietly.

There was no time for Ranulf to reply because they were interrupted when William de Roumare intruded. "Ranulf I would speak with you," he said leaning over.

"What is it now brother?" Ranulf said getting to his feet. Ardron turned and watched with some relief as William led his younger brother away. Ranulf's wife, Maud, leaned over and touched his hand lightly.

"Sir Ardron," she said. "I do hope that my husband is not irritating you. It seems that these days he is not happy unless he complains."

"Not at all," Ardron lied for the sake of politeness.

She paused looking up towards the elite on the top table then said thoughtfully. "Do you think that my father looks a little tired?"

Ardron looked over to where Earl Robert sat. In truth, he agreed that he did look a little weary, however, he replied, consolingly, "I think he looks fine." He waited a moment. "No Prince Henry here today?" he posed the statement as a question.

"No__," Maud almost drawled. "I believe he is back in France with his father. Perhaps he will return in the spring."

"Perhaps," he nodded agreement without further comment. His eyes then strayed down the table to where Rohesa's sat with her husband and just for a moment they looked at each other. Then she looked away coyly. Aware that he still watched, she deliberately touched the elbow of her husband with a trace of a smile upon her lips. Ardron knew he was being teased. He sighed quietly, then looked around for distraction. The distraction was immediate and from an unexpected source.

"Sir Ardron," Robert Fitzedith said leaning over his shoulder. "We have something important we wish to discuss with you. Is it convenient?"

Of course it was convenient. It was more or less an instruction. "Lead on Sir Robert," he said getting to his feet.

Fitzedith led the way out from the room and up the stone steps to a small chamber. Inside the candle-lit room Reginald de Dunstanville sat at a small table with Sir Roger Fitzmiles at his side.

"Sit there," Fitzedith invited Ardron to take a seat. before he went and sat opposite alongside the other two. Ardron took the seat appraising the situation as he did, this must be important. Facing him were two bastard sons of King Henry, both half-brothers to the empress, and Roger Fitzmiles, son of Miles Fitzwalter. Now a lead Angevin general. As he sat down some movement over to his right, in the window bay, caught his attention. In the gloom, and seemingly, taking no part in this meeting he saw Humphry de Bohun. He nodded a brief acknowledgement to Ardron.

"We have something of a dilemma, de Dunstanville began. "We hope you can help us with."

"I am at your service," Ardron replied dutifully

436

De Dunstanville nodded then gathered his thoughts, perhaps, wondering how best to explain the dilemma. "You know, I suppose, that Phillip Fitzrobert is, at his father's instruction, building a castle at Faringdon on Faringdon Hill."

"I had heard so," Ardron affirmed.

"Well__. The Empress has declared that you should be made its Castellan. She thinks that you have not been rewarded adequately for her Oxford rescue."

Ardron was both surprised and elated. Another castle estate would double his income, perhaps even more than double. And the prestige that would go with it, would promote him amongst the elite of the Angevin cause. "I would be greatly honoured," he said.

"Not so fast," de Dunstanville said. "Earl Robert has commissioned its building and his son Phillip is building it. Therefore, when it is finished, he is of the opinion that Phillip should be its castellan."

Ardron's hopes were dashed. "He would have a point," he admitted nodding slowly. Silence protracted before Ardron added. "I am in knights service to Earl Robert, therefore, whatever he commands of me I will do."

"We hoped you would see it that way," Fitzmiles spoke for the first time.

"But here is the dilemma," de Dunstanville said. "You cannot refuse the empress's offer on the grounds that Sir Robert commands you. That would, seemingly, proclaim that the earl's instructions over-rule hers. She is after all the empress."

"I see," said Ardron. "If I refuse the post the empress is offended. If I accept the earl is displeased."

"Exactly," de Dunstanville announced with some relief. "We hoped you would understand. The last thing we want is disharmony between Empress Maude and Earl Robert,"

"What do you want me to do?" Ardron asked.

"There is the crux of our dilemma. We don't know! We have to find a solution that will not upset either."

Ardron spread his arms shaking his head in confusion.

Fitzmiles leaned forward. "We need you to find a very believable reason why you would refuse the promotion."

"How?"

De Dunstanville shook his head. "We need you to think on the matter. The castle will not be finished for some months yet, so you have time to consider. For our part, we also agree that you did not get enough of a reward for your actions. So, we intend to look around to see if we can find an alternative promotion for you. A promotion that will be acceptable to you, and at the same time satisfy her Majesty. That would leave young Phillip as castellan of Faringdon as his father wishes."

That seemed like a solution to Ardron. And perhaps he would still get a promotion of some sort in the end.

"Are you enjoying the feast?" Fitzedith asked, indicating also that the discussion was closed.

"Very much so," Ardron lied diplomatically.

"Come," de Bohun said as he emerged from the shadows. "I will walk down with you."

De Bohun led the way down the narrow twisting stairs, and it was not until they reached the bottom he spoke. But first he glanced around furtively to see if he would be over-heard.

"If the empress offers you Faringdon you should take it," he said.

Ardron stared at him more than a little surprised.

"A castle at Faringdon will be more than just strategically important, it will be vital. The loss of Oxford was something of a disaster, it left an open route right into the west. But a castle at Faringdon will in effect put a gate across that route. King Stephen will know that, and he must try to move it."

"You think the king will attack Faringdon?" Ardron asked.

"I'd bet my estates on it."

"Perhaps the gift of Faringdon is something of a poison chalice," Ardron said.

"Undoubtedly there will be a struggle, but it is essential that it stands. If the king were to take Faringdon as well, then he will be close enough to almost piss over us."

"Philip Fitzrobert is his father's son and bred as a fighter like his father.," Ardron said.

De Bohun scoffed. "I don't think he has his father's characteristics,"

"He did alright at Malmesbury," Ardron said.

"At Malmesbury he wasn't tested," de Bohun replied.

"But at Tetbury," Ardron countered. "He stood against the king until his father came."

"Stood against the king? He wasn't even there," de Bohun said with derision.

"He wasn't there? Ardron was puzzled.

"No, he wasn't. Fitzedith smuggled him away to his other castle in Cricklade, fearing that if he were to fall into the king's hands then Earl Robert would have to dance to Stephen's tune."

"That would seem like a sensible tactic to me." Ardron responded.

De Bohun snorted with derision. "Picture a situation," he said with a sigh. "The king instead of attacking Tetbury came to Norwood with the intention of seizing you along with your castle. Now picture that situation where I came to your aid with re-enforcements. Now picture that same situation where I suggest you retreat to Trowbridge Castle and leave me to defend your property." He paused for effect. "Would you go?" he asked.

"No," Ardron replied resoundingly.

"No, you wouldn't. But Fitzrobert did. And he will do the same when the king comes to Faringdon."

"Surely Earl Robert would soon come to his son's aid."

"Aye, I expect he would," de Bohun said. "But could he get there in time?" He paused. "No, it will need someone with a lot more backbone to be the castellan of Faringdon. Someone proven, like you. Those three, back there can't see it," he said jerking his thumb over his shoulder.

"And Earl Robert?" Ardron asked.

De Bohun shook his head sadly. "It would seem that he has a blind spot when it comes to his youngest son. Either he can't see, or doesn't want to see, the weaknesses in that boy. You take Faringdon if it's offered to you. For the good of the cause as well as for your own benefit, take it." He pushed open the door into the great hall. "Think on, my friend," he said as he walked in.

He had given Ardron much to think on. He could understand the strategic importance of Faringdon, and if de Bohun was right, and there was every reason to believe he was, it would be a tough and dangerous assignment. He wasn't even sure he wanted it now!

"Sir Humphrey," he called after him.

De Bohun stopped and waited.

"What happened to the Grey Wolf outlaws?" he asked.

"Hanged every one of them."

"Every one?"

"Yes. Cousin Patric made a spectacle of it. Hanging five every day until there was only Grey Wolf left."

Ardron stood silent.

"He was the last one to die." De Bohun added.

Ardron nodded a little sadly. A bad ending for the man he had saved in the battle of turnips. There was of course still the question of his son, Adelfrid, and a promise made.

The celebrations were becoming noisy and lively with a minstrel cavorting and singing bawdy songs. But the festivities had no attraction for him. He decided to leave.

***

Norwood

"You have an irate village elder waiting to see you," Luc said holding the horse's reins as Ardron halted at the foot of the mote.

"An irate village elder?" he queried as he dismounted.

"Yes Sir. Calls himself Rothgar.

"Is he alone?"

"No, he arrived Christmas Eve with Adelfrid.

"Where are they now?

"Rothgar waits in the main hall. Adelfrid I have put into one of the cells."

Ardron nodded approval, as he handed the reins over to Jacques. "Tend the horses," he instructed. "What exactly is he irate about," he asked Luc.

"Because I wouldn't release the girl and her brother without your permission."

"I see," Ardron replied.

"Did I do right?" Luc asked.

"You did," Ardron affirmed. "Have him, the girl Edwina, and her brother attend me in the council chamber, if you please."

"Adelfrid?"

"Leave him where he is."

He ascended the steps into the keep. This day it had been a cold and bleak journey back from Devizes to Norwood. The conversation with his squire Jacques had been limited. He had much to think on. The Faringdon situation was a real conundrum. Vitally important strategically, but so very obviously perilous. Whilst the castellan position brought increase in both status and wealth, it might be a position precarious, and any advantages ending as an illusion. On the other hand, if successfully held against the inevitable royalist attack, the benefits would be enormous. His concentration was not absolute, however. His thoughts continually strayed over to his huge disappointment over Rohesa.

In his private chamber he found that Hildi had already laid out a casual change of clothing for him. He wriggled out of the heavy hauberk, just letting it drop to the floor. He thought to pick it up but then just left it where it lay. Hildi would clear up behind him! Just for a moment he considered just how much he would miss her dutiful attentions when she left for France with Luc. Undoubtedly, he would miss both of them. He pulled on the red tunic and using a long belt gathered it about his waist. It was time to face the irate village elder Rothgar.

He walked into the chamber to find the three Saxon villagers already waiting. He strode past the trio to where Luc and Maurice waited at the end of the room. After he settled in his large imposing seat, he took stock of the three villagers. Rothgar stood at the point, a stern expression betraying his mood. The other two flanked him a pace or so behind.

"Good day to you Rothgar," Ardron said. "I trust you have been well attended in my absence."

"Not the point," Rothgar responded angrily. "We have languished here two days waiting to be released. Your word was that these youngsters would be released within one hour of delivering Adelfrid. Is it that your word is not worth the spit in a man's mouth to utter the words?"

"Have a care Rothgar," Ardron warned in a low voice leaning forward. "You are in my domain now." He allowed some moments silence for the man's temper to ease. "The timing of your arrival was unfortunate, in-as-much that I was summoned to be elsewhere," he went on. "My constable here did what he thought was right and proper. And his action, I approve." He took a deep breath and leaned back in the chair. "You may leave this very minute if you wish," he said. "However, I would point out that the day wears down and you can never make it to Boks before nightfall. A night under the stars at this time of year can be harsh. I would advise that you take advantage of our hospitality for one more night and leave first thing in the morning."

"We'll leave right away," Rothgar affirmed still an edge of anger in his reply.

"As you wish!" Ardron replied turning to Luc.

"Wait!" Harold, Edwina's brother, spoke up. A whispered conversation then started among the three villagers. Ardron waited patiently glancing once up at Luc who gave a slight shrug. The discussion eventually settled, Rothgar moved away staring dubiously at the other two before turning back to face Ardron.

"Sir," he said with more contrition in his voice. "We have decided to accept your gracious offer."

"Sensible," Ardron responded. "And tomorrow I will provide you with a sergen escort of Saxons."

"What of Adelfrid" Rothgar asked.

Adelfrid? He stays here," Ardron replied. "I have a message of a personal nature to deliver." He paused. "Also, that young man has questions to answer on the murder of three of my villeins. One a mere boy of ten." Obviously surprised, Rothgar stared back with belligerence. Ardron thought he was about to protest, but under his harsh gaze Rothgar thought better of it.

He did not rise early the next morning, indeed did not rise until mass was over, and then took breakfast in his room. Many thoughts occupied his mind and at the forefront was Faringdon. In the end he decided that he had no need to mull on it, at least until the offer was made. If indeed the offer was made. Then there was the boy outlaw in one of his cells, Adelfrid. If it was confirmed that he was guilty of hanging three then what should his sentence be? The only sentence would of course be to hang also. That would, however, renege on his promise to Welfwulf. He thought to put off the interrogation for another day, but that was only avoiding the issue. Better get it over with this very day, he decided.

Later that afternoon he assembled a small board of four. In addition to himself, Luc, as castle constable, Maurice as constable in waiting and Swidhurn as a Saxon representative and a valued voice of reason. Adelfrid was brought in, sandwiched between Pique and Roland, his wrists and ankles in chains. The proceedings he intended to conduct in English anticipating that perhaps Adelfrid's French was not good. Luc, he knew, would understand what was said, but Maurice would perhaps struggle a little. Nevertheless, in fairness to the boy he just had no choice.

He looked up from his notes and studied the young man. More than five years had passed since last he had seen Adelfrid, and the change was remarkable. He had grown tall and straight with wide shoulders and a man's beard clipped tidy. So marked was the change, that if he didn't know that this was he, before him, then he doubted that he would have recognised him.

"Adelfrid? You are Adelfrid son of Welfwulf?" he said.

"I am," he replied confidently.

"Do you remember me?"

"Of course," he said.

"Do you know why you are here?"

"No, I do not! I was told that I should present myself here, Edwina would then be released, and I would hear a message from my father." He spoke confidently, with a little edge of pique in his reply. He held up the chains. "I didn't expect this," he said.

"No, I suppose you didn't, Ardron said. "I will tell you why you are here. Around eighteen months ago there was a raid upon my estate. Three raids in fact. In each raid villeins were made to draw straws, and the one who drew the shortest was hanged. Three were hung that day. One of which was a boy of ten." He paused studying Adelfrid's face; he was obviously taken aback. "I have reason to believe that you, in fact, led those raids."

"No! Wait a moment," he said concerned and perhaps feeling that he was already judged. "I remember the raids. They were reprisals for your own similar actions some days before."

"My action was against outlaws. Those beyond the protection of laws," Ardron replied. "The outlaw reprisals were against law abiding people." He waited. "Did you or didn't you lead those raids? Think carefully before you answer, young man and be aware that after speaking with your father I already know the answer."

Now he was not so confident. "Sir," he said. "It was all a mistake. An error right at the very beginning, and from there it got worse. After that it all went beyond my control."

"Of course it did," Ardron replied sarcastically.

"It did. Sir, it did." Adelfrid almost pleaded.

Ardron nodded. "Better you try to explain your actions."

"My father had a plan. A good plan that would get landowners to pay us to leave their estates alone. But first we needed to terrorise those estates before offering the deal. And it worked."

"I know all that," Ardron replied impatiently.

"Aware of the dept my father owed you, his strictest order was that your estate be exempt from any attacks." he quickly went on. "However, whether twas deliberate, or accident, William the Fletcher and a small band did raid your estate. You gave chase, caught up with the band, killed one and hung another. The rest, including Will, were humiliated and sent on their way with a warning message."

"I know all that too," Ardron said.

"At first my father was furious that he had been disobeyed," Adelfrid went on regardless. However, when the hanging was revealed he then came under enormous pressure from all others to do something. So__, bowing to pressure, he agreed to remove the protection from your estate and just to show your vulnerability he organised the triple raids. For those raids he did place me in charge. But at no stage did he suggest, or sanction, retaliating hangings."

"Are you saying that the hangings were on your orders?" Ardron interrupted.

"No Sir, I did not suggest it, nor did I approve it. It was William the Fletcher's idea, a suggestion at the campfire the night before the raids. It would be a fitting revenge, he said. The others were for it and the idea was keenly accepted. My counter orders were ignored. I was disregarded." He spread his arms in hopeless appeal. "What could I do? At that point I was no longer in control. Command had been taken from me, simply by them all wilfully disregarding my instructions. William had assumed control. I could do nothing."

Ardron was thoughtful. He could see how a mere callow youth might have trouble establishing authority when all were against him. "Is this true?" he asked dubiously.

"Yes, Sir. I swear by God."

Luc scoffed noisily. "Sir," he said. "It would seem on that day we hung the wrong man."

Ardron nodded agreement. "It would seem so," he said. He turned his attention back to Adelfrid, he was not yet fully convinced. "Go on."

Adelfrid licked his lips nervously. "When I reported to my father what had happened, he was furious and expelled William from the camp. Then trying to put right the wrong, he ordered all the contraband be returned."

He paused a moment. "Sir__," he said. "We did not know that a boy of ten was hanged."

Luc leaned forward again. "That would account for the returned stock a couple of days later, he muttered." Ardron nodded agreement.

"Then explain this young man," Ardron said leaning back in his chair. "If William Fletcher was expelled from the camp, how then was it that I saw him there and indeed questioned him?"

Adelfrid was stunned. "He was expelled, he was." He beseeched. "For a number of weeks he was." There was desperation in his explanation. "One day he came back pleading forgiveness. Eventually, he convinced my father that he was sorry and promised that he would be more obedient in the future. So, my father gave him a second chance."

Ardron studied him a few moments then asked, "Where is this William Fletcher now?"

"He was sent to Salisbury along with the others," Adelfrid replied. "Hanged I suppose."

"Little good that second chance did him," Swidhurn commented sardonically.

Ardron had heard Adelfrid's story but wasn't sure whether he should be believed or not. If it were true that the decision to kill had been taken out of his control, then there were mitigating circumstances. On the other hand, it seemed he had blamed people who were no longer available to contradict his story. He was thoughtful a moment, then decided to hear other opinions. "Return him to his cell." He instructed Pique and Roland.

He waited while Luc translated to Maurice what had been said. It seemed, however, that Maurice had understood most of it. He leaned back and looked at the others questioningly. "How much of that do you believe?" He asked, but no one offered a ready opinion. "Luc?" he prompted.

Luc squirmed a little looking a bit uncomfortable. "Well__," he said after a long sigh. "He seems plausible. But even if he did not order the killings, nor could stop it, he was, nevertheless, present. Guilty by association. He should hang."

"He couldn't have been present at all three." Swidhurn countered. Outnumbered and a mere stripling of tender years, I can't see how he could have stopped it."

"We have no evidence, other than his word, that he was actually against it," Luc said.

"No, Swidhurn agreed. "But then we have no evidence that he was for it either."

Ardron nodded agreement, both men were right. "Maurice?" he sought his opinion.

"If we say not guilty and let him go. We could be setting a killer free. If we say guilty and hang the boy, we could be killing an innocent," he replied in halting English.

"And there we have the dilemma," Ardron said with a sigh. "It was Welfwulf's last wish that his son gives up the outlaw life and return to his brother in Newbury and there a farmer be."

"To be a farmer or hang?" I know which I would choose if I had the choice." Luc said.

"That, however, is not the question." Ardron said. "Was he complicit in the guilt or just a helpless by-stander?"

"Whichever. How much more guilty is he than others?" Swidhurn asked. "There are high ranking barons in exalted positions of influence that have done deeds much worse. Earl Chester! Did he not pillage and rob his own citizens at Lincoln? And the king himself is he not guilty of mass death and destruction at both Winchcombe, Winchester and Malmesbury? Even our own Earl Robert, did mercilessly raze Worcester to the ground." He paused a moment. "It seems to me that we have stared into a castle shit-pit, swarming with rats, and pointed at one and said. 'There, that little one over there. We will punish that one."

His words were greeted with stony silence. Ardron turned to look at the others waiting for some reaction. Eventually, it was Luc who spoke sucking in a noisy breath and nodding as he did. "He's right," he said then added a shrug.

"But," Maurice spoke. "We cannot just let him go without some punishment. We could just turn him over to Earl Salisbury and excuse ourselves from this dilemma."

"That would be a death penalty for certain," Ardron said. "Patric de Evereux would hang him without compunction." He paused a moment. "But, Maurice, you are right, there must be retribution of some sort."

"You could simply make him a slave and take him in service to the castle." Luc suggested.

Ardron leaned back in his chair the idea had some merit. "Hmm," he said thoughtfully stroking his beard. "I will consider on that," he muttered. "Perhaps a slave with a prospect of release when appropriate."

"A slave?" Swidhurn screwed up his face in doubt. "He is a young man. Strong and quick. He might well make a break for freedom the first chance he gets."

Ardron smiled ruefully. "It seems there are impediments to every alternative," he said. His fingers tapped the table as he thought. "Thank you, friends," he eventually said. "It seems the final decision has to be mine. "

It was mid-morning immediately after Mass the next day when Ardron went to see Adelfrid in his cell. He found him sitting on the ground his knees bent up to his chest seemingly an abject of misery. The gaoler's keys rattled noisily as he unlocked the door to let him in. Adelfrid started to get to his feet but Ardron waved a nonchalant hand. "Stay there," he said.

From somewhere the gaoler produced an empty cider cask and after brushing off the top with his sleeve placed it on the ground for Ardron to sit on. Nodding his gratitude, Ardron took the seat. Then waited until the gaoler had left re-locking the cell as he did. For a few moments both men silently stared at each other. Adelfrid's silence due to apprehension and anticipation, while Ardron's not sure how to start.

"Well young man," he said eventually. "We are completely undecided what to do with you." He paused for effect. "As an outlaw, we should have you hung! And we might do yet," he added. "It will all depend on these next few minutes." Adelfrid's expression brightened as a glimmer of hope was born. "We could," Ardron went on, "Commit you to slavery. You have no rights you are still an outlaw."

Sir," Adelfrid said. "Slavery is preferable to hanging."

"Yes, I dare say it is," Ardron replied. "However, before he was sent to Salisbury, your father asked a favour of me and that was: that I find you and to give you a message. That message was, that I should deliver you to your brother in Newbury, and there you were to become a farmer. That was his last wish for you." He waited for that to sink in.

"A farmer is even better than slavery," he said.

"Aye it is," Ardron agreed. "However, before we decide on that I need to be sure that you do not revert to outlaw ways."

"I can only give you my word," Adelfrid said.

Ardron stroked his beard thoughtfully rolling his eyes upward. "Setting that aside for the moment," he said. "What would be your preference if I were to set you free?"

"First, I would go to Rathgar and ask his permission to settle in Boks. Then I would take the maid Edwina as my wife. After that I would strive to become a good husband, and a valued villager," he replied without hesitation.

"It would seem that you have thought on this."

"I have. Sir. And for a long time. Even before the quarry was attacked."

"What about your father's wishes?" Ardron asked.

"It would seem that my father's main intention was for me to give up the outlaw life, and that is what I would be doing."

Ardron nodded agreement. "How old are you?"

"Nineteen, Sir."

"Plenty of life to come, he muttered. "Unless of course I have you hung."

"Yes, sir," Adelfrid replied softly.

"Are you repentant on those hangings?"

Sir, I am." he replied. "Though I was powerless to stop it. And I wasn't at the killing of the boy. I knew nothing of it," he added shaking his head.

Ardron was thoughtful for a few moments then his mind made up he said. "Very well. I will take a chance that you will mend your outlaw ways. But I will have you watched, and if you should play me false then I will find you. And if I have to come and find you, then my retribution will be mercilessly horrendous, and terrible to behold. A hanging death will seem pleasant in comparison."

Adelfrid sunk to his knees and kissed Ardron's fingers. "I will be your true servant onto death," he said.

"Gaoler!" Ardron called. "Open the door." Then helping Adelfrid to his feet he said. "Young sir, you may go."

Chapter 19

Bristol Castle, April 1145

Standing atop of the castle tower, Ardron gazed out over the urban sprawl of uneven dwellings that was Bristol. However, it was not the myriad of abodes nor its wide substantial harbour snaking through its very middle, or even the array of ships at anchor there, that was his interest. His eyes instead, were turned towards the heavens and to the night sky. His object of fascination was the Tituli Star. Glowing with a lustrous iridescence of white whilst trailing in its wake a wide track of shimmering silver, this star moved almost imperceptibly across the sky, contrasting vividly against its inky blackness as it did. For more than a week, from dusk onto dawn, this phenomenon of astronomy, had been clearly visible, causing elements of fear among the superstitious. With almost thirty years stretching behind him Ardron had never seen its like before. He had, however, listened to accounts by village elders of its rare and unwelcomed appearances.

The sighting of the Tituli Star was, for the Saxon populace a portent of doom. For the Norman's, however, it was the complete opposite. The last sighting was reported to have been in 1066, and to William of Normandy it was interpreted as a message from God that he should cross the channel and claim that which Edward the Confessor had promised him, the English throne. Motivated by the star's appearance, Earl Gloucester had convened a meeting to discuss and arrange a re-vitalised summer campaign against King Stephen.

"Tis a sight to see!" a voice behind him muttered. He turned to see John Fitzgilbert standing behind him. "Even with one eye," Fitzgilbert added with an ironic grin.

Ardron turned back to look at the star again. "Yes, it is," he agreed.

"It's a good omen," Fitzgilbert said. "It was for William of Normandy and it will be for our Empress."

"Not for Harold Godwin it wasn't," Ardron replied.

"No, it wasn't," Fitzgilbert agreed. "But that was because it was, he who was the usurper. As is Stephen of Blois."

No Saxon would ever agree that King Harold was the usurper, but not wishing to be contradictory Ardron let that go. "Let us hope you are right," he said instead, "God knows we need some successes to bring this wretched war to a successful end."

"Amen to that," Fitzgilbert agreed.

For a few moments both men were silent watching the spectacle in the sky before Fitzgilbert spoke. "Scorrenstone," he said. "I know what is being planned. And as far as I am concerned in a fight there is no man, I would rather have at my side than you. I would be much obliged to you, if you can work your preference to get yourself assigned to my force."

Ardron stared at him quizzically. "Can you tell me what is being planned?"

Fitzgilbert shook his head. "I can say no more," he said. "I might already have said too much. But you will find out soon enough. Just bear in mind what I ask."

"Alright," Ardron said dubiously. "There is a condition though."

"What is that?"

"It's time you started calling me Ardron or Norwood."

Fitzgilbert grinned broadly. "I'll try to remember," he said.

Activity below inside the bailey caught the attention of both men. They leaned forward for a better view. Amid bustle and shouted instructions, guards hastened to open the main gate. When it was, a party of around two dozen riders rode in.

Oh good!" Fitzgilbert muttered more to himself. "Phillip Fitzrobert! Tomorrow," he said turning away, "Plans can be finalised."

Ardron stared after Fitzgilbert a few moments watching him walk away. No explanation would be forthcoming, and so with a slight shrug he turned back to watch the Tituli Star.

It was just after noon the next day, when all knights and barons were summoned into the great hall. Empress Maude sat somewhat aloof on a highchair, with her half-brother Earl Gloucester standing at her side. Fitzgilbert was prominent also, standing close by, but a step or two down.

Empress Maude opened the proceedings with a welcoming address and an expression of gratitude for all the continued support. She continued with rhetoric on the legality of Prince Henry, her son, on his right to the English crown. She was patently gratified when she received noisy support. Then it was the earl's turn to add more rhetoric, before he got to the real reason of the assembly, the plans for a re-vitalised campaign against King Stephen.

The plan, initially, was to raise a large army to relieve Wallingford. Since the fall of Oxford Brien Fitzcount at Wallingford had come under consistent attacks from William de Chesney, the Oxford Castellan. These regular raids attacked and pillaged villages and homesteads on the estate, even onto laying short sieges upon the castle itself. These sieges served a double purpose, whilst the castle inmates were locked inside, then the estate could be robbed and pillaged at leisure.

The Angevin plan was to split the raised army, when assembled, with half under Fitzgilbert's command at Marlborough and half under Fitzrobert at Faringdon. When de Chesney ventured out to attack Wallingford, he would find himself being pursued and attacked by the force from

Marlborough, whilst the force at Faringdon would attack a weakened Oxford and cause wide-spread devastation. If de Chesney, then decided to turn his attention to Faringdon the force at Marlborough would attack the attackers, whilst Fitzcount's own force would attack Oxford. It seemed therefore a reasonable assumption, that de Chesney would soon learn to keep his forces within his boundary to protect his own interests. However, the flaw in the plan was Faringdon. The castle was not yet complete. Earl Robert, however, assured all that although not yet complete, it would still be defendable. Particularly so because it would not have to stand very long before aid arrived.

"What of King Stephen?" someone asked.

"Stephen spends most of his time at Winchester," the earl replied. "We anticipate that he might attack John Fitzgilbert's castle at Ludgershall to relieve the pressure on de Chesny. However," he went on. "There is a pact between Patric, Earl Salisbury and Sir John which establishes one will aid the other in such an event. It was not lost on Ardron, that Fitzgilbert having wed Sybil de Evereux, Patric's sister, could count on his support. A pact that guaranteed an alliance, where once there had been aggravation.

The plans now described only the detailing remained and the pledges of numbers. Ardron found himself assigned to Fitzgilbert's strength without having to make any request. He assumed that Fitzgilbert had influenced that decision, it seemed likely. Because he had only a modest estate and this campaign might be a long one, he was reluctant to pledge too many sergens to the taskforce. To his relief his offer of just two score was accepted without cavil.

***

Wallingford, June 1145

Fitzgilbert's force of around two hundred breasted the hill opposite Wallingford Castle. It was from this high ground vantage that Fitzgilbert had intended to use his archers to rain sheets of arrows down upon William de Chesney's siege force. However, were it not for a few locals going about their mundane chores. the meadow below would have been deserted.

"Looks as if the quarry has flown," Reginald de Dunstanville said cynically, leaning forward onto his horse's withers.

"It would seem so," Fitzgilbert agreed.

Ardron was first to spot the small company of horsemen exiting the castle starting in their direction. "There, my Lord," he said pointing.

De Dunstanville raised his right hand to his face shading his eyes from the low sun. "They sport the red and white Fitzcount banner," he said.

"And I do believe," he added after a short pause. "My Lord Brien is riding with them."

"Then let us go to meet him," Fitzgilbert replied. "Wait here," he said over his shoulder to his captain of horse then added. "You may stand the men down." After glancing at Ardron he said. "Come Scorrenstone, join us." as he spurred his horse forward.

"Norwood," Ardron rectified almost inaudibly before urging Rattlebone after the two men.

At the bottom of the hill, they crossed the shallow brook and moved across the meadow at an easy canter towards the castle. Reining in as both parties met, they greeted each other by exchanging polite salutations.

"You're too late," Fitzcount declared. "Sometime during the night, they withdrew."

In response Fitzgilbert heaved a heavy sigh and shook a rueful head. "We should not have halted over-night," he bemoaned.

It had been late afternoon three days previously, when word had been received that de Chesney had once more laid siege to Wallingford. Early the next day Fitzgilbert had led his force towards Wallingford, travelling in excess of twenty-five miles to arrive at Dudecota in the early evening. Within four miles of Wallingford he had, nevertheless, chose to rest his troops rather than press on. Deciding, not unreasonably, that it would be better to attack this morning with troops that were fresh. That delay now seemed to have been a mistake.

"They must have received warning that we were close," de Dunstanville suggested.

"Aye," Fitzgilbert agreed.

"What now?" de Dunstanville asked.

"We go after them." Fitzgilbert replied.

"We won't catch them!"

"Perhaps not. But at least we can chase then back inside their own perimeters." Fitzgilbert replied. "By all the saints," he then cursed. "They have the luck of the devil."

"Maybe not such a disaster," Ardron ventured. "We go after them and we will have chased them back. If Phillip Fitzrobert has done his job, then a corner of Oxford will have been attacked and pillaged. It's still a considerable cost to de Chesney."

"He's right," Brien Fitzcount agreed.

"He is," de Dunstanville endorsed.

"Gentlemen. Take breakfast with us before you leave," Fitzcount offered.

"May as well," Fitzgilbert allowed grudgingly. "We're not likely to catch em now."

Ardron surmised that if de Chesney had retreated back to Oxford during the night, then in so doing, he could have passed within less than two miles to the north of Fitzgilbert while they rested at Dudecota. Not a comfortable thought. But he kept that conclusion to himself.

It was almost two hours later, when the half-hearted pursuit began. In no particular hurry they casually followed the tracks of de Chesney's force until insight of Abingdon. It was here, and well inside the Oxford estate, that Fitzgilbert called off the pursuit. After a short rest, for the horses benefit, and in the early part of the afternoon, they headed south west back to Marlborough. There was a general air of anti-climax among the upper echelon of the force, but Ardron saw it differently. They had successfully lifted the siege of Wallingford, shepherded the de Chesney force back to Oxford and all achieved without a single casualty.

It took only three weeks before de Chesny retaliated against Phillip Fitzrobert and attacked Faringdon. Once again, Fitzgilbert assembled his force and set off to relieve Faringdon. The early morning start, and at a forced pace, saw them cover the seventeen miles in quick time and close in on the target by early afternoon.

Working to a pre-plan, and just out of sight of the castle, Fitzgilbert split his forces sending Ardron south of the town. He was to advance northwards through the town and approach the castle from its south. With the remaining force, under the command of Reginald de Dunstanville, Fitzgilbert planned to attack the de Chesney siege force direct from the east.

At the head of a force of around twelve dozen, Ardron breasted a bluff south of the town and took a few moments to study the landscape. Faringdon was a town like any other, with a multitude of bucolic houses and dwellings. Its significance was that it had been granted market status and as such was perhaps more populated than most. The result being that the dwellings were tightly packed, separated by a myriad of narrow alleyways and streets. Beyond the town and the open common, was the castle itself.

Faringdon Castle was erected atop the high ground known as Faringdon Hill, just north of the town itself. Around the foot of this high circular mound, a deep trench had been excavated with the access across to the main gate via a draw bridge. When raised, as it was now, that drawbridge represented an extra layer of protection to the gate. A stout timber palisade wrapped all the way around the base of the hill, with three stone towers strategically inbuilt. At the hilltop, and although not yet complete, a significant stone-keep dominated not only the whole complex, but well beyond also. To Ardron the castle looked formidable. Obviously, the construction advice tended by William Peverel was a sound investment. If there was a fault, then it was perhaps that the town dwellings were situated close enough to be comfortably within the range of archers, while at the same time providing them cover. Ardron accepted, however, it wasn't possible to move the hill, and maybe once the castle was completed those dwellings would then be razed.

His immediate problem was to advance through the town along all those narrow passages and streets. Hopefully, the townspeople would stand off, and not interfere. Even so, it was probably infested with de Chesney's siege troops. Once in among that complex then it would become each man for himself, because within that maze, it would be impossible to keep touch with all except the men close by. It would be rugged and bitter hand to hand fighting without knowing where the rest of the troops were.

He glanced along the line spread either side, by now everybody in the town would be aware of their presence. "Dismount," he ordered. Fighting from horse-back in that warren would be awkward. "You will stay here and tend the horses," he instructed Jacques, his young squire. Then satisfied all his sergens were on foot, he lifted his shield, drew his sword and shouted. "God protect you all." Waving his sword, he then pointed it forward and led the advance, at a walk, down towards Faringdon.

They encountered no resistance as they entered the town, indeed the locals had all gone to ground, lowered their shutters and sealed their doors. The resistance came when nearing the opposite end of the town. Ardron found himself in one of the wider streets with about two dozen other Angevins for company. At the opposite end of the street, a similar number barred their way standing with swords drawn ready. A slight hesitation and then the Angevins continued their steady advance. From somewhere within the de Chesney ranks a signal was given, and responding as one, they charged forward shouting, growling and waving swords. There was no time to form a defensive line, they would have to fight hand to hand. "Stand men," there was just time for Ardron to shout before the first charging man was upon him.

He came at him with sword raised high above his right shoulder to send it crashing down upon Ardron. But Ardron had his shield in position and the sword clashed on steel with the reverberating ring of metal on metal. With his sword up, still on Ardron's shield, his lower body was exposed and Ardron thrust his sword beneath the shield jabbing fiercely into the man's mid-rift. The man gasped and staggered backwards. In all probability, the sword had not penetrated his hauberk. Nevertheless, the thrust had done enough to probably puncture and wound the flesh beneath. Either way he was out of the fight, at least for now. Ardron stepped forward to engage the next man. That man came at him in a rush and again Ardron raised his shield this time they clashed shield to shield and for some moments they pushed hard against each other, faces only inches apart. Ardron suddenly stepped back allowing the other man to stumble forward. It was only a step or two but was enough for Ardron to spin around and swing his sword down onto the man's exposed back. He did not have the protection of a hauberk and the blade cut into flesh sending him sprawling to the ground. Ardron stood over him and mercilessly thrust the sword into his back penetrating the kidneys area. Glancing round he saw, close by, another standing over a fallen Angevin. Moving quickly, Ardron engaged before the man had time to deal the death blow. This man was no novice with a sword. For a while it was thrust and parry, parry and thrust as swords clashed sword to sword and sword to shield. Just for an instant Ardron saw an opening, and leaned forward to thrust at the exposure, but the exposure was gone and instead he left his left side open. The other man laid his sword across Ardron's left thigh just below the cover of his hauberk, slicing deep into flesh. Using his elbow, Ardron swung his shield to hit the man hard across the head and shoulder sending him staggering backwards, eventually falling. Tossing his shield aside, Ardron leapt forward and using both hands on his sword he smashed downwards once, twice, three times. Desperately, the man using his elbow tried to shuffle away along the ground whilst forced to parry blows that continuously rained down. His eyes held no fear as he stared upwards dealing capably with the onslaught, but in lifting his head, he opened a narrow gap between the hauberk hood and his chin. Ardron saw it, and quicksilver-like, thrust his sword through the gap and into the man's throat. The shock and surprise in his face was evident. He let out a grunt and a gurgle, then dropping his sword grasped despairingly at his throat. But blood oozed between his fingers as he looked up with astonishment at Ardron. A moment or two later he rolled onto his side to die. No time to think, no time to reason, another was upon him. This time a man with a lance. As he charged and thrust Ardron deftly leapt sideways and used his sword to deflect it away. He then used his fist to punch the man hard in the face as he stumbled past. When he turned to face the man again an arrow thudded into the ground close by. But there was no time to worry about that, the man with the lance was charging again. Yet again, he dodged inside the thrust, but this time he grabbed the shank of the lance and held on to it. Then, with a backhand swipe of his sword he sliced deeply across his face. Someone leapt on to his back and tried with a dagger to cut his throat. But, by God's mercy, Ardron's hauberk resisted the slice. He spun round and round trying frantically to dislodge the man, if he were to change his grip on the dagger and stab instead, then his hauberk might not hold. Suddenly, he was gone, pulled off by one of his own. He spun round to see his rescuer atop the man with his hands around his throat strangling the life out of him. Yet another arrow thudded this time into a wattle wall close by. Taking a moment to investigate, he saw yet another in the sky passing above. Looking round quickly, once more for danger, he was relieved to see the ferociousness of the onslaught was waning. Most of the men around him sported the red arm bands that identified Angevins, and any remaining de Chesney men were withdrawing. Another arrow thudded harmlessly into the roof of a nearby dwelling.

"They are coming from the castle!" The Angevin, who had been his rescuer just moments before, said as he got slowly up from the now the strangled dead man.

"The castle?" Ardron said.

"Aye the castle."

"God's truth," Ardron swore. Then remembering that he might owe this man his life said. "I would know your name, Sir."

"Algernon, Sir Ardron." He replied.

"I owe you my life, Algernon" Ardron said.

"And I owe you mine twice over," he replied.

Ardron frowned not understanding.

"I was with you at Wherwell in that smoke-filled crypt," Algernon said.

"Ah! Then you must be in service to Sir John Fitzgilbert," Ardron said.

"Indeed, I am, Sir."

Ardron nodded and glanced up the road, which was now clear, except for his own men now moving forward. "Let us then see how goes the attack."

They emerged into the clearing between the town and the castle, in time to see de Dunstanville and his men giving chase to the siege force, who now retreated hurriedly away to the west. Glancing along the clearing, he could see men of his force had already emerged from the town ahead of him. Others were still emerging. Either way Faringdon had been cleared of de Chesney sergens.

"Sir, you are wounded!" Algernon said, pointing down at Ardron's leg.

Ardron glanced down. He was right, his whole leg below the wound soaked blood, it was bleeding profusely. "Not too bad," Ardron made light of it. But closer inspection revealed a long and deep gash across the thigh of his left leg. Certainly, it would need stitching and perhaps even cauterizing. 'Perish that thought,' Ardron thought to himself. Ripping the red Angevin cloth from his arm, he used it as a temporary bandage, wrapping it as tight as he could bear. When finished he stood and stamped his leg a couple of times to test the pain level. Bearable, but now it seemed to hurt more than before, it would hold for now. Across the clearing the castle drawbridge was being lowered.

"Let's just see which fool launched those arrows upon us," he muttered more to himself and set off towards the castle with a pronounced limp. He had reached around half-way when he heard approaching horse hooves. He turned half expecting danger. But it was his squire Jacques, mounted, but leading Rattlebone on a halter.

"Sir. Your horse." From somewhere Jacques had found him and brought him his charger

"Good man," Ardron readily approved. To mount he had to use his left leg in the stirrup, causing him to grimace when he hauled himself up and swung his other leg over the saddle.

With Jacques following, he rode through the castle gate and was greeted by loud cheering. Ignoring the accolade, he made straight for the mote.

"Welcome, welcome and welcome again," he was greeted by a Norman knight dressed in a long red and yellow robe standing at the foot of the mote.

"Thank you," Ardron said curtly. Who might you be, Sir?"

"I am Brien de Soulis. Constable of the castle in service to Sir Phillip Fitzrobert."

"Sir Brien." Ardron acknowledged leaning forward onto his horse withers. "Tell me Sir, upon whose order was it to fire arrows into the town?" he demanded.

"Truly sir, that was a mistake." De Soulis replied. "I regret if any of our allies were injured, but we didn't know that Fitzgilbert would advance through the town. As soon as I realised, I ordered it cease immediately." He spread his arms disconsolately. "Confusion of battle, Sir. Confusion of battle!" He lamented.

"Fitzgilbert didn't advance through the town, I did," Ardron replied somewhat piqued

"You are?"

"I am Ardron of Norwood,"

"Ah, Sir Ardron. I have heard of you," de Soulis replied. "Your reputation precedes you."

Their conversation was interrupted by the sounds of horses galloping into the compound.

"Where is Phillip Fitzrobert?" Reginald de Dunstanville demanded almost before he had brought his horse to a standstill.

"Sir Phillip?" De Soulis queried.

"Yes, Sir Philip. My nephew!" De Dunstanville demanded again.

"He's not here, Sir."

"Not here? Then, where is he?" de Dunstanville snapped

"He's at Cricklade," de Soulis replied.

"What is he doing at Cricklade?"

De Soulis shrugged. "Castle business."

"It had better be important castle business for him to desert his post here." De Dunstanville said clearly angry.

"I believe it was," de Soulis said.

"Explain yourself."

"Four, five days ago, Sir Philip received word from William Peverel at Cricklade that he had captured Walter de Pinkney and held him prisoner at Cricklade Castle. Sir Phillip decided that the best plan would be to take de Pinkney to Devizes and hand him over to the empress. She could imprison him, and demand he surrender Malmesbury Castle in exchange for his freedom.

Clearly this was new to de Dunstanville. "How did Peverel capture de Pinkney?" he asked.

Ardron listened with interest as de Soulis went on to explain. "It seems that Peverel was out hunting and came across de Pinkney also hunting, but with only four for escort. Peverel, with considerably more, had no problem arresting the man. He took him back to Cricklade and imprisoned him there. Then sent the message to Sir Phillip"

"And Phillip decided to move him to Devizes," de Dunstanville added derisively.

"Yes, Sir."

"A good excuse to escape from here, and at the same time ingratiate himself to my sister."

De Soulis did not reply.

After sighing with clear exasperation, de Dunstanville changed the subject. "There are casualties," he said. "We will have them brought in here to be tended," He did not seek permission. "Have your men help," he added with authority,

"At once, Sir." De Soulis left to issue the orders, probably relieved to be excused.

De Dunstanville watched him go a few moments then turned his attention to Ardron. "Well done Norwood," he said. "Your men performed bravely today. You have casualties?"

"Most certainly," Ardron replied. "The extent I do not yet know."

De Dunstanville nodded without comment, then after a thoughtful pause said more cheerfully.

"Providing Fitzcount completed his attack on Oxford, then De Chesny will not readily leave his estate again. All in all, I think a good day's work." He turned and for a few moments watched de Soulis issuing orders. "What think you of his story about de Pinkney's capture?" He asked.

"Not a story to be made up, I think," Ardron replied.

"No___." His drawled agreement. "If true then it's good news indeed. De Pinkney will have to trade Malmesbury Castle for his freedom, and that will be a major thorn removed from our Angevin arses." He pulled on the reins turning his horse's head. "I must report this to Fitzgilbert," he said.

Ardron watched him go. He didn't exactly share his optimism. Even if Walter de Pinkney agreed to trade Malmesbury Castle for his freedom, then it still needed brother Roger de Pinkney to co-operate. If Roger were

457

an ambitious man, which Ardron had little doubt he was, he might be prepared to sacrifice his brother's freedom to realize personal power and status to become castellan of the castle himself.

***

Marlborough Castle, July 1143

"I would address all," De Dunstanville said to Fitzgilbert as soon as he had dismounted.

"All?" Fitzgilbert queried.

"All," he affirmed.

This was the first time in almost a month de Dunstanville had set foot in Marlborough Castle. Just a week or so after the relief of Faringdon he had left for Devizes, presumably to involve himself in the negotiations for Malmesbury Castle.

"To address all it will have to be in the bailey forecourt." Fitzgilbert said.

"That will do."

"One hour?"

"One hour will be fine," de Dunstanville agreed. "Now," he said less urgently, "My throats as dry as an old witch's twat."

"Come, Sir Reginald," Fitzgilbert replied. "I will see you refreshed." He stood aside inviting de Dunstanville to ascend the steps to the keep. "Ardron my friend. Will you see all are assembled within the hour?" He said before he followed de Dunstanville"

"Of course," he replied.

Ardron watched the pair climb the steps. Clearly something important had happened, but he could not even begin to speculate just what it might be. He sighed inwardly all would be revealed in an hour. However, he could not contain his curiosity and as soon as the message was circulating, he ascended the mote into the keep and its main chamber. Sergen commanders stood around the main chamber in small clusters in quiet discussion, seemingly there was no alarm nor jubilation. Neither de Dunstanville nor Fitzgilbert was among the assembly, presumably having retired to a private chamber. Close by Ardron could see De Bohun in conversation with his cousin Patric. He didn't wait to be invited, instead sauntered across and interrupted their conversation.

"Has something important happened?" he asked.

"Yes_," de Bohun drawled. "It seems that last week Bishop Henry presented himself at Devizes Castle under a white flag. His news was that the new Pope, Eugenius, in response to the fall of Edessa, has decreed that a new crusade should be launched. The French King, Louis, has responded by declaring he will lead the army to the Holy Land and take the city back from the Muslims. His call to arms has the blessings of the Pope, and he in turn has declared all who take part will be absolved of all sins."

"Don't we have our own war to fight?" Ardron said.

"Indeed, we do," Patric responded. "However, Bishop Henry appeals that all Christians should stop fighting amongst themselves and instead turn their aggression against the Muslim."

"But that will only work if both sides agree to stop fighting." De Bohun took up the conversation.

"Of course," Ardron agreed. "Have both sides agreed?"

"Not yet," Patric re-engaged. "The Bishop is trying to organise a peace conference in Coventry."

"Ah," Ardron muttered. He didn't care too much about a war that would be fought three thousand miles away whatever its religious morality, but a peace pact in England? That did seem attractive and no doubt would be welcomed by the common populace.

"What are the chances?" He asked the question more of himself than anybody.

"Chance of what? A conference or peace?" De Bohun enquired.

"Well, both I suppose."

"The chances of a conference are probably good. But of peace? Well that I don't know."

"Well, you never know," Patric put forward his opinion. "If enough of the nobility decide that God is more important than loyalty to their sovereign, there may not be enough knights remaining to continue this war."

De Bohun shook his head. "No matter how many leave, there will always be another ready to step up to take their place."

"And__" Ardron added thoughtfully. "If one side is so weakened then the other might well endeavour to press home the advantage."

"Quite!" De Bohun agreed. "I cannot see any knight leaving his estate vulnerable unless a strong and lasting peace is arranged. Otherwise, he might well return after three years to find himself a pauper."

Ardron was thoughtful a moment. "How long will it take for Louis to get a sizeable army to Edessa?" he asked.

Both men scoffed. "More than a year I would say," Patric said.

"A year?" Ardron questioned surprise in his voice.

"Yes, I would say," Patric confirmed. "Even after an army is assembled then Louis will need ships. Lots of ships. When he has them then he will have to operate a shuttle service of men and supplies down the Mediterranean to land his army at Antioch. Some, of course, will make their own way to Antioch across land," he added.

"Antioch?" Ardron queried. "That's a long way from here."

"Indeed," Patric agreed. "When eventually Louis has all assembled, and only then, would he dare move north-east into Edessa. Yes, I would say at least a year! And__," he went on, "What do you think the Muslim leader, Zengi, will be doing during this time?" The question was rhetorical. "He won't be waiting until Louis is ready to march. That's for certain."

Ardron nodded." For certes," he said.

"Why?" de Bohun asked. "Are you thinking of going?"

"Perish the thought," Ardron responded with cynicism.

"We'll have to wait and see what develops," Patric concluded, as de Dunstanville and Fitzgilbert returned to the chamber. The pair moved down the hall to the far end, and to the seat which Fitzgilbert usually occupied when conducting proceedings. Neither sat, both stood on the dais and after exchanging a few quiet words faced the assembly.

"Good baron's and knights." De Dunstanville addressed the gathering. "By now you all know why I am here. It is true that the Pope has decreed a crusade into Edessa to recover its castle and lands and to push the Muslim back into Mesopotamia. Each man must decide for himself if, or not, he wants to venture into this crusade. It is also true the Pope grants absolution of all previous sins to any who crusades. However, I must urge you to balance this against conscience and sworn fealties to the empress." He waited for effect

"In a few minutes I will address the rank and file waiting outside," he started again. "Before I do, however, I have to impart another order this time from our Supreme Commander, my Lord Robert Fitzroy, Earl of Gloucester. The army standing at readiness here in Marlborough will, over the next few days, be gradually reduced and eventually stood down." He waited for the murmuring to cease. "It is our belief that de Chesny, fearing any reduction in his force will result in Oxford being attacked will, therefore, be wary about any venture outside his own hide areas. But, if by chance we have miscalculated and he should attack either, Wallingford or Faringdon, then the estate not under siege, be it Sir Brien or Sir Phillip, will attack Oxford. Meanwhile, Sir John's own personal force here at Marlborough will stand ready to lend assistance if and where needed."

Ardron picked up readily on the remark which indicated that Phillip Fitzrobert was to be master of Faringdon Castle. Even though he knew the post itself might well be a poisoned chalice, he still felt a pang of disappointment.

Meanwhile de Dunstanville had paused and was searching the faces before him. "Ardron of Norwood. Are you here?"

"Here my Lord," Ardron responded.

De Dunstanville cast around and found his raised arm. "I would talk with you before I leave today," he said. He then leaned back slightly, spoke to Fitzgilbert, before stepping from the dais and with Fitzgilbert alongside, made his way out to address the waiting others.

It was mid-afternoon and the de Dunstanville escort party preparing to leave before Ardron was summoned in Fitzgilbert's private chamber. He found both Fitzgilbert and de Dunstanville seated across a long table in earnest conversation. Fitzgilbert's Constable coughed loudly to attract their attention.

"Ah," Fitzgilbert acknowledged. "Ardron, please come in," he said. "Have a seat," he invited with an arm wave.

Ardron moved into the chamber and selected a seat alongside Fitzgilbert.

"You are well?" de Dunstanville enquired.

"Yes Sir. I am well"

"And your leg wound?" he asked.

"Stitched and mending," Ardron replied somewhat surprised that he even remembered. Then he slapped his leg to demonstrate its progress.

"Good," de Dunstanville muttered clearly only half-interested. "Now," he said gathering his thoughts. "We spoke previously about Faringdon Castle," he said. "We asked you to find a believable reason to reject the post in order not to offend the empress."

"I remember," Ardron said.

"Yes. Well you are relieved of that problem because Phillip Fitzrobert has been appointed to the post."

Ardron nodded without speaking.

"We found a way to appease Empress Maude while satisfying Earl Robert's opinion that his son should have the post. At the same time, I believe that you too will be satisfied with the proposed arrangements." He paused to gather his thoughts. "You are, I believe, local to Malmesbury."

"Yes, I am."

De Dunstanville nodded. "Are you aware that currently we have Walter de Pinkney as a prisoner at Devizes?"

"Of course," Ardron replied.

"Well," de Dunstanville went on. "A condition for his release is that he surrender Malmesbury Castle, and when he does then the empress will be pleased to offer you the post as its castellan."

Ardron was surprised. Without doubt it was a veritable jewel of an offer. To be castellan of an estate, where previously he had been a lowly villein, was beyond any possible aspiration that he could have dreamed. Both men waited for his response.

"Truly, Sir that is a very great honour," he replied.

"Yes," Fitzgilbert agreed. "But truly a deserved one. You have done great service at Wallingford, Lincoln, Winchester, Malmesbury, Oxford and here."

"Not many have done more," de Dunstanville added.

Slightly embarrassed, but massively elated he allowed himself a deep satisfied breath. "Is there any indication when this might come to pass?" He asked.

"As soon as de Pinkney capitulates," de Dunstanville said. "He is stubborn and standing firm at this time but, eventually, he will have to give in, if he ever wants his freedom. But be assured Malmesbury will be yours."

Satisfied with the answer Ardron allowed in his mind's eye to see himself as lord of Malmesbury. But even as he thought the shadow of Roger de Pinkney, Walter's brother, momentarily passed across those jubilant thoughts.

***

Norwood, Early September 1145

The great stag had run itself to a standstill. For around four miles twisting and weaving in all directions he had led the hunt a lively chase. Finally, hardly able to raise a gallop it had stumbled into a blind gulley and now trapped, snorting and panting breathlessly, it turned to face the hunters. Although the animal was completely exhausted, he lowered its head and pointed its great antlers threateningly towards the hunters. There was still some fight left.

From horseback, Roland wound back the string of his crossbow, placed in an arrow and took careful aim. There he remained for several seconds frozen still as a sculpture. Slowly he lowered the bow and looked at Ardron apologetically, "I can't do it," he said. "He has run too well, and even now exhausted and cornered, he stands to fight. He doesn't deserve to die," he said shaking his head.

"That'll feed the castle for nigh on a week," Fique protested.

"Then you do it," Roland replied offering him the bow.

Fique ignored the bow, instead he leaned forward to stroke away lathered sweat from his horse's neck.

"The stag lives," Ardron decreed in secret sympathy with Roland. "I know not where we are," he went on looking around him. "But I suspect we are no longer on Norwood estate. So, to kill the animal would make us poachers." He found a practical excuse to spare the animal. "Come," he said dismounting from his tired horse, leading the animal away from the cornered stag. His four companions followed his example and dismounted also.

"How do we find Jarcot?" Roland asked walking alongside.

"Well_, Ardron replied. "We have no kill to add to the cart, so we won't try. He'll make his own way home."

It was early afternoon and the September sun past its zenith. Even so it was not easy to calculate its setting direction. Instead he looked to the greenery forming on north side of the tree trunks to establish a bearing. "That way," he said pointing in a westerly direction.

"Where do you think we are?" Cerdic asked, moving up to walk alongside Ardron.

Ardron made a wry face. "I don't know for certain, but I would say we might be somewhere south of Cricklade but north of Suindune."

"We're a long way from home."

"Ten, twelve miles perhaps," Ardron replied. "Don't worry we'll be back at the castle long before dark."

His estimated position proved not to be too far out when they came across a well- trodden road and a little way to their right, the village of Cricklade. The village itself, lay on a gently sloping hillside with the castle on the ridge above. Having been on foot for almost half-an-hour, Ardron considered the horses now sufficiently rested and permitted the remount. At a leisurely pace they made their way across the meadow below the village. A continuation in this direction would see them back at Norwood within two hours.

"Ardron, Sir." Fique called as he moved from the rear to ride alongside. "Who is the castellan of the castle?" he asked.

"Phillip Fitzrobert."

"And is he for the king?"

"Fitzrobert?" Ardron was surprised by the question. "Fitzrobert is the youngest son of Earl Robert and therefore staunchly for the empress."

"That is what I thought." Fique said. "So, why is the king's flag flying from the tower?"

Ardron reined his horse to a stop and stared across to the castle. The flag was slumped hanging down lazily along the flagpole, and at that moment unidentifiable. It took a little while before a whisper of wind half unfurled the flag. Although only half floating it was, nevertheless, still clear to see that the flag was red with the yellow livery of half-man half lion emblazed across its centre. It was indeed the kings ensign.

"I don't understand," he muttered to himself. There had been no word of a siege, nor was there any evidence that one had taken place. "I need to find out just what has happened," he said.

"How? Fique asked.

Not sure exactly how to answer that Ardron said. "I'll go into the village and ask." It was more of a suggestion than any definite plan.

"You can't do that," Fique replied. "You are too well known. If it is that now the king holds Cricklade you will be taken prisoner and held for ransom."

"Ardron scoffed. "The king held me once before but didn't see any value in me as a ransom."

"No," Fique agreed. "But you did escape, and it may be that given another opportunity he might, next time, imprison you. If he did and he put a price on your release it might also be the empress would feel morally bound pay." He paused to let the point sink in. "I'll go," he then said.

"No," Ardron was thinking now. Cerdic will go. "He is Saxon and will be less suspicious than a Norman." He looked to Cerdic. "Cerdic," he said. "You will go into the village posing as a traveller trying to buy food. Casually, work the conversation round to why the king's flag fly's above the keep." He waited for a response. Cerdic nodded compliance. "We will wait here." Ardron went on. "You have just half-an-hour. If you are not back by then we will come in and get you out. Do you understand?"

"I do."

"Good. Remember half-an-hour."

Lazing in the afternoon sun they waited beyond half-an-hour. Ardron was edgy and close to the point of effecting Cerdic's rescue. But then, he was spotted leaving the village coming in their direction. "Mount up," Ardron instructed.

The news is bad, Sir." Cerdic said even before his horse had stopped. "Faringdon has fallen to the king, and Phillip Fitzrobert did swear fealty to him.

"God's piles," Roland cursed. "That's bad."

Certainly is, Ardron silently agreed. "I wasn't aware that Faringdon had been attacked," he muttered. "Perhaps it wasn't." he added. "I smell treachery in this," he said aloud. "We must make all speed to Norwood and get this word out."

They rode hard, and a little over an hour later they rode into Norwood and were greeted by Maurice de Prevuer, "I wondered what had happened to you," he said. "Jarcot and Jacques arrived back here more than two hours ago."

"Good," Ardron muttered tersely. "Have my charger Rattlebone saddled, I have to leave for Devizes right away."

For the first time Maurice noticed the lather on the horses. "What has happened," he asked as he wiped some of the froth from the horse's neck.

"Faringdon has fallen to the king," Ardron said as he dismounted.

Twenty minutes later Ardron re-emerged from the keep. Rattlebone was saddled ready for him and waiting alongside, Maurice and Swidhurn.

We're coming with you," Maurice said.

464

There was no argument from Ardron. Twas not a good idea to travel alone in the current climate, the forests harboured desperate outlawed men.

***

Devizes Castle

After convincing the castle constable of the urgency of the news he had to convey, he was kept waiting four or five minutes only, before he was brought before Empress Maude. Inside the chamber he was a little surprised to find Roger Fitzmiles, Reginald de Dunstanville, Humphry de Bohun, John Fitzgilbert, and William Peverel all in attendance. Their faces betrayed little as all seated at a long table looked at Ardron expressionless. The empress was seated at the end, although not actually at its head. Could it be, he wondered, that the news he was about to report would not be a surprise.

He walked down the side of the table to stop exactly opposite Empress Maude. "Your Majesty," he acknowledged her with all respects due.

"Sir Ardron," Maude acknowledged. "You have important news?"

"Yes, I have. But I fear it is not welcome news."

"Tell it," she said.

"Earlier today," he went on. "I was returning from a hunt and by chance passed close by the village of Cricklade."

"Yes?" Fitzmiles queried.

"I was surprised to see King Stephen's colours flying from the tower."

Nobody spoke! Nobody looked surprised.

"I sent a man into the village to discover why. He returned reporting that Faringdon had fallen to the king. And Phillip Fitzrobert had joined the king's cause." It did not have the impact he expected.

"Yes," de Dunstanville was first to speak. "It was definitely the king's flag?"

"Oh yes."

"Did you see a mass of the kings sergenti," Fitzmiles asked.

"No, I did not."

Fitzmiles turned his attention to the others. "No king's army, and yet his flag flies over Cricklade. The reports must be true"

"How know you that my nephew has joined Stephen?" Maude asked.

Ardron shrugged. "Word from the village, my Lady."

"Sir William here," Fitzmiles waved a hand towards Peverel. "Reported yesterday that Phillip Fitzrobert surrendered Faringdon Castle to Stephen after five days. Five days? Five days only he withstood the siege." He almost spat in disgust. "Then his constable, de Soulis, negotiated surrender terms throwing the gates open. Open without a fight!" He paused a moment. "Some brave souls did try to resist, barricading themselves in the keep. But they soon realised their position was hopeless and they too surrendered. They weren't so lucky, however, and are held prisoners, while all the rest are considered allies."

"We didn't want to believe that Fitzrobert had sworn fealty to Stephen, but with your report we are forced to that conclusion," de Dunstanville said.

"We thank you for your diligence," Maude said to Ardron. "This news must be forwarded to my brother, Earl Robert, immediately." She went on addressing the others.

"Not a message I want to deliver. His favourite son turned against him. It will devastate him." Fitzmiles said.

"Yes, it will," Maude agreed. "So, the message must be delivered by a close relation. She paused. "Sir Reginald, it will have to be you."

"As you wish, my Lady," De Dunstanville replied. "Sir Ardron," he said looking up at him. "Would you accompany me?"

"Not a good idea." De Bohun cut in before he could reply. "With the fall of Faringdon and the defection of Fitzrobert, the king controls a line of castles. Oxford, Faringdon, Cricklade and presumably Tetbury also. With Walter de Pinkney still refusing to cede Malmesbury, that too. The next castle in line is Norwood. I think Sir Ardron will need to look to his defences urgently."

"You're right," de Dunstanville agreed. He smiled at Ardron. "Regrettably, I will have to do without your company on this trip." He turned his attention to Maude. "I will leave at first light tomorrow, he said.

"Did I not tell you?" de Bohun spoke quietly to Ardron as the meeting broke up and they filed out from the chamber. "It should have been you as castellan at Faringdon. I'd wager that it would not have fallen so easily."

"What's done is done," Ardron replied.

"Aye, it is! Nevertheless, it's a bad-bad blow. Earl Robert invested much, building a formidable castle in a very strategic position. Only to see it gifted to Stephen." He sighed heavily. "I rather think that we might be losing this war."

Ardron said nothing, but deep down he feared he might be right.

"Look to your defences," de Bohun continued. "You're practically front line at Norwood now."

"Yes," Ardron agreed a little gloomily.

"Good luck, my friend," he said as he turned away.

For a moment Ardron stood and watched him walk away, reflecting as he did, that the sighting of the Tituli star was really a portent of disaster after all.

Chapter 20

Norwood, November 1145

"Riders coming in, Sir."

Ardron turned to look to where Roland pointed. A dozen or so riders approached the castle at an easy canter under a green and white banner. He recognised the banner. "Hmm," he grunted with surprise and wondered what it was that brought Patric Earl Salisbury to Norwood. He dusted off his hands and handed the heavy lump hammer to Roland. "Be sure they keep this palisade line straight," he instructed, glancing along the newly erected line. For a moment he wondered if he ought to change into something more presentable to greet his guest, but instantly rejected it. Instead, they would have to accept him as they found. Hard at work strengthening the Norwood castle defences. He reached the foot of the mote just as the riders entered the bailey. It was indeed Patric of Salisbury and riding alongside, his cousin Edward d'Evereux.

"Gentlemen," he greeted. "You are welcome."

Both men acknowledged the greeting. "It seems you are busy, Sir." Patric said glancing around at the building activity.

"Yes," Ardron agreed. "A second bailey will strengthen our defences if it is ever so needed."

Patric leaned forward onto his horse's withers. "This place is unrecognisable from when I was last here." He said it with a degree of surprise.

"That must have been some time ago," Ardron replied, knowing full well that he had never been while he was castellan.

"Indeed, it was," he replied. "As a mere boy I used to visit when it was owned by my uncle. He dowered it to my cousin Matilda when she married Humphry de Bohun."

"Our cousin Matilda," Edward d'Evereux corrected, perhaps feeling left out of the conversation."

"Of course," Patric acknowledged.

"Please, gentlemen step down and let me offer you some refreshments," Ardron invited.

Sitting afront of a flourishing fire blazing in the inglenook, the three men supped gingered wine and nibbled oat cakes talking of nothing in-particular, while Ardron wondered, silently, the purpose of their visit.

Eventually it was Patric who broached the subject. "Has Sir Humphry asked you to provide an escort to Coventry?"

Puzzled, Ardron frowned. "No__," he muttered. "What's at Coventry?"

"The peace talks. The peace talks," Edward exclaimed with an irk of frustration.

"Ah," now he understood. "No, he hasn't," Ardron confirmed. "I didn't know Sir Humphry was going."

"He is to be part of the negotiating team," Patric explained.

"I didn't know," Ardron replied.

"Yes," Patric went on. "The team is to be led by Robert Fitzedith and supported by Baldwin de Reivers and Humphrey de Bohun. And the meeting, in Coventry, one week from today."

"You're not going?" Ardron asked Patric.

"No," he said. "I did offer my services, but it was declined."

Ardron was not surprised. Until recently Patric had been the king's man, and to place a turncoat on the opposite side of the negotiating table, might have been provocative. But he said nothing, instead asked. "How is their safety guaranteed?"

"Safe conduct is assured by Bishop Roger de Clinton." Patric answered.

"Is that reliable?"

Patric scoffed. "Your guess is equal to mine," he said. "That is why I thought de Bohun would have asked you to accompany him. I know he thinks highly of your company."

"I'm flattered to hear it. But no, he hasn't asked me, but then his constable, d'Aumale is a capable man."

"I suppose," Patric allowed.

"What are the chances?" he asked after a pause.

"Of peace?" Patric queried. Ardron nodded. "Slim I would say. The side in the strongest position make the demands the weakest look for compromises. And with the fall of Faringdon, I would say, it will be the royalists who will make all the demands."

"Do you know who will make those demands on the king's behalf?"

"Aye. I hear it is to be the poison dwarf himself, Robert de Bossa

De Bossa?" Ardron queried. "The hunchback," he translated into English.

"Yes," Patric agreed. "Robert de Beaumont, Earl of Leicester. A man no taller than a miller's grain sack with a hump as big as his ego."

"Not heard of this man," Ardron admitted.

"One of twins," Patric went on. "His brother has not a hint of deformity about him. Which I suppose does nothing to ease de Bossa's ill disposition."

"Is the king taking these peace talks seriously?" Ardron quizzed himself more than a directed question.

Edward snorted. "Perhaps not," he said. "If he thinks he's winning, why would he?"

468

Ardron smiled inwardly as he noted Patric glare at his cousin. If the king did prevail then his earldom would most certainly disappear also.

***

Late November 1145

The snow was not deep. Deep enough, however, that nothing could move without leaving tracks. The roe deer had, therefore, been easy to track and as it contentedly grazed on the grass tufts poking through the snow, it was oblivious to Ardron and Fique close by.

"Easy now," Ardron breathed as Fique levelled the crossbow at the animal.

The arrow whispered through the air striking the deer with a dull thud and causing the animal to leap before falling on its side kicking the air in death throes.

Fique lowered his bow. Surprise scorched across his face as he looked down on the arrow still resting in his crossbow. His mouth opened to speak but nothing came out. Ardron rested his hand on his arm and bade him to silence. Then they waited. From a thicket away to their left a sallow youth emerged, camouflaged in white and dangling a long bow from his left hand. Soundless but with gestures Ardron ordered Fique to move across and behind. He waited a few moments before drawing his sword and emerging from cover.

Intent on binding the deer's legs together the boy did not hear Ardron's approach until he spoke. "Stand up," he said prodding the sword point at his back.

As startled as a panicked rabbit, the boy jumped and tried to bolt only to run straight at Fique's sword point. "Poacher," Fique accused.

"I, I__," the poacher started to speak. Then unable to think of any justification fell silent.

Only an utterance, but the voice was too high pitched. Ardron reached forward and pulled back the hood. Hair the colour of ripe corn tumbled down about her face and steely blue eyes stared back.

"By all saints in heaven, it's a girl." Fique muttered.

"It is, Ardron confirmed. "But nevertheless, still a poacher. Where are you from?" he asked in English. There was no answer. "Alright, then tell me your name." Still no reply. "You do speak English?"

"Of course."

"Then I ask again. Where are you from?" There was still no answer only defiance in her steely eyes. "Never mind," Ardron said. "Tie her hands," he instructed Fique. "Use that rope," he nodded towards the rope that half bound the deer's legs. "Tie them well. We'll take her back to Norwood."

"The deer?" Fique asked when the girl's hands were bound.

"Take it. Load it across your horse's back."

Fique lifted the carcass and slung it over the horse's back. The smell of blood momentarily spooked his animal causing it to twist away and shy. "Easy there," he soothed holding tight to the reins while calming the horse with pats down its neck.

Meanwhile, Ardron had looped a rope through the girl's tied hands and secured the other end to his own saddle. With an unsympathetically attitude he intended to make the four-mile walk back to Norwood not comfortable for her.

"It was a fair shot, though." Fique allowed as he mounted his horse.

"It was that" Ardron agreed.

Little over an hour later they passed through the gates into the castle bailey, attracting many silent and curious stares.

"What have you there?" Maurice queried, as he held Rattlebone's head while Ardron dismounted.

"A poacher."

"A poacher?" Maurice's surprise was evident.

"Yes. Felled that deer with a good a shot as you will see from any archer."

"What do you want done with her."

Ardron glanced at her. Although he had subjected her to many heartless tugs during the trek back to Norwood, she refused to show any distress, standing erect and defiant. "Put her in a cell for now," he said. "Maybe a couple of hours in such a place will make her a little more communicative."

He let her languishing in a dark dank cell for more than three hours, until the evening meal was coming to its end. He then had her brought before him in the great hall. Standing isolated and flanked on both sides by the seated castle sergens. he had expected her to be intimidated. But if she was, it wasn't evident. Her blue eyes framed by long unruly fair hair stared back undaunted.

"Gentlemen," he addressed the gathering of sergens. "This young girl was caught poaching on the Norwood estate contrary to forest law."

"Poaching?" Jarcot queried undeniably surprised

"Aye, poaching. She has refused to reveal her name or where she is from," Ardron went on. "Ignoring the fact that she is a girl dressed as a boy, she is obviously Saxon." He paused. "So, I ask, does anybody here know her?"

From the long table a voice said. "I know her."

Ardron sought the speaker and found Beldwine with a half-raised hand. "She is the maid, Claennis daughter of Modig from the village Cloatly." He said in halting French.

"Cloatly?" Ardron uttered. "By God girl not only do you steal from me you're not even one of my villeins. You steal to feed the villeins of Malmesbury."

"I don't steal." She spoke for the first time. "I take what God put on this earth for all to share. Not just the privileged few." She turned towards Beldwine. "Yes," she said. "And I know you Beldwine of Minety. You are lapdog to Norman masters. And you also Osric. You too Penda," she sought out more Saxons with a pointed finger.

"And you speak French," Ardron said.

"Of course, I speak French. And I also speak Latin as well as English. Do you do as well, Norman?"

"No, I do not," Ardron replied. "Obviously, you are well studied. How so?"

"My father is a Saxon Geneat, a Freeman with an estate of his own. In generations past we probably owned this land on which your castle stands. That is until you Norman bandits robbed us of it."

"That is history," Ardron replied. "Now you cannot wander the area claiming this was once my land, therefore, I can do as I will. You are subject to Norman law as am I, the son of a Saxon Thegn."

"You're a Saxon?"

"I am a Saxon."

Her surprise was fleeting, she immediately recovered belligerence.

Ardron stroked his beard thoughtfully. "What to do with you?" he said sucking through his teeth noisily. "I would speak with your father," he decided. "Swidhurn,"

"Sir," the reply was immediate.

"Make a slaves collar and put it about her neck."

"You would make her a slave?" The disproval in his question was evident.

"I would." He didn't bother to elaborate that he thought it more desirable than confining the girl to the misery of a cell. At least with a slave's collar she could wander freely about the castle. "Take her now," he overruled Swidhurn's hesitation.

"Beldwine," he addressed the Saxon after the pair had left. "You know this girl's father, Modig?"

"I know of him," Beldwine stood and corrected.

Ardron nodded acceptance. "Tomorrow before the sun has cleared the horizon you will carry a message to this Geneat that his daughter is safe here at Norwood, and that she is being held for breaking forest law. Then tell him that I would be honoured if he would deem to visit to discuss the situation."

Beldwine nodded acceptance. "Yes Sir," he said and sat.

The meal finished and the diners dispersing to allow the servants in to enter and pick over the remnants, Ardron made his way to his private chamber. He poured over his rough-hewn drawings that strengthened the Norwood defences and at length declared himself satisfied. The second bailey was all but constructed. It squared off the area in front of the original bailey. Now it required only that a substantial entrance gate be positioned. Whether or not the castle would withstand a determined siege he could not be sure, but at least the modifications did give it a better chance.

His thoughts turned to the maid Claennis. Without doubt she was easy on the eye possessing an obvious beauty. But her indomitable spirit knew no bounds, and that could be a future problem for her if she didn't learn to temper it with tact. However, she was still young, perhaps in early twenties or perhaps younger, and perchance it would be, that life's experiences would wear down her sharp edge of audacity. No doubt someone somewhere would become a husband to the maid, but whoever that be he would, without doubt, face challenges from her forthright outspoken perspectives. He smiled to himself thinking of those challenges. Next, he pondered if she was in fact already betrothed. To promote alliances and treaties, marriages are often arranged while girls are still in infancy.

"Sir," his thoughts were interrupted by Maurice. "A messenger has just ridden in."

"A messenger?" The hour was getting late and the cold weather outside testing, therefore, it must be important he reasoned. "Messenger from where?"

"From Trowbridge."

"Where is this man?

"He waits in the hall, Sir." Maurice replied.

Ardron found the courier waiting in the hall trying to warm himself from the hot ash that was the remnants of an earlier searing fire.

"Sir," he said turning his attention to Ardron. "I have despatches from Sir Francis de Aumale."

"Maurice, get the man some gingered wine." Ardron said as he took the leather pouch. "Poke the fire. See if you can spark it into a little life," he encouraged the courier. Then he moved over to the long table to open the pouch.

"God's piles," he swore. This is the devil's own treachery."

Maurice froze waiting expectantly, wine decanter poised in his hand. "Bad news?" he asked.

"The worst," Ardron replied. "All the Angevin team negotiating peace at Coventry, have been seized and arrested by none other than Phillip Fitzrobert."

"Fitzrobert? The earl's own son? What's he doing at the peace conference?" Maurice questioned.

It was a good question. His attendance representing the crown at the peace conference could be nothing except provocation.

"So much for Bishop de Clinton's assurance of safe conduct." Ardron muttered tossing the despatch to the table. "This is an outrage."

There was silence for a few seconds then Maurice asked. "What will you do?" as he poured the wine and handed it to the courier.

Ardron was bemused. What could he do? "I don't know," he said shaking his head ruefully. "I could go to Bristol and offer my support to my liege lord." He said it but he couldn't see what Earl Robert could do either. Even if he assembled an army in double quick time, the prisoners would probably no longer be in Coventry. Most likely moved to London. To attack the capital, would take a massive army. "Is there no honour left in this war," he muttered rubbing tired eyes. "I'm going to bed," he declared. "Find this man somewhere to sleep," he added indicating the courier.

With morning mass completed, the superiors of the castle sat for breakfast. The news was out, and breakfast was a subdued affair, each man sensing Ardron's dilemma. Although he could see no practical point in reporting to Bristol, he had decided that it was his duty, as a knight in service to Earl Robert, to do so, if only to show moral support. He had yet to announce his intention, but he would make the journey tomorrow, at the head of an escort of around half-dozen. Only the sergens who would make up this six was undecided, but he would make that decision in consultation with Maurice later today.

Ardron climbed to the top of the newly erected tower and found Roland posted lookout. The pair exchanged acknowledging nods without speaking. Ardron looked out across the open area towards the wooded area beyond. The light covering of snow had all but gone, clinging only to those areas that were shaded. As he gazed out a small band of riders emerged from the trees and walked their mounts unhurriedly towards the castle.

"Riders approaching," Roland needlessly informed Ardron.

"I see them," he replied. He counted a total of nine in orderly pairs under a yellow banner. A flag that he did not recognise.

"Below the gate." Roland leaned over the barrier and alerted the gate-guard below. "Riders approaching." He glanced back at Ardron.

They didn't seem to offer any threat. "Let them pass," Ardron allowed then made his way down to greet the arrivals. He took position half-a dozen steps up the mote as the riders entered the inner bailey and came towards him.

"I am Modig the Geneat of Cloatly," the lead rider said as he brought his horse to a halt.

"Welcome Modig," Ardron replied. The man before him had a presence about him. He was a big man, barrel-chested with a robust physique. His long grey hair, centre parted, hung down onto his shoulders and a full-face beard completed the grey frame around a well-lined face.

"Sir, you hold my daughter, Claennis," It was more an accusation then a question.

"I do Sir," Ardron replied. "Be assured., she is well, and no harm has come to her."

"Good," Modig said. "Then I will pay her fine, and we'll be on our way troubling you no further."

Ardron shook his head. "No Sir," he said. "Please step down, sample my hospitality and we will discuss the issue." For a few moments Ardron feared the man was about to refuse and become belligerent. Then perhaps realising his vulnerable situation he nodded acceptance and dismounted.

Inside the hall polite pleasantries were exchanged while servants busied themselves supplying refreshments. Eventually banalities exhausted, Ardron approached the subject for which they were now gathered.

"Modig, I have to inform you that your daughter, Claennis, was witnessed killing a deer on my estate, contrary to forest law." He said.

"Who was that witness?" Modig challenged.

"I was." Ardron said. "Before my very eyes she brought the animal down with an arrow."

"There can be no doubt?" Modig queried.

"None."

He took a deep breath resigned to his daughter's guilt. "Name the fine," he said. "I will see that she is chastened."

"Not that easy, Ardron said. "It was a deer she killed. Not a rabbit nor a partridge. A deer! And that is an offence which could actually see her declared outlaw."

"You wouldn't do that?

"No, I wouldn't." Ardron agreed shaking his head. That would be an extreme penalty. "She must, however, face some personal penance. An easy fine paid by a doting father on her behalf, will not be a future deterrent."

"Sir. I will deal with it." Modig insisted.

"No, I will deal with it." Ardron countered.

Modig leaned back folded his arms and stared hard at Ardron. "What do you propose?" He asked suspiciously.

"I propose that she work as a kitchen maid in my kitchens for a month."

"A kitchen maid? My daughter?"

"Yes,"

"Sir, she is my daughter. The daughter of a Geneat. She cannot be expected to labour as a kitchen maid. That would be too humiliating. I will not allow it."

"Nevertheless, Ardron said. "A taste of humiliation lasting a month, will give her time for reflection and, hopefully, she will learn that laws do apply to her also."

Modig sighed heavily. "I don't like it," he said.

Ardron waited, offering no alternative.

"One month?"

"One month," Ardron confirmed.

Modig looked down at his spread fingers counting. "That would be the second day of Christmas the day of Saint Stephen Feast." he said.

"It would," Ardron agreed. "Very well," he said relenting a little. "Twenty-eight days and I will have her returned her to you on the day before Christmas."

"Modig was silent a few moments probably still trying to think of an alternative suggestion. Then he gave a reluctant capitulating nod. "You must give me your word she will not be harmed."

"You have it," Ardron said." I promise she will not be harmed at all."

"May I see her?"

"Of course," Ardron replied. "Maurice," he addressed his constable who had stood silently by door. "Have the maid Claennis brought in."

Some minutes later she was brought in still retaining that defiant air. "Father," she said with an element of relief when she saw him.

"What's this," Modig demanded angrily when he spotted the slave collar about her neck. "You said no harm would come to her. Is this your idea of Norman promises."

Ardron calmly held up his hand. "The collar is there to stop her running away. It also means that she does not have to be kept in a cell. She can move freely within the castle precincts. Now explain to her what we have agreed, and if she is willing to give me her solemn promise that she will not try to escape during this twenty-eight-day period, I will have the collar removed." He got up from his chair. "I will leave you alone to talk," he said. A meaningful nod towards Maurice and they left the room together.

***

Bristol Castle

Ardron waited in the ante room of Bristol Castle. He had arrived in Bristol the evening before but did not come to the castle. Instead he had taken lodgings in a boarding house close by. Anticipating now that breakfast would be finished, he presented himself to the castle constable.

"Ardron of Norwood," de Dunstanville walked through the large double doors and greeted him warmly. "It is always good to see you."

"Thank you, Sir Reginald," Ardron replied.

"The earl will be pleased to see you, and I am sent to bring you to him." He made a gesture with his arm indicating the direction. "You fare well?" he asked politely as they walked.

"I do, Sir Reginald," Ardron replied.

"Good," he said as he pushed open the door to Earl Robert's private chamber.

He found Earl Robert sat behind a desk, studying papers before him through a magnifying glass. "Ah," he said when he looked up. "Ardron of Norwood, please come in and take a seat." He invited with a wave of his hand as he himself got to his feet. A glance down and to his side, Ardron took the nearby seat at the end of a long table while the earl moved and sat himself opposite. Pleasantries were then exchanged as de Dunstanville took it upon himself to pour wine.

Assuming that the earl would most certainly know the news from Coventry, Ardron opened the subject which had brought him to Bristol. "Sir," he said. "On hearing the alarming news from Coventry, I have come to put myself at your disposal."

"Ah yes, Coventry," Earl Robert said with a sigh. "The situation may not be as bad as first feared, there have been developments. I am soon to address all my knights gathering in the great hall. You are invited to join us, where I will reveal all I know." He stared into the light slanting in through the portal. "Which may not be very much," he added quietly.

"As I recall," de Dunstanville interrupted. "You met the Faringdon Castle constable, de Soulis?" It was a question.

"Yes, Sir I did."

"What was your impression?"

Ardron shrugged. "We met only briefly hardly enough time to form an opinion."

"Even so?" de Dunstanville pressed.

"Seemed efficient and loyal to his castellan." He deliberately avoiding mentioning Phillip Fitzrobert's name, knowing full well it was the earl's disloyal son.

"We assemble in the great hall at noon," Earl Robert said wearily.

He had been dismissed, Ardron knew. "Yes," he said getting to his feet. "Thank you for seeing me."

"Thank you for being such a loyal servant." Earl Robert muttered. "I remember it was you who bought me news in the middle of the night that my sister had landed in England eight years ago."

"Six, Sir." Ardron corrected

"Six?"

476

"Yes, Sir. Six years."

"Seems much longer," the earl said tiredly.

Standing behind the earl, de Dunstanville indicated with a silent head flick that Ardron should leave. At the door Ardron looked back. The earl still sat in the same position and still stared wistfully into the shaft of light. Ardron looked questioningly at de Dunstanville who stood holding the door open.

"He's alright. Just a little tired." He answered Ardron's unasked question.

In the great hall most of those assembled stood around in small groups chattering, while others had seated themselves on benches lining the side walls. Ardron stood by the entrance door and for a few moments scanned around looking for familiar faces. There was not many he could actually call friends. No Fitzcount no Fitzgilbert, both he assumed, staying in attendance at their respective castles which were now frontline and vulnerable. Patric Earl of Salisbury was there and as their eyes met across the room, he gave an acknowledging nod. Another one recognised, Albert Casteneau with whom he had twice crossed swords in combat. From him, a stony glare. Which was no more than could be expected. Ardron held the stare a moment then allowed the hint of a dismissive smile as he turned away.

"Sir," a servant moved at his elbow offering a platter of drinks.

"Thank you," Ardron said taking a small pewter of wine. Glancing down the side of the room he spotted a vacant seat and shuffled towards it.

For a moment he paused in front of the vacant seat and stared up appreciatively at the expansive tapestry above.

"Impressive, isn't it?" the man seated next to the vacant seat said.

"Most certainly," Ardron agreed. This man was not a young man, probably had seen as many as fifty winters. But he was a man of status, being expensively dressed wearing a long gown of brown and an elegant cloak of red, held across his shoulders by a large brooch of silver.

"Excuse me sir," Ardron said. "Is this seat available?"

"It is,"

"May I sit here a while?"

"Of course, Sir Ardron," he replied.

"You know me, Sir?

"I do."

"Then you have the advantage of me Sir," Ardron said has he sat.

"I am William Fitzrichard, High sheriff of Cornwall." He paused a moment. "My daughter is married to Reginald de Dunstanville."

"Ah__," Ardron said. "Sir Reginald is your son-in-law." As he said it, he felt rather stupid blurting out the obvious.

"Yes," he agreed passing over the inanity. "Reginald holds you in high regard."

"Nice to know," Ardron replied.

"It seems that you have distinguished yourself many times over in the cause of the empress."

"Only doing my duty, Sir," Ardron glossed over.

Fitzrichard scoffed slightly. "Gallantly modest too," he said. "Commendable. But," he went on, "I'm sure you'll have your reward."

"If God wills," Ardron muttered.

"I believe you have been promised Malmesbury?" Fitzrichard posed the statement as a query.

"I have," Ardron confirmed. "That is if Walter de Pinkney ever concedes."

"Surely, he will eventually. If he values his freedom that is."

"Perhaps," Ardron said. "But I fear that with each day that passes his brother's position as temporary castellan strengthens."

There was shuffling movement in the crowd as the double doors were pushed open and locked back.

"Ah," William Fitzrichard said. "Something is about to happen." Both men got to their feet.

Accompanied by de Dunstanville Earl Robert walked purposefully down the room to the dais at the far end. By the time he had reached the dais all the chatter had died away, and the room waited expectantly.

"My loyal knights, Friends. Comrades," Earl Robert began. "The news is mixed." He paused gathering his thoughts. "The good news is that the team of negotiators we sent to Coventry have, by order of Stephen Blois, been released. Even as I speak, they are making their way home."

The news was greeted by enthusiastic cheering. Ardron noted that the earl had not, could not, refer to Stephen as king.

Earl Robert held up his hands to quell the cheering. "It is reported that someone did plunge a knife into Brien de Soulis chest, killing him."

This news also brought a smattering of cheers also. "So should all traitors meet that end." Someone shouted.

"It was my own son, Phillip, who accused our negotiating team of harbouring a murderer and placed them all under arrest to reveal the culprit." Earl Robert went on. "Bishop de Clinton appealed to Stephen Blois that there was no proof that a murderer was harboured in the Angevin team. It was he who ordered their release, so that the peace talks could continue. However, upon their release, Robert Fitzedith decided that it be not prudent to stay, and that very evening ordered the team's departure." He paused a moment. "Friends," he went on. "I have to report that the peace talks did not proceed beyond the first day and have, therefore, failed." He paused a moment. "Consequently, I have to tell you the war goes on." There was mixed reaction to that statement some cheered while others looked despondent.

"Hmm." Fitzrichard uttered. "That will be a major disappointment to our good earl," he said. "Since his son's betrayal he has lost much enthusiasm for the fight."

Ardron studied the earl as he was leaving the hall. Truly, he did seem to be much subdued. That smouldering anger at Stephen's audacity to usurp seemed to have become much diminished. Perhaps it was that the many discouraging setbacks of late, had been over-whelmingly depressing. There was no doubt in Ardron's mind that the Angevin's needed a victory of sorts. Any victory of sorts.

"Are you stopping in the castle?" Fitzrichard asked.

Ardron glanced through the open portal. Outside the day, though cold, was bright and not yet midday. "No." He decided that he could still be at Norwood before the night was too old. "I return to Norwood within the hour."

Fitzrichard looked disappointed. "I was looking forward to your company this evening. Oh well," he said. "Perhaps you will attend Empress Maude's Christmas celebrations at Devizes."

"Almost certainly," Ardron said.

***

Norwood, Mid December 1145

This day Ardron had not risen early, having missed morning mass, but deliberately so. Nor did he intend to join the communal breakfast, instead he had ordered a light breakfast to be brought to his chamber. While he waited, he opened the daybook which Maurice had placed on his table. This morning was to be a day when he presided over disputes. The arguments were usually petty and easily resolved, and sometimes amusing. Even so, he appreciated, that to the plaintiffs involved, these arguments were not a cause of amusement. According to the book there was a single application to hear and two disputes to be settled. Both disputed between neighbouring villeins. Only three hearings, he did not expect that these would take a lot of time today.

The knock on his door was a shy one, and only just audible. "Enter," he called. Claennis entered his chamber modestly. He was surprised, a retiring attitude was not in her nature.

"I have your breakfast," she said. Then as an afterthought added, "Sir."

"Thank you," he said. "Lay it down here." Then as she did, "No, I think it would be better over there." She gave him a hard look before picking up the platter. He waited until she had set it down then said. "No, I think I will have it here after all." He managed to keep a dead-pan face. Claennis didn't, however, her exasperation was patently obvious. But as she laid out his breakfast once more, she said nothing.

"I am charged to chore your room," she said.

"Continue," he said nonchalantly, then turned his attention back to the daybook. However, he was not studying the book, he only pretended. Covertly, he watched her go about her task.

"Do you wish me to light a fire?" she asked before adding "Your Lordship."

Ardron hid a smirk. 'Your Lordship' had been added mockingly. He thought to say yes, just to see her scrape around in the fire grate clearing yesterday's ashes. "No. It's too early yet," he eventually said. He thought to fill the silence "How does it go in the kitchen?" He asked.

"Slowly," she bit back.

"Slowly?"

"Eight days and fourteen hours to go."

"Oh, I see," Ardron said with a nod. "I hear you have been critical of our arrangements."

"Arrangements? You have nothing like arrangements," she retorted. "Your wastage is criminal."

"We allow wastage deliberately, so that the servants can dine after we have finished." He explained.

"And the servants know it. So, in order that they too can dine royally they deliberately produce a big surplus. Do you know some of the dishes prepared don't even reach your table?"

Ardron leaned back in his chair. "I suspected as much, but I allow it."

"You need a housekeeper," she said.

"I had a housekeeper."

"What happened to her?"

"My constable went back to Normandy last spring and took her with him."

"If you had a good housekeeper you could reduce the amount of your wastage considerably. Then you could take less from your villeins and they would benefit."

Her forthrightness rankled him, probably because she had a point. "Are you applying for the position?"

"That's not likely," she scoffed as she began ripping the bedding off his bed.

"You are plainspoken to a point of rudeness," he snapped. "I suppose your father has a better system."

"I think he does," she replied.

"And that is?"

480

She paused from stripping off the bed. "He uses the estate to grow crops and to raise livestock. Of course, he doesn't do the work himself. He pays good coin to workers to do it for him. Then he encourages those workers to buy our surplus which returns the coin. Or at least most of it." She continued pulling off the bedding. "Surpluses to surplus," she went on. "Are sold on the Malmesbury market. And of course, things like grain he sells to the miller, or meat to local village Thegnes." She paused with an air of self-satisfaction and faced him." From all this we live comfortably and so do our workers and customers."

Ardron stared back at her thoughtfully. It seemed like an efficient arrangement, and whilst not openly agreeing with her, he wondered if there was possibly something to be learned.

"You sleep alone!" she said looking down on the bed and pile of bedclothes. It was not a question but an observation.

"I do," Ardron confirmed.

"Surely there is a queue of local village girls eager to share the bed of their lord and master." Once again, she was cleverly taunting with disguised disrespect. "Unless of course you have one of those perversions," she added.

"There is no perversion, "Ardron replied evenly. "But, if you are so curious you may join me in there tonight and find out," he invited.

She scoffed. "There will be frost in the devil's kitchen before that happens," she retorted.

Ardron laughed. "Who knows," he said. "If the Almighty has a mind, then one day, he might make it happen. What will you do then?"

"I will report to the devil's kitchen with kindle and flint."

He chuckled and shook his head ruefully. This girl was always going to have the last word. "Get on with your chores," he said and returned his attention again to the daybook.

The conversation dried as Claennis busied herself with her chores and Ardron thumbed idly through the book looking back on previous disputes. The silence was broken when Maurice came to the chamber.

He took a brief dismissive glance at Claennis before turning his attention to Ardron. "All is readied for you in the main hall. At your convenience, Sir," he said.

"Very good," Ardron acknowledged. "I'll be there in twenty minutes," he added, eyeing his breakfast.

"There are two disputes and an application to hear," Maurice confirmed before he left.

All that remained for Ardron to do now was to dress himself in official Norman dress to lend authority to the proceedings. "Have you finished?" he asked Claennis.

"Not quite," she said.

"Then you will have to come back later," he replied.

"I wonder__," she said ponderously."

"Yes?" Ardron said warily.

"I wonder if I might be allowed to watch."

"Why?"

"I would like to see how Norman barons handle disputes," she answered.

"I am not a baron," Ardron replied

She just shrugged. "Alright," she said. "How Norman castellans handle disputes."

"Neither am I Norman."

"You're castellan of a Norman castle." She argued pointedly.

Ardron shook his head ruefully. He was then thoughtful a moment, wondering if he was leaving himself open to more harassment if he granted her request.

"On one condition," he said.

"That is?"

"That you stand at the back and stay silent. If you utter a sound then by God, I'll add fourteen days to your incarceration."

She smirked. "I'll be as timid as a church mouse."

"Oh really," he muttered.

In the main chamber Ardron sat on a high seat positioned on a dais raised a little from the floor. Positioned so, to emphasise autonomy over the petitioners. Spectators there were, but only a handful, and all were castle inmates with no particular interest in the outcomes, only a bored curiosity in proceedings. Briefly he browsed those spectators, finding Claennis standing among them towards the back. He scowled as she gave him a cheeky little wave. He feared he might have made a mistake allowing her in. He sighed inwardly, nothing to be done now. He glanced to his right where his treasurer, Louis, readied himself with ledgers and registers. On his other side, in his role of constable, stood Maurice, acting advisor and security. Ardron gave him the nod to proceed.

"Mildgyd," Maurice said aloud. "Step forward." A dapper little man, approaching senior years shuffled forward among the spectators. "Sir," Maurice went on. "He makes application to increase his beehives from eight to twelve."

Ardron frowned and leaned towards Louis. "Does he need my permission for that?" he muttered.

"Yes Sir, it is for the record," he replied slapping his ledger. "We need to know so that we can increase his tythe of honey." Ardron nodded acceptance and turned his attention to the man before him

Sir," the dapper man presented his case. "I have eight productive hives, but I would like to erect four others at a different site overlooking the meadow of Swill Brook."

"The Swill? Isn't that on Malmesbury land?" Ardron queried.

"Yes, Sir. It is," the dapper man replied. "But I would place the hives inside your boundary and let the bees forage across the meadow. It is a meadow that is always carpeted knee height in buttercup during August."

"Is the meadow part of my estate," he asked Louis.

"No Sir, I fear not," Louis replied.

"The bees won't know that though, will they?" It appealed to Ardron that he could have insects gathering nectar from Malmesbury estate to make honey for Norwood. "Permission granted." he said. "Next."

"A charge of theft, Sir," Maurice said. "Eadbetht of Kemble Wick charges his neighbour Hrothgar of stealing apples.

"Stealing Apples?" Ardron queried a little despairingly, it seemed so petty.

"Yes Sir," Maurice confirmed. "Step forward Eadbetht and Hrothgar."

Ardron recognised both men immediately. "You were with me at the battle of Lincoln." he said pointing at Eadbetht.

"I was," he replied.

"And you were also at Lincoln," he said to Hrothgar.

"Yes Sir. I was. And also, at Malmesbury, where you were wounded."

He leaned back in his chair. "Then you are comrades in arms and are falling out over apples." He sighed with some exasperation. "Alright," he said resigned to pettiness. "How many apples do you claim he stole?"

Eadbetht shrugged. "Perhaps two barrels full."

"Two barrels? Why that must be every apple on the tree."

"Yes, Sir."

Perhaps this wasn't quite so petty after all. "Do you deny it?" he asked Hrothgar.

"I never took a single apple from his tree, Sir."

"Then you deny you took the apples."

"No Sir, I did take the apples. But I took those only that lay on the ground and had laid there for weeks and were beginning to rot."

"Beginning to rot! Why would you want rotten apples?"

"I planned to make a little cider for Christmas celebration."

"I see," said Ardron. "You took them believing that he didn't want them."

"Yes, Sir."

"But you took them without asking?"

Hrothgar nodded.

"Then technically it is stealing." He turned his attention to Eadbetht. "Did you want those apples?"

"I did, Sir."

"For what purpose?"

"To make cider also."

"Then why had you not gathered them earlier?"

"I just hadn't had the time." Eadbetht replied.

Ardron was dubious. He suspected that he didn't really want the apples, but because Hrothgar had taken them without permission he had decided to complain.

"How goes the cider fermenting?" he asked Hrothgar.

"It goes well, I have almost two gallons." he replied.

"I am pleased to hear it." Ardron said. "Even though the apples were rotting you did take them without consent. Therefore, you did steal them. My judgement is that you will give the two gallons of cider to Eadbetht." Hrothgar was taken aback, then just looked disappointed.

"Eadbetht," Ardron turned his attention to the other man. "You will give one gallon of cider back to Hrothgar, as a reward for his labour. And that is my decision. Next case," he said turning towards Maurice.

The next and last case concerned a man who had damned up a small stream. His intention was to create for himself a reservoir in order to fill irrigation channels, which he dug across his rented land. However, in so doing, he had drastically reduced the amount of water available to his neighbour downstream. Not wishing to dampen the man's enterprise Ardron allowed him to keep the reservoir, but to lower the dam, adding a promise to the complainer, that there would be a further review of the situation at a later date.

As he left the chamber, he could not help but to glance at Claennis. She gave what passed as an approving half nod with a half-curled lip which hinted at a verdict; satisfactory.

***

Christmas Eve

"Is the maid ready?"

"She has been ready since first light," Maurice confirmed.

"And Jacques?"

"Your squire is with the horses."

Ardron nodded and glanced around his chamber looking for something, anything over-looked. Seeing nothing he was satisfied all was ready. "I will attend the Christmas celebrations this evening and tomorrow. Then make my return on the morning of the day of St Stephen," he informed Maurice.

"You should take the maid with you." Maurice said.

"I intend to, and drop her off at her father's estate Cloatly."

"No," Maurice said. "I meant to the empresses festivities."

"To the festivities?" Ardron echoed surprise. "Within thirty minutes she would have offended half the people there and would have berated Empress Maude for food wastage."

Amusement twinkling in Maurice's eyes as he drawled "Yes___."

Ardron could not help but snigger at the thought.

"She's going to be missed around here," Maurice added.

"Missed like a bad headache," Ardron muttered, dismissing Maurice's comment although secretly agreeing with his constable.

In the bailey and mounted on Rattlebone, Ardron glanced around at the other two. "Ready?" he asked.

"Lead on my lord," Claennis responded with an extravagant hand wave.

Ignoring the jibe, he looked at Jacques who responded with a brief nod.

Ardron glanced down to Maurice who stood at Rattlebone's head. "How far is it to Cloatly?" he asked.

"Five miles."

Ardron sighed. "Could be a long five miles," he muttered.

Maurice only chuckled.

The morning was as is typical for late December, gloomy and overcast. Even so it could not dampen Claennis's spirits and soon into the journey she began to sing. At first quietly but gradually strengthening

"She's happy," Jacques said.

"She's happy," Ardron confirmed, glancing back, but suspected it was just as much an attempt to irritate. To tell her to be quiet, however, would acknowledge some success. So, he kept quiet and endured it. Instead, he turned his thoughts to the imminent festivities at Devizes castle. All these empress's feast followed the same tried and tested pattern. A feast designed to impress, as extravagant and highly decorated dishes would be trundled out. Some of them so audacious it required a servant at each corner to bring in. Wine, mead, cider and beer would flow to excess. Then the dancing would follow. Refined and sophisticated at first, but later due to alcohol excess some over-indulgers, with inhibitions gone, would allow enthusiasm to over-rule dignity.

His thoughts turned to who would be there. All the usual high-ranking dignitaries he could anticipate with a degree of certainty. Earl Gloucester, Brien Fitzcount, Reginald de Dunstanville, Baldwin de Reviers, Robert Fitzedith, Roger Fitzmiles, John Fitzgilbert, Humphry de Bohun to name some of the obvious. The latter, however, he did look forward to seeing. Perhaps, from him, he would get a full account of what went amiss with the Coventry peace talks. Then he thought of Rohesa. Would she be there along with her husband Payn de Beauchamp? He didn't especially look forward to that. Maybe, he mused, they wouldn't be there. After all

Bedford is a long way east of Devizes. But if she was? What then should his reaction be? He might ignore her completely. That wouldn't do. Not only would it be rude, it would suggest resentment. Better that he behaves politely but indifferent and carry on as if there had never been anything between them. That, he decided, would be the best policy.

Engrossed in his thoughts he hadn't realised that Claennis had stopped singing. Curiosity made him glance over his shoulder. She flashed a half-smile and a reassuring nod in his direction. From the nearby thicket two pheasants took to wing, screeching loudly in alarm as they did. With panicked flight, the birds passed between the riders causing the mare that Claennis rode to shy violently then to rear onto her hind legs. Claennis was an adept rider, and instinctively leaned forward onto the horse's neck while squeezing her legs into its ribs for balance. She would have kept her seat and control, except on landing the horse stumbled and fell over onto its side. Fearing she was partially trapped beneath the horse Ardron whirled his own mount about. However, the horse got to its feet rather quickly and trotted away. Claennis got to her feet ruefully dusting herself down none the worse for being flung.

"Are you alright?" Ardron asked.

"I'm fine. I'm fine," she said dismissively.

"Jacques catch the horse," Ardron instructed, then dismounted to lend any assistance that might be needed.

"Don't fuss," Claennis snapped. "Not the first time I have been thrown nor will it be the last I suppose."

Ardron nodded then, instinctively, began to help her brush away some of the December mud.

"What do you think you are doing?" she asked.

Realising what he was doing he lifted his hands as if they had been scorched. "I beg your pardon, my Lady."

"My Lady?" she queried.

Ardron spluttered, not sure whether to make a correction and call her Claennis. In the end simply said. "Yes. My Lady.

Further embarrassment was spared when Jacques returned on foot leading both horses. "Sir, he said. "I'm afraid the mare is lame on her front leg."

She was indeed lame, limping pronouncedly. A quick inspection by Ardron revealed that, although the animal could not be ridden, the injury did not look to be life-threatening.

"Now what?" Claennis challenged.

Ardron continued to look down at the injured leg while he thought through his options. "You'll have to ride double with me," he said.

"That'll be cosy," she said. "And what about the horse?"

"She'll follow,"

486

"Follow to where?"

He could see her point. "How far are we from your father's manor?" he asked.

She looked about her. "Three miles she said with a shrug."

"In fact, we are nearer Norwood," he said thoughtfully.

New plan, he decided. "Jacques I'm going to ask you to take the mare back to Norwood on foot. Take your time, lead her slowly. Can't be much more than two miles. When you have done that, then get yourself a fresh mount and follow me to Devizes. We have rooms at the Travellers Rest outside the north gate."

"I know it," he said.

"Of course you do." Ardron said. "And you, my Lady," with a hint of sarcasm. "Can ride Jacques horse."

"Oh, what a disappointment," she said. "I thought I was going to get my arms around a noble knight."

It took just a few minutes for Jacques to get organised, then with a brief glance at Ardron he set off with the mare hobbling behind on a long lead.

Ardron watched until his squire was out of sight. It would be slow progress for the boy, but he would make it alright. "Mount up," he charged Claennis. For a few minutes they rode on in silence before she spoke.

"So, this feast you have to attend tonight is it compulsory?" she asked.

"Not compulsory, but attendance is expected."

She was silent a few moments before she asked. "Empress Maude, what is she like?"

"What is she like?" Ardron paraphrased while he gathered his thoughts. It was not an easy question to answer. "Well__," he drawled. "She is very regal, very refined. Certainly, single-minded and she does not suffer fools at all. I suppose," he went on, "She's quite formidable."

"I have some admiration for her," Claennis admitted. "She was denied what was her birth-right simply because she was born the wrong sex. If she had a pair of balls instead of a pair of tits, she would be ruler and there would be no war throughout the country."

Ardron looked at her sharply, surprised by her forthright explication.

"Well it's true," she responded to his look. "How many bastard sons did the old king sire?"

"A few," Ardron replied with a shrug.

"Aye a few. It's a shame he didn't spend a little more time in his own marriage bed then, perhaps, he would have sired more than just William and Maude as legitimate heirs."

She had a point. "The past is history and the past cannot be changed," he said with a sigh.

"No," she agreed. "What are they like, these royal feasts?" she asked after a few moments.

"Extravagant,"

"I would like to see one," she said.

"No, you wouldn't,"

"Why?"

"Why? Because you would be appalled at the over-indulgence."

"Is it that bad?"

"From aristocracy point of view perhaps not. However, from a peasant point of view, positively indecent."

She stared at him hard. "You said that the way a son of a Saxon Thegne would see it."

He laughed out loud. "You interpret things your own way, don't you?" he said.

"Take me with you," she said.

"No."

"Why not?

"Why not? Because you're too opinionated! You just have no idea when it is better to keep your own counsel. Within an hour you would probably have cost me half of my friends, and the regard that I currently enjoy among the elite, would have nose-dived."

***

Devizes Castle, Christmas Eve

Shuffling very slowly forward Ardron arrived at the head of the line where he was greeted and welcomed to the eve celebrations by Earl Robert.

"Welcome, sir Ardron," he said. "I trust you are well."

"Indeed Sir." He half turned. "May I present the maid Claennis from Cloatly."

"My Lady," the Earl said, as Claennis bobbed a curtsy. They shuffled on until Ardron faced the empress.

"Ah, Sir Ardron, my loyal knight. You are welcome," Maude greeted.

"Thank you, your Majesty, he said.

"Fare you well?" she asked.

"I do,"

"Enjoy the festivities," she said. He was dismissed.

"May I present the maid Claennis, daughter of Modig the Geneat of Cloatly," he said half turning and desperately hoping that Claennis responded appropriately. He need not have worried.

She made a deep respectful curtsy. "Your Majesty," she said with head bowed.

"You are welcome, young lady." The empress said. "Have you journeyed far?"

"Twenty-five miles, your Majesty."

"Not too far then." Maude replied. "Enjoy our festivities." To Ardron's relief she too was dismissed, as the empress turned to greet the next person in line.

"What now?" Claennis whispered, taking his offered arm, as they moved into the vast space that was the great hall of Devizes castle. He paused a moment to survey the spectacle. The walls were decorated with long red and yellow streamers interspersed by evergreen foliage. At the other end, the traditional yule log smouldered with hot embers. Just beyond that, and above in the narrow gallery, a combo of half-a-dozen musicians played seasonal music. It was still comparatively early and perhaps only half of the expected guests were yet in attendance.

"What now?" He echoed Claennis's question. "Now we pay our respects to the kitchen staff's supper presentation," he said. Then he guided her towards the long bench, where laid out for all to admire, was the evenings fare.

At the near end were a selection of solid and cream cheeses, then moving along into array of cold meats, all laid out with imaginative decoration. Along the back was a tower of shrimp, and alongside that, a tower of ocean fish. The fish entangled and twisted together to form the tower. Bread there was in abundance, but all carefully re-shaped into items of amusement. At the centre piece, of course, a roasted boar, decorated with apples, oranges and trimmed with olives.

"What are they?" Claennis asked pointing at the olives.

"They are olives from Italy" Ardron explained. She shook her head bemused.

"And those?"

"Bananas"

"Bananas?" with her finger she poked one. "How do you eat that?"

"You peel it."

"You peel it?"

"Never mind," he said. "Perhaps later you can try one."

They moved along into an area of pastries and sweets. When they reached the end Claennis looked back along the bench. "Your right," she said. "Awful self-indulgence."

Ardron looked back philosophically. "This is just Christmas Eve supper. You will see the real indulgence tomorrow when the feast really begins."

She didn't reply, but her face said it all. "What do we do now?" she asked.

"Well I suppose we mingle." Not too far away he could see Fitzgilbert with his wife Sibyl. "Let's go and talk to Sir John," he suggested.

"What happened to his face?" she asked,

"I'll tell you later," he replied as they made their way over.

The conversation was light-hearted and pleasant as they discussed the skilful food presentation of the kitchen staff, the masses of decorations hung around the hall, and onto the results of the autumn harvest. Over Fitzgilbert's shoulder, Ardron spotted Humphrey de Bohun pass. He wanted to speak with him, and so after a moment's hesitation he said. "I wonder if you would excuse me just for a few moments? I need a quick word with Sir Humphry.

"Of course," Fitzgilbert said after a brief confusion.

"Can I leave Claennis here with you? I promise I'll be back promptly."

"Twill be our pleasure," Sibyl said.

Stepping out hurriedly he soon caught up with de Bohun. "It's good to see you back Sir Humphrey," he said.

"It's a relief to be back," he replied.

"You are none the worse for the experience?"

"Good God no. It'd take more than a hump-back dwarf and an immature traitor, to rattle me." He scoffed.

"Glad to hear it," Ardron said. "The peace conference ended in failure!"

"It did!" he said. "The conference was doomed to fail from the very onset. Our primary demand was the return of Faringdon Castle and the release of all those held as prisoners. With Phillip Fitzrobert at the right hand of de Bossa, that was never going to be accepted. Their counter demands were the release of Walter de Pinkney, and a guarantee of sovereignty for Malmesbury Castle." He paused shaking his head. "And that could never be agreed. We couldn't even agree on the start time for the next day. Bishop de Clinton insisted that we must all attend morning mass to seek divine guidance before renewing negotiations. Of course, when, during the evening, someone knifed de Soulis to death, all the priority's changed. Fitzrobert immediately accused us of having his constable murdered, and arrested us, demanding that we surrender his killer."

"Who did kill him?" Ardron asked.

"Who knows," de Bohun replied. "Stabbed in the chest, so I would guess it was someone he knew. But who? We'll probably never know. Anyway, when the king intervened and had us released, Fitzedith decided that we should make good our escape while we still could."

"The war goes on," Ardron muttered dispiritedly.

"The war goes on," de Bohun agreed.

De Bohun looked over his shoulder. "The girl," he said nodding in Claennis's direction. "Who is she?"

Ardron turned to look at Claennis, eight or nine paces away and seemingly in deep conversation. "She is the daughter of Modig the Geneat of Cloatly."

"Of course she is!" De Bohun said. "Now I recognise her. It has been many years since I saw her last. Then she was just a ruffian adolescence with freckles. My she has turned out to be a real looker, hasn't she?"

"She has," Ardron agreed looking approvingly at her. With her long gown of light blue, beneath a full-length over-dress of darker blue, and a wimple matching the light colour of her gown, she had begun to turn heads.

"If you will excuse me Sir Humphrey, I ought to return to her side." Ardron said to excuse himself. Although she had been a model of good behaviour so far this evening, he was still wary of her suddenly expressing a radical viewpoint.

"Of course," de Bohun allowed his excuse.

Lifting two goblets of wine from a waiter as he did, he made his way back. He reached the trio at the same time as did Ranulf Earl of Chester who was accompanied by a younger man.

"Good evening to you," Ardron said to him as he handed Claennis a goblet.

"Good evening to you. Are you well?" Ranulf replied politely.

Ardron had time only to nod concurrence before Chester had turned away. "Sir John," he said. "I would speak with you urgently before this evening ends." Fitzgilbert nodded a somewhat reluctant agreement.

Ardron studied the man standing behind Chester. He was tall, in his prime years, perhaps twenty years younger than Chester. With thumbs hooked, nonchalantly, into his waist belt, he stood aloof looking disinterested, but the watchfulness in his eyes revealed the opposite.

"When?" Chester pressed.

Fitzgilbert looked at Ardron. "Will you be here a few minutes with the ladies?" he asked.

"I will," Ardron said.

"Let's do it now," Fitzgilbert said to Chester with a sigh.

"We must find somewhere private," Chester said looking around.

Fitzgilbert pointed towards a terrace door. "If you can stand the cold, let's do it outside," he said. "Excuse me ladies," he added then allowed Chester to lead the way.

"That man is so intense," Sibyl said as she watched her husband go.

Before Fitzgilbert returned, they had been joined by Sibyl's brother, Patric Earl Salisbury, Baldwin de Reivers and his wife Lucia. With the arrival of newcomers the conversation had been somewhat repetitive. Ardron's concentration became somewhat limited, and he casually looked around the hall. His nerves took a jolt, when he saw Payn de Beauchamp and his wife Rohesa moving slowly along the food table admiring the presentation. He returned his focus back to the present company, then smiling and nodding agreement with Lucia's comments, he slowly altered his position to be less exposed. It was unlikely that he could avoid the pair all night, but at this moment he wasn't ready. He then saw Fitzgilbert crossing the room returning. He studied his face trying to gauge the man's mood, but his expression betrayed nothing.

"Everything alright, Sir John," he asked when he re-joined the company.

He nodded with slight exasperation. "Ranulf just being Ranulf. We'll talk later." he said briefly turning his attention to greet the newcomers.

The hall became more crowded as the number of guests swelled through the evening. Ardron had circulated casually, introducing Claennis to many of the Angevin dignitaries, and in all cases the maid had behaved impeccably. It was only when the young Roger Fitzmiles had persuaded Claennis to the floor to dance a carole, that Ardron had chance to speak again with Fitzgilbert and raise the subject of Ranulf of Chester.

"He is convinced that we are on the verge of losing the war," Fitzgilbert said. "He feels that we need a victory of sorts to regain the initiative. He proposes that we raise two armies and lay siege to both Ludlow Castle and Warwick Castle. He wants me to use my influence to persuade his father-in-law, Earl Robert, to raise and fund his venture, then to give him overall command."

Ardron whistled softly. "That's ambitious!" he muttered.

"Too ambitious," Fitzgilbert replied. "Notwithstanding that both are formidable stone-built castles, it would take very long sieges indeed to bring about their downfall. The cost of maintaining two sieges for any length of time would be enormous. As the Empress's Marshal, I know only too well the state of our finances, and we just do not have the resources to fund such a venture," he added shaking his head. "Whilst I do agree that a victory of sorts is what we do need right now, it would be more prudent to find softer targets."

"Why Ludlow and Warwick?" Ardron asked.

"Hmm. That too is interesting," Fitzgilbert said. "Ludlow I can see the attraction for him. If he could annexe that estate so close to his own at Chester, what a power in the land he would become."

"Then why doesn't he fund it and go ahead himself?"

Fitzgilbert smirked. "Because he has made himself so unpopular with the Welsh on his borders that he has to keep his own sergenti at a state of permanent readiness. 'Those troublesome Welsh,' he calls them. He daren't withdraw from his borders, if he does the Welsh would pour across his estate like a flood."

"As I recall they were his allies at Lincoln," Ardron said.

"They were," Fitzgilbert confirmed.

"Will you approach, Earl Robert?"

"No, I will not," he said firmly. "I will report Chester's approach, but I could not recommend such a venture."

"The young man with him, who was that?" Ardron asked.

"That was his nephew, Gilbert de Claire."

It was not helpful to Ardron, he hadn't previously heard of him.

"Ah," Fitzgilbert said looking over Ardron's shoulder. "Your Lady returns." He touched his brow to Claennis and muttered, "My Lady." After glancing at Fitzmiles added, "Sir Roger," then he withdrew.

"Are you having a good time?" Ardron asked when they were left alone.

"I am," She readily agreed.

"You sound surprised," he said.

"Yes, I am. Tell me," she went on. "That man there hasn't left the Empress's side all evening. Is that her lover?"

He looked to where she had indicated and to Brien Fitzcount. "Her lover? I doubt it. They are fond of each other because he has known her since she was an infant. Lover? I would say not. More like uncle and niece, and as a devoted uncle, he looks out for her welfare."

"But he is not really her uncle?"

"No."

"And that lady over there? She constantly looks this way?"

He had no need to turn and look, he knew exactly who she meant. But he feigned ignorance and turned anyway. "Oh," he said. "That is Lady Bedford, and her husband Payn de Beauchamp, Lord Bedford."

"Are they special friends of yours?" she asked.

"Erm. They are friends of mine, yes. Special?" he sniffed. "Not especially."

"I think Lady Bedford wants to talk with you. Why else would she keep watching you?"

Ardron raised an eyebrow. "I'm sure I don't know," he said dismissively. He had been avoiding the pair all evening, but now it was time to face up. It would be indecorous to continue to ignore them for the duration of both feasts, and it might even pose curious and awkward question. "Come," he said. "Let's go and talk with them."

He saw Rohesa watching him with interest as they approached. "Good evening my Lord," Ardron said.

"Ah good evening Sir? __," clearly he couldn't remember.

"Ardron," Rohesa helped him out.

"Ardron. Of course."

"Lady Rohesa," Ardron acknowledged.

She held out her hand, which he took and allowed his lips to brush her fingers. "I understand congratulations are in order," he said.

"Our daughter, Beatrice?" De Beauchamp took up the conversation.

493

"Yes," Ardron confirmed. "Born sometime during the summer, I believe."

"August," Rohesa interjected.

"Where is the infant now?" He asked.

"We left her at Bedford with her wet nurse," she said.

"Yes, just a little too far for such an infant to journey, and particularly so at this time of year," de Beauchamp added.

Ardron nodded agreement. "May I present Maid Claennis. Daughter to the Geneat of Cloatly," he said half turning towards Claennis.

"Geneat? That's Saxon nobility I believe."

"It is, Ardron confirmed.

"Charmed, my dear," de Beauchamp said turning his attention to Claennis

Claennis gave a smile and a polite bobbed curtesy in response.

"Is this your first time at one of these Norman feasts?" Rohesa asked.

"Yes, it is."

Rohesa nodded. "You probably find them a little overwhelming, at the moment, my dear. But you will get used to them." She said with a hint of false sympathy. "If of course, you get the opportunity to attend another," she added

"Decadent, would be a better description," Claennis countered with a smile.

"Claennis will be here tomorrow," Ardron said. "And perhaps sometimes in the future she might do me the honour of accompanying me again." He was being defensive.

"What sort of year have you had?" de Beauchamp enquired changing the subject.

"Eventful," Ardron replied with a sigh.

"Profitable?"

"Yes," Ardron replied nodding, after a moment's thought.

They were joined by the young man who had accompanied Chester earlier.

"Oh," de Beauchamp uttered a little surprised by his appearance behind him. "Have you met Gilbert de Claire, Earl of Pembroke?" He asked Ardron.

"Er," Ardron wasn't sure how to answer. "We almost did earlier but were not introduced."

"Then let me do it now."

Polite pleasantries exchanged, Ardron asked de Claire about Pembroke.

"I own the barony of Pembroke but spend very little time there. It is a little too remote," he said. "Perhaps a couple of months in the summer," he added with a wince. "No," he went on. "I prefer to spend time much closer to the action."

"And where would that be?"

"Pevensey Castle."

"You own Pevensey Castle?" Ardron asked.

"I do."

"Forgive me," Ardron said. "That is south of London, isn't it?"

"It is! And is the very spot on the coast where William Duke of Normandy landed his army in 1066."

"But isn't that deep in King Stephen's territory?"

"Yes," he replied off-handed, before turning his attention to de Beauchamp. "Payn when you have a few moments my Uncle Ranulf would like to talk with you."

Ardron watched de Beauchamp's reaction closely, having a fairly good idea what Chester wanted to talk about. But there wasn't one. Clearly, he didn't know what the subject would be.

"What about?" de Beauchamp asked.

"Er_. Matters of war strategy," de Claire hedged.

De Beauchamp nodded and with a sigh said. "I'll be there presently."

De Claire hesitated, then finally accepted that matters of war strategy were not top priority for de Beauchamp at that moment. "You'll find us over in the far corner," he said with a vague direction wave. "Excuse me ladies," he said backing away.

"We didn't come here for a war counsel," de Beauchamp muttered, as he watched de Claire walk away. "We came to enjoy the Christmas celebrations." Then after giving Ardron a brief smile said, "Please excuse us Ardron. We have to pay our respects to Sir Reginald." A vague pointed finger indicated Reginald de Dunstanville a few paces away. "It was nice to see you again," he added. "And it was a pleasure to meet you Claennis."

The evening wore down and Claennis seemed to be drawn more and more into the festivities as she received many invitations to dance. There was no doubt, she was having a good time. On this occasion, Ardron watched from the side as she took her place in a large circle as the next carole was played. She clapped her hands and flashed a large smile at him before she made a spin.

Somebody whispered in his ear. "She is a delight, isn't she?"

"Yes, she is, Rohesa." he replied.

"How did you find her?" she asked.

"A chance meet while hunting." He didn't expand.

The was a long pause before she asked. "Do you love her as much as you loved me?"

It was an awkward question, and he wasn't sure how to answer. He was reluctant to reveal the circumstances of their relationship, and so he hedged. "Not yet," he said.

"Not yet!" she echoed. "Funny answer." There was a protracted silence before she said quietly. "You can still have the ring back. You have only to say the word."

He understood precisely what conditions that would bring. "You're married now," he replied.

"I was married before," she said.

"You were. But now you have a child as well." She stared at him without speaking. "He seems like a good man, your husband," he said.

"He is," she agreed.

"Where is he?"

"He went off to talk with Earl Chester."

"Then he won't be long," he predicted.

"How do you know that?"

"I have a pretty good idea what he wants."

"Tell me," she said.

"You can ask him yourself," he said looking over her shoulder seeing de Beauchamp returning. Even before he had actually joined them, he could sense the man's exasperation. "Is everything alright?" he asked.

De Beauchamp shook his head ruefully. "The man's mad," he said.

"Could be," Ardron agreed.

He stared at Ardron quizzically. "You know what it was all about. Don't you?"

"If it was about attacking Ludlow and Warwick castles, then yes."

"It was. And what I told him to do is a physical impossibility. But he might have fun trying."

Ardron grinned. "A response I applaud," he said. "But be wary., Chester would make a bad enemy." The carole was finished and all the dancers stood politely applauding. "If you will excuse me," he said. "I must find Claennis, I think she has had enough excitement for one night."

"Of course," de Beauchamp said. "Will you be here tomorrow?"

"We will. Goodnight to you both," he said

It was a mere fifteen-minute journey to the Travellers Rest and was just a few minutes after midnight when they arrived. A handful of Christmas Eve revellers still patronised, but by this hour they were themselves somewhat subdued,

"Did my squire arrive?" Ardron asked the landlord.

"Yes Sir, about two hours ago."

Ardron looked around but could not see him. "Do you know where he is?"

496

The landlord looked around. "I haven't seen him for a little while." he said. "He sat himself over there by the fire for a while, but I must assume that he has gone to bed."

Ardron turned away a muttered a quiet curse.

"What is the problem?" Claennis asked.

"Jacques has gone to bed.

"So?"

"He will have gone to bed in your room." He sucked noisily through his teeth. "I'll have to get him up."

"Why?"

"Unless." A thought occurred to him. He turned back to the landlord. "Do you have another room?"

"Christmas Eve and an empress's feast at the castle? No," he said with a hint of amusement and a head shake.

"We'll just have to get him up," he concluded.

"Leave him," Claennis replied sympathetically. "We can share a room."

Ardron looked at her hard. "OK," he concluded. "You take the bed and I'll take the chair."

"Of course," she said.

The chamber was not big, but big enough. The large four poster bed occupied the greater area, positioned as far away as was possible from the shutters. The room was lit by two half-burned candles, and the fire in the grate had by this time burned through to glowing ash. Ardron found one remaining log in the bucket, and with a bit of poking, managed to revive the fire enough to give the log a chance of burning. Claennis had leapt onto the bed and dropped the curtains to give herself some privacy while she undressed. Ardron moved the only chair as close to the fire as possible and, with poker still in hand, stared into the fire grate watching tiny flames struggling to gain a hold.

Alone with his thoughts he reflected on the evening. It had gone far better than he could have possibly hoped. Claennis had not only behaved impeccable, but had, if anything, enhanced his status. She had attracted admiring glances all evening, and to have such a good-looking young filly in his company had surely enhanced his reputation. His encounter with Rohesa had also gone better than he hoped. Where he had anticipated unhappiness there had been none. Where he had anticipated awkwardness there had been a little, but not that much. The fact that he had found it easy to reject her offer, of some vague illicit reconciliation, had proved that. Self-satisfied, he considered that he had successfully closed the door on that affair.

"Everything alright out there?" Claennis said.

"Fine," he responded looking round to see her leaning out from behind the curtain.

"Here, you will need this," she said tossing a blanket towards him.

"Thank you."

"Goodnight," she said disappearing back behind the curtain.

He got up slowly from the chair and picked up the blanket. "Goodnight," he said wrapping it around his shoulders.

The chair was not a comfortable place to sleep. He tried, at first, a normal sitting position but as sleep began overtaking, his head would suddenly drop waking him abruptly. He tried to half curl on the seat but before long his folded legs began to ache. He tried an unconventional way of looping his legs over the back of the chair with his torso on the seat, but his head draped over the edge. And all the time he wrestled with the blanket. Eventually, he gave up with the chair and stretched out on the floor in front of the rapidly dying fire. The floor was hard, but that was not the major problem. Although the shutters were closed, they were an ill fit. And, as the fire died away the cold of a December night began to seep into the room, eventually creeping into every corner. Finally, with the fire gone and the cold dominant he, shivering, tried the chair once more with the same results.

He looked with envy at the bed only feet away and thought, 'if he could just curl up in a bottom corner it would be softer, and with the heavy curtains protecting from draughts things would be so much better.' He wouldn't even need to get in. But instantly he rejected the thought, that action might be misinterpreted. So, he tried yet again to find a comfortable position in the chair. Minutes later he gave up, and after staring towards the bed for a few more moments decided to yield to temptation.

Lifting the curtain in the nearest corner he peered in. He couldn't see Claennis clearly, only the hump in the bedding under which she lay. Cautiously, he climbed on the bed and slowly crawled further in.

"What are you doing?" she demanded.

He withdrew hastily muttering, inaudibly, "It's cold." Wrapping the blanket around him tightly, he went back to the chair.

A few moments later, Claennis drew back the curtain and partially folded down the bedclothes. After a moment's pause, she said. "Come. Get in." After a moment's hesitation, he hurried across to the bed and in one movement slid under the blankets. "I'll stay over on this edge," he muttered.

Comfort was instant, but the cold took a little longer to ease. Gradually it did so. He lay on his back staring up into the darkness truly thankful to be out of the cold, drowsiness gradually started to come. But he suddenly snapped alert when Claennis turned towards him and cast a leg across his thigh. For a few moments he lay still, not daring to move. Turning his head slowly, he looked at her. She appeared to be still sleeping. Nevertheless, the closeness of her, the scent of her, and her leg across his nether region began to have an effect and he began to get aroused. Through embarrassment, he sought to move away and rolled over slowly to lay on his shoulder at the very bed edge. Almost instantly, she followed him snuggling up to his back, throwing an arm across his hip as she did. Wide awake now and hardly daring to move, he lay perfectly still trying to control his carnal urges. But clearly, she was not asleep, as her hand moved slowly over his hip and her fingers sought his manhood. When she found what she sought, she gripped him tight. Greatly surprised, he rolled over and looked down at her, she stared back without speaking. As if by strong magnet force their lips pressed together with hungry desire. There was no foreplay, nor hesitation, just burning need between them. He lowered himself down onto her and coupled instantly. She responded only with a gasp.

Now joined together as one he, supporting his weight on his elbows, looked down at her. "There must be frost in the devil's kitchen tonight," he whispered with the hint of a smirk.

"And here am I, without kindle or flint," she giggled.

Chapter 21

Norwood, January 1146

"There are two Templars in the bailey," Maurice informed him.

Ardron looked up from his papers. "Templars? Here?"

"Yes Sir."

"What do they want?" He muttered to himself as he got up from his chair and walked over to the window. From here he had a good view down into the main front area of the bailey. Immediately identifiable by their long white robes emblazed by vivid red crosses, there were indeed two Knight Templars in the bailey. They stood, by their horse's, waiting at the foot of the mote steps. "Have them brought up," he said a little apathetically.

He went over to his desk and gathered the papers he had been studying and placed them neatly to one side to be re-studied later. Soon after, Maurice entered with the visitors.

"Welcome mon chevalier's," he greeted as he directed them towards comfortable seats by the fire. "Have you come far today?"

From Malmesbury," one replied. He turned and indicated his companion. "This is Faramund and I am Adelhard," he said in French with a heavy guttural accent.

"Can I get you some refreshments?" Ardron offered.

"Nein, danke." Adelhard said.

"You're not French," Ardron said.

"No, we're from Saxony," Adelhard answered.

Ardron nodded. "What can I do for you, mon chevaliers?"

"You know that after the fall of Edassa to the Muslim, Pope Eugenius called for volunteers to take up the cross on a second crusade?"

"I do."

"Well," he went on. "The number that has come forward from England is disappointing, and on the initiative of Abbot Bernard de Claivaux, a team is assembled to come here to promote God's cause."

"You surely know that a war of succession rages throughout England." Ardron said.

"Of course! And Pope Eugenius has asked all to lay aside their parochial quarrels and turn their attention to rescuing the holy land from the Muslim heretics."

"An easy request to make when the consequences do not concern you over-much." Ardron's comment was greeted by stony silence and hard glares.

"We are just two of Bernard de Claivaux recruiting party," Faramund said, easing the tension. "Today we are here to invite you and all your sergens to a service in Malmesbury Abbey, this coming Sunday."

"Malmesbury Abbey?" Ardron queried. "Do you know that I and all here are in the cause of Empress Maude. And Roger de Pinkney, the Malmesbury Castellan, is for Stephen?"

"We do."

"Then it would be extremely stupid of us to surrender ourselves to a de Pinkney's promise. Don't you agree?"

"We will guarantee safe passage for all," Faramund said.

"You will? How can you do that?" Ardron asked.

"In this instance, we are the voice of the Pope and any who defies us, defies the Pope, risking damnation." Adelhard said.

Ardron sighed heavily. "You will have to forgive me," he said. "But I will not take the risk for myself or any of my sergens." It would, he concluded under the circumstances, be particularly stupid because it would give Roger de Pinkney a golden opportunity to seize him, and then demand exchange for his brother Walter, who was still being held prisoner in Devizes. He could imagine the anger it would generate if he were to put himself in that position and present the empress with such a dilemma.

"However," he went on. "I will permit you to address a congregation here in the main hall one hour from now. And you have my word that I will not stand in the way of any who desires to follow the cross to the holy land."

Both Templars looked disappointed to the point of exasperation. But then they began to converse in German. Eventually, realising that it was perhaps the best deal they were going to get, accepted Ardron's offer.

In the days that followed only two of his sergens were inspired enough to follow the cross. With reluctance, Ardron said goodbye to both men and wished them well as they left to join the crusading army of Emperor Conrad in Germany, and from there, travelling on to join the French King Louis.

***

Norwood, February 1146

For the depth of winter, these last few days had been unseasonably mild, and as Ardron sat in his chamber honing his sword edge it caused him a contemplative mood. On such a day as this, many years ago, and as a young teenager, he had romped with friends in the river Avon, just below Scorrenstone. He recalled how they had attempted to build a fish trap and then to catch the fish that had swam unwittingly into it. Even though trapped in a restricted place, the fish had proved to be quick and elusive. However, there had been some successes, although limited. He smiled as he recalled how in the end, they all stood on the bank counting their triumphs and as soaked as any water rat could be. But that was in the days of King Henry before this conflict between Stephen and Maude had erupted.

It was in the days when life was uncomplicated, and he a simple village Saxon. He wondered what he was now? He was a Norman Castellan and lived a Norman life. He dressed as a Norman, fought in a Norman war and followed Norman rules. He mused that, in truth, he had perhaps become more Norman than Saxon. Then instantly he rejected that. He was the second son of a Thegne and no matter how he dressed, nor the comrades he fought alongside, it was Saxon blood that filled his veins and would ever be so. He thought on the words of the young Prince Henry. 'When I become king there will be no Normans or Saxons there will be only English.' Noble words indeed! However, it could only come to pass if Henry became king, and now, that looked to be a remote possibility. The Angevin momentum seemed the have died away, and as far as he knew, there were no offensives planned or being planned. The policy had become one of hold onto currently held possessions and properties. There was no doubt that the downfall of Faringdon Castle was a severe blow, extenuated by the defection of Phillip Fitzrobert to Stephen, taking with him the additional castles of Cricklade and Tetbury. That was a line of castles that now supported the previously isolated Malmesbury.

Thinking further, he realised that he now had no realistic hopes of becoming castellan of Malmesbury. Even in the unlikely event that Roger de Pinkney did agree to trade Malmesbury Castle for his brother's freedom, then King Stephen would not. That castle had gone from an isolated outpost in Angevin territory to the very point of front line. Perhaps there was some merit in Earl Chester's fears that the Angevin's were losing this war. Even so Chester's schemes of laying siege to both Warwick and Ludlow castles were unrealistic. He sighed heavily as he carefully rubbed a finger down the honed edge of the sword. Satisfied that it was as sharp as could be he turned his attention the other edge.

He became aware of the sounds of light-hearted banter drifting in through the open shutters. Mildly curious he turned and looked towards the window. Stirred curiosity then made him lay aside his sword and go to the window to investigate. In the bailey and at the foot of the mote steps, a group of four in jovial mood, surrounded the maid Claennis and her horse.

"Swidhurn, you old iron clanger. Are you deaf yet?" she jested.

"What's that?" he responded cupping his ear in jest.

Next, she turned her attention to Louis, "Louis," she greeted with a smile. "You must be a wealthy man by now all those years handling the account books."

"Alas," he responded. "Complete honesty is the terrible cross I have to bear."

"Of course," she joshed sarcastically.

His own delight at seeing her again was tempered with some embarrassment. It had been eight weeks since he had returned her to her father's house, and he had left with a promise that he would call on her very soon. However, at first the castle business had demanded his attention, and time had slipped past. Knowing full well that he could have temporarily laid that aside and honoured his promised, he had tried to think of a better excuse for his tardiness. But then even more time had elapsed, and because of that, he felt he then needed to find an excuse to make the visit. But here she was, standing below in the bailey, surrounded by enthusiastic sergens who were so obviously pleased to see her. The situation was now that he couldn't avoid the issue, he could only make grovelling apologies and ask forgiveness. However, the fact that she had come to Norwood was perhaps cause for encouragement. Taking only enough time to check his own appearance in a mirror, he left the chamber to greet her. Halfway down the mote steps and still unseen he stopped and looked down on the small gathering. They were still in high spirits.

"I'll take you on in an archery contest at any time and at any purse." She challenged Jarcot amid giggles.

Ardron smiled to himself at the thought of the one-armed Jarcot struggling to draw a long bow. It was then that Maurice drew attention to Ardron watching from the steps. The hilarity faded a little as Claennis turned towards him and acknowledged with a wave, before turning back to the group speaking quietly. Having made her withdrawal excuses, she turned away and came up the steps towards him.

"Good day to you Sir Ardron," she said formally.

Ardron nodded. "I am pleased to see you Claennis." He replied stiffly. He stepped aside and then said. "Would you please come in," and indicated with a wave towards the keep. Nodding briefly, she moved past him and led the way up the steps.

Inside his private chamber she stood awaiting his guidance. He hurried past and removed his sword from the seat where he had left it. "Please," he said, "Take a seat." Sheaving the sword and placing it out of sight he asked. "How have you been?"

"I have been well," she replied as she took the seat.

The atmosphere was a little awkward and charged with an amount of unease. It shouldn't have been! He was more than just happy to see her. In fact he was positively pleased. Her happy banter of a few moments ago had dried up, perhaps revealing her unease also. "Can I get you anything?" he asked to ease the tension. "A little wine or cider, perhaps."

"Nothing for me," she answered. He nodded without speaking and then there followed a pause. It was, he decided, time to make his grovelling apologies for the non-delivery on his promise to visit.

"I had thought that you would have come to visit." She said before he could speak.

"Ah yes," he said. "I had always intended to do so, and I do earnestly beg your pardon. I can make no excuse other than at first, I was busy with castle business and then as time elapsed, I became embarrassed that I had reneged on my promise. But I would have eventually found an excuse of some sort. Be assured of that." He waited for a re-action but at first none came, and he wasn't sure if that was a good or bad sign.

"Well," she eventually said. "Perhaps I have one for you. Next week is the end of shrove-tide and the start of Lent. On that day, my father arranges a feast for friends and servants. It will be modest fare compared to the Christmas feast of Devizes Castle. Nevertheless, I am here to invite you."

Ardron was inwardly delighted. Here on offer was a possible way back into Claennis's affections. "Tell your father it will be my pleasure to attend."

"I will tell my father," she said, "But the invitation is from me."

"Then I will be doubly delighted," he beamed.

"Good," she said. "I think I will take a little cider, if you don't mind?"

"Of course." From the decanter on the table he poured a little into a pewter and carried it over to where she sat. Even dressed in masculine attire it was obvious that she was a sensual beauty. She curved in and out deliciously in all the right places, and her golden hair, although bundled up tight, still complimented a pretty face.

She took the pewter and as Ardron turned away to take the seat close by she muttered almost inaudibly. "I am with child."

Ardron momentarily froze as he moved to sit. He stood upright and turned back towards Claennis. "I'm sorry," he said. "What did you say?" he asked unable to believe his ears.

"I am with child," she repeated this time a little more firmly.

"Are you sure?" he asked stupidly.

"I'm sure."

"Well," was all that confusion would let him mutter. Recovering after a few moments, he took her hand. "Don't worry, "he said, "I'll make everything right."

"How?"

He took a breath. "I'll speak with your father and ask for your hand in marriage." He hesitated a moment then added. "If that's what you want."

She looked down into her lap. "You don't have to," she muttered.

"Of course I do, I want to."

A simple nod of agreement was her only re-action.

"You do want to?" he sought confirmation.

"Yes."

"Then if your father agrees we will be married as soon as possible."

He lifted her up and wrapped his arms around her. "You will make me the envy of all men." He whispered. He looked down the chamber as she snuggled her head into his neck. 'Me! With a wife and child,' he thought. It was a thought that left him with as much trepidation as did the eve before battle. But then, it might just as easily turn out to be wonderful.

***

Cloatly Estate, April 1146

The wedding had taken place amidst the apple blossom of Geneat Modig's estate orchard. It had been a traditional Saxon wedding with a Weodfodthegn appealing to the Saxon Gods to look favourably on the wedding pair. Then he went on to appeal to Frige to bless the bride with fertility. At that point Ardron had fought off a smile and maintained a stony face even after the meaningful glance from his bride. Only he and she knew that she was already fertile, but it was a secret that would not remain long. Ardron had accepted the traditional ceremonial sword presented by Modig symbolising the passing over of responsibility for protection of his daughter. Now as the afternoon began to wane, and early evening took over the real festivities were about to begin.

Modig had spared no expense to exalt his only daughter on her special day. Troubadours strolled around the grounds mingling amongst the guests as they strummed their instruments and crooned little ditties. Mead, beer and wines flowed as if easily gathered from a nearby brook, and although the evening feast was yet to begin, the delicious smells that oozed from the kitchen promised something exceptional.

"Well brother," Redwald said with his arm across Ardron's shoulders. "My young brother weds at last. I had begun to think this day would never come. I suppose you do know what you have to do tonight in your wedding bed." He added with a tease sparkle in his eye.

"Redwald, stop it," his wife Acha scolded.

Redwald squeezed his brother's shoulder and laughed heartily. "Congratulations," he said. "You have done well." Then added, with an approving glance across the lawn at Ardron's new wife. "Very well."

Ardron said nothing but gave an agreeing and a slightly smug nod.

"And the Christian wedding?" Acha asked.

"Tomorrow in the village church," he replied. "Just a modest affair with close relatives only." After a pause added. "You are of course invited if you wish."

"If you don't mind, we won't." Redwald said. "We'll go back to Scorrenstone tonight, and Cloatly is just a little too far away to return again tomorrow."

Ardron nodded understandingly. "Of course," he said.

"Who stands with you?" Acha asked.

"Swidhurn, of course. Who else?"

"Good," Redwald approved nodding.

Raucous laughter across the lawn attracted attention. It had come from the four Norman's that Ardron had invited along as token sergen representatives. Probably feeling a little isolated by the language barrier they had naturally hung together. Nevertheless, Jarcot, Fique, Roland and Jacques seemed to be in good spirits. Maurice, his castle constable, he had left at Norwood to over-see the feast celebrations he had arranged for the rest of his castle staff.

"If you will excuse me, I must move on," he begged leave to circulate.

"Of course Redwald said. "You must bring your bride to Scorrenstone at your earliest opportunity," he added.

Ardron nodded ascent. It was an instruction of a Thegne politely wrapped in a request. He wandered across the lawn and stood behind Claennis who was in conversation with Saxon relatives. After joining the conversation for a few moments, he then made excuses to capture his bride. "There is someone I want you to meet," he said to Claennis, then he led the way to a small group where his younger brother Esmond and his wife Edyo stood. He was particularly pleased to see that Cerdic was in their company, both he and Esmond had been friends from boys. Only the rivalry for the hand of Edyo had soured that. Perhaps not all that *l'amitie* was lost after all. The conversation was light with questions passing backwards and forwards as strangers tried to familiarise themselves with each other. However, it was interrupted by a servile servant touching Ardron's elbow before stepping back a couple of paces.

"Excuse me Sir," he said politely. "Geneat Modig would like to see you both in his chamber."

"Thank you," Ardron responded. "We'll be there right away." It took another three or four minutes before Ardron was able to withdraw from the conversation.

"What do you think he wants?" Claennis asked as they crossed the lawn towards the manor.

"Probably found out that you're pregnant and wants to bury that ceremonial sword in my chest," he joked.

"And you would deserve it!" she replied with a smirk.

It was a typical chamber of a Geneat, with heavy tapestries covering walls intermingled with a flamboyant assortment of weapons. Quite possibly each weapon carrying its own folklore. For Ardron, however, the real surprise was standing next to Modig, Humphrey de Bohun.

"Sir Humphrey!" he uttered.

"Sir Humphrey has made a special journey from Trowbridge to bring you wedding gifts," Modig said.

"Always a pleasure to see you Sir Humphrey," Ardron said. Then half turning towards Claennis said. "My wife, I believe you have met."

"Indeed I have. And long before those Christmas celebrations at Devizes." Switching his attention to Claennis added. "It was many years ago when you were nought but an adolescent tomboy." He took her hand and kissed her fingers. "You look absolutely stunning, my dear," he said. Straightening up he turned his attention back to Ardron. "I have here," he said holding up a rolled parchment. "A commendation from Empress Maude. She cites all your acts of valour in her cause, and acknowledging her dept she has, on this special day, great pleasure in promoting you to Baron."

Ardron was stunned. "I didn't expect anything like that," he spluttered.

"It is well deserved," de Bohun said. "You will of course have to attend an official ceremony to be awarded the title, but that is just formality."

"Oh my God." Claennis said. "I have married a baron," she paused. "Baron Ardron," she addressed her new husband, satirically.

"That, my daughter, makes you a baroness," Modig said.

"Well," she giggled shaking her head. "Now I can be <u>really,</u> irritating."

"Yes, my Lady Baroness," de Bohun agreed. He waited a few moments for the excitement to wane before going on. "There is more," he said. "A baron must have his own estates. Therefore, it is my personal pleasure to hand over these deeds." He picked up another rolled parchment from the table and offered it to Ardron.

"Deeds?" Ardron queried. "Deeds to what?" he asked taking the parchment.

"Deeds to Norwood estate. The estate the castle and all buildings including chattels contained there-in are now yours by title."

Ardron was stunned. "Then I don't." he didn't finish the sentence.

"No, you don't have to pay me anymore fief," de Bohun said. "It's all yours."

***

Ardron stood beside his charger, Rattlebone, fondly patting his neck. "He won't pull a cart, nor drag a plough." He sought assurance from his brother Redwald.

Redwald sighed resignedly and reluctantly agreed. "He won't pull a cart nor drag a plough," he granted.

"Then he is yours for two months. But two months only."

"He is a horse, "Redwald reminded him. "And you are over-protective of the animal."

Ardron nodded stroking the horse's muzzle. "Many times he has protected me, and many times I have protected him. To me he is not just a horse."

"Stallion duties only," Redwald confirmed. Then after a moments silence. "How old is the animal now?"

"Eleven, twelve," Ardron replied with a shrug.

"He is not a young horse, and his best athletic years are probably gone. He would probably be happier here in the village pulling carts and pulling ploughs, with the occasional stallion duties, than charging across a battlefield with all the dangers that go with that." He waited for the point to sink in. "You should very soon think about giving him back to the village."

Ardron didn't reply. His brother had a point. "When the time comes, I'll retire him to a Norwood paddock," he said,

"The horse is an asset and would be invaluable to the village. He would be more use here than lazing around a paddock." Redwald countered.

He had a point. "Father gave him to me, and I intend to look after him even unto retirement and beyond."

Redwald nodded surrendering to Ardron's determination then added. "In the Norman world you may be a baron, but in the Saxon world I am your Thegne," he reminded him. "You need to heed me more than you do." But he put his arm across his younger brother's shoulders. "Come," he said. "Let us see if your charming wife is yet ready to leave."

Four days he and Claennis had spent in Scorrenstone. It had been extremely pleasant introducing his new wife and renewing old friendships. Also, it had provided temporary escapism from the stresses and strains of castle business, and the anxieties of the conflict, which was not going well.

There was still an hour before noon when he and Claennis left the village to return to Norwood. In no hurry, they circled to the north of Malmesbury and passed south of Tetbury. By the time they approached Crudwell, the morning sunshine had been replaced by dark rain clouds with a heavy mist rolling up behind them, signifying rapidly approaching heavy rain. Seeking shelter they angled away towards a thickly wooded area and settled to wait out the storm. Very soon the wind became fierce, and the rain lashed almost horizontally. But huddled together beneath the thick canopy of a mature chestnut tree they were dry and snug. The torrential rain pelted upon the surface of the nearby brook creating miniature fountains across the water's fast flowing surface.

"That's the Swill, isn't it? Claennis looked for confirmation.

"It is," Ardron confirmed.

"Fast flowing," she muttered." That village," she said nodding in the direction of Crudwell, "Should have a water mill."

She was right. "It should," Ardron agreed."

"How far are we from Norwood?" Claennis asked.

"Three miles."

"Three miles?" She echoed. "That close?"

"Yes."

"Why don't you annexe the village?" she asked.

"Annexe the village?" He paraphrased with a chuckle. "It's on the Malmesbury estate and I don't think de Pinkney would allow that to pass."

"The villagers would!"

"They would? How did you arrive at that conclusion?"

"Well," she said. "First it would be new money to you, so you could accept a much lower fief. They would like that. And then you could build them a water mill, and they would love you for that."

"You have it all thought out, don't you?" he replied with a chuckle. "The idea, I suppose, does have merit," he allowed. "But I think the opportunity for that has passed. If it was ever there."

"How so?" she asked.

"When Malmesbury was isolated in the midst of Angevin territory, it might just have been possible. But now Malmesbury Castle is in a line of castles all sympathetic to the king's cause and is, therefore, much stronger. De Pinkney would most certainly retaliate and ferociously I would wager."

"Seems to me that you Angevins should have taken Malmesbury when it was more vulnerable."

"You are right," he agreed. "But it wasn't for the need of trying. "Two years ago we attacked Malmesbury."

"I remember," she said. "What went wrong?"

"What went wrong? Well__, Fitzmiles took the town easily enough and then laid siege to the castle. But the king brought an army to its rescue and we, outnumbered, were forced to withdraw. That is why Faringdon was so important to us. It would have put a barrier in the king's way west. In any future incursions he would then have to have taken Faringdon before he could progress. Strategically, he couldn't leave it in his rear."

"No," she agreed. "I can see that. He'd get a red-hot blade up his poopa."

"His poopa?" he queried with a chuckle.

"His poopa," she confirmed.

For a Lady Baroness you have a colourful vocabulary," he said putting his arm around her and giving her a squeeze.

"Wait until I am a countess," she said. "Then I'll say, arse."

He slapped his hand to his face and shook his head with a giggle. "I think the rain is stopping," he said looking up. Getting to his feet he took her hand and pulled her to her feet. "We should carry on," he said.

Well inside an hour later they arrived back at Norwood, where they were greeted with welcoming nods and grins.

"Anything I should know about" he asked Maurice as he dismounted.

"Mostly routine stuff, but there was one message that you might find important." Maurice replied. "It's all on your desk."

Ardron moved to help Claennis dismount, but she ignored his helping hand and leapt down unaided.

From somewhere his squire Jacques appeared and readily took charge of the horses. "Welcome back Sir," he said brightly before he led the horses away.

"Jacques," Ardron called.

"I know, Sir," he replied over his shoulder. "Tend and feed them well."

"Exactly," Ardron said. "Do you think I have him trained?" he asked of Maurice. "This important news is it good or is it bad?"

There was a definite reluctance to answer. Eventually he said with a sigh. "It's bad, Sir. But I'll let you read for yourself."

Ardron groaned silently. The past four or five days had been an enjoyable diversion but, there is always a sting in the tail, and wasn't that ever so. He put it off for now and followed Claennis up into the keep and to their private chamber.

***

"When did you get this?" He asked Maurice holding out the despatch.

"Two days ago?"

"You didn't think to get this to me?"

"I did. But I couldn't see what you could possibly do about it and as it is only information, I decided to let you continue to enjoy your leisure."

Maurice was right. There is not a damn thing he could do about it. Ardron nodded acceptance. "How many others know of this?

"Just Jarcot,"

He dropped the despatch on the desk and fell silent with bowed head while he thought on. "All should know of this," he said. "Call an assembly," he instructed. "I'll make the announcement in an hour."

His mood was black, and his body language showed it as he returned to his private chamber. Claennis picked up on it as soon as he entered. "What's wrong?" she asked.

He sat down heavily looking at the floor in silence. After a few moments he looked up sadly. "I will have to go to Bristol tomorrow," he said. "It seems that Ranulf de Gernon, Earl of Chester has sworn for the king, and at this moment has joined him and laid siege to Bedford Castle."

"Earl Chester? Isn't he the man that was advocating attacking Warwick and Ludlow castles at the Christmas celebrations?" she asked.

"The same,"

"But isn't he married to Robert, Earl Gloucester's daughter?"

"He is. Earl Gloucester is his father-in-law."

"Oh that poor man," she said. "First his son in betrayal, now his son-in-law."

Chester is a greedy man," Ardron said. "I would guess that he sees the king as the probable victor in this war, and with self-preservation in mind has decided to ally himself to Stephen. And with, of course, potential for huge rewards."

"Or perhaps it was that he felt piqued about not being taken seriously." Claennis suggested.

"Perhaps," Ardron allowed. "Whichever, it is still a bad business."

***

Bristol Castle

It was a sombre mood, spiced generously with anger, that settled over the assembly in the great hall of the castle. There was only one topic and that the defection of Ranulf, Earl Chester.

"It's a bad business," Reginald de Dunstanville said. "Not only is his defection shamefully disloyal, but it cedes to Stephen vast estates areas. The Welsh borders, southern parts of Lancashire and across the West Midlands too," he went on, sighing heavily. "That means a significant loss of revenue for the empress."

"Not to mention the huge army that Chester has at his disposal," Roger Fitzmiles added glumly.

"Was there any indication'" Ardron asked.

"None," de Dunstanville answered. "But I suppose," he went on, "With Chester one always knew that he was as about as reliable as a whore's promise of fidelity."

"What happens now?" Ardron asked.

De Dunstanville snorted derisively, "What can we do?" he replied somewhat hopelessly.

"We should attack Chester Castle while he is at Bedford and take it from him," Fitzmiles intervened angrily.

"Would that we could," de Dunstanville said sadly. "But it would be a formidable objective and a lengthy siege, and at the moment we have neither the resources nor the money."

"So he gets away with treachery."

De Dunstanville sighed without replying.

"Will Bedford hold?" Ardron asked.

"Payn de Beauchamp is no easy push over," de Dunstanville said. "So it might, or for a while at least."

"And the lady Rohesa, she is with de Beauchamp?"

Both men looked at him with blank expressions as if the question had no relevance. "She is his wife," Fitzmiles said. "Where else would she be?"

Ardron shrugged. "I wondered if perhaps de Beauchamp would have moved her to safety." He pulled a face seemingly agreeing that the question had no relevance.

The trio fell silent for a few moments and Ardron took the opportunity to glance around the great hall. It seemed that most of the Angevin nobles were there. The room buzzed with low conversation as men stood around in small clusters talking. It took no massive intellect to guess the topic all discussed.

"And Earl Robert?" Ardron asked. "How is he taking it?"

"Not well," de Dunstanville replied. "He is blaming himself and wondering if he could have done things differently on not only this issue, but the issue of his youngest son also. Of course," he went on. "There was absolutely nothing he could have done to prevent any of it."

"We need some sort of lift to raise his spirits." Fitzmiles added. "A victory of some sort no matter how small." He shook his head ruefully with a sigh.

"We are working on it," de Dunstanville said. "In the meantime Earl Robert is preparing to travel to Devizes to talk with Empress Maude. He will try to persuade her to sanction another mission to Anjou to persuade her husband, Geoffrey Plantagenet, to support her claim with money and men."

"It wasn't successful last time," Ardron commented.

"No, it wasn't," de Dunstanville agreed. "But we will have to try once more. After all it is his son that we strive to put on the English throne."

The circumstances remained the same as they were in the summer four years ago when they last appealed unsuccessfully to Count Geoffrey. It wasn't successful then and Ardron couldn't see why it would be more successful this time., but he made no comment. Instead he casually glanced around the hall and watched as one of the castle servants shouldered and weaved his way in their direction.

"Sir," he said, addressing de Dunstanville when he reached the trio. "Earl Robert would see you in his private chamber. You too Sir," he went on to Fitzmiles.

"We'll be there right away," de Dunstanville replied.

"The servant glanced at Ardron. "Sir, would you be Ardron of Norwood?"

"I would."

"Then you too are asked to attend."

"Thank you." De Dunstanville dismissed the man. "I wonder what's afoot," he muttered as the servant moved away.

"Only one way to find out," Fitzmiles said.

The earl's private chamber was atop the castle tower affording a panoramic view across the rooftops of Bristol and its harbour beyond. Earl Robert stood by an open portal hands clasped behind his back gazing out into the sunshine of a May afternoon. "Ah" he said turning around as the trio entered. "Come in, come in. Everybody knows everybody here," he went on indicating the two men sitting at the long table. Ardron recognised Robert Fitzedith and Baldwin de Reviers. Both greeted the new arrivals with friendly nods.

"Find a seat," the earl said with a wave of his hand as he made himself comfortable at the head of the table. He then paused a few moments while all others settled. Ardron took the opportunity to study Earl Robert. On the last occasion Ardron had seen him, he had seemed distant, tired and dispirited. But even though the Angevin cause had suffered further setbacks since then, he did appear to be in better spirits.

"Tomorrow," he began. "I intend to journey to Devizes with two propositions to lay before my sister Maude. The first will be to suggest that she set free Walter de Pinkney." Ignoring the obvious surprise around him he went on. "There will be of course certain conditions. In fact strict conditions! De Pinkney must first swear fealty to the empress and her cause. If he does, he will then be allowed to recover his seat as castellan of Malmesbury Castle from his brother Roger. This in effect will deliver Malmesbury to us, and at the same time blunt the spear of Stephen's advance west. If this comes about, we could then turn our attention to mopping up Tetbury and Cricklade bringing them both back under our control without the need for a large siege force. He paused before going on. "Of course, it all depends on Walter de Pinkney agreeing."

"What are the chances he will agree?" de Dunstanville asked.

"Well__," the earl drawled. "He has been incarcerated in a Devizes dungeon for some time now, so I suppose it will depend on how sick he is of prison life and how much he craves freedom."

"What about his brother Roger de Pinkney?" Ardron asked.

"Yes," the earl said. "What about his brother? And that my friend is why you are here. You are his near neighbour, and I would that you tell us what you know of this man."

Ardron spread his arms out over the table and looked down while he gathered his thoughts. "Not a lot," he said eventually." I have met the man on only three or four occasions. On all those occasions he was acting as an advisor to his elder brother. However, he did counsel a hard line every time. I would say that Walter is the more conciliatory of the pair. I personally think that Roger would not give up his new position willingly."

"Do you think he would defy his brother if Walter turned up to reclaim his seat?" Earl Robert asked.

Ardron was cautious. What he had as thoughts, were not what the earl wanted to hear. "I think it is probable that he would," he said quietly. Then adding after a pause. "But that is only my opinion."

"Thank you," the earl said. "Comments please," he asked from the others.

"Would it be so terrible for us if open conflict developed between the de Pinkney's?" de Dunstanville asked. "I think not," he answered his own question.

"I think the idea has merit," Fitzedith said. "If Roger de Pinkney falls in line then the plan has worked. If he defies his brother and conflict develop, then it is still possible that Walter will win. If he doesn't then we have still lost nothing."

"Except a ransomable prisoner," de Reviers ventured."

"Except a ransomable prisoner," Earl Robert echoed.

"What if he swears fealty to the empress and as soon as he is set free reneges on that promise?" De Dunstanville asked.

"And that is a real possibility," Fitzmiles agreed.

"Maybe," Earl Robert said. "However, he might still need our help to wrest his castle back from his brother. In which case he would not renege until he has control back. But before we help him there can be certain extra conditions levied. So we would still have influence."

"If he refuses to swear fealty and prefers to stay prisoner, then the plan doesn't even begin." Fitzedith said.

"No it doesn't," Earl Robert agreed. But in that situation, we have lost absolutely nothing."

"So!" Ardron summed up. "Worst case scenario would be that we set the man free. His brother welcomes him back and steps aside. Then back in control Walter de Pinkney reneges on his fealty."

"Precisely," Earl Robert agreed.

"It's still worth a try." De Dunstanville concluded and no one disagreed.

"I just need to convince my sister then," Earl Robert said.

"And the second proposition?" Fitzedith asked after a pause.

Ah yes! The second proposition," the earl said. "Well if that fails then I can see no other alternative except to go once more to plead for help from Geoffrey Plantagenet. I know my sister will feel the humiliation in having to ask Geoffrey once more for help, as will I. But we do badly need an influx of fresh money and fighting men.

"Will she agree?" de Dunstanville asked.

Earl Robert only shrugged.

"Perhaps if the other scheme is successful then we won't need to go to Plantagenet for help.

"Let us hope so," Earl Robert muttered.

It was straight after morning mass when Robert Earl Gloucester left Bristol for Devizes. Within an hour Ardron also left but he, for Norwood. Accompanied by his squire, Jacques, the journey through the English countryside was pleasant. The warm spring weather, the song of contented birds and emerging fresh green foliage contradicted completely the trouble and discord which currently traumatised England.

Just after they passed through the small hamlet of Westerleigh and re-entered the dense forest the fresh spring air became polluted by the stench of putrefaction. As they progressed the obnoxious reek became much stronger and forced them to use hands covering noses to effect relief. Just a few yards further and the cause of the stink became apparent. Just off the track, and hanging from the same tree, were three lifeless corpses. From the clothing on the bodies Ardron could tell one was woman, and all were Saxon. Their faces were deeply pallid yellow with skin already turning to leather. The tautening of that skin had dragged back flesh from mouths to reveal teeth, which gave the impression of hideous grins. He could not tell just how long the corpses had hung there, but without doubt it had been some time. Perhaps deliberately so, to enhance a warning. Suddenly, from the undergrowth a boy of adolescence years emerged and began to throw stones towards them. Ardron put spur to his horse taking them out of range before bringing the animal back to a walk.

"Sir? Jacques said enquiringly.

Ardron shook his head. "Ride on," he said sharply. There were questions. Many questions. But there would be no answers.

By noon they had reached the small hamlet of Sodbury, recently renamed Chipping Sodbury, after a royal charter had granted permission for a market. Today was not a day for a market but, nevertheless, in a relaxed mood and in no hurry to return to Norwood, Ardron dallied at the Wild Boar Inn, taking a light lunch.

Breaking off a piece of bread Jacques hesitated before taking a bite. He fixed Ardron with an enquiring look and said. "Sir, do you think Prince Henry will ever become King of England?"

Ardron took a breath and let out a sigh before replying. "If desire was all, then he would already be king. However, desire counts for nothing when faced with reality." He paused a moment, "But he is an impressive young man, the son of Geoffrey Plantagenet and Geoffrey is a man who knows how to win. If he learns well from his father, he will be formidable indeed. He will eventually, inherit his father's lands and estates making him rich and immensely powerful. It is then, I can imagine, his eyes will turn to England and the crown that is his by God's divine right. With greater resources, he will surely come for that crown as did his Great Grandfather William. And, by God, Stephen will find him ten times more formidable than his mother. Yes, I believe he will be King of England one day. But I'm afraid, my dear squire, it will not be soon.

"A long time then?" Jacques queried.

"A very long time."

"So what do we do?" Jacques asked.

Ardron shrugged. "We do our best to hold on to what we have. I fear that's all we can do." He studied his squire for a few moments. "You grow weary of this war?" he asked.

"It seems to have become so one sided," he replied. "Almost every day we hear of yet another crisis, another set-back."

"Where are you from?" Ardron asked.

"A small village in Anjou." He looked away wistfully. "At this time there will be cherry blossom on the trees and primroses beneath the canopies. The shallow river nearby will be teaming with roach. Hares will be running in the fields and leaping in courtship while the does in the forest will be spawning their young."

Ardron studied the young man before him. It had been almost five years since the ordeal that was Wherwell Priory. Five years since that battle when Jacques a mere boy of tender years had blundered into his life and into his service. In all that time he had never heard the boy complain. "How old are you," he asked.

"Nineteen, Sir."

"When were you last at home?"

He shrugged. "Six years."

"Then its time you made a visit home. My God boy, your mother will have forgotten what you look like. When we get back, we will make arrangements for you to take a holiday."

"No Sir," he said. "You need me in your service."

"Yes, I do need you. You are a fine squire. But perhaps I don't need you as much as you may think. My God! Do you think I can't saddle my own horse or sharpen the edge of my own sword?"

"No Sir."

"Then its settled. When we get back, we will make your travel arrangements. You will yet see those cherry blossoms and the roach in the river. Who knows perhaps you'll be running and leaping in the fields in your own courtship with some local wench?"

The afternoon had worn down to early evening by the time they reached Norwood. Maurice was there to greet them and held the horse's reins while Ardron dismounted.

"How was the trip?" he asked.

Ardron scoffed. "Not particularly informative," he replied.

"You have a visitor?"

"I do?" Ardron said. "Who would that be?

"Your brother Esmond. He arrived this morning and has waited all day."

"Oh? Where is he now?"

"He waits in your private quarters," Maurice replied.

"Sir," Jacques sought his attention. He nodded towards the keep as he took his horse's reins to lead him away.

Ardron turned his attention towards the keep. Claennis stood at the top of the mote waiting to greet him.

"Your wife waits to greet you," Jacques needlessly informed him.

"So she does." He agreed and then made his way up the steps to join her.

"Did you miss me? She asked as she wrapped her arms around his.

"Like the flowers would miss the morning sun," he answered.

"Which flowers?

"Mushrooms of course," he said.

"Mushrooms? But they grow in the dark?"

"Oh do they?" he feigned surprise.

She playfully hit him on the shoulder as they entered the keep.

Taking out a little time to freshen up and to indulge Claennis's excited chatter, he eventually went to find his younger brother. He found Esmond in the reception area with Swidhurn and Maurice. Customary polite greetings were exchanged before Ardron's curiosity compelled him to ask the reason for his brother's visit.

"Something rather strange," Esmond said. "Perhaps nothing, but very strange," he added with a frown. "I really don't want to be wasting your time."

"Brother," Ardron said a little impatiently. "Tell us what it is you have on your mind. Don't worry if it's nothing it doesn't matter. I am always pleased to see you."

Esmond nodded. "Two days ago I was at the market in Malmesbury. As I walked down the hill Edward de' Evereux came riding up with an escort of around a dozen.

"De Evereux in Malmesbury?" Ardron was puzzled. "He would be taking an awful chance."

"My thoughts exactly," Esmond said. "But it gets even more curious. He didn't stop in the market nor did he go to the abbey. Instead he rode through the castle gate into the bailey."

Ardron leaned forward in his chair resting his elbows on the chair arms. "That is curious," he muttered. "He wasn't seized or anything?"

"No, he rode through the gate like he was expected."

Ardron was thoughtful. "How long was he in there?" he asked eventually.

Esmond shrugged. "I was at the market for at least another hour-and-half, and he never came out."

"You're right, brother. That is strange." He turned to Maurice. "What do you think, constable?"

Maurice shook his head. "Not good," he said. Then was thoughtful for a few moments. "Couldn't be anything to do with those Templars that came here some months back recruiting for the crusade."

"Surely if it was, de Evereux would have gone to the abbey and not the castle." Swidhurn said.

"I agree," Maurice said nodding.

"So do I," Ardron endorsed. "Can't see de Evereux signing up for a fight of any description."

"Then can it be that de Evereux is looking to defect to the king?" Maurice added.

"Looks likely," Ardron said.

"That's not good," Swidhurn muttered.

"No," Ardron agreed. We have Malmesbury to our south, Tetbury to the west and Cricklade in the east, if de Evereux signs over South Cerney to our north, we are boxed in."

There was silence around the table. "What are we going to do?" Maurice broke the silence.

"I won't let it happen," Ardron said. "What we have discussed in this room stays in this room for now. Say nothing to anyone." he paused a moment. "I will have a decision in the morning." He turned to his brother. "Thank you, Esmond, we are indebted to you. I have to ask you also to say nothing about this to anyone."

"Of course," he said.

518

"You will of course stay here tonight, it's perhaps too late to return to Scorrenstone."

Gradually all began to shuffle thoughtfully out of the room. "Oh Maurice." Ardron stopped the constable. "I intend to send Jacques back to his home in Anjou for a short while. I would be obliged if you could find me a temporary squire while he's away."

Maurice paused in thought. "I think I have just the man," he said.

"Oh?"

"How about Cerdic?"

"Cerdic? Yes! Cerdic will do nicely," Ardron agreed.

The next morning straight after morning mass Ardron convened an emergency meeting with four of his most trusted sergens. "I have thought long and hard on the matter and I have come to a decision," he said pausing. "I intend to take Castle Cerney by force!" The announcement was greeted with silence. Whether it was due to astonishment or expected approval he couldn't tell.

"Can it be done?" it was Roland who broke the silence.

"Yes I believe it can," Ardron replied.

"It will have to be done quickly," Maurice said. "If we get into a long siege then a weakened Norwood will become vulnerable to attack from the king's supporter at Malmesbury."

"Yes." Ardron agreed. "And I think I have just the plan." He paused a moment. "I think we can take the castle by deceit. Perhaps not honourable but effective."

"Effective if it succeeds," It was Jarcot interjected.

"Quite!" Ardron agreed.

"So how will this deceit work?" Fique asked.

Ardron leaned back in his chair. "Some years ago I had the misfortune to tangle with a man called Robert Fitzhubert. He was the master of cunning. This man had a plan to take Marlborough Castle by deceit. It was a good plan, but it came unstuck due to two mistakes. I intend to use that same plan, except to eliminate the mistakes he made." He paused. "His first mistake was a lapse of security. He mouthed off to his offices in front of me assuming that I was just a Saxon plebe who did not understand French. I will not make that mistake. Therefore, everything discussed in this room will be top secret." He looked across the table. "Is that clear?"

Each man nodded acceptance.

"Fitzhubert's second mistake, he approached Marlborough on the pretence of a friendly visit with a significant force. I also intend to make the pretence of a friendly visit except with a small compliment of around twenty."

"Twenty?" Maurice queried.

"Yes twenty." Ardron confirmed. "The visit will be timed to coincide with morning mass when most will be in the castle chapel. Whether it is de Evereux who greets us or his constable I expect to be invited to wait somewhere inside the keep. I will take four men. No more. The rest will casually stroll over to the gate area to seemingly wait out the service. The onus is then on those of us inside the keep. We must take it and secure it. When that is achieved a signal will be given to those who loiter around the gate. There are always three guards on duty two on the gate and one above. We must overcome those gate guards and secure the gate to keep it open. Not forgetting the guard house where the relief guards await their shift. That must be locked keeping them trapped inside. When all is secure, from above the gate, a signal will be given to the main assault force who wait hidden in the nearby woodland. That force will come at speed to occupy the castle bailey. If luck is with us, we will have occupied the castle while the majority are at prayer." He leaned back to gauge the reaction around the table.

At first no one spoke, instead they just looked at each other, some with raised eyebrows.

Maurice was first to speak. "My," he said. "You must have been awake all night to think that through." He paused before adding. "It could work."

"Yes it could," Roland agreed. "How likely is it that five men inside the keep can take it?" If they don't the whole plan falls flat.

"Yes," Ardron agreed. "It will be my judgement call. If it doesn't look possible then the plan does not even start." He shrugged. "We will have lost nothing".

"What about the rest of the castle sergens not all will be at mass." Jarcot said.

Ardron nodded. "The seizing of the sergen barracks will be a priority for the main force when it arrives in the bailey. Hopefully, those not at mass will be completely unprepared for an attack."

"It's a good plan. With a good chance of succeeding." Jarcot said approvingly.

"Aye," the others agreed.

"Good," Ardron was pleased. "We'll have a better chance if we practice," he said.

"Practice?" Fique queried.

"Yes practice. For exercise purposes this castle becomes Cerney Castle. Send out riders this afternoon to call in all our villeins. They are to report tomorrow morning. Practice will then begin tomorrow afternoon and continue the day after. The following day is Sunday. Sunday is a good day to attack."

Maurice held up a cautioning hand. "With all this practicing how do we keep our intentions secret?"

"Good question," Ardron answered. "We let it freely known that we are preparing an attack. But_, we declare Tetbury to be our objective."

Maurice shook his head in admiration. "That man Fitzhubert taught you well," he said.

***

South Cerney Castle

The gates at South Cerney castle were closed. Ardron had not anticipated that. Still mounted, and along with an escort of twenty he waited for the castle constable to appear. Eventually he arrived and from the platform above the gate he looked down on the group.

"Sir Ardron," he said recognising him. "What business do you have here today?"

"I would speak with Sir Edward," Ardron replied.

"Sir Edward? Sir Edward is not here! He left yesterday on a hunt."

Ardron heard Maurice groan. "We should abandon and try again in a couple of days," he whispered.

He might have a point, Ardron allowed, but even so, he was not ready to give up just yet. "Do you have power of attorney in his absence?" He asked.

"I do."

"Then perhaps I could talk with you."

"What about?" he queried.

"A matter of mutual alliance for the defence of both castles. This one and ours at Norwood." Even from this distance he could see the man's unease. "I wouldn't expect you to make the final decision," he went on. "Perhaps I could lay out my proposal before you, and you could then relay the proposition before Sir Edward when he returns." He tried to make it easy for him. But still he hesitated. "You don't have an alliance already in place with someone else, do you?" he put the pressure on.

"Cleverly done," he heard Maurice's approval.

It was cleverly done. If there already existed an agreement of sorts in place with Roger de Pinkney, they could not, at this stage, let it be known. In order to avoid suspicion he would have to go through the motions of being interested.

The constable took a few moments to think things through, then without speaking disappeared.

"What's happening?" Roland muttered. There was no time to answer before the castle gates were opened.

They rode through at a semi hurried pace, leaving the constable at the gate. At the foot of the mote, Ardron halted the group. Not waiting to be invited he dismounted quickly. At the same time he motioned to the others to do likewise. By the time the constable had caught up with them they were standing waiting. Not allowing the man to wrest any sort of control, he said firmly. "Lead on, if you please," waving an arm up towards the keep.

Perhaps confused and a little shocked the constable obligingly began to do as bade.

"Maurice, Roland, Beldwine and William come with me. The rest of you wait here," Ardron instructed, then gave a secret nod to Fique. "It's alright if these four come with me. Isn't it?" he asked the constable. But he didn't wait for an answer, instead keeping up the verbal barrage, said. "I'm sorry. I don't know your name."

"Alphonse," he meekly replied.

"Alphonse!" Ardron repeated. "How long have you been constable here?" He went on.

"Two years."

"Two years!" Ardron said, then looking round the bailey. "Where is everybody?"

"Er__. Most are at mass." Alphonse replied.

"Two years? And is it a good position?" Ardron kept up the babbling.

"Yes."

"But you're not at mass. Aren't you religious?"

"I am, but."

Ardron gave him no time to answer. "When do you expect Sir Edward back?" He asked.

"Maybe later today, or perhaps tomorrow." Alphonse replied.

By now they had reached the top of the mote. As they approached the door, the apathetic sentry sitting there, hauled himself to his feet using his pike as an aid. Seeing the castle constable leading the way, he stepped aside without challenging. Alphonse led the way into Sir Edward's private area.

Once inside, Ardron's attitude hardened. "Is there anyone else within the keep?" he asked.

Alphonse was confused, and suspicion began to grow. "Why?" he asked.

"Answer the question," Maurice demanded menacingly drawing his sword.

For the first time Alphonse realised all was not as it seemed. But he was unarmed. Turning quickly he made a grab for the sword hanging above the inglenook fireplace. However, feeling the point of Maurice's sword pressed hard against his ribs, made him slowly release his grip, leaving the sword where it hung.

"I ask you again," Ardron said. "Is there anyone else in the keep." Alphonse took a deep breath and stubbornly refused to answer. "Never mind," Ardron decided. "Take a look around. Anyone you find bring back here." He tasked William and Beldwine.

"What do you hope to gain from this?" Alphonse asked quietly.

"Simple, my dear constable. Occupation of this castle." Ardron answered.

"Why?"

"For my security and peace of mind."

"Security?" But we are on the same side," Alphonse responded.

"Are we?" Ardron queried. "It is on the suspicion that we might not be, which has brought me here today."

"What do you mean?"

"I mean, that I know of Sir Edward's meeting in Malmesbury Castle. A secret meeting with the enemy!" Ardron shook his head. "It probably means that there is treachery afoot, and I mean to ensure that I am not on the end of it."

Alphonse scoffed. "You'll never get away with it," he retorted.

"We'll see!" Ardron muttered. "Ask the guard to come in," he added after a short pause.

"I will not," Alphonse was defiant.

"It matters not," Ardron said. "Maurice, tell the guard that Constable Alphonse wants to see him."

A few moments later the guard walked in ahead of Maurice and straight onto the tip of Ardron's sword. "Sit over there with your constable," Ardron instructed. "Behave and no harm will come to you."

Just as Ardron was beginning to fret about the extended absence of William and Beldwine they arrived, bringing with them four chamber maids. "This is it," Beldwine said. "We have complete control of the keep."

Please be seated ladies," he said, indicating that they should join the guard and the constable. Satisfied that, so far, all was under control he went out onto the mote.

Across the bailey he could see Fique and the rest of the company had positioned themselves in close proximity to the gate. They seemed to be noisily pre-occupied, gambling enthusiastically on the toss of a coin. But Fique was alert and acknowledged Ardron's signal immediately. Almost instantly a furious argument broke out amongst the gamblers. Two of the gate guards moved forward to watch the fracas. Taken by surprise, they were instantly overwhelmed and disarmed. Satisfied that Fique would now seize control of the gate, Ardron went back inside.

"All goes well." he reported.

"What now?" William asked.

"Now! We wait, as planned." Ardron replied.

Eventually, after what seemed an age, but in fact was probably less than five minutes, Jarcot rode through the gates at the head of more than a hundred sergens. "Now," Ardron said, with some relief, "We can set about taking the rest of the castle."

The resistance came in small pockets, but being disorganised, had little chance of meaningful resistance. It took only minutes for the Norwood sergens to take control of the bailey. Ardron descended the mote to be met by Jarcot and Fique.

"All goes well," he reported.

"Good!" Ardron replied. "What's happening over there?"

Jarcot turned to look where he pointed. "Castle sergens," he said. "They came out of their barracks fighting, then as they were beaten back, they retreated into their barracks and have barricaded themselves in."

Ardron nodded. "Leave them there for now," he said. "Fique have the gate closed. No one goes out. No one comes in."

"What about the guards locked in the guardroom?" He asked.

"Leave them locked in, for now."

"That just leaves the chapel," Jarcot said. "They too have locked the door and barricaded themselves in."

Ardron looked away towards the chapel. "Alright," he said. "I'll deal with that." He paused. "Casualties?" he asked.

"Light," Jarcot said. "Half-a-dozen wounded. One likely to die."

Ardron pulled a face. "What about the Cerney casualties?

"Seven or eight." Jarcot replied.

"Any likely to die?"

"Two already dead," Fique said.

"And another one might." Jarcot said.

Ardron sighed heavily and said. "Regrettable."

Thirty minutes later Ardron faced the chapel. The chapel door was substantial. Made of stout oak and strengthen by broad brass banding, it would not be broken down easily. He glanced over his shoulder to Maurice and a score of ready sergens. He hoped that he could coax the congregation out peacefully.

"Hello in the chapel," he shouted. But there was no reply. He tried again.

"Who's out there?" a voice from within.

"I am Baron Ardron of Norwood," he replied.

"What's your business, Ardron of Norwood?"

"I have taken charge of the castle. You must come out and I will guarantee safety for all within." There was no reply. "It is pointless to remain in the chapel." Still no reply. "You can't stay in there indefinitely," he went on.

He turned to Maurice. "What do you think," he asked. "Can this door be broken down?"

Maurice sucked noisily through his teeth. "Not easily I think."

A voice from the chapel side of the door. "We will let the women and children out, if you will guarantee their safety."

"No!" Ardron replied firmly. "All come out together or none come out." There was a long silence. His patience was wearing thin. "You have two minutes to make up your mind. After that I will set fire to the chapel."

"If you set fire to the chapel you will surely burn in hell," said an outraged voice from within.

"Very likely. But I'm sure I will see lots of familiar faces," Ardron replied nonchalantly. More than two minutes elapsed and still there was no response. "Very well," he said. "You leave me no alternative. Gather some straw bales and place them around the chapel." He instructed his sergens loudly so that all within could hear.

"What guarantees do we have?" The question from within.

"You have my promise."

The promise of a man who arrives under a banner of friendship then by treachery attacks castle inmates?"

Ardron sighed exasperated. "Yes. The promise of a man who arrived under the banner of friendship then took the castle by treachery," he said. "But then, you have no choice except to take my word." The silence protracted. "Set fire to one of the bales and make sure smoke enters the chapel." He instructed Maurice.

The straw bale was dry and ignited readily with a generous amount of smoke.

"Alright. Alright. We are coming out." The voice from within said, when the smoke began to drift inside.

Slowly, sullen and cautiously the chapel congregation began to emerge into the morning. With the exception of Lady d'Evereux and her two children, who were escorted to her husband's private chamber, all were assembled in the bailey in front of the mote. Added to these were the guards from the guardroom, and eventually the barricaded sergens were also tempted from their barracks. In less than two hours the castle was secured, and all its inmates subjugated.

"The castle is yours." Maurice reported.

"Ours." Ardron corrected. "The castle is ours."

He left the keep and descended to about halfway down the mote and surveyed the gathering. Some were seated on the ground, some stood, others had managed to find more comfortable vantage points, but all waited gloomily, to learn their fate. Ardron had no desire to deal harshly with any of these people. After all, in almost all cases, they had merely performed their duties to the best of their abilities.

"From today, I, Baron Ardron of Norwood, will be the castellan of this castle," he began. "That does not mean that any of you have anything to fear. All are welcome to stay, or leave, just as you wish. For all you tradesmen, who operate inside the bailey, you may continue to do so. For those who carry out servant duties, you too may continue to do so." He paused to gauge the reactions. Was there an easing of tensions? He couldn't tell. "Now I come to you sergens. The fighting men of this castle. You too are free to stay or leave. However, for those who wish to stay there will be some changes. You may find that you stay here at Cerney, but not all. Some may find themselves moved to Norwood. Those who stay will find that a contingent of Norwood sergens joins them here at Cerney." He considered that by diluting those of unproven loyalty with those of proven loyalty it would reduce the risk of a counter coup. "Those who do not wish to stay," he went on, "Will have themselves one hour to gather personal possessions and to leave. There will be no malice, no resentment. However, it is my sincere wish that most of you will stay." He paused. "Any questions? He asked.

"What of Sir Edward?" a sergen asked.

"When Sir Edward arrives with his hunting party, he will find there is a new situation, and he will be refused entry." Ardron answered.

"And Lady d'Evereux?" the same sergen asked.

"Lady d'Evereux, and her children, are quite safe. And at this very moment is gathering together her belongings, so that she may leave with her husband when he arrives."

"Those of us that choose to leave, where will we go?" another sergen asked.

Ardron shrugged. "Wherever you please. Back to Normandy if you so desire."

"What about us villeins?" another asked.

"Ah yes. The villeins." Ardron answered. "If you live on the estate then you will be tied to the estate. That means that you will serve me in all respects. However, once again. If that does not suit, then they too will be allowed to seek alternative arrangements at some other estate."

Another sergen got to his feet. "Do you really expect Sir Edward to simply walk away and leave his castle to you?"

"Yes," Ardron replied flatly. Although he did not believe that himself.

The sergen shook his head not accepting Ardron's reply. "There will be fighting," he challenged.

Ardron sighed quietly, the man was probably right. "If there is to be fighting, then each man must decide where his loyalties lay. If it is not behind me, then there is the gate," he said pointing.

He waited a few moments. There were no more questions. So, with a brief nod, he turned and walked back up to the keep. Pausing at the top of the mote, where Maurice waited, he looked back to see the assembly breaking up into small groups and begin to disperse.

"What do you think?" he asked. "Will they stay?"

Maurice shrugged non-committal. "We'll know in an hour," he said.

"What about me?" Alphonse challenged when they were back inside. "Am I still constable here?"

Ardron smiled as he shook his head. "Oh no," he said. "I will put my own man in here."

"So I am dismissed?"

"As constable? I'm afraid so! However, I can find a position for you at Norwood if you wish. But it will not be as constable. I will make a concession though. That will be, to keep your pay at its current rate for six months. After six months if you have performed well and proved your loyalty then we will review the situation."

Alphonse stroked his chin thoughtfully. "I will think on," he said.

"Good," Ardron said. You have one hour." He paused a moment. "Now leave us."

Maurice stared after the man watching him leave. "I will respect that man a lot more if he decides to leave and stand with Sir Edward," he said.

"Me too!" Ardron agreed. "Regarding the position of constable here. I would consider it a favour if you would take the position."

"Hmm," Maurice mused. "It could be a poison chalice."

"It could, if not handled right. That is why I have chosen you. You have some experience as constable, and you have the capacity for diplomacy. I can think of no one better."

"If that is what you desire of me, then I am at your service." Maurice replied. "What of the position constable at Norwood?"

Ardron bit his lip in thought. "I think it is past the time I rewarded Jarcot."

"Jarcot?" Maurice echoed. "I think he'll do," he concurred.

Chapter 22

Devizes Castle, June 1146

"If glares were arrows, then you would resemble a large hedgehog," Cerdic whispered.

Ardron smiled grimly and knew precisely what he meant. He returned the hostile stares across the ante room as they waited to be summoned before Empress Maude.

Two days ago Sir Humphrey de Bohun had delivered by hand, a written summons that he should attend the Empress's court to explain his action. De Bohun had left that day with a warning that he would need a pretty good reason for seizing South Cerney Castle. Ardron still believed that he had that good reason.

For a petty sessions day, the ante room was unusually quiet. Among all the trivia the main event, without doubt, were the charges that Edward d'Evereux had levelled against Ardron. He had appealed to Empress Maude claiming that by taking Cerney Castle, Ardron's action were tantamount to treason against the empress herself, and to her allies. He demanded that the castle be immediately returned into his keeping, and that Ardron should face the ultimate punishment.

Again, Ardron glanced across the room. Unsurprisingly, he was still the object of those aggressive and hateful stares of Edward d'Evereux and his cousin Patric Earl Salisbury. Unconcerned he gave a slight nod and allowed a flicker of a smile to curl a lip.

It was nearing noon when they were eventually ushered in before Maude. On her right stood Reginald de Dunstanville and on her left Roger Fitzmiles.

"Sir Ardron. You are brought here today to answer charges of disloyalty, in as much as you did attack the castle and estate of a loyal subject of her Majesty, Empress Maude." Roger Fitzmiles read out. "Have you anything to say?"

"Ardron nodded. "I did what I had to do for the security of my own estate and the protection of her Majesty's properties," he said.

Fitzmiles said nothing and was expressionless as he stepped back.

"Lay your charges, Sir Edward." Empress Maude invited.

"Baron Ardron of Norwood is a close neighbour to my own estate at South Cerney, and was regarded, before this attack, to be an ally," d'Evereux began. "But, by the most deceitful and treacherous means attacked and seized my castle." He paused. "He timed his attack to a time when he knew that I would, personally, be absent on a hunt. It was timed also to correspond with morning mass when most of the castle personnel would be at prayer. By devious deception he persuaded my constable to allow him access. Once inside he proceeded to seize control of the gate. When that was achieved, he was able to allow his, not insignificant force, entry and take control of critical castle points. Those who were at prayer in the chapel, including women and children, claimed right of sanctuary. But he callously disregarded their pleas, and ordered the chapel set afire. All those inside, were then forced to come out. By then he had complete control of the castle, and all personnel who would not bend the knee to him he had evicted. The resulting cost to me was, my home, my castle, my estate and a dozen loyal sergens killed. Your Majesty," he went on, "I petition that my estate and castle be returned to me without delay. And, that Ardron of Norwood experience the full wrath of your outrage."

There was something of a pause before Maude asked. "What say you, Baron Ardron?"

Ardron hooked a thumb inside his belt and bit a lip in thought. "Your Majesty," he began. "Somewhere in Sir Edward's claims there are elements of truth. But so distorted that they be hard to find."

"Well!" she said. "Let us hear your version,"

"I agree the attack was planned to proceed during morning mass, and that was because I considered it to be the time when the castle would be most vulnerable. I didn't know Sir Edward was away on a hunt. But it would have made no difference even if I had. Nor did we set the chapel afire, and I never had any intention of doing so. We did set alight a straw bale to alarm those inside the chapel. I make no apologies for that action. It achieved its purpose to get the people out without a single casualty. On the subject of casualties. Sir Edward's figures are so wide of the mark they are ridiculous. The actual number that died was four. Three from Cerney and one from Norwood. Every death under such circumstances is regrettable and negotiations for some form of compensation with those victims dependants are ongoing. Now regarding__."

"Stop there." Empress Maude interrupted. "We have no interest in, Your account, his account arguments." She paused a moment. "Our only interest is, why? The facts are that you did attack and seize South Cerney Castle and we want to know why."

"Your Majesty," Ardron acknowledged with a subservient nod. "I had good reason to believe that Sir Edward was in negotiations with Roger de Pinkney."

"Absolutely ridiculous." Patric interjected with scorn.

Maude held up her hand to silence him. "And the reason is?" she asked.

"It was reported to me on good authority, that Edward d'Evereux was seen entering Malmesbury Castle where he stayed for at least one and a half hours."

"What do you say to that?" Maude questioned d'Evereux.

"I don't deny it," he replied.

Patric's expression betrayed his surprise and that this was news to him also.

"May we know the reason?" Maude asked.

"A trade agreement."

"A trade agreement?" she queried.

"Because we have different loyalties," d'Evereux went on, "Doesn't mean that we cannot discuss mutual trade benefits between our estates."

"Sir Ardron?" Maude invited his comment.

Ardron shook his head in disbelief. "I can't and won't accept that," he said. "Two men on opposite sides of a war, agree a trade agreement?" He said with disdain and a head shake. He waited a moment allowing the remarks to ferment. "You know of course," he went on. "I have hostile castles south, east and west of Norwood. The only reason I can stand, in fact the only reason both I and Sir Edward can stand, is because of mutual support. If one or the other were to withdraw that support, then the remainer becomes isolated and extremely vulnerable to attack. I have never been convinced of Sir Edward's resolve, and when I learned of his meeting with de Pinkney then I smelled treachery afoot. So, I decided that to take Castle Cerney would be the only way I could rely on that continued situation." He paused a moment. "My Angevin support is well proven, and while I hold both castles then the Angevin cause holds both castles also." He pointed out.

"Do you have any proof of Sir Edward's possible treachery?" De Dunstanville asked.

"Proof? No, not proof, only a conviction. But one does not wait until after the adder has bitten before killing it."

"Enough." Empress Maude said forcibly. "It seems that you took the action you did on suspicion only. Suspicion that may or may not be justified." She looked towards the window. "It is past noon. We will adjourn while we consider the situation. "We will re-assemble in two hours, when we will let you know our decision."

* * *

There are three watch towers to Devizes Castle. Two above the main gate. It was from one of these gate towers that Ardron now stood gazing out over a countryside that fell away steeply to flatten out to a lowland plain. He was contemplative and more than a little anxious about the pending decision. He had previously made up his mind that under no circumstances would he surrender Cerney Castle back to d'Evereux. But if it came to open defiance of the empress, he was under no illusions what the penalties could be. She could be an intolerant woman, demonstrated by her vengeful punishment metered out on the London Merchants five years ago.

"There you are." de Dunstanville said emerging from the spiral stairs. "We need to talk." He said joining him at the castellations.

Ardron nodded, turning his attention back to the view. "This is some view to command," he muttered.

"Most certainly," de Dunstanville agreed. "Probably one of the reasons my half-sister chose this castle for herself."

"Half-sister?" Ardron mused. "How many half-brothers does she have?"

"Many," de Dunstanville replied with a smirk. "Probably more unknown than known. Old King Henry was an avaricious womaniser."

"Would that he spent more energy into his marriage bed then perhaps this war would never have happened." Ardron muttered.

"Aye," de Dunstanville agreed. "Would, also, that the white ship had never sunk in the channel, then Prince William, Henry's heir, would have been alive today and undisputed King of England." He shook his head sadly. "But I am afraid the situation today is what it is. However, at this moment we need to concentrate our attention on the situation that you have created."

"I have created?" Ardron questioned, then leaning over the castellation he spit with an element of disrespect. He watched the spittle all the way into the moat below.

"Yes, a situation that you have created." De Dunstanville replied firmly. "We can, however, still retrieve the situation if you agree to hand back South Cerney Castle to Sir Edward, accompanied with a meaningful apology.

"What?" Ardron uttered with disbelief. "That will never happen."

"You would defy your empress?"

Ardron sighed heavily. "If I hand back Cerney Castle to Sir Edward then it is inevitable that Norwood Castle would fall to the royalist soon after. Currently, I am as good as besieged on three compass points. By handing back Cerney to d'Evereux that would add the fourth, because d'Evereux would also be hostile to me. Roger De Pinkney is not a fool, and would recognise instantly, my vulnerability. The pressure he could bring onto Norwood from three sides alone would be enormous. And without aid to come from anywhere then Norwood would eventually fall. Next in line to fall would be Cerney Castle, because d'Evereux will not stand. I suspect that he has already begun negotiations to defect to the king anyway. Or at the very least, he has agreed a non-aggression pact with Roger de Pinkney. Which gives de Pinkney the go-ahead to attack Norwood? When Norwood does fall then the empress will eventually lose two castles, and Stephen's relentless creep westward will continue.

"That is supposition," de Dunstanville said.

"It is, Ardron agreed. "But I believe it is an accurate supposition."

"But if the empress tells you to hand back South Cerney you will have no alternative."

"No alternative except one."

"What would that be?" de Dunstanville asked.

"If Norwood and South Cerney are destined to fall under the kings banner then I may as well go with them and keep both castles."

"You would defect?" de Dunstanville's tone revealed his surprise

Ardron turned and gazed unseeing out across the Wiltshire landscape. "Regrettably!" he muttered.

"No! Not you," de Dunstanville said. But Ardron continued to gaze away into the distance without replying. "Let us hope it doesn't come to that." De Dunstanville added as he turned and walked away. "Yes. Let us hope," Ardron muttered to himself, and wondered, if he had, perhaps, said too much.

As de Dunstanville walked away he passed close to Cerdic coming the opposite way. Perhaps in deep thought he failed to acknowledge him.

"What's wrong with him?" Cerdic said to Ardron looking back over his shoulder.

Ardron shrugged. "Something I said," he muttered dismissively. "Did you get any food?" he changed the subject.

"Yes," Cerdic replied. "I was able to get bread and a little cold chicken. And," he said producing an onion from in his pocket, "Something for flavour. Also," he added with a hint of triumph, "This to wash it all down" He fiddled down the front of his tunic and produced a stoneware jug of wine."

* * *

It was in the early part of the afternoon when Maude re-convened the session. Ardron was surprised to see they had been joined by Robert, Earl Gloucester. Whether that was a good sign for him, or not, he was undecided. They did, however, acknowledge each other with curt nods. The empress was last to join the room, taking her time to make herself comfortable in the presiding chair. Only when she was good and ready, did she fix the appellants, standing before her, with a non-committal scrutiny.

"We have reached a decision," she eventually said. Ardron waited with bated breath, as she paused, perhaps taking a last reflection on the decision. "Baron Ardron of Norwood. We have decided that you may keep South Cerney Castle.

Whilst Ardron breathed a heavy sigh of relief, he heard both Edward d'Evereux and Patric Earl Salisbury groan.

"However," Maude went on. "There are to be reparations."

Isn't there always a sting in the tale? Ardron questioned himself without speaking.

Maude had moved on to address d'Evereux. "Sir Edward," she said. "You will be found another castle, another estate, to replace South Cerney and in addition will be adequately compensated to replace your loss."

"Where will this castle be?" he asked.

"That is still under discussion," she replied. "But be assured a decision will be made very soon."

D'Evereux bowed subserviently without speaking.

Maude turned her attention back to Ardron. "Baron Ardron," she said. "Notwithstanding, that you took it upon yourself to seize, by force, Cerney Castle, you will be allowed to keep it, under the condition that the reparations are honoured in full."

"Yes, your Majesty. And these reparations will be?" he asked.

"The full income value of the fief on the South Cerney estate for the next twelve months will be paid in coin to Sir Edward."

Ardron was taken aback. "All the fief?"

"In its entirety," Maude confirmed.

"For the whole year?"

"Yes."

Ardron was stunned. It meant that for one year he would have to fund the castle wages, expenses and taxes from his own personal reserves. He nodded obediently accepting the decision.

"No further business?" Maude queried. After a quick glance around, she went on. "Good. All business and disputes being settled the session is ended." All bowed dutifully as she got up from her chair and left the chamber.

"This is not ended," d'Evereux quietly growled to Ardron as they filed out of the room. "You got away with it because you have influential friends in high places."

Ardron nodded agreement. "Perhaps I have," he said. "If that is true, then it is because I have earned their friendship with deeds." He stood and watched the disgruntled pair stomp bad humouredly away.

"Baron Ardron," he turned to see Robert, Earl Gloucester behind him.

"Sir Robert." Ardron acknowledged the earl.

"Accept this verdict as a reward and the only reward." Earl Robert said.

"A reward?"

"Yes a reward."

"A reward for what?" Ardron asked.

"Oxford!"

"Oxford?"

"Yes Oxford. We were heavily indebted to you for our empress's rescue from the besieged castle, and I know that my sister wanted to reward you with Faringdon Castle. When that did not happen, she had hopes that it could be Malmesbury Castle. But that hasn't worked out either. So consider your reward to be South Cerney Castle and estate. The debt is now paid in full!"

"Thank you," Ardron said accepting his explanation.

Earl Robert nodded. "But be warned. Curb your aggression and do nothing like this again."

"Sir." Ardron agreed.

* * *

Late afternoon on the following day, Ardron convened a meeting in his private chamber at Norwood. It was a select meeting concerning only Maurice and Jarcot as castle constables, Louis as castle treasurer and Swidhurn as advisor. Claennis had persuaded her husband to allow her to eavesdrop but promised she would sit at the back and listen only.

Ardron explained the pre-conditions for the continued occupation of South Cerney Castle. There were some surprised expressions, some puffing of cheeks and some shaking heads.

"Can I make those payments? "Ardron asked Louis.

"You are saying that the income on this castle will have to fund the expenses of both castles?" He sought clarification.

"That's about the sum of it." Ardron said

"I would need to examine the Cerney Castle ledgers to get an idea what those castle expenses are likely to be." Louis said. "Even without examining those ledgers I can say, with some certainty, that there will have to be some severe cuts."

"Do we have a surplus?" Ardron asked.

"We do."

"Without seeing those ledgers, here and now, from the top of your head, is it a possibility?"

"Louis sucked in noisily as he thought. Then hand stroking chin and nodding slowly. he said. "We'll just have to make it possible. But it will not be easy, there will have to be savings and perhaps some fiefs will have to be raised.

"No, I don't want to do that." Ardron said. "I don't expect Norwood villeins to pay for my South Cerney acquisition."

"Then, it might be that, at the year end, you will find yourself in debt." Louis warned.

"There must be another way," Maurice ventured.

"Perhaps you could sell a hide of land to cover any shortfall," Jarcot suggested.

"Sell to who?" Swidhurn asked. "We are surrounded by hostiles. They won't want to negotiate to buy. They'll want to take."

"There is another way," Claennis interrupted.

Ardron fixed her with a hard stare, she had broken her promise.

"Let her speak," Swidhurn said on her behalf.

She got to her feet and approached the table. "We." Or you," She corrected herself eyeing her husband compliantly. "Will have to pay Edward d'Evereux every penny that comes into Cerney Castle coffers?" she sought confirmation.

"We do," Ardron allowed.

"Then," she went on. "We make sure that the amount that comes in is greatly reduced."

"Whilst I can see that would be a very satisfying thing to do, I cannot see how it helps to meet the expense bill." Ardron said.

"She held up her hand. "You go amongst your villeins and proclaim that you will allow them to keep a bigger chunk of their fief this year. Providing, they invest the extra income on improvements. A new barn, new buildings, more livestock, pigs, sheep, oxen, or extended cropping." She suggested examples with a shrug. "Anything that will be an investment for future increased yields."

"That would certainly make you extremely popular amongst your vassals. If nothing else." Jarcot said.

"But, what about d'Evereux he would be furious and be certain to protest. Ardron said."

"Well," Claennis continued. "You could claim it was necessary investments due to many previous years of neglect."

Ardron raised his eyebrows. It might work, he thought.

"Then the next year the yields would be much improved as would the income," she continued. "So, if by chance we do finish in debt, then we should be in a good position to pay off quickly." She stood back waiting reaction.

"One-year reduced income, followed, by big improvements after." Louis mused thoughtfully. "In effect, Edward d'Evereux indirectly finances the improvements."

"Exactly!" she agreed.

"It's devious," Louis said. "So devious it borders on being dishonest." He paused a moment shaking his head. "I don't like it," he said gloomily. Then, a grin spread across his face. "I love it," he declared loudly.

"Me too," Ardron said with a good deal of pride in his wife. He paused, thoughtful a moment, then decision made, said. "Maurice, tomorrow you and I will go among the villeins of South Cerney and pass the word. While you Louis, will get together with Maurice's castle treasurer and review the ledgers."

***

Scorrenstone, July 1146

Being Sunday morning, most of the villagers were still in church when Ardron, accompanied by Swidhurn, arrived at the village. Anxious to spend time with his own family, Swidhurn had left him sitting quietly waiting for his brother Redwald to arrive back at his house. The weather had been kind this year, and the crops in the fields surrounding the village looked bountiful. That was pleasing to him, even though it benefitted him, personally, not one jot.

It was just a little over seven years ago when those violent events right here, had set him on a path that had changed his life so very much. Changed so much so, that he could hardly identify to those memories of that previous village life. It almost seemed to him as if those memories belonged to another person and not to him.

The day was pleasant, the sun warm, and only the busy twitter of rising larks disturbed the quiet. Completely relaxed, and at this moment at perfect peace with the world, he closed his eyes and allowed himself to drift into a semi-conscious state. For a little while he dallied in this trance-like state until he became irritated by a bothersome fly on his face. Without opening his eyes he wafted the fly away, but it returned almost instantly. Three, four times he wafted it away, but always it returned. He gave up and opened his eyes, to find that by using a long piece of grass, he was being tormented by Redwald's children. Surprised, he leapt to his feet growling bad temperedly, as he did. The children quickly retreated to a safe distance, giggling.

"The big bad Norman Baron scares the little children," Redwald chided as he approached.

"The little pests." Ardron muttered with a snigger.

"Come inside brother," Redwald said as he led the way. "What brings you here today?" he asked as he poured beer from a pitcher.

"I am here to retrieve my charger," Ardron replied. "You have had him three months."

"Almost!" Redwald corrected.

"Almost!" Ardron allowed.

"Well," Redwald went on as he handed Ardron a pewter. "He is well. He has covered a dozen or more mares, and probably some of our own stock too, that we don't actually know about just yet. Yes, He has had a good summer," he added nodding. "The horse is happy and content." He paused a moment. "Are you sure you want to take him away?"

"Quite sure," Ardron replied.

Redwald nodded resigned. "We will go and find him when you've finished your drink."

At the top of the bank they paused and looked down into the meadow below. A rough-hewn paddock contained the contentedly grazing village horses. Ardron scanned quickly and soon spotted Rattlebone in their midst. His attention was drawn away a little distance from the paddock to a familiar two wheeled cart by the river, with a small smouldering campfire close by. He glanced sideways at Redwald.

"Yes," Redwald answered the unasked question. "It is the pedlar Hengist. He arrived yesterday and asked to dally a while to rest his weary horse."

Ardron nodded without comment and swinging a halter at his side he descended down the bank to the paddock. Moving the cross beamed panel, that served as a gate, he entered the paddock. For a moment he hesitated then gave his usual low whistle. Rattlebone did not respond. He tried again. This time something stirred in the big horses memory and he looked in Ardron's direction with ears pricked. It took a third whistle before the horse recognised him and he began to casually stroll towards him.

"Hello big fellow," Ardron said affectionately as he stroked the horse's neck. Fishing in his pocket he produced a carrot treat for the animal, then as Rattlebone munched noisily, he began to fit the halter. When it was fitted, he led the horse towards the gate, where Redwald had been joined by Hengist.

"A very fine horse, brother of Thegne," Hengist commented.

"He certainly is that." Ardron agreed. Then looking critically back along the horse's length added. "Perhaps carrying a little too much condition though," he said glancing at Redwald.

"Well," Redwald said defensively. "You instructed that he does not work as a village horse, and so I honoured your instructions. He ate well and lazed a lot. Hence the fat belly."

Ardron nodded agreement. "Three weeks and we'll have that off. Wont we boy?" He addressed the horse for all to hear as he led him from the paddock.

"Well Hengist," he addressed the pedlar as Redwald replaced the crude paddock gate. "How do you fare?"

"I fare well," he replied.

It had been six years since Ardron had last seen the pedlar, and to him it seemed the years had not been kind to him. The familiar gnarled face and grey streaked beard was now replaced by a very much aged version. That gnarled face remained but so very much thinner and had developed a sallow complexion. The beard also remained but that had aged even beyond grey to white and was now thin and straggled.

"Isn't it time you gave up your travelling days?" Ardron suggested.

"And do what?" Hengist asked.

Ardron shrugged. "Find a village you like and settle there, maybe."

Hengist laughed. "Who would have me?" he asked with a grin. "I have no particular skills to contribute. My physical strength is on the wane and I would be nothing except a burden on the village. No__," he concluded. "I was born a pedlar, the son of a pedlar, and I will die a pedlar."

Ardron shrugged. "I just wondered how much longer you would be a traveller."

Hengist grinned. "I know exactly what you mean, and I thank you, brother of Thegn, for your concern. I expect that at the end of one of these hard winters somebody, somewhere, will stumble across my winter camp and peek inside my cart to find me long since dead." He shrugged. "All I hope then, is that whoever it be, set fire to my cart and belongings with me inside."

"A cheerful subject," Redwald cut in. "Do you have any other news?"

"I passed through Wallingford some days ago and couldn't get in the castle because it was under siege." He shrugged. "No matter to me. I do as much business among the siege force as I would inside the castle."

"Wallingford, under siege?" Ardron queried. "Who by?"

"The king's forces," He replied.

"The king was there?"

"The king? No, he wasn't there. He was residing nearby at Oxford castle."

"Then who headed the siege?" Ardron asked.

"There were two banners. Waleron de Beaumont and Ranulf Earl Chester."

Ardron was confused. Could it be that Bedford had fallen to the king's men, and that they had now moved onto Wallingford? "What of Bedford?" he asked.

"Bedford?" It was Hengist's turn to be confused.

"Aye Bedford. Last I heard the king with Earl Chester had laid siege to the castle."

Hengist shook his head. "I don't know," he said. "I travel and trade along the Thames valley and into the west country. I never go as far north as Bedford."

There were many unanswered questions whirling around Ardron's head, and at this moment none that could be answered. "When were you at Wallingford?" he asked.

"Some days ago," Hengist answered with a shrug.

"Days? How many days?"

"Twenty? Thirty, perhaps." His answer was vague.

"Does that concern you, brother?" Redwald asked.

"Yes it does," he replied not expanding. If Bedford had fallen to the king, then not only would it be yet another blow to the Angevin cause, but he wondered what fate had befallen Payn de Beauchamp and in-particular his wife Rohesa.

***

It was early evening by the time Swidhurn, and he arrived back at Norwood. They were greeted by Jarcot who informed him that he had a visitor.

"Oh!" Ardron said not expecting anyone.

"Yes. Sir John Fitzgilbert with an escort of a dozen seeking shelter for the night." Jarcot paused. "I allowed them access. I hope I did right." He added.

"You did," Ardron confirmed as he dismounted.

Swidhurn, still mounted, took his horse's reins, and the long halter on which Rattlebone was fast, then with a brief murmur led the animals away to the stable area.

"Where is Sir John now?" Ardron asked.

"I believe he is in your private quarters, where Lady Claennis sees him comfortable."

He found Sir John in the chamber but alone. However, with his head on his chest he was asleep. Deliberately noisy, in order to rouse him, he went to the table and poured a tumbler of water.

Fitzgilbert snapped alert. "Ah," he said, perhaps slightly embarrassed. "Ardron, my friend. It's good to see you"

"Sir John," Ardron acknowledged. "Have you been looked after?"

"Indeed I have. And royally, by your charming wife, Claennis."

Ardron glanced around needlessly, "Where is she now?" he asked as he offered the water to Sir John.

"She left some time ago to attend some kitchen business, I believe." He refused the water with a head shake. He waited a moment then said with a brief smile, "By the looks of things you will be a father very soon."

"Yes, eight or so weeks," Ardron replied pulling up a seat opposite Fitzgilbert. "What brings you to this area, Sir John?" he asked.

"Ah yes," he almost groaned. "I am," he went on with a sigh. "Requested to attend Earl Robert at Bristol to discuss a way to relieve the siege at Wallingford."

"The siege at Wallingford?" Ardron said. "What happened to the siege at Bedford?"

Fitzgilbert shrugged. "It didn't last," he said. "After about six weeks Stephen gave up and moved on to Wallingford."

Ardron frowned. "Why?"

Fitzgilbert shrugged. "I don't know. Perhaps Stephen decided that it just was not that strategically important. And I'd have to agree. If he intends to monopolise the whole of the Thames valley then Wallingford is much more important." Perhaps," he went on, "he decided that while he had a siege force assembled, it could be better used trying to bring down Brien Fitzcount's Castle."

Ardron nodded agreement. "Bedford Castle did not fall?"

"No, Bedford Castle stood. Not so the town, however. That was savagely plundered as they left."

For a moment Ardron thought back to Lincoln and remembered, Ranulf, Earl Chester leading the charge down steep hill to rob and plunder his own townspeople. He knew, precisely, where to lay the blame for the Bedford outrage. "What will it take to lift the Wallingford siege?" he asked.

Fitzgilbert shook his head. "More than we have," he said. "We just don't have the resources to raise an army to march on Wallingford."

"And you would know, being the Empresses Justiciar." Ardron said.

"Yes," he replied. "The empress has a personal regard for Brien Fitzcount, and it is she who says we must relieve the siege. Clearly, she is allowing her concern for the man to disregard the practicalities. But I'm afraid it is just not feasible."

"Perhaps," Ardron suggested, "we should consider attacking somewhere else to drag the king away from Wallingford."

"Such as?"

Ardron shrugged. "Winchester," he suggested.

Fitzgilbert laughed. "That would certainly bring him storming to its protection. But it would take a force just as large."

"How about Faringdon?" he suggested an alternative.

"Yes." He allowed. "But it would still take a large force. No, I'm very much afraid the basic situation is that we desperately need a big influx of sergens and money. And there is only one place where we might get it." He paused. "The empress needs to swallow her pride and appeal to her husband Geoffrey Plantagenet and ask him for help."

"She would never do that," Ardron said.

"She has to! And it will take Earl Robert himself to go to Anjou to broker the deal. That is the procedure I will be advocating when I get to Bristol."

"It won't make you popular,"

"No, it won't. But it's the only alternative I can see."

Ardron was thoughtful a few moments then asked. "What happened to Earl Robert's scheme of releasing Walter de Pinkney to cause conflict between him and his brother, over the ownership of Malmesbury Castle?"

Fitzgilbert shook his head sadly. "Didn't work," he said. "He was released. Although he did make straight for Malmesbury, the expected conflict just never happened. It simply went quiet for about a month, then, surprisingly, Walter left these shores for France. Leaving his younger brother in sole charge of the castle. It rather seems as if all that time in prison dented his appetite for the stresses and strains, and he opted instead for a quiet life back in Normandy."

"The outlook for the cause seems a bit bleak at the moment." Ardron said gloomily.

"I'd have to agree" Fitzgilbert said. "But it would only take a decent investment, followed by a victory of some sort, to restart the initiative. All is not lost. Not yet. For now, each of us has to hold on to what we have."

The pair fell silent a few moments until Fitzgilbert spoke, changing the subject. "I hear that you have recently acquired a second castle," he said.

"I have," Ardron confirmed. "South Cerney."

"Good. You certainly deserve it."

"I'm not sure Edward d'Evereux would agree," Ardron said.

Fitzgilbert laughed out loud. "Ah, the d'Evereux's," he said, shaking his head. "They are a complex bunch. "For years Patric d'Evereux and I ferociously banged heads. Now, because I married his sister, Sybil. he is my brother-in-law. Despite having been a resolute king supporter, he has been granted an earldom by our empress. Now he actually out-ranks me." He shrugged, "But as things stand my youngest son, William, is the heir to his estate and title. Unless, of course, he marries and produces a brat of his own. The irony of life." He added with a shrug. "But my friend," he went on. "You don't have to worry about Edward d'Evereux. In fact you did him a favour."

"How so?" Ardron asked.

"Why? Don't you know? He has been made castellan of Castle Cary."

"No. I didn't know."

"Sir Walter Douai died earlier this year and his son, Robert, took over the care-taker duties of his estate. Because of this vacancy the empress was able to pass the castle on to d'Evereux. I imagine he is highly satisfied."

Ardron nodded agreement. "I imagine so," he agreed. "He lost a castle in the front line of this war and gained one sitting safely and snugly in the heart of Angevin territory."

"You have it," Fitzgilbert said.

"Doesn't seem fair on Douai's son though," Ardron said.

"Oh. Robert did alright," Fitzgilbert said. "Walter Douai had two estates, the other at Bampton. Robert was elevated from caretaker to castellan of Bampton."

***

Devizes Castle, September 1146

Once again Ardron was summoned to report to Empress Maude at Devizes castle, to answer yet another complaint by Edward d'Evereux. However, this was a complaint that he had readily anticipated.

There was a definite air of exasperation about the empress when both men stood in the chamber before her. "We had thought that we had settled the dispute between you two," she said frostily. For God's sake!" she cursed. "You are grown men can you not settle your differences without involving me?" She took a breath then said. "There are more important issues that need my attention then to sit here and pass judgement on petty squabbles."

"I offer my apologies your Majesty," d'Evereux said. "But I am forced into this procedure because of the dishonesty of Norwood. The man has no integrity at all, absolutely none." He added with a glare in Ardron's direction

Ardron remained silent trying to remain aloof. It had been a few days since he had forwarded the first of four quarterly fiefs to d'Evereux, and this was exactly the response he had expected.

Reginald de Dunstanville stood at the empresses side. "Explain yourself." he said.

"This man tries to cheat me," d'Evereux said. "I received the first of the four fiefs that you, your Majesty, had decreed I should receive in compensation for the loss of South Cerney Castle. It is much less than I expected, considerably less."

"Sir Ardron," The empress sought his comment.

"I have no idea what Sir Edward was expecting," Ardron said. "All I can tell you is that was the exact sum that was collected."

"I was castellan of Cerney Castle for six years and I know roughly by past experience the amount of fief that would have been paid. This sum comes a long way short of that amount," d'Evereux countered hotly.

"Oh I see," Ardron said. "You based your expectations on your own past performances."

"Of course," he snapped.

Ardron addressed the empress, "Your Majesty," he said. "There is an obvious explanation."

"Which is?" she queried.

"My attitude to the estate vassals is quite different to Sir Edward's. Soon after the acquisition of Cerny I toured the estate, and it was patently obvious to me, that there had been a neglect of investment. So I allowed many of my tenants a fief reduction in order that they would have the means to carry out their own improvements."

"Nonsense!" d'Evereux barked.

"There were two villages without a suitable barn in which to store their winter goods, and to shelter their animals through the winter." Ardron went on ignoring d'Evereux. "There was a small farm hamlet with only a single compound to grow their crops. As a result, through crop exhaustion the land was played out. It needed to lay fallow for a year. I allowed them to purchase another compound and suggested a method of crop rotation. Many other owners had work animals that were old and very tired. Because of their exorbitant fief they could not purchase newer ones. I reduced their fief to allow them to purchase new stock. Many of the villeins abodes where dilapidated and run down. I allowed some to harvest some of the estate timber and also reduced their fiefs so that they might purchase other needs to make themselves more comfortable. He paused, "The list goes on," he added.

"Your tenants must find you very agreeable," Maude said.

Ardron was not sure whether the comment was genuine or sarcastic. "Your Majesty," he said with modesty, deciding to take it as a compliment. Then he took a moment before going on. "Waiting outside, I have the castle treasurer armed with the estate ledger," he said. "We are more than happy to hand these ledgers over for inspection. I am sure you will readily see that we have satisfied the terms of compensation, and Sir Edward has received every mark due."

D'Evereux stood with folded arms, muttering to himself and shaking his head in denial.

"We will inspect your books, Sir Ardron," Maude said, before turning her attention to Sir Edward. "Your recent acquisition of Castle Cary, that goes well?" She asked.

"It does your Majesty."

"Good," she said. "And you will have received a fief from those tenants?"

"D'Evereux hesitated, anticipating where this line of questioning was heading. "Er, yes," he agreed.

The proceedings were interrupted when Robert Fitzedith entered at the back of the room. Clearly, he was agitated, but even so waited to be acknowledged.

"What is it Maude?" demanded.

"I have an important despatch," Fitzedith said.

With an air of irritation, she motioned him forward. The chamber was silent while she read. "When did this come in?" She asked.

"Just now," Fitzedith said. "I brought it straight up."

She nodded and turned her attention back to the matter before her. "The case is dismissed." She proclaimed. "Now clear the chamber."

Ardron was amongst the last to leave, glancing back before he did. There was an air of excitement between the three. The news he surmised, was good.

"How did it go?" the waiting Louis asked.

"It went alright. I think." Ardron replied still not completely sure what the abrupt dismissal meant.

"Do they want to see the ledgers?" Louis asked.

Ardron wasn't really concentrating, his thoughts were on the unknown developments and what they were. "What? he asked. Then he realised that he had heard the question. "No I don't think they do."

"Then you won?"

Ardron nodded, then seeing de Dunstanville emerge from the chamber, he raised a hand towards Louis. "Wait here," he said and moved to intercept de Dunstanville.

"Sir Reginald," he sought his attention. "The news, was it good?"

"It was," de Dunstanville replied.

"Can you tell me?"

De Dunstanville stopped and looked around thoughtfully. "Yes," he said dubiously. "It'll be all round the castle within a few minutes, so I suppose I can."

Ardron waited.

"It seems," de Dunstanville said. "The king has arrested Ranulf, Earl Chester, and put him in prison."

Ardron was puzzled. "Do we know why?" he asked.

"He was abusive to the king, accusing him of having no honour and reneging on his part of the alliance."

"Why would he do that?

De Dunstanville took a breath. "Taking advantage of Chester's absence Madog of Gwyneth and Cadwaladr of Powys plundered along the borders of his estate," he said. "For Chester, the problem became serious, forcing him to consider a return to deal with the problem. As part of the alliance, he expected the king to join him. However, Stephen refused. Chester then became angry and abusive. So much so that the king had no alternative except to arrest him. After Chester was imprisoned his sergens deserted the king in their hundreds, leaving him with a very much weakened force. So much so, that he could no longer carry on the siege, and he retreated back to London. The siege of Wallingford is ended."

544

"That is good news," Ardron agreed. He was thoughtful a moment. "It was very fortuitus though that those Welsh Princes invaded Chester's estate at that time, Wasn't it?"

"Indeed it was," de Dunstanville replied. He turned to go, but after only a couple of steps stopped and turned back a moment and winked at Ardron.

He watched him walk away thinking of that wink. Perhaps it wasn't fortuitous after all, but more arranged. If it was, then it was a stroke of genius that had worked out perfectly for the Angevin cause. Not, however, so perfect for those innocents on the receiving end of the Welsh savagery.

"Sir" somebody said behind him. Then repeated, "Sir."

Ardron turned. "Cerdic! What are you doing here?"

"You should get back to Norwood," he said.

"Why?"

"The Lady Claennis,"

"The Lady Claennis?"

"Yes, Sir. She went into labour this morning just after you left."

Chapter 23

Bristol Castle, Christmas Eve 1146

Ardron could not believe his eyes as he looked over John Fitzgilbert's shoulder and watched Ranulf Earl Chester strut nonchalantly into the main hall.

"I don't believe it," he muttered.

Fitzgilbert turned to look where he looked. "Oh," he said. "Didn't you know that he had been brought back into the fold?"

"Yes, I had heard that, but I didn't think he would have the chutzpah to attend these celebrations."

"That is Earl Chester. The man has the arrogance of the devil." Fitzgilbert said.

Ardron shook his head slowly in disproval. "Far be it from me to criticize Earl Robert, but how could he forgive so easily?"

Fitzgilbert shrugged. "He is, after all, his son-in-law, and perhaps it was that he was considering his daughter's welfare.

Ardron shook a bewildered head. "She wouldn't be the first wife that found herself a better husband," he said.

"Fitzgilbert shrugged again, "Families," was all he said.

"Last I heard," Ardron went on. "Was that Chester was in the east midlands creating havoc."

"He was," Fitzgilbert confirmed. "The price of his release from Stephen's prison was that he surrendered Lincoln. His brother William Roumare agreed, and so the king took back Lincoln. Then, after extracting a promise from Chester that he would not take arms against him, he let him go. However, true to form, the moment Ranulf arrived back at Chester he assembled his army and marched on Lincoln in an attempt to get it back." He paused a moment. "He never even got into the town. The townsfolk did not want him and closed all the gates. Then stood too in their hundreds to repel any attack.

Chester gave up, deciding there was an easier target to the south and marched on Coventry. That siege didn't last long either. An angry Stephen arrived with an army of superior numbers and drove him off. So, he retreated back to Chester to sulk and kick his dogs," he added with a smirk. "Then supposedly, full of contrition, he allowed his wife Maud, to approach her father and request that he be allowed to re-join the Angevin cause. He claimed that the king is a dishonourable man without principles."

Ardron could not help but scoff loudly at that remark. "I could find it easier to trust a half blind drunken archer to shoot an apple off my head, much more than I could trust Chester with anything."

Fitzgilbert laughed loudly.

"Seems like a poor exchange to me, Lincoln for Chester," Ardron went on. "And what of his obnoxious nephew?"

"Gilbert de Claire?"

"That's him," Ardron confirmed.

"I believe," Fitzgilbert said. "That he was taken prisoner at Coventry and is still held at the king's convenience."

Ardron shrugged. "I have no sympathy for such turncoats."

"Nor I!" Fitzgilbert agreed.

At that point they were joined by Humphrey de Bohun. "I understand," he said addressing Ardron. "Congratulations are in order. Your wife presented you with a son some months back."

"She did, Sir Humphrey," Ardron replied.

"Isn't she here?" he asked glancing around.

"Regrettably, no she isn't. She decided that the infant was too small to leave."

"She wouldn't use a wet nurse?" he queried.

"Not my Claennis," Ardron replied. "Anything she decides important, she will always deal with herself."

He nodded approvingly. "Very commendable," he said. "And what did you call the infant?"

"We called him Wolfstan, after my father." Ardron said.

"Noble," de Bohun said. Then glanced around the hall. "There seems to be less people here each Christmas that passes," he muttered.

Ardron glanced around. Perhaps he was right. He wasn't sure whether it was support for the Angevin cause, that was waning, or perhaps it was the enthusiasm to celebrate when there was little to celebrate. He himself did not intend to stay throughout all of these celebrations. Personally, he saw this assembly as a duty, and as a duty he would, therefore, attend. However, as soon as the duty was satisfied, he intended to return post haste to Norwood. His plan was to attend this evening supper, then tomorrow's Christmas Day Mass and midday lunch. After that, he considered his duty satisfied, and could be on his way back to Norwood, not staying for the grand evening feast. To him, personally, the attraction of wife Claennis and infant Wolfstan waiting for him at Norwood were much more preferable. As he scanned around aimlessly, he noticed Roger Fitzmiles making his way through the crowd stopping briefly to impart some information before moving on to the next group.

"Has something happened?" he asked of no one in-particular. Both Fitzgilbert and de Bohun looked confused. "Over there," he said nodding in Fitzmiles direction. "He seems to be passing messages."

Both men turned to where he looked and watched for a few moments. "I do believe you are right," Fitzgilbert agreed. All three watched in silence as Fitzmiles slowly worked his way towards them.

It didn't take long for Fitzmiles to reach them and with his hands resting on the shoulders of both de Bohun and Fitzgilbert he leaned forward and said. "Good Sirs. May I interrupt for a moment?"

"Of course," de Bohun permitted.

"Before we go through into the dining hall," he said. "There is to be an announcement by his Grace Earl Robert."

Ardron could not help but groan. Every snippet of news of late had been bad.

Fitzmiles grinned and held up a hand. "This time the news is good," he said. Then smirking he moved on.

"Good news?" de Bohun muttered as he watched him go. "You're the Justiciar," he said to Fitzgilbert. "Do you know what it could be?"

"No," he replied looking a little puzzled. "I have been told nothing. However, I do know that Earl Robert has spent a month in France negotiating possible help with Geoffrey Plantagenet."

"He has," Ardron agreed. "But he's been back some two or three weeks now."

"He has," Fitzgilbert affirmed.

De Bohun shrugged. "We won't have to wait too long to find out."

In fact the wait was only a few short minutes before Robert Earl Gloucester entered the hall and stepped up onto the raised dais.

"Ladies, gentlemen, knights," he began. "Most of you, if not all, will know that in recent weeks I spent a full month as guest to Geoffrey Plantagenet at his castle in Anjou. The purpose was to negotiate some practical and financial aid in our cause to place his son, Henry, on the throne of England. Henry's right to the crown, as grandson to King Henry Beauclare, is indisputable. But I don't have to tell you that." He paused a moment. "The negotiations were long and protracted and, yes, sometimes bad tempered. Nevertheless, I persevered and in the end a semblance of a possible agreement was reached, but not agreed. With no further progress to be made, I left and returned to England leaving the proposition open on the table. I have no need to tell you just how badly we need Plantagenet's help." He paused again. Then waving a scroll in front of him, he went on. "Yesterday I received these despatches from Sir Geoffrey. He has provisionally agreed to send an expeditionary army of two-thousand men to our cause." The cheering and clapping were immediate. Earl Robert waited patiently for the euphoria to die away. "This army, he expects to send when winter's bite has eased. By that, I expect he means March or at the latest April. I have no need to impress on you just how devastating an army of two thousand strong marauding around the south of England would be to Stephen. He would be forced to deal with it. While he tries to deal with that, then we could be advancing elsewhere. Or__." He waited for effect. "If Stephen decides on open confrontation then, with us adding strength to Plantagenet's army, it just might prove to be another Lincoln for him." He smiled a smile of satisfaction. "This could be the very initiative we've waited for," he said.

As he stepped down the wave of optimism that swept through the room was palpable. After months of bad news and stalemate the morale lift was as good as any tonic could be.

"You had something to do with that," Ardron said to Fitzgilbert.

He smirked and wobbled his head in modesty, "At our meeting in August I did advocate that we appeal to Geoffrey Plantagenet for help. Despite Empress Maude's extreme reluctance the suggestion was eventually accepted. I can't take a great deal of credit though. It was the only sensible course of action remaining. But it is a tribute to Earl Robert's negotiating skills that he was able to pull it off. Plantagenet is just not interested in his wife's predicament."

"Well!" de Bohun said. "It does give us all something to hope for now."

He was right, Ardron silently concluded. Even Earl Robert's disposition seemed to have received a boost. For months now he had seemed like a man in deep depression. The responsibility of promoting a war that had limited funds, and was devoid of prospects, was visibly exacting a toll on his physical well-being.

At the far end, the doors into the banqueting hall were opened wide and the guests began to shuffle through, talking excitably as they did.

***

Norwood, April 1147

Although the sun shone this morning, the day held that slight chill that is typical of April. Ardron settled down at the long breakfast table among his rank and file. Because of the pleasantness of the morning, the servants had laid out this morning's breakfast in the open. Taking breakfast with his sergens was a habit that he tried to do at least twice during a week. It was, he believed, a habit that made him approachable and cemented good relations with men that he relied upon to receive unsolicited loyalty. To this end, he always took care not to seat himself at the table head. Instead he always found a seat somewhere along the side deep amongst his men.

The banter was, as always, light and amusing. This day most of the chiding was levelled at Jacques. The squire had recently returned after spending the better part of a year at his home in Anjou. During his time at home he had met and become betrothed to a local girl. This was the subject of most of the teasing.

Ardron placed a consoling hand on his shoulder. "Keep smiling Jacques," he encouraged. "They like you. They wouldn't do it if they didn't."

Taking as good as he was getting, Jacques raised a pointed finger in the air and waved it slowly around in all directions with a huge grin. No one took insult, instead it provoked raucous laughter.

Ardron's attention was then drawn across the table, and beyond, towards the bailey gate. A rider had just ridden in, his horse lathered in sweat. Clearly the animal had been hard ridden. He watched as Jarcot approached the rider and held the horse's reins while the rider slid off. The rider handed to him a pouch containing despatches. Jarcot looked across to Ardron.

With a brief arm wave, Ardron indicated that he had seen. He got to his feet and held up outstretched arms. "Carry on gentlemen, please," he said as he stepped back and turned to leave.

"I have urgent despatches from her Majesty, Empress Maude." The rider said.

Ardron nodded taking the pouch from Jarcot. "Please go and take yourself some breakfast," he said with an arm wave. "We will have your horse tended."

The rider looked uneasy. "I am ordered to return immediately with your reply," he said.

Ardron nodded. "You will have my response presently. And we will find you a fresh horse. Now go take breakfast," he added firmly.

Ardron took a few moments to scan the despatch, as the rider did as he was told. He could hardly believe what he read. Without comment he handed the despatches to Jarcot.

"God be praised," Jarcot uttered as he read. "It seems the Almighty smiles on us at last?"

"Maybe so," Ardron agreed taking back the despatch and rolling it up. Then he wandered back to the breakfast benches. "My friends. Can I have your attention a moment," he said.

All eyes turned in his direction.

"I have here," he said, waving the rolled despatch, "Good news." He paused a moment. "The young Plantagenet Prince, Henry, landed at Wareham some days ago, at the head of an army. He now lays siege to Cricklade Castle." The news brought immediate response of cheering, some getting impulsively to their feet to do so. He waited until the jubilation calmed a little. "Empress Maude," he went on, "Has tasked me to go to Cricklade to render whatever support I can. This I fully intend to do." He scanned around seeking the despatch rider. "As soon as you are rested you may return to Devizes and inform the empress that I will gladly do as she asks, and that I intend to go to Cricklade early tomorrow." He looked to Jacques. "Jacques when you have finished breakfast then look to my hauberk and my weapons."

"Sir," Jacques acknowledged formally.

He then looked to Jarcot, and with a head sign indicated that he should follow as he began to walk away.

"Well this is a pleasant surprise." Jarcot said when they were inside the keep.

"I can hardly believe it," Ardron agreed.

"How old is the Prince?"

Ardron shrugged. "Fourteen? Not more."

"Fourteen," Jarcot muttered with a deal of incredulity.

"Right!" Ardron became business like. If Geoffrey Plantagenet is as good as his word the Prince will be at the head of near two-thousand men. So, he will not be wanting for numbers. Therefore, I intend to take with me only an accompanying force of two-dozen. Select for me twelve good sergens. Also send word to Maurice, at Cerney and inform him of the new situation. Inform him also that, I will be arriving tomorrow before mass, and will be in want of twelve good sergens from him also."

"I will go myself," Jarcot said.

Ardron nodded agreement.

"I have a request, Sir," Jarcot said.

Ardron waited.

"I would like to go with you and be one of your number."

Ardron thought a moment considering his constables one arm handicap. Then decided that, assuming the Prince was at the head of a substantial force, Jarcot probably would not become involved in close combat fighting, he permitted his request.

As he turned to leave, he looked back at Ardron. "One thing puzzles me," he said. "Why Cricklade? Wareham must be all of seventy miles from Cricklade, and yet the Prince made directly for Cricklade. And, seemingly, in all haste."

"I have pondered exactly the same thing," Ardron replied. "Perhaps it is, that Henry is more than just a little peeved at his cousin, Phillip's disloyalty to his father. I know that Prince Henry holds Earl Robert in high regard. Whatever, I confess that, personally, I am pleased. If the siege is successful, and with the numbers advantage young Henry has, it should be, Then, it will in effect clear the enemy away from our eastern doorstep."

"Yes, it will," Jarcot agreed as he left.

Cricklade

Although little more than five miles from South Cerney, Ardron led his small party through a roundabout route in order to approach Cricklade from the south. Now as they emerged from the woodland to the south, the scene that they surveyed was not as they expected. All seemed calm and pastoral.

The small village lay south of the river and its populous appeared to be casually going about its usual daily activities. The castle itself, north of the Thames, also seemed to be under no stress. The main gate into the bailey was open and patrolled by two guards who casually monitored any traffic going in. Above the keep itself, although mostly hanging limp, Phillip Fitzrobert's flag could clearly be seen. Ardron, baffled, glanced sideways at Maurice. His response to the unasked question was a silent shrug.

"There is no siege going on here," Jarcot stated the obvious.

"There isn't," Ardron concurred.

"So where is the Prince?" Jarcot muttered.

Ardron shook a puzzled head.

"Perhaps," Maurice said. "He hasn't arrived yet. After all, Wareham is a long way south of here."

Ardron took a long breath. "Withdraw," he said turning Rattlebone's head about. For half-a-mile or so they retraced their steps until Ardron was satisfied that they were well clear. He then called a halt and dismounted bidding the others do the same. He then called for Beldwine his loyal Saxon.

"I want you to discard your armour and go back to Cricklade, posing as a traveller passing through," he said. "Find out what you can. We will wait here for your return." Beldwine nodded compliance. "Take Cerdic with you," Ardron added, as Beldwine prepared to leave.

It was pleasant in the forest glade, the April sunshine warm. With nothing to do but wait, Ardron found a small grassy bank on which to repose. 'Where could the Prince be? Perhaps it was as Maurice said, he had not yet arrived? Perhaps it was the despatch was wrong, and the siege was elsewhere? There were, at this moment, just no answers. In the background the low muttering of his companions faded to a hum, and he was overtaken by shallow sleep.

A little over an hour later Maurice roused him. "Beldwine returns," he said.

"Thank you, Ardron responded using his hands over his face to rub away any sleepiness.

"Well," Beldwine began. "It seems there was a siege of sorts some five days ago. But it was a half-hearted affair consisting only of a blockade and a few arrow storms over into the bailey. There was no actual assault on the castle defences, and by the third day the assault force did nothing except laze around and get drunk. When the sun rose on the morning of the fourth day they had gone."

Gone! Gone where?" Ardron asked.

Beldwine shrugged and spread his hands. "South. Back the way they came."

Ardron glanced skywards. The afternoon was wearing down with perhaps two maybe three hours daylight left. "Have the men mount," he instructed Maurice, "We will follow."

It was not a difficult trail to follow. An army survives on scavenging as it travels, and so they needed only follow the reports of destruction. It had begun to get dark when somewhere to the west of Suindune Ardron called a halt. "Tomorrow, we will catch up to them." He announced as they prepared to bed for the night.

It was an early start the next morning, without provision for breakfast there was no reason for delay. By mid-morning they were confronted by a steep bluff that rose fully a thousand feet above the flat land beneath.

"That's Clacks Mount," Beldwine informed him.

Clacks Mount?" Ardron queried as he sat his horse surveying the steep embankment. "What's on the top?" he asked.

"The village Clack and an old ruin of a Norman castle."

"Beyond that?"

"Beyond that?" Beldwine stroked his chin thoughtfully. Well, I suppose that eventually you would come to the hamlet of Calne."

"Calne? I know Calne." Ardron replied, feeling a little more comfortable as he managed a rough fix on their location. He studied the bank a few moments mapping the rough-hewn roadway that snaked its way to and fro up the side of the hill.

To spare the horses they dismounted and led their mounts up the steep hill, however, in full armour the climb was taxing. Eventually the top was reached, and taking a few minutes recover, they were able to enjoy the remarkable outlook across the flat land below. There were still appreciating the panoramic view when Roland came back riding excitedly into their midst.

"Sir," he called before he had pulled his horse to a stop. "The prince and his army."

Ardron was on his feet. "What about the prince and his army,"

"They are but a few yards ahead in the ruins of Clack Castle."

"Mount up," Ardron ordered immediately.

They were able to ride unchallenged into the castle ruins. It was not until they had halted in what remained of the castle bailey that anyone even approached them. Security was lax, in fact non-existent.

"I would speak with the prince," Ardron demanded.

A lazy arm wave directed him towards the pile of rocks that was once the castle keep. It was at the rear of the rubble where he discovered the sizeable bell tent. It was constructed eye catching green and yellow stripes, the identifying livery, Plantagenet. Further frivolous decorations included streamers and flags. There was no doubt to Ardron, this was the boy prince's tent. He slid from his horse and approached. However, he was halted by two burly pike-men crossing their pikes barring his way before he got within ten yards of the tent. He stood still waiting for a further reaction from the guards. None came.

"I am sent by the Empress Maude, and I would speak with Prince Henry," he said.

"Sir Helias," one called.

After a few moments, a knight emerged from within the tent. Not a young man probably in his mid-thirties. He was dressed smartly in a short tunic patterned into quarters of red and yellow. He stood outside the tent a few moments and stared at Ardron.

"I am Sir Helias Count of Maine," he said brusquely when he approached. "State your business!"

"I am Baron Ardron of Norwood, and I am here by the Empresses bidding, to aid Prince Henry.

Helias studied Ardron a few moments. "Do you bring men?" He asked.

"I do."

"How many?"

"Two dozen."

"Two dozen?" he scoffed.

"Two dozen," Ardron re-affirmed.

"Why so few?" Helias asked.

"My brief is to lend assistance, which I assumed to be as an advisor."

"Well Sir. We don't need an advisor!"

Ardron sighed heavily. "I would speak with the prince." He demanded.

"Wait here. I will see if he will see you."

During the exchanges Jarcot had moved to Ardron's elbow. "Sir," he said in a low voice, as Helias moved away. "There is no army here."

Ardron glanced sideways at him. "No army?"

"No Sir," Jarcot said. "At least not of any size. Most certainly not that numbers two thousand, or even close."

Moments later Helias re-appeared. "The prince will see you," he said. Ardron was allowed past the guards, but when Jarcot tried to follow he was abruptly halted by curt instructions from Helias. "You, with one arm.

Wait there." Then turning his attention back to Ardron said. "Hand your weapons over to one-arm." Ardron passed over his sword and his dagger to Jarcot. Now satisfied, Helias lifted the tent flap allowing Ardron inside.

Inside, the tent was regaled with cushions, curtains, and other luxury items of paraphernalia, even to the extent of a high wooden seat representing a modest throne.

"Your highness," Helias raised his voice. "That baron is here."

Pulling back a dividing curtain, Prince Henry appeared from beyond and greeted Ardron with a wide smile. "It is, as always, a pleasure to see you Sir Ardron," he said as he made his way to the high seat. "Please find a seat."

Ardron glanced around. His alternatives were cushions or stools. He decided that he preferred to stand, but decorum demanded he choose as he was bade. He chose a stool. Seated low with his knees tucked high he wasn't particularly comfortable, and considerably lower than the seated prince. Probably planned that way. Helias, meanwhile, took a position standing slightly to the rear of Prince Henry's chair.

"Your highness," he began. "I was tasked, by your esteemed mother, to lend whatever assistance I could to you at the siege of Cricklade. But when I arrived you were not there."

"No. We were obliged to call off the attack."

Ardron waited but he did not proffer an excuse. So, he let the topic go and instead asked, "Can I ask? Where is your army?"

"Outside. In and around the ruins."

"I could not see two-thousand men at arms."

"Two thousand men?" The prince repeated with an element of surprise.

"Two thousand men at arms that your father Geoffrey promised." Ardron said.

"Oh I see," the prince replied as he leaned back. "These men are not here at the directive of my father. At this moment he has enough problems of his own to spare an army of two thousand. King Louis's Queen, Eleanor of Aquitaine, has initiated a border dispute along the southern region of Anjou, and my father stands there to protect his assets."

"Ah," Ardron said feeling a little foolish. "You were not sent here by your father."

"No," Prince Henry confirmed. "He doesn't know that I am here." He held up his hands. "Or at least he didn't know. By now, however, he probably does."

Ardron was confused. "So, where did you get these men?"

"We recruited our own." It was Helias that answered.

"Recruited from where?"

"Here and there," Helias replied off-handed.

"Mercenaries!" Ardron accused.

"Yes," Prince Henry confirmed.

"How many of these mercenaries do you have?" he asked.

Henry glanced up over his shoulder and allowed Helias to answer. "Four hundred. Plus or minus a few."

"The loyalty of mercenaries is bought with money and when the money runs out so does their loyalty." Ardron responded.

"Yes," the prince said. "These men have not been paid since before they left France and are overdue payment."

Ardron's body language said it all. "I see," he said with a sigh. "At Cricklade they refused to fight until they were paid."

"There you have it." Helias said. "What we need is money."

Ardron looked up curiously at Helias. "Excuse me Sir," he said. "What exactly is your connection here?"

"Sir Helias is my advisor, and he is also my uncle. Younger brother to my father." The prince answered.

Ardron rubbed his eyes tiredly, wondering if the prince knew exactly how vulnerable he was at this time. He decided to spell it out for him. "Sir," he said. "If King Stephen hears of your current situation, he is certain to gather, without delay, a substantial force and march on you at the double. When he gets here, he will, with the offer of immediate money, recruit your mercenaries for himself. You, then, defenceless will become his prisoner. All your aspirations to be England's King will end right there. Your mother, at the fear of your life, will be obliged to do as Stephen commands. The Angevin cause is then defeated." He paused a moment allowing the thoughts to mature a little. "You must, retreat to the safety of Devizes Castle at once." He asserted.

"Must?" the prince responded clearly irked.

Ardron held up a hand. "Sorry Sir," he said. "Perhaps, should, was the correct word."

"Do you think that we don't understand that?" Helias said with a smirk. "Therefore, the responsibility has now fallen on you, Sir, to make sure that does not happen. You will go to my sister-in-law and persuade her to support her son by funding us with both money and an army."

"It can't happen," Ardron said. "The very reason your father's help was sought was because at this time there is neither the resources nor the finance to raise an army."

"But," Helias, interrupted. "Once the army is active, on the rampage, it will fund itself. There are riches to be taken from the defeated."

"Yes," the prince agreed. "We will return to Cricklade then on to Faringdon heaping vengeance onto my treacherous cousin, Phillip. After that, the glittering prize that is Oxford."

"Oxford." Ardron cut in with surprise. "Oxford is almost impregnable. Ask Robert d'Oyly. Ask your mother. Oxford can only be starved into submission. That will take several months. Have you any idea how much it will take to fund a siege army for that length of time?"

"The prince shrugged. "Alright miss Oxford. Instead advance into the midlands on to Coventry and Leicester."

Ardron could see the boys mind had been filled with near fantasies. There was little point trying to reason. It would need a heavy dose of realism to bring the boy back to reality. He glanced at Helias standing smug and wondered his part. Clearly the man had his own agenda. He was actively encouraging a massive gamble from which he, personally, had much to gain and little to lose. With a heavy heart Ardron conceded for the time being.

"I will go to Devizes and I will speak with your mother on your situation." He said quietly. "However, my young prince, you need to, at least, consider that disappointment may be the most likely outcome." He looked up at Helias as he made the last remark.

***

Devizes Castle

"Not one mark nor a single sergen will I send." Maude was angry. Ardron had not seen her this irate since she had confronted the London merchants six years ago. "I will not be blackmailed by my own son. He is behaving like a__. Like a." Words failed her.

"Like a king?" Reginald de Dunstanville suggested. Then even he withered beneath her angry glare.

"Spoiled brat," she finished for herself.

The room was silent. Ardron glanced sideways at Fitzgilbert looking to him for a lead, but he remained silent.

"Your Majesty," Ardron spoke up. "The boy is but fourteen and is being heavily influenced by Helias, Count of Maine.

"Count of Maine indeed," she spat. "Since when? Last I heard was that the title belonged to Geoffrey. Unless my husband as changed a great deal, then I can see no way that he would relinquish that title to his brother."

The point was not particular relevant. "Nevertheless," Ardron went on. "Helias does manipulate the young prince."

"Yes," She agreed. "He is a scheming bastard, and as ever been so. That man is so base that he could comfortably wriggle beneath the belly of a snake." She paused a moment. "Reginald," she said. "Can you not take a troop and arrest him?"

"That would be a bad idea," Fitzgilbert cut in. "The man will be amid four hundred mercenaries. Whilst the loyalty of those mercenaries might be questionable, their ability is not. Most, if not all, are experienced fighters."

Momentarily closing her eyes she sighed heavily. "What's to be done?" she asked.

"We do nothing," Fitzmiles said.

"Nothing?"

"Nothing." Fitzmiles confirmed. "It can often be the best policy."

"What about the king?" Maude asked.

"The king, we know, at this time, lays siege to Pevensey Castle. In the south east corner of the country. He couldn't, at this moment, be any further east. He will of course know by now that Henry has landed in England. Like us he might believe his army is much bigger than it actually is."

"It won't be long before he knows that it is not." De' Dunstanville said.

"No it won't," Fitzmiles agreed. "But he may not know that his army is refusing to fight until they are paid. Meanwhile the prince waits at Clack Castle for your assistance." He indicated towards Maude. "Likely he will remain at Clack waiting and waiting. We still do nothing. As time wears on some of his mercenaries will realise that the money is just not going to come. When that happens some will give up and drift away. At first it will be a mere trickle, later it will become a definite flow. When his force is weakened enough then the young prince will probably see reason."

The room was silent pondering his scheme. "And Helias?" Fitzgilbert asked.

"He too will realise the plan has failed and might leave. If, however, he continues to wait around, that might be the time to arrest him." Again the room was silent.

"It's a good plan," de Dunstanville said.

"I agree," Fitzgilbert echoed.

"But!" Maude cut in. "What if Stephen does come?"

"In that case, we will have to act before he actually arrives." Fitzmiles said. "We step in and lift the prince to safety. Even Henry will realise he cannot stay."

Maude nodded acceptance. "Then it is agreed. For now we do nothing." The silent pause indicated all were satisfied. "Thank you, gentlemen," she said. Then accompanied by de Dunstanville she left the chamber.

"I didn't know the king had laid siege to Pevensey," Ardron said to Fitzgilbert as they left the chamber.

"Yes. These two weeks past now." He answered.

Ardron was puzzled." But what of Gilbert de Clair, isn't that his castle?"

"Indeed it is."

"The king holds him prisoner from Coventry, does he not?"

"He did," Fitzgilbert confirmed. "The price of his freedom was to surrender Pevensey to the crown. Which he agreed. However, as soon as he was freed, he reneged his word, hurried to Pevensey and fortified the castle. Stephen was, of course, furious, and immediately marched against the castle. While he remains furious and concentrating his wrath against de Clair, it buys us precious time."

"It would seem," Ardron said thoughtfully, "That to be a friend to this king is a hazardous station. Earl Chester found it so to his cost, as did Mandeville, and even the Salisbury Bishop before them."

Fitzgilbert sniggered. "It would seem so," he agreed.

***

Norwood, June 1147

Gazing from a portal in the castle keep, Ardron looked down into an inactive bailey below. It was yet another hot afternoon, just as hot as it had been for more than a week. Once past noon personnel in and around the castle sought the comfort of shade, and their chores finished, there was no reason why they shouldn't. The civil war, it seemed, had slipped into a welcome state of suspension.

There had been no significant news for a few days. As far as Ardron was aware the king still laid siege to Pevensey Castle, prince Henry still waited on Clack Mount for his mother to do something, and there were no advances from any of the Angevin supporters. One could almost believe that the war had just petered out. But that was a forlorn hope he knew. Somewhere, and soon, something would flare up. Selfishly he hoped that when it did it would by-pass him, leaving him in reserve.

"Ardron," Claennis sought his attention. He turned away from the portal. "Come. I have something to show you," she said.

"What is it?" he asked.

"Come, I will show you."

Obediently, he followed her higher up the keep into their private chamber. His infant son, Wolfstan, sat on the floor amongst cushions and wooden toys.

"Kneel," she said pointing where he stood.

"Kneel?"

"Kneel," she said again. Warily he did as instructed.

She sat on the floor next to the baby just a couple of yards away. She picked up the infant and set him on his feet, then lined him up. "Call him," she said. Once again, he did as instructed. "Hold out your arms" She charged, then let go of the infant. Tottering and stumbling the boy took his first steps until he fell into his father's arms.

"Wow," Ardron grinned with delight as he grabbed the baby and scooped him up. "Again," he said handing him back to his mother. Once more he scooped him up with delight, and this time spun him around playfully. Jarcot knocked shyly on the open door. "Did you see that?" Ardron asked proudly.

"Yes, Sir," he answered. "How old is he?"

"A little over nine months," Ardron answered smugly.

"He has done well," Jarcot answered, mildly interested. "I have despatches here, just in, from the empress."

Ardron nodded. "Once more," he said handing the baby back to Claennis. Eventually satisfied at last, with the development of his son's progress, he turned his attention to the despatches.

"What?" he spluttered as he read. "I don't believe it!"

"Bad news Sir?" Jarcot queried.

"No. Er, I don't know," Ardron's confused reply. "It seems," he said, "Prince Henry has accepted a bribe from the king to return to France."

It was Jarcot's turn to be confused.

"King Stephen has paid Prince Henry to return to France, and the prince has accepted. He is on his way back to France."

Jarcot did not know what to say. "Is it good news?" he muttered.

"Well," Ardron drawled. "It does at least take him out of harms-way, and it does relieve Empress Maude of a knotty problem. But it might be posing awkward questions about the boy's resolve." He sighed heavily. "Have the men assemble, I will announce the news." He handed the scroll back to Jarcot. "Have this sent on to Maurice at South Cerney," he said.

***

Norwood, September 1147

The summer had worn away and evidence of autumn was all around. The nights were colder, the trees were shredding leaves, and the hours of daylight were much less.

For Ardron, it had not been a bad summer. In fact in the Angevin struggle he seemed to have been side-lined, and he was not at all dismayed by that. Left alone to tend his own personal interests he had glimpsed into what life could be like without the civil war. With a wife that was the envy of most, and an infant son to dote over, his life was idyllic.

Improvements across the South Cerney estate had progressed a pace. Many villeins had benefitted from his benevolence, and just about all had voiced contentment with their new master. There had been two incursions by Fitzrobert's hunting parties. But a warning letter and the installation of regular patrols had put a stop to the Cricklade trespasses. Perhaps, Ardron allowed, they had been accidental incursions. There had been another reduced fief payment to Edward d' Evereux. But it had passed without a challenge. Why would there be a challenge? Ardron had thought. D'Evereux had himself a new castle away from the front line with a regular fief income. These extra payments he was receiving from South Cerney were added bonus. The loss of South Cerney had worked out well for him. Very well, indeed.

On the war front, Pevensey Castle had eventually fallen to King Stephen. The inmates had held out for months, but eventually starvation forced their surrender. Gilbert de Clair had, however, escaped and took refuge at Chester Castle, the home of his uncle. John Fitzgilbert had brazenly started to build himself a new castle at Newbury. The strategic importance of placing a fortification at that location was obvious and would have been a vitally important asset to the Angevin cause. However, also appreciating its importance, the king sent an armed force to wreck the construction and drive away all the workers. Probably as a result of Fitzgilbert's audacity, the king had laid siege to Marlborough Castle. It was, however, a half-hearted attack because before a month had elapsed the king withdrew his force.

"How long will you be gone?" Claennis asked as Ardron tossed a travel bag onto the bed.

He shrugged, "Four days, maybe five. Not more." He hazarded a guess. He had been summoned to attend a gathering at Bristol Castle. With no added invitation for spouses to attend, he guessed the meeting to be a war counsel of sorts. "I don't know exactly what there is to discuss," he added.

It seemed to him that the Angevin cause was wedged in unfathomable impasse. There was no denying the critical shortage of funds. That promise of aid from Geoffrey Plantagenet had proved to be as empty as a dead man's ambition. Motivation to promote any offensive had all but withered. Seemingly, all that was left were desperate men, desperately holding on to personal possessions, with only scant hope of assistance should they be attacked. The main objective to place Prince Henry on the throne of England seemed now to be nothing more than a false illusion. The mystery to Ardron was, why the king had, so far, failed to press home his advantage and launch a significant offensive into Angevin territory. The only conclusion he could draw was that the king had no appetite for the hardships of winter sieges. But come next spring, things could be different.

***

Bristol Castle.

All were there. The direct male descendants of King Henry, significant cause leaders, the titled, the barons, the knights and even some squires. Anyone of consequence to the cause was in attendance. There were faces that Ardron had not seen for some considerable time. William de Keynes was one. He was a man that he had not seen actively in the cause since he had taken possession of the king as prisoner at the Lincoln battle. Another was Hugh Bigod. A man Ardron considered just may have started this war with his statement the King Henry had declared Stephen his successor. He was a man who, when the situation suited his purpose, had switch his loyalties to the empress.

Speculation was rife. The pessimistic feared the prelude to complete surrender. The optimistic predicted a revival of fortunes. For himself, Ardron decided not to speculate but to wait and see. The entire assembly were instructed to be in place by the early part of the afternoon, at two-thirty. Well before that appointed time Ardron had found himself a niche close to the front, his back against a stone pillar.

"Well," Humphrey de Bohun muttered as he sidled up alongside Ardron. "The announcement must be significant. All the good, the mighty and the meek are summoned into attendance."

Glancing sideways at him, Ardron only nodded and snorted agreement.

"How is that pretty wife of yours?" he started conversation.

"She is well. Very well.

"And the infant? You have an infant now?"

"I do," Ardron said. "He is well. Just had his first birthday."

"My Lord!" de Bohun exclaimed. "Is that a year since?"

"It is." Ardron just had time to mumble before the doors at the far end were opened admitting   Reginald De Dunstanville and Robert Fitzedith. Both men made their way to the raised dais and began to make themselves comfortable. Ardron didn't actually see Empress Maude enter the chamber, but the clapping and cheering alerted him. She too took her place on the dais. He focussed his attention on her. She looked somewhat austere, but then that was her usual posture. He could glean nothing from that. He turned his head when movement in the doorway attracted his attention. Earl Robert of Gloucester began to enter. By his side Roger Fitzmiles held the Earl's elbow steadying him. Somewhat piqued, Earl Robert snatched his elbow clear. Then determinedly, he too made his way to the dais and took his place on Maude's right. There was no doubt in Ardron's mind, the earl looked decidedly affected. For some time now he had noted his steady decline, but here and now that steady decline looked as if collapse was imminent.

De Dunstanville opened the meeting with a cheery and warm welcome. This welcome was endorsed when Empress Maude took over and added her own personal welcome. Then there followed a routine progress report by Fitzmiles. Although his report was somewhat protracted there was no disguising that the content really revealed that there was no proper progress to report.

It was when Earl Robert got to his feet to make his contribution that the whole reason for this assembly was revealed.

"For seven years now," he began. "I have been the Supreme Commander of my sister's cause. God above us knows full well that her claim to England's throne is just. If it were not, I would not have taken up this cause. A cause in which many of our comrades and friends have, regrettably, given their lives. There is among us many acclaimed heroes, and there just as many heroes who didn't get acclaimed. But you, whoever you are, know what you have contributed. To each and every one of you I stand here today and proffer my deepest gratitude for your support. We could not have achieved all that we did achieve without you."

He paused to drink some water and to steady himself." I have promoted this war with all the energy and vigour that I could muster," He went on. "But now I fear my strength is worn and I fear that I am in need of rest. So it is my intention to step back for a little while to recoup my strength. In my absence, I." He paused correcting himself. "We intend to make Sir Roger Fitzmiles acting Supreme Commander in my absence. He will be responsible for promoting Prince Henry's claim to the throne. To this objective all attack or defend plans will emanate through him. You all know him as a fearless fighter and a clever tactician. I could not leave the promotion of the war in more capable hands. I trust to you, my comrades, that he will receive from you all the same loyalty and co-operation that I have enjoyed. I still remain Supreme Commander and I will receive regular reports from Sir Roger. I will, of course, offer advice and encouragement, if so needed.

So! My friends. On behalf of my sister and myself, all that is left is to declare our eternal appreciation to each and every one of you. If it were in my power, I would make you all earls of the realm." There was emotion in the last words he uttered and then, to resounding cheers, he sat down.

***

Bristol Castle, Early November 1147

Dressed this day in full military armour, with the added addition of a broad black sash, Ardron took his place in the slow-moving column that filed toward the coffin of Robert Earl Gloucester. The earl's body lay in state inside the small castle chapel. As he neared, he briefly nodded acknowledgement to the earl's eldest son Richard, who along with three of his brothers, stood sentry at each corner of the dais. To the rear, the chapel priest stood muttering prayers, whilst his server swung a smoking lamp, filling the air with the smell of incense. The coffin itself was draped in the earl's colours of vivid blue, spotted with golden sheaves.

It had been the last day of October when Earl Robert had succumbed to the illness and had slowly faded away. Today, a week later, his body was to be laid to rest in the nearby Priory of St James. It would be a fitting resting place because it was he who had founded the Priory. After a sad respectful dip of the head, Ardron shuffled on past and made his way back towards the door. At the door he was offered a goblet of wine by a posted servant. A nod and a muttered thanks he took the wine and made his way to the main hall.

Inside the hall it was crowded. Voices, speaking softly, resonated as a low hum throughout the room. For a few moments he remained standing in the doorway casting around for Roger Fitzmiles face. It seemed that everyone who was anyone was in attendance. A waving hand away to his right caught his attention. Fitzgilbert beckoned him over. For a moment he hesitated because among his company was Patric Earl Salisbury. 'What the hell? He swept away reservation. Today would not be the day for old scores or scenes. He joined the company acknowledging John Fitzgilbert, Baldwin de Reviers, Robert d'Oyly and finally Patric Earl Salisbury.

"A sad day, gentlemen," he said. All muttered agreement.

"He should have been king," de Reviers said. "He was Henry's eldest."

Fitzgilbert shook his head. "Maybe you have a point. But he was a bastard and no bastard can be made king." He said.

"His grandfather, William was a bastard too. But he was king." de Reviers countered

"Yes he was!" Fitzgilbert agreed with a shrug. "But he took England's crown by force." He paused a moment. "But I do agree. Robert would have made a good king."

"He was unwavering loyal to his father's last will," De Reviers said sadly. "He supported Maude, unselfishly, right unto his last breath. No father could have had a more dependable son."

"Doesn't matter now." d Oyly muttered with a sigh.

"No it doesn't," Fitzgilbert agreed.

De Reviers eyed Ardron up and down examining his military dress. "Do you have a role to play in today's ceremonies," he asked.

Ardron nodded. "I am tasked to provide a guard of honour outside the Priory."

"Why?" Earl Patric asked.

"Why?" Ardron was confused.

564

"Yes. Why you?"

"Because he has earned the privilege by loyal and outstanding service to Earl Robert." Fitzgilbert answered for him, staring hard at Patric. The insinuation was clear, Patric's own loyalty had to be bribed with a title. Clearly, although the two men were brothers-in-law, they were not bosom friends.

Ardron looked beyond Patric and spotted Fitzmiles. "Excuse me," he said. "I must speak with Sir Roger." He made his excuse to leave.

"Ah, Ardron," Fitzmiles said as he approached. "Are your men in position?

"They are, Sir Roger. We await only further instruction." Ardron answered.

Fitzmiles gave a satisfied nod. "I am about to close the chapel and organise the procession," he said. "I would say that one hour from now we will arrive at the Priory."

"Then I will leave right now. We will be ready when the cortege arrives."

In the event it was more like an hour-and-half before the slow-moving procession arrived. Ardron had placed twenty men either side of the curving footpath. They stood too, each with an upright lance at his right hand, and each man bowing his head as the carriage bearing Earl Robert's coffin passed. Following on foot, behind the carriage Empress Maude and Mabel, Earl Robert's wife, walked side by side. Immediately behind them came the earl's two daughters and his six sons, including the outcast Phillip. Then came the multitude of mourners. So many, in fact that a prodigious queue to enter soon formed at the narrow Priory door.

Once all were inside, Ardron allowed Maurice to stand the guard of honour down, with the instruction that they were to make their way back to Norwood and South Cerney. But not before he had handed across a few marks for the company to socialize a little on the way.

He watched until his sergens had disappeared, then turned towards the priory door trying to decide whether or not to go in. He decided not. Instead he settled down, in contemplative mood, beneath a tree in the priory grounds.

There was no doubt in his mind that with the passing of Earl Gloucester something significant had ended. He reminisced on the time when he had disturbed him from his bed, bringing him the news that Empress Maude had landed in England. Although the hour late, he had roused the whole castle instantly, and rapidly began to organise his sisters rescue. Most certainly he was a man of action. Proof, if it were needed, confirmed at Lincoln when his invading army was confronted by a flooded Fossedyke. Without hesitation he had, himself, plunged his mount into the freezing waters. Setting the example for all to follow. Without doubt he was a man who had led by example. Ardron's thoughts then strayed on to Hedingham Castle and the arena where he had been forced to fight for his life. It was Earl Robert who had ridden in and stopped the event. It was probable, Ardron allowed, that he actually owed his life to that intervention. There was no doubt the Angevin cause had lost its supreme champion. And at this moment he could not see how its loss could be covered.

***

Norwood, Christmas 1147

Unsurprisingly, there had been no official Christmas celebrations this year. The reports were that the empress had become withdrawn, spending long hours in her chamber alone with only her close ladies in waiting. Even her quick temper and sharp tongue seemed to have mellowed. Clearly, she was feeling the loss of Robert, her main confidante and the commander in chief of her enterprise.

Instead, this Christmas Ardron had stayed at Norwood and had, personally, joined in with the celebrations that he always organised for all the castle staff. In the event he had found that staying at home to be equally as enjoyable, if not more so. But now, three days past Christmas Day he prepared a carriage to take Claennis and Wolfstan to visit his father-in-law at Cloatly, where they intended to stay for a few days.

"Sir," Jarcot sought his attention. "There is a rider coming in."

Ardron groaned inwardly. 'What now?' he thought. Standing together, staring towards the gate, they waited for the rider to appear. When he did, he entered calmly his horse walking leisurely. Ardron took a breath of relief. The man's casual approach could only mean the news was not important.

"Step down," Jarcot invited taking the horses bridle.

The rider slid from the saddle then fiddled in the saddle paniers producing the rolled scroll. "Despatches from Sir Humphrey de Bohun," he said as he handed it over to Ardron.

"Good or bad news," Ardron asked staring into the rider's face as he took the despatches.

"Oh. Good I believe," he said.

Ardron only nodded. "See him comfortable," he muttered to Jarcot as he broke the seal.

"Of course," Jarcot said.

He scanned the despatch. "Jarcot," he called after his disappearing constable. "Have the men assemble in thirty minutes. I have an announcement to make."

The news was good. Good enough to be a desperately needed morale booster. Soon after the death of Robert, Earl Gloucester, King Stephen's General, William de Ypres, had led a force deep into Angevin territory to attack and lay siege to Sherbourne Castle. Why Sherborne had been selected for this attack was not clear. Probably for no better reason than to demonstrate that the Royalists, if they so desired, could venture, at will, deep into the Angevin territory. However, what these despatches informed Ardron, was that some days before Christmas de Ypres had been forced to withdraw back to Winchester. It seemed that Fitzmiles had not, as was expected, raised a large force to relieve Sherbourne. Instead he had gathered a smaller force and positioned it east of Sherbourne, effectively cutting de Ypres's supply line. The siege force, short on supplies, had then been forced to brutally forage among the local populace. Soon that too became exhausted because the traumatised people fled, taking with them all they could carry. Without supplies and no easy means to re-stock de Ypres was forced to withdraw.

Ardron bounded up the steps to his private chamber. "I saw the despatch rider come in," Claennis said with trepidation. "Does it mean our visit to Cloatly will have to be cancelled?"

"Not at all," he replied in high spirits. "The news was good. There is no need to disappoint your father. I know just how much he is looking forward to entertaining his grandson."

***

Bristol Docks March 1148

The overnight rain had cleared away. Chased away by strong winds that, even now, rushed dark clouds across the morning sky. A small sombre crowd of around five dozen had gathered on the dockside to see the empress leave. The small ship that was to take her to Rouen in France, rocked against the harbour wall on a gentle tide. Sailors on board the ship busied themselves, making sure all was ready to begin the voyage that was to take her into exile.

"I never thought I'd see this day," Humphrey de Bohun said. "A bad end to a righteous cause."

Ardron made no reply but did nod agreement.

"Perhaps her reward awaits in heaven," Fitzgilbert muttered.

A clattering of coach wheels on the harbour side cobbles attracted attention. "What is he doing here?" De Bohun almost growled when he recognised the crest of Bishop Henry on the coach door.

"The eyes of the king," Fitzgilbert said. "Making sure that Maude does actually leave."

"The conniving scheming troublemaker," de Bohun snarled. "For just a pinch of salt I would take four men and have him tossed into the waters."

"Had I a pinch of salt on me, I would hand it to you right now," Ardron said. They all sniggered just as cheering broke out a little further along the harbour. "I think Empress Maude arrives." Ardron added.

She came on foot, attended by two maids and escorted by four burly protecting sergens. Her quest was in tatters. A bitter situation to accept, nevertheless, she still walked with dignity and a head held proud. She moved through the gathering slowly, acknowledging all as she did.

"Gentlemen," she said with a nodded greeting when she reached Ardron's company. she then passed on to the gangplank. Halfway up she paused. "I have no words to lessen the disappointment I feel," she said. "But it is not your fault that I failed to achieve that which my father willed. You have served me well and no monarch was served better. The fates, it seems, conspired against me. Now, I must leave you and hope that cousin, Stephen does not judge you too harshly." She paused. "Good luck and may God bless and protect you all." With that she turned and continued up the gangplank onto the ship.

It was not lost on Ardron that she still could not call Stephen, King. "What now?" he asked.

"What now, indeed," de Bohun said.

"I guess we carry on and try to hold what we have. Then hope that Prince Henry invades soon," Fitzgilbert said.

"After last year's debacle, I imagine he will have learned the lesson that he needs a good deal of money to make a successful invasion." Ardron said.

"Exactly," de Bohun agreed. "But where is he going to get it? His father, Geoffrey Plantagenet, is not interested in England, so I can't see him funding an expedition."

"Nor me," Fitzgilbert concurred. "So there are only two ways for him to obtain that amount of money. First is to inherit. That will take Geoffrey's death for that to happen."

"He is a comparatively young man and so that's not likely to happen soon." Ardron said. "So what's the other?"

"The other to marry a rich woman." Fitzgilbert said.

"Not so many of those around," Ardron replied.

"No," Fitzgilbert mused.

"There is Eleanor," de Bohun said.

"Eleanor?"

"Eleanor of Aquitaine."

"But she's married to Louis. The French King." Fitzgilbert pointed out.

"Yes," de Bohun drawled. "More's the pity." He paused a moment. "At this moment it looks unlikely that there will ever be a Plantagenet on England's throne."

Over by the ship, the gangplank had been pulled. Sailors, using long poles, began to push the ship away from the harbour wall. The three fell silent watching the ship slowly drift out.

"If that be the case, where do we stand with Stephen?" Ardron asked.

"It looks as if Stephen is in control." Fitzgilbert said. "I expect he'll try to find ways to bring us to heel."

"Negotiations or occupation?" Ardron queried.

Fitzgilbert shrugged. "Oh. I do hope negotiations. At least that way we might end up with some dignity."

"I suppose that would depend on the minus and plus you have in his ledger," de Bohun said.

Fitzgilbert scoffed. "I for one will have many minus and probably not a single credit."

"What about you?" de Bohun asked Ardron.

Ardron was thoughtful as he watched the sailors on the ship heaving on ropes to haul the sail up the mast. "Me?" he said remembering the question. "I might have a couple of credits."

"Oh!"

"Yes. I did once come to his rescue when he was beset by bandits in the forest just beyond Lacock."

"Really?" both were surprised. "That is a definite credit," de Bohun replied.

"And again at Lincoln," Ardron went on. "He fought for his very life to the point of collapse. I felled him from behind with one blow, then stood over him defending him until help arrived. But I don't think he knows that."

"Well," Fitzgilbert said. "If you stand before him to be judged, then I suggest that you had better enlighten him."

"Certainly," Ardron said with a grin. The ship's sail had caught the wind and slowly began to glide down the harbour. "Shall we walk down the harbour with the ship?"

At first the ship moved down the harbour sedately, but gradually gathered speed under a fresh wind. The three men were forced to increase their pace to stay with the vessel. At the end of the harbour the ship turned away, and they had gone as far as they could go. They watched in silence as it got gradually further away. Eventually it turned again, this time to disappear and make its way to the Avon Gorge and out into the open sea.

"That's it then, "Fitzgilbert said with finality in his voice. All stared after the disappeared ship in silence. "We have grown much poorer fighting this war," he added.

Ardron could not suppress a scoff. Fitzgilbert's version of poor differed greatly from his own.

"Not all," de Bohun said. "You have done quite well from it." He suggested, looking at Ardron. "From a simple village Saxon pilfering firewood in Melksham Forest to a baron with two castles and two estates."

Ardron nodded. "It's true," he said. "I have. Now I have a wife who deserves the best, and a son who will have every right to expect an inheritance. Therefore, I will do whatever it takes to keep my estates." His determination was evident. He looked down the harbour to where the ship had disappeared. "Henry will come," he said doggedly. "Sooner or later he will come." Both men looked at him dubiously without comment. "He will," Ardron affirmed. "He once said to me, 'when he becomes King of England there will be no Normans, no Saxons, there will be only Englishmen.' And I will not believe that he has given up on that ambition."

"Noble thoughts," Do Bohun said. "Noble thoughts indeed."

"Hold onto those thoughts," Fitzgilbert said. "Hold on for as long as you can."

Ardron felt the first spots of rain on his face. He cocked an eye skywards. A bank of dark cloud, pushed along on a strong wind, rolled up above them.

"We should seek shelter," Ardron said. "There is a storm brewing."

*****

Other Books by This Author

Double Time

A time travel fantasy in which a struggling bookmaker hatches a scheme to get rich using a time travel machine. Nothing works out as he planned.

Dust and Fury

A story of an Omani mountain family torn apart by different creeds and different loyalties during the bitter conflict known as the Dhofar Insurgencies.

Fair Winds to Perdition

A story of about 18th century Welsh smuggler William Owen

Ingram Content Group UK Ltd.
Milton Keynes UK
UKHW010134060623
422929UK00015B/710/J